Dogs in the Cathedral

David Megenhardt

To Helen m Rick,

We're so happy to spend time with ya and have great conversations.

Love

D

red giant books

For Sarah

I got to keep moving, I got to keep
moving
Blues falling down like hail, blues
Falling down like hail
Mmmm, blues falling down like hail,
Blues falling down like hail
And the day keeps on remindin' me,
there's a hellhound on my trail
Hellhound on my trail, hellhound on my
trail

-Robert Johnson

Circuitry

Orange and blue flame roared from the mouth of a brick smokestack. Acrid smoke curled and lolled against the pale afternoon sky, seeping across the city, slipping around the patina of St. Basil's domes, and lying like gauze over the roof of the rotting cathedral. It tumbled onto an expressway and mingled with gasoline exhaust, then spiraled back to the sky from the rush of cars. It roiled over hermetically sealed burritos and pizzas lined on a convenience store shelf. It grazed on the front yards of dirty clapboard houses. With slow, deliberate hands it patted and probed the wooden facades, windows, and doors. It found a crack, an open seam, a broken window, and slid over hardwood floors and ragged oval rugs. Creeping over a sagging and stained couch, brushing the glass of a picture frame holding the frozen echo of a smile, the smoke crawled across a tile floor, around the legs of an aluminum kitchen table and up a dress, around flowered underwear, under two fleshy arms, and through the fingers of a woman reading a Hungarian newspaper. She wrinkled her nose and scratched a downy moustache. Over her head, through glossed and sprayed hair, and down the back of her neck, licking lightly a brownish black mole, the smoke slid through the back door, sailing over the upturned nose of a dog that growled as it passed.

The smoke rose hard with a powerful gust and stretched itself into a haze over Cleveland like a putrid, toxic blanket swaddling a colicky baby. On an expressway that lay north to south a 1988 Monte Carlo sliced through the stench. The smoke jimmied loose the trunk and coiled around an oversized purple and aqua gym bag. It jiggled the zipper until it slowly split open and picked through a hundred or so plastic bags tightly packed with cocaine. Some of the smoke lay gently down on the powder, expended from its long and exhausting course, while the rest picked itself up and squeezed into the back seat, where it found crumpled fast food bags, half of a dried-up hamburger, scraps of browning paper, a couple of supermarket novels with garish covers,

1

split and torn porno magazines, and three used ballpoint pens. Over and under the seat, the smoke rubbed itself on a pair of stale socks, massaged the temples of a sweaty head and loosened the buttons of a shirt draped over a sunken and sweaty chest. Finally, it tickled the stubble on an upper lip and fluttered down over a revolver with electrical tape wound around the handle at rest on the vinyl seat. There, the smoke closed its eyes and fell into a nightmarish sleep.

Nelson Munroe scratched his lip and grimaced against the stench. He lit a cigarette and blew smoke hard against the windshield, hoping to diffuse the smell of sweat and smelted ore. Flicking up the sun visor, which had been squeaking slowly down into his eyesight every five minutes since he had left Tampa Bay, he yawned. The visor began its descent, blocking his line of sight, and he smiled weakly to himself. He rubbed his eyes and slapped his right cheek, then his left. He opened his mouth wide and shouted. His head drooped and his eyes fluttered. He flicked up the visor. He closed his left eye and leaned his head back on the headrest.

His mind drifted from the road and his tired and failing body. Thoughts and ideas trapped inside a moist, exhausted carcass. Man encased in metal and glass, throwing himself along a black asphalt plane, driving within himself for himself. The slick polished sheen of a car's exterior masks the panoply of oscillations, surging fluids, sparks, explosions, belts, fans and pumps. Cars are inscrutable. Machines built in the image of man, skin stretched across a structure, covering the violent synapses, the crude bones. Under the skin the final electric truth lies. Man is the final electric truth, a surge waiting for a circuit, driving within himself on a road poured down for himself by himself. Until, until, a car headed north will not stop until it runs out of asphalt somewhere above North Bay or if the pulse of energy is fortunate it will spark out in one of the Great Lakes... and Nelson Munroe....Nelson Munroe...His forehead bounced off the top of the steering wheel. He regained his senses long enough to shoot a glance at the revolver on the seat. A pulse of adrenalin surged through him.

"Christ on the Cross...shame and retribution...Jail, jail, jail," Nelson said with his mouth stretched as far as it could go. He gave his cheeks two more slaps.

In the distance a train rolled through the tops of trees. Brake lights flashed. Other solitary human beings carried through the circuit, waiting for the spark to die. In a valley open pools of sludge were being agitated by rotating aluminum hooks. Nelson jerked the steering wheel toward an exit sign. A horn blasted, rubber screeched, and broken glass fell on the pavement. He didn't look behind him to see what carnage he may have caused.

Driving west on Harvard Avenue, he pulled into a driveway next to a seven foot wooden bear that wore a derby and raised a massive paw in greeting. Long black factories, separated from the road by sooty, brown gravel parking lots and sealed with chain link fences, lined the street. A remnant of a neighborhood, seven houses painted with smoke, front yards chewed to a

2

few square feet by the expanding road, scattered with immobile cars, hoods up, doors off, engines picked clean from their cavities, huddled around a small motel called the Wander Inn. The motel, once a double house, had been converted into rooms with beds for truckers to sleep off the asphalt buzzing in their eyes. A concrete block wing, painted a deep brown, extended into the back yard, housing an additional six rooms. Nelson parked his car near the back of the concrete wing and walked to the front porch. Industrial grinding, a din of melting iron, stamping plants, cargo pounding on the bottom of trailers, steel coils rattling, shouts and curses, emanated from the sky, the ground, and the road.

Nelson entered. The office was dark and smelled of stale smoke. A television set crackled and hissed behind a wall. He leaned heavily on the counter and accidentally rang the bell. He lit a cigarette and let it burn between his fingers. An attendant hobbled to the counter. He had a large yellow wad of gauze taped to his cheek, covering a patch of torn or surgically removed skin. He performed the transaction without words but two or three simple hand signals, pointing to a hand written piece of paper on which had been written "24 dollars a nite," pointing to the key, giving Nelson change, and pointing to another piece of paper that read "Cheakout Noon." Before he returned to the television he nodded his head about four degrees in Nelson's direction.

After he completed the transaction, Nelson retrieved the gym bag and a small suitcase from the trunk. He picked up the revolver from the seat and slipped it behind his belt. He opened the door of the room and a thick swirl of aged humidity greeted his face. Stepping in, he slammed the door behind him and clicked the cheap knob lock and placed a thin hook in a brass eyelet that had been screwed into the door frame. The heat pressed him from every direction as if he had stepped into a wet, hot pillow. He opened two screenless windows on either side of the door. He stripped off all of his clothes and threw them one piece at a time to the farthest corner of the room until he had created a soggy mass.

He carried the gym bag to the bed, ripping off a nappy wool blanket before he sat down. Unzipping the bag deliberately, he brushed his dripping hair from his eyes and used hand, forearm and shoulder to clear the sweat from his face. He burrowed through the contents and caressed the plastic stretched over the cocaine, still unbelieving that he possessed it, however briefly. After placing the gun on an acrylic doily draped over the nightstand, handle toward the pillow, he returned to the bag, counting with his index finger one hundred and twelve tightly packed squares. He zipped it closed and stuffed it under the bed, using the pile of the wool blanket to shield it from a door view. He lay back on the bed, spread-eagle. A musty breeze slid across his body.

It was almost over. Make the connection. Jet back to Tampa. Call Montenegro. Make the connection. Close the circuit. Sleep came upon him in a rush.

3

Mice and Leather

When Nelson woke, the sun had dipped below the horizon and the day had cooled into a pleasant summer night. Crickets had risen and sang from small islands of grass pushing through the concrete and gravel. Engines rattled by on the street, shaking the room and making the brass hook on the door vibrate. He lay on the bed blinking his eyes, taking inventory of the regions of ache and stiffness down the length of his spine and through his legs. Even his toes on his left foot ached from clawing the insole and sock throughout the drive. His fingers remained bent from the hours of squeezing the steering wheel until his knuckles had turned white.

Dim light seeped through the windows. He followed the sloppy brushstrokes of paint on the ceiling. The paint looked splashed on as if to mask some violence. Fear and nausea crept through him. The image, the sensation, of a quick and bloody death had followed him since he picked up the shipment. Somewhere in North Carolina he had developed a knot in his neck and had convinced himself it would be the spot where the bullet entered. What poor maintenance man would be given the task of covering his life's last spatter sprayed upon the wall?

He lurched off the bed, fumbling for the light switch and the bathroom door. The shower head dripped to life and he lathered himself with a nub of soap that resembled a toe. He stood under the showerhead and water drizzled onto his head. Rivulets of soap and water snaked their way down his legs and feet and leaked into the drain. He stayed until the water ran cold. As he stepped from the shower and dried himself, he inhaled his new soapy scent, so different from the musk of the road that it reminded him that he could live. Maybe a faint and pulsing ember of will glowed underneath his fear, and maybe with will came a form of courage and with this form of courage maybe a chance of success could be possible. The closed circuit. The end of this business. Sweat moistened his temples. His stomach felt like he had eaten something hot and leaden. Maybe the ember was nothing more than another tumor of fear.

From his suitcase he retrieved a razor and shaving cream and a set of fresh clothes. After smearing his face slowly with the cream, he cut perfect swaths down his cheeks and under his chin with the blades. He splashed his face with water and dug in his ears to find any stray cream. In the medicine cabinet he found a greasy comb and carved neat furrows into his thick black hair. He stared into the mirror, which reflected a man with a pink flush in his face, the hollow disturbed eyes, and a long and square and freshly razor scraped jaw. If nothing else he would make a striking cadaver, if they were able to reconstruct his face with plastic and putty.

He slipped on the fresh clothes and found a scrap of paper in his suitcase. In pencil he had written in a tight scrawl: M 216-566-1799, 5992 Maypole Avenue. A tremor passed through his hands because, technically, the possession of this paper could have him killed. Otter had told him never write anything down and never program the number into his cell phone. Be a shadow creeping along the highway, untraceable, unnoticeable. The paper proved connection, but he had decided to run the risk because his recall, given the anxiety, had all but vanished. He had to remind himself of his name throughout the length of Virginia and West Virginia. He thought, if asked, he may not be able to recite the alphabet. He folded the paper in half and slid it in his front shirt pocket.

He found his cell phone in the sodden pile of old clothes, nestled in his pants pocket with coins, a watch with no band and a disgorged packet of gum he had chewed through early in the trip. He flipped open the phone and as his finger pushed the first nine in the number the LCD display went blank. He pushed the power button and the phone briefly came to life before falling back into darkness. Nelson gathered a chunk of his lower lip between his teeth and clamped his teeth together until pain radiated through his jaw. He checked the room with a quick scan, and put the gun on the mattress, handle pointing toward the door. He fell to his knees and reached a hand under the bed, groping until he felt the nylon of the duffel, rolling the fabric between his fingertips, proving its existence.

Retrieving his car keys from the bedside table, he slipped from the room and quietly clicked the door closed behind him. He held the cell phone at his side like he wielded a gun and unlocked the passenger side door of the car with a key. He opened the door, leaned in and plugged the phone in the car charger. As he moved the cord it separated into two distinct pieces in his hand. Holding it up against the dim dome light he could see where the cord had been burned through. On the wood grain plastic of the console lay the ashes of a burnt cherry end of a cigarette, resting in a fragile heap next to the other end of the cord. How could he not of smelled burning rubber and wire? What are the fucking chances?

He bounced out of the car, seized with a sudden panic of exposing his back to open space. Spinning around, he found the same brown gravel parking lot on the edge of an industrial valley. The steel mills below rose in a cluster of black masses, forever burning.

Nelson stepped back into the room and looked for a phone. The jack in the room had been destroyed and the wires burst from the wall in a small explosion of red, blue and green. The corner of his lip twitched and he calmed it with the end of a thumb. He fell to the floor and reached a hand under the bed to touch the cocaine. After slamming and locking the windows, he pulled on a jacket and slipped the gun in the front zippered pocket. He stepped outside the door, locking the knob but knowing that one good kick would send the door off its hinges. He lit a cigarette. The glowing ember acted as a small lantern in the deepening night. He rested his free hand on the handle of the gun and exhaled. A little spark in a vast blanket of darkness. He walked past the car. Leaving it in front of the dark room would give the appearance that he waited inside, would give an assassin pause and give him enough time to make a phone call and return. As he walked, he listened to his feet scuffling the gravel. A lobster scuttling under a black sea, unnoticeable, untraceable. A skeleton running through the desert at midnight, alone and bone clean. Near the road headlights flashed on his legs. To the west and a hundred yards distant, a knot of cars cooled under a yellow and orange illuminated sign.

Nelson had arrived early. They expected him in the morning. The operation never wanted a mule to rush. He had been told repeatedly by Otter to never drive straight through. Otter had told him this and a hundred other pieces of advice. Since Otter had recruited him to be a mule he had some responsibility for Nelson's ability to deliver the drugs. The advice came so fast, delivered in a frantic, drug-fueled scat that Nelson tried to focus on the main points. Never chance falling asleep at the wheel. Even a minor fender bender could waste thousands and thousands of dollars, not to mention jeopardizing the operation and risking a lengthy stay in a backwater penitentiary. Stay on schedule. Never arrive early or late. Montenegro had choreographed the schedule into a perpetual ballet, molding a many limbed monster stretching two thousand miles into an engine, an engine that relies on every part listening to commands and performing their small tasks. Think of yourself as a pulse of electricity on a circuit. Bribe cops whenever possible and kill pirates if they try to hijack the shipment. Nelson laughed at the word pirate and Otter's eyes flashed anger.

"It's not the patrol going to get you. Maybe the boys from Fisher's Fly or Zune blow your head off. Maybe Gutterman break your neck and throw you in a ditch, keep it all for himself. There's spies and assassins everywhere, tracking you and watching you, trying to get the shipment. What you think? You can just take a million dollars worth of goods up the gut of the country and somebody not notice, somebody else not want it? Laughing don't make me think you taking this seriously."

"I take it seriously. It's just the word pirate has long been abused. You can't say that word without thinking of a Halloween costume party."

"OK, Nelson, you like the words hijacker, scumbag, butcher, assfucker any better? How about shark-eyed motherfucking psychopath? You need some more words? If I thought about it I could probably come up with more."

So against Otter's advice, against one of the operation's commandments, Nelson drove straight through, knowing that he couldn't reverse the decision to become involved but that he could shorten the duration of the run and his involvement. Close the circuit and retire. Find a job nestled in a cubicle amidst humming office machinery and climate controlled air, avoiding all human contact not directly related to survival.

He thought a working man's bar in the heart of industry would still have a public phone, so he walked to the edge of the road toward the cluster of cars as semi-trailers rumbled and growled past.

"So I'll be a smart mule with eyes in the back of my head."

"Mule?"

"That's what I'm called, right?"

"Maybe you got something wrong with you. Can you deliver this or not?"

"Isn't that what it's called, a drug mule?"

"Call yourself whatever you want to call yourself if it makes you feel better. Maybe just get the shit to Cleveland and don't worry about what we call you. I'll call you fucking Sea Biscuit if that helps, otherwise just get the shit there."

Nelson walked toward the bar and flicked his cigarette into a ditch. It tumbled in the air and slowly extinguished on the edge of a black pool of water and grease. He turned into a shadow, crunching gravel under his feet.

The bar glowed amber from wood paneling on the walls and naked yellow bulbs hanging from the ceiling. Every surface had been saturated by smoke and beer. Two men, their heads wrapped in bandanas, shot a game of pool in the back. A miscue twanged and a guttural voice cursed the ball until it spun to a stop. Two men in baseball hats sat at the bar, slurping foam off their drafts as they watched a baseball game on a faded TV. Three others sat at a table playing poker, each in a studied attitude of indifference. The building rattled as the trucks passed. Everyone had a burning cigarette in their hand or resting close to them in an ashtray as tendrils of smoke crawled along the ceiling.

The woman bartender, a veteran of the bar for over a decade and who over the years had taken on the mannerisms and dress of the clientele until she looked like neither man nor woman, barked at Nelson to order. He ordered the most common American beer he could think of and asked her if the place had a pay phone.

"Last one in town. Won't let the phone company take the sombitch. It's over by the shitter," she said as she pointed a vague direction with her chin.

Nelson gathered his beer and change and made straight for the phone. He set his beer on top of it and slipped a quarter down the slot. The receiver had been smeared with chewing tobacco and ear wax, several times. With a rigid finger he dialed, holding the buttons down so the tones blared through the speaker. It rang twice before a recorded message told him the number had been disconnected. He found the note, reread the number and dialed again. The same message began. He hung up and his quarter bounced to the return. He cradled the receiver between his shoulder and chin and used his left hand to plaster the paper against the phone just above the buttons. He jammed the quarter in the slot and dialed with precision, holding each number down for five seconds. The phone rang twice and the message began once again. The voice rambled on as he waited for someone to answer after it concluded. Instead, the phone clicked and a dial tone hummed. He called information but the operator told him the number as given was a non-working number.

He gently placed the receiver back on the hook and backed away from the phone, rubbing his chin. His strength began to weaken and his knees strained to keep him upright. He fumbled for a stool at the bar and sat, holding the bar with both hands. He ordered a beer and the bartender squinted at him.

"You don't like the other one I served you?" she said through an inch gap in her teeth.

"What?" Helpless, Nelson stared at her mouth to make sense of her words.

"The other beer. You just going to leave it over there?"

"Where?"

"By the phone. How drunk are you pal?"

Nelson spun on the stool and spied the beer atop the telephone, giving the bartender a weak thumbs-up on his way to retrieving it. The men at the bar watched him as he walked to the phone. Nelson brushed his hand against the gun in his jacket pocket as it banged against his hip. Maybe one of them had been sent by Zune or Gutterman. He doubted his ability to find the gun, pull it free from the pocket, vaguely aim and send a bullet in the vicinity of Gutterman's chest or belly. An assassin could slice his throat with a pocket knife before he readied himself to shoot. He essentially had no protection in the bar, but what alternative could he devise? He couldn't go back to the squalid little room, nothing more than a cage, a humid, dirty cage where he could only look out the filthy windows and wait for his death. The image of his corpse, forgotten and bloating in the heat on the brown carpet next to the hideous bedspread, came clearly to him. He could count the entry wounds of the bullets and saw the aftermath of some unspeakable violence committed against his mouth. He picked up the beer and drank half the bottle in a few swallows. He leaned against a machine that sat near the phone and the bump woke it from its dormancy. Through the blue haze of a failing monitor a woman with auburn hair, dressed like a lawyer or accountant with horn-rimmed glasses and a slate gray business suit blew oval kisses and rubbed her shoulder with red claw-like nails. The image faded and the instructions came on to the screen. She would take off an article of clothing for every right answer a player could guess. Ten questions, ten articles of clothing. He fed two dollars into the machine and picked Arts and Literature as his category.

1) Who dies in *Death of a Salesman*?
   a) Willy Loman
   b) Jay Gatsby
   c) John Proctor
   d) Popeye Doyle

Where did Montenegro go? What happens if he finds an abandoned building at 5992 Maypole Avenue? What happens then? The address is written in the same handwriting as the phone number. Who wrote that number? How could it get into his wallet with his very apparent, very apparent fingerprints smudged all over it? He thought he wrote that note. But is it his handwriting? He doesn't make fives like that and even that M look suspicious. Munroe. He'd had years of writing the letter M and that M in Maypole simply did not look like one of his M's. How did Willy die anyway? With a bullet in the back of the head? What is it about life that eludes him? Gutterman peering around the corner, left eye squinting, a slight pressure from a finger and then a release. Assassination? Could you even call it an extermination? A car crash. He killed himself for the insurance. What did the car hit? A telephone pole? An abutment? A tree? Gutterman standing in the street pointing a gun at his head through the windshield?

   a) Willy Loman

With a whirl and a compression of eyes that hinted at an Asian influx somewhere in the bloodline, off came the glasses.

2) Who is the author of *Revolutionary Road* ?
   a) Henry Roth
   b) William Gaddis
   c) Richard Yates
   d) John Cheever

Why hadn't he stayed in Tampa with Jules? Lounging at the beach or poolside, drinking at Nick's or Jocko's or the Rest in Peace Tavern. A life discarded. Another picked up at random and half-lived. He could have found another job, selling insurance, folding tacos, cleaning teeth, washing cars, bookkeeping, tanning hides, writing cutting-edge articles on beekeeping in blank verse. Anything. What did it matter? He needed a little money, a poolside drink and Jules. She sipping her drink, top off, watching her belly tan. Wisps of pubic hair crowning the top of her bikini bottom. The faintest trace. He watching her lithe body at rest, feeling the sun's radiation slowly warm his penis.

c) Richard Yates

With a click, the band of the Rolex unfastened and slid into the palm of her hand. She dangled the watch in the air, sticking out her bottom lip in a mock pout before dropping. She flinched as it made a sickening, broken sound when it hit the floor offscreen.

.

3) Who was Paul Gauguin's first mentor?
   a) Charles Gleyre
   b) Pierre Auguste Renoir
   c) Paul Cézanne
   d) Camille Pisarro
   e) Frédéric Bazille

Something brushed against Nelson's shoulder and he spun on his heel, scanning the open bar behind him. Distracted by the sudden movement one of the pool players raised his torso from the table and eyed Nelson. Satisfied it had nothing to do with him, the player lowered himself and squinted along the stick at a chipped cue ball. Nelson gulped the rest of the beer and wiped the seepage from his lips. He touched the gun, thinking that by the end of the night his pocket would be matted and slick from the grease of his fingertips. He turned back toward the video machine. The question began blinking, warning him the time had nearly elapsed. He read the question again and pushed:

c) Camille Pisarro

Her crisp gray jacket slid from her shoulders and limply fell away. She arched her back and stretched as if she had been held in chains. She looked at Nelson and brushed her hands against her ample breasts, making the nipples rise.

4) Who painted *Portrait of Alof de Wigancourt with a Page*?
   a) Peter Paul Ruebens
   b) Michelangelo Merisi da Caravaggio
   c) Annibale Carracci
   d) Agostino Carracci
   e) Rembrandt van Rijn

Otter must have been addled to entrust this enterprise to him. Jules had drawn Otter to them at the apartment complex pool. She, with her top lying bunched on the concrete, sending a beacon to all men. Otter padded over, jabbering, offering lines of coke and an opportunity. Why did Jules smile? Had she seen him before? Did his fingertips touch her thigh when he greeted her? Wouldn't most women put on their top when a stranger loomed so close? Why did she lean back, supplicate, make herself more open, more supine? Wouldn't most women sit up and at least cover their breasts with their knees? Would they just about now be slipping into bed, madly pawing each other, blotting out Nelson with each kiss.

b) Michelangelo Merisi da Caravaggio

The woman with the auburn hair kicked once and a shoe sailed into view before crashing in a clatter. She kicked again, a full punt, and the shoe shot through the air end over end.

5) What is the central paradox in Zeno's "Achilles and the Tortoise?"

a) There is no motion, because that which is moved must arrive at the middle before it arrives at the end, and so on ad infinitum.

b) The slower will never be overtaken by the quicker, for that which is pursuing must first reach the point from which the fleeing started, so that the slower must always be some distance ahead.

c) If everything is either at rest or moving when it occupies a space equal to itself. If the object moving is always on the instant, a moving object is unmoved.

d) Consider two rows of bodies, each composed of an equal number of bodies or equal size. They pass each other as they travel with equal velocity in opposite directions. Thus, half a time is equal to the whole time.

Why close the circuit? Why even jet back to Tampa after the shipment is delivered? The construct of his life had culminated in a mad dash north with a trunk of cocaine. Maybe he should accept the car as payment and drive to a town bypassed by the highway, forgotten and dying. Buy a little house with oxidized aluminum siding and drafty windows. Stay there for the next fifty years, curtains drawn, television unplugged. Grackles and jays screaming at dawn. Raccoons thieving garbage and building colonies in the attic. A slow invasion of mice beneath the floorboards, gnawing at the wood, creating small holes behind the couch or refrigerator, a maze of tunnels and connections, pilfering his food hidden away in cupboards, one mouse bite at a time. Mice running across his legs as he sleeps. Mice stuffing his mouth with lint gleaned from the clothes dryer. Mice covering him like a quilt, their bellies and the thumping of their little hearts on his flesh, retaining warmth.

b) The slower will never be overtaken by the quicker, for that which is pursuing must first reach the point from which the fleeing started, so that the slower must always be some distance ahead.

The woman hiked up her skirt, revealing thigh-high hose fastened to a garter. She unclipped one leg and peeled the hose down the thigh and calf. She unclipped the other and pushed the hose down with a spasm of longing. Her hands clasped her thighs, then traveled upwards to the curves of her hips. They slid across her flat belly then downward, circling her groin. Mock ecstasy contorted her face and her mouth fell open.

6) What is the name of Pietro Santi Bartoli's important publication of engravings detailing classical sculpture, which is often cited as an influence in the rise of Neo-Classical art?
   a) Le Pitture antiche delle grotto di Roma (1680)
   b) Romane magnitudinus Monumenta (1699)
   c) Admiranda Romanorum antiguitatum (1685)
   d) Veterum lucernae sepulcrales, collectae ex cavermis et specubus subterraneis (1691)
   e) Pitture Antiche Di Roma, E Del Sepolcro De' Nasoni (1702)

Hadn't the same impulse driven him to Houston, Phoenix, Colorado Springs, Memphis, Portland, Sioux City, Minneapolis and finally Tampa Bay? What would be different inside an aluminum clad house? The first day of any new city felt like the last. He had become expert in setting up camp, finding cheap apartments, jobs and girlfriends weeks after arrival. To what point? His constructs always seemed to collapse no matter how he approached the work. He would probably never see Jules again. His possessions would be thrown away after a respectful interval or Otter would inherent them. Her number would change and her warm tanned body would rot away from his memory. How many times had the pattern repeated? Did he run on a circuit or had he begun the same infinite chase as Achilles? Always arriving at a point where the tortoise had already been, a faint groove in the sand where the shell had been dragged, an indentation of where a claw had tread, but no turtle, ever. He would have to resign himself to living the life of a shadow slinking across the surface of the world, except he couldn't be sure what he chased.

   b) Admiranda Romanorum antiquitatum (1685)

She reached behind her head and unclipped her hair. It fell to her shoulders and with both hands she mussed the formality from it. She smiled at Nelson's acumen.

7) In Herman Melville's Moby Dick, what is the name of the preacher who

delivers the sermon in Chapter 9?

a) Father Ishmael
b) Father Maple
c) Father Starbuck
d) Father Stubb
e) Father Flask
f) Father Madlen
g) Father Marple
h) Father Maypole
i) Father Mason
j) Father Friar
k) Father Freeman
l) Father Freemon
m) Father Morple
n) Father Mission
o) Father Masen
p) Father Masson
q) Father Mayridge
r) Father Barston
s) Father Barrow
t) Father Below
u) Judge Holden
v) Father Mapple
x) Farther Farther
y) Father Smithton
z) Father Jameson
aa) Father Fisher's Fly
bb) Father Lost
cc) Father Found
dd) Father
ee) Father Gutterman
ff) Father Zune
gg) Father Brother
hh) Father Booth
ii) Father Guiteau
jj) Father Czolgosz
kk) Father Oswald
ll) Father Lawrence
mm) Father Schrank
nn) Father Di Giovanni
oo) Father Zangara
pp) Father Collazo
qq) Father Torresola

rr) Father Pavlick
ss) Father Byck
tt) Sister Fromme
uu) Sister Moore
vv) Father Harvey
ww) Father Hinckley
xx) Father Ray
yy) Father Siran
zz) Father Chapman

Insensible. Chasing a tortoise across the world, touching the remnants of a shadow, the whisper of its claws scuttling over stones. Why wouldn't he agree to Otter's proposition? Hadn't some logical progression of factors led to this point? Even though he could tell Otter had kept Jules high and had extracted favors in the form of payment, even though he could tell by one of her gestures, or a certain look, both helpless and filled with rage that she really wanted him to rescue her from a trajectory that could only end with her dying frantic and confused, perhaps in a fiery crash amongst a small, dark copse of trees. Even though other possibilities lay open before him, he chose to accept Otter's offer. He could be hauling orange juice, cigarettes, milk or Snickers bars. Where could the distinction be drawn, really? Gutterman or Zune wouldn't assassinate him for juice or candy, maybe cigarettes, before considering their value and how much they valued money over life. But considering his inability to ever find the tortoise, he may have been the worst person Otter could have ever picked. Did Otter's desire for Jules push him to convince Nelson to hop on the circuit? Did Otter want him out of the way, any way? Throw the shipment in the trunk and drive. He would only need a few days to turn Jules' head completely and enjoy her body. It didn't matter that the likelihood that he'll ever find Montenegro is slim, quite possibly a paradox all of its own.

v) Father Mapple

She walked on to the screen from the right. She centered herself and wagged a finger at Nelson, a playful scold. She placed her hands on her hips, pondered her options and decided to unbutton her blouse. The silk blouse fell open, revealing a snug black lace bra covering her ample breasts. She slid off the shirt and dared Nelson to get another question right.

8) What was the painter's name who painted the blue sky and gold stars on the ceiling of the Sistine Chapel, later covered by Michelangelo di Lodovica Buonarroti Simoni?

a) Filippo Lippi
b) Bernardino di Benedetto di Biggio

c) Giovanni fi Francesco del Cervelliera
d) Piermatteo d'Amelia
e) Giusto d' Andrea

There were better ways to end this endless chase. Tomorrow he would find Montenegro or someone from the operation and deposit the shipment. He would trade in his one-way ticket back to Tampa. Play roulette with his destination. Buy a ticket of equal value no matter where. He would have his payment and a suitcase full of clothes. Random clothes though, stuffed in the suitcase more for props than practicality. Abandon the construct that led to this decision. One way out of the labyrinth is to never return. He would survive by chance. Maybe Gutterman had been asleep in the bushes when he passed. Maybe he lost him in traffic outside of Jacksonville. He had to hold the duffel for a few more hours then he could slink back to a life without assassins.

d) Piermatteo D'Amelia (1481-83)

She rose from the bottom of the screen as if she had been crouching out of sight. She twisted her arms behind her back, pretending to unhook her bra. She laughed a silent laugh. She found the zipper of her skirt on her right hip and pulled it downwards. Even unzipped the skirt clung tightly to her, but she pushed it down her thighs and stepped out of it. Her black lace panties matched her bra. She turned and presented the thin string of her thong to Nelson, then turned back to face him. She squeezed herself with both arms and danced off screen.

9) What is the beginning dialogue of the First Keeper in William Shakespeare's *King Henry The Sixth Part III*, Act III, Scene 1.

a) O' I have past a miserable night, so full of fearful dreams, of ugly sights, that as I am a Christian faithfull man, I would not spend another night, though 'twere to buy a world of happy days: so full of dismal terror was the time.

b) Under this thick-grown brake we'll shroud ourselves: For this laund anon the deer will come; And in this covert will we make our stand, culling principal of all the deer.

c) The gaudy, babbly, and remorseful day Is crept in the bosom of the sea, and now loud-howling wolves arouse the jades that drag the tragic melancholy night who with their drowsy, slow and flagging wings clip dead men's graves, and from their misty jaws breathe foul contagious darkness in the air.

d) Here's a stay that shakes the rotten carcass of Old Death out of his rags!

Here's a large mouth, indeed, that spits forth death and mountains, rocks and seas; talks as familiarly of roaring lions as maids of thirteen do of puppy dogs!

If nothing else he discarded a life he couldn't live. Having carefully avoided violence his entire life, he now had stepped into a world ruled by it. Go back to the room. Spend a sleepless night staring at the drawn curtains and the locked door. Listen to his own breathing. Count the seconds it takes for a bead of sweat to form on his forehead, seep down his nose and drip to the floor. How many drips would it take to reach morning?

    b)   Under this thick-grown brake we'll shroud ourselves: For this laund anon the deer will come; And in this covert will we make our stand, culling principal of all the deer.

She popped on screen, reached her hands behind her back and unhooked her bra. She slipped the straps from her shoulders, revealing natural, perfectly formed breasts. Inspecting them, looking for the smallest flaw, her hands followed the natural curve of their weight and lifted them as an offering. She produced a bottle of baby oil, squirted a pool on the top of each breast and slowly, slowly worked it down the slope.

10) Complete the sentence from Fyodor Dostoevsky's novel *Crime and Punishment*. "The

    a)   …day before her birthday he was in a fever of agitation.
    b)   …room was nearly in darkness, for the candle was flickering, and throwing stray beams of light which suddenly illuminated the room, danced a moment on the walls and then disappeared.
    c)   …large books he could not afford at all; he could only look at them wistfully, fumble their leaves with his finger, turn over the volumes in his hands, and replace them.
    d)   …hysterical outbreaks and sobbings on my shoulder that recurred at regular intervals did not in the least mar our prosperity.
    e)   …carelessness of the apology was almost equivalent to a fresh insult.
    f)   …room felt stuffy, the candle burnt dimly, the wind howled outside, a mouse scratched somewhere in a corner, and the whole room smelt of mice and some kind of leather.
    g)   …Grandmother was in an impatient, irritable form of mind.

"Whelp, let's see some video pussy," Nelson said under his breath. He rubbed his eyes, which suddenly felt dry and tired.

a) …room felt stuffy, the candle burnt dimly, the wind howled outside, a mouse scratched somewhere in a corner, and the whole room smelt of mice and some kind of leather.

The screen flashed wildly. A roar erupted behind Nelson's head. The woman began twirling in place with her thumbs embedded under the black lace straps of her panties. Just as she slid them down her hips, the bar began spinning and Nelson felt glass crunching underneath his belly. He rolled under a table, smashing his head against the leg of a chair. A cache of change burst from his pocket, rolling and twirling with him. He stopped, face down in a puddle of Budweiser fifteen feet away from the machine.

"The sonofabitch did it!"

"Go baby go!"

"All the way! All the way!"

"What's this shit about a mouse and leather!"

"S and M! S and M!"

"That would be L and M wouldn't it?"

"Look at that pussy! Awwwwwwww!"

"Ouch!...Mother!"

"Such a pretty face masking such a dirty mind."

"Damn, how much of that can she take?"

Nelson looked up to see five jean-clad asses crowded around the front of the machine. Fists were raised. Three baseball hats flew through the air. Backs were slapped and hands were shaken. Five faces that all seemed to share the same beard turned and rushed toward him. Ten hands shot at him, grabbed him, shook him, lifted him, and propped him up on a bar stool. The hands kept coming as they slapped at his spine and the back of his neck. A set of yellow teeth grinned two inches from Nelson's nose.

"You're the first to crack that box in five years! What are you drinking?! What's your name?! You know your mouse and leather! You made the poor little girly give it up, to a stranger no less. Mice and motherfucking leather! That's a new one on me!"

Gray whiskers, a trace of a lip and a flash of yellowed teeth. A face and then air. Two fatherly hands picked off the peanut shells and shards of glass from Nelson's hair and shirt, flicking them behind the bar as he went. The bartender looked up as a shard landed near her feet.

"What the fuck, Jack?" she howled.

Ignoring her, he continued his work.

"The boys got a little carried away. They didn't mean no harm. It ain't often a genius comes through those doors," and he leaned emphatically, pointing his large scarred forehead in the direction of the cool black night outside the open door. "Good thing we didn't cut you any worse. But if it's any consolation you won't be paying for any drinks the rest of the night."

A fresh beer and a shot of whiskey landed in Nelson's hand as he looked down at his paunch. His belly and chest felt injured. He unzipped the coat, unbuttoned two of the buttons of his shirt and peered inside to see his pale skin blotted with a spiderweb of deepening redness. Two men still roared about the woman on the video screen, her shape, her abilities, and her dirty mind.

"They call me Cactus, Cactus Jack of Montana."

"Cacti are not indigenous to Montana."

Cactus Jack squeezed together his eyebrows that sprouted in divergent directions.

"That is a fact. Not many people pick up on that. Don't know where the fuck Montana is, I suspect. Actually, to be perfectly truthful it's Jack of Montana Avenue. The cactus had been added later for reasons better left unsaid."

"Then why use it as your name?"

"Well son, that there is a story for another time. That story would take the night and most of tomorrow to explain with enough detail and drama to be sensical."

He leaned away from the bar, stuffing his hands in his pockets, jingling his coins. Cactus Jack's belly, covered in a t-shirt stretched beyond reason, poured over his belt. His belt, a hand-tooled leather job he commissioned from Cherokee Slim's Leather Shop at the end of a mad road trip that had lasted three years, had scenes of the prairie, of western mountain ranges, of dust and sun, horses and buffaloes, fat children with oval heads, of coyote and prairie dogs, long eared jack rabbits and their kin, drunken cowboys and dancing Sioux and a crystal lake filled with frothy mountain streams with ducks and geese drinking the cool water and supping on thick rainbow trout with a hulking mountain glowering in the background, basking in a full assault of the sun's radiant power. The buckle, a hand-painted representation of a prickly eight-armed giant, frozen in time in a sandy wasteland like the upraised arms of a dead octopus, a green gargantuan posed like two prominent and defiant middle fingers, a cactus, peeped out from under his hanging flesh as if ducking under a heavy storm cloud. The leather and metal mosaic was being constantly turned inside out by Cactus Jack's shaking girth. He considered the belt and buckle a removable tattoo. Who the hell wanted some blue or green scar on their arm, back or ass years after you've outgrown that particular symbolism? With leather a person can add to it, change it, let it metamorphose as he blooms to the flower of soulful adulthood. Cactus Jack wore a long, unkempt mustache that obscured his entire upper lip. Thick lines crisscrossed his face and Nelson couldn't tell if they represented the normal process of aging or a collection of scars from past lacerations.

"What's your name, genius?"

"Nelson."

"Family name or did your parents pluck it off the tube without a thought to your suffering?"

"Neither. But I can't say I know the exact origin."

"You never asked."

"No. Never thought to ask about it."

"Makes me think of Ricky Nelson. Remember that godawful show, black and white, where they walked around like zombies sucking on suburban utopia. If you were named after a show like that it would have serious ramifications."

"I think I saw the show a couple of times late night."

"Who the fuck watches something like that late night?"

"I don't know. I know Ricky Nelson. Turned into a country singer. Died in a plane crash."

"Like a friend of mine always says when a celebrity dies in some horrific fashion, *une mort imbecile.*"

"Your friend is Camus?"

"No, my friend is a sweet lady in Tulsa who skirts the existential question by baking perfect bread, with a crusty exterior and a cloud-like fluffiness on the interior, and fucking until one of us passes out. And that would usually be me."

Nelson drank his beer with the quick, furtive movement of a rodent, letting the thread of conversation drop. Jack bought round after round, starting with bottled beer and whiskey, then shots of vodka and then draft beer. Once Nelson passed the third drink he felt his body and mind flooded with welcome relief. Montenegro must take a dim view of his mules getting drunk, but if tomorrow he walked into his own slaughter shouldn't his last night be spent in the thrall of something outside his own anxiety. Without a woman, easily had, he settled on alcohol and the fellowship of Cactus Jack. He would drink everything placed before him and forget for a few moments his execution.

Jack continued with shots of Wild Turkey, shots of Jack Daniels, shots of Jose Cuervo, shots of Paramount gin and when the lights flickered for last call and Jack's money had nearly all been spent, the two ended with 25 cent shots of raspberry schnapps from an unlabeled bottle, pounding down five a piece before the bartender could take the bottle away with a disgusted scowl.

They stood and staggered toward the door. Jack lurched over to the video striptease and gave the machine a powerful bear hug and kissed the greasy side panel where a giant sticker of a buxom cartoon had been placed to entice would-be players.

"Lovely, darling, lovely, thank you for your gifts to mankind"

He turned to Nelson and encased him in a more powerful hug.

"And thank you for stumbling in and unlocking the riddle of the Lady Sphinx. I'd say the boys were ready to push this goddamn thing in the river. She's safe for awhile. The boys might hit the books and see if they can duplicate your effort, but they have a long way to go. She has a sweet pussy."

Jack released him. Nelson, in turn, tried to bow, but the rush of blood to his head and the roiling alcohol in his stomach cast him forward and, even though his hands responded by shooting forward and bracing his body against the force of the fall, his forehead bounced off the floor with enough energy to snap his head back and cause a sharp pain to ripple down his spine.

"Jesus, Ricky, careful with that brain of yours. I'd hate to see you turn into a slobbering idiot after your performance."

Jack picked him off the floor by yanking on a fistful of jacket and shirt. He righted Nelson and held him until his dazed equilibrium found the horizon.

"Jack.....Jack......Jack....thank you for the cure...the balm...the elixir....I will go back to my room."

"No, the night is not over. The night is far from complete. We will travel in my homely truck to the land of afterhours, where the party still rages. We will drink until dawn when her rose red fingers reaches for the sky."

"But Cacti, Jacks...ich bin stinking drunk and tomorrow...or today... this morning...later this morning...this pathetic lonlihood of a man faces his hour of reckoning. All of this man's past indiscretions...mistakes...his desires and futilities are poured into a funnel to create a...vortex...let's say...a whirlpool...a sludge...to be washed away...drained...A man to be cleansed."

"Schnapps will make a man philosophical right before he vomits."

Jack led Nelson by the arm out of the bar. Nelson offered no resistance and could barely bend his knees in a rhythm that resembled walking. They stopped in front of a dented and rusting pickup truck with wooden sides encasing the bed. A green refrigerator rose high above the cab with a matching stove pushed against a side. Stacked and ordered to use every square inch of available storage, Jack's collection included a massive window air conditioner that looked like it needed its own generator to run, three doors (two solid cherry inside doors with crystal handles and one mahogany entry door carved with a Medieval motif), 20 cured two-by-fours, a moldering mink coat-ankle length, spools of black, red and green electrical wire, a bundle of copper pipes tucked near the side, a garbage disposal still in the box, three tube televisions plucked from the lawns of families dedicated to staying on the electronic innovation curve, six lamps (two ceramic lamps, painted to resemble Greek lekythi, one wrought iron floor lamp with four pigskin shades, one carved wooden bear with a paw raised and conduit bursting from the top of his head, and two iron ingots, capable of smashing a skull just with their own weight, that had been fashioned into light bearers) a mattress carefully wrapped in plastic, worn box springs once home to a family of mice, three cardboard boxes deteriorating from several cycles of rain and sun, carrying real silver flatware and two sets of dishes, (a formal set of obscure French origin with silver and gold leaf filigree, depicted a gang of randy satyrs chasing a flock of nubile beauties around and around the edges of the plates and bowls, as the center of each piece had been dedicated to a position a mythical satyr may place said beauty should they be lucky enough to catch one), four overstuffed hard-shell American Tourister suitcases, in an array of faded colors (red, yellow, orange, aqua) that held every article of clothing Jack still owned, except the clothes he wore, a gang box of tools and hardware, everything from screwdrivers, sockets, hammers, chisels, measuring tapes, levels, scissors, chalk lines, trowels, saws, wrenches, soldering kits, blueprints for a belfry, a warranty card for a bidet, and a brand new cordless drill with a set of gleaming bits, a set of six dining room chairs fashioned out of hardwood maple and holding the remnants and stench of rotted cushions, a dozen unlabeled wooden apple crates from Skookum Orchard that held a small collection of books (leather bound classics of Dickens and Tolstoy and yellowed paperbacks with titles like *Young Stewardesses* and *Ginger at Play*) a collection of photographs, one set his family's entire history since the beginning of photography and another set of photos from the 60s of a family with three small boys traveling across the United States, a family Jack didn't know and had never met, but when he found the box next to a dumpster some small impulse to save the family from obliteration made him throw the box in the back of his truck and carry it with him for over a decade, a box full of ballpoint pens, colored pencils, No. 2 pencils, chalk, mechanical pencils, crayons and pink erasers that looked like dirty thumbs, a couple of boxes of computer parts, keyboards, mice, memory chips, wireless cards, three hard drives, a tiny orange-hued monitor, printer cables and power cords, audio cables and speaker wire all wrapped in a thick jumble, three telephones with cords because walking around with a phone made Jack nervous as he liked to have one spot wherever he lived to be dedicated to telephone conversations, near a kitchen table preferably, and the rest of the house, apartment or hotel to be free of chatter and everything outside that place an opportunity to be lost, and a box of all his important documents including his original Social Security card, draft card, honorable discharge papers, birth certificate, copies of all his tax returns since he had begun to file taxes at the age of eighteen, three sets of divorce papers, negative results of a cancer screening, a certificate of completion for OSHA training, all of his old driver's licenses that he never turned back in to whatever state government where he had been living at the time so not only did the eleven cards provide an existential flipbook but a brief travelogue as well, x-rays of his teeth (should he ever need to be identified without the help of his face or hands) and a nearly complete set of all his paystubs from companies that paid him legally and a notebook ledger of all the companies that paid him under the table, because Jack knew that governments are fueled by paperwork and if he didn't want to be hassled or audited or thrown in jail he would be prepared to fight them with their own fuel.

Cactus Jack spread his arms wide and twirled in place with a steady spin, an amazing feat considering the amount of alcohol he had consumed.

"A lifetime, Ricky. I'm a goddamn Bedouin!" he shouted over Nelson's head.

Nelson leaned against the truck and sucked air and, even though it carried traces of poison, it cooled his blazing lungs. Jack pushed him into the cab and bounded behind the wheel. The truck started with a roar, more like an explosion than anything else, and the seat shimmied with the grand mal rattle of the engine. They descended along a winding road into the valley of the steel mills. Flatbed semis passed them going up the hill, carrying coils of stainless steel chained to the beds, in shadow looking like imprisoned ogres recently clawed from the earth. A brown haze blotted out the moon as fire belched from the smokestacks, casting a flickering orange light on the road. Grinding and shouts echoed from the mills as if an army of men were being forged behind the brick walls. Through thickly stained windows they could see traces of molten steel flying through the air. The jumble of dirty buildings with tubes and conveyer belts connecting the structures in an overhead labyrinth, seemed designed to contain something violent underground, a cap or plug straining to hold an eruption, that if unleashed, would bury the city in red molten death, swallowing Jack's tiny truck in a blinding flash.

Men in yellow suits, peeled to the waist, stood by warehouse doors smoking cigarettes, the glowing tips satellites of the glowing fire behind them, over them, below them. Jack blew air from his lips audibly.

"Goddamn work! We've got to build shit!"

"Yes, *that*, Cactus, is work," Nelson mumbled, revived by his uneasiness of descending into an alien landscape.

They passed under a trestle cradling an immobile train filled with glowing pieces of scrap metal. Further down the road the valley flattened and the road passed abandoned black hulks of buildings crumbling back to the dirt. Through these tombstones the road straightened, creating a half-mile long drag strip with no obstructions. A line of twenty cars gleaming in the cast of headlights idled by the side of the road. The thought of ambush flickered in Nelson's mind before being extinguished by another random thought of Jules asleep on a pillow, her hair fanned over her eyes. A group of young men and their girlfriends stood by their cars drinking beer, passing joints and waiting for some super-charged motherfucker to come to the track and demand a race. Jack honked his horn, which sounded like a tired bleat and waved his hand out of the window. The group raised their beers and cheered. Jack popped the truck into fourth gear and punched the gas. The tires squealed, sending the truck zigzagging down the road. A plate for casual dining dislodged itself from its rotted box and rolled off the back, shattering on the asphalt. Someone whistled a shrill salute.

They drove over a one lane bridge, skimming low across a muddy brown river, and passed tall wooden houses squeezed onto dirt lots the size of their foundations. The air smelled of burnt coal, plowed earth, and fetid water, a thread of each weaving through the houses in an invisible tapestry. Silhouettes moved on dark porches, disturbed by the beams of light from the truck. The street lights had been shot out one by one over the years. City crews no longer came into the neighborhood to replace them. They turned six or seven times, down a one-way, up another, never moving in a straight line, traversing streets designed as a scribble. Jack made a final turn and coasted to a stop behind a car parked on the edge of a broken sidewalk. They exited the truck and followed a snake of cars and trucks to a house with a single naked bulb illuminating the porch with a dim yellow glow. Nelson looked around at the row of black houses. The bulb was the only outside light on the entire street. Even the moon had withdrawn its cast. If he listened closely, without breathing, he thought he could discern a faint drumbeat, like a heart beating deep within a cave.

"Look, Rickey. You're with me. These people don't like strangers," Jack wheezed when they stopped on the sidewalk in front of the house. "They'll cut your gizzard out and feed it to their kids if you give them a reason."

"Do you think Montenegro will be there?" Nelson said in an attempted whisper that echoed down the street.

"Who?"

"Mon-te-neg-ro."

The Cactus hooked his thumbs in his belt, conjured phlegm onto his tongue and spit a wad in a high arc toward the street. He inspected Nelson, squinting one eye like he looked through a monocle with dizzying magnifying powers.

"And why are you asking about that stinking lizard dick?"

"Do lizards have dicks? How we would think of a dick? You'd think they just rub 'em right off. They's so low to the ground."

"Look," Jack stepped forward until his lips almost grazed Nelson's chin. "If you're a cop, tonight's the night you die. Some of them people inside might work for him. Something bad in their heads, some kind of frenzy."

"A cop? Cacti, please, Polizist! A joke."

"Why'd you ask about him?"

"In college we were on the crewing team together. Slipping through the early morning mist on the Charles river. We shared girls, lockers, jock straps. He's a fine man and I thought I'd look him up and share a brandy or two with him during my brief visit."

Fury blazed through Jack who channeled the energy into his arm and fist and sent a club of a punch onto Nelson's jaw. It landed with a fleshy slap. Nelson staggered backward toward the street, his balance blasted into a million little shards, and he fell hard against the door of a parked car. From inside, his tongue felt for loose teeth. From outside his hand probed the swelling knot on his jaw. With his other hand he felt for the gun, but his coat had twisted in the fall and he sat on the lump of steel.

"Fuck, Jack."

"If you get killed it ain't on my head."

"I can take care of myself."

"What? With that piece-o-shit gun you have in your pocket?"

"What gun?"

Jack walked to where Nelson sat against the car, grabbed a handful of shirt and coat and lifted him to his feet with a jerk.

"I ain't taking you in there if you ain't clean….or dirty….you know what I mean?"

"What the fuck? Are you taking me aboard a pirate ship?"

"Pirates? I imagine there's a few in there."

"No shit."

"No shit."

"Don't worry about me."

"How do you know that name?"

"I just heard it somewhere."

"Right…and my dick wiggles when you sing to it."

"You must listen to the radio all day."

Jack cuffed him on the ear. The shock doubled over Nelson and he put his hands on his knees for balance.

"You do that again I'll shoot you."

"And I'll break your neck in six places before you touch the handle of the gun. Just give me a reason not to think you're a cop."

Nelson straightened himself and managed to maintain a wobbly stance.

"I got in business with him…I have a package….several little packages for delivery."

"You're in the wrong line of work. I can get a general sense of people pretty quick and my sense tells me that's the last fucking thing a guy like you should be doing."

"After tomorrow that won't be an issue."

"Right. After tomorrow everything turns to gold."

"How do you know his name, Jack? How come we're about to board a pirate ship?"

Jack thought about the question, tumbled words in his mind until he found a deliberate combination.

"Sometimes a man gets his hands dirty. Sometimes it can't be helped."

"I need Lava soap for my hands. Remember that shit? Take the skin right off with the dirt. Oh, I have dirty hands Jack. Dir-ty hands."

Nelson raised his hands to eye level. They were actually filthy from crawling on the bar floor, touching the interior of Jack's truck and falling in the dirt after the punch.

"Look at that. They're actually dirty. I don't fuck around with my metaphors."

"Well, Ricky, not many men whistle on their way to the gas chamber. I'll give you credit."

"They don't still gas people, do they?"

"Who?"

"The gas chamber. Are there still gas chambers?"

"I don't know. Maybe my references are a little dated. Something new comes up everyday so they probably have new ways to kill by now. But I'm sure there's a gas chamber somewhere in the world."

Jack turned and wobbled toward the side door of the house. Nelson staggered after him with sources of pain emanating from the back of his neck, lower spine, his right knee and the left side of his face. Each spot swelled at a different rate, blood surging in spirals, creating the first strokes of black, blue and yellow bruises. Jack entered without knocking and paused at the threshold until Nelson caught up.

A plump woman, wearing an apron loosely, stood near an open refrigerator, holding a pitcher of freshly squeezed lemonade. The misshapen lemon rinds, disgorged of juice and pulp, lay in a cluster on the counter. Her face, framed by straight black hair streaked with swaths of gray, ignited into a broad smile as Jack and Nelson climbed the three steps leading to the kitchen. She set the pitcher down and opened her arms wide, creating a cove with her arms and breasts where Jack couldn't help but land.

"Mr. Jack Cactus," she said as his head nestled on her warm neck. "Has decided to pay us a visit and he brought a visitor."

The last words of her sentence trailed off as she turned her head to a table where two men, both old and worn, played Scrabble. Neither had broken their concentration from the wooden squares of letters standing in the respective trays. She kissed Jack on the ear and pushed away.

"Ben, Jack Cactus is here. AND HE BROUGHT A VISITIOR!"

Her look swept across Nelson and catalogued his swollen face, the blood on his shirt, the hole in the knee of his pants, and the unfocused stare of a barely conscious man.

"I see the two of you must have had quite a night."

Jack pretended to inspect himself, turning his hand over, craning his neck to catch site of his feet and the back of his legs.

"Well, I don't look worse for wear."

"You never do."

One of the old men pushed back his chair, used the table to lift himself and once standing adjusted his belt. He shuffled over to Jack and peered into his face over his reading glasses.

"Well, Jack, is he our type of folk?"

A shudder of fear traversed through Nelson. The Cactus had shown his temperamental side. His fate hinged on the words Jack readied himself to speak. What would these people do to him if Jack turned on him? Hours and hours of talk about gallbladder trouble, reruns of shows popular two decades before, strangely tasteless and soggy food, even more hours of watching the Scrabble board fill up with three letter words and drinking lemonade until even his feet felt bloated. How many days had he spent at relatives' houses entombed in the same atrophy?

After a long pause during which Jack dug at the kitchen floor with the toe of his boot, he said, "Ben, you don't think I would bring him here if he weren't?"

The old man made little agreeing noises in the back of his throat and shuffled back to the game. Nelson leaned over and whispered into Jack's ear.

"Watch my back while I get a piece of banana bread."

"Where's the party tonight?" Jack asked the men at the table.

Both pointed downward with their thumbs. The woman blew him a kiss and Jack led the way out of the kitchen and into the living room where he found the door, leaden with massive rivets holding the panels together, leading down. He opened it and the weight swung easily on massive steel hinges, releasing a blue cloud of stale vapor, the thump-thump-thumping of a bass guitar, a unified cheer of a hundred voices, the whisk of paper money passing hand to hand, the grinding crunch of masticated popcorn and the wheeze of nostrils inhaling. Jack turned and smiled into Nelson's blanching face.

They descended and stopped halfway down the stairs to survey the scene. Men and women formed a cheering, jostling circle around the walls, some with money clenched in their teeth while others waved cash wildly above their heads. A bet would be made with a chirp or click using an indecipherable language and a hand would come slashing down, loudly smacking an upturned palm. Some kneeled down in the front row, arching their backs so those behind could snort cocaine off their shirts. A haze of smoke hung over their heads. Jack and Nelson couldn't break through the circle so they sat on the steps, seeing only the backs of sweating heads, that is, until an entwined couple directly in front of them fell to the floor in a moaning heap, creating a narrow canyon into the inner circle. A muscular Rottweiler danced on its hinds legs. The dog hip-hopped to the thumping bass, landing on beat. His trainer, on his knees with his cheek flush to the floor, shouted, "Blood! Blood! Blood!" and slapped his hand on the concrete each time the dog's toe nails scratched the floor. A tense, thin faced man with a greasy moustache held a stopwatch in one hand and beat the rhythm with the other. Tiring, the dog's legs wobbled and spread with each successive hop. Saliva dripped from its teeth, dribbling along its black lips. Money flew through the air. The crowd began stomping and clapping to the beat. The dog's spirits rose. Its jumps became a little crisper, a little higher, but its straining body betrayed it would only be a temporary rally. A joint fell into Nelson's hand and he sucked a long, thick breath, then flicked it into the circle, where it continued from mouth to mouth. Blackness closed from above, and his brain decided to close up shop and receive no more information, except the pounding rhythm of dog, trainer, bass and crowd.

Disinterested, Jack walked up the stairs to the Scrabble game and lemonade. Passing Nelson, who had shut his eyes and had a thin stream of drool hanging from his lip, Jack shook his head, witnessing the last peaceful moments of a man's life before the dirigible he's riding bursts into flames and the man falls from the sky in a rain of fire.

"A goddamn shame," Jack said to himself. "With a brain like that."

In the kitchen all eyes were on the game board, which had two new additions since Jack had left. The woman squeezed Jack's neck with both of her hands and planted a kiss on his forehead.

"Jack Cactus, Jack Cactus, where have you been?"

"A man falls in love with the chase, sometimes forgets what he's supposed to find."

"Remember my hair? First it coarsened into wire then turned black and now the black won't even hold. I've lost the looks I had."

"Not to these eyes."

"Jack, I know you spent decades holed up with some immortal beauty without a thought to what could have been."

They each drifted to a separate moment in their shared history that had spanned forty years. Each time they met, first one, then the other, would begin following the thread back to regret, humiliations, unanswered letters, and minor betrayals that always seemed to thwart them from spending their lives together. The thread always ended in a tangle, confused in a murk of decisions tethered to no discernible reason. When Jack looked at her he ached to take her by the hand and lead her to a spot on a patch of grass and make love to her under the smattering of stars bright enough to glimmer through the haze of the city's lights. Anne Marie watched as her husband leaned back in his chair, cleared his throat of a mighty knot of phlegm in preparation, she knew, of pronouncing an important piece of news or an opinion that had been mulled over, turned over in his mind a thousand and two times, until the perfect sequence of words had been found to fit the thought.

As he stared at the Scrabble board, he said, "Jaaaaaack, I hear you've been looking for a house. There's one been foreclosed on a few streets over. County took it for taxes. Old woman lived it in. She pretty much lived on the porch at the end after the County boarded it up. Anne Marie even tried to take her some food, but she ran away like a stray cat. A guy from the County told me you could basically get the house for back taxes. There's so many goddamn empty houses nobody wants them."

"Probably get that house for under ten thousand. be my guess," piped in his opponent.

"Where are all the people going? It's like whole neighborhoods are disappearing. They're just leaving these houses to rot," said Anne Marie.

"Nothing permanent in this country. In a hundred years maybe this will all be forest again. Even a city like Vegas is one sandstorm away from obliteration."

"Jack must have got religion. He's starting to talk about the end of days," Ben said as he looked up and directed his words toward Anne Marie.

Jack laughed at the thought of him sitting in a church pew listening to the Word. He didn't even own a shirt with a collar let alone pants that could be pleated. He stroked his mustache with the palm of his left hand, a habit meant to signify he had kick-started his imagination and ideas now rumbled through his mind. He had just over ten thousand dollars saved in a pouch securely taped to the back of the seat in the truck. A house. Even at his age, when most of his generation were divesting their properties, titles and offices and trudging to warmer climates and perfecting the hook and slice of their miserable golf swings, the prospect of owning a house hung like bait in the water.

"Jack Cactus settling down to die? Lord-have-mercy on the old and beaten," Anne Marie shook her head in playful sorrow. "What's next? Jack siring offspring and raising babies?"

Jack leaned over and grabbed a handful of her fleshy behind.

"Is that an offer?" he whispered in her ear.

"I'd say that's been a standing offer for forty years," she hissed back.

Jack released his grip and raised his voice to address the kitchen, "You have to die somewhere. It might as well be in something you own."

"That's why I always thought you'd die underneath the sky with dew settling on your peaceful eyes."

"Ah, now you credit me with too much poetry."

"No, Jack, I don't"

Their faces leaned toward each other, their eyes shining with the memory of intimacies stolen by circumstance.

"The county man said the place is not far from the bulldozer. Nobody wants to take it on. But I remember you're handy with a hammer and when I heard about the house I said to myself that it sounds like a place Jack has been looking for and I've kept thinking that I needed to tell you next time I saw you. Last I heard the auction is this coming week."

Jack leaned forward enough to smell the scent of her neck and closed his eyes as if overtaken by a dream.

"How far you say it's away from here, Ben?"

"Just a couple of streets. It's about a minute and a half to walk there in a straight line.

Jack turned from Anne Marie and walked over to the table. He towered over the two decrepit old men and looked capable, suddenly, of crushing their heads with his hands.

"Well. hell! If I'm going to live around here I better learn this goddamn game!" he said as he slapped Ben hard on the back.

The left hind leg of the Rottweiler skidded on the concrete, wildly throwing off its balance. It leaped to the right and landed in a semi-crouch. Jumping backward, it skipped four or five times until its two hind legs crossed each other, sending the dog crashing to the floor exhausted. The referee clicked the stopwatch. Raising it above his head, he shouted, "I have the official time!" All fell quiet. Fluidly, he lowered the watch, turned his wrist, and brought the watch close to his face.

"The official time is! Sixteen minutes- forty-five and three-quarter seconds!"

Most of the crowd groaned. Blood had barely moved into third place, a disappointing performance, because everyone knew the time wouldn't hold up with so many dogs yet to perform. The official scorekeeper yelled, "Dog twelve, Blood, trainer Guy Florentine, with an official time of sixteen minutes, forty-five and three-quarter seconds is now in third place."

Conspiracies flew. Somebody made the dog slip, somebody threw oil on the floor, the dog had aged too rapidly. They should have retired the damn cur long ago. Others dug into their pockets looking for money to bet on the next dog. Nelson picked at a piece of loose skin on his finger. Dry and hard, it came off easily. He picked it clean, but he didn't stop. He dug into his living skin and began to pull. It came off in long moist strips and he made a pile of it around his feet. After pulling off his hair and dropping it to the floor, he stepped out of the skin on his legs like a pair of pants. Clawing at his muscles and fat, he threw heaping piles to the ground. He popped out his organs and kicked them into a corner of a room. He picked every last piece of living tissue from his skeleton. He felt clean, reborn. He sat in first class of a 747, drinking a martini with a bright green olive in it. The first skeleton among men.

He awoke to the growl of Blood as it passed by and walked up the stairs unattended. The dog had murder and sleep in its eyes and Nelson watched it climb the stairs and disappear through the door. Down came the beagle, Druid, a somber, almost lugubrious, dog that wore a scowl and looked through slits of its barely opened eyes. Druid stopped by Nelson on the stairs, turned, and subtly bared a long glistening fang, then continued down to the arena to the cheers of the audience. It took a position in the center of the circle, arched his toes in the ready position and waited for the signal to begin. Druid's trainer, Marques Johnson, had his cheek to the floor and his hand raised. Marques slapped the floor and began the count. Druid hopped high into the air and his performance began. Money burst from pockets and arms waved furiously in the air.

Nelson sipped a beer that had been passed to him. The embracing couple had stood up, pulling clothing over their bodies, so Nelson could no longer see the jumping dog. Alone with the pot and alcohol buzz jumping and sparking in his mind, he watched the word Cleveland as it floated, hovered, slowly illuminated like a summer flight of a firefly, above the echoing tumult of dogs and cacti, of drugs and skeletons. Horror and shame crept across him. How could he make his dream a reality? How could he jump from his skin and become a pure white skeleton. He had two essences, two beings. The human, veins and blood, pulpy gray matter, wet eyes, sweating feet and cracked lips, farting and shitting, the copulating being with hunger propelling him forward. The skeleton, dry clean bones, teeth without gums masticating air, fingers cracking and popping around a handful of sand. The sloppy veins and blood, carrier of fear and desire, had walked him into a trap. He would walk the desert with a simoom slashing his face until his flesh dissolved and the red wind carried the dust away. He would make amends to the skeleton, the sublime construction, the pure frame, the tortured being wrapped in moist evil.

Exasperation and hate erupted from the crowd. A knife flashed briefly in the light and sounds of capitulation and reason erupted. The knife disappeared, safely tucked inside a pocket. A man in a tightly stretched shirt hurried up the stairs with a bundle of money five inches thick. Druid broke through the crowd, limping badly with its nose scraping the steps as it ascended. It stopped on the step above Nelson's head, turned, lifted its eyes, and considered something, then said:

"Montenegro." The words came out in a low howl. Druid then jerked his head in the direction of the door as if to entice Nelson to follow.

Nelson jumped to his feet and backed down a few steps. Druid languidly closed his eyes, looked at the door, then turned back to Nelson.

"Montenegro," it repeated, wallowing in and enjoying each syllable, as it continued the journey up the steps, hopping on three legs.

Nelson followed at a distance of about ten feet as they made their way to the back of the house through a long and narrow hallway, bypassing the kitchen. Druid nosed through the back door and yelped a command. Chow-chow Beanie jumped up and trotted past Nelson in the hallway. Nelson reached the back door and looked over a dirt swath of yard fenced in with chicken wire. Druid sat down stiff with pain, rolled over on its side, and let the kinks flow out of its body. Two mutts lay like lions in the center of the pen, staring at the back door. Behind them some twenty dogs of mixed breeds, a German shepherd, a collie, various retrievers, two poodles, mutts of untraceable heritage, an English bulldog, and the Rottweiler, Blood, stood nose to nose in a semi-circle at the back of the pen. The two guard mutts howled in chorus. The circle nonchalantly broke up, each dog looking and walking in different directions. The collie came over to Druid and nosed his ear, turning back the long brown flap, and made guttural growling noises into the pink interior. Druid nodded as the collie continued. The collie lifted its head and barked crisp short barks to the pack, which met the commands with nods of approval. A line of twelve dogs formed and they began scratching the dirt with their paws.

Nelson stood behind the screen, lighting a cigarette as he watched. There seemed to be some organization to the dirt scratching, as the collie mounted the steps and yelped now and again to one of those pawing. The line stretched from one side of the pen to the other, pawing, backing away, cocking their heads at what they had done, then diving back into their work. All of them stopped at once. The collie produced a long, sorrowful howl and jumped from the steps. In a single file line, the dogs trotted to the back of the pen, with Druid bringing up the rear. The dogs, all twenty of them, sat down in unison with their backs to the fence, staring blankly at Nelson. His eyelids drew back as far as they could go, causing a slight distortion, his nostrils flared and his mouth formed an ugly grimace. In the dirt the dogs had pawed and scratched:

MONTENEGRO IS DEADTH

Nelson eased the screen open and entered the pen, taking vicious drags from his cigarette. He walked over to the "M", then followed the sentence to the other side. With the toe of his shoe he dug a period. The collie barked once, then twice and on the third bark the pack pounced on him. He crashed to the ground in a blanket of fur. Nails dug at his clothes. The dogs were strangely silent as two wet noses covered his mouth. His shouts ended mute on the interior of his lips. Jaws snapped on his clothes, not drawing one drop of blood. Lifted into the air, his back to the ground, he began moving. He tried to turn his head, but dogs had taken clumps of hair into their mouths, keeping his head immobile. Moving faster, he could hear the unified gallop of the pack as they ran over grass and cement. Silhouettes of trees and busted streetlights flowed past. Slobber seeped into his clothes as the dogs took hard, sharp breaths. Nelson closed his eyes and relaxed his muscles. The dogs ran and Nelson dreamed of a skeleton flying through a desert.

A House on a Dirty City Street

Cactus Jack snared his thumbs into the belt loops above his hips and ran his tongue over the uneven edges of his front teeth. He leaned against his truck, forced to acknowledge the sharp pain radiating from both kneecaps and ankles, relieving some of the pressure by transferring his weight to the fender. He couldn't tell which injury had risen up in anger this morning. Could it be one of the old work injuries? Was it a scrape from gravel, a burn from molten iron, the repetitive torque on his knees and hips as he scrambled up ladders, the strain of lifting concrete block or bricks or bags of cement or furniture or timber or sacks of grain, the squatting behind the plate in the deep minor leagues when he still didn't have to shave every day, or the time he spent digging trenches on his knees like a muddy supplicant? Did the pain emanate from the broken and frayed vessels, flaring at the memory of kicks to the legs, violent, crazed wrestling or the bullet that shattered his shin bone? Or did the pain pulse from the dead area around his ankle where that drunken asshole Randy Reamer ran him down from behind with his Corvette, clipping his leg, snapping the ankle and leaving him to crawl across an empty mall parking lot in the middle of the night in the middle of winter just for having the audacity to touch the fine downy pubic hair and tender labia of Randy's sometimes girlfriend Darlene? Or did it represent after all an accumulation, a debt, his legs a credit card statement detailing a history of unwise purchases made without the thought of their actual cost.

His house loomed in front of him. He had bought it the previous day at the county building during a sad auction where dozens of houses were sold, the addresses enunciated in a flat monotone by a twenty-five year bureaucrat enlisted for the duty because of the inherent gravitas of his voice. As Jack waited for his address to be announced he imagined the list to be a recitation of the war dead, the government deciding to use addresses and parcel numbers instead of names to prevent rioting. When he made his first bid of $5,316.19, the exact amount of back taxes owed on the property and the starting bid for it, he expected a flurry of bids to come flying over his head, but he heard only the shuffling of papers and a sneeze. After he paid from his weathered roll of cash, a clerk gave him a copy of the deed to the house.

There it stood, a massive colonial built around the turn of the previous century for a rollicking brood of working class children. Three floors, a wide front porch with thick columns but the porch roof sagging in the middle nevertheless, about forty windows with those on the first floor covered with gray sheets of plywood warped from a few seasons of snow and rain and the upper story windows all broken, irresistible targets for rocks and bottles, clapboard siding with a halo of paint chips lying in the grass around the foundation, a collapsed garage and a driveway, once smooth black asphalt but now so broken it could pass for gravel.

A shadow, an arm, something passed in front of a window on the second floor. Jack watched the spot but could only see the play of sunlight on the shards of glass remaining in the window frame. He kept his eye on the window as he walked to the side door along the driveway. Each step felt like a fresh violation, like someone had poured gravel into his joints. The door had been blasted from its hinges and wood lay on the ground and on the two interior steps leading into the kitchen. He stopped at the threshold and inspected the frame. Ruined by an act of a bored, teenage chimpanzee. He stepped into the kitchen which smelled like rot and wet dog fur. Cabinets, paint splattered and carved with initials, aphorisms, and scatological blasts that all revolved around the word "dick," hung precariously from the walls. The sink held several strata of dried vomit. On the floor between patches of linoleum shone constellations of cigarette burns and the heads of rusty nails rising. A dripping red swastika rambled across the ceiling and down a wall, created with a mammoth can of spray paint. The counter held an array of cheap beer, wine and liquor bottles filled with soggy cigarette butts and ashes. One wine bottle had been crowned with a used condom. Jack thought the kitchen, probably the entire house, could use a good cleansing burn, a raging white hot inferno to rid himself, his home and the world of such obvious disease.

A muffled shout drifted down from above. Jack shuffled over to the counter and tested the bottles one by one, avoiding, however, the condom, until he found the one with the right mass and distribution of weight, opting for a thick, rectangular bottle with a heavy bottom. Holding it by the neck, he left the kitchen, following the rumbling human tones that crept along the damp plaster walls. He pirouetted through the dining room cluttered with swollen porno magazines, the stench of diesel fuel and smears of Vaseline shaped into abstract genital designs, making sure his massive boots didn't disturb the clutter and give his presence away. He stopped at the foot of the stairs, catching the bouncing cacophony of squeals and grunts.

"The exit, my trespassing friends, is blocked by the prickly pear himself, mighty Jack Cactus," he whispered.

For emphasis he slapped the palm of his free hand with the bottle. He had never passed up a fight or a situation where one could develop and he could feel the old energy, however degraded, passing through his limbs. He hadn't been in the house for five minutes and already he had to defend it or die trying.

"The Cactus frowns upon uninvited guests."

He crept up the stairs, shifting his weight in a coordinated ripple of heel, ball, and toe that massaged the steps and didn't betray him with a creak or a groan. On the first landing he waited for another sound to help locate his prey. He released his breath slowly through his nose as he watched a tremor pass through his thumb. Breathing that way had not been easy or natural since the nose had been broken and not properly set three of four times. A lady friend he hitchhiked with across the Plain states through a whistling October wind told him his nose looked like a meandering river. A giggle rolled through the smashed banister above. He continued up the steps, trying to levitate his mass with a rising fury, attempting to gather himself into a coordinated, violent machine.

At the top of the stairs stood four doors nestled around a small landing. Two doors were firmly closed, one had holes kicked and punched through it, and the fourth hung open a quarter of the way and through it Jack could see a wrestling of flesh. Rising and falling buttocks grasped and clawed at the air. A tanned back, sliced with thick vertebrae and alive rotating shoulder blades expanded and contracted with deep, pleasurable breaths. Two thin, pale hands tugged at curls of thick, black hair. Four sets of toes danced in a primitive rhythm. Jack almost turned and descended the steps, thinking it close to a crime to interrupt lovemaking under any circumstance. A philosophy he had once put into practice the day he caught his first wife screwing a neighbor in their bed. He had waited outside the trailer in a folding lawn chair, smoking an unfiltered cigarette. Once his wife cried a final, desperate moan Jack crushed the cigarette out with his boot and waited until her lover, hurriedly dressed, came bounding out of his home with his dick still wet from his wife's vagina, to beat the living snot and piss out of him. But the truth be told, Jack could have watched this coupling all day long. Something about the softness and newness of their feet. The unblemished skin of their legs and the rising and falling back. The desperate clawing and wrestling against pain, the search for fulfillment through an erect dick.

The fluid motion turned spasm and the head with black hair lowered. The buttocks squeezed in a final, brutal clench, then softened as the back collapsed. The body listed, then rolled out of sight behind the door, uncovering a girl's body and a small wisp of downy pubic hair. She stretched her arms towards the ceiling, working the stiffness from her hands. Her hair lay in a fan about her head as she stared past her hands to the ruined plaster. Her breasts, heavy and full, had rolled from each other and now she moved her toes to a syncopated beat of a pop song rumbling through her head.

Jack considered falling to his knees and weeping for this beautiful world, but they were trespassing, afterall, on his property and they may have even sprayed the swastika in his kitchen, such was the treacherous nature of beauty. He had to make an example of them, root them out and humiliate them so they would tell their stupid friends that a crazy fuck now lived in their party house and they needed to find someplace else to swill and piss and vomit and rut. The girl bent her knees and raised herself to a sitting position, arms wrapped loosely around her legs. She looked at the boy behind the door, admiring his lithe body, inclining her head in the direction of his penis but not committing herself to the act. She smiled and let her gaze drift around the room and through the open space between the door and its frame.

To Jack it seemed like their eyes met, but the girl did not reveal any sign of recognition. He looked through her eyes for a brief moment and realized that the sight of an old man wielding a bottle while staring at her and her naked boyfriend, post coital, would give most young girls, at the very least, the creeps and probably would elicit terror in most. Even Jack believed he stepped into territory he never wanted to occupy and for the second time almost turned heel and left them to their passion. He stayed, because of a strong impulse towards sexual perversion or fighting. He stood rooted and watched the girl take a cigarette and inhale long deep breaths like she had been smoking since birth. She lay back down and blew smoke into the air. The two began talking, but Jack couldn't pick up what they were saying. The girl sat bolt upright, squinted directly at Jack and let out a scream. Jack made his move.

Waving the dirty bottle above his head, Jack leapt and kicked the door hard. The door bounced against the wall and swung violently back, pinching Jack against the frame as he passed the threshold and knocking both the air from his lungs and the bottle from his hand. He staggered into the room, clawing at the air for balance, and tripped over the girl's legs as she scuttled away from him. He fell hard on a knee and then his forehead. Reflexively, he rolled on his back in time to see the boy arching through the air above and land with all knees and elbows on top of old Jack. The boy with smooth, hairless skin seized Jack's throat and squeezed until his knuckles turned red, all the while bouncing Jack's head against the hardwood. Jack felt spent. These new violations of his body, the throbbing knee, the scraped forehead, the sore ribs, pushed him close to not giving much of a damn. Through calm eyes he watched the blood gather in the boy's face, pooling into death grip hatred. Jack stretched out his arms to form a cross and wait for death. A fitting end, somehow, to his life, dying at the hands of a crazed naked devil as a beautiful nymph looks on as his life passes from him. But as his brain began starving the old panic set in, released from a reservoir of will or death fear, and his hands became fists and his arms became wooden axe handles and his shoulders newly machined, greased ball bearings, creating two efficient machines that when swung smashed onto both ears of the boy's head, sending a buzzer through his brain.

The boy released his grip and breath returned to Jack's lungs. The boy cradled his head with both hands, making sure to cover his ears to keep his unglued brain from leaking out, as he straddled Jack's waist. Jack considered the boy's body, a body without a paunch or misplaced gathering of fat, a thick rope of a penis, a frame all sinew and bone and energy, and he couldn't believe he hadn't died in his hands. Had the boy learned a few tricks, a defense or two, Jack would have been dead on the floor. He pushed the boy from his body and he landed on his side, moaning because the shock had subsided and clear vision hadn't returned to his eyes.

Jack lifted himself to his feet, holding his ribs and wincing with every new breath. He spied the girl cowering in the corner wearing the boys pants low on her hips and her bra which had both straps dangling at her sides.

"Don't worry honey. I ain't no Ghengis Kahn."

She looked back at him with a squint, unsure what he meant.

"I'm not going to touch you. Just get dressed properly."

She turned toward the corner and slipped the dangling bra straps over her shoulders and quickly pulled on a tight t-shirt. Realizing she had the boy's pants on she ripped them off and stepped into her own, even though she wore no underwear. Jack shook his head, trying to clear sensation and desire from his mind by turning to the window and looking at his truck parked in the driveway through the jagged edges of the broken glass.

"This is my house now. Go tell your friends there ain't no more partying here. You need to find some other place to do your business."

"We're not from around here. Never been in this house before," the girl said as she kneeled to check on the boy.

"Where are you from?"

"California."

"That's a big state. Whereabouts in California?"

"Bakersfield."

"Ah, I spent a season or two making product in Bakersfield. I remember eating at a Basque restaurant that almost made me faint."

"Wool Growers. All the tourists go there."

"I've never been a tourist."

"I'm just saying."

"You get a lot of tourists in Bakersfield?"

"Some. On there way to somewhere else mostly. People from L.A."

"I think I can still conjure up the taste of their oxtail stew."

The girl helped the boy sit up and stroked his bare back and petted his hair. The boy released one hand from an ear, inspecting the palm for blood or gray matter. He released the other hand and gently shook his head and blinked his eyes.

"Bastard sonofabitch," the boy muttered.

"I've been called worse and have been in better fights."

"Can you just leave us alone? We'll get our stuff together and get out of here. We didn't think anybody lived here. We've just been here one night," the girl pleaded.

"Where are you going?"

The girl shrugged her shoulders and the boy looked at his toes.

"You don't know where you are going?"

"No, not really. What does it matter?"

"Yes, we do. We know where we are going," the boy chimed in.

"Well, I'm not a hard man. If you need a place to stay you can stay here. How long have you been on the road?"

"A month or so."

"And when was the last time you've eaten?"

"Probably a couple of days. We don't need much to eat."

"This can be your room. I'll go get some food and make breakfast."

"We don't want no breakfast," the boy grumbled.

"I'm going to get food. If you're here when I get back I'll make it for you. I just can't imagine walking away from breakfast when you haven't eaten in a few days."

Jack walked from the room and shut the door behind him. On the landing he picked up the liquor bottle he had dropped, holding the spot on his ribs where one of the boy's knees had landed. Behind the door a spirited conversation erupted between the couple, weighing hunger against mistrust. Jack heard them agree the old man must be crazy and probably a pervert and did they really want to eat something he had prepared for them. He bet on hunger.

Jack descended the stairs, clinking the bottle on the banister and walls as he went. He weaved his way out of the house, punting debris on the floor and replacing the bottle on the counter where he had found it. He jumped in the truck and it started with a shudder. He circled the neighborhood in search of a supermarket, but he only found a couple of corner stores that specialized in cigarettes, beer, lottery tickets and spongy white bread. Other businesses had been boarded-up with sheets of plywood painted dark brown or green. He found an art gallery, a coffee shop called Red Star and a trendy bar created out of an abandoned machine shop, but no supermarket. He passed the green onion domes of St. Basil's, a brooding Greek Orthodox cathedral built on the ridge above the valley of the steel mills. A cluster of worker cottages genuflected in its shadow. Jack lowered his head and admired the stonework of the cathedral's façade.

He drove through a housing project where a cluster of kids smoked weed and kicked a dirty basketball around. Pulling over to the curb, Jack rolled down the passenger window and called the group over to his truck. They turned their backs to him and pretended not to hear his call. Jack listened to the rough idle of the engine for a moment and called again. He noticed they all wore the same baggy white t-shirts that hung to their knees with the right side tucked under a thick black belt and the same brand of white sneaker and the same brand of overly large dark blue jeans and the same red bandana hanging from their right back pocket. After another minute two broke off from the group and approached Jack's truck. They stopped ten feet from the open window and eyed the heap of his possessions in the bed.

"Whacht you want," the larger of the two barked.

"Your crew like to destroy things?"

"Who don't? Whacht you need destroying?"

"It's a house. A complete fucking rehab. Top to bottom. Rip out the old shit, put in the new. I need a lot of hands. I've got crowbars, but I need arms and I need fucking hands! I need the fury! I need to smash the shit out of this house and I want your crew to help."

"You paying?" the other one asked.

"Pay? Honestly, you won't get paid shit, but it's a hell of a lot more fun than kicking a goddamn basketball around in a dirt patch. You help me and you'll always have a place to stay. How about that? And it won't be owned by the goddamn county either. And it won't have bars on the doors or windows either."

"What kind of bullshit is this?"

"No bullshit. You come over for a day and then you tell me you don't want to come back and do some more."

"We're not doing it without getting paid."

"C'mon. I'll throw in Thanksgiving dinner with real cranberry sauce. None of that canned cranberry jelly. You just have to come and give it a try."

"It's the fucking summer you crazy fuck. Why you telling us about Thanksgiving?"

"I like cranberry jelly from a can," the larger spoke up again.

"Then we'll have canned jelly and real cranberry sauce. I'll give you a slice two inches thick."

"Come back when you need us. We'll see."

"All them guys available?" Jack nodded toward the group who watched the conversation from afar.

"What the fuck else they be doing?" the smaller one piped in.

"Wasting all that muscle. Wasting all that gray matter. Goddamn shame."

The two turned toward the group to consider them.

"So I can find you here?"

"Where else?"

"Who should I ask for if I don't see you?"

"Al K-wood el," the larger one responded.

"What?"

"Al K-wood el."

"Right."

"Just ask for Wood. Somebody find me."

Jack jammed the truck into gear and lurched away. A hand mirror slipped along the wood of the truck bed and under the gate, landing on the asphalt in a splintering crash. Wood walked to where it had landed. Glass lay in a small splatter around the handle and the remaining shards rained to the ground when Wood picked it up. The mirror had once lain on a rich woman's dressing table or had been the prized intimate object in a poor woman's life. The handle had been crafted with gold leaf and a string of delicate flowers wound around the frame to gently hold the visage of the owner. Wood inspected it for damage other than the shattered glass and polished a scuff on the top edge with a finger and a dollop of spit. He slipped it in his enormous back pocket, opposite the red bandana underneath his oversized shirt.

Jack found a foul and dingy supermarket fifty blocks away. A man with unlaced shoes and no shirt under a greasy sports jacket walked the aisles pushing a cart half-filled with cans of beef stew, humming the television jingles of the food he passed. Two cashiers were heavily tattooed with overlapping doodles up and down their arms. The air smelled of freshly baked pastries and bread though, and Jack weaved his way through the store until he found the bakery and its ancient attendant, withered and humped with a dusting of flour covering her arms and cheeks.

"You made all this?"

"I have help. My recipes," she said in a heavy Italian accent.

"Why are you still working? Haven't you earned a rest?"

She squinted at him and rubbed the flour from her palms.

"Because the wolf still clawing the door."

Jack bought a load, three loaves of Italian bread, a dozen donuts, a dozen muffins, cookies and a lemon meringue pie, thinking the hard work may bring on a craving for carbohydrates. He zipped through the rest of the store, filling the cart with the best ingredients he could find and thinking ahead to what he could whip together on a propane camp stove. They wouldn't have gas, electricity or water for weeks so the food had to be planned carefully. Nothing that needed constant refrigeration. Nothing that had to be baked. Meat would have to be bought and eaten the same day. He would find a cooler and stock it with ice because god knows they would need some cold beer at the end of the day.

He sped back to the house, coasting through stop signs and rolling through stoplights. After carrying the groceries into the back yard and placing them on a concrete slab that once had passed for a patio, he scaled the bed of his truck and rummaged through the boxes until he found a propane stove, skillet, knife, spatula, grater, a camp style percolating coffee pot, utensils and plates. He couldn't properly digest food under the shadow of a swastika and, until they properly cleansed the house of its disease, meals would be made and served on the concrete slab. He needed a big white tent, the kind people used for outdoor weddings and garden parties and set it up as protection against the weather. It would be a lovely place for them to take their meals, at least until winter. He walked inside and called for the couple. No answer. He called again, this time standing at the foot of the stairs. Still, no one responded. Climbing the stairs to the second floor landing, Jack became more disappointed with every step. He shouldn't have expected that they would have stayed, especially after he had been caught spying on their lovely act of coitus. They were probably miles away in the backseat of their first ride of the day. On the landing he heard giggling and grunting coming from behind the shut bedroom door.

"Breakfast! Breakfast! Breakfast! " he bellowed at the door before he turned to descend the steps.

"We locked the door!" the boy said, stifling a laugh.

"Glad to hear you two are working up an appetite! Now finish up and get yourselves downstairs to eat some breakfast."

Jack made the propane stove sing. Bacon, crisp, but tender and chewable. Omelets, fluffed and folded like idealized sculptures of omelets, with cheese, ham, mushrooms, red and green peppers tucked within the sizzling egg blanket. Hashbrown potatoes, simultaneously crisp and fluffy, heaped on the plates in airy mounds. Coffee percolated black and rich, with enough kick to keep a worker working all day off of one steaming cup.

The dew of the morning had begun to dry in patches where sunlight slipped through the trees. Sounds of the waking world rose from the neighborhood. The boy and girl, wrapped in blankets they had found in one of the rooms, stumbled out of the side door. Their hair stuck out tangled and matted and the boy had forgotten to put on his shoes. Jack set down two plates on the concrete, each loaded with an omelet, bacon, hashbrowns next to two tin cups of steaming coffee.

"Don't ask for sugar. We don't have any."

"What if we don't drink coffee?" the girl asked.

"That would be a crying shame and I'd suggest that today would be a good day to start."

"Why are we eating outside?" the boy asked, but the question sounded more like a complaint.

"That house maybe mine by title, but I can recognize bad mojo when I see it. There ain't no way to properly digest food in a place like that. You've got to be careful. Can't start this project by eating disease. I'd never make it to the finish."

"That's crazy. What disease is in the house?"

"No, prudent. I can even smell it on those blankets you're wearing. Not quite death. Not exactly life either. I wonder why the natives couldn't smell smallpox when the white devils gave them wool as a gift?"

"Are you a white devil?" the girl asked.

She smelled the blanket and slipped it from her shoulders, letting it fall to the ground and gather around her hips. Jack's heart doubled its rate, but she had dressed and Jack dismissed his anticipation by giving his eyes a deep rub.

"You believe that?" the boy said in the same tone as the first two questions so that Jack thought maybe the boy had a hereditary whine to his voice.

"It smells weird. Kind of like puke or a dirty mouth."

"That's the least of it. Eat your breakfast before it gets cold."

They attacked the food and even though they didn't give Jack the honor of a compliment he knew by their reaction they were surprised by every mouthful. They had no intention of thanking Jack, because he owed them something for seeing them naked and watching them fuck. They agreed to wait for breakfast because they were starving and because they wanted to extract some payment from Jack for his violation. Certainly a breakfast was a small price in a life of regular schedules, clean sheets, jobs and paychecks, but to them, lost and hungry, they wouldn't have been able to come up with better terms of the transaction than what Jack had provided.

They cleaned their plates efficiently and topped off the meal with two donuts apiece. They sat on the concrete, letting the sunlight play on their faces, silent, meditating over their still steaming coffee. The girl blew ripples across the black surface of her cup and took tentative sips from the rim. Even though she screwed up her face as the bitterness touched her tongue, she seemed determined to like it or at the least finish the cup. Jack openly watched them as he put his cup to his lips. He felt and smelled the blood pumping underneath their skin. Skin that had never known a scar or disease. Hands that had never shaken so much they felt like they may come loose from your wrists because you wake up in the morning with the sweats and you're wondering why the front of your shirt is covered in someone's blood and why did you decide in the night to tape all your money to the ceiling and you're lying in some dirty ass mattress and there's a pounding on the door and in comes some ape of a cop just smiling his cocky, self-satisfied smile because he's going to put you away for some seven odd years. Too many goddamn years. Mottled, ruined skin collapsing in folds, soon to be a pile around his ankles. Home is a crate to pack away the years.

"I don't generally eat a meal with someone if I don't know their names."

"Glover," muttered the boy.

"Estonia Marble."

"Are you Basque?"

"No," the boy responded.

"I meant her. She's got a look I can't quite place."

"American mutt, I suppose. My great grandfather raised sheep I think, but I don't know where he came from."

"Well, Glover and Estonia Marble. Let me get right to this. I've been thinking about this since I found you in the house and I'm thinking it might work. I need some hands around this house of mine. You can see how big of a job it is and I ain't likely to be able to do all of it myself. I can feed you and give you a place to stay, if you're willing to do some work and down the road I may be able to give you some money if I make some myself."

"We're going to New York, then maybe Boston," Glover cut in.

"The devil lives in New York, son. He'll chew you up and spit you to

Boston where you'll land in a pile of fish heads. And there, son, is where you'll likely die."

"Better than living in this shit hole."

Jack rose to his feet and spread his arms wide.

"A shit hole now, yes, oh God yes, this is a stinking shit hole. Probably the sensible thing would have been to bulldoze it to the ground. But in a matter of months!" he lowered his arms and pointed at Glover. " In matter of a few months this is going to be a goddamn palace! We're building from scratch Glover! We're going to rip it all down and build it back up again! We're going to rip out walls. We're going to blast away all the pain and confusion. We're going to build a belfry! We're going to have a hot tub! The floors are going to be shined and polished and slick as ice! We're going to eat in the dining room under a motherfucking chandelier. And that awful kitchen, the shitty kitchen filled with vomit and trash is going to have sparkling new appliances that a goddamn French chef would envy. You'll open the refrigerator and you'll have more choices that you know what to do with. We'll find farmers and get our food fresh. Flat screens will hang from every wall. We'll find chairs so comfortable you'll think you're back in your mommy's womb. And you know who's going to do it? You, me and Estonia. Maybe get some help from the neighborhood and with a little luck we'll create a house that just isn't a house. More like a manifestation of desire. How could you walk away from that?!"

"No," Glover said staring at his toes.

"What?"

"No, why should we build your house so you can live in it? What'll we get out of it?"

"You're not building it for me."

"Then who are we building it for?"

"You're giving your life some purpose, some direction. You're finally going to use those goddamn hands of yours. Hell, I might not even live long enough to settle down in the house. Maybe I'll exit like Moses on the threshold of the Promised Land. You have to think of it more like a sculpture. A product of your mind and back. A statement that you have lived on earth."

"No, we're going to New York."

"We don't have any money. I'm sick of sleeping on floors and under trees," Estonia piped in.

"This is better?"

"We can't even take the bus."

"We'll hitchhike."

"And what happens, Glover, when you're in the middle of Pennsylvania." Jack directed his words to Estonia because he knew once he convinced her Glover would have no choice but to stay. "And your belly feels like its touching your spine and a thunderhead comes rolling over the hills and you're deep within the state and there's nobody on the road. Will your next thought be about old Jack's house? Will you be saying to yourself you turned down the best offer you ever had since your mommy presented you with this beautiful life?"

"New York is the next state."

"No, son, P.A. is the next state and it's long and filled with trees and hills. I'm not going to lie to you. You've got about 500 miles to go and that might not seem like a lot considering how far you've come, but it's not the journey that troubles me. It's the destination. New York is not for kids with no money and no connections. You think the two of you are just going to tramp into the city and have it lie down before your feet? In a month you're going to be letting some random bald guy suck your dick so you can afford a meal. And this beautiful girl right here. Lord, the things that will happen to her. You have to sell whatever you got and you two know what you'll be selling."

"Estonia, he's just trying to scare us because he wants us to work for him."

"True. I do want you to work for me. I've told you that, but you're not even the first to get the offer. Don't get too full of yourself because Jack knows where to find people. I'd say I have my pick of castaways. You turn down the offer then I'll move on to the next."

"Ya, I'll bet they're all lining up at the door, begging to work for you."

"You're a cocky kid for having no food, no money, no prospects and no plan," Jack counted out Glover's deficiencies on his fingers as he went.

"I'll stay for a few days and see if I like it. I don't know how you're going to fix up the house but it might be fun to see it happen," Estonia spoke without looking at Glover, fearing her resolve might collapse once she saw his eyes.

"All right! The wisdom of woman prevails again," Jack slapped his hands together and rubbed them warm. " Throw off them goddamn blankets and follow me to the truck. Estonia, you'll start by clearing out the kitchen and dining room. I'll get a broom, garbage bags and the thickest rubber gloves you've ever seen. Glover, you and I have to build a shitter. You dig the hole and I'll build the structure. Start with the necessities."

"I'm not staying," Glover asserted.

Jack laughed deeply.

"Glover, your love just told you she's staying for a few days. Now, what are your choices? Walk away from her to what? Hunger and loneliness? Or stay with her and hear her breathing in the night and wake up next to her in the morning thinking life just might not be so bad. That ain't much of a choice. You just got to hope she hates the work and agrees to leave sometime when I'm sleeping."

Glover looked to Estonia, but she still wouldn't meet his eyes and she started walking toward the truck.

"Where's that broom you were talking about?"

"Agreed?" They both watched her walk down the driveway. "You're not leaving her, yet. So let's get to work."

Glover exhaled loudly through his mouth and walked with Jack to the truck.

"See, here's the thing. I've been thinking about this plan for days now. We're not going to have any plumbing for a while so we need a shitter. I also need a place to store all my wares. Doesn't make sense to have them in the house. We'd just have to move them room to room when the rehab gets going, so we need a garage. But our poor garage has given up the ghost. It's a pile of rubble. So, I'm thinking I'm going to use the scrap, whatever useful wood I can find from the rubble to build the outhouse, then we get to building the garage. I can put my stuff in there and have a workshop for working on the house."

"Why don't you rent out a storage unit and put your stuff in there."

"No, no, I want the stuff near me. It can't be in some unit. No, can't do that."

"Why aren't we going to have plumbing?"

"Son, you're going to have to get that whine out of your voice. We're not going to have plumbing because there ain't a bit of copper left in that house. Crackheads stripped it out and sold it for seventy bucks a long time ago."

Jack gave Estonia a broom, ten thick ply garbage bags and gloves so thick she wondered if she would be able to bend her fingers with them on. She slipped through the side door without a word. Jack found the shovel, hammer, nails, circular saw, saw horses and hinges and he and Glover carried them to a spot near the collapsed garage. They paced about the back yard looking for the appropriate spot for the shit hole. The yard felt small and houses loomed on all sides. The house behind Jack's house had also been boarded up and looked in bad shape. The two houses on either side seemed fit for habitation, but by the condition of the trash strewn lawns and the general disrepair of the structures whoever lived in them teetered on the brink of ruin. They chose a spot near the back corner of the lot far enough away from the concrete slab so their meals wouldn't be spoiled.

"Dig it wide and dig it deep. Wait!"

Jack jogged to the truck and returned with a can of orange spray paint. He sprayed a circle in the dirt and grass five feet in diameter.

"Follow that line and make it six feet deep."

"That's a lot of shit."

"We don't want to have to dig it again. Pile up the dirt here where we can get at it. We'll cover our shit like cats. It won't smell so bad then."

Glover jammed the shovel into the earth. Jack attacked the collapsed garage, yanking boards from the pile, inspecting them and throwing them into two piles, usable and rotted. He hacked the tar paper and rotted wood from the ceiling joists, thick beams hand cut a century ago, and dragged them to the driveway where he piled them in a neat stack. Even though the rot had progressed extensively and he found remnants of termites, he salvaged enough usable wood to build a couple of latrines. He briefly considered the idea of building a his and hers, but he dismissed the idea quickly as a luxury they could ill afford. When would he be unable to temper the million ideas pressing from the inside against his skull? When would his imagination consume him? As he cleared the final wall of debris a colony of mice bolted across his feet. He raised his boot to smash them but they had disappeared into the grass and bushes before his foot began its descent.

He used the joists to create the floor, making a seven by seven square by nailing together six joists for support and topping them with ¾ inch plywood from his truck. Luckily he owned a cordless circular saw, but the charge would only last the day so he would have to search for a source of electricity as well as water. He cut a hole a foot and a half in diameter in the center of the floor. It would be the biggest damn latrine he had ever seen. Plenty of elbow room. No need to shit in a closet. Around the hole he built a stand out of two by fours and plywood, capping it with the only remaining toilet seat left in the house. He dragged the completed floor with the stand and seat to the hole, where Glover hadn't made much progress. The area looked more like a spot where a giant animal had clawed at the ground than an actual hole.

"Sweet Jesus, put your goddamn back into it. Fill the shovel. Now do it again. Do it until you can't straighten your back."

"Why didn't you just get a port-o-potty?"

"So, that's what's bothering you? You're not going to work because you got a better idea? First minute on the job the boy already has ideas. Listen, if I start spending money on a temporary shitter we won't have much chance of finishing this house. Now dig the goddamn hole!"

Glover stabbed the ground and gouged out a heavy shovelful.

"Good. Now do that about seven hundred more times."

Jack framed the walls and covered them with the clapboard siding from the garage. He fashioned a door out of plywood and thick steel hinges he had taken from a job in a ketchup factory. Glover stood in a hole as deep as his thighs. He had taken his shirt off as he had found a shoveling rhythm that looked both efficient and violent.

Jack crept away to check on Estonia. When he entered he found her on her hands and knees picking up soggy cigarette butts from the floor. Most of the trash from the kitchen and dining room had been cleared away and tucked into five mammoth garbage bags lined against the front dining room wall. Estonia had taken off her shirt too and worked in a black sports bra. She jumped to her feet when she noticed Jack had entered.

"What happened to your shirt?"

"Well, I don't have many clothes and the clothes I do have I don't want to stain with this mess. This is pretty disgusting."

"Yes, I do know it is disgusting."

"Do we have any water?"

"No."

"Great. How long am I supposed to smell like this?"

"I can get water to the house, but we got no plumbing. I guess I can fix up a little wash room in the basement."

"Have you seen the basement?"

"No, I can't say I have."

"I made the mistake of opening the door and looking down there. Creeeee-ppppy."

"Why?"

"Just look. I can't explain it."

Jack walked to the basement door and yanked it open. He descended the stairs and stopped half way down, where trash eddied over the steps and blocked his way. He expected to see the detritus of a meth lab or a homemade dungeon or even the traces of past butchery. Bending over, he looked through the dim light over a solid mass of debris four or five feet high that had been packed so tightly it looked liquid. Jack sat on the steps and ran his fingers through his hair. Thank God it still clung to his scalp in thick wiry curls. At that moment it felt like the only part of his body that had retained a hint of youth.

"Well shit, it'll give the girl something to do for a month," Jack mumbled to the tide of trash before he bounded up the stairs. "I've seen worse," he shouted to Estonia as he exited the side door.

She didn't hear him as she had become preoccupied with crushing a colony of ants that had swarmed over a sticky remnant of spilled beer.

By late afternoon Glover stood in a hole deeper than his head, the walls cut straight and clean in a vertical line from the circle Jack had painted. Jack had finished all the pieces of the outhouse and had laid them in the yard in a chronology of assembly.

"Alright! Alright! Get out of that hole. Let's put this thing up."

Jack reached down a hand. Glover pitched the shovel out of the hole and grabbed Jack's hand. Jack jerked him out and deposited him on his feet. Dirt and sweat covered Glover's chest, arms and face.

"That's a pretty hole, son."

"We got a shower? I think I got dirt in my underwear."

"There ain't no goddamn shower. You and your girlfriend better get used to being dirty."

"This is more than dirty. I've got clay on my balls."

"That's a little rough. I'll jerryrig something. Mean time, shake it out."

They pulled the floor over the hole and Jack pounded iron stakes along the edges to keep it from slipping or being tipped over in a high wind. They erected the walls and roof in an hour. Jack thought about leaving off the roof, but remembered having to shit in the rain once or twice and once having a swarm of flies descend upon him while he squatted, so they added a plywood roof with a vent.

As they stood with their hands on their hips, pausing a moment to witness their creation, Jack scrutinized his sloppy carpentry. Though the wood had come from a structural failure and even the best pieces had warped and rotted in spots, Jack knew he could have done a better job. He had rushed, had known the structure to be temporary, and the outhouse reflected his impatience. The whole structure tilted a few degrees to the left and the door scraped the frame when it closed.

"Once we get running water we'll burn it anyway," Jack said aloud, but he addressed himself more than Glover.

Glover picked up the shovel and slammed it into the yard, leaving it sticking from the ground.

"What the fuck! Put that goddamn shovel back where it belongs. You don't leave my tools out to rot. Show a little goddamn sense."

Glover pulled the shovel from the ground and carried it to the truck, picking up his shirt along the way. He suppressed a thought of planting the shovel in Jack's face, remembering the hammer blows that had sent his brain reeling. Estonia came out of the side door holding her arms from her side at an odd angle, like she carried a bag of groceries in either arm.

"I'm about to freak. Did you ever have maggots run down your arm?"

"I think roll would be the proper verb. Maggots aren't equipped to run."

"Whatever. They were on my arm. Actually both arms."

"Glover, run up and get some cleaner clothes for both of you. I have a place where you can shower. You'd think a couple of homeless tramps would be use to dirt by now."

Glover returned with a small rucksack and they followed Jack through the backyard and past the outhouse. They stepped over a rotted fence and continued through then yard of the house behind Jack's house. Jack stalked the perimeter, searching for a gap in the plywood to spy the interior. Partiers and vandals had worked on this house as well. An entrance had been made from a side window. A makeshift stair of concrete block rested against the side, giving trespassers enough height to slip through the loosened plywood. Jack poked his head through and wanton devastation greeted him. He jumped back down.

"How come you didn't pick this house to sleep in?"

"Believe it or not, that house is creepier than your house," said Estonia.

"And the stains look fresher. We thought people might be coming back. Your house looked like the party had moved on a long time ago."

They walked across a narrow street and down the driveway of another house and through its backyard and the backyard behind it and up the driveway of the adjoining house. Jack paused on the sidewalk before crossing the next street to Anne Marie's house. Her husband had been right. The two houses stood two streets apart, almost in a straight line. They crossed and Jack knocked on the side door. Anne Marie greeted them with a puzzled look.

"The party has moved on, Jack Cactus."

"I bought that house Ben told me about. The one where you said the lady lived on the porch. I can see the roof line from here."

"Well, that information certainly livens up the neighborhood," she said as she stepped out of the house and joined them in the driveway.

"I found two feral children who've decided to help me out. They are in desperate need of a shower and probably a laundry. Think you could help an old friend out?"

"If I didn't think you were teasing me I'd be offended. I have hot water for your dirty children and I'll even make you a hot supper." She turned and addressed Glover and Estonia. "You'll find that Jack's cooking talents don't extend much beyond breakfast and grilled steaks."

"Ben home?"

"No, he's at the bar, where else?"

Jack nodded his head and let his eyes drift in the direction of his house.

"I'm Anne Marie. Never count on Jack for introductions."

"I'm Estonia."

"I'm Glover."

"Pleased to meet you. Follow me and I'll get some towels and if you give me your dirty clothes I'll throw them in the wash."

The three of them entered the house as Jack shuffled to the backyard. The chicken wire had been rolled up and stowed away. The dog prints had been raked from the dirt, but the scent of wet fur still hung in the air. He unfolded a lawn chair, inspected the dingy nylon straps for tears, and sat down. He pulled a small greasy notebook and a nub of a pencil with a worn away eraser from his shirt pocket and he began calculating the wood he would need for a new garage. His mind ranged over plywood, two by fours, ceiling joists and then concrete, electrical wire, and shingles. Soon, several notebook pages were filled with indecipherable notations that looked either Arabic or like some personalized system of shorthand. After his performance with the outhouse the thought of building a garage seemed foolish, but he had to bet his talent would return, his focus, his ability to build something exactly how he imagined it. A warm hand touched his shoulder.

"You know Jack you're welcome to take a shower too," Anne Marie whispered in his ear.

"If I start taking off my pants in your house I'm pretty sure where that will lead."

"And why exactly do you see that as a problem?"

"It's not a problem. Maybe we should think before we start up again."

"Think. About what?"

"Is it what we want? We've had our chances before."

Anne Marie unfolded a lawn chair and sat down facing Jack, their knees touching.

"Those two kids seem sweet. They're not going to steal my jewelry are they?"

"I don't vouch for anyone. Every person I've ever met is more devilish than I could have imagined and kinder than I could have ever hoped for."

"Maybe that's the limits of your imagination talking."

"Maybe so. Them kids seem alright, but I wouldn't put it past them to cut my throat one night to steal the money I got left. I think the girl might be pregnant. I think she knows but doesn't want to know and the boy definitely doesn't want to know yet."

"How do you know?"

"It's a hunch, but I can't quite come up with any other reason why she agreed to stay. I ain't delusional. I can be pretty persuasive, but she gave in way too easy without even consulting her boyfriend. What other reason could there be?"

"My, my, my, Jack Cactus a grandpappy. Will wonders ever cease? Or maybe these are the plagues of Moses raining down on poor Jackie's head?"

"You remember that guy I came to the party with?"

"You mean the one who looked like be had been in a car accident?"

"Yes, that one."

"I'm likely not to forget him."

"Did you see him leave?"

"No."

"He just vanished. He could have walked away I suppose, but I don't see how he could have gotten that far."

"You need a better class of friend, especially now that you are going to be raising an infant."

"We'll have to figure out how to get her to a doctor without spooking her."

"We?"

"C'mon Anne Marie, you'll help."

"I'll have to ponder whether or not it's what I want," she answered.

"You know what I'm saying."

"No, I don't know what you're saying. I'll move in to your house tonight if you ask me."

"I don't even have water yet."

"Water or no water, I'll come. Ask."

"I want to talk to Ben first. I ain't going to sneak around his back."

"How many days do we have left Jack?"

"I'm not going to tell him at the bar. Drunks don't like those kind of conversations. When he sobers up I'll tell him."

"Better catch him early then.

"Tomorrow."

"I guess you're not going to ponder it anymore."

"Forgive me for that, Anne Marie."

"If I'm living with you tomorrow, then maybe," she reached out and placed both hands on his thighs. "I'll forgive everything."

"I don't expect that."

"What's done is done. Let's just think about the days we have left."

Jack placed his hands on top of hers, but he could barely feel her skin through his calluses. She cradled his right hand and lifted it to her lips, kissing the knuckles. She stood up and let Jack' hand fall.

"I better make supper for them kids."

Jack accepted a kiss on the forehead and watched her leave. Through an open window he listened to the sounds of her preparing their meal, running water, chopping vegetables, clanging pots, the efficient dance of her feet, like he had become a solitary audience member for a choir of thirty full-throated birds. He would crush Ben if he showed a moment of resistance. The man had slept with her for decades, but now he drank himself to oblivion as his imagination had run dry or he had solved all the mysteries of life to his limited satisfaction. Jack would make him see reason, convince him that with so few days left on earth he had no purpose to live one day in misery and certainly no purpose to recuperate in a full body cast with no visitors at your bedside, eating from a straw.

Jack heard Anne Marie talking to Glover and Estonia so he heaved himself out of the chair and entered the side door. The three stood in the kitchen. Estonia wore a loose fitting dress patterned with tiny cornflowers, belted at the waist, and Glover wore giant black pants held up with suspenders and a white button down shirt. They looked like two freshly scrubbed Amish kids, wearing hand-me-downs from their older siblings and chatting with their mother.

"Look at you two, all sparkly and dressed like you're going to church."

"I'm washing their clothes. I can't say I had appropriate loaners."

"They look cute."

"Thank God suspenders went out of style."

"I feel ridiculous," Glover said as he twanged the suspenders for emphasis.

"Your clothes were ready to crawl away."

"Thanks to Jack and his dirty house."

"I haven't worn a dress since my confirmation."

"Anne Marie, does she look Basque? It's driving me crazy."

"I couldn't say."

"How come you don't know where your family comes from?"

Estonia shrugged her shoulders for an answer.

"Your parents never told you?"

"It never came up."

"Jesus, they did you a disservice. You've got to know where you're from."

"That's not all they did."

"I assumed or you wouldn't be on the road for a month, half-starving to death."

Jack didn't want to hear a litany of abuses delivered just before dinner should Estonia feel the need to open her past to them, so the intonation of his delivery severed the conversation and left them in silence for a minute or two, giving Anne Marie enough uninterrupted time to finish preparing the meal. She served them grilled vegetables, brown rice, crusty whole wheat bread and grilled chicken breasts, delicately seasoned. It hadn't taken her long to start serving pre-natal meals, Jack thought. What would he do with the gift of her generosity, her kindness, her thoughtfulness? Based on his history, he couldn't trust his instincts, his nature. How many times had a woman given herself to him, asking only that he become a humble supplicant to the love they shared? Each time he rose from his knees and walked away.

They ate the meal, drank coffee, and left well after the sun had set. Anne Marie had touched Jack's hand before they left and he found himself, as they weaved through the yards back to his house, holding the spot where her fingers had touched with his other hand. They reached the house and Jack pulled a flashlight, three sleeping bags and three pillows from the truck. They each carried a set to the door, but only Glover and Estonia entered the house. Jack handed them the flashlight.

"I'm not sleeping in there tonight."

"What?"

"After I smash that fucking swastika from the walls I'll sleep in the house, not before."

"Why?"

"It's a matter of principle. Go sleep in your room. You're immune. I'm going to sleep outside."

Glover rolled his eyes to Estonia and they disappeared in the darkness. Jack walked to the back of the house and threw the sleeping bag and pillow on the concrete pad. He shimmied into the bag and lay on his back, staring at a handful of muted stars. He fell asleep mulling over the sequence of work and dreamed of a world where everything looked like a blueprint and everything around him he had built with his own hands.

Under the Ladle, a Heart Sparks

When Nelson awoke the smell of wet clay overwhelmed him, so much so that he thought the dogs may have buried him alive. He could feel his eyelids open and close, but he could not discern a difference in the amount of light entering the eye in either position. Craning his neck in search of some clue to where he lay, he spotted a small circle of light above him and he watched it to determine its source. Clear blue and white passed through the circle and Nelson wondered if it could be a projection of random patterns on a wall or ceiling. Moving his arms he found he could nearly unfold them entirely before he touched damp clay walls. Then he straightened his legs that had been folded under him to their full length. Dampness played on his toes, but he couldn't see his feet to understand why cold radiated up his legs. He wiggled his toes against the floor and realized his shoes and socks had been taken from him. Drawing his legs against his body he raised an arm to see if he could touch the top of his cubby and with a slight reach his fingers grazed a clay ceiling, knocking free small chunks of dirt that landed in his mouth and eyes. His sputtering and spitting and the quick jerk of his arms to protect his face awakened another presence in the darkness.

"You best be still. Sometimes these holes are unstable," a voice rasped from somewhere behind Nelson's head.

"Why the hell am I in a hole?"

Silence answered Nelson's question. He tried, but he couldn't hear breathing or any movement that betrayed the location of the voice. He asked his question again.

"Are you in a hole?"

"It looks like it to me."

"That'd be something you'd have to answer."

"Is that the way out?" Nelson said as he pointed to the circular play of white and blue, then realizing his mistake of using hand gestures in darkness.

"Toward the circle, up there? Is that the way out?"

After another long pause the voice said, "That way leads to the outside, but I haven't found a way out yet."

"What are you talking about?"

"They track you."

"Who?"

"You know who."

"I'm tracked by hallucinations."

"By demons."

"Why would they bury me in a hole? It doesn't make much sense really?"

"Doesn't matter where you go, what you do, they'll find you. They'll always find you. Sometimes I think it's just best to stay in the hole."

"Who are you?"

Again, the answer came in silence and Nelson waited until it drove him mad before restarting the conversation.

"What is your name? What are you called?"

"Pez," came the answer like an exhalation of breath.

"Well, Pez, let's get out of here. My feet are freezing."

"They always take your shoes and socks. I think they believe shoes to be an abomination."

"Did you take my shoes, Pez?"

"What did I just tell you?"

"You told me that the dogs always take my shoes. They seem to have some philosophical disagreement with the wearing of shoes."

"Then why would I take your shoes? What good would they do me?"

"I don't know."

"Before you start accusing people maybe you need to gather all the facts."

"I'm sorry. My feet are freezing. I've woken up in a hole with no shoes and I'm talking to a voice disembodied from its owner. I could be wrong, but something just doesn't seem right."

"Sometimes they joke. They like jokes."

"What kind of jokes?"

Pez withdrew into silence and Nelson wondered if he had been talking to a turtle who periodically felt the need to return to the safety of its shell.

"Are you a turtle?

Once the words became audible he flushed with embarrassment.

"What?"

"Nevermind."

"How far gone are you?"

"Forget it."

"Jesus."

"I'm going to the surface. Are you coming?"

"No, I've just about given that up. They just bring me back down here. There's not much point of going to the surface. I'd just be back before sunset with a broken heart."

Nelson pointed his body toward the light and started crawling. The floor of the hole had been smoothed with repeated comings and goings and the slope inclined gradually enough that he made it to the surface without slipping, so that by the end of the crawl he decided that it would be more accurate to call it a tunnel rather than a hole even though, as far as he could tell, the terminus lay underground. When he climbed out, the fresh air and sunlight smacked him to the ground, where he lay on his back with a forearm draped over his glowing eyelids for added protection, breathing air impossibly laden with oxygen. After a few breaths he realized that although the air may be life-sustaining it smelled far from a gentle breeze rippling over a grassy slope carrying the scent of new growth. Something acrid and rotten hung in the air.

He sat up and dropped the arm from his eyes, opening a slit in his lids and flooding his sight with white light. Slowly, his brain found the proper aperture for his pupils and patches of color began to appear, followed by incomplete masses dashed on a sketchbook. Finally, after an interminable length of time, during which Nelson began to believe he had damaged his sight through the volume of alcohol he had consumed or one of the other violations to his body, distinct shapes popped into focus. Brown weeds, bent and dry, lay at odd angles, each one determining a path for its own survival but dying together en masse. Black buildings connected with tubing and walkways, erected in a jumble, rose in the distance. A savanna of weeds dotted with piles of bricks, broken concrete slabs tossed in heaps, and the glint of shards of glass casting razor light from large swaths separated Nelson from the buildings. Behind him a highway overpass carried traffic high in the air. A brand new barbed wire fence protected the underbelly of the road from incursions of the dispossessed. The remnants of a homeless jungle spilled down the concrete slope. Pants, cardboard, a street sign, a shoe. Nelson wondered if the shoe still protected the foot of its owner.

Head down, trying to spot obvious detritus that could possibly puncture his feet, he began walking his way across the field. The blaze of the sun pricked his neck and after no more than twenty-five yards he took off his jacket, which felt heavier than he expected. Holding the coat by the collar and patting it with his free hand, he found the gun. He unzipped the pocket and extracted it and for a moment its presence rallied him. He twisted around, spotted a pile of bricks fifty yards away, took aim and fired off a round. The explosion thrilled him even though the bullet disappeared without reporting back where it had landed. The bricks were obviously whole and obviously massive. Not even a wisp of dust gave him encouragement. He dropped to a knee, cradled his gun hand with his equally shaky left hand and pulled the trigger. The bullet skipped in the dirt ten yards in front of the pile and ricocheted off the brick. The shot would have taken out one leg of one dog.

Nelson stood up and raised his free hand to his brow, shielding the sun from his eyes. He dropped the gun to his side, feeling both the power and the sound of its power wane. Next time, if he could believe Pez that there would be a next time, he would be prepared to fight. They had to expect it, want it, demand it, because hadn't they left him the gun? Why take his shoes and leave the gun? He would wait until they were close to shoot, and once he fired a shot, whether it hit one or not, they would likely scatter.

He returned the gun to his coat pocket, zipped it closed, and carried the coat over his shoulder. They were unlikely to return so soon and he couldn't risk being noticed, walking back to the motel with a gun in his hand, wearing no shoes. The motel. A wave of nausea stopped him. He had lost track of the days. How long had he been in the hole? He had assumed it had only been a few hours, considering the alcohol still in his blood, but how did he know? What would Montenegro do to him if he were late? And the cocaine lay in his motel room behind the cheapest of locks. Did Gutterman have the shipment slung over his shoulder laughing at the ease of the theft, thinking of the torture his rival would inflict on his addled mule? Nelson tried to step faster, but the glass made it impossible for him to walk faster than an infantryman walking through a mine field.

The sun felt hotter than he remembered it ever feeling even in Florida. Alcohol tainted sweat coursed freely from his pores, soaking his clothes and hair. He sat down several times, his concern growing with each rest that he would be unable to stand again once on the ground. After the last rest, when he had to rock himself to gain enough momentum to fall on his hands and knees, then push against the ground with both arms and legs, actively fighting gravity, just to get back on his feet, he decided to take breathers by placing his hands on his knees, stand doubled over, and watch the sweat drip from his face to the dirt.

Nelson came upon an abandoned road, the asphalt chewed by time. A shoebox lay in the middle of the road resting on a small pile of rocks arranged in a ceremonial pyramid. He fought with the zipper of his coat and turned the pocket inside out trying to extract the gun. He fired a shot without careful aim and knocked the box off of its throne. Out spilled a pair of shoes filled with tissue paper but already laced. First, Nelson nudged them with a raw toe, then kicked each one over several times before bending over and retrieving one of them. The bullet had blown through this shoe, leaving a hole in the sole and through the toe below the laces. The shoe had been crafted of some kind of vinyl and he supposed the pigment had been meant to be a variation of burgundy but came across more like fire engine red. A pair of dress socks still lay in the shoebox, undisturbed by the bullet's path. He stowed away the gun and risked sitting down, reasonably sure the discovery of the shoes had brought enough life back to his legs that he would be able to get up. After brushing dirt and small embedded stones from his feet he pulled on the socks. The polyester felt scratchy, suffocating and hot against his tender skin, akin to wrapping plastic bread bags around his feet. He dug the tissue paper out of the shoes and slipped them on. They were at least three sizes too big and stiff as lumber. He laced them tight and lurched to his feet, giving them a trial run by flapping back and forth on the broken road. After a few steps he could feel potential hot spots growing on his feet, so he figured if he had to walk a mile back to the motel a host of blisters would blossom on his toes and heel, but blisters were better than bare feet considering where he had to walk.

Nelson followed the road until it led to another abandoned road, where he had to decide which way to continue. Both directions looked like they ended in a choke of weeds. The black buildings of the steel mill stood no closer than when he started. Could the new road be just a larger concentric circle of the one he had been walking? By definition concentric circles could not intersect, right? Did he walk an imprint of a spiral created by a tribe who built circular roads with no exits? The sunlight turned whiter, blanching the faint color of the field. The shoes felt leaden, like massive ingots tied to his feet, and he stumbled with every other step, causing him to take twice as many rests than when he had been barefoot. Sweat soaked through his shirt, dried, and soaked through again. His belt hung sodden, and rocks kept finding a way to jab through the bullet hole in the sole of the one new shoe. The road crumbled to dust and gravel, then all traces of its path vanished. He kept a straight line toward the buildings, dodging stray car tires, remnants of homeless shanties, and charred circles where fires had burned. His breath came in gulps, and his vision retracted to a distance no more than five feet in front of him. He kept his line by letting the heat push him, offering as little resistance as a walking man could against its flow.

Another road, newly paved, sliced through the field. The new paint of the white edge lines and a broken yellow line in the middle gleamed in both directions. Nelson scanned both ways but each way seemed to lead directly to nowhere or one direction acted the mouth and the other a tail and somewhere unseen the mouth swallowed the tail. Nelson eased himself to the pavement, knowing that without a pint of water and a rally from his increasingly leaden legs his chances of standing again were dim. He lay on the road, but when his cheek touched the burning surface and the smell of baking tar flooded his nostrils, he revived enough to roll to the side in a stubble of weeds, where he lost consciousness.

He awoke to the rumble of an engine idling near his head and his shoulder being jerked back and forth by a large mitt of a hand.

"Wake up! Wake up! How close are you to being a corpse?"

Nelson couldn't bring himself to open his eyes. The voice sounded deep and old.

"C'mon, let's get you in the car. I can't leave you out here to die in the weeds."

The giant fingers pawed at Nelson's shoulders until they found a grip and pulled him across the asphalt to an open car door. With a heave and a grunt Nelson landed on the seat, knocking his skull against something hard and unforgiving. The hands bent his legs and jammed them under the dash. A door, large and long, slammed shut. Suddenly, the voice barked on the other side of his head.

"Where can I take you?"

Nelson heard the words, but he didn't realize they formed a question and that at some point the man expected him to formulate an answer.

"I bet my wife can fix you up better than a hospital."

"Thanks, Jack," Nelson whispered.

"Name's not Jack, friend. Never has been."

"Take me to the Wander Inn."

"Ooooo booy. You are a down and outer. The only creatures I've ever seen walking out of the Wander Inn are whores and corpses, and you, if you wished to look in a mirror, are probably a few steps closer to the second than the first. But I wouldn't suggest it- looking in the mirror that is- because an image can warp your sensibility, make you think times are more desperate or more beautiful than they really are. Keep an image of the last time you looked good in your head and it'll get you through. And imagine me, driving leisurely down a newly paved road, a smooth track that's highly unlikely and so tragically transitory up here in the North with freezing and thawing ground. I find a man lying face down in the dirt and I'm thinking I found another body but this man revives and wants to be taken to the funeral home of the dispossessed. I want my wife to check you over. She has a talent for nursing. You've involved me and now I've got to resolve my conscience one way or another. If my wife can't help you then nobody can. I can't be wondering at night what happened to that one stray I found in the dirt. I'm not going to be looking for a little blurb in the back of the Metro section that tells the truncated story of another unidentified corpse hauled out of the Wander Inn. I need to be absolved of this."

Nelson open his eyes but darkness rushed in from all sides. He regained consciousness in the middle of a song.

Find me a place where the trees grow high,
Find me a place where the bushes don't die,
Find me a place where the rent is low,
Find me a place where my liver won't glow.

Is this place near or far?
Can this place be reached by plane or car?
It doesn't matter in the least to me,
Because I have a pension.

Nelson carefully cocked open an eye and watched the man seated behind the wheel finish the tune. The man sensed Nelson had awakened and turned his head toward him.

"Welcome back. Friend, you are quite the mess."

"What day is it?"

"The question is do you remember what day it was when you started losing time?"

"What?"

"What day did you check into the Wander Inn?"

"I don't know. Friday?"

"Exactly, so when I tell you it's Wednesday I imagine it won't make much sense since you have no frame of reference."

"I have business. Important....very....very....important."

"There's no more business! Money is dead! Nobody makes a goddamn thing anymore. No work! It's just you and me and my pension."

"There's business. My business.....there's the circuit and the dogs."

"Well, of course, we can't forget about the circuit and the dogs." The man nodded in affirmation as the car shuddered under the growing torque of the racing motor. "I find the circuit very oppressive."

Nelson began to collect and process images in an orderly pattern that looked not unlike a crude black and white television screen receiving programs through a coat hanger. He sat on a front bench seat patterned after massive couches slung into faux wooden dens. An opened pack of cinnamon gum lay in the ashtray. The smell reminded him of his dad's truck and the car trips that began with resolve and purpose but ended always with a paper bag wrapped around a bottle of Jim Beam. Trips to the dingy Kmart to buy cheap fishing poles and to the bait shop to buy thick night crawlers when the rain hadn't coordinated its fall with the setting sun. Family-time pantomimes used to mask the true purpose of their mission. Nelson would content himself to jamming stick after stick of cinnamon gum into his mouth until he had a chaw resembling a baseball player's wad of tobacco. The can of night crawlers sat in the bed of the pickup until the dirt dried and the worms resembled scraps of unused string.

"Do you know the circuit?" Nelson asked.

"No, no, can't say that I do. Just making conversation. I've heard it's quite oppressive.

"It's not oppressive."

"That's not what I've heard."

"Once something is done, once there is closure, the circuit is complete."

"There are open circuits. Broken circuits. And the purpose of the circuit is repetition. Electrical charges bouncing back and forth until the conductors just plain wear out. It's simple oppression."

"But there is clarity. Understanding your purpose as a small electrical charge."

"Broken engagements, broken marriages, bankruptcies, broken arms, disunity, chaos and war. That's how human life operates, through a fog of

ificial circuits smashed by our lust, greed and violence. Circuits?
You probably wear a wrist watch as well. Feeble!"

son's neck slackened and the back of his head landed on the headrest,
the images he had delicately constructed. His thoughts went brown.
When his eyes opened again a chipped white coffee cup and saucer filled to
the brim with coffee and a swirl of cream rested close to his cheek, the steam
warming his face. A brilliant silver spoon lay cocked on the saucer, holding a
drop of coffee. Wisps of steam climbed over his head only to lose resolve and
dissipate. Raising his head and wiping the drool from his mouth he saw a red
and silver flecked linoleum table yawning in front of him and holding at bay
two ghastly pale heads, a man and woman, lurking behind coffee cups of their
own.

"We thought we lost you," the man said as he leaned over his cup.

"Did the dogs bring me here?"

The man and woman exchanged a meaningful look through the steam
of their coffee.

"What do you know about the dogs?" said the man as he raised himself
erect and cocked his head to one side, indicating suspicion and fear.

"Nothing. They attacked me and left me in a hole."

A cat landed on the table from below and skipped past Nelson's coffee,
brushing his hand. A piece of twine trailed from its mouth. Two others landed
on opposite shoulders of the woman and began licking her ears. Behind the
woman's head on the sink a tabby tilted its head under the faucet and caught
drips as they fell. Nelson shuffled his feet and caught the corner of a newspaper
lying flat under his chair. The section around his feet had not been stained,
but as he inspected the balance of the floor he saw areas darkened by urine
or holding tidy parcels of feces, covered in scraps of newspaper the cats had
clawed from the floor.

"We don't like talking about the dogs."

"No, that's not a topic we discuss much."

"They exist?"

"What put you in the hole?"

"Can't you hear them at night? They're massing. Something is afoot."

"I've been known to hallucinate," said Nelson

"Don't we all, son, don't we all."

"Bill says you like the circuit," said the woman without flinching as the
cats continued to tongue her ears.

"Like?"

"Doris, now don't put words in my mouth. I didn't say like."

"Yes, you did. You said this boy likes the circuit."

"You don't listen to what I say."

"Bill, I listen. I listen. All day I listen to your stories and your theories. I
can't help listening because you're always talking. What would I do if I didn't
listen? What would I do?"

"You'd find things to do, I'm sure."

"What does that mean?"

"You know perfectly well what it means."

A Persian cat, muddled through several generations of random cross-breeding, knocked four magazines to the floor from a pile of fifty scattered on the kitchen counter.

"You've always found things to do, haven't you Doris?"

"I've kept myself busy."

"Well, I brought the man here to be nursed. Take a look at him and make sure its nothing terminal. He looks like he's bled from several spots."

"It's not necessary. I'm sore….a little stiff and…."

"Unable to remain conscious for more than ten minutes at a time. Doris, take a look at him."

"Yes, it would really be for the best," said Doris as she set her cup down and shuffled to Nelson's side of the table. She pinched the collar of his coat and extracted it from his lap, throwing it on the chair next to him. Three cats jumped from the seat before the coat landed on them.

"There's a gun in the coat pocket, Bill. Our guest has brought a gun into our house."

"What do you expect of him? He's a man the dogs are after. I wouldn't expect kibbles to be in his pockets."

"True. Take off your shirt and scoot back from the table."

Nelson slid the chair on the floor and held his feet in the air until he found a spot for them to land free of shit and soaked newspaper. As he unbuttoned the shirt pulses of pain shot through his arms and pooled under his shoulder blades.

"You're sliced to ribbons."

Doris retrieved a dusty bottle of Mercurochrome and cotton balls from a cabinet and began dabbing the wounds, beginning with this neck.

"Bill, look at how tan our guest is. He must not be from around here."

"Do you ever wear a shirt?"

"I live in Florida."

"Shameful. A man walking around without a shirt on. Why do you need to be tan?"

Doris hit a deeper wound and Nelson gasped from the sharp pain. With steady fingers she pulled a shard of glass from his skin. Her papery, translucent hands looked even more ghostly against his darkened skin.

"Bill, he's simply cut to ribbons."

"How can you tell with all that tan?"

"I think it looks good."

"Of course you would."

"What does that mean?"

"You know perfectly well what it means."

"No, I don't."

"You've kept yourself busy"

"As I've told you."

"I remember a day, '58 or '59. It must have been '59 because I was driving a Pontiac. Smitty covered for me and I slipped out of the mill. It was winter and I remember driving through the snow. That horizontal snow that keeps coming at you. I suspected a few things. I wasn't blind and I had a pretty good nose when things were awry. I parked along the street five houses away and snuck through the backyards. I saw you. Don't think I didn't see you."

"You saw nothing," Doris said to Nelson's chest as she expertly worked on a series of nicks on his ribs.

"I saw it all. Never the same after that. Never the same."

"You didn't drive a Pontiac in '59. We didn't buy the Pontiac until '60. You were driving a Buick in 1959."

"No, that's ludicrous."

"Yes, when we bought the Pontiac we drove it to Indiana first thing. Forty miles an hour the whole way because you insisted on breaking the engine in the right way. That was 1960 because Mary just had little Mike and that's why we went down to Indiana, to see the baby."

"I remember the Pontiac in the snow."

"We had it five years! That's a lot of winter. You did drive it in the snow plenty of times." Doris had reached Nelson's belly and crouched on her knees to ensure a thorough inspection. Four cats began to lazily circle her legs, backs arched in anticipation of a friendly hand as they rubbed their faces on her stockings.

"I think you're right. I remember the Indiana trip."

"I hope you remember little Mike?"

"Do I remember little Mike?"

"Wasn't that the trip when we ate at that restaurant?"

"I kept telling them to take back the steak!"

"Take it back! Take it back! If I wanted it that bloody I would have killed it myself."

"Take it back!"

"Take it back!"

"Take it back!"

"We were a couple of six-shooters."

Doris straightened up and exchanged smiles with Bill who took a sip of coffee and frowned at it bitterness or at the fact it had gone cold. His face further collapsed as he withdrew the cup from his face.

"Still it was never the same after that day."

"What was never the same?"

"Us....this.....me."

"Did you have doubts about us?"

"How could I not, after what you did? It was shameful."

"You've had doubts all this time?"

"Not really doubts, not reservations, it was different...I was....ruined."

"I ruined you?"

Bill slid out of his chair and onto his feet. He jammed his hands in his pockets and began an aimless pace.

"Yes, you ruined me."

"What did I do? I never slept with the postman. I believe the man was a eunuch. The milkman was fat and smelled like cottage cheese. I was faithful."

"If you would have slept with that milkman. Then there would have been hell to pay. I wouldn't have been able to touch you after that. Isn't the world free of eunuchs? Doesn't seem possible in this day and age to have eunuchs roaming about. Of course, there are accidents and disease."

"If he would have thinned down he would have been a good looking man. He looked like....oh...who was it..."

"A lard ass."

"Hush...he looked like....Vic Damone."

"He was obese! Vic Damone! The milkman was three hundred pounds if he weighed a pound."

"OK, if he was thinner, then."

"He wheezed and huffed and damn did that man sweat."

An orange cat with a blind marbled eye chased its tail and fell over in confusion. Once on the ground it began chewing a corner of the newspaper on the floor.

"OK, OK, maybe he wouldn't have made a good looking man even if he was thinner."

"I can't imagine why you slept with him."

"I didn't. I've been sleeping with you all these years. "

"No? You didn't?"

"Of course not."

"It still doesn't make what you did any better."

"No, I suppose it doesn't," she said as she looked up at Nelson, "Take off your pants."

"That's not necessary."

"This is a full-service check-up. Do as Doris says."

Nelson slipped off the shoes and unbuckled his belt. He let the pants fall to his ankles and he stepped out of them. A handful of dirt fell to the floor also.

"Look at your legs. Nothing but cuts and scrapes. Take off the briefs," Doris said behind a clinical eye.

Nelson hooked his thumbs under the elastic waistband and slipped them down his legs. More dirt cascaded past his knees and ankles and landed in little piles at his feet. Once he kicked them off he steadied himself by holding the back of the chair. Doris began working on a red spot over his right hip.

Bill walked over to the refrigerator and swung open the door. Inside, the weak light cast its shine over mounds of opened envelopes, coupon books, advertisements, circulars, bundles of receipts bound together with rubber bands, check books, deeds, stock certificates, utility bills, tax returns, birth certificates, credit card offers, and Christmas cards of twenty holidays past. Dollar bills had been crushed, pressed and shaped into egg-like shapes and sat in a double row in the egg tray. Black and white photos of small children and infants were taped on the inside walls and on the interior of the door shelves, making a time-lapse film. Bill peered over the contents and found a carton of milk in the far corner. Cats from around the house had heard the refrigerator door open and began massing at his feet, on the counters, on the chairs, everywhere they thought might be an advantageous spot for the culling of a scrap of food or a lick of milk. Bill swished the milk, listening closely to the splashing sounds before opening the top and smelling for sourness. He grimaced, smelled again, and drank straight from the carton. After two swigs he poured the rest in a bowl and set it on the counter. Two cats, a black-and-white and an orange were winners of the lottery. They dove at the milk and growled together to ward off any interlopers. Yowls of protest came from the losers who paced away their fury and anguish across the floor before leaving to the places from whence they had come.

Doris picked up Nelson's penis and inspected its underside. She lifted his testicles and cleaned it all thoroughly. The clinical hand hesitated and with an exploring index finger she traced the length of his penis, then rotated her hand, fingers underneath, thumb on top, and stroked from base to head. Nelson felt the first stirrings of an erection. He looked at Bill who stared at the floor at the disappointed cats who straggled and turned up their best begging faces to him.

"What did she do?" Nelson felt the words come out moist and heavy.

The hand jumped to his thigh. Bill looked at him, annoyed that Nelson had interrupted his reverie.

"What did you say?"

"What did Doris do? In 1959. What did she do?

"That's a mighty personal question, son."

"You brought it up.

"He always brings it up." Doris' breath skimmed across his thighs.

"It was 1959. I was driving a Pontiac…"

"Buick."

"Buick. Toomer covered for me and I slipped out of the mill. It was winter and I remember driving through the snow. A strange vertical snow that smacks you on top of the head. Black snow and new snow. Slush and grime and the whitest of powder this side of Aspen. I suspected a few things. Things, as they say, were not right. I parked along the street five houses away and snuck across the backyard. A dog was barking, standing up to his neck in snow. The drifts were five, six feet high…"

"Impossible," Doris interjected as she caressed Nelson's inner thighs as close to his genitals as she could come without touching them.

"...two, three feet high. My socks were wet. I remember thinking you had taken a shine to the milkman because you said he looked like Victor Mature..."

"Right! Why was I thinking about Vic Damone? Was it the butcher who looked like Vic Damone?"

"So I snuck home and crept up the stairs thinking that if the milkman looks like Victor Mature I should have brought a gun. I'm still in my mill dungarees and my face is smudged black. I look like a real monster from the pits of hell. Completely out of place in the house walking through the furniture we bought on the lay-away plan and up the new carpet I laid myself on the stairs. But I saw you. I saw you. Don't think I didn't see you."

As Doris continued working down his legs wisps of her hair brushed against the tip of his penis.

"You saw nothing," she said to Nelson's feet.

"I saw you standing there. Naked. Fresh from the bath. No towel. Naked. Even though it's winter and the house never stayed that warm. No goddamn insulation. You're standing in front of the mirror singing to yourself. It was a tune we both liked. Your hair was wet. This was before the kids so your body was your own. So young, fresh and clean. New skin. You sat on the bed with your back to me. A perfect back. Now, just the top of the crack of your butt visible over the covers. You get lotion from a jar, raise a leg and stroke yourself, the length of your legs, slowly, inspecting, analyzing, enjoying the lean muscle. Then the other leg. I can feel your humidity and smell freshly lathered soap. There I am standing in the doorway in cold and wet socks, wearing mill dungarees with a dirty face, feeling every inch the monster, the intruder. It's a wonder you didn't smell me, hear my breathing. You had a separate life, an internal, beautiful life. I slunk back down the stairs like a miserable slug. I didn't even have the gumption, the will, to bed you whether or not I was stained by the mill. I should have spread your legs and dirtied all that lotion and soap. But I crawled away."

"What did you expect?"

"I didn't expect from there on in to think about you naked and clean while I'd slave away in that mouth of hell. Everyday, I'd think of you. I'd think, maybe she's at that moment singing to herself, sitting on the bed, rubbing lotion on her thighs."

"Everyday?"

"Everyday. Maybe at noon when I'm choking down a goddamn bologna sandwich, the image of you might come to mind and I'd be ruined."

"You didn't like bologna?"

"Hated it. I would think how I'd rather be with you than in that pit. As I walked through the smoke with sparks raining down upon me, jumping rivers of molten steel, always aware that one misstep could lead to death or disfigurement, I thought it an appropriate place to work given my state of mind. I was given that glimpse of you, so young and smooth and perfect, as punishment. It's a wonder I didn't kill myself in the mill, not because of suicide, even though that did cross my mind a few times, but it's surprising I lived because it wasn't a place you wanted to think about anything else but survival. For thirty years I thought of you naked and wet and singing while I was in the belly of the beast. That is ruin and rot."

"That's a beautiful story, Bill," Doris said as she wiped away tears.

"What? You think my story of torture is beautiful?"

"You were thinking of me."

"I was nuts. I was obsessed. Thirty years. What kind of life is that? Now, I'm here and you're no longer young and I haven't seen you naked in ten years and you're always in that housecoat screeching at me."

"I think it's beautiful."

"Of course, devils always think their torture is beautiful. It's beautiful because you were the agent of my ruin."

"Oh dear, look at that," Doris said as she pointed at Nelson's very erect penis. All human eyes and even a few cat's eyes looked to Nelson's groin and considered the penis for a moment. Nelson looked away first, casting his eyes toward the sink where in the nook underneath lay an exhausted Siamese, a new mother who chomped on a mass of placenta as her six kittens bobbed their slick heads for the first time.

"Jesus, do you have something to say for yourself. That woman is old enough to be your grandmother."

"It's lovely, Bill."

"Get your fill."

Doris grabbed the base of his cock and her head started to move toward the tip. Nelson leapt backwards, but she held on. The force of his leap pulled her forward and as she fell she reasserted her grip and pulled him down. Both of his feet had landed on piles of cat shit so she easily brought him to his knees, given that he couldn't secure his footing. She put his cock in her mouth before he could decide what to do.

"Let her get her fill. It's not going to kill you."

Bill stalked off behind Nelson, who watched the pink scalp underneath Doris' wispy cloud of white hair as it bobbed up and down. Nelson expected his cock to go limp from disgust or shame but Doris' technique kept it firm. He closed his eyes and imagined a woman sitting on a bed, her back to him stroking lotion on her arms and legs. First one leg in the air, then the other, revealing a tender pink labia crowned with a tuft of hair. The woman resembled Jules, a perfect, mute Jules, momentarily content and rested, free of drugs, neurosis and the irresistible urge to vomit her meals. Perfect hips. Her head turns and she acknowledges his voyeurism with a wink.

The room cleared of cats, except for the newly born kittens and their mother. Bill had somehow pied-pipered them to another room. Doris kept a balance between keeping him erect and making him cum until she developed a crick in her neck some fifteen minutes later. Then, with a flurry of strokes and licks she had him cum in her mouth. She wiped the saliva and ejaculate from her lips and chin.

"Oh look! Pearl had her babies! Help me up dear. I have to get Pearly some milk for all her hard work."

Nelson yanked on his clothes and as he buttoned the second-to-last button of his shirt Bill returned, followed by a troop of cats walking behind him in a ragged line. Bill dropped treats as he walked. Every time one would drop a cat would catch it, break from the line and slowly chew it to paste.

"So, Pearly has dropped her load!"

"Six beauties, Bill"

Bill walked over to Doris and engulfed her in a bear hug. He gave her a long passionate kiss. Nelson suppressed a flutter of nausea at the thought of Bill tasting his cock on his wife's lips.

"I'm running out of names. We're going to have to start using numbers."

"Look, I have to be going. I need you to drive me to the motel."

"Well, wham, bam, thank you ma'am"

"I have business."

"I'm sure my wife was looking forward to having that in her pussy sometime tonight."

"What day is it?"

"I told you, we don't keep track of those kind of things around here. I've had enough Mondays and Sundays to fill two lifetimes."

"I'm sure I'm late."

"Can't stand in the way of progress."

"I am disappointed, Bill."

"Of course you are. I didn't think I was bringing home a business man."

"I just need to get back to my motel."

"The Wander Inn. I remember. C'mon Rockefeller. Can't keep the shareholders waiting."

"I just need to get back."

"Some gratitude. I pick you up half-dead by the road and you treat my wife like a whore."

"Don't forget I nursed him too."

"You look like a new man."

"His penis tasted like dirt."

"You might want to spare me a few details. Let's go before Doris starts crying."

Nelson followed Bill through a doorway toward the front of the house. Across the threshold the room narrowed into a serpentine path not quite three feet wide. The walls were towers of paper in all forms, newspaper, cardboard, parchment, circulars, utility bills, pension checks uncashed, social security checks, dollar bills, five dollar bills, ten dollar bills, hard cover books, paperbacks and books with no covers, magazines, catalogs, reams of unopened copier paper, notebooks, diaries, phone books, milk cartons, egg cartons, cereal boxes crushed flat, layered in a solid construction from floor to ceiling. Dim light from naked overhead bulbs illuminated small burrows cut in the tower facing, large enough for solitary cats to sleep. Yellow, green and blue eyes blinked awake as they passed, revealing the room to be a vast cliff-dwelling community. In a crevasse off the main path sat a black-and-white television and an overstuffed armchair. Nelson choked on the stench of moldering paper, but the chair looked surprisingly free of debris and cat hair. An antennae made of several coat hangers straightened and twisted together at their ends snaked its way up one of the paper towers from the television to the ceiling where it had been taped several times with black electrical tape. They turned three more corners. A set of color photographs, faded to a point just between full color and sepia, had been taped on another tower from the floor to about eye level. The photo series contained a start to finish documentation of a western driving trip sometime in the last two years of the 60s. A picture of dawn in front of the very house where Nelson now stood, three children clustered around a young, shapely Doris in cat eye glasses with first light tinting their faces as they look both exhausted and expectant. The same grouping in front of Mount Rushmore, standing in the Badlands wearing Indian headdresses, in front of Devil's Tower, in front of a spouting Old Faithful, in front of a family of bears eating marshmallows tossed from the windows of passing cars, in front of a pool connected to a roadside motel, Doris modestly clad in a one piece bathing suit but revealing enough of a body worthy of being called torture, a blurry coyote running across the frame, miniature moose eating grass in a meadow, the orange glow of a magnificent dawn inexpertly caught on film, the family in the pool, a motel room before the family settled in for the night, a random woman bending over on the periphery of a view of a river valley, the family wearing cowboy hats, a cactus reaching toward the clouds, the family on ponies staked to the ground, the family in Las Vegas huddled underneath a sign for the Tropicana, a private moment of Doris in the car applying lipstick, and finally a picture of the car, a 1968 Oldsmobile Delta Eighty-Eight alone and dusty back in the driveway of the house.

Nelson broke into sunlight and found himself standing on the front porch. The cats that had trailed them stopped at the threshold and turned back as Nelson and Bill crossed the porch and continued toward the car. Once Bill started the engine and pulled the gearshift into reverse, he gave Nelson a piercing, analytical look.

"The day a man turns down pussy he may as well just climb back into the hole he came from."

"You know about the hole?"

"What are you talking about?"

"The hole. The hole the dogs put me in."

"You told me about that."

"Yes, but did you know about it before I told you?"

"I've had enough of this wordplay. Doris is very disappointed."

Bill released the brake and the car lurched backward. Once in the street, he cranked the steering wheel hard to straighten the wheels and they sped off toward the Wander Inn.

"I saw the pictures of Doris hanging on the…wall…she was beautiful."

"All the more reason to give her what she wants. Look what she lost."

"Yes, but…"

"It wouldn't have killed you."

"No."

"You could have showed a little gratitude."

"I know. I have business. Maybe I'll come back."

"Why are you still talking? Rubbing salt in the wound?"

"No."

"I'll have hell to pay tonight. Thanks to you."

Nelson suddenly couldn't muster the energy to ask what form hell would take. He felt the apertures of his eyes closing to pin holes before his brain processed the actual loss of light. He blinked awake, but his head bobbed. He tried to shake it clear but only managed to begin a dull headache.

"You were probably done for the day anyway. I'll tell Doris you couldn't even stay awake during the drive."

Unconsciousness came upon with the insidious force of anesthesia as all went dark and the engine rattle faded to silence.

"Get out of my car," Bill shouted as he shook Nelson's shoulder, rattling his head from side to side.

"What?"

"Get out. We're here."

"Where?"

"Son, what the fuck? What have you done to your brain? We're at your motel."

"I think I'm paralyzed."

"I've had more than my fill of you. Get out."

"I don't know if I can move."

"Jesus."

Bill jumped out of the car and walked with purpose to the passenger side where he yanked open the door and placed a no longer friendly hand on Nelson's shoulder.

"Get out."

'I want to, but…"

Two hands grabbed his jacket and with a violent jerk Nelson toppled out of the car. He landed on the gravel of the lot, still unable to coordinate his limbs or break his fall. Wheels spun through the gravel, pelting him with stones and the car disappeared in a cloud of slate gray dust. After the stones stopped bouncing and the dust, after a slow, meandering descent, finally settled, Nelson pushed himself to his hands and knees, then stood up and staggered to his room, resembling someone awakened from a deep sleep by the need to take a piss as they stumbled to the bathroom in pitch black. He touched every pocket of his clothes twice, but he couldn't find the room key. Then, after completing a third round he remembered the flimsy door lock, so he gave the door a feeble kick and it popped open without a splinter. He closed the door behind him and made sure it was locked and he even placed the tin hook back in the eyelet. Falling to the floor he retrieved the duffel of cocaine and crawled into bed. He wrapped his body around the canvas as if spooning a tiny, coarse woman and fell to sleep almost immediately. His last conscious thought settled on Doris by the pool, wet and smiling for the camera with children and cats at her feet.

*   *`                    `*

Nelson slept until the crickets had tired and sat mutely between blades of grass, some twelve hours after his head had hit the pillow. He still held the cocaine against his body and he had nuzzled his cheek into a fold of the duffel. He rolled to his back and blinked at the ceiling. His body felt as if it hadn't moved the entire twelve of hours of sleep, temporarily atrophied into an S, but thoughts tumbled through his mind at a pace faster than normal. So, with a quick, logical progression informed by a catalog of sensory information, he realized he had missed his appointment, meaning that the operation had sent emissaries to look for him, to find him and in all probability to kill him. The question he now posed orbited the terrifying reality of the shipment being past due, but how many days, and had he entered a sliding scale of punishment based on the lateness of the delivery? Had he given Gutterman enough time to track and catch him? He tried to blink away his decision to walk to the bar. Stay in the room. Watch the clock tick by second by second. Concentrate on the earth's rotation and the slow rising of the sun. Reel back the hours and change the decision. Stay in the room.

He eased himself off the bed and plodded into the bathroom, where he pissed in the dark, splashing the floor and the back of the bowl with a thick rope of urine colored with a trace of blood. After washing his hands under a trickle of lukewarm water, he patted his pockets in search of his car keys. Pants, jacket, pants, and then again. Jumping over to his discarded clothes in the corner of the room, he shook them, hoping to hear the familiar rattle of key against key. He heard nothing but the dry rustle of cotton clothing being shaken and the clink of a few coins bouncing together. His hands burrowed into every pocket, and when he found nothing but the coins, he slammed the shirt, then the pants, then the socks, then the underwear, to the carpet. The violent swings ended with soft and completely unsatisfying thuds near the wall. He yanked the drawer of the nightstand completely out and turned it upside down. A Tic Tac and a receipt to Arby's fell to the floor. Retracing his steps to the bathroom he switched on the light and looked at every crevice, including the shower, toilet tank and under the sink. Returning to the side of the bed, he lifted the duffel off the mattress and gently set it out the floor. Then, he ripped off the covers and shook them. The comforter, sheets, and pillows flew through the air and landed in a jumble over his dirty clothes. No keys.

Standing near the doorway, hands on hips, Nelson gave the room one last scan as the rate of his breathing began to quicken. As a last gesture he rifled through his suitcase even though he knew he would never think of depositing the keys inside such a logical place. Finally convinced the keys could not be found in the room, he slipped out of the door. In the darkness he couldn't tell if they were in the ignition so he retrieved a brick from a patch of dead weeds near the back of the building and smashed the rear driver's side window. It sounded like a small grenade had been detonated and Nelson waited until the echo died on its way down the valley until he reached in and unlocked the door. The keys were not in the ignition, so he searched the glovebox, the floor mats, the loose visor, the crevices of the seats, underneath the seats by groping with a blind hand, the dashboard and then all again before he remembered he had a small toolbox in the trunk of the car, courtesy of Otter, who told him a dozen times that a million dollars could be lost for the lack of a screwdriver.

Nelson popped the trunk by pressing a switch on the dash. Otter hadn't thought of packing an extra set of car keys, but Nelson did find a hammer and screwdriver which he used to hack apart the steering column, peeling the plastic away to expose the wiring. He yanked on what he thought might be the ignition wires and connected them together. Nothing happened. He pulled them apart and then touched them again. He connected the headlight wire to the ignition wires, but the car still sat dead. Twining the wiper wire with the headlight wire to the ignition wires caused an electrical shudder as if the car had caught a chill, but the starter did not crank. Stripping the radio wires, wrapping them around the headlight wire, connecting those to the ignition wires and using the wiper wire as a ground made the dome light flicker. He massed the wiper wire, headlight wire, ignition wires, radio wire, antennae wire, blinker wire, and dome light wire together in a lump, but the car sat mute. He jumped out and opened the hood, pulling at any wires or belts he could find. He checked the battery connection to make sure it remained secure, but he knew he had just killed the car. He slammed down the hood and lit a cigarette. He would call a taxi.

The old problem of a working phone returned. The bar would not be open for a couple of more hours when breakfast vodka would start flowing and he didn't want to give the motel clerk another look at him should the police or Gutterman ask for a description, so he tried the knob of the adjacent room with his gun drawn. The door popped open with a hard twist. The place sat empty except for two spent whiskey bottles and the smell of humid, dead air. On the wall hung a phone jack but no phone. Nelson retraced his steps and tried the door to the next room. He had to use his shoulder to produce enough force to open it but it gave way after three times. A heavy scent of sex had been trapped in the room for a week and it came rushing past him when he opened the door. A broken lamp lay in the middle of the floor and a perfect handprint made by painting lipstick over the palm and fingers of a slender hand hung on the wall just above the headboard. On the nightstand sat a base of a phone and a cord dangling to the floor and terminating on the carpet, but with no receiver. No jack hung on the wall, or any trace there had ever been one on the wall. He carried the phone base to the first room with the jack and returned to try the third door. Her shouldered the door as he had with the previous one, but it caught on a deadbolt much stronger than the hook and eye of his room. Looking around at the parking lot he saw only his mutilated car. Drawn curtains masked the windows of the room. Tapping the gun on his forehead as he paced in front of the door, he thought about his options: kicking the door down, knocking politely or giving the clerk another look at his face and the chance for him to ask for another night's rent, or week's rent or however many days he had been away. A different clerk may be on duty than the afternoon he had checked in, but the likelihood the motel had more than one employee seemed slim.

He knocked sharply with a knuckle. No answer. He used a knuckle again, waited a minute, then pounded with a fist. Another minute passed with no sound coming from the room. Nelson kicked the door hard, three, four times. The frame cracked with a small splintering sound on the fourth kick. A light popped on in the room. Feet padded to the window and the curtain was pulled aside the width of an eye. The light went off. Nelson knocked again.

"Give me your phone receiver," he ordered calmly in a forced baritone.

"What?" squealed the occupant. Nelson couldn't tell if the voice came from a man or woman.

"I said, give me your phone receiver."

"I don't have a cell phone."

"I didn't say cell phone. I want the receiver from the phone in your room."

Something fell to the floor that sounded like it broke when it hit.

"OK, I've got it."

"Open the door and give me the receiver."

"I don't have any money."

"Why else would you be staying here?"

"I don't have anything to take."

"I want the phone receiver."

The feet came to the door again. Nelson could hear the occupant breathing on the other side. He paused, hand on the deadbolt, as it rattled with a tremor. The deadbolt slid back and the door opened far enough for the hand to hold out the phone receiver with a cord hanging from its end.

"That's all I need," Nelson said as he reached over and took the receiver from the still shaking hand.

"AT&T thanks you. If you have any suggestions concerning our service please call our customer care line."

He assembled the parts in the second room and a dial tone surprised him. Opening the drawer of the night stand he found a fairly new phonebook and looked up taxi services. He picked the largest ad with the best graphics, a sleek looking cab slicing through the city streets like a rocket. Dialing the phone, increasingly excited as each number he pressed worked and sensing a kernel of relief glowing deep within his chest, he raised the gun and pointed it at the open door, hoping in a small way that someone might try to enter, to try to stop him from completing the task so that the growing sense of elation could find expression in a fired bullet. The operator told him a cab would pick him up within ten minutes.

Throwing the duffel over his shoulder he paced in the room, checking twice to make sure the whiskey bottles were indeed empty. He decided to stash the gun back in his jacket pocket and zip it closed. The cocaine weighed three times as much as it did the previous day as his knees wobbled as the full weight pushed down his spine. He shut his door and the doors to the rooms he had broken into, as well as his car doors, all four of which had been left open so that the car looked like a flightless bird with an extra pair of useless wings.

An orange taxi cab pulled into the gravel lot and slowly rolled to where Nelson stood by his car. The driver opened the passenger side window and leaned over the seat to get an unobstructed view of Nelson.

"Car trouble?" said the driver as his smile betrayed the wariness he felt.

"You could say that."

"Where do you want to go?"

"Are you going to let me in the car?"

"I just asked where you want to go."

"5992 Maypole Avenue."

"What was that?"

"5992 Maypole Avenue."

"Quit fucking with me. You can't take a cab there."

"Why not?"

"Are you fucking stupid or crazy?"

Nelson reached out and pulled at the door latch but the door had been locked. He aimed his hand to the door lock on the inside, but the driver hit the automatic window button and the glass had risen just high enough to block his fingers.

"Let me in!"

"No fucking way am I going to be involved in that," the driver shouted, but most of the force of the voice was muffled by the glass as he slammed the accelerator to the floor, causing the car to jump away from Nelson's hand.

Nelson fumbled for the gun and by the time he had extracted it, the hammer having caught somewhere inside the pocket, the cab had made a wide arc in the parking lot, kicking up stones as it went, and its brake lights flashed briefly as it entered the deserted road. Nelson raised the gun and aimed but stopped himself from taking a wild shot that would serve very little purpose.

He marched to the occupied room, walking in not a particularly straight line because of the weight of the duffel. At the door he took three deep breaths and kicked it open with one vicious kick. He jumped into the room and grabbed at the spot where the light switch should have been based on the layout of his room. By luck the builders had maintained some consistency and the room exploded in light. On the bed someone with hair down to their shoulders cowered underneath a sheet.

"That was all the phone I had!"

"I don't want more phone."

"Don't shoot me. Please don't shoot me. I don't have anything."

"Do you have a car?"

"No, no, I don't"

"How did you get here?"

"We came in a van. Log has it. I don't know where he is."

"When will he be coming back with the van?"

"Late. When he gets going there's no telling."

"It's already late. It's almost early. Shouldn't he be coming back soon?"

"There's no telling."

"Really? Well, you and I are going to wait until Log returns with the van. Get dressed and ready to go. Take me where I want to go and nobody gets shot."

When the occupant crawled out of bed Nelson saw he possessed a body of all elbows, knees and cock, adorned with a series of tattoos up either leg and down both arms. His pale, thin, torso without hair or ink looked like a trapped soft animal inside a blue, green and red cage. Three or four piercings in his cock and scrotum glinted in the harsh light. The kernel of hope born by the working phone had been extinguished and Nelson thought of a silver piercing the size of a javelin thrust through his heart, adorning his beautiful corpse.

The man slipped on a black t-shirt, black underwear and faded and ripped jeans. Then he laced up a pair of massive work shoes with unbendable soles. After dressing he stood against the wall near the nightstand, his hand fluttering about, looking for a comfortable spot to land.

"What's your name?" Nelson asked as he stood in the middle of the room, the strap of the duffel creating a crease in his shoulder.

"Treg."

Nelson spotted a tiny dinette set framed by the window, consisting of a circular table that looked like it could barely hold two coffee cups without saucers and two metal folding chairs, nicked and pocked with rust. He dragged one of the chairs to a spot on the floor where he could watch the door and the bed and dropped the duffel next to the chair as he sat down heavily, nearly toppling over backwards before he righted his balance.

"Sit on the bed, Treg."

Treg complied quickly and jammed his hands under his thighs, palms downward.

"Who is Log?"

"He's what's left of my band. We started out from Madison with five but we've lost three along the way."

"On the way to where?"

"We've been touring. Been on the road for three months."

"What happened to the other three?"

"They took off. No note, nothing. They left the van and their amps. Fuckers. Now, Log and I have no choice but to play acoustic shit until we find a drummer. People hate that shit. People want to throw shit at you when you bring out an acoustic."

"You work for Gutterman?"

"We don't have a label."

"Zune?"

"No," said Treg as he realized working for either would garner a bullet or a beating. "I don't know those people."

"So, you thought you'd splurge on a hotel tonight? Is that your story?"

"This is splurging?" Treg looked around his shabby room. "Besides, I've slept in a van with an amp in my back for two months straight."

"I thought you were on the road three months."

"The first month we stayed in motels until the money ran out and we needed to use the gig money for gas and sometimes food."

"What's the name of your band?"

"When we started out we called ourselves Free Fall Stooges, but that was when we had a fucking great rhythm section. When they took off we changed our name to Buttered Toast. We were kind of pissed so we took it out on ourselves. People hate that fucking name but managers of coffee houses seem to like it. We've been living off tips and free lattes. Girls will sometimes sneak us a stale croissant or some awful tasting shortbread, but it's enough calories to keep going."

Nelson stared at the pale face spotted along the chin with pimples. He withheld the urge to release his frustration on the boy's body, casting a complicated series of suppressions in the form of false patience and deep breathing over the need to commit violence. The look on his face must have released some of the urge because Treg grew increasingly nervous as the silence lengthened. Sensing some crack or impending collapse of Nelson's resolve, Treg tried to disarm him with a weak smile.

"You want a beer?"

"Sure. One beer."

Treg reached to the floor and twisted off a cap of a lukewarm beer, a lower rung domestic they had found for half-price at a wholesale store. Nelson took it from him and took a long, hard swallow.

"Logic, Treg, logic saved you from the grave."

"I always thought that, you know, logic," he said as he looked at the door for help that wasn't coming. "So, did that phone work OK?"

Headlights flashed in the window and the sound of tires on gravel trickled to a stop. A laboring engine shuddered off. A car door clicked open and then slammed shut, sounding like someone had closed a door of a giant tin can. Footsteps, first on gravel, then on the small patch of cement before the door. Nelson raised a finger to his lips as a signal for Treg to remain quiet as he pointed the gun at the door. In walked Log, a paler, thinner version of Treg, wearing all black with black-dyed hair hanging over his eyes, giving the general impression of a morose sheepdog. Nelson trained the gun on Log's stomach and waved him toward the direction of Treg. Log slunk over to the bed and sat down. Drawing his knees to his chest, his body collapsed into a small black spot. He pulled a small moleskin pad and a pen from his pocket and began writing furiously with jerky hand movements.

"Stop that," Nelson growled.

Log looked up briefly, then returned to his work.

"Stop that now."

Nelson aimed the gun at Log's chest. Log waved a hand weakly through the air as if dissipating a musty pocket of odor, but he didn't take his eyes off the pad. Treg nudged him with an elbow, recognizing the return of the deeply violent look on Nelson's face, and Log grunted in return. Nelson jumped to his feet and stalked over to him by the edge of the bed, glowering at the top of his black-dyed head and wanting to squeeze it until it exploded in red and gray through his clenched fingers.

"Give me the pad."

Nelson offered an open palm in front of Log's face. Log howled in fury and pain and lunged forward, trying to bite Nelson's hand with a full set of bared teeth. Nelson stumbled backward and pulled the trigger. An explosion shattered their senses as the bullet blasted away the top of Log's pen and lodged in the mattress. Ink covered his hand and dripped on the pad and to the floor. Log shut the pad, found the tattered cap on his lap and replaced the cap over the tip of the pen and then returned both to his jacket. He then cocked his head downward and stared at a small spot near Nelson's shoes. Blue sulfur smoke hung in the air and their ears rang from the concussion of the blast.

"Log, man, there's a time and place for poetry," Treg whispered.

Log stood up and walked toward the wall behind the headboard.

"Sit the fuck down!"

Log turned his back to Nelson and Treg, reached out his ink-stained hand and placed a nearly perfect palm print on the wall in indelible ink. The top knuckle and above of his middle finger had not printed, so that the line of his fingers looked ragged. Once done, he retuned to the spot next to Treg, inhabiting the same indentation his body had previously created.

"Do I not look desperate, you fucks? I could leave your goddamn corpses in this room so Gutterman could come and sodomize your cold dead assholes!"

"What is he talking about? Log asked Treg.

Treg shook his head, now convinced they would both be dead within minutes.

"You know what I'm talking about! I need a ride and you two assholes are taking me. It's simple. So goddamn simple. Don't write poetry. Don't fingerpaint. Just drive me to the fucking address and you won't die."

Log reached inside his jacket pocket, wetting his forefinger with fresh ink, and drew a thick, comic moustache on his upper lip, curving the ends toward his eyes.

"Now I'm in disguise. Maybe I'm the Gutterman. Maybe my moustache is a protective shield. Impervious to bullets. Shall we try?"

"Jesus Christ, Log, since when are you on a suicide trip?"

"That fucker shot my pen."

"Buy another pen."

"I wrote 'Driving with the Grotesque' with that pen and he just comes in here and blows it away."

"That's a good song. You know I like that song. Not really appropriate for Buttered Toast."

"God, I hate that name."

"Everyone hates it."

"Except for managers of coffee houses," Nelson chimed in.

"Exactly," they returned in unison.

"Get the fuck off the bed and get into the car."

"Van," Log corrected.

Nelson grabbed him by the back of the neck and pulled him to his feet. Treg followed and the three trooped out of the door, Nelson in the rear with the duffel over his shoulder.

"Give me the keys," Nelson said as he held out his hand again, raising the gun into Log's line of sight should he have the idea of biting him again.

"I drive," Log answered.

"Give me the keys. Treg is going to drive."

"I drive."

"We made a deal that Log is the driver."

"Right. Give Treg the keys."

"Dude, he almost killed me for a phone. Just do what the fuck he says."

Log reluctantly surrendered the keys. Treg slid behind the wheel as Log and Nelson entered through the sliding side door. The backseats had been taken out so the back of the van acted as cargo hold and bedroom. Two musty smelling sleeping bags, an opened bag of stale corn chips, a small pile of black underwear, three empty two liters of Coke, a ziplock bag of guitar picks and a novel with the cover torn off lay in a coffin-sized space in the middle of a collection of Marshall and Fender amps, electric and acoustic guitar cases, a battered drum set, a synthesizer, bundles of cords, and three microphones and stands. It smelled of burnt oil and soiled underwear as Nelson could tell the van hadn't been aired out since the tour began. Log sat in the front passenger seat and Nelson kneeled behind them on the sleeping bags with the gun pointed at an angle that would have sent a bullet through the floor and into the gravel lot.

The engine wheezed to life.

"Go downtown," Nelson commanded.

"Where's that?"

"How the fuck should I know? Look for big buildings."

Nelson had memorized the directions from the center of the city, a place called Public Square. From there he knew how many lefts, rights, and stoplights to go to find the drop location. The incongruity of knowing the directions by heart but having to write down the address had not been lost on him. His life had been riddled with examples of knowing the process but being unable to come up with a reasonable answer.

Log slid a CD into the dash player, obviously added long after the van had been manufactured. Screeching guitars and garbled moaning, products of a bad recording more than purposeful song construction, exploded out speakers that had been installed the length of the van. A synthesizer squealed and a bongo riff came up but drowned under the banging and smashing of another drummer who sounded like he played his set with his fists. Feedback warbled and whined. Treg found a freeway entrance and headed north, toward a small cluster of skyscrapers that looked green and sickly. Nelson let the music play because it kept the two quiet and focused on their task. The intensity of the sound increased and Treg steadily pressed on the accelerator until the roar of the engine blended with the song.

Nelson followed the serpentine path from Public Square to Montenegro's warehouse as if he traced a thick red line on a computer screen. Still unsure of the day, he didn't know how late he would arrive. Only under torture or the threat of torture or any concrete threat at all to his well being would he tell them about the dogs. Montenegro had to be the type to kill anyone for any reason and surely fantasy and tardiness both had to be high on the list. He could fashion a convincing series of misfortunes, a gun battle with Gutterman, striking a herd of deer with his car, falling in a deep hole and finding a man named Pez at the bottom. He would leave out the dogs. They would muddle his excuse. If he delivered the shipment intact. That had to be worth something.

In the distance a dark spot appeared in the road. The three saw it simultaneously, leaned forward and squinted to try to get an extra yard or two of sight from their eyes. Log lowered the music and Nelson raised his gun. Two more spots appeared and occupied the other two lanes. Treg eased off the gas and let the van coast. Nelson cocked his gun. Treg flipped on the brights and six yellow dots flashed as the beams hit three pair of eyes.

""They're dogs! Hit them! Hit them! It's the fucking dogs! Nelson screamed.

Log turned off the music as Treg applied some brake and weaved back and forth across three lanes. The dogs followed the movement of the van like cornerbacks shifting with a receiver.

"Don't fucking stop! Hit them! Hit them!"

Their speed steadily decreased.

"What are you talking about? They're dogs."

"I know! I know! Hit them! Don't stop. I still have bullets motherfucker. Don't stop!"

Nelson pounded his fist against the back of Treg's seat, the roof, the back of Treg's head. He stomped his feet and screeched with all the power of his lungs.

"I can't do it! I love dogs, man!"

Nelson fired two bullets through the roof, but the action had the opposite effect that he had been hoping for. Thinking the bullets must be cutting through him, Treg slammed on the brake pedal with both feet. The wheels locked and the van slid sideways, teetering on two wheels before bouncing to a stop between two lanes. Knocked to the floor, Nelson lost his gun. Treg fell into the passenger seat and lay on top of Log in a tight embrace. Nelson scrambled to a sitting position and a slow, inevitable black curtain slid across his vision. After a few moments his sight returned and with his left hand he found the rising knot above his eye and pushed against it. He squeezed behind the wheel. The van had stalled so he turned the ignition key. On the third try the engine started. Nelson gave a quick look out the window and in the side mirrors, but he couldn't see what had become of the dogs. He jammed the gear shift in drive and pressed the gas pedal to the floor. The tires managed a squeal and the van fishtailed down the road, at one point heading directly towards the guardrail with enough speed to crash through and end up in the valley below, but Nelson cranked the wheel hard to avoid it. Treg tried to stand but Nelson grabbed him by the belt and threw him on to the sleeping bags. Something clutched his sleeve. The dogs yanked Nelson toward the window and he had to grab the steering wheel to keep himself on the seat. His left arm had already been pulled past the plane of the window when he saw that a Maltese and a foxhound had a mouthful of his coat and were hanging from his arm against the side of the van. Driving with his knees he reached for the shoulder belt and clicked it in place. The cargo door had opened and a Chesapeake Bay retriever had crawled over Treg's legs toward Nelson. Treg, misinterpreting the dog's intent, kicked wildly at its face until it became angry and caught Treg's ankle in its mouth. A third, heavier mutt caught Nelson's arm, pulling him farther out the window, enough that his foot no longer could touch the pedals.

The van lost the speed it had been gaining. Treg was being pulled out of the door as the dog's teeth had broken through the skin. More dogs ran along beside the van and a chocolate lab, tail wagging, with enough speed and a good angle managed to jump through the open cargo door with the purpose of helping its mate with Treg's other ankle. Log spotted Nelson's gun resting against one of the amps. He scrambled over Treg whose arms were frantically searching for a secure hold to counteract the force of the pull. Log pressed the gun against the Chesapeake's chest and fired. Later he would remember the dog's eyes holding laughter before they were extinguished. The dog's body collapsed and rolled out of the van. The lab released its grip and followed the corpse. Log slid the cargo door shut and locked it.

The van rolled to a stop. Log aimed the gun at Nelson's back and pulled the trigger, but the act ended with a disappointing click as all the bullets had been shot. Two more dogs had taken hold of his sleeve. The coat pulled taut against his throat, effectively strangling him. He hooked his feet under the dash and let go of the steering wheel. He lurched further out the window. A dog sailed through the air and caught hold of a clump of his hair. The dog dangled momentarily before the clump ripped away from his scalp and the dog fell back to the ground. The pain gave Nelson a shot of strength so he found the zipper of his coat and ripped it down. Contorting his torso so that the weight of the dogs pulled the jacket off his shoulders, he freed his right arm. The dogs sensed they were losing position so their jaws found flesh and bone and they seized upon it. Nelson found he could touch the gas pedals and he pushed as far as his toes could reach. The van began to roll with even acceleration. The foxhound and mutt ran to keep up, but soon became airborne as the Maltese cast worried glances at the road as it rushed by below its feet. Nelson screamed in pain as the thought of his arm being ripped from his shoulder became a distinct and immediate possibility. The weight pulled him from the seat and his foot lost the pedal. The van began coasting. Nelson heard a click and looked over in time to see Log's ink stained hand releasing his shoulder belt. Suddenly, Nelson's head and shoulders hung outside the window and his back acted as a fulcrum on the edge of the door as the weight of the dogs bent him backwards.

A squeaky brake stopped the remaining momentum of the van. Nelson flipped out of the window but was fortunate in the fall as he landed on the four or five dogs attached to him. Their bodies broke his fall and the force of the landing knocked the air from their lungs and momentarily stunned them. Nelson regained his feet and opened the van door before Log could drive away. Nelson grabbed him by the shirt and pulled him to the road as he reclaimed the driver's seat. He ripped off his jacket, hanging by one arm, and threw it on the passenger seat. The dogs slowly revived as Log ran past to the cargo door and pounded with his fists until Treg let him in, just as Nelson had started to pull away.

The van sped to eighty miles per hour in a few moments. A few dogs tried to block the road again but Nelson purposely hit them and they died instantly on the grill of the van or under a tire, their bodies flung to the median or crushed. A great mournful howl echoed over the city. Started by the stray pack, the threnody soon gained steam from the domestics, dogs behind gates, lying on pillows, dogs fat and slow and unable to run without wheezing, dogs snoozing between their masters dreaming the same ancient dream that all dogs dreamed as they all walked to a window, a gate or door, and howled because a crushing sadness for the loss of irreplaceable life now dominated their thoughts.

Lights in the neighborhoods blinked on and a few bursts of angry protests and epithets came from the human beings living with them, but as spontaneously as it started, the lament ended with a crisp high note. The echo reverberated, then faded, but the emotion that hung in the air remained far from resolved.

"You think that many people would sing at your death?" Log pointed the question at Nelson.

"Not a one."

"We'll sing for you, sir, as Buttered Toast, if the news of your death is ignored."

"They won't kill me."

"You're as good as dead too, Log. You shot one," Treg reminded him.

"They didn't want you."

"Obviously, Treg will have to sing solo at both funerals. Call yourself Butter."

"Who the fuck are you?" Treg ignored Log's last comment because since Treg had come up with the Buttered Toast moniker, Log never missed a chance to remind him of it.

"You don't need to know who I am."

"What's in the bag?"

"Touch the bag and I'll kill you with my hands."

"I'm thinking its not boxers with shit stains, eh?"

Log found the zipper and pulled it enough to fit two fingers through the seam. When he touched the plastic and could feel the powder underneath he withdrew his hand like he had touched a piece of broken glass. Sweat had made the ink moustache run so now he looked like he had a shaggy goatee or like he had attacked and eaten a creature with black blood. He told Treg through a complicated series of pantomimes what he had found in the duffel. Treg rolled his eyes and moved away from the bag and stared through the holes Nelson had shot in the roof. Log curled up much like a potato bug, staring at the bag but being unable to reconcile its existence in his life. Treg hoped by being silent and still he could avoid further notice and execution. If it wasn't for all the equipment, he would have jumped to the pavement no matter how fast the van moved. It had taken him years to accumulate enough equipment to outfit a band through a series of dishwashing, car washing, landscaping, painting and roofing jobs, so he couldn't leave the treasure just to start the accumulation all over again.

Nelson unfolded the map in his mind and followed a path of six left turns, four right turns, a circle and a dead end street, an alleyway squeezed between two warehouses where once ladies' garments had been sewn. At the end of the alleyway a rutted gravel road turned to the left and the van scraped past overgrown bushes, gnarled and brown from carving out a brief life in the city. After splashing through three craters filled with opaque brown water, they came to a squat black building with a beaten and rust-pocked door. On the side of the building a ghost of a painted sign clung to the brick, announcing the building as the new home of Charles Waverly Chocolates, Smooth and Dark Chocolate Treats. Filigree framed the words and a large mustachioed head missing eyes and half of its mouth, no doubt the once idealized visage of Charles Waverly himself. Tall arched windows that once let sunlight pour over the shoulders of Waverly workers had been bricked up so the building sat black and mute, unable to tell him who might be inside.

Nelson stopped the van and turned off the engine. He tried to smooth the wayward ends of his hair over the small bald patch with little luck. His arm bled, but the jacket could cover the wound. The jacket, unfortunately, had several tears running up the sleeve and the seam along the back had all but burst. The tears seemed preferable to blood so Nelson put it back on. Jumping out of the seat he pocketed the keys and ran to the cargo door. Log opened the door and handed him the duffel. Nelson threw it over his shoulder, tried to tuck in his shirt, hitched up his pants and dug the underwear out of his crack. The shipment remained intact and that would count for something. He would show up late and torn up, but he had somehow been successful. Montenegro would release him from further deliveries once he saw his disheveled state, no doubt. Who would ever trust him with something of value?

Walking to the door, he noticed both of his shoes had become unlaced, but he didn't bother to stop and tie them. He knocked on the metal and the door swung open without a sound, revealing a huge, barren room lit by a series of dim twenty-five watt bulbs hanging by long cords from the ceiling. It smelled of paint and mortar. The floor had been newly poured and painted dark gray so the surface was slippery smooth. The walls had been scrubbed clean and repointed. Nelson continued walking and the heels of his hard shoes sounded like a chain being whipped against concrete as he walked. He tried to call out but words ended in a knot at the top of his throat. He stopped, afraid his knees would give way, and he reached out a hand but found nothing to hold in his immediate vicinity. He caught himself in a crouch and leaned his elbows heavily on his knees until a pulse of strength returned. When he stood up he saw a dim ghost of a stool squatting on the floor some thirty feet in front of him. He checked the impulse to light a cigarette, considering the importance of having both hands free and not carrying a burning object that could so quickly be turned against him.

He circled the stool twice, first in a circle of about fifteen feet in diameter and then halving it so that his approach looked like a last spiral, before he stepped close enough to see an envelope lying on top of the seat. He picked it up and weighed it in his hands before opening it. It seemed to weigh nothing more than the envelope itself but Nelson hooked a finger under the flap and ripped a ragged line across the top. A single yellow post-it note sailed to the floor. He bent over and picked it up. In typewritten letters the note read:

Never wear another man's shoes,
Never bite more than you can chew,
Never make me wait.

-J. Montenegro

Nelson let the note fall to the floor and then threw up a pint of stomach acid on his shoes and the floor. He wiped his mouth, but his stomach clenched in another spasm, forcing him to his hands and knees. After four more spasms his stomach settled, satisfied that anything offensive had been pushed out. He smeared the beads of sweat across his forehead with the torn sleeve of his jacket and he picked up the note again, the edge now soaked with his vomit. He read it again, but found no hidden hope, no possibility of reprieve. He flipped it over and on the backside it read:

Nelson, we've missed you.

-Dog

Nelson jumped to his feet and ran in a sprint toward the back of the building, but he found only a remnant of a garage door long ago bricked-up. He ran along the perimeter of the room but the only exit seemed to be through the door he had come. He bolted through the still open door and slid to a stop at the side of the van. When he threw open the cargo door, twenty dogs jumped on him from inside the van. Nelson fell under a mass of fur and before he could struggle his limbs were pinned to the ground. He gave his muscles a flex to test the possibility of escape but the weight of the dogs proved too much to budge. He closed his eyes and relaxed as he felt their mouths taking hold of his clothes. They lifted him and galloped away, heading south.
Log and Treg who were leaning against the front of the building threw down their cigarettes and watched as Nelson disappeared around the corner of the warehouse. On the ground lay the keys and the duffel bag. Both looked in all directions before crouching over the bag. Log unzipped it and pulled out a white square of cocaine and held it between them.
"Have you ever seen anything like this?"
"No."
"What is to be done?"
"Let's take two and leave the rest in the warehouse where he was supposed to deposit it and drive the fuck out of this city."
"His people aren't here."
"Still."
"This is life altering, Treg."
"Did you see that fucking guy?"

"What about him?"

"You saw him."

"Yes, and?"

"He's not somebody I want to be."

"He's a lunatic."

"Still. Let's take two and leave the rest. It'll be more than enough."

"You're handed a lottery ticket and you refuse the cash."

"No, I'm handed a knife and I don't want to cut my throat to the bone."

"I'll take the responsibility. I can't walk away from this."

Log stood up and threw the duffel over his shoulder.

"You drive."

Treg picked up the keys and they headed to the van, passing three security cameras embedded in the façade of the building as they walked.

Conflagration

When Jack awoke he found that dew had settled on his eyelids and his body felt better than he had expected after a night sleeping on concrete. He kicked off the sleeping bag and stretched. The day's work list began forming in his mind and after he reached twelve possible tasks to complete he shuffled them first in order of most difficult to easiest and then from most important to least important. He settled on the second order of the list, because at the top two spots were fetching Anne Marie to live with him and gutting the kitchen of the fascist residue. After breakfast he would go talk to Ben and Anne Marie would come live with him until he died. Actually, fetching Anne Marie sat at the top of both lists, because he believed nothing more important than searching for lost time and correcting the folly of idiot youth, but how could anything be more difficult than destroying another man's life by informing him he never had his wife's heart, never measured up to what they once had, who would be now left with the cold comfort of both realizations? Smashing the kitchen would not only be a pleasure but a necessary step toward habitation. Maybe, after hacking out the walls and ripping down the cabinets and wrestling out the broken appliances, some of the uneasiness would be gone from the house.

A sharp, piercing beep, the kind used to warn pedestrians and drivers of small cars that a truck backed-up and probably would not be stopping, sounded from around the corner of the house. Jack scrambled to his feet and hobbled to the driveway. A semi sat idling on the street attached to a flatbed carrying a huge blue dumpster. Jack walked until he stood below the door and called up to the driver.

"What's this?"

"A present from Kaufman who tells me to tell you to go fuck yourself."

"You didn't really want to say that did you?"

"I'm Seventh Day Adventist. No, I don't like talking like that."

"Sounds like Kaufman."

"He likes to hear me swear or think of me swearing."

"That's Kaufman."

"I stopped carrying a picture of my daughter. The man is a menace."

"A picture?"

"There are incidents in life that don't need repeating. That is one of them."

"Let me move my truck."

"Where do you want the dumpster?"

"Back edge of the house."

Jack drove the truck on the front lawn and watched as the driver expertly maneuvered the flatbed down the narrow driveway and deposited the dumpster with a boom on the concrete. He gave the driver a twenty dollar tip.

"Can you get a message back to Kaufman?"

"It depends. I don't work for you."

'Tell him to pray for his soul and that not one of those whores he's so fond of are going to be part of the welcoming committee at the pearly gates, should he choose to go ascend to heaven."

"I can relay that."

"And tell him thanks. Part of his debt is repaid."

The driver nodded and rumbled off. Jack had worked for Kaufman for years until the tirades and alcohol binges grated on him so much he felt like he had lost his top two layers of skin. The debt referred back to a contract steering investigation conducted by the FBI on a small municipality with a crooked mayor. Jack knew Kaufman had paid off the mayor for a trash hauling contract, since he acted as the bagman and even had the misfortune of watching the mayor receive a blowjob in a dark back room of Kaufman's favorite strip club. Jack mustered his best look of incredulity and played the role of dopey workingman to the FBI agent's slick investigator. After a series of interviews the agent felt better about his superior education and career, but he gathered absolutely no useful information for the investigation. From that day Kaufman loved Jack like a favorite brother, so he warmly received a phone call from old Jack Cactus to hear he had taken on an impossible renovation in a neighborhood that had sunk past the level of a ghetto.

"I'll do anything to keep you out of my neighborhood. Keep you down there with the rats where you belong, you nasty old cocksucker." Kaufman broke off with a hoarse laugh and a coughing fit.

Jack hadn't asked specifically for the dumpster, but he knew Kaufman would figure out a way to help him with the job.

Jack brewed coffee over the propane and ate a muffin in four vicious bites. Glover and Estonia came from the side door, which exited directly to the dumpster.

"Now we know what the banging was," Estonia said as she jumped to see if anything was inside. "It's empty."

They continued walking toward Jack who downed a cup of too hot coffee.

"Guess who's going to fill it."

"I think we know."

"Goddamn right you're going to fill it. I want all that shit out of the basement. When I come back we'll rip out the kitchen. There's coffee, muffins, anything else you can find."

"Jack, where's the eggs, the bacon?" Glover implored.

"Not today. I have some business. I'll be gone for a couple of hours. Start with the basement."

"He's done dating us, Glove. No more time for making impressions. Now he's just taking us for granted."

Jack left them by the coffee pot as he walked past the outhouse and past the vacant house in the back. A fresh trail of beer cans and vomit lay in the yard and he soft-shoed his way around it. He had heard the thumping bass of muted music, the shrieks and screams of girls looking to be laid and eventually a fist fight during the night from his concrete bed. Jack finally fell asleep after the loser of the fight stopped moaning and four of his friends dragged him to his car. He crossed the street and cut through the yard of another dormant house or the home of an elderly shut-in because in the daylight the structure looked relatively well-maintained and the lawn recently mowed. Anne Marie had given him an ultimatum in her own quiet way. How many days did he have left on earth? How many more days could he live without her? His life sometimes felt like an empty wallet and the days like spent cash with nothing to show for the buying.

He knocked on the side door and hooked a thumb in a belt loop. Anne Marie came to the door wiping her hands on a dish towel. Color slowly rose to her cheeks as she stepped onto the driveway.

"It's tomorrow."

"I see that."

"You best go pack a bag if you are coming."

"Why wouldn't I be coming?"

"I slept on concrete last night and listened to a pack of animals drinking and fighting all night. I've go no running water and the prospect of getting some is dim. And I'm late."

"We'll figure something out. Water is the least of my worries. I'll go pack and I hope when I come down with my bag you'll still be here. I have to tell you, Jack, I didn't expect you this morning or any morning. I've learned never to expect what you want and I stopped waiting for you a long time ago."

"Based on previous observations you would have been a fool to expect otherwise. I can't honestly say I expected to be here myself, but I think I've fooled around long enough."

"My life with and without Jack Cactus."

Anne Marie opened her arms and they embraced. She lay her cheek flush against his chest and flexed her arms to tighten the hug. In truth she hadn't slept all night, wondering if he would deliver on his promise. She had been disappointed so many times before by his best intentions and his promises that she audibly cursed herself for mooning over him and waiting for him like the teenager she had once been. How could she tap a reservoir of foolishness without the slightest evidence that Jack could suddenly change and take her when he had refused the opportunity again and again?

"Is Ben here?"

"He's eating cereal. I don't know how he holds his head up. He looks like somebody drank all of his blood last night."

"Do you want to send him out here or do you want me to come in?"

"Come in. There's no reason to make him move, because I don't know if he can."

Anne Marie held the door open and Jack bounded in, ascending the three steps with a long stride. Ben looked up as Jack approached, a dribble of milk hanging on his chin. He flinched as he caught sight of Jack's eyes which bore through his skin and skull to the soft violently throbbing mass deep in his brain, but he regained his composure when he saw Anne Marie trailing Jack across the kitchen floor. Ben looked at Jack's hands to determine if he had come to strangle him.

"Morning Jack. What brings you by?"

"I wanted to talk to you, Ben. Thought it would be best to do it in the morning."

"I can't say that my head agrees with you, Jack. It's all I can do to keep my eyes open. I have the best intentions each night and it seems it always ends up the same. You want some coffee? I'm having some whiskey myself. Otherwise I think I'm going to die."

Anne Marie had already poured a cup of coffee and handed it to Jack. Ben leaned over his bowl and pulled a soggy spoonful of cereal to his mouth, dislodging the dribble from his chin. Once he pushed the cereal around his mouth and swallowed, he chased it with a sip of low grade whiskey from a coffee cup.

"It's the only way I can keep that down, the cereal that is. So what is it you want to talk about that can't wait until a body is awake and not feeling half-dead? Anne Marie tells me you bought that house I told you about."

"Yes I did. I thank you for the lead. It's all potential right now. One day maybe it'll be as nice as this house."

Ben raised his eyes to the ceiling and scanned the balance of the kitchen, considering the state of his house. Jack's compliment made him wary of his intentions, because he had never known Jack to compliment him and he hadn't tended to the house over the past decade and he thought it obvious to everyone's eyes, including his own, that the house had turned into a shithole.

"Don't use this house as your guide. It's a goddamn rattrap. The next strong wind is going to send it to the ground."

"I've got my work ahead of me."

"You need money? Is that what you want? Is that why your standing over me watching me eat my cereal?"

"No, Ben, I've come to tell you that Anne Marie is coming to live with me. I didn't want to sneak around and behind your back. I thought I'd come here and tell you to your face. This has been a long time coming and I've been in love with that woman for close to forty years and now it's our time. It might not seem fair or right in your mind, but we're going to live out our lives together. I thought you should know."

Ben submerged his spoon in the milk and flaccid cereal left in the bowl.

"So you just come into my kitchen and say you're going to blow-up thirty years of marriage? Just like that? And I'm supposed to tell you it's alright? I'm supposed to sit here and watch it happen?"

"No, I don't want your blessing. I wanted you to hear it from my mouth so you know exactly what's happening."

"Well, I heard it and it's not going to happen."

"It's not something you can stop."

Ben placed a palm on the table so he could push himself to his feet.

"I'd stay in the chair, Ben, if I were you."

He stared at Jack and eased himself back into the chair, not really convinced he could stay on his feet once he stood upright.

"Is this what you want?" Ben asked Anne Marie who had been poised to jump between them should the words escalate into a fight.

"It is. I've loved Jack since I've been seventeen. There's nothing to be done about that. This was something I always thought could happen, but I stopped hoping for it a long time ago."

"He never married you."

"No, he never did and I don't expect he will now either."

"And he didn't stick with you for thirty years, did he? He didn't give you children and help you raise them. He didn't pay your goddamn medical bills. Didn't buy you cars and watch those goddamn TV shows with you. He didn't watch your looks fade and still stay with you, did he?"

"No."

"What's he done? What's he have? He's nearly in the grave and he's buying his first house. This goddamn shithole has been paid for for ten years. It's all a bunch of bluster and nonsense that won't amount to nothing. Always the big talker, the big dreamer with the big appetites and the big belly with not a goddamn thing to show for it. You think he'll finish that house? There's no goddamn way it'll ever be done. That man is a shyster, a kook, a fucking con. And look at you falling for it again. He blows into town and you open your legs, thinking that old Jack is going to save you from misery, the misery you yourself created. It's a goddamn pathetic show to watch and you ought to be ashamed of yourself. What do you think you are doing? Where is this going to lead? He ain't going to stay with you or that house. You'll be on the street in a year. What are you going to tell your children?"

"I'll tell them that for once in my life I followed my heart and I'll tell them to do the same, because sometimes listening to your head and reason can lead you where I've been and that's about as close to misery as I ever want to come. You're right, Ben, I'm leaving misery for a chance at something that isn't, not yet anyway. I at least owe that to myself and I'm sorry in some sense that I'm leaving you but it has more to do with habit than with any true emotion. You stopped loving me twenty years ago and if you're honest with yourself you'll admit that."

"I hear you talking, Anne Marie, but all it is is talking. There's no sense in it."

"What is it you're wanting me to say? I think we've been pretty clear and I told you I'm sorry about it but this is something I'm doing for myself, not you, not the children, and not even for Jack. This is for me and I'm starting not to care whether you understand it or not."

"Your lips smell like his cock."

"Alright now, that's about enough of your talking," Jack jumped in and drew himself erect, looming over Ben menacingly. "The way I look at it you got thirty years with her and now it's my time. I ain't ever going to catch you, because I'm not going to have thirty years with her. It's not my problem how you used your thirty years and if you wasted it, or abused it, it's a goddamn crying shame, because if you would have used those thirty years like you should of we wouldn't be having this conversation. I would have come back into town and Anne Marie would have laughed me right back out again. She would have told me about her man Ben and how their love has grown over thirty years until now we're pretty much one person with two bodies. She would have told me to put my tail between my legs and run along and cry over the lost opportunity you squandered when you were no more than a child. The fact is you opened the door and I'm walking through and taking her back out. I've told you to your face and that's more respect than most people get."

"I'm suppose to thank you for that?"

"You're not supposed to do anything. I don't know what you want to do, now that you've been told."

"I know people, Jack, that might break you up just for the fun of it."

"I know the same people."

"This doesn't end today."

"The fuck it doesn't. Listen. I told you it's my time now and I don't want you fucking with it. I don't want you near my house and I don't want you bothering us. I'll break you over my knee. You got lucky! You happened to be there to pick up the pieces. You've had a lucky thirty years, the luckiest thirty years a mortal on this earth has ever had! If you step a foot near my life I'll snap it off and shove it up your ass! You don't live in a goddamn bubble. It's not about you. You had a thirty year head start and you pissed it away drinking it that hole-in-the-wall and playing your bullshit. If I see you on the street I'll rip your heart out!" Jack's face had flushed with blood and his massive hands had clenched into fists ready to smash anything in their way. "Do we understand each other?"

Ben stared at the table, his spoon, and the flakes of cereal pasted to the side of the bowl.

"You're nothing but a bully. Just cause I can't fight you don't make what you're doing right."

"Why don't you take a walk and let Anne Marie pack in peace and let me enjoy this cup of coffee while I wait for her? And it wouldn't be a bad idea to start doing that right about now. Like you said, I ain't above bullying or fighting when the situation calls for it."

Ben pushed himself up using the table and wobbled to his feet. He limped across the kitchen floor holding his coffee cup of whiskey and yanked a set of car keys off a hook by the door. Jack and Anne Marie listened to his footsteps on the concrete, the slamming of the car door, the starting of the car and his backing into the street before they took their next breath.

"I could use a warm up of this coffee," Jack swished the coffee in the cup. "How many guns does Ben own?"

Anne Marie took the cup from him, poured it in the sink and filled it with fresh coffee.

"I don't know. I wouldn't call it an arsenal, but he has a collection."

"What are you thinking about?" Jack asked as she handed him the cup of coffee.

"I'm thinking that thirty years is a long time to live between blinks."

"I think you lost me on that one, darling."

'You blink once and you're at the Justice of the Peace and you blink again and you're standing in a kitchen feeling old and excited and you're wondering where thirty years has gone."

"Right. I'm a little off my game. There's still adrenaline in my head."

Anne Marie filled two suitcases with the essentials, clothes, hairbrush, extra pair of shoes, toothbrush and walked out of the door without even turning off the coffee pot. She had changed into jeans, a denim shirt and thick work boots with scars and dirt on the toe of each. She had pulled back her hair in a ponytail and her face shone clear of makeup. Jack thought the clothes made her look slimmer and younger by years. He took the suitcases from her and she walked away from her house of twenty-eight years. She and Ben had lived with Ben's parents the first two years of their marriage, two years that she bad blotted from her memory long ago, before buying this house with a borrowed down payment and no furniture to fill the many rooms. She did not take a look back as they crossed the street and already those thirty years were lived by another woman who's name she couldn't quite remember.

Jack walked her down the street, forgoing the shortcut through the neighbors' yards, probably so it wouldn't be too obvious how close the two houses actually were and to provide Anne Marie a moment to consider the transition and turn around if she thought better of walking away from her previous life. When they arrived at the house they stopped on the sidewalk in front and Jack encompassed the scene with a wide stretch of his arms.

"There it is. It's not much to look at and the inside is probably worse. I wouldn't begrudge you if you decide this isn't for you."

"I see that. I can't imagine the inside. It must not be very comfortable."

"No, it's not comfortable. It smells a lot like rot. The basement is filled with trash and there's an uneasy feeling in there. I told you I slept outside last night. I didn't want that uneasiness creeping into my head through my ear when I was sleeping."

"We better get to work then."

"I wish it was done and you could walk into a brand new home with every comfort you've ever desired."

"If you would have waited to come for me until after the house was done I would have never come to live with you."

"Why not? It would have been for you."

"It would have meant you didn't trust me. Like you were trying to impress me or like I was a porcelain doll. Who the heck am I to demand comfort? Anyway, Jack, I appreciate the sentiments but we both know this house was never meant for me. I'm glad to come live in it with you but I imagine you had the idea of settling before you saw me and even if I wouldn't have come you still would have fixed this up. I'm a willing addition, but I'm no muse, so stop talking that nonsense, right now."

"I still have a lot to learn about you."

"I know that to be a fact. You might be surprised and hopefully you're not too disappointed."

They walked to the back of the house and found Glover lying on his back in the grass with Estonia on top of him, straddling his belly and stroking his arms. Two muffin wrappers and two three-quarter full coffee cups lay at their feet. The grass around them looked trampled and flat.

"Are you done with the basement yet?" Jack barked.

Estonia slowly turned her head in the direction of Jack's voice.

"Why are you always watching us, Jack? Are you some kind of pervert?"

"What about the basement?"

"The basement?"

"You're supposed to be working on the basement."

"We haven't finished our breakfast yet," Glover piped in.

"I see that. It looks like you're planning on seconds."

Estonia slid off Glover and sat on the grass next to him, taking a quick inventory of her clothes to make sure everything had been buttoned or zipped.

"You remember Anne Marie."

"Can I please take another shower?"

"That's not possible anymore," said Anne Marie.

"Our shower source has been cut off. Anne Marie's going to be living with us now, so we can't go back to that house. We'll have to think of something else. Maybe we'll just not worry how we're smelling and just get the work done. All you got to do is make sure your asshole is clean and the rest is manageable."

'I know a few people on this block. I'm sure if I go ask one of them will let us use a shower every now and again.

"Anyway, there's no showers before you start picking up trash. That's a ridiculous notion. You have to be clean for the maggots and roaches? They don't give a good goddamn."

"You were busy this morning," Glover still lay on his back and his words were directed toward the sky.

"Unlike you."

"Well...."

"I'm talking about the basement. Get off your back and let's start hacking out the kitchen."

"I thought the garage was the next step?"

"It should be but that kitchen has to go. Estonia cleaned it pretty well but it's in the walls and floors. Plus, I haven't secured the lumber for the garage yet. Got a couple of leads. It's a lot of wood, wire, shingles. Plus, if we pour a new driveway it's going to get all beat up if we do it first, so we'll build the garage and rehab the house and the driveway will be last. That concrete will be so white you won't be able to look at it when the sun is up. You're thinking, Glover, that's a good sign. Maybe you're starting to get it. The garage is important. It'll be a shelter, a workshop, a storage unit, maybe I'll build a little room on top like a study or a studio, a little place to go on a winter's night. We'll see when we start building. It's all a matter of doing and following the muse."

"What's in the walls of the kitchen?"

"God knows. But no doubt it's something that needs to be burned. I'm not even sure fire will take care of it but at least it won't be in solid form after being burned. We'll release it into the air and let it infect another place. Anne Marie and Estonia will work in the basement. Glover come with me and get yourself a crowbar and a sledge hammer."

Jack sprinted to the truck and Glover rose from the grass, stretched and plodded after him.

"You don't mind him giving orders like that?" Estonia asked Anne Marie.

"It's not an order if you don't have a better idea. I'll tell him if I have a different idea. For now let's take a look at the basement."

Jack and Glover worked throughout the day hacking at the kitchen walls with crowbars and exploding the cabinets and countertops with swings of the heavy sledges as Anne Marie and Estonia made a hundred trips up the steps clutching trash in their arms. By the end of the day the dumpster had been filled. They had cleared the basement of debris, except for a rusted iron bed, revealing hand-cut stone walls, a boiler that looked like it could power a steamship, a rusty circle where the hot water tank once stood, and a cracked and damp floor that looked on the verge of disintegrating into mud. Estonia amused herself throughout the day by imagining the object she carried as new and the owner proudly bearing it in their hands as they brought it home to use. Some items were easier to imagine than others. A rusty and dented silver lamp five feet tall with a smashed shade held a remnant of its past elegance, but a plastic yellow table with green legs attached to casters could not have been a good buy in any era as its main purpose seemed to be to elicit buyer's remorse. To Estonia, whose personal possessions didn't quite fill up a small backpack and who when she lived under her parent's roof owned a collection of objects that could fit on the top and in two drawers of a chipped white dresser, the mass of discarded items looked like all the unhappiness of a person's life settled at the bottom of the house like silt on the bottom of a river. How many things did a person need? Who read all the boxes of moldering paperbacks and where did the knowledge go? The buyer once desired this trash so intensely they spent their money earned in dreary, dirty jobs and it ended up rotting in a basement and will now be buried in the ground along with the rest of our cast off desires. A false promise. A shed skin. Anne Marie and Estonia worked in silence. Whether Anne Marie had the same thoughts she did not know. When they knew each other better she may ask her about the purpose of things bought and lost.

Glover stood in the kitchen, surrounded by the gutted walls covered with crumbling and yellowed newspaper. They had ripped off the plaster and lathe and exposed the paper insulation tacked and stuffed against the exterior walls. He found a readable front page near the door and saw the date of July 7, 1927 on the upper hand corner over the two cent price.

"We have to take all of this off," Jack said.

"Listen to this. Seize $30,000 drugs as part of cult store. Morphine and cocaine found Thursday hidden in bushel basket. Federal Agents claim narcotics object of raid on temple."

"OK, that's enough."

"No, listen, listen. Morphine and cocaine valued by federal narcotics agents at $30,000 and declared to have been in "Dr." Homer Thompson's alleged mystic cult temple at 2905 E. 55th Street when it was raided Monday night, was found Thursday. A stone's throw down the alley from the alleged cult house is the grocery store of Abraham Bolmar at 2803 E. 51st. Street. Thursday morning, Bolmar called Third District Police and told them he had found the narcotics in a bushel basket beside the garbage can. Analyzed as Drugs. Patrolman John Miller and Frank Holacek took the basket to the Forest City Drug Company 37th Street and Woodland Avenue, where the contents of one bottle were analyzed as cocaine and of one can as morphine. There were 55 bottles and ten cans. Dr. W.W. Wolders, chief federal narcotic agent for Ohio and Michigan, who has taken personal charge of the case against the alleged mystic cult head and Federal Narcotic Agent Robert Artis, who participated in the raid on the alleged temple Monday night, seized the basket of drugs. Armed with a federal narcotic warrant, Detectives Joseph Hartman and Victor

Plopp have searched houses in the neighborhood of "Dr." Thompson's house for the basket ever since Monday. Detectives had positive information that the basket of drugs was in the house 20 minutes before the raid, Hartman said Thursday. Three cans of opium and a small quantity of cocaine were seized. A man known to have been in the house 20 minutes before the raid was missing with the basket, Hartman said. The cans of morphine found in the basket each contained 383 grains. The powdered cocaine was packed in ounce bottles. Youngstown enters probe. Youngstown Police have entered the investigation of the alleged mystic cult temple. They believed they had found a connection between a 16 year-old girl held in the Mahoning County jail and "Dr." Thompson's establishment. The girl had been found by friends after having been missing from her home several days. She said she had been doped and then mistreated, but refused to name the persons implicated. Captain Dorothy Doan Henry devoted her day off Thursday to the search for young Cleveland girls alleged to have been habitués of the establishment. Five Under Bond. "Dr." Homer Thompson, alleged head of the cult, and Robert Burlingame in whose room in the cult temple three cans of opium were found, are now in County Jail in default of $2,500 bond and after each had pleaded not guilty to a federal narcotic charge. Mrs. Helen Chaslyn , "Dr." Thompson's daughter is held in default of $2,000 bond. Three men and two women, held as suspicious persons following the arrests as visitors to "Dr." Thompson's establishment are held under bond."

"Are you done?

"No, not by a long shot."

Glover scanned the rest of the page and in a series of small stories on the lower right, between a paragraph reporting that General Wood looked feeble on his return to Washington from the Philippines and one stating the actor, socialite and chum of Edwin Booth, John Drew had taken to his death bed and was near his final reckoning was a small paragraph entitled "Man's Best Friend Turns Beastly."

"And listen to this…residents of the City have reported activity among our canine friends never before witnessed. Several complaints have been lodged at City Hall, all of the police districts and several fire stations concerning large packs of roving dogs. No injuries have been reported but officials at the Catholic Diocese have reported that one such pack of mongrels befouled the sacred ground of St. John's Cathedral. When asked about these complaints, Dog Warden Heath Slocum suggested a citywide sweep could be planned. 'We haven't seen activity of this kind before but I would like to remind you that several European breeds have recently become popular. We think they may have befuddled our native dogs.' Slocum has asked money be set aside in the budget to increase manpower to capture the offending dogs."

"Take it down. Read it later if you want to. I have to check this floor."

"What do you make of that?"

"What? The pack?"

"Roving packs of dogs?"

"Do your research on your own time, goddamnit! Take it down," Jack waved a hammer at him before he left the kitchen in search of another tool.

Glover tried to save what he could but at least half the newspaper shattered into dime-sized pieces when his fingers touched it. After he had cleaned the walls he had a pile a foot thick on the floor. Jack strode back into the room holding a sledgehammer.

"This floor is nothing but goddamn rot. We've got to take it up."

"What? Now?"

"Yes, now. When else would be appropriate? Do you have a schedule you're not sharing? You got some other goddamn place you have to be?"

"No, but haven't we done enough for today?"

"Here," Jack tossed a claw hammer at Glover, who let it sail past and land with a thud on the floor. "Watch me."

Jack raised the sledge over his head, paused and coiled his body, then brought down the head hard against the floor. A hole opened which a sickening crack and swallowed the sledge like the floor had been crafted from paper maché.

"That is what you call 'not good.' Let's hope this is the only floor in this shape. Otherwise I'd say we better put this old house out of its misery and burn it to the ground."

Jack picked up a long handled tool with a massive blade on the end and slipped it under the linoleum. He pushed with all his weight and the linoleum popped and curled like pencil shavings as Jack ripped a gouge the length of the floor

"Grab that end," Jack pointed to the edge of the linoleum and he and Glover pulled one section up in a single piece. "That, son, is shoddy work. It shouldn't come up that goddamn easy."

They pulled the rest off the floor in pieces and hauled it all to the dumpster. Glover moved the pile of old newspapers to the dining room, hoping to salvage some of the history to read later. The floorboards were black with rot and mildew. The sledgehammer made a bull's-eye in a particularly black and rotted part of the floor.

"Get your hammer and start pulling these boards up and don't fall on Anne Marie or Estonia. They're working below and they don't need you landing on their heads. Let's start from the far corner away from the door," Jack barked.

"Can you stop being a dick for like one second? By the end of the day my ears feel like they're going to start bleeding. Enough with the orders."

"If you knew what you were doing I wouldn't have to order you around. Once you can walk without tripping over your dick I'll keep my mouth shut."

They pulled board after board and Glover threw them in the dumpster as they went. With each board they revealed a little more of the basement and they could hear the women walking back and forth carrying armfuls of trash. Glover caught sight of the top of Estonia's head and a knot of nausea brewed deep in his stomach, which resembled a cross between a hunger pang and terror, but he recognized it for what it really had to be, an urge to take her behind the outhouse and fuck her until he lost sensation in his cock. He had been continually surprised at the frequency these urges had been coming since they left home, but Estonia never refused him even when she lay half-asleep or aching from a night of sleeping on another floor or under a tree. He had never had access to a girl at anytime of every day. When they lived with their parents they had to find hidden places in public or wait until their houses emptied to hurry through sex and never fully take their clothes off. Now that the shackles had been taken off, his libido burned night and day.

"Son, there'll be time for that once we finish for the day."

"What?"

"Quit ogling your girlfriend and take these boards to the dumpster."

Glover's neck flushed as he snatched up five or six boards and stomped his way out of the door, hoping his stomping would tame his erection that had become obvious under his jeans.

Within three hours they had finished ripping out the floor and Jack had conducted a careful inspection of the exposed floor joists. He propped a ladder on the basement floor and ascended the steps until his torso poked through the floor in the kitchen. Some rot had touched the top of half the joists. The boards would hold a floor until the walls turned to dust but nailing in a sub-floor would be a challenge. Nails or screws would try to sink their teeth in the wood but would come away with a mouthful of rot. Within months they would have a trampoline as a floor so he would have to nail new wood on either side of the joists to give the screws new fiber to hold. He added the length and dimensions of the needed wood to the growing list of materials.

To this point he had avoided any serious thought to how he would obtain the needed wood, plumbing, shingles, siding, cabinets, sinks, toilets, receptacles, electrical boxes, switches, shower heads, bathtubs, cement, windows, drywall, joint compound, light fixtures, plywood, wire, countertops, faucets, not to mention a boiler, hot water tank, washer, and dryer. He knew he would need all of it, had guessed at the problems and surprises he would come across once he started, held a swelling monetary figure in his head accurate to a few hundred dollars that swelled out of synch with the reality of his budget, but no firm plan of acquisition had ever formed. He would call Kaufman. He already needed another dumpster and the man knew everybody and their children in town. Kaufman may be able to give him a lead or may even contribute to the cause. The problem wouldn't be solved with one phone call, but Kaufman knew the trailheads to most solutions.

"I haven't put in a day's work like that in a decade or two," Anne Marie said as she pulled a strand of hair from her eyes and tucked it behind an ear.

"You get all the trash out of there?"

"Yes, and it's been down there a long time. I didn't throw away an iron bed we found. I don't know, it was a little rusted, but with some sanding and paint it should be alright. I'm thinking before it's all over we might need an extra bed or two."

Glover and Estonia lay back side by side, their heads resting on the grass.

"Does anybody have a cell phone?" Jack asked.

"That was turned off six weeks ago, so I threw the fucking thing in some river we crossed. I tried to hit a rock that was sticking out but I got nothing but water," Glover said as he pressed his hip against Estonia's.

"I need a phone."

"Believe it or not there's still a pay phone over on Merriweather in front of the convenience store," Anne Marie told him.

"Does it work?"

"It might. You really can't trace calls on pay phones. The owners of the store think it brings in business."

"I'm starving." Glover grabbed the skin over his stomach as he could find no fat above the wall of muscle.

'I think a plan is forming. I'll make my call. You three start dinner and we'll be asleep before the sun sets. Tomorrow will be just as brutal as today. We'll all want to sleep."

Jack winced as he gained his feet and he limped his way to the truck in front of the house. His right knee felt like the femur and tibia might be grinding bone on bone and the left knee felt like the patella may have slipped down his shin on its way to his ankle. Two neighborhood kids about eight years old stood on the refrigerator in the truck bed, the highest point of Jack's possessions. They had been playing a variation of King of the Mountain but were now exhausted as they decided to share power and soak in the view from this dizzying height.

"That won't be much fun when I start driving. Better hold on tight or you'll end up splattered in the street."

Both leapt from the refrigerator to the grass, tucking and rolling to stop their momentum, and shot down the sidewalk without looking back. Jack considered their agility and chuckled to his throbbing knees, thinking about the boys in a few years time when they were stronger and mean and would be able to knock him off his crippled legs without much effort.

Jack drove to the pay phone and a lusty dial tone greeted him. He dialed Kaufman's number and Kaufman's voice barked into his ear before the first ring had completed its cycle.

"Kaufman, how are you?"

"Jack?"

"Yessir,"

"How the fuck would I be? I've got too many broads trying to blow me and my golf game is for shit. Suddenly, I can't get off the tee. I swing like a pussy and I'm lucky to make it to the broad's tee, honest to God. I'm thinking to myself, when did I become a pussy? When did I get a cunt and when did my muscles turn to flab? I think I'm going to start paying somebody to play the game for me and I'll stay in the clubhouse and get blown. They can tell me what I shot and if they suck I'll get somebody better. Look at me, Jack, I'm a thousand years old and I still don't have time for all the broads who want a taste of my dick, honest to God."

"Sounds about the same as always."

"Nothing changes except your skin and your bones and sometimes you grow a cunt when you least expect it. Did you get my present?"

"I did. Perfect timing, but I'll need another one for tomorrow if you can swing it."

"Jesus Christ, Jack! You filled that cocksucker up already? What the fuck did you fill it with? The corpses of dead rats?"

"I'm ripping out to the studs. Plus the previous inhabitants left a few things. The place is pretty much filled up with junk."

"Why the fuck are you living in that neighborhood anyway? I haven't been through there in twenty years, but it was fucked up then so I can't imagine what it's like now. Why didn't you go to the country and get some fucking cottage and finally pick-up golf so we could play once in awhile, so I could take your money and we could get some broads. Maybe you could teach me how not to play like a pussy and knock the cunt smell off of me."

"You go where you can afford. The neighborhood is not that bad. I've seen worse."

"Where the fuck have you been living? The Gaza-fucking-strip? Inside a missile silo? Honest to God, you're better than those animals down there."

"I can't see how anybody is better than anybody else. That's not clear thinking."

"Clear thinking? There are strata my friend. There are higher orders and lower orders. You've chosen to nestle yourself in with the lowest of the low. It's disappointing."

"They wouldn't let me live in your neighborhood. The cops follow me when I drive through it. Your neighbors wouldn't abide my presence."

"You've got to maintain order, my friend, or else everything gets fucked up and everybody lives in shit. How many dumpsters are you going to need?"

"I've only torn out the kitchen. All the walls go. There's still a lot of debris. I'm thinking three more that size."

"Jesus, fuck, Jack. I do a good deed and now you want to violate my asshole. I'm tender down there Jack. I guard it pretty closely. I'm no virgin back there. God knows I've had my share of ass fucking at the hands of animals and pirates, but I can't have everyone sticking their business in my asshole, because you'll start thinking of me as another dirty old cunt to be used and thrown away."

"Where else am I going to go? Who else has connections and resources like you?"

"Exactly. Jackie wants and I'm supposed to wag my asshole in the air and wait for him to call his shot."

"Kaufman, goddamn, I'm not asking for your first born."

"You should have taken my first born. He was born with his heart outside his chest. They didn't have the imaging they have now so delivery day was a nice fucking surprise. The little chap only lived three days and after he died I named him after me. My wife didn't understand that." He lapsed into silence for a breath or two then continued. "Consider it done, cocksucker. Tell the driver to give you his number. Call him directly when you need another one. That way I don't have to hear more bullshit messages from you and I won't know when your dick is inside me."

"The driver seems like a decent man. Seemed a little out of character for you."

"I know. I usually hire ex-cons and animals like you. Did you notice his face? I think that cocksucker must shave with a straight razor. His face is completely fucking clean and his ears are the cleanest I think I've every seen on a human being. The man is old enough to have a crop of hair growing out of his ears but I'll be goddamned if there is a single strand on his lobes. Who the fuck can respect that?"

"I don't follow the problem with clean ears."

"Who spends that much time on their face that they get around to cleaning and clipping their ears besides broads? I haven't looked at my fucking ears since I figured out what they are. Comb your hair, brush your teeth, shave your face, great, now where are the fucking broads?"

"One more thing. Do you know where I can get lumber?"

"You don't have that worked out yet?"

"This happened fast. I acted on impulse. It's only been a week."

"You rush in to buy a shithole and now you're making a plan?"

"That's about right. I can't argue."

"Stupid cocksucker. Why didn't you call me before you jumped in. Sometimes you need help, Jackie, with your decisions. I would have told you to stay away from those shitholes down there. I would have told you they look tempting. They look like a deal. They look like maybe a place to hunker down and die a quiet death, but you are in for a shitstorm. Call this guy. Big, giant cocksucker, um, he has no short game, pounds the ball off the tee like a goddamn ape but he gets twenty yards from the green and becomes like a fucking maniac. I've seen the ape throw the ball at the tee because the sticks are useless in his hands. He's never had goddamn touch, Charlie Cavano, tell him I told you to call and tell him what you need and what you're looking for. He'll know, but I'm warning you it won't be free. Charlie doesn't give away anything for free. Honest to God, I think he sells his gism to the broads he fucks."

"Do you have his number?"

"Goddamn, do I look like the fucking yellow pages. Honest to God, hold on a second."

After five or six muffled curses and a prolonged shuffling of papers, Kaufman came back to the phone and gave Jack the number.

"Is that about all? My hemorrhoids are flaring up. If you don't stop I won't be able to sit for a month."

"C'mon Kaufman, you know you like hearing from me."

"Every time you call it costs me money. I feel so dirty when you're done with me. I didn't accumulate all this cash to give it away to the likes of you, so how about leaving me the fuck alone for awhile until I heal up and can take it balls deep, honest to God."

"One more thing."

"No more things. Bye-bye."

The phone clicked and Jack waited until the dial tone sounded until he hung up. He'd call Cavano tomorrow, giving time for Kaufman to smooth the way, because he figured Kaufman would obsess on the possibility of Jack taking the wrong approach or Cavano being less than receptive and the deal collapsing and having Jack come back with the same request. Just then, five guys tumbled out of the convenience store, each holding a bottle wrapped in a brown paper bag. Al K-Wood el led the group past Jack. The group chattered and laughed, but K-Wood looked morose and had already opened his bottle and taken a swig of liquor. Jack nodded his head as he came close. K-Wood stopped and wobbled a little as he tried to find his balance.

"Do I fucking know you?"

"You don't know me. We had a brief conversation a few days ago," Jack answered as he took inventory of K-Wood's state and surmised by the look of his red eyes, the stale smell of his skin and the gasoline fumes pouring from his mouth from a near-lethal concoction brewing in his stomach that the drinking had been uninterrupted for a few days.

"Ah, you're the crazy fuck in the truck," K-Wood had caught sight of Jack's truck parked along the street.

"That would be me. The offer still stands."

K-Wood took three rapid swallows of liquor and watched his friends walk away down the sidewalk.

"Look at them fucks. They don't fucking wait."

K-Wood let out a quick and loud shout but the group laughed too hard to hear him so they continued on their way.

"I'm leaving if I can walk."

"I live on Whitman Avenue. I'm not going to tell you the number because I don't even know it. Look for my truck."

"When I got nothing else better to do."

He tried to jog after his friends, but after a few strides he realized he had better walk or he'd end up with his face on the concrete and it even took him a few measured steps at a walking pace before it could be determined that he would remain upright.

Jack jumped into his truck and rumbled back to the house. The three were gone when he returned, no doubt searching for a place to wash before starting dinner. Maybe he needed to start the plumbing, he thought. They needed to be self-sufficient because all this hunting for hot water just pushed the schedule farther back and made it even more unlikely that the house would ever be finished. They would start dinner later, finish dinner later, go to sleep later and wake-up later and get less work done tomorrow all because of a little hot water and soap. Over the course of a month, hours, if not whole days, would be wasted if he logged and calculated all the lost time. He picked up a crowbar and swung it hard against one of the dining room walls. He pulled down and a section of plaster and lathe fell at his feet. Working his way up from the jagged hole he threw the claw against the plaster again and again until he needed a ladder to reach the area near the ceiling. "Shit," he half mumbled, half breathed. He had not planned on the ceilings. They would have to come out too, of course, because they had been damage by water, mildew and smoke. How many plumbing, radiator and roof leaks had soaked them, swelled and yellowed them until the plaster hung heavy from the joists like rotten fruit barely clinging to a branch? Jack reached high with the crowbar and touched a section of ceiling that looked especially rotten and a four foot section crashed to the floor and sprayed him with mildew and dust. Why not buy a coffin-sized condo on the edge of a chlorinated lake that even thirsty geese refused to land on or swim in? Kaufman had the knack of throwing out some thought or phrase that stuck with Jack like a virus, worming its way silently from the inside until his thoughts were skewed toward Kaufman's thinking or his resolve wavered in the face of such rational opposition. He thought about dying in front of the shitbox, watching some show that could have been written by chimpanzees or, in an undetermined way, followed the trials and tribulations of chimpanzees or presented a masquerade of human beings who acted like guffawing, prancing, hairless and horny primates, in a climate-controlled, freshly carpeted living/dining/kitchenette room with his pants around his ankles and a can of beer emptying a tepid brew on the new carpet compared to dying with a crowbar in his hand, falling to his knees, clutching his chest that suddenly felt like someone had turned a screw and twisted his heart inside out and toppling onto a pile of spoiled plaster, his last breath a lungful of rot. The claw smashed again on the plaster and lathe. It made a difference how he planned on dying, if the moment could at all be planned. He should die on the job, his shirt soaked with sweat, his body finally worked to its limit. How else could he sum up a life of work? He wouldn't mind dying on the shitter or in his sleep as long as the death occurred in the context of work, meaning that if he died tonight or in the morning while he squeezed rock hard crap through his sphincter he honestly wouldn't have minded much because whoever found his body in its last embarrassing position would know the work had ultimately killed him. At least, they would say, he worked right up until the end. His last great joy and achievement would be hacking out a ruined wall.

"Jesus, Jack, give it a rest," Glover said as he walked through the front door. "The sun is about to go down and I don't think there's any electricity in here."

"Don't you look pretty. You must be addicted to showers. What the hell did you do when you were on the road?"

"I stank. I stank worse than I have ever stank. One night we were convinced our skin was rotting. I stank worse than Estonia, but she was no picnic. She and Anne Marie are out back. I think they want to eat."

Jack dropped the crowbar and he and Glover walked to the backyard. He thought about going through the kitchen and skipping across the bare floor joists like an ironworker high in the air, but his throbbing ankle told him not to try it unless he wanted to end up in a broken heap in the basement. Instead, they went the long way around through the front door. Anne Marie gave him a long look as he approached, because she felt a little stunned that he had continued working after he had returned. The man seemed to have inexhaustible energy. She would never be able to keep up.

"Seven houses down on the other side of the street lives Mary Kelly. She's expecting you. She said we can shower and do laundry anytime. I know her from the neighborhood. Her husband used to come over to play poker with Ben and I think he bet the dogs. She came sometimes. She lives with her son, but he doesn't come out of his room much, she said. I think her husband was killed in a foundry accident. I remember it being gruesome. She said we could cook in her kitchen, but honestly, as long as the weather holds out, I'd prefer to cook outdoors because her kitchen is past filthy. I'll stick with the camp stove. I'd be afraid to catch a disease otherwise. The house seems too much for her, poor thing. And then put a dead husband and a disturbed son on top of that. I guess I'd probably have a dirty kitchen too. But you need to go, Jack, your stink is going to spoil our stew."

Jack opened his mouth, but he turned on his heel without responding other than an acquiescing nod. He fetched a clean pair of jeans and a flannel shirt from the truck and walked to Mary Kelly's house. The house looked identical to Jack's in structure, but it had been continuously inhabited since it had been built in 1917 and had been better maintained by the series of owners. He knocked on the door and a woman in her mid-40s, unnaturally pale, with a worn, beautiful face and red hair streaked with gray answered.

"Mary Kelley?" Jack ventured because he had imagined a woman in her 70s, caring for her idiot son and stooped from bearing the world on her back.

"You must be the new neighbor. Anne Marie said she'd send you by. Been working?"

"Why?"

"Not much for mirrors are you? I mean you're covered in dust and you're as white as a sheet and you ask how I can tell you've been working? It didn't take a whole lot of detective work."

"I'd hate to track dust through your house."

"There's a shower in the basement. Come to the side door."

She let him in and led him to the corner of the basement where a shower head hung from a floor joist over a floor drain. Rusty hot and cold levers stuck out from pipes running up the wall.

"Somebody who owned the house before must have worked like you. Why else would they need a shower like this? My husband sometimes used it."

"This was a factory town. Lots of dirty work. Had to protect the few possessions they had."

"I'll leave you to it. Let yourself out when you want to leave."

She bounded up the stairs and closed the door to the basement. She seemed athletic as she moved quickly with powerful strides. Jack undressed and washed himself under the trickle of the shower. He found a sliver of hard soap wedged behind the cold supply line, and wondered if her dead husband had used it. He scraped it across his body, smearing a thin residue of soap rather than working up a lather. Mary Kelly had obviously let Glover use the upstairs shower, because the corner had been dry and the water brown when it first came out of the pipes. Old men wash in the basement under a spider's web and a rusty shower head while the young buck plays above, Jack mused as the water turned cold because the small hot water tank, squatting few feet from the shower hadn't had time to replenish its supply. Jack's shower had been the fourth in an hour, so he could do nothing but turn off the hot water supply completely and not pretend the water would be anything but ice cold. Jack added a jumbo hot water tank on his wish list. The tank would be capable of boiling enough water to heat fifteen showers and a couple of baths an hour should the need ever arise.

After letting the cold water drip on his body for a few minutes, Jack turned the water off and dried himself with a crusty hand towel he found hanging on the edge of the slop sink. Once he dressed he left by the side door without acknowledging his exit since that's what she seemed to prefer. He felt soapy and cold, his skin alive and tingling over knotting muscles, but some of the stink had been washed from him even though by carrying his dirty clothes over his arm some of the stench had been transferred back to his person. Mary Kelly, with that athletic build and her ability to leap up the stairs, hung in his mind. He cast backwards, but he could find no woman in his past that exactly resembled her. Some had pale skin, others had varying shades of red hair whether natural or from a dye, and one liked to jog in the mornings and the evenings, but her body tilted toward anorexia rather than sculpted muscle and sinew. Mary Kelly stood alone in her uniqueness and that troubled him, as it raised the specter of him reverting back to a destructive habit he had developed since his first erection, something so natural and easy that it could almost be called an instinct, namely pursuing every opportunity, exploiting every attraction and consummating every flirtation whenever and wherever possible. Annie Marie had yet to sleep her first night in his house, she being the only woman he had ever remembered sobbing over when he lost her the first two times, the only woman whose scent lingered with him for decades, and he now pondered the various approaches he could employ against Mary Kelly and the chances for their success. He knew he should confess to Anne Marie when he got home, tell her he thought he had been reformed, but he had been gravely mistaken. Tell her to ask for Ben's forgiveness and for her to forget this search for lost time. He thought of another possibility for his death. He saw his pants around his ankles as he humped a broad-hipped waitress in the back of a cinder block building by a greasy dumpster. Maybe a rat would be eating garbage but keeping one eye peeled on their intercourse. Maybe that's when the heart attack, stroke or aneurysm occurred and he would die with his erection pointing up to the vapor light and the stars above.

Anne Marie had made a big pot of thick stew and even though the potatoes had been undercooked and she had used too much pepper and not enough salt the food tasted so good they bolted down heaping spoonfuls until they couldn't burp without tasting the stew rise from their stomachs. They sat on the concrete slab with their plates on their laps, using the light of the propane to see.

"Jack, don't you have lawn chairs?" asked Anne Marie.

"I believe I do."

"Could you pull them out tomorrow so we can be more comfortable?"

"I didn't think of it."

"You missed your calling. If there was ever a man suited to be a monk it would be you."

"There's one really big problem with that calling."

"Chastity?"

"I can sleep on concrete, wear hair shirts, not talk for weeks and eat a fistful of worms but that is one torture I could not endure."

"Lucky for me."

Jack looked at the blue flame of the propane and stopped himself from sticking his fingertips in it. He very nearly confessed at that moment to the infidelity brewing in his mind that would find its expression with Mary Kelly or a surrogate.

"Don't get your hopes up."

"It's not your hopes I want up."

"Alright, alright," Glover broke in. "I know that old people have sex and everything but it doesn't mean I have to hear about it. We're going to our room and we'll leave you two to do whatever you need to do. Right Es?"

Estonia's eyes didn't signal recognition that she had been spoken to and fluttered further closed.

"Es, let's go, Jack's about to get wild and I don't think we should be anywhere near him."

Estonia rose to her feet but looked already asleep. She wobbled until Glover placed a hand on the small of her back and guided her to their room. Anne Marie had given them a flashlight to navigate the house in the dark. She had packed it with her underwear and comb and she remembered buying it with Ben after they had lost power in the house and they had lived without electricity for over a week. Jack followed the beam until it disappeared around the corner.

"I think they might stay," Jack said.

"They're not bad kids. She's a little quiet around me."

"Our first night in a long time."

"The first of many."

"None of the bedrooms have been cleaned."

"We'll sleep out here tonight. I'll take care of the rooms tomorrow. We'll have a nice nest."

"Two birds at rest."

"I feel like a girl Jack. I don't know if it's the thrill of doing something for myself or doing something that nobody expected. I've been naughty and I don't care who judges me. It makes my skin tingle and I feel like I could grow two more feet and grab everyone I see in a giant bear hug and proselytize my discovery. Do yourself a favor and listen to your heart. I guess it's close to the feeling I had when I gave birth. You can't believe this thing has happened. In one moment you're a different person and the skin of the old person you were lies at your feet or if you're like me the skin hangs neatly on a hanger in the closet next to all the other old skins. You hope someday to donate the collection to a resale shop for poor orphans, but it's hard to give away the overstock of yourself. I feel so good, so full of hope and love that I can't believe the feeling will ever end."

"It never does end, right? Once you feel it?"

"It ends. It always ends. The perfect wee babe grows up to torture your resolve and patience. But I think once you've opened that path, once you've let yourself feel true horror and joy, you can always return to it whenever you want. I think its like once you've blazed the trail through your brain it always remains open. Sometimes I've thought I lost it forever, like when I saw how my kids actually turned out and I realized that maybe all that hope was misguided and sometimes I felt sorry that I unleashed them on an unsuspecting world and I felt a little embarrassed, I guess you would say, that I once thought I could bear children who would be part of the good side of the world. Then you come back with your offer and the path is clear and open and ready for me to walk down. Thank you, Jackie."

"What have I done? I've really done nothing."

"Kept your word. Came back for me. Given me a chance to walk down the path again, even for a short time. At this point in my life I'm happy with a short walk. My expectations are realistic I think. Seems strange to say but leaving my house was worth this night. I cashed in a lot of years, but I feel like I'm on the planet again."

"I'll do my best. Our life will be nice."

"It already is. What's not perfect about a concrete pad, a cup of tea and you?"

They kissed for a long time until Anne Marie pushed him to the ground and mounted him. She kissed his belt buckle before unhooking it and loosening his belt. He fumbled with the rivet and zipper of his jeans, but his fingers were too stiff and swollen to be of much help. He let his head fall on the stiff grass while his body remained on the concrete as he arched his back, no small feat given the girth of his midsection, so she could pull off his pants. She stood up and wriggled out of her jeans. She laid a scratchy blanket, smelling of mildew, over the concrete and pointed for him to move on top of it, giving him a small hard pillow for his head. His penis became erect without much of a struggle because the sight of her efficient and swift movements in making their bed as she bent over naked below the waist excited a man who honored work. They both paused after she had guided him into her, enjoying the first moment of warm, deep sensation. She lurched and he thrust and their bellies slapped against each other together before they found a smooth rhythm.

He closed his eyes and let his body relax, letting her drive the act and guide him. Over the years the feeling in his penis had been worn away to the point where he could now last a day and a half in a woman if she desired it. When the woman looked exhausted or frustrated he could concentrate and close the deal, usually with the aid of a memory culled from a vast library of sexual experience. A hundred times the image of Anne Marie as a young girl, maybe fifteen, came to him and allowed him to release and the older the memory had become the more it grew in stature so that she transfigured from a young girl in the first flower of womanhood to an adolescent priestess guiding his sexual life. His first memory of her began in a black field furrowed for corn. She wore a blue skirt dotted with cornflowers and a loose white top. The top two buttons of her blouse were unbuttoned, revealing the breastbone of her pink chest. She picked small round stones from the clogs of dirt and collected them in the palm of her hand, even though the purpose of the hunt had been to find arrowheads from a rummaged native encampment. He had thrown his shirt on the field and it acted as a marker for how far they had searched. The sun had reddened his neck and back and he could feel his skin beginning to tighten and protest the exposure. He watched her pick her way through a deep furrow, bending scissor-like, precise and efficient. They had grown up five houses away from each other. He had seen her at school year after year, at church on Sundays, at the river with bare legs and downtown at the market buying flour or gum. He had teased her, chased her, probably at some point pulled her hair and punched her in the back or tripped her during a game of tag. He had kissed her once, but it had been on a dare and they met each other with hard, pressed lips. How had they managed to be alone in a long black field? Were there others who had been edited from the scene or blotted out by an old man's sentimentality? She stood up and wiped her forehead with the back of her hand, placed her hands on her hips, and stretched her back, a pantomime meant to show the lithe body of a young girl shaking off the pain of work. Her hand dove toward the ground and plucked a chip of quartz from the dirt. The white side of her breast flashed in the sun. Jack jammed his hand down his pants, but after rolling his penis between his fingers he decided to leave it alone. He watched her come to the end of the furrow, where she twice counted the stones. She pitched each one back to the field, except for the quartz, which she slipped into the pocket of her shirt. She looked at him looking at her and she laughed. She ran away taking long strides and flashing her tan legs. He wanted to run after her, tackle her, tickle her, make snot come out of her nose, and ignore her shrill screams and desperate begging. He stood and watched the sun drop below a distant hill.

Even though he would come to know her body better than any other woman's body, Jack could never find another moment with the ability to stretch across time and knock him off his feet or to provide the unfailing key to orgasm. In his more contemplative moods he tried to find reasons for the memory's power over him. Had the intensity of a youthful thrill burned itself indelibly in his mind? Had that been the moment when a swirl of confusing male instincts had coalesced, found a slim organization and revealed their purpose to him for the first time? Did the mature man like to hold up his younger self for mockery and derision because he stood rooted to the ground and couldn't run after her and couldn't consummate the attraction because he had been shocked by the opportunity and befuddled with sentimentality? He held out the possibility that the scene had never happened and that he had constructed it out of other fragments and longings, but even this couldn't douse the memory's significance. He had never asked her if they had ever been in a freshly plowed field collecting arrowheads because he felt little hope that the day held as much importance to her as it did to him and he had no interest in details being filled in by another perspective. All the edges of the memory had been worn down from use and time and the colors were vibrant and highly polished. The scene, as it existed, seemed too perfectly sentimental, with the visage of Anne Marie's lithe figure being the central figure and conducting the scene with the smell of fresh dirt, the azure sky, the light breeze tumbling in from the south and the ache of young muscle stretching and contracting. Why try and change it now or get closer to the truth of things since the memory had served him so well? Of course it didn't matter to Jack that even if it did happen exactly the way he remembered, the best that could be said of his attraction is that it led to a lifetime of coming together and parting, of false promises and broken oaths, with the girl in the scene bearing the brunt of his wanderings. This slow, gentle fuck under the high, drifting clouds in the backyard of his only house may be related in some way to the memory, given the worn and beautiful woman straddling him may be the same girl and they had shared many such moments since she had accidently flashed her breast and moved like a fluid machine across the field, but after decades chasing the possibility that he may one day feel the same intensity he had resigned himself to letting it reside in this fragment and calling it forth when he needed it.

Anne Marie bowed her head and let a shudder pass through her. Jack came back to the moment, armed with remembered intensity and desire, and placed his hands on her hips. She twitched as if receiving an electric shock. She leaned over and kissed him and he came inside her. They heard a loud crack of plywood and drunken laughter. Anne Marie rolled off and wrapped a blanket around her hips and Jack sat up. He saw the silhouettes of a group of people climbing through the side window of the house behind him. Within minutes the throb of muted bass and drums began as more shadows piled in.

"It's just kids getting into that house to party."

"Should we call the police? Maybe they need some kind of notice that people are living here again."

"By the time the cops would get here those kids will be sober. If they keep it over there I don't mind I guess. They'll probably find another spot in a couple of weeks. Tomorrow Glover and I will nail the plywood shut and that might stop them. I'm thinking if you throw a little barrier in their way they'll get discouraged."

Anne Marie hugged Jack from behind and kissed him on the ear. He kissed her hand and stood up to put his pants back on.

"You're going to sleep in your jeans?"

"I'm thinking I best be ready with all the nonsense going on back there. I won't put my boots on though. Never could get use to sleeping in shoes even though it probably would have been a good skill to learn. More than once I've left shoes at the scene of the crime. No worse way to wake up than running on gravel or a chip and seal road in your stocking feet."

"I'm thinking I don't want to hear the first part of those stories. There's only so many reasons you have to run in the middle of the night."

"True, I lost some damn fine shoes in my day."

"Tomorrow we'll sleep in a room inside and we can sleep together properly, even though there's something fitting to us spending our first night together sleeping on a concrete pad under the stars."

"I think I can sleep in there. I think we cut all the Nazi out of there."

"You better learn how or perform an exorcism because it's going to get awfully cold out here in a couple of months. You'll be sleeping in a snow bank."

"Right now it's nothing but shelter. We have a long way to go."

They fell asleep with their sleeping bags pushed together and their heads inches apart. Sometime after midnight Jack awoke to voices mumbling close to where they lay. He sat up and saw two shadows pissing on the grass in his backyard, so close he could hear the splash of urine on the ground.

"Get the fuck off of my property!" he roared.

Anne Marie snapped awake and the shadows clamped off their streams and shuffled off of the property. A bottle flew over Jack's head, but he didn't know of its flight until it smashed against the foundation of the house. Jack kicked the sleeping bag off of his legs and began to scramble to his feet when Marie grabbed his arm.

"Not on our first night. It's not a good way to start things."

"Anne Marie, if you don't mind me saying, you're choosing sentimentality over a very obvious course of action.

"There's no need for conflict tonight."

"Would you be saying that if you were picking shards of glass out of my forehead? I can't let that pass. They'll think they can do anything."

"They're gone by now. Board up the house tomorrow. Problem solved, right?"

"It's never that easy."

"Maybe this time it will be. You don't know."

Jack lay back down and placed his hands under his head with the sleeping bag still bunched near his feet. Anne Marie placed a hand on his chest.

"I can't guarantee there will be the same resolution on the second night of our life together."

"Fair enough. Are you going to get back in the sleeping bag?"

"I'll stay like this awhile to make sure they don't come back."

In the upstairs bedroom Glover read the newspaper article he found in the wall by the light of a candle stub. Estonia lay curled on the floor as she drifted to sleep, watching the candle flame.

"Do you think this place still exists?"

Estonia didn't understand that Glover addressed the question to her so he had to repeat it three times before she roused herself enough to respond.

"Didn't that happen like eighty years ago?"

"Ya, about that."

"Don't you think they're all dead?"

"Right. You think places like this still exist?"

"Drug houses? You're serious? Aren't we sleeping in one? Isn't this whole neighborhood filled with them?"

"But this was a mystic cult. This doesn't seem like an ordinary drug house."

"I wouldn't know anything about that. What does that mean?"

"I don't know. That's why it doesn't sound like an ordinary drug house. They had something else going on."

"Like underage prostitution from the sounds of it."

"Probably, it just sounds different, like it was a community or something and cocaine and prostitutes were part of their ceremony."

"Don't read too much into it. I think it was just a drug house with a fancy name. Maybe people eighty years ago had to make up names for their sins that made them sound like something other than a sin."

"I think we should still check it out."

"Check what out?"

"Check to see if places like this exist. Sounds like it could be fun or interesting."

"The place doesn't exist. Dr. Thompson was arrested eighty years ago.

He probably died in prison."

"Maybe his son or daughter took it over."

"Like a family business?"

"Ya, maybe he passed it down and now it's legitimate and they sponsor softball teams and a litter prevention program on the side of the highway."

"I think you're spending too much time thinking about this."

"Probably."

Jack awoke stiff and frozen. His back and shoulder had been exposed to the air most of the night as the bag had never been wrapped around him properly. Anne Marie had ducked her head inside her bag and curled against the cold and the dampness in the air. Jack heard hydraulic brakes hiss and the deep rumble of a diesel engine. He staggered to his feet and hobbled to the front of the house where the truck idled, carrying a new dumpster. The same driver as the day before sat behind the wheel.

"You've been busy," the driver said as he surveyed the loaded dumpster from his perch in the cab.

"I can barely walk and my hands feel like claws more than anything else."

"Life's not easy if you want to do something in the world."

"What did Kaufman say when you delivered my message?"

"The man invents swear words. I've never heard some of them that come out of his mouth."

"Yet, here is the dumpster."

"Mister, either he really likes you or you got something big on him. I've never seen him give away anything free and he hates debts. The man will froth at the mouth if he thinks he has a debt to be paid."

"Sometimes luck falls in your lap. Sometimes you need to know when to keep your mouth shut and good things can happen."

"He told me to give you my cell phone number. Call me directly when you need another."

"That'll streamline the operation and eliminate the abuse."

"For you. I have my own cross to bear."

"And you must be heavy in debt to him to put up with him talking to you like that."

"Up to my eyes. I wasn't always Adventist. I'm working off a lot of past stupidity."

"Amen, brother."

The driver exchanged the dumpsters by dropping the empty one on the front yard next to Jack's truck and dragging the full one onto the flatbed by connecting chains to two knobs on either side and flipping on an electric motor that slowly turned the knobs, collecting the chains onto two spools.

"I'm sure I'll be seeing you soon."

The driver nodded and rumbled away with the debris. Jack started his truck, backed it off the lawn and parked it in the back of the house. He pulled out a policeman's flashlight, black and long with the dual purpose of providing illumination and serving as an alternative to a billyclub when needed. Anne Marie stayed asleep through the wheeze and cough of the truck motor, the grinding of a full dumpster being dragged across concrete, and Jack walking past to the house behind them. He twirled the flashlight in his hand to limber his fingers.

First, he walked the perimeter and checked the boards covering the basement, the first floor windows and the front and back doors. One sheet had been pried open, covering a side, first floor window, so he climbed up two makeshift steps and squeezed under the loose plywood, flopping to the floor on the other side. He clicked on the flashlight and swept the room with a beam. He stood near a fireplace that held a mouthful of blackened aluminum and shattered glass. Two mattresses lay on the floor and a collection of rusted and dented folding chairs sat grouped in a ragged semi-circle, the remnant of an audience who had witnessed a lewd exhibition. Jack walked through the house to make sure no stragglers, asleep or dead, remained in the house before he fixed the loose sheet. Glover and Estonia had been right not to stay in this house. The house had been abandoned more recently and still held some of the possessions of the previous owners: a wedding photo hanging on the wall, a laminate dresser, a toothbrush holder with two frayed toothbrushes sticking from the holes, a yellowed and swollen book on how to raise a puppy, several shoes without their twins. The skinheads had not yet marked it as their territory and Jack had to admit the structure felt more solid than his own house. He could feel an active habitation in the house. His house had been abandoned by its owners, then the banks, and then the partiers. It had been exhausted of all its uses, had found a sullied and uneasy terminus until someone walked in, fool enough to come and try to reclaim it. This house careened downward on the same track but still supported some life, no matter how base. Whoever had left had planned to return and Jack had to make sure they couldn't.

By the time Jack returned to his yard Anne Marie had awakened and had been joined by Glover and Estonia, who watched her with dazed eyes as she prepared the coffee. Jack jumped onto the bed of his truck, suddenly agile once his mind had latched onto a project. He threw ten eight foot long two by fours to the ground. He hated using such beautiful wood on a board-up, knowing he would need every scrap he could get his hands on, but ultimately his house would only be as good as the neighborhood and what would be the point of cutting the disease out of his house when more incubated a breath away?

"Jesus, Jack, before breakfast?" Glover whined.

"Work doesn't wait for you to have a full tummy."

"Some kids threw a bottle at us last night," Anne Marie explained.

"They were pissing on my lawn, our lawn."

"And are they still alive?" Estonia piped in.

"They are because of the grace and commonsense of Anne Marie. If she wasn't there there's no telling what would have happened."

"He attacked us," said Glover. "While we were naked."

"We were minding our own business and in charged this rabid dog waving a bottle over his head."

"You were in my house. Fucking in my house to be more precise."

"Thanks. I had gathered as much when Glover said they were naked," Anne Marie said.

"We didn't know. It looked like an old rundown house. We didn't think anybody could possibly own the place. Anybody alive, at least."

"Right, and I had to demonstrate that we had reached the end of bullshit and there would be no more foolishness. Banks own half the country and they're just letting it rot. Glover, grab some of these two by fours and let's get this done."

Jack and Glover carried the wood to the house and threw it through the opening were it clattered against the hardwood floor. Jack also carried a cordless drill, a hand saw, a crescent wrench so rusty it looked like it had been salvaged from a sunken ship and had been forged before the invention of the automobile, a flashlight and a collection of bolts as thick as his thumbs, which would be extraordinarily wide even for thumbs. With Glover holding the light Jack cut the two by fours into four foot lengths with the hand saw by pinning the wood against the kitchen counter and ripping it with four or five strokes. Then, Jack drilled a hole in the center of each board wide enough for a bolt to pass through and a corresponding hole in the plywood sheets covering the windows.

"Before we entomb ourselves in this goddamn place we better go get a ladder," Jack said as he tried to plan the right sequencing for the completion of the job.

They retrieved an aluminum extension ladder and Jack instructed Glover on its use and the plan they were going to follow. Glover would stay outside and push the bolts through the drilled holes in the plywood and Jack would be inside and match the bolt with a two by four. Jack told Glover to extend the ladder to the second floor when he wanted to leave. So they set to work. Glover slipped a bolt through the hole in the plywood sheet, Jack guided it through the hole in the two by four, braced the board against the inside of the window frame, put the nut on the end of the bolt and tightened it with the steel crescent wrench. As the nut tightened it pulled the plywood taut against the outside frame and made it so a vandal, crackhead or Nazi couldn't easily pry the board off unless they brought hand tools. Not one of the three ever thought far enough ahead to carry hand tools, so Jack thought the place might stay secured. Jack used an extra board and bolt on what had become the main entrance and wrenched the nuts until the wood started cracking. They made quick work of the rest of the windows and in an hour's time the extra security had been completed. Jack climbed the stairs to a second floor bedroom window facing the street and smashed out the remaining glass from the frame and waited for Glover to extend the ladder. The ladder banged against the house and Jack caught the last rung before the ladder gathered enough momentum to slide off the house and smash to the ground. He yelled to Glover to stand on the first rung to keep it secure, threw his leg out the window and scrambled down the ladder. He showed another surprising burst of agility, something his bulging and worn body should not have been able to perform, thought Glover, but here he half-slid down the rungs and on the grass before Glover had time to consider just how easy Jack had made climbing out of a window and sliding down a ladder look, like a distended acrobat falling back on years of training.

Jack and Glover carried the ladder and tools back to the house.

"We've already eaten our breakfast. What would you like? Asked Anne Marie as she hugged Jack's sweaty head and kissed him on the ear.

"Coffee. I've got to run and track down a guy about a shipment of wood."

"Kaufman again?"

"Somebody he knows. Charlie Cavano."

"Oh, you have to watch that one. I don't like you doing business with a man like him."

"You know him?"

"You know half the town. I know the other half."

"How do you know him?"

"Through Ben. He worked for Cavano for awhile. He didn't last long. Almost killed the poor man."

"What does he do?"

"What doesn't he do? Once he owned a junkyard, that's where Ben worked, but most of what they had in the lot wasn't junk or previously owned. Then, I think there was a trucking company, a Teamster outfit, and a small manufacturer where he employed nothing but Albanians and Poles who couldn't speak English. Once they learned enough English to ask for a raise or to go to the bathroom he fired them. Old women, young girls, didn't matter. I don't know what he's up to now. I know he had poor Ben so twisted up and confused he stopped being able to make decisions. I couldn't ask him what he wanted for dinner or what TV show he wanted to watch because he would just stare at me afraid to open his mouth. I did all the deciding there for a awhile."

"I hope he can get us a load of wood."

"He can get it. The question is how much is it going to cost you. We might be better off just living in the house like it is before we start making deals with a man like Cavano."

Jack kissed her on the mouth as she handed him a cup of coffee. He headed for his truck.

"What do you want me to do?" Glover asked as Jack passed him.

"Clear that goddamn garage debris. That'll keep you busy until I get back. Anne Marie is in charge. Do what she says."

"What about the kitchen floor?"

"I don't have the proper wood, son. We can't build a floor without wood."

"Then why'd we rip it up?"

"Sometimes you have to see the problem before you know the nature of it."

"Now you have a giant hole in the kitchen. The kitchen is a hole."

"And there's a goddamn hole in your head. Suddenly you've turned into a straw boss and you're telling me how to proceed?"

"I know what makes sense."

Jack dismissed the conversation by continuing to walk to his truck and driving to the pay phone in front of the convenience store, where he dialed Charlie Cavano's number. Cavano answered the phone by sucking a persistent nasal drip back up his nostrils with a sharp inhalation and clearing his throat of the reclaimed phlegm.

"Kaufman gave me your number. He said you might know where I could get lumber."

"I've spoken to Kaufman."

"Then you know I need lumber."

"Are we talking about lumber as in wood? Just for clarification."

"That's what we are talking about."

"You've tried lumber yards, hardware stores, do-it-yourself superstores? They don't got lumber?"

"They do."

"You don't have cash, credit, debit or a checkbook."

"No, I don't."

"No money at all?"

"Not the kind of cash I need."

"So you want free lumber? Is this what we're talking about. Kaufman sends me a maniac who wants free lumber."

"Doesn't have to be free."

"But it can't involve money?"

"No, it can't involve money."

"So what are you offering exactly? Want can you give in return?"

"I don't know."

"So you were hoping that dropping Kaufman's name would be like dropping an aphrodisiac in my drink or that drug that all the young cocks are using today to dope their dates. You were hoping that magical name would make me drop my pants and spread my cheeks, after, of course, assuming the position to grant you easy access."

"I didn't think it would be quite that easy."

"But, in the end, at the conclusion of our little tête a tête that would be the preferred outcome from your perspective."

"I don't want to think about spreading your cheeks."

"Now you're going to insult me?"

"Not an insult, just a fact. I try to stay away from imagining disturbing images. They have a way of piling up and sticking with you until you're just fucking nuts. Spreading your cheeks would fall into that category."

"So what is it you're offering me for this pile of lumber?"

"I've done jobs. Assignments. I can fix almost anything."

"I have a mechanic and a carpenter and a handful of drunk plumbers. What kind of assignments?"

"I've done everything. I worked for Kaufman for five years, but I won't kill no one and I don't mule drugs."

"A man has to know his limitations. These are parameters in which the deal must be done. The parameters are very constricting, however. What do you think goes on out there that doesn't involve killing and drugs? You think I need you to wash my car? Polish my goddamn golf clubs. Have you ever caddied?"

"No, I don't know the first thing about that game."

"Jesus, there's not much to recommend hillbilly culture."

"Those are my limits."

"Two days from now the back gate of Weber Lumber will be open. You'll have about two hours to load up. You better bring a list and an extra pair of hands. Start at one ante meridiem and be done by three. I'll figure out a payment with the guard. I can give a box of cookies to that one and he'll look the other way."

"What's my payment?"

"You're on retainer until something comes up that doesn't involve killing or drugs."

"I don't like debts."

"You don't like money and you don't like debts. You're building a house with your good looks, charming personality and the size of your scrotum sac. I'm not a fucking temp service or hiring hall. Something will come up and when it does you'll do the job. And if you get caught and mention my name I'll have you killed with a knife."

"I don't need a disclaimer. I know how it works."

"Right, because you worked for Kaufman for five years."

"Among other jobs."

"If you're stupid enough to get caught, should the assignment be outside of the suffocating laws of this nation, you'll still owe the debt."

"How much lumber can I take?"

"Whatever you can take in two hours."

"I don't have a phone by the way."

"Kaufman told me where you're living. Down among the animals. I don't think I would put a piece of clean wood down in that neighborhood. Somehow I think the wood deserves better. I'll find you when I need you."

Cavano clicked off and Jack hung up the phone. He mulled over a collection of half-formed strategies to get the wood he needed that didn't involve Cavano, all dead ends because each strategy involved stealing in one form or another and didn't hold the promise of an open gate and two hours load time. He would have liked to have done a job for Cavano before receiving payment. Everyone knew about the trap of compounding interest and debts of service were no different than credit card debts, except debts of service compounded more quickly under a system of subjective regulation. By the time Cavano gave him a job he would be convinced Jack owed him his life or at least a thick slice of it, and the job, no doubt, would be ten times more difficult than a pile of lumber could ever warrant.

When he got back to the house he found the three busy at work. He parked in the street to give them a clear path to the dumpster and he walked into the basement. Estonia pushed hard against a mop to scrub the concrete floor, but she had little luck in getting it clean since sections of the floor were crumbling and sticking to her mop. She wore cut-off jean shorts and a tank top with no bra and Jack felt his legs quiver when he spotted her. She spun around when she heard Jack's footsteps.

"Jack is back," she said as she pushed hair from her eyes and then crossed her arms over her chest.

"If I was forty years younger I'd kill Glover in his sleep and take you for my bride."

"That's just a little creepy, Jack. I appreciate the compliment, I guess."

"I didn't look like this forty years ago."

"Show me a picture. Maybe I could imagine you looking human then. Even monsters can be hot when they're young, huh?"

Jack felt the walls and inspected the corners and the seam where the wall met the floor. The stone and concrete were damp, but he could store his possessions down here for a week or two without the threat of ruin. The truck had to be cleaned so he could haul the lumber, and since the garage had collapsed the basement stood as the only real option.

"It's clean enough. Go help Anne Marie."

Estonia stopped mid-stroke and analyzed the floor.

"The floor is still filthy."

"That's because it's crumbling under the mop and you're just making new dirt. Give me the mop."

Jack held out a hand and Estonia flicked the handle to him, angry that she couldn't see the job to its conclusion, just another example of an adult bossing her around just because they could. She stomped up the stairs, adding an extra sway to her hips in hopes of torturing Jack.

For the rest of the day Jack unloaded the truck, placing everything on makeshift wooden pallets he had crafted out of scrap wood. Glover helped him move the refrigerator, stove and air conditioners with the aid of a hand truck. Jack asked Anne Marie what room she had picked for their bedroom. She had decided on the front bedroom, facing east, that would catch the early morning light and that would be the first room to darken in the evening. Anne Marie obviously considered herself a morning person. Jack and Glover moved the mattress and box springs to the room and set them on the floor.

"You don't have an extra one of these do you?" Glover asked.

"Mattress? No, just one."

"Estonia is tired of sleeping on the floor."

"Then one of you should have strapped a mattress on your back when you left home."

"Don't be a dick."

"We'll keep an eye out. We'll find something. I always do."

Glover made twenty trips to Mary Kelly's house to get fresh water. Anne Marie and Estonia removed all the remaining trash, swept and mopped every floor so that the house smelled like oil soap and revealed for the first time a glimpse of its hidden beauty. Jack imagined that if the house had become a stripper she would have raised her dress and revealed a white and creamy ankle with a promise of more to come.

They ate again on the concrete pad, slumped in a circle around a small propane flame and eating with their plates on their laps. Jack passed on seeing Mary Kelly's athletic build and he fell asleep in his chair as the rest tromped to her house to shower. At some point while they were gone he awoke and stumbled to their room where he slept face down on the bare mattress, still wearing his clothes.

He awoke some eight hours later in the same position with a sheet thrown over him and Anne Marie lying next to him. He rolled off the mattress and onto the floor and blinked at the ceiling. A blue jay, a grackle, and a mob of chickadees chirped in a ragged chorus to the rising sun. They sounded so close they may have been in the room, but Jack remembered that most of the windows no longer had glass so inside or outside made no difference to the quality of sound. He pushed himself up and creaked his way down the stairs, making his way to the outhouse. When he turned the corner of the house he noticed his extension ladder propped up against the house in back, leading to an open second floor window. As he emptied his bowel and bladder he retraced his steps the previous day and watched Glover and he retract the ladder and carry it to the backyard. He remembered thinking as he dozed in the chair that he should lock up the ladder because if nothing else it would fetch a good price at a scrap yard for someone looking for quick money to buy drugs or a bottle. After he completed his morning purge, he walked over to the ladder to make sure they had used his and a quick scan of the nicks and paint splatters confirmed it. Walking to the side of the house, he found the main entrance had been reopened as the plywood sheet and his two by four braces lay broken in the grass.

Jack climbed through the window and nearly fell on two bodies sleeping on one of the filthy mattresses. He stumbled to his feet with elephant steps, but the two didn't stir, not even altering the slow and deep rhythm of their breathing. A couple of liquor bottles, something sweet and cheap, lay at their heads and they looked like they had been poisoned by a carbon monoxide leak as they lay twisted in permanent repose. They were a boy and a girl and for a moment Jack thought of Glover and Estonia and whether or not to extend the same offer to these two castaways, because Glover and Estonia had turned out to be pretty good kids who were just looking for their way and this couple could have been of the same crop. But Jack couldn't shake his anger at them and their friends for sneaking into his yard and toting off his ladder when he had absolutely and unambiguously signaled through his security measures that the party at the house had been closed. Jack kicked a shoe of the boy and shouted for him to wake-up, but other than rolling on his side the boy didn't respond. Jack kicked again and produced an eye lid flutter. He leaned down and grabbed a handful of pants and shirt and lifted him into the air with a jerk. The boy opened his eyes as Jack raised him over his head and threw him against the wall. The back of the boy's head smacked on the floor and he let out a howl. The girl woke up and witnessed Jack spring into the air and land on the boy's chest with both knees. He cocked his arm and sent a fierce blow to the left side of the boy's head and then another to the right side. The girl sat up and cast a line of curses in a rising scream. As Jack inflicted more punishment, he barked out his own epithets to spice up a curt lecture on never using a man's ladder without permission. The boy stopped defending himself as blood streamed from his mouth and nose. Jack stood up and grabbed the boy the pants and shirt again. He lifted him and ran toward the window, releasing him as the boy's shoulders broke the plane of the opening, slinging him out of the house. His legs caught on the sill, causing his waist to scissor and his face to smack against the siding. He landed on his shoulder and neck and flopped to the grass. Jack turned his attention to the girl who had been incoherently wailing once she had exhausted her dictionary of curses, deep as it had been. Jack grabbed her by the arm and she tried to scratch his face with her free hand. He spun around her, pinned both arms to her sides and marched her to the window. He released her arms and pushed her in the back. She swung a leg out of the opening and scrambled free. Once on the ground, she tried to get the boy to stand on his feet, as she started swearing again.

"Never mind how much cock I suck. Just tell your friends to stay the fuck out of this neighborhood and to stay the fuck specifically away from this house. I'm not tolerating another fucking night of your bullshit. You got to respect a man's tools and where he lives or you can expect a shitstorm to come down on your heads."

Jack watched them stagger away toward the front of the house and then he climbed out. He walked to the ladder and brought the extension down. He carried it to his yard and berated himself for not chaining it to a tree the night before. He had been lucky to get it back. Three of his knuckles on his right hand were cut and bleeding so he wrapped a greasy rag around his hand and tied it. He would keep it on until the blood clotted, but he expected the wounds to open again once he started working. Cuts on the knuckles always seemed to take the longest to heal. He filled the percolator up with water and coffee, using three too many scoops, and lit the propane burner. He set the pot over the flame and sat down in a lawn chair. It didn't seem possible the neighborhood still lay asleep as a thick knot of rage still coursed through him. His hand throbbed and the old ache in the knees had turned sharp and intense. Adrenalin started to thicken and slow and he could feel his body relaxing into the nylon straps of the chair. The percolator started popping coffee through the clear knob on the top of the pot. Jack waited for his family to rise so he could start hacking out the walls of the house as he contemplated the consequences of his brief violence.

When they did awake they found that Jack had cooked a breakfast of pancakes, eggs and bacon. As he cooked he wondered how long the food would last and decided not to worry about inevitable developments such as the running out of money and hunger. He dodged all the questions about his bloody hand and his hobbled gait, preferring to map out the day's plan. Jack had already boarded up the opening to the house again, this time using a piece of his own plywood, which added to his dark mood. Glover and he would continue chopping out the plaster and lathe and Anne Marie and Estonia would come up with their own plan, since he believed Anne Marie more than capable of designing and completing a project.

"Unless you want to grab a crowbar and start swinging, you can see what needs to be done around the house."

"I'll need the truck," Anne Marie responded.

"I don't need it today."

"I'll work on getting some materials."

"What?"

"Materials, for building. I know you have that deal brewing with Cavano, but I have my own connections."

"Anne Marie, I'm pretty particular about the stuff I build with. In a couple of days I'll have wood for a garage and a kitchen floor."

"Then you'll need tile and cabinets and appliances and light fixtures."

"We have appliances."

"I love those antiques of yours, but I'm not cooking on them. I'll blow myself up using that stove. I mean it looks more like a piece from a gas chamber than anything else."

"That's a low blow. You know my disgust of Nazis. How am I going to eat food prepared on that stove now?"

"You won't. Since I'm going to be the one cooking most of the time I get my say. Leave the kitchen to me."

"I can't stand cheap stuff. Old is OK, but there's so excuse for cheap."

"Goddamnit, Jack, I know walnut from plywood. Who do you think you're talking to?"

"I never said you didn't. I have a vision of how I want it to look."

"So do I and I'm going to be using it mostly. Trust me. I'm not going cheap. I have my own visions."

"What should I do with my refrigerator and stove?"

"That would be up to you."

Jack walked away, crowbar in hand, making a small noise of agreement by sucking air between his front teeth. Glover followed in his wake, trying to twirl his crowbar like a baton and nearly smashing his toes more than once. Anne Marie and Estonia hopped into the truck and roared away from the house. They had not found a rhythm of small talk as they had spent the past two days together in vast stretches of silence, and this ride began no differently. Anne Marie had raised three boys so she knew young women through their roles as girlfriends or wives, and these relationships were clouded by her varying degrees of disappointment and pride in her sons. The women they had chosen merely confirmed their personalities and paved the paths they had chosen to follow, so the women bore little individuality outside of confirming one son's solid and respectable manhood and two sons' dissolution and fear. So, when faced with a girl not connected with a son she came up blank each time she tried to start a conversational thread. Three minutes into the ride Anne Marie decided to treat the whole situation much like she would if she had found a injured bird on the side of the road.

"Do you think you're pregnant, Estonia?"

"Pregnant? No, I don't think so. I mean probably not," Estonia stuttered to a stop and a sob caught in her throat before she could finish.

"Have you done a test?"

"No. I don't have any money. Glover might have a little, but I didn't want to ask him."

"Did you think of stealing one?"

"Most places have them locked up in a glass cabinet or have them behind the counter." By now tears were running down her cheeks and she crossed her arms over her breasts, hoping to contain a modicum of control as the stress of secrecy and aloneness released.

"How long has it been?'

"Awhile."

"Glover?"

"He doesn't know or even suspect anything. He'll flip."

"I mean, you're sure it's his?"

"There's never been another. Maybe a blowjob here and there, but not sex."

Anne Marie found herself so hunched over she looked through the steering wheel to see the road. She slowly straightened her back and tried to remain conscious of her posture as she thought through the next steps.

"First, let's confirm the diagnosis."

They drove to a superstore, lighted like a hospital and just as clean, and wandered past lawn mowers and jewelry, soft drinks and televisions before they found the pharmacy section. Anne Marie pushed a red button near the cabinet of pregnancy tests and a laconic woman's voice, maybe with an edge of sarcasm, announced that a patron needed help in the family planning aisle, even though it had been recorded and approved in a distant corporate headquarters and decisions such as what voice to use for pre-recorded announcements skewed toward neutrality. Maybe, Anne Marie thought, the corporate bosses thought sarcasm could pass for condemnation in most parts of the country and could quell their moral objections to making money off of devices employed in pre-martial sex. Estonia fingered the condoms, lubricants, oils and gels and realized she had begun to cry again or had never stopped crying once she had begun. She wiped her face just as a clerk, clad in a red smock with downy muttonchops spilling along his jaw line and a wallet connected to a chain bouncing on his thigh, turned the corner of the aisle. He produced a bundle of keys, unlocked the cabinet and stood back as Anne Marie made the choice. The novelty of beautiful young women needing pregnancy tests had worn off for the clerk long ago since he had seen twenty-five to thirty a day for the past three months of his employment. During his first week he rated their bodies, imagined what position they may prefer, guessed at the smell of their necks and the shape of their nipples, but after the onslaught he came to see his job as keeper of the cabinet keys as depressing because most of the girls seemed distraught and desperate, and he didn't give Estonia a second look, preferring to stare at the row of overhead light fixtures instead.

Anne Marie made her choice and the clerk locked the cabinet again and carried the test to the checkout line. After Anne Marie paid for it she made Estonia double back to the restrooms at the rear of the store to take the test in one of the stalls. Anne Marie waited nearby in an aisle of lawn chairs, tiki torches, decorative porch lighting and garden gnomes. Ten minutes later Estonia came out of the bathroom and handed Anne Marie the wand. A very clear blue plus sign had developed in the middle of a white circle.

"There's two in a pack. Might as well do the other one."

Estonia pulled the other wand from the box and gave it to Anne Marie. If possible, the blue looked a little brighter and the plus sign a little thicker than the first one she had seen. Anne Marie placed a hand on Estonia's shoulder and she collapsed against her chest. Anne Marie brought her other hand, holding the two wands, around her waist to hold her. She felt an overwhelming sadness for every child who had ever made a mistake and she knew, from bungling many such moments with her own sons, that the only thing that might help is if she stayed close and kept her mouth shut. Estonia needed a beating heart and a warm hand and not a single word, because any word would be a recrimination, a lecture, another beating.

They found a lunch counter in the store and sat down at a plastic table. Anne Marie sipped a cup of weak coffee and Estonia stared at the carbonation rising to the top of her Coke.

"Do you want to go home?"

"Bakersfield?"

"Yes."

"No, the day before I left my dad told me I'd be pregnant in six months and not to come back if I was."

"People say things. When it becomes reality they change their tune. I don't know anything about them, but I bet they wouldn't turn you out."

"No, he meant it. That's how he is. My mom said the same thing. She called me all kind of names. They really hate Glover."

"Now they have another reason."

"They'll never forgive me. I'm on my own."

"Maybe things aren't so cut and dry. Anger gives way to forgiveness most times when it involves your child."

"I'm not going back to California."

"Jack is loyal. You have a place to stay. You don't have to go anywhere. We're not going to turn you out into the streets."

"Has he always been this crazy?"

"The man I fell in love with decades ago was seven times crazier than this version."

"God."

"There's a reason it's taken this long for him to settle down."

"This is settled?"

"This is settled for Jack."

"Glover thinks he's killed people. More than one."

"Maybe. If it happened it would be closer to manslaughter than murder."

"I don't know the difference between the two."

"Jack's a good man."

"He beat somebody up before 6 AM."

"Are you talking about his bloody hand?"

"Why else wouldn't he talk about it?"

"Jack is a good man to have on your side."

Estonia finally took a sip of Coke through her straw.

"Let's go see about our kitchen cabinets," Anne Marie said, hoping to sum up the conversation and move Estonia out of her torpor.

"We passed the kitchen aisle on the way over here."

"Honey, the cabinets here are not much more than painted cardboard. If I brought these home Jack might throw me on the street just for having no construction sense."

Estonia hoped her dilemma could have held the attention of the world for a moment, at least until she finished her drink, but shoppers strolled by with loaded carts and were oblivious to her pain. Even Anne Marie looked suddenly impatient as she swallowed the dregs of her coffee and waited for Estonia to move. Estonia put her hands over her eyes and she wanted to play peek-a-boo with the unsuspecting shoppers, except that when she obliterated them with her hands they would actually disappear from the earth to some formless and airless world of her imagination. Maybe she could use her hands to blind her own eyes then mute her mouth and deafen her ears and continue to destroy all the functions of her body one palm print at a time.

"You can terminate the pregnancy."

"I can't believe this is my life."

"It might be time to start believing."

Estonia finished her drink in silence and they walked out of the store. Anne Marie drove the truck deep into the city to a neighborhood west of where they lived. They passed abandoned slaughterhouses, tanneries and a couple of miles of empty sidewalk. She found a narrow alleyway that skirted a hulking black building with green plywood over the windows. Behind the building a short row of three worker cottages sat in shadow and gloom. The houses were so close to the building they could have sheltered a function of whatever industrial process the building had once housed. She parked in front of the middle house and knocked on the front door, unleashing a cacophony of barking and growling dogs chained in the backyard. Estonia stayed in the truck and stared at her knees. A dirty kid with a red ring around his mouth from having eaten a package of popsicles answered the door. The boy told Anne Marie his father worked in the workshop and pointed to a door, propped open with a cinder block, at the back of the black building. Anne Marie nodded and told the boy to wash his face before jumping off the porch and making her way to the door. Estonia didn't acknowledge her as she passed so Anne Marie reached out two fingers and lightly dragged them across Estonia's arm resting on the edge of the window. Estonia jumped and briefly smiled before her thoughts retreated back to a narrative akin to a disaster film. She imagined herself cradling a baby in her arms, standing in a field recently leveled by a tornado or bomb with houses piled around her like a jumble of sticks and cars lying on their hoods and Glover and her family dead in the rubble. The baby clawed at her breast, but when she looked down her nipples had disappeared and the baby sucked a mouthful of skin. She wanted to scream, but who would hear her? In what pile of rubble could she possibly find food for such a small infant?

Anne Marie ducked inside the door and let her eyes adjust to the dimness before walking further. Fifty yards ahead in the gloom she could see her brother working at a bench, two floodlights on either side illuminating his work. As she walked toward him she could hear animals, most likely rats, running in the shadows. Her brother slowly caressed a thick slab of mahogany with a piece of sandpaper. He wore safety glasses with yellow lenses and greasy overalls. A coating of dust covered his face, hair and torso.

"You have room for expansion," Anne Marie said as her brother finished a sanding stroke.

He looked up from his work and, seeing who had come to visit, he took off his glasses and tried to straighten his hunched back. She had always been his favorite sister, and probably favorite sibling, but the competition for the title had not been fierce or inspired.

"I own the whole block. I'm a real estate mogul. I bought this building for a song. Literally, I went down to the courthouse and sang *In-A-Godda-Da-*

Vida and they gave me the title to this building. If I had some more money or I knew a few more songs I'd buy up the entire west side."

Anne Marie walked around the bench and gave him a hug and a kiss on the cheek.

"My nephew is filthy and fat."

"I can't keep that one out of the refrigerator. Never have a kid late in life. The others I battled and kept them on the run. I don't have the energy for this one so I just let him sit around and watch TV and he's always hungry. He's going to be enormous, but I don't see how I can change any of it."

"What about his mother?"

"She's already enormous and watches TV all day. What help is she going to be?

"I left Ben."

"Why? At some point doesn't inertia take over?"

"You remember Jack?"

"Not the Cactus? He's still alive?"

"And kicking."

"When did this happen?"

"A couple of days ago."

"Jack was never the marrying kind."

"I'm not going to marry him. I want to take one last ride."

"My big sis still has some fire in her. You best be careful, Anne Marie, you might have thirty years left in you. That's a mighty long time to take a ride with Jack."

"I have embers left. Don't flatter me with talk of fire."

"How's Ben taking it?

"I don't know. He just needs someone to do his laundry once a month and clean up his vomit in the morning. Other than that I can't see him missing me much."

"That's pleasant. I wouldn't underestimate Ben, though. He was once capable of performing his own misdeeds."

"It hasn't been pleasant for fifteen years."

"But Cactus Jack? The chances of that ending bad are pretty high."

"It's going to end with one of our deaths, so I'd have to agree there's a hundred percent chance of it ending badly."

"I mean before his demise."

"I'm already living with him, so it's a little late for the warning."

"Where are you living?"

"Two blocks from the old house. Don't say I'm not a world traveler. It's a beat up old house. Do you remember the story of the woman living on her porch?" She paused to see if her brother remembered the story that had made the newspaper and a couple the television stations. When he showed no sign of remembering she continued. "Anyway, it's beautiful and rotted and we're going to rehab it."

"Does Ben know all this?"

"Why are you so worried about Ben? He should know it, depending how drunk he was when Jack told him. He told him straight out. It was almost like Jack was asking Ben's permission for my hand in marriage."

"Really?"

"No, not really much like that at all other than it seemed like part of a ceremony. I felt like I had been passed off between two alphas or an alpha and a zeta and they had to perform this little dance to make the transaction complete. Something to eliminate hard feelings and revenge."

"At least I understand the reason for your visit."

"Don't I visit you when I don't want something? I don't always have my hand out."

"That's why you're my favorite sister. The others can't say the same thing."

"I want you to build the cabinets for our new kitchen."

"Jack's a good carpenter. What does he think about this idea?"

"Jack's a different kind of carpenter. I don't think he can build cabinets like you. I want yours in my last kitchen. I have money. I've been keeping it away from Ben for years and years, so I can pay for what I want."

"Like I would charge my big sis. I won't take your money and if you insist I won't do the job. What kind of wood?"

"Cherry."

"Thank you. Inspired choice. Nobody orders cherry much anymore. Everybody wants sleek and blonde. I try to sell them on cherry. I tell them they can see the past in the grain. I tell them there are songs inside the wood. I think I freak them out more than anything, but I feel I have to try."

"I've heard the pitch often enough that you've convinced me."

"You didn't come to this decision on your own?"

"Of course I did. I picked it in spite of your selling techniques."

"Good, you really have to pick a wood after carefully thinking about it. It'll drive you crazy otherwise. Never invite a wood into your house unless you can't imagine living without it, because otherwise every morning it will stare you in the face and you'll feel like taking a hatchet to it. When do you need them?"

"Couple of months will do. No rush really. Cabinets are the least of our worries in that house."

"I was hoping for a year. If you want them done right. I'm a mogul, remember. I have people and property and headaches on top of headaches. But I'm already thinking about what they are going to look like and I think I know where I can get a load of cherry."

She gave him the address so he could come and measure the dimensions of the kitchen, and she walked toward the white rectangle of the open door. Her brother watched her silhouette recede and called to her when she had neared the door. Her name echoed through the empty space and the rats sniffed the air as if the words carried a scent.

"Any ideas for my fat son?"

She stopped and turned, blocking most of the light from the door.

"Stop buying popsicles."

He waited for the echo to stop before responding.

"It's the wife. She buys them for him and for herself."

"Maybe it's time for a new wife."

He coughed a short burst of hysterical laughter that carried twice as much bitterness as joy.

"That's not likely."

Anne Marie waited to see if he had more to say, but he buried his head back in his work as he started scraping the sandpaper across the mahogany. She turned and took the last two steps out of the building, shielding her eyes against the harsh light with a hand across her brow. She found Estonia asleep in the truck, her head jammed in the corner between the seat and the door. She awoke when Anne Marie started the truck and a fresh whiff of burning oil filled the cab. Her unfocused gaze roamed from her knees, through the windshield and to Anne Marie before her eyelids narrowed and a glint of recognition forced its way through the fog.

"I take it I'm still pregnant."

"Unless you took care if it yourself. You didn't sleep it away."

"That's too bad because in my dream I wasn't pregnant anymore and I could still fit into these cute little shorts I have. I get the most comments when I wear those shorts."

"You'll wear them again."

"With a baby on my hip. It won't be quite the same."

"No, but you'll still be cute."

"With a baby on my hip."

Anne Marie sighed and gave Estonia a long look.

"Or not," she said.

Estonia closed her eyes against the mounting pressure in her head. A migraine had taken root and in a matter of minutes it would overtake her body.

When they returned to the house they helped Glover and Jack haul chunks of plaster and lathe to the dumpster. Estonia begged off the work after two trips carrying the moldy plaster and walked to her room, where she lay down and cried the rest of the afternoon. Glover and Jack had chopped out the walls on the first floor and the stairwell leading up to the second. Anne Marie made a light lunch of sandwiches and apples. Jack ate standing, having not bothered to wipe the dust and grime from his hands or face, and finished both the sandwich and apple in under ten bites. He washed it all down with a couple of swigs of tepid water and picked up his crowbar. As he climbed the stairs to the second floor he thought he should consider quitting for the day and conserving his energy for what would be an entertaining evening, if he knew anything about the inability of some people to walk away from a situation, no matter the degree of humiliation suffered, that they had no chance of winning or salving their past defeats. But what if he stopped and let four or five productive hours go by and the punks didn't show up? What if it took them three days to regroup and build up enough anger to come give the Old Cactus another try? He couldn't let his life be controlled by if-comes or the house had no chance of ever being completed. He sank the claw end of the crowbar into a soft patch of plaster and chunks fell to the floor. He yanked and a sickening break sounded, akin to the sound of breaking fingers, as the lathe splintered. By the time the claw hit the wall a second time he had forgotten all about the fight to come and conserving his energy for it.

They worked until the light in the house turned gray. They pried off their gloves and tried to straighten their finger with little success. Anne Marie and Estonia had already showered and were preparing dinner by the time Jack and Glover tromped downstairs. Jack sent Glover ahead to Mary Kelly's as he swept the floors one last time, even though all the dust would settle in the night and leave a thick blanket for them in the morning, and he picked up stray pieces of plaster that had been dropped on the way to the dumpster. Glover returned with his hair slicked back and flushed skin, but plaster dust still clung to the interior folds of his ear. Anne Marie handed Jack a plastic bag of clean and folded clothes with a towel and he made the walk to Mary Kelly's.

She answered the door wearing spandex running clothes and she had pulled her hair back into a pony tail.

"You're dirtier than you were yesterday. I didn't think that was possible."

"And I'll be dirtier tomorrow."

"What are you planning to do tomorrow?"

"Whatever is thrown in my way."

"There might be a gallon of hot water left. Glover likes long showers."

"You don't run in this neighborhood, do you?"

Mary Kelly inspected her body and Jack's eyes followed. Even clad in material as unforgiving as spandex her body looked almost perfect to him.

"I have a treadmill. I'm just another hamster in a cage."

Jack thought to say something like, "If hamsters looked like you, I'd consider them something better than rats," but he left it unspoken because he thought he might be trying to advance the ball too far too soon in this new game with his neighbor. Launching an attack too soon ran the risk of losing access to water and never seeing her in her running clothes again and that would have been a shame on both fronts.

"Glover said he'd run with me if I ever want to get out of the house."

"That might be awhile. He's not going to feel like running over the next couple of months."

"That's what he said."

"Your son interested in doing any work?"

"Interested? No. I'm sure he wouldn't be. Should I send him your way, though?"

"He can always come back and lay on the couch if it doesn't work out."

"It's getting him off the couch in the first place that's the problem."

"If you can get him to come, send him. We have so much work, I'm probably going to kill poor Glover."

"That would be a shame." She backed from the door to allow Jack to enter. As he started downstairs she stopped him. "If you want to use the upstairs shower. It's a lot nicer."

"No, I don't want to track up your house. I'd prefer to wash up down there. Hopefully, Glover at least took off his shoes."

Mary Kelly shrugged, a response that snapped close the line of inquiry of Glover's movements in her house, and she disappeared around the corner leading to the kitchen. Jack walked downstairs and slowly peeled off his clothes, feeling like he shed a crust, and washed himself deliberately. Either Anne Marie or Mary Kelly had set out a fresh bar of soap and cheap shampoo that could have been used on hair or carpet so the washing proved more effective than the previous day. He shampooed his hair twice and let the water drip into his ears, using Glover's inattention as a guide. After he dried himself and dressed, his clawed hands, which refused to straighten past sixty degrees, existed as the only reminder of the day's labor. He noted to ask Glover when he had taken up an interest in jogging. Was he going to run in his tattered jeans and army boots? He had to give the kid some credit though for casting his line in a river even though he had no idea of its current or depth.

They ate a meal of chicken skewers, roasted red peppers and brown rice, as Anne Marie focused her attention on the proper nutrition for Estonia's maternity. Jack drank three beers before he felt the slightest pressure on his stomach and thought that either the work had made his taste less discriminating or Anne Marie had become a better cook than he remembered her being. Glover built a small circle of cast off bricks and built a fire. Jack watched closely, but Glover's technique worked competently enough so Jack kept his advice to himself. They all leaned back in their chairs and let the fire warm the soles of their feet. Anne Marie had checked on Estonia periodically since they returned with the results and now watched her through the orange glow of the fire, but she did not betray the turmoil within, even though her face had remained puffy from an afternoon of crying. She held Glover's hand and looked contemplative and resigned. Glover stared at the side of her face as she looked into the fire. He thought the few days work or the regular food had made her even more beautiful. If he had ever dreamed he could be tramping across the country with a girl as beautiful as Estonia he may have attended a few more days of high school and seriously attempted to earn a diploma. Until Estonia his girlfriends had been fat or acne-scarred or both and they always seemed to represent to him his very real lack of opportunity or his complete confusion concerning how the populace at large maintained themselves in successful and productive lives. He could imagine being trapped by one of them and buying a trailer near some work and slowly being driven insane, drinking hard and fast for an early exit from his life. So the day Estonia came to him, like she had been sculpted out of clay just for him, made to his specifications and his desires, planted a seed of despair and regret, because he started thinking the first day he met her that he should have prepared himself for her entrance and not have been beguiled by his acne-scarred sluts into thinking life offered nothing better than trailer parks and bloat. Had he been prepared he would have had a fighting chance to keep Estonia and make a life for them, but as it was, each additional day she stayed with him seemed more incredible than the day previous. She could do better than him and he had no doubt that one day she would.

By the time night deepened they all were asleep in their chairs, except for Jack who tended the fire and watched the dark house behind them. He gathered more wood and his scuffling woke Anne Marie, as she watched him strategically place lathe in the tongues of flame.

"You can't help yourself," she said in a hoarse whisper.

"What?"

"You have to build. The fire looks like a five-pointed star. Most people would have been content to throw the wood in a heap."

"Most people don't take the time to learn anything. They'd rather pay somebody else to do it for them or they are content to just do it wrong."

Estonia and then Glover roused, stretched and shuffled off to bed to sleep in the haze of plaster dust, mumbling their good nights as they rubbed the smoke out their eyes. They reminded Jack of sleepy children up past their bedtimes, and he realized the image stood closer to their true selves than they wanted to believe. Anne Marie leaned over and dialed down her voice just above an inaudible level once Estonia and Glover were in the house.

"She's definitely pregnant. Confirmed by two tests."

"Is she keeping it?"

"Probably. The girl is in a fog. She's not the easiest person to deal with, but it's always a shock to run smack into the end of your childhood."

"I suppose we can figure out a way to help either way."

"I thought I was going to throttle her in the truck. She's not quite in reality yet, because what she really needs to do is go home, but she's saying that's not an option."

"You have to know some people who can help."

"I do."

"It shortens the time frame when all this has to get done."

A piece of wood cracked, sounding very close to a shot fired from a small caliber handgun, and a horrible wrenching and splintering sound followed. Another window or door had been opened in the house behind them. Next came a solitary burst of drunken laughter and a chorus of hushing sounds. Jack stood up and heard a sharp rustle in the grass, but he stood too close to the fire to see much beyond the perimeter of its cast light. From above came a hail of bottles and rocks. A bottle glanced off his jaw and a rock struck him in the thigh. Anne Marie crouched low, covered her head with her hands and missed being hit. Jack took a step forward and a bottle caught him in the mouth, splitting his lower lip and knocking out an incisor. He fell to his knees and a third wave rained down upon him and then a fourth. Blood poured from his lip and pooled on the dirt below his chin. A chunk of brick hit Anne Marie on the back of her head and she placed a palm over the throbbing wound and tried not to pass out. Jack made it to his feet, sucked the blood from his lip, and spit a mouthful into the fire. He had been hit eight or nine times besides in the mouth and on each spot a welt had begun to rise. He helped Anne Marie into a chair and lightly touched her forehead with a solitary finger before turning toward the black house. He considered his options as another bottle skimmed past his head. Anne Marie had to be taken from the line of fire, so he gently lifted her by the arms and guided her into the house and up the stairs to their room. Jack's thumping and cursing woke Glover who opened the door and stood naked on the landing, holding a flashlight. The knot on Anne Marie's head had kept swelling and the effort to climb the stairs had made her dizzy.

"Sheath that pecker of yours and get that light out of my eyes. Go to Mary Kelly's and get some ice. Wake up Estonia and have her sit with Anne Marie until I get back. Tell her not to let her fall asleep."

"What happened to her? What happened to your lip?"

"Never mind. Just look after her," Jack said, holding blood inside his lip like a wad of chew. "Give me the goddamn flashlight."

He guided her to the bed and tried to prop her up with all the pillows without bumping the injured part of her head. He heard Glover run downstairs and Estonia came into the room wearing nothing but an oversized tank top, obviously Glover's, that gave the illusion of her being dressed without really covering anything. She fell down on the mattress beside Anne Marie who squinted an eye against the pain.

Jack left the room smacking the flashlight against the palm of his right hand. His mouth had filled with blood and he had nowhere to spit, so he swallowed it. He walked to the basement and sorted through his possessions until he found a five gallon gasoline can filled to the top and four rags, old t-shirts with faded writing and graphics that advertised car parts, chewing tobacco, a sports team, and beer. Outside near the fire he found an unburned piece of construction wood and soaked the end in gasoline. He wrapped the car parts t-shirt tightly around the gas-soaked end and he soaked the shirt in gas as well. He touched the shirt to the fire and he raised a torch, the likes of which hadn't been seen since ignorant villagers chased a frightened monster through plowed fields and tangled forests. He picked up the gas can and remaining rags and headed for the house. Their attackers had long gone and Jack stepped over a small pile of ammunition they had forgotten to throw. He threw the torch into the open window and scrambled in after it. By the time he retrieved the torch it had blackened a small circle on the hardwood floor. He dragged a mattress with one hand, carrying the torch in the other, to the second floor and placed it on the landing in the middle of three bedrooms. He descended the stairs and fetched the can. He splashed a trail of gas up the stairs and soaked the mattress. He touched the torch to the trail and a line of fire blazed, terminating at the mattress. He splashed gas throughout the living and dining rooms and on the second mattress. He threw down the torch and both rooms filled with orange light. After picking up the empty gas can, he climbed out the window. Outside he found the broken piece of plywood and bracing and threw them into the fire. He walked back to his house and stowed the gas can in the basement and returned outside, where he turned a chair to face the coming blaze. He sat down heavily and spit a clot into the dying embers of the campfire.

The boards over the windows and doors kept the fire a secret long enough for it to spread throughout the three floors and ensure the house's doom. Smoke started pouring out of the open window and holes were soon burned through the roof. The smoke spread through the neighborhood and the back of Jack's throat began to feel raw from breathing it in. Sirens warbled over the rooftops and through the narrow streets. By the time a fire truck and police car stopped in front of the house the roof had turned into an orange and black column of flame, tossing fist-sized embers on the house next door. Several small fires burned on the roof and porch of the second house and some embers were landing in Jack's backyard, threatening the outhouse more than the house. As firefighters hooked the hose to a fire hydrant and planned an attack, a small explosion rocked the second house and the whole façade succumbed to the flames. Two firefighters chopped open the side door of the second house and ran in. A second set of sirens whistled through the streets. The second house burned faster than first. The other firefighters tried to shoot water on both houses until help arrived, but the one hundred year old wood burned faster than the water could be sprayed and within another ten minutes both houses had been lost. They switched their plan and tried to keep the fire contained to just the two houses, because the whole block could easily be lost. A second and third truck found the street and soon half a dozen ropes of water blasted the houses. The two firefighters emerged from the second house carrying an elderly woman between them. They brought her to the sidewalk where they placed an oxygen mask over her mouth and checked her pulse. Small clusters of neighbors stood in their yards or on the street and watched the firefighters swarm around the houses. Two came into Jack's yard, saw him sitting in the chair, and asked if the fire had spread in this direction. Jack mumbled through his swollen lip that the fire had missed him. Once the houses had been torn down he could plant a small orchard or a vegetable garden in the footprint of the foundations. He would more than likely have to build a high fence around the land to keep the neighbors from stealing his food once the trees bore fruit. But what could be better than growing tomatoes and corn, apples and peaches in your own backyard? In the spring he could look on the blossoms of the trees from his second story windows and he could walk among them, breathing the sweet and thick scent. He pushed himself off the chair and hobbled into the house to check on Anne Marie as the fires continued to rage.

Another One of Life's Holes

"No, you were going to be different. You weren't coming back to the hole. Wouldn't listen to Pez. You were leaving and never coming back, no siree," Pez rasped through the darkness. "I told you it would do no good to leave. They just bring you back and they keep bringing you back until you just don't leave no more. I told you, but you wouldn't listen to me. Nobody listens to Pez. That's alright. Sooner or later you'll understand by yourself then you'll say to yourself that Pez knew what he was talking about."

Nelson blinked his eyes open and the small circle of light shone above him again, but this time it seemed more distant than he remembered it. He tried to scratch an itch on his nose, but when he tried to raise his left hand, his itching hand, it wouldn't come away, when using the force he thought he needed to raise a hand and scratch his nose. He clenched his fist and found that his hand lay submerged in a reservoir of viscous goo. His other hand remained free, fortunately, and when he moved his toes, really more to take inventory of the situation than a need to employ his feet in freeing his hand, he discovered his right foot had been trapped by the same viscosity, although in a separate and distinct pool.

"Damn curs took my shoes again."

"It's always the same. You end up in a hole of their making with no shoes. I told you this, but who would listen to a little man like Pez. There's no reason to listen to me. I'm a man without information and form. I'm a man whose very existence is in question."

"That's true, Pez. I'm not particularly comfortable in believing in your existence."

"Well, here we are again. Maybe you can believe that. Smell the dirt around you. Grab a handful and put it to your nose. Maybe you can believe in dirt, eh?"

Nelson made his trapped hand into a flat plane and pulled against the jelly. At first he thought he may be pulling the skin and sinew off his fingers, right down to the clean white bone, because the goo wouldn't release its hold and he used a considerable amount of strength to free himself. Suddenly his hand popped free and for a moment he wondered which had given way first, his skin or the goo, until he clasped both hands together and he didn't feel anything abnormal, except a few traces of the substance lodged between his middle and index fingers and matted in the hair on the back of his hand. Three of his fingers felt close to dislocation and throbbed in protest, but he cracked them back to place without much trouble. Pointing his toe, he straightened his foot and tried to pull his leg free. Even though it should have been easier given the superior strength of his leg compared to his underdeveloped arm, the jelly would not give up its grip. He clawed at the earthen floor above his head, creating grips for his hands, and pulled with both arms, as he used the ceiling of the hole to push off with his free leg. By keeping up a constant pressure he made progress, as the trapped foot began to slide out a centimeter at a time, and he pushed and pulled until his arms began to shake from exhaustion. Nelson thought he may have to relax his effort and lose the gains he had made. He could gather his strength and breath, now knowing the length of time he would have to employ his muscles in the extraction, and chalk up the first attempt as a pilot mission during which necessary information had been collected, but right before he gave up the jelly released the foot with a loud slurp. He crawled up the slope of the hole, away from the traps and fell on his back, breathing the moist, earthy air into the deepest nook of his lungs.

"That was fine technique," Pez's voice almost whispered into his ear, as Nelson had obviously crawled toward him instead of away or Pez had somehow scrambled past him as he extracted himself.

"Do you know this city, Pez?" Nelson asked between breaths.

"Lot's changed since I've been down here. Sometimes I wonder what's left, if it's even the same city at all. Maybe I've been buried under a different place without my knowledge. Maybe the dogs have played one final joke on old Pez, buried him under a strange city and a strange people who old Pez doesn't know. All the time I've been dreaming of the life I once knew being played out above my head, but that old life is miles away, maybe in a different state or country and what's above my head bears no resemblance to what I once knew. Maybe the people speak without using their tongues. Maybe I wouldn't recognize the shape of the buildings or the spray of stars in the sky. Maybe Centaurus and Musca twirl in the sky in a northerly direction."

"Assuming for a moment it is the city you left would you know your way around?"

"Of course, if it resembles the city I left, then it follows that since I've lived in or below it my entire life I could find my way around. I think I still have the grid memorized. They haven't changed the names of streets, yet. I could draw it in the dirt, but an outsider might not find it terribly compelling since it is, after all, a grid, like most American cities. If the dogs have had their fun and the city that sits atop of us is a different place than the one I've left, then I would not know the streets or the people. But if it's an American city, it stands to reason that we could find our bearings by deciphering the grid, but I couldn't be sure where I would want to go or how I could apply my grid knowledge since I find it hard to believe I would have a destination in an alien town."

Nelson turned over on his hands and knees. He reached out a hand, the one that had not been in the jelly, in the direction of Pez's voice, but he touched nothing but air. He squinted against the darkness, but he couldn't find a silhouette or any movement to tell him where Pez might be sitting precisely.

"Are you there, Pez?"

"What do you mean?"

"Where are you?"

"What does that matter? The only thing you need to know is that I'm in a hole with you. You're lucky to have my company at all. I've spent years down here by myself with only my thoughts to keep me company. The dogs never saw fit to bring down another person that might keep Pez from going crazy. I sometimes wondered if I was going to lose the power of speech. My throat got so balled up and stiff it felt like I had swallowed a sock and it had wrapped itself around my larynx. I surprised myself when words came out when they dropped you down here."

"How come I don't remember being put down here?"

"I can't speak to that."

"Do they steal your breath? Do they put you into some kind of suspended animation?"

"I'm not sure why you're even talking right now. You should take a breath and try again when you can make sense."

Nelson crouched and sprang as best as he could at the direction of the words, having briefly thought he saw the darkness disturbed by moving lips and having smelled the taint of rancid breath slip past him. He crashed against something small and soft and they both flopped onto the dirt. Nelson lay on top of Pez, who smelled of urine, shit and a pungent dirt odor more akin to a steaming compost pile than the damp clay around them.

"You're coming with me."

"Where? Where would you go that you need me? I'm not used to it up there anymore, even if it is the city of my memory. What's the point of bringing me? What help can I be to you?

"Maybe you'll recognize a street or someone you know. Someone that can help me," Nelson stopped his thought because he became conscious of their size difference and he thought he may be lying on a small child or a large doll.

"Everybody I ever knew is dead."

"You can't say that. You're still alive. There may be a whole herd of your contemporaries still walking about."

"I'm pretty sure I'm last of the Mohicans, and even this, I suppose, wouldn't constitute much of a life. I do live in a hole that's deeper than most graves."

"It's a grave with a door," said Nelson.

"Lately I've been thinking about miners trapped in a collapse. Sometimes they just dynamite the shaft closed, place a wreath at the crumbled entrance and call it a grave. Maybe the town bows its collective head at the shattered mouth for a month or two until the wreath turns brown and blows away. Within a year there's talk of reopening the shaft and extracting all that pretty black coal, but it doesn't help matters that the widows mope around town with tears rimming their eyes and their children looking skinnier and more sickly by the day, because the widow's pension couldn't keep a family of rats fed. All she can think about is her husband's bones crushed by the mountainside and knowing that even though he's in dirt and rocks like every other grave it's not what you would call a proper burial."

"You've thought this through."

"What else would I do, deprived of light except for a small circle far above my head, with only the sound of my own breathing to keep me company and my larynx wrapped in a sock."

"Come with me. Once I leave the city you'll be free to return here. I'll never bother you again."

Pez laughed and the laugh had no hint of mockery or sarcasm, but he did think Nelson's statement one of the funniest combination of words that he had ever heard. Nelson's anger grew as he waited for Pez to regain his composure and he became aware that he still lay on top of him and had been for an uncomfortably long time, a position usually reserved for a woman he had just finished fucking.

"I'll give you credit. You are dense and bordering on ignorant, but you still have the fire of persistence in you. How could I not accept your offer? How could I not see where this fantasy leads? I'm sure I'm in line for an entertainment. Lead the way! Lead me to another hole! I've worn this one out with my dreaming."

Nelson crawled off Pez backwards and made him go first up the slope as he followed closely behind. He watched Pez's silhouette in the circle of light as he progressed with methodical rhythm. When they broke the surface of the ground they both sat down with tightly shuttered eyes, stunned by the light. Nelson adapted first, having seen a full sky of sunlight just the day before, and he expected to see the same barren field near the steel mills where the dogs had buried him the first time. Instead, he found himself standing behind a two story building that housed a restaurant and an office supply store that sold dried-up ink pens, sun bleached construction paper, and paper figurines of most of the traditional holidays including Memorial and Labor Days that were easy-to-construct dioramas of slaughtered soldiers and John Henry racing the steam drill respectively, from their display window facing the street. On the second floor were two roach-infested apartments that had housed a series of renters willing to smell fried eggs and pulled pork throughout the day. On the ground near the entrance or exit of the hole a puddle of bacon fat had solidified and resembled a tiny, murky and possibly frozen lake. Fresh smoke and steam rolled out of a vent in the back and carried with it the smell of frying meat and burning grease and Nelson's stomach began doing flips in anticipation. He caught a movement in the periphery of his sight and when he turned he saw Pez halfway down the hole. Nelson leapt and caught a foot just as it was about to disappear. He trapped the other foot with his free hand and jerked Pez upwards. Pez slipped out of the hole easily, since he weighed next to nothing, and Nelson dragged him a few yards at such an angle that his face scraped the ground before dropping his feet and kicking him over onto his back.

"Don't do that again," Nelson said as he wagged a finger at him.

"I forgot my car keys."

"You have a car!"

"My assumption that you are some kind of an idiot is gaining the upper hand."

"So, you're still capable of jokes?"

"Not jokes so much as mildly amusing witticisms."

Pez stood up and brushed the dust and dirt from his sleeves. Ringed with a halo of coarse gray hair, the pink dome of his head looked vulnerable and newly born in the sunlight. His face collapsed around rheumy gray eyes, five yellow teeth, and a nose that looked like a football pointing downward. A small, elfin man, not much more than 5'1" tall, he wore matching green work pants and shirt, a type of uniform with over-sized flaps buttoned over two matching pockets on either side of his chest. The only things missing were a white oval with Pez's name embroidered over his left breast and shoes, for Pez stood on the ground barefoot like Nelson. His feet were monstrous, not only gnarled and hairy with wild, unclipped toenails curling like corn chips from his toes, but they were large and out of proportion with the rest of his body. They were no shorter than size eighteen, sixteen once the nails were clipped, and Nelson toyed with the notion that Pez had been bred to be a clown given his natural proportions looked like the ideal that most clown's only achieved, if ever, with a dexterous hand for make-up and an eye for wardrobe, not that Nelson had ever seen a clown dressed like a workingman, but who, even children, could stand the traditional patchwork garb of most clowns?

"We need shoes," Nelson said as his stomach roared in protest. "And breakfast. I wonder if I still have any…" Nelson touched his back pocket and found he did still have his wallet with all his credit cards and cash intact. "Why would they leave me my wallet?"

"They're not thieves. What would they do with money anyway?"

"They stole my shoes!"

"That's different. That's just to remind us we have tender feet."

Nelson looked at Pez's feet. "I'm not sure you can say that anymore."

Pez also looked at his feet.

"They are a marvel. My daddy told me I nearly ripped my mother in two when she pushed out my feet. She thought once she got past my head it would be smooth sailing, but she had not counted on these. They had problems in the marital bed long after the wound had healed. I found out later he hated my feet because they were a constant reminder of his loss of pleasure. He would say things like, 'Look at those little demons scuttling across the floor' or 'Pez, my boy, you're goading me into violence by leaving those feet unshod.' He would buy shoes too small either as a punishment for my habit of walking barefoot or as a low-grade revenge for his poor wife's gaping vagina or, I've entertained the possibility recently, as an attempt to stunt their growth, a kind of homespun foot binding. Either way, it didn't make much difference. My feet always prevailed. I learned to walk with curled toes, but really no shoe could contain them. They would always burst through in the end. Leather, vinyl, canvas, rubber, didn't matter. I came to regard them as a blessing. I destroyed my father with one kick to my mother's vagina before I even took my first full-fledged breath. I accomplished what it takes most sons twenty or thirty years to do while I was still attached to mommy's placenta."

"Shall we eat?" Nelson broke in, because he sensed now that Pez realized his larynx still worked, that his voice had become clearer with each sentence and he may never stop talking.

Pez nodded, letting the words flow but terminating them at his closed lips, so he sounded like he growled. Nelson led them to the front of the building and they entered the restaurant. Two eggs shimmied and spat on a yard long griddle. Koo Koo Beatrice stood poised, spatula in hand, waiting for the right moment when the softness of the whites showed the first signs of hardening. She stood behind a counter populated with half a dozen people looking in no hurry to leave. Three tables had been set-up on a small patch of floor between the counter and the side of the building and it looked like Koo Koo ran the whole operation herself as the griddle faced inward so she could cook and take orders simultaneously. Toast popped up from the depths of a toaster and she assembled a plate of bacon, hashbrowns, eggs and toast with the clean, efficient movements of a person so practiced in a particular operation as to produce wonder in the viewer no matter how mundane the task. She slid the plate with a spin and it stopped in front of a uniformed policeman planted on a stool. His partner, with a grapefruit half and a small bowl of granola in front of him, eyed the plate with a look of mocking shock.

"Hayes, I pity that poor heart of yours. How many years have you been making it pump fat?"

"That's between me and my arteries and Koo Koo. She takes care of old Hayes and she don't preach. Can't stand a goddamn sermon before I take my first bite of egg."

"I just give the people what they want, officer." Koo Koo said as she noticed Nelson and Pez had slunk to a table in the farthest corner and that

140

neither were wearing shoes, but she decided not to make a stand for the sake of hygiene. Bare feet were the least of her worries or anyone else's in this diner. "You two shout to me when you're ready to order. Menus are on the table."

Nelson nodded his head and tried to read the menu. Either he couldn't focus or the menu had been written in Aramaic, because he could not decipher a single word of it. Pez held his upside down and gave each menu item serious consideration. By now Nelson's stomach rose in open revolt, throwing a tantrum much like a two year old who had been told toys cost money and money doesn't grow on trees and because money does not grow on trees and toys are not free, they will not be playing with a new toy after every trip to the shiny fluorescent airplane hangar known as the Stupendous Superstore. He set the menu down and concentrated on the back of the cops' heads, the bulging, masticating jaws, and the unreal black pistols strapped to their hips. A scenario came to him in which he snuck up behind one of them, grabbed the pistol and began shooting until the other cop subdued and arrested him so that some foul-breathed judge with a wandering eye could throw him in the darkest prison cell in the state where he could await lethal injection because really that might be preferable to what Montenegro might do to him for losing a big and expensive shipment. He suddenly felt like he had dunked his head in a cup of steaming coffee as he flushed and beads of sweat broke out along his hairline as he remembered he lived under a death warrant.

Koo Koo dropped a plate of pancakes in front of a man with a face covered in short gray whiskers. He raised a pair of 3-D glasses, one red lens and one blue lens, to his eyes and inspected the plate methodically.

"Anything suspicious, X-Ray?" Officer Hayes asked without sarcasm.

"Well, officer, there are no radium particles, a dash of arsenic and a smidgen of barium. Barium is good for cleansing and we all need a good cleansing now and again. And Miss Koo Koo seems to have folded in a quantity of rat hairs far over the FDA mandated ratio, but other than that the cakes look clean."

"It is my special recipe," Koo Koo added.

"The manna of the nuclear power plant," Hayes quipped.

As Siddharta Gautama once said, 'Let us find Nirvana, but after we eat breakfast," Hayes' partner added.

"Brankowski, how did you get from rat hairs to Gautama? Are you trying to lay a Buddhist trip on me?"

"No, the link was breakfast. Free association."

"Because I know the bacon and fat dharma. I live by the four Noble Truths."

"Which are?"

"Number one, eat when you are hungry and again when you are not. Number two, reject a long life if it means sacrificing today. Number three, keeping your cock in your pants, sorry Koo Koo, is like never planting seeds in the field, and number four, choke any living motherfucker who stands in the way of the other three."

"They are noble."

"One tries to be perfect."

"What do the two of you want?" Koo Koo shouted at Nelson and Pez.

"Two number fours and two coffees."

Koo Koo set to work and Pez leaned forward across the table and asked, "What is the number four?"

"I have no idea, but how many variations can there be?"

"Good choice, just what I wanted, but I thought number seven might be a dark horse and win at the tape."

The screen door banged open, viciously rattling a small silver bell hanging from the knob and providing a tinny fanfare for the entrance of Ellen Oglethorpe. She hobbled to the counter and stood, waiting for Koo Koo to turn her way. When Koo Koo did notice her she walked to the other side of the counter across from Ellen. Ellen leaned forward and cupped a hand around her mouth.

"May I please borrow two pieces of cotton, Miss Koo Koo? There is a terrible storm today, electrical, I think, in nature. So many frequencies crisscrossing through the sky like a web-that is what they call it, right? A worldwide web, a spider spinning her web catching all the poor little flies, giving chase to the flesh, so many people riding the frequencies into my head, too many people trying to enter my private chambers. Cotton is anathema to them. It gums up the works. The pulses become entangled and confused and they eventually move on to another victim who is not so prepared. There are so many willing and waiting victims and all they need is a small discouragement to move along. Of course, this has stricken me with considerable guilt because my preparedness is another victim's doom, but self-preservation is a strong motivator that even trumps guilt in my case."

Koo Koo reached under the counter and pulled out two fresh cotton balls and set them before a stool two seats away from X-Ray. She poured a cup of tea and set half a packet of sugar and a spoon on the saucer.

"Who is trying to gain entrance in the chamber Mrs. Oglethorpe?" Hayes asked through a mouthful of potatoes.

"You like this, don't you?" Brankowski asked.

"I am a man of the people, if nothing else. Tell me you don't like this."

"They are terrible people bent on violating me, if you would allow me to be so graphic. They change shape and form, but their preferred entrance is through the ears. They fetishize ears and have been known to violate ten or twenty an hour. It's like a thunderclap or the open maw of a band of apes. Sometimes they ride your sirens and the blare of television. Radio seems to be some kind of super highway for them with cloverleaves and marginal roads. I don't know who they are so I expect they could be anyone. I feel them skulking about, licking their teeth, waiting for me to let my guard down."

She sat on the stool and placed the cotton balls apart on the counter the exact width of her head. She would wait until she left the diner and walked into the gale of their voices or when she heard the telltale signs of their approach inside. They often didn't enter Koo Koo's diner and Ellen had long considered the place a safe harbor.

"You're all crazy! Crazy as loons!"

They all turned to look at a man sitting at a table near the door. He wore a powder blue sports jacket and his face looked peppered with pock marks as if someone had fired a shot gun at him with purpose. He parted his white hair just above his left ear and it swept upward and across to inadequately cover his bald head. Across the table from him sat a woman whose face had been smeared with make-up without much concern for proper placement of the powder or cream or stick being used. She grabbed his arm and contorted her face in an attempt to hush him.

"They need to hear it." He pulled his arm away from the woman's grasp. "You need to dig to the roots, the cause, and stop blither blathering about what's above. Too much nonsense and effect. You have to dig your hands deep, get them good and dirty, besmirch yourself. You need empirical evidence to prove a theorem. It's not going to be found in fried eggs no matter what meaning you insert using the constructs of religion and the cage known as realism. Once you start chasing the real you're living in world of trouble. I know why people are disappearing."

"Now the kitty has slipped the sack," the woman said through hands which covered her face.

"Meaning the truth is the cat and the bag is the fog of ignorance, of misunderstanding, of disease and intolerance and the act of jumping or 'slipping' as you say is my very own act of spilling the beans, of pulling back the curtain, of raising the hem of the skirt to reveal a most glorious truth."

"I'm not an idiot Checkers."

"I'm just clarifying the meaning of your use of the saying, even though you chose to employ a version not often used."

"Who's disappearing? Why haven't I heard about this?" Hayes asked.

Brankowski shot him a look that asked the questions 'why are you encouraging this maniac?' and 'how exactly did you get to be such a sick fuck that you would delight in utter nonsense?' simultaneously.

"Officer, don't humor me. I'm part of the information age. I'm a current citizen with an email account. We know people are disappearing. Maybe the paper doesn't report it all the time or maybe they create stories about migration to the suburbs or the Sun Belt. They euphemistically write about population loss, lost tax revenue, bad weather, a shrinking manufacturing base because the corporations have figured out how to employ slave labor around the world to produce their products. This is no time to be a free man. I know we're not to concern ourselves with these matters. I know we're suppose to wait to be taken, kidnapped and disposed of when they see fit. I know we have the pretense of freedom, but we're just chattel in our little shacks asking to be abused and killed. Seven have disappeared this month already, seemingly unrelated and at random."

"Seemingly?" Hayes coaxed Checkers as Brankowski stared at his grapefruit.

"They were all in the same area code. It's no wonder really because when you play with fire you usually end up with fewer digits than you started with, so what could we expect other than these scofflaws disintegrating amidst the ropes of electricity. All the same code, all the same result."

Ellen mumbled to the cotton balls that Checkers may have been possessed by the voices in the wind. This may be their new approach in preparing for an assault on her sanctuary. They figured out how to use proxies in the war. Hayes turned on his stool and faced him to better hear the explanation.

"All different occupations, different economic classes, different parts of the city. Same code. Men and women, a jumble of races and creeds. They disappeared at different times of the day, some from their jobs, some from their houses, some from their cars. Some had reason to disappear and some left their wives scratching their heads or fearing the worse. I know all of you are saying, 'Where's the pattern, Checkers? What's the link, man?' And you would be right to ask these questions because that's where I began when I started considering the question. It's elegant and insidious in its simplicity. The clue sat right before me. They act like they want to be caught. They flaunt their arrogance and dare someone to put the pieces together. They all had one thing in common."

All leaned forward, despite their better judgment, waiting for an answer. The griddle popped and spat and the toaster shot two pieces of toast in the air.

"How did I know they were in the same area code? They all used telephones. Follow the lead. All used phones. Who provides the phone service other than the phone company? The phone company is taking people, enslaving them or executing them. I've heard they have a barge on the river that takes the poor souls away. I don't know where they take them from there. Could be anywhere. Could be they are dropped to the bottom of the lake for the walleye to sup on their flesh. I've heard tell a second barge may be coming because the program is so successful. They need more capacity."

The diners exhaled. Koo Koo turned to the toast and slathered a swath of butter across its face. Hayes and Brankowski exchanged looks and then Brankowski refocused on the grapefruit. Hayes had not yet given up, so he asked:

"What about the two we found this morning in the river?"

"Yes, a disturbing development. They were headless, I believe?"

"That's the talk. Nothing official yet."

"And they found a burned out van under a bridge near the river?"

"So I hear. Brankowski and I were not there."

"You said 'we found' so I assumed the 'we' in this case was you and your partner."

"I'm part of a fraternal order. I slide into 'we' naturally."

"Hayes, they've upped the ante. This is a new phase in the game. When they start murdering their slaves everything is in play. I've feared this day would come. Maybe the two in the river fell off the barge. Maybe it's a mistake, sloppiness, or a well-placed threat should any of us think of getting out of line as we await our fates."

"So you think the phone company chopped off their heads? Which phone company? We don't live under a monopoly any more. Ma Bell was dissected long ago. Your conspiracy might be fraying at the edges or has gone a little yellow with age."

"There's only one that has the world tethered to its wires. There's only one that matters. Yes, they've waited a coon's age to run the world and now is their time, now they execute their plan."

"Your lack of discretion has killed us. We're as good as corpses," his companion cried as tears washed black and blue canals down her cheeks. "You always have to shoot your mouth off, displaying your wisdom and intelligence like some cheap conjurer performing magic tricks at a children's birthday party, wearing a soiled cape. You don't think you can spread the truth about these monsters without them coming for us? Which one of these people is their spy? How long do you think it will be before we're being herded onto the barge ourselves? You'll have no one to blame but yourself. I hope you've enjoyed your little performance since it will be your last."

Hayes flipped cash on the counter and he and Brankowski lurched off their stools.

"I'll pass along the info to my superiors, but they're a skeptical crew. You need some ev-i-dence, not theories, for the detectives to get involved."

Hayes and Brankowski walked toward the door, acknowledging Koo Koo with nods before they left. Their massive bulk and the clean, sharp lines of their uniforms tore the room in two as they passed through and the wound didn't heal until the last of the witnesses left the diner an hour later. X-Ray raised his glasses and analyzed their forms as they left.

"Hayes has a hot prostate. It's as big as an apple and just as red. Nothing but problems ahead for that man. Urine stream will shrink to a dribble, impotence. Brankowski on the other hand looks to have trouble with his gallbladder and his left testicle looks malformed." X-Ray gave a furtive look at the backside of Koo Koo before lowering the glasses.

"You still looking at the tattoo on my butt, X-Ray?"

"It's lovely artistry. A butterfly, no? An explosion of color and radiance. It makes me want to dance in my seat." His neck and ears turned a deep crimson.

"Close. It's actually still a caterpillar in its chrysalis state, a moment before transformation. Any stupid girl can get a butterfly, can marvel at its beauty and grace. I'm interested in transfiguration and potential. It's always more interesting. The butterfly state is the end, the highest and purest expression and deadly boring. Give me the hope that something can be better, but I really don't want to know how it turns out."

As she turned back to the griddle X-Ray gave another look, but he had lost the image and now could only see the gauze of her cotton underwear. Koo Koo walked the plates over to Nelson and Pez and set them down on the table in front of them. The number four turned out to be a monstrous load of food with potatoes, sausage, bacon, three eggs, grits, pancakes, yogurt, sliced apples, pears and a dollop of sour cream. The unofficial name among the regular diners for the number four had become the Annapurna Sanctuary. The size and scale of the plate in relation to the other combinations on the menu felt akin to the Himalayan range compared to the Appalachian so someone who had read a book on Nepal or had traveled through it in search of mystic lands had tagged it with the name. Nelson and Pez stared at the plates in wonder.

"I added a little extra, so next time wear shoes. The health inspector would shut me down the second he saw those monsters," she said as she pointed toward Pez' feet.

"Do you know where we can buy shoes? We are in unfortunate circumstances," Nelson asked as he looked Koo Koo in the face and realized he stared at extraordinary beauty, faded maybe, or a little worn, but the weariness and wrinkles gave her a context that made the remaining beauty radiant.

"Actually, there's a new Shoe Horn opening down the street. The grand opening is today." She gave a look at Pez's feet again sticking out from the table. "I don't know if they'll have anything for those. You may want to try a blacksmith."

Instead of withdrawing his feet under the table in shame or embarrassment, Pez pushed them forward and gave Koo Koo a fully display.

"Like I said, thank God the health inspector is not here. I'd be looking for work in this crappy economy. There would be no reasonable defense I could muster."

Ellen Oglethorpe worked a cotton ball into her right ear, then her left. She searched her coat and found a flattened cola can and a superball and placed them next to her empty tea cup. She hoped the superball would be enough of a tip, but she thought one of Koo Koo's children would enjoy throwing it at people on the sidewalk or cars on the freeway, because children employed themselves in such destructive behavior. The first wave of the tide of frequencies had begun, which sounded like a siren warming up with several decibels of static added on. Through the cotton the noises were just below a roar. She had to get home. No one should be on the streets when the plague descended. Now the phone company had been set on the loose and there could be no way of knowing how close the end could actually be. Some called it the end of days and she heard someone else call it the second Passover, but when she asked for the symbol that would allow the terrible angels to know whom to spare he scoffed at her and said he hadn't been authorized to release the classified stuff.

Nelson started on the left side of the plate and worked his way to the center without much thought to the taste, texture and combination of flavors passing his tongue. His stomach wouldn't stop complaining even after he had begun eating so he sped up the delivery of food in a flurry of forkfuls without considerable chewing. His chances of survival had dipped below impossible with the news of Log and Treg. Who else would have a reason to be floating headless in the river? Now that the terminus of his life had become visible like a building on the horizon that seemed incredibly distant until the moment he pulled to its front door, he really wanted nothing more than to be made comfortable. His feet were sore and cold and a chill had taken up residence between his shoulder blades that even the coffee and hot food couldn't warm. Koo Koo's face and voice reminded him of Jules and how he hadn't talked to her in days or weeks, if she had ever existed at all, because how he felt now had slipped a long way from how he felt when he last spoke with her, so far that a gap of disbelief had developed concerning almost everything that had happened to him before the moment he stepped into the car and began his trip to Cleveland. If he could hear her voice maybe he could believe something existed before this moment and he could loop a tether to it to keep it from floating further away. He had never counted on Jules for her reason or intellect, but her voice as he now remembered it would keep him from disintegrating, because she had assumed all of his knowledge and experiences, all of his faith and emotion as a singular totem to the past. The rising and falling tones would provide the frame in which to exist. Her voice lay a boundary, benign and soft, and it constructed a perch on which to sit while staring into the void. He noticed a pay phone hanging on the wall of a hallway leading to two closet-sized bathrooms, and he grasped at the idea of hearing Jules' voice. He didn't care if Otter answered the phone or listened to the conversation a foot away from Jules naked in bed. What would he tell him about the shipment? What could he say really? 'Sorry, I'll do better next time. I'll pay Montenegro back on a monthly installment plan with a reasonable one percent plus prime interest rate covering the next two hundred years.' He pushed through his hesitation and pulled out a phone company calling card from his wallet. Pez gasped when he saw the logo.

"Are you the spy?"

"What are you talking about?"

"Will you send us all to our doom?"

Nelson looked at the card and made the connection between Checkers and Pez' real fear and waved it away with impatience even though he began to consider that Montenegro may have infiltrated the phone company himself and might be monitoring every call speeding along the wires, waiting to ensnare him. He warned Pez that if he tried to run he would break his legs to which Pez responded:

"Why would I run now? I'm addicted to catastrophe."

Nelson dialed his old home number, now inherited by Jules and Otter.

After three rings Jules answered the phone. He waited until she said hello a third time before he spoke. She may have even decided to hang up the phone, but given the early morning hour her memory of the process to hang up had slowed and gave Nelson the time he needed to recover and launch into a conversation. She had become, after all, a totem, the last surviving figure of an era who had to be approached cautiously lest she be scared away.

"Jules, it's Nelson."

Now that she fully understood the mechanism for ending calls she considered employing it fully but anger or curiosity held her hand.

"Where are you?"

"In a diner. I'm not in Florida."

"Nelson, Otter is missing."

"Missing how?"

"Like here one day and gone the next kind of missing."

"Did he say anything before he left?"

"Two things. Fuck Nelson and kill Nelson. Something along those lines."

Nelson sucked air between his teeth which produced a whistle that sounded like the beginning of a classic melody.

"What have you done? What's going on?"

"I called to hear your voice. I may be on the verge of disintegrating."

"You hear me asking you a question, don't you?"

"Yes, it's all I could hope for."

"Then answer it."

"I lost a shipment I was carrying for Otter, so Otter will probably he held responsible."

"What does that mean? Lost?"

"As in can't find, gone."

"What does that mean to you?"

"Nothing good. I'm alive by luck, but it won't hold. These people won't let this go. It was a major fuck-up."

Nelson rattled off the whole story: the squeaking visor, the awful motel, video pussy, Cactus Jack, the dogs, the hole, the cat house and the blow job from a septuagenarian, the disabled car, Treg and Log and their betrayal and their untimely but deserved end, his inability to stay conscious, and Pez who he had found in the hole and who may be able to guide him from the city. He finished with a litany of possibilities for his death, all horrible and slow and involving torture in some part of the process. Jules couldn't help to pause when the words stopped. She thought breathing easier than trying to untangle the story, but she tried after a dozen or so breaths.

"Is any of this true or have you just cracked up?"

"True."

"What does this mean for Otter?"

The fact that her concern had already moved along to her new lover felt especially crushing given that Nelson had hoped Jules would allow herself to be tethered. Even a token nod to past happiness would have been enough to complete the job. Now, all had been lost.

"I wouldn't expect him back."

"Do you think he's dead?"

"Or running under a new name and look or driving to Cleveland to cut my throat."

"He's not like that."

"Which one is he not like?"

"What?"

"A runner or a killer?"

"He's not a killer"

"But he's a better lover than me?" The question sounded absurd coming out of his mouth since his concerns had taken a much graver turn since he had guessed at her infidelity, but he couldn't let the opportunity pass for form's sake.

"Let's not get into that. You don't believe he broke up something between us, do you? You don't believe there was anything left between us, right?"

"I think he convinced me to do this job so he could get in your pants. I believe that. I didn't know I was committing to a murder-suicide pact. Of course, it may have come as a surprise to Otter as well."

"He's not like that either."

"Otter, the drug-dealing saint."

"Are you drunk"

"Don't stay in Tampa, Jules. Cut your hair, gain thirty pounds, grow back a nice bushy thatch on your crotch, buy a little dog for your lap and move to a dark corner of the country. I worry you won't be spared. Otter may have whispered something in your ear, something innocuous and trite but, Jules, you never know where a death sentence can come from. It may be written on a gum wrapper or on the bottom of a shoe. It may come the mouth of a dog or from the inside of your own eyelids. Find a bungalow next to a waste treatment facility. Wear a mask and never open your windows. Don't pluck the hairs from your moles and stop the infernal tanning. Never show your tits in public again. Those are like GPS. Show them again and you're dead."

"I'll get right on that."

She hung up the phone. Nelson considered calling her back to finish his point, but the probability of her picking the phone up again seemed very low, so he walked back to the table instead. Pez had cleaned his plate and held a coffee cup between his hands an inch or so from his face.

"I'd forgotten about food. Lovely, really."

"Have you ever tried to leave the city?"

"Once early on when I still believed I could exert my will on them. When I thought the purpose was the struggle and the more I struggled, the more I fought, the sharper and more distinct my existence became. What else do I have but my struggle? I asked. I tried every trick you're likely to ever think of and I remember saying to myself that the pack may only have a limited geographic range. For instance would they really want to live in the desert or try to eke out an existence in the mountains? I even looked into buying a houseboat and casting off permanently and when I needed to stop dropping anchor a hundred yards from shore and signaling for diesel and supplies. Somewhat like a self-imposed quarantine. So I tried to leave and they caught me. I tried to leave again and they caught me again. I developed a mania for the geographic solution and then they made it hard on me. No food, no water, no light, no air, suffocation and paralysis, delirium and shingles. They treated me no better that a chattel slave. They would allow me a peek at the sun now and again or a waft of fresh air. Mostly I could feel tumors growing deep within me. Once I abandoned the geographic solution and I gave them full credit for environmental adaptability, guessing correctly they would hound me no matter where I went, once I understood their nature and mission, their single-minded purpose, then I could breathe a little easier. I had no expectations of freedom, so they granted me a little more room. Not freedom exactly but at least the perimeter of the fence had been enlarged."

"If you were to try it again what would be the best way to leave?"

"A boat."

"You think a boat is the best way?"

"An airplane is the best way, but you'll never get to the airport. They'll understand what you're thinking before you think it."

"Do you think a boat will work?"

"No, but there's a better chance with that than the others."

"Does it have a better chance of working than trying to leave by car?"

"If there are no dogs onboard when you shove off there's a chance, but what makes you think they won't follow you and climb onboard when you're not looking? Haven't you heard a word I said? A boat is a better chance than a car, but a car is no chance. That is a dead end not worth even trying. A hundred of them will lie across the road and sacrifice themselves before they would let you drive away."

"What am I suppose to do? Wait until they figure out what they want to do to me? Or crawl in the hole myself? This city means nothing to me."

"It's the food talking. I remember always feeling like I could conquer the world after I ate a good meal."

"First we need shoes."

"Defying them only makes it worse, like I have been trying to tell you. They don't want you wearing shoes."

Nelson pulled out his wallet and extracted a twenty dollar bill that would pay the check twice over with change left. He threw it on the table and noticed a piece of paper wedged between a five and a single. He grabbed all three and had to peel the paper off the five because they were stuck together with syrup or a low-grade glue. He turned the paper over and read:

Montenegro is Alife.

He slammed the paper on the tabletop, making Koo Koo jump.

"There was a time before the dogs!" he screamed.

"Easy partner. We draw the line when you start breaking up the place," Koo Koo growled.

'No, dogs predate human beings, I'm sure. Certainly not in the mutated forms we have now bred them into for our own pleasures and needs, but we are guests on their planet." Pez drained his coffee cup. A rivulet drained from the corner of his mouth and dripped onto his legs. "My God, with all this caffeine and calories coursing through me I feel like I could throttle one of them, guest or no guest."

"First, shoes."

"The time of shoes is upon us!"

"It's a new era!"

"We shall clad our feet in hides of leather or a reasonable facsimile of such. We shall march with a newfound confidence and power. We shall be chattel slaves no more, but men with manifest destiny. Jesus, I think I'm drunk."

Nelson helped him up and directed him out the door. He left him on the sidewalk and returned to the diner to ask Koo Koo directions to the Shoe Horn. She told him to turn left and walk a few blocks as the store stood on the same side of the street as the diner. Nelson tried to catch her eye, make her consider him, but her mind hurried on to a thousand tasks surrounding her as the lone operator of a dying, smoking machine.

"You are beautiful," Nelson said and he surprised himself in two regards. One, that he could be so easily distracted from the task at hand by a faded beauty and two, his old self, handsome and arrogant, remained somewhere inside him and it had been waiting for a woman to provide the fuel for the rally. The talk with Jules had stirred a desire for contact with a woman, any woman other than Jules, but what purpose such a detour could take he couldn't guess. "With a face like that why isn't somebody taking care of you? How did you end up here?"

Koo Koo tucked a strand of hair behind her ear and arched an eyebrow at him.

"First, I prefer my dates to wear shoes. I'm picky like that. Second, I'm assuming by the question you believe this type of work to be lowly and awful, which may not be the right approach to piquing my interest since I am employed doing the very work you find disgusting. Third, I'm ten years past beautiful. I hold no illusions. I have a fluorescent light in my bathroom and I don't shy away from the mirror."

She moved on to her tasks and left Nelson standing by the counter. He waited a few moments before retreating, wondering what he must look like given the ease of her dismissal. Back outside he turned toward the Shoe

Horn and motioned Pez to follow. Pez charged ahead on his calloused feet as Nelson stepped his way around broken glass, stones, cigarette butts and spills and stains of undetermined liquid. Pez made it to the store minutes ahead of him and when Nelson finally caught up he dozed against the side of the store. A weary traffic cop directed traffic in and out of the small parking lot on the side of the building. Cars jammed both sides of the street a block either way. A mammoth, half-inflated gorilla had been tethered to the roof and shook his mighty fists with the wind at patrons entering the store. Nelson couldn't tell if the gorilla protected his horde of shoes or threatened passersby with death in his grip should they fail to take advantage of the outrageous deals inside. Shoppers streamed out of the store carrying bags in both hands. Eight foot tall numbers saying 2-4-1 had been applied to the storefront windows. Pez slept under the weight of the number two and it looked like it might crush his head. Nelson nudged Pez' feet with his own toe and regretted it once their bare feet touched.

"I don't have the strength to face a place like this," Pez said as he popped open an eye. "I think that food has turned on me. I feel like there is lead in my veins."

"Face it we must. It is a place of shoes."

"I'm agile on my feet. I beat you here by ten minutes at least. I'm past shoes. Keep the extra pair for yourself. Hide a pair where you know where you can find them again. That's what I use to do. Don't waste a pair on me. I'm long past shoes, long past."

"You'll have shoes. It's a matter of principle. Besides, we don't know where we are going. You might need shoes."

"I know where I'm going. I'm going right back in the hole. There can really be only one conclusion to this little misadventure. A breath of air, a spot of sun, new shoes, back in the hole. You've planned nothing. We're wandering about, wasting time, chasing shoes. We'll be lucky to make it past the next corner before getting caught."

"Get up. We are wasting time. They probably found out we left by now. They have to be furious."

"They don't have emotion. They simply perform tasks and one of their jobs is to remain always and forever relentless and persistent."

"That's a little redundant."

"After so many years it feels redundant. But maybe I can give one last run, why not? They won't be expecting it from me, right? One more chance, maybe? If they catch me this time they'll be hard on me. I can't imagine surviving it. Try on some shoes, feel briefly new, give it a run, leave by boat, sail right across the lake and watch the shoreline slowly dissolve. That used to be a dominant image of my dreams, but I haven't conjured it in years. You've contaminated me with hope. Nothing good can come of it, I can tell you that."

Pez scrambled to his feet and they entered Shoe Horn. A child of two lay prostrate on the carpet, shrieking to the fluorescent light above. Another sibling, a year older, kicked the two year old in the shins as his mother tried to yank him to his feet. A greeter stepped around them and welcomed Nelson and Pez into the store. When she noticed Pez' feet her smile collapsed and she forgot lesson eighteen of the Shoe Horn Customer Service Training Guide that explicitly stated that no matter who came in the store, in whatever condition, whether harboring a gripe, a bitterness toward life, an attitude unrelated to the Shoe Horn experience, mischievousness, ideas of sabotage or terror, the greeter must maintain a friendly countenance complete with a smile that connotes sincerity, helpfulness and the inability to condemn or judge the state the customer has carried into the store. The smile could not be suggestive, lascivious, sarcastic, or intended to convey anything but the greeter's desire to help. So, when the greeter, her first day on the job and admittedly with not much capacity to retain training materials in the first place, saw Pez' curled corn chip toe nails and tufts of ape hair dragging on the floor she stepped backwards and raised a hand to her mouth and said, "Oh, for fuck's sake. What kind of fucking job did I get into?"

She waved them into the store and continued backing up until she stepped on the foot of a cashier who tried to bag two shoe boxes in a bag too small.

The aisles squalled with women shoppers, their children and lonely men drawn to the crowd to spy on the young mothers. The din of squealing children, exasperated adults elbowed, jostled and stepped on to the brink of explosive anger, of softly playing piano music proven to encourage buying, especially during a 2-4-1 special (if the results from the test store in Tulsa, OK were to be believed) of squeaking vinyl shoes and shouts of pain as shoppers tried to ram their sweaty and swollen feet into shoes of any size to find the 2 in the 2-4-1 special, of lights so bright the illumination they cast seemed to make a sound (akin to a faint whir of a dentist's drill) of the smell of cardboard and new vinyl with traces of new leather, of air struggling to stay conditioned with the rising heat from the tops of the angry shoppers' heads and the odors from their bodies, both natural and chemical, of the scents from their breath including peppermint, curry, spearmint, garlic, cigarettes, coffee, alcohol, tartar and plaque, of the whisk of polyester blend uniforms chafing the thighs and underarms of the workers hired as sentries and docents to the horde of shoes who were pummeled for hours by the grand opening waves and shoe buying fever and now loudly complained about the hiring tricks the management had used to entice them to take this abuse, tore at the knees of Nelson and Pez like a powerful undertow, trying to pull them under the level of consciousness or just drown them so their bodies would be found washed up in the slipper aisle, bloated and unrecognizable, at closing time.

The shelves had been picked clean. A few disgorged boxes remained, ripped and smashed, the shoes relieved of the tissue paper jammed in their toes. Nelson walked through a pocket of perfume that smelled like rotting apples and cottage cheese and staggered to an open bench. A clerk, crouching low in the aisle, looking like she had just been discovered in a day long game of hide-and-seek jumped when Nelson landed. Pez sat down quietly next to him, their bare feet pointing directly at the clerk. She wore a too tight smock with the top two buttons undone so that her breasts were crushed and pushed upward, creating a long line of cleavage. Six earrings graced each ear and tattoos poked out from the collar of her smock at the back of her neck, at both wrists and on the small of her back and hips, so that the uniform looked more like a drape over a cage teeming with exotic animals. She looked overweight, as if succumbing to a disease that caused a pasty bloat, with a rash of pimples on her forehead and neck. Nelson surmised that any man willing to take a chance on her would be surprised by her willingness to do anything and everything to please and pleasure him. She chewed a wad of gum as if trying to dislocate her jaw. Faced with their four dirty and hideous feet she leaned against the shelf and looked down either direction of the aisle, no doubt mapping out her best escape route.

"We need shoes." Nelson explained.

"I (pop, crack) see that."

"Do you want to know our sizes?"

"Not particularly, but fire away."

"I'm a size ten and my friend here…what size do you think you are Pez?"

"Sixteen sizes of glorious feet."

"We don't carry size sixteen," she said as she got a really good look at Pez' feet and a look of revulsion and fear crept across her face. "Besides, what shoe is going to go over those nails."

"They're beauties, aren't they?" Pez mused as he wiggled his toes, creating tiny arabesques in the air.

"A sandal (pop, crack) might work (pop). It'd be small though."

"Get the largest sandal you have left," Nelson instructed.

"What shoe do you want (pop, crack), sir."

Nelson mulled the question over longer than he needed to since any shoe would be better than bare feet.

"I want a running shoe."

"Gone (crack)."

"Tennis shoe?"

"Gone (pop)."

"Cross trainers?"

"Gone."

"Any kind of athletic shoe? I'd even consider baseball spikes."

"Gone (crack, pop)."

"Hiking boots?"

"Never had them. Don't carry them."

"Work boots?"

"First to go. Missed it by a half an hour?"

"Anything good for walking?"

"We never had anything good for walking. You know you are in Shoe Horn, right?"

"Bring me something in size ten. Whatever you have left."

She returned in about ten minutes holding two boxes, looking stunned at running the gauntlet of shoppers.

"Alright, a lady tried to pull these out of my hands. Accused me of hiding the best shoes. She wouldn't let go until I showed her so don't expect much (pop, crack). I mean this is opening day, right? We sold a lot of shoes and the second truck never came so the stock is pretty low. The rumor is the driver is selling them half-price, I guess 4-4-1, a couple blocks away to get a little extra cash in his pocket. (crack, pop). First, the sandal." She pulled out a pair of flip-flops, the soles of which were shaped like surfboards, and dropped them in front of Pez as she didn't want to risk getting close to his feet and picking up a pathogen from a nail scratch. "And these are the only size tens we have left in the whole store." She said as she lifted the lid like she expected the stench of a rotting corpse to be released from the box. She placed fire-engine red loafers on the floor in front of Nelson. "And before you ask I'm not messing with you. It's really the only thing we have left in your size."

"I told you. They love jokes. I wouldn't put it past them to have stopped that second truck just so you had to buy those monsters," Pez said as he maneuvered his toes through the straps of the sandals. The extra rubber of the surfboard point gave enough room for his toes to stay off the ground. Had they been on the beach the new sport of foot surfing may have taken root.

"I need socks."

Nelson felt both soles to see if he could find a bullet hole, but these shoes were new and smelled like recently cooked vinyl.

"I thought of that (pop, crack)."

Out of her pocket of her smock came a pair of baby shit brown dress socks dotted with small bursts of orange stitching.

"You think this is funny, don't you?"

"Those are the only socks we have left. I had to smuggle them to get them across the floor. Without me you would have left this store barefoot."

"They're fine. I used to own a pair just like them."

"That's a little sad. I might think of that the rest of the day. Somebody picking these when they had a choice."

"I owned them less than a day, I think."

"That makes it less sad, I suppose. What will your method of payment be?"

"Don't we take these up to the check out line?"

"Half the cashiers quit already. Never came back from break. We've been told to help out, so follow me."

They walked to a deserted cash register. Pez walked as slowly as a tightrope walker with a twisted grimace on his face.

"How much do I owe you?"

"I don't know. I need to know the method of payment first. I have to push one of these little touch screen squares before I proceed. I know it's weird and backwards, but it won't let me scan the items if I don't push a square first. They want you to commit to paying before ringing it up."

Nelson told her he would use credit, but he had no idea what money he had left in his bank account, what bills were now seriously overdue, what usurious default interest rates the cards were now charging him, or if the bill collectors had picked up the scent of his trail and had joined Montenegro, Zune and Gutterman in a lynch mob. She pushed the credit button with a flourish of a hard won victory. She scanned the items and in a scripted voice said that with the 2-4-1 low cost pricing both pairs of superior grade shoes cost sixteen dollars. Nelson reached into his back pocket and found his wallet no longer there. He slapped the pocket three times and searched the three other pockets of his pants and the three pockets of his jacket with no luck. He remembered pulling out a twenty to pay for breakfast, reading the note from the dogs and setting the wallet on the table and from that point his memory grew vague. He had no corresponding memory of putting the wallet back in his pants.

"Pez, did you pick up my wallet?"

"I know better than to pick up another man's wallet."

"I don't think I have my wallet."

"Of course you don't. We've had a plague of lost and stolen wallets today. Misplaced cards, forgotten expiration dates, one dollar bills magically turning into ten dollar bills once the cashier touches it. Incredible."

"I'll run up to the diner to get it. I'll be right back. I'll leave him here as collateral."

"That would be the definition of an unsecured loan."

"I'll be right back."

"Look, I don't know what happened to you, but look at those shoes. I can't imagine that things could ever get so bad, that your life could become so awful and pathetic that a grown man would come into this rat lab of a store and try to steal these shoes. They cost, like, eight bucks! They're red vinyl shoes! There was never a need for them. They never had a real purpose, yet here they are. Manufactured in Malaysia, shipped by boat, unloaded by dockworkers, loaded onto a truck and driven to this very store for you to try to steal. They made shit! You are stealing shit! They are red pieces of shit! You can't steal shit! It can't happen. It's bad enough that someone's labor was used in making red vinyl but if people are going to make a habit of stealing red vinyl shoes I give the fuck up. What is the point?" She leaned forward on the counter and rubbed her temples. "I need a cigarette."

A narrow-faced man with his hair cut to stubble stepped up to Nelson and the clerk. He wore a burgundy smock that coded him as the manager.

"Something wrong?" he said as he caught sight of Nelson's shoes. "Excellent choice, sir. You liked them so much you had to wear them out of the store. I had my eye on them myself, so I'm hoping more come with the next shipment."

"Baaaaaa," the clerk groaned as she began walking to the back of the store.

"May I speak with you a moment," the manager called to her in a practiced voice that conveyed fairness with sternness and command.

"Blow it out your red vinyl ass," she tossed over her shoulder.

The manager followed her, throwing commands that she stop and that she stop acting like a child and that in difficult situations she should rely on her training as a guide. She lit a cigarette and blew smoke towards the ceiling and disappeared into the bowels of the store and the crush of patrons picking over the scraps and waiting for the second truck to arrive. Nelson stepped over two children who still writhed on the carpet, sobbing and insanely pounding their fists on the floor while their parents stood disinterested or defeated several feet away. As the red monster rose above them, they quieted and followed its ascent with keen interest and watched it make a deft landing on the other side of their heads. Whether it had been a bird or an amphibian with powerful legs that could launch the mass of red skin into brief flight they could not tell. Just as they began to truly consider its nature and origin another followed and landed closer to their ears. A flock may have dropped around them while they were protesting against their parents' bad decisions, and they hoped for a mass launching into flight. A pink light reflected onto their tear-stained and swollen faces. Then, two menacing, naked mutants soared above them, blocking the pink light and threatening to crush their heads. One of the children gasped as if to say, "Too soon, too soon, bring back the light." Their worst fears never came true as the naked mutant landed on the other side with a squeak and another followed more hideous than the first. The mutants acted as predators, looking to dine on the red birds. They tread away without touching or further disturbing them and the children sought solace and peace in their parents' arms, humbly apologizing for their sudden outbursts.

Nelson and Pez slipped out of the door and onto the sidewalk where they took breaths of humidity as they tried to clear their lungs of the conditioned air.

"I don't like these shoes," Pez said as he stomped onto the cement. "They squeak every time I step and I think the soles are made of wood or anthracite."

"You have to break them in."

"My feet will break first. Do you think these are real surfboards?"

"I don't care if you wear them, just don't throw them away. You may need them later on."

"Or you may need them. With each passing minute I'm convinced I should have stayed in my hole. Why am I out here? To what purpose?"

"You just have the Shoe Horn blues. It will pass. Before we went in there you were ready to conquer the world."

"I want to sleep. I feel pummeled and bruised. Remember, I lived in silence for years."

"We're going to get my wallet and then put the plan in place."

"You conjured a plan? What plan is it? Share."

"We are going to leave the city by boat."

"That's a plan?"

"It'll pass for one."

"You cribbed that off me. That's not original to you. I doubt you even knew there was a lake and a waterway to Ontario and the ocean beyond before I mentioned escape by boat. This is nothing but pure plagiarism."

"I'll credit you in the footnotes. A full citation with a picture if you want."

"Who reads the footnotes?" Pez said as he took off his sandals and flexed his toes against the cement. "I think my feet are still broken"

They walked back to the diner. When Koo Koo saw them enter the door, she reached into the front pocket of her apron and pulled out Nelson's wallet.

"Forget something?" She held the wallet in front of her and he took it from her hand. "Florida? You didn't seem like you were from around here. Do you always visit strange cities with no shoes?"

"I have shoes now. We could have dinner tonight."

Koo Koo looked at his shoes.

"They are shoes, but really, where could we go with you wearing shoes like that? We couldn't go anyplace I would ever want to show my face again. I don't want to be known as the lady who brought the guy with the red shoes. No offense."

"I used to have black shoes. Most of the time I only wear black shoes."

"I usually date men who wear black shoes, but those definitely are not black."

Pez opened two packets of sugar and poured them directly to the back of his throat as Koo Koo and Nelson talked. He grimaced as if swallowing a shot of whiskey. Koo Koo moved the remaining sugar away from him as she looked at Nelson.

"Come back with black shoes sometime and I'll consider the request."

"Hope is a tether holding me from the void."

"I'm happy to be of service, I guess."

"Cognitive dissonance is filling my head with static. How is she part of the plan? Does she own a boat of some kind? Have we abandoned the plan already with the first sniff of a lady?" Pez said as he tried to reach the sugar carousel but Koo Koo had moved it just out of his reach.

Nelson asked Koo Koo for directions to the docks, but she could only tell him vaguely where downtown and the waterfront lay in relation to where they stood. They turned toward the downtown skyline that looked more distant than Nelson had remembered. He asked Pez how far they would have to walk and he told him about a hundred and twenty blocks. So they walked. They walked past an elderly lady dressed in a pantsuit and smoking a cigarette riding a bike with a little dog and cat in a handle bar basket, an abandoned neighborhood movie theater that had rolled *'Crocodile' Dundee II* as its last film, a street ministry called Jesus Speaks, You Should Listen Ministries whose congregation sat on mismatched folding chairs and whose minister preached through a karaoke machine, an old orphanage built on a hill when the area had been covered with sumac and ash trees (the building had been converted into an adoption center and social service agency because the orphanage busted the county budget as well as a fire that killed a dozen orphans while they slept and a series of well-publicized strangulations perpetrated by the head groundskeeper doomed the reputation of the facility in the eyes of the public), a check cashing and money lending establishment that stayed open eighteen hours a day and looked cheap and dirty a few moments after it opened its doors, an Arab grocery store whose owner refused to translate any of the signage or daily specials into English, a karate studio run by an ex-cop with bad knees and fifteen pins in his arm from when he tried to break up a street brawl that had spilled out of one of the bars, a bargain carpet store where seventy-five percent of patrons and pedestrians walking past sneezed when they inhaled their first full breath fiber-laced air with Nelson and Pez being no exception, a bar that had undergone seventeen name and ownership changes in the past twenty years with The Marble Faun, The Lead Parachute and Binky's Wee Winky Hut being the name highlights over the two decades, past Ellen Oglethrope as she weaved down the sidewalk and clutched her hands in front of her as she walked to an unknown destination, past a discount auto parts store that had adopted a caricature of a geek as their mascot who had either bitten off his first chicken head or seen a woman's breasts for the first time given the startled and crazed expression of his eyes, past a family style restaurant serving American classics like open faced turkey and gravy sandwiches with mashed potatoes and Lebanese classics like rolled pita shistawook and kebobs, where half the city had eaten after the bars had closed when they had drunk too much and the buzz still coursed upward and would continue eating until the owner would be shot in the head at 4:00 AM one Sunday morning after an argument over a patron's vomit splattered shoes and pants, past recently built national chain pizza and donut shops and a suburban style strip mall with a vast asphalt parking lot in front of a row of single story stores that sold everything from clothes for really big women to movie rentals, hairstyling where the stylists were not pretty and the styles stayed at least a decade out of date, a sandwich shop hawking pulled pork and fat, processed groceries, paint, and more shoes (different chain), past a trophy shop specializing in the old-style keepsake with a glittering column (the height determined by price and the importance of the event won, sporting a figurine, sometimes indeterminately nude or lightly clothed, playing the sport whose champion it honored), a barber shop with a broken barber pole where the reading material consisted of years old copies of *Playboy*, *Penthouse*, *Fly Fishing Today*, and *Gear Box Quarterly*, past gas stations that had begun transforming into mini-grocery and knickknack stores, pharmacies that had already transformed into larger grocery, sundry and knickknack stores, resale shops that sold used knickknacks, placemats, salt and pepper shakers, mugs in the shape of German and Dutch heads, wobbly lamps and dirty crystal, a beauty supply store with an inventory of every kind of hair or skin product knock-off that a low end salon might want to carry, several closed storefronts that briefly housed a collection of bars and strip clubs where the bars were known for their brawls and wild danger and the strip clubs were known for completely nude women who displayed constellations of track marks and who taught each other how to spread their legs in front of a man's face and push their vaginas inside out so that it looked like a small pink mouth sang along to the lyrics of the heavy metal soundtrack so that even the most desperate of men, even after paying seven dollars for a coke, couldn't help but tip the little singer with what money they had left, over a bridge that spanned a highway, past a massive lumber company with a high, barbed wire fence around its perimeter, a plumbing supply store, an electrical supply store, past storefront contractors who practiced the look of stability but who were always one or two jobs away from skipping town with a homeowner's deposit money, who are sometimes descendents of Pavees or Irish Travelers, past cheap furniture stores where pine constructed furniture sheathed in upholstery could be bought or rented for interest rates higher than the worst default rates of vulture credit cards, past used car lots that always displayed the stud of the lot on a spot close to the street, whether it be a Porsche, Jaguar or Cadillac, in front of a couple of dozen beaters polished to a buy-me shine, so that the buyer could feel good about purchasing a wheezing, leaking hunk of scrap from the same lot as the stud, past a surgical supply store with cages on the windows and doors, no doubt protecting the boxes of hypodermic needles but also guaranteeing muddled junkies who thought the supply might include anesthetic, Percodan or methadone would be deterred from breaking in, more bars that looked to be on the brink of closing because of too much blood having been spilled, antiques stores that held collections from people who died or fled or sold off their heirlooms to buy food or to gain entrance in a nursing home, a fire equipment store that sold oxygen tanks, masks, fire suits, graphite handled axes, and every other tool a firefighter would need to run into a blaze, including a GPS body retrieval system and salves for minor burns, past a newly built recreation center constructed like a fortress amidst a raging urban war and named after a councilman who died in council chambers of a heart attack while listening to a speech from one of his colleagues concerning the need for new taxes to support a new professional sports stadium (the death did not stop the council from steamrolling the legislation through as it passed the morning of his funeral), two hot dog restaurants, side by side, both boasting of serving the largest 100% all beef hot dog in town (the first restaurant looked clean and bustling with new neon signs and a designed look while the second copied from the first, except the owner hand painted the signs and mopped the floor half as much), a radiator repair shop where radiator had been spelled with an "e" instead of an "o" and remained that way since it had opened years ago even though half the customers pointed out the mistake, a small manufacturing shop that made gaskets and that had also adopted a geek-like character, except he had gaskets for eyes, past a funeral home known for being able to paste together the most gruesome corpses and presenting them for one last showing to family and friends with some of the most extreme cases being car accidents and gang slayings, which came in with a high degree of mutilation and left being remembered as good as, if not better, than Madame Tussaud's wax likenesses, past a massive stone bank, all ten floors empty and awaiting redevelopment, a cluster of fast food restaurants that kept this section of the street blanketed in a mist of grease, a Catholic high school dominant in football with the academic buildings crowded around an immaculate field with new stadium lighting and crisp white striping, past a storefront soup restaurant that ladled out the best jambalaya and chicken noodle in town from cast iron pots that looked like they could have come from the Bronze Age, past a once bustling twenty-five story office that now housed a dozen social service agencies, a Chinese herbalist and acupuncturist, a comic book collector, a couple of artists who slept in their offices and gave themselves and sometimes each other sponge baths in the common restroom, a bike messenger service that had started as a lark but had grown into a fascist bike-first organization promoting bike access on all roads including superhighways, a laudable goal but internal debates had grown increasingly fantastic and the messengers now openly talked of sabotage and terror, and a computer design company that had no customers other than the social service agencies who needed a quick fix of a computer, which usually involved an anti-viral cleansing or replacing a hard drive, and finally they walked past the tall clock tower of the Westside Market where distributors brought their fresh produce and meats and sold it under the brick, barrel roof inside or under canvas tents that had been erected in the alleys when the market had grown larger than the building. They walked through the parking lot of the market jammed with cars and came to a line of sick trees, stunted with leaves that were neither green nor brown, but a pale gray like they had been boiled for hours. They fought through the branches and a thicket that had filled the space under the trees and came to a grassy embankment on top of the valley carved by the meandering river below.

"If we're leaving by boat we have to get to the water," Nelson said as he looked for a path leading down.

"You have a firm grasp of strategy. And you're logical too. Several streets lead down to the river. You can have your pick of any one of them. Makes sense, right. The whole purpose of the city being where it's at is the meeting of the lake and river. The first settlement was on the river. All roads began there."

"I haven't seen the dogs, have you? Let's keep out of sight."

"But they've seen you. They've been following us. They know where we are. All they have to do is lift their noses into the air and take a whiff."

"Have you seen them?"

"I don't have to see them to know they're there. I can feel them. They're close. They're always close."

Nelson plunged forward down the bank, stepping blindly into the long grass and holding onto saplings sprouting from the hillside. Pez followed with measured, sure steps, jumping at times like a mountain goat, and easily passed Nelson. They crossed a train tracks carved into the side of the hill and passed a small cluster of cardboard and milk jug shanties. A pair of feet stuck out of one and cigarette smoke filtered out of another. The milk jugs had been filled with sand, laid on their sides and stacked to make walls. Pieces of scrap two-by-fours had been driven into the ground to hold the wall from rolling and saplings had been bent to provide extra support and cover. The roofs were made of scrap corrugated metal, road signs and flattened cans laid like shingles. Cardboard lined the inside like drywall and if a man paid attention to the detail of the construction he could pass a leisurely winter within its confines without fear of freezing to death. The inhabitants only had to worry about keeping out of sight of the commuters aboard the transit train, who, if they witnessed this shocking display of poverty for more than a few days straight, would call the police and have the men rousted from their nests and their neighborhood torn down.

They came to a road at the bottom of the hill and followed it around a bend. Pez refrained from saying they could have just as easily descended on this road without risking breaking their necks by climbing through the grass and trees, which had made a more obvious trail for the dogs to follow. On one side of the road stood manufacturers and boat storage facilities. On the other side a ten acre square had been cordoned off with a rusting barbed wire fence. The land inside the fence had been left to grow, but the tress looked gnarled and twisted, choked by high weeds and poison in the ground. The areas without weeds and trees looked torn and blasted and imperfectly put back together. Large piles of broken concrete lay within circles of gouged, barren earth. Two pillars from a lost building tilted toward each other and as Nelson and Pez walked under them they quickened their step to avoid being crushed under a rain of bricks and mortar. They came to another chain link fence, rusted through and leaning from the weight of small trees, shrubs and a thicket of weeds and brambles. Pez stopped and sniffed at a branch of thick blackberries. He plucked them one by one and popped them in his mouth without a thorough inspection for dirt or insects.

"They're good," Pez said through a mouthful.

Nelson held a berry in his hand, brought it to his nose and inhaled the scent before dropping it to the dirt and crushing it with his shoe.

"Waste not, want not."

Pez wagged a finger at him, but Nelson walked away and along the fence until he found a break in the trees and weeds and spotted the edge of the river twenty feet away on the other side of the fence. Nelson grabbed the links and pulled himself up, struggling to find a toe hold as his shoes kept slipping out of the chainlink. He pulled himself up until he gained the top and he used his stomach as a fulcrum to swing his legs over. His right foot landed on a root which caused his ankle to roll. A shot of pain seized the lower half of his leg and he crumpled to the ground. Pez climbed the fence in three coordinated movements of arms and legs and landed on the other side in a balanced stance reminiscent of a gymnast's dismount.

"See if you can put weight on it," Pez said as he pointed to Nelson's ankle.

Nelson stood up and expected to collapse in agony, but the ankle held and when he gave it a test walk it remained stable, if a little loose.

"Lucky. That would have scuttled our plans, eh? You would have begged the dogs to take you back."

"Not likely. Those goddamn shoes made me slip."

"I'll keep repeating what I know until it sinks into your consciousness. They like tricks and jokes. Nothing makes them happier. They are cousin to the coyote you know. Scratch the surface of Native American myth and the coyote will come up as the trickster figure."

Pez turned and broke through another line of trees to the edge of the muddy brown river. He waited for Nelson to gingerly step around the roots and bottles. They stood over the river's offerings: muddy plastic bottles and rotted branches, a fleet of cigarette butts and a fish head, three condoms balled and twisted and a fishing bobber hopelessly entangled around a log. Across the water the downtown skyscrapers rose and Nelson imagined a pair of eyes in each of the thousands of windows, peering through binoculars or telescopes, scanning the trees and streets as they looked for a flash of his red shoes. Above them a tangle of bridges spanned the river. Massive concrete pillars stained with grime and rust held the road deck and cast a deep shadow over them. To the left a truss bridge stepped over the river and its crisscrossed beams looked like a steel cat's cradle. An old viaduct started from the bank but terminated at the water's edge as if a flood had washed away the remaining span. Close to the ground, bridges that split or rose for ship traffic had all cleared as a tug pushed a barge toward the steel mills downriver.

"That's how you get out of town."

Pez pointed at the barge, non-descript as barges go with its brown and beige paint, its featureless hull and its block-like cluster of shapes on deck, except for its enormous size in relation to the river. It looked big enough to displace all the water from the banks and to flatten a skyscraper should the tug captain let his concentration wander. On the stern the name of the boat, *The Red Laugh,* had been painted in white letters over a series of numbers.

"How would we get on it?"

"It'll stop at the mill to unload the iron ore. I've seen a thousand of them come and go. There must be lots of places to hide on a boat like that. Small crew not thinking about stowaways. I think they would notice dogs massing on deck, too. It could be the ticket. I bet we could almost just walk right on."

"Shouldn't we just steal a car?" Nelson said as the size of the barge made him think the task too large and complicated to be completed successfully.

"Ever stolen a car before?"

"No."

"Know how to hot wire one?"

"No, definitely not. I have no idea."

"Don't get me wrong. There are always options. You can try anything. It's just that I've tried everything except this, except a boat. I don't know if they've figured out boats yet."

"Then I suspect we'll be trying to get out of here by boat. Where's it going to stop?".

"The steel mills. It's loaded with iron ore."

"I'm not going back there."

"It's a comfortable hole. Dry most times even though it's below the level of the river and is in a valley. Sometimes I think they have the engineering skills of the Romans."

"It took me most of the day to get out of that area."

"That's because you were not suppose to leave. That should be obvious to you. But I bet you walked right past a boat. You passed your ticket out without even knowing it. Pez had to tell you."

"Where do these barges go once they've unloaded?"

"Michigan, Huron, Superior. That one will stop in Wisconsin. It's an ore boat on a circuit from the ore fields to the mills."

"That's not any closer to Florida."

"You think you're going back there? That door is closed, friend, shift your paradigm. Throw a dart at a map and start over or change your thinking about what is possible and prudent. Retracing your steps backward never works."

"We have to follow the river?"

"What else would we follow to trail the barge? Maybe he can take us?" Pez pointed to a man wearing a faded baseball cap motoring by in an aluminum fishing boat with an outboard motor. The boat bounced over the wake of the barge as the man steered it away from the worst of the turbulence. Pez whistled using a finger on either side of his mouth and caught the fisherman's attention. He snapped his head in their direction and they motioned for him to come to shore. He turned his boat toward them and slid up next to the steel bulkhead that lined the shore, prevented erosion, but eliminated the spawning areas of the lake fish. He clicked the motor off and peered at them from under the bill of his cap.

"What are you doing on this side of the fence?" he said, using an inflection usually employed by guards or policeman.

"Aren't we allowed here? After all, it is a public waterway." Pez asked.

"Fences usually mean stay out or stay in. What do you think this one means?"

"I understand the intent. I disagree with the law or the philosophy behind the intent."

"Can you give us a ride down river?" Nelson broke in before a non-productive debate could be launched.

"Actually, that's considered up the river." He pointed to the barge as it turned the bend and disappeared. "And that's downriver." He pointed to the section of river that sluiced through a field of ruins that used to be a jumble of bars and restaurants.

"Upriver, then."

"Where?"

"The steel mill."

"Late for a shift? Going by road doesn't interest you?"

"We were chased by a pack of wild dogs to this side of the fence. They've taken the road," Pez said in a measured and liquid voice meant to convey a rational mind with no cognitive gaps. "Otherwise we wouldn't be on this side of the fence."

"I'm going that way anyway. They say there's bluegill biting over by Kingsbury Run. They must be some tough goddamn fish. Thought I'd like to see how one of them tastes, probably have enough mercury in them that I'll be able to rent myself out as a thermometer. Slide down the bulkhead and get in. Don't jump. You'll flip the boat over and we'll all be in the river."

"That would ruin my shoes," Nelson said without a trace of humor so the fisherman couldn't help but take the statement seriously.

"That would be a shame to ruin those beauties. Besides, there's about a hundred and fifty years of industry in this river. The water might dissolve the shoes right off your feet."

"But you're going to eat the fish out of here?"

"What's the difference? Something has to kill you. Might as well be by your own hand."

Nelson and Pez lowered themselves into the boat by holding on to the edge of the bulkhead and stretching until their toes touched the seats. Once the fisherman held their legs for stability they let go of their grip. The fisherman started the motor once Nelson and Pez settled in their seats and he made for the middle of the river.

"Not just anybody would pick up a couple of guys at the side of the river," the fisherman said. "Especially when they're on the wrong side of the fence." Nelson and Pez nodded because they were unsure how to respond or if the fisherman expected a response. A long silence followed. "Do you have an interest in knowing why I picked you up?"

"First, let me say thank you for inviting us into your boat and second, I would be interested in knowing why you decided to pick us up, given that we were on the wrong side of the fence," Pez figured the fisherman had kept talking to elicit a thank you from them so he obliged by yelling over the thacking engine.

"The reason isn't all that interesting, I suspect. Maybe a little crazy. I was on the other side of the river chasing a couple of stray perch when the barge went by and when it passed suddenly you two show up on the bank flagging me down. It looked like you had fallen off the barge. I thought 'that'd be funny if they fell off the barge,' but as I got closer I could tell you weren't wet so my theory went out the window. By then I was committed to finding out why you were on the wrong side of the fence."

"I suspect you didn't expect the reason to be a pack of wild dogs," Pez said with a smile on his face that looked deranged given his lack of teeth and the hair sprouting from his ears."

"I've heard that before. Goddamn city."

"We have to get on that barge before it sails."

"Barges don't sail. No sails."

"Before the barge floats away."

"So I was right. You are from the barge. They've exiled you."

"No, we're supposed to report to the barge today. This is our first trip."

"It's not easy to stick with that outfit. I've seen the exiles on the bank before. They always looked dispossessed like you two. Some of them can't even speak anymore."

"Possible victims of the phone company, yes?" Pez inquired.

"No, those people are never thrown in. They're just taken away."

They passed mountains of limestone and gravel that looked like piles of ground up skyscrapers and passed under two more bridges. A cluster of chemical tanks, each at a different height, sat on a low hill overlooking the river. A tangle of black graffiti near the base defaced the largest one and made the tank seem more dangerous because it added a sense of abandonment to the inscrutable sheen of metal containing liquid capable of dissolving bone. More bulkheads had been driven into the banks on either side and made the river look like a man-made canal, tamed and poisoned. They turned a bend. Low flatlands and the barge came into view. The familiar black mass of the steel mill dominated the horizon. They passed under another bridge, modern and functional, constructed out of concrete and steel without distinctive features. Some of the concrete had fallen away in chunks, exposing the rebar, as the bridge teetered a few years away from a massive reconstruction.

"They found those two headless corpses right over there along the bank. They say it was a pretty clean cut, almost guillotine clean. Who has a guillotine in their basement or backyard? How do you get a cut like that? We're talking thick muscle and bone."

"Decapitation isn't all that rare. A good sword will do it," Pez asserted.

"At first I thought the dead may have come from the barge, but that's not really their style. They wouldn't want to attract that much attention. Headless corpses spawn too many questions. They destroy their people in different ways."

"Were the corpses young kids wearing black?" Nelson shouted.

"They're not saying. They're saying it could be related to drugs. They always say that to kill everyone's interest. Tell the viewing audience it was drug-related and they'll yawn, tell their wives the little bastards had it coming if they were stupid enough to mess with drugs, and turn off the light believing that justice always prevails. Sometimes delayed, sometimes harsh, but you always get what you have coming. I don't believe a goddamn word of any of it. I don't believe anything anybody says. For all I know the cops cut off their heads. How will we ever know? Who's actually going to tell the truth?"

Nelson thought he recognized the barren flatland and the distant mill. He turned to Pez who had been staring at the back of Nelson's head and smiling.

"Feels like home, doesn't it?"

"Not really," Nelson said, but if he had been honest he would have admitted that he felt a surge of comfort and familiarity when he recognized the river basin.

"Makes me feel regret again." Pez cleared his throat and spit into the swirls of the river, then continued, "A man has to have a home. He needs the cocoon, the shell, the womb. A man has to have an address. When a person asks him, 'Where do you live?' he can't return a blank stare or point to the sky or the horizon. He can't hem and haw and mutter an incomprehensible string of syllables. Understand? Why am I running? What am I running to? Where am I going? After forty years it shouldn't be this easy, right? I know my home isn't much to look at, but it's mine, it's unique and for a brief moment in the history of the earth's rotations I've claimed it as my own. Now, I decide to abandon it on a whim. I destroy the only shelter I know and I expose myself to the storm. I've cast myself out to what? Where are we going? Why did you drag me out here? I'm beyond adventure and hope."

"I heard about every third word you said, but I think I heard enough to understand. It does no good to run. You feel better being in motion, but it's always the same outcome. I made it to Nebraska once, then New York City. Another time it was Tennessee. None of it mattered. Look where I am. Fishing for mutant bluegill," the fisherman shouted.

"What are you talking about?" Nelson shouted.

"Don't act like it's a secret. Everybody knows. Everybody has their idiosyncratic way of dealing with it. Right over there at the bend they tell me the bluegill are practically jumping out of the water, acting just like the water is a blazing hot griddle. I'll swing back over there after I drop the two of you off."

Neither Nelson nor Pez could muster the energy to ask the man for specifics and chose to remain ignorant of his meaning. The boat puttered down the river until they reached the stern of the barge, its hull rising straight up like a factory wall. The skin of the barge, pocked and rusted, looked like it had been under mortar or machinegun fire. The tug had stopped and the crew on shore tethered the barge to a dock.

"Which side?"

"Of what?"

"Of the river. Where do you want to be dropped off? There's still time to change your mind."

Pez pointed to the side of the river where the crew secured the barge. The fisherman received the instructions with a shrug. Then, he swung the boat around, pointed it toward the shore and gunned the motor. Steel bulkheads lined this portion of the river as well so no spot existed to beach the boat, but the fisherman increased the speed anyway and the boat bounced over the choppy water. The bulkheads rushed toward them and Nelson considered his options, which were two in his estimation, either staying in the boat and crashing headlong into the steel wall or jumping in the river and swimming to a spot where he could climb out. Before a decision needed to be made the fisherman yanked the steering lever and turned off the motor with one movement so the boat violently jerked and slowed down, drifting alongside the bulkhead with no damage to the boat or personal injury to the captain and his passengers. The fisherman grabbed a steel ring welded on to the bulkhead and brought the boat to a stop. Pez stood up, bounced on the boat seat and hoisted himself onto the shore. Nelson followed Pez' technique and by the time he stood up the fisherman had pushed off and started the motor.

"Remember," the fisherman shouted. "Sometimes the cur is worse than the disease." He opened up the throttle and the knocking of the motor drowned out his laughter.

"Did he say what I think he said?" Nelson asked as he turned toward Pez.

"They love jokes. I've never seen such a silly pack of dogs."

A large crane had swung from the deck of the barge and a conveyer belt drew iron ore from the storage holds. The belt carried the ore down the length of the crane and it flew off the end to a pile on the ground, a foothill to a range of ore mountains already established onshore. To the right a white mountain of crushed limestone rose alongside the black ore range. A staircase had been extended from the deck of the barge to the dock below. Three men stood smoking cigarettes at the bottom of the staircase as they engaged in a fractured conversation, interrupted by their watching the ore fall to the ground.

"We wait until night and sneak on," Pez said as he crouched in the weeds, then lay down spread-eagle. "That's the most I've walked in years. I feel like my legs are going to fall off."

Nelson crouched down beside him, but he couldn't force himself to lie down. So, for the next four hours he watched the pile of ore grow from a foothill to something more substantial, nothing close to being considered a peak of the range, but growing. When he lost interest in the ore he watched for dogs or followed the muddy brown churn of the river or gazed at the windows of a skyscraper illuminated in a random pattern that didn't create a recognizable geometric shape or a number or letters that spelled a word that would give him a clue about his fate as the sky turned from blue to crepuscular brown. The men near the staircase eventually drifted away, either up the stairs or through the mountains. He waited until they sensed no movement except the falling ore, and Nelson shook Pez awake and they crept along the bank until they came to the foot of the staircase.

Nelson went first, keeping his eye on the top of the stairs and expecting the head of a security guard or a guard dog to pop up and detach the staircase from the barge. From below the sailors would push it to the river's edge and dump them both in the muddy water and throw rocks at their bobbing heads until they slipped under the surface of the water. But no one appeared to block their entry and they stepped on to the deck. They were near the back of the barge. The pilot house rose behind them and in front along the span of the deck sat a jumble of mechanical systems, protrusions, small towers and pipes covered in a grimy patina. A chorus of motors rumbled from below. The crane still hung over the bank, but the rush of ore had slowed to a dribble. Pez found a series of cabinets along the base of the pilot house that held life preservers, flares, ropes, tool boxes, discarded overalls and a forgotten lunchbox that entombed a petrified lunch. Two cabinets were empty and Pez charaded Nelson into understanding they should hide in the cabinets until they reached their destinations, wherever that may be.

"We need to hide out of sight. The dogs can't find us if they can't see us," Pez said in a whisper as he pointed to the cabinets, unable to come up with an appropriate silent gesture to communicate this last thought.

"Dogs track by smell. My God, Pez, no wonder you never escaped. Did you learn nothing about them in the last thirty years?"

"The crew won't find us unless they are looking for this lunch they packed ten years ago."

Shouldn't we go see if there's a more comfortable place to hide than this? It might be a long trip."

"If you want to get caught that's up to you. I'm hiding in this cabinet," Pez said as he scrambled inside. "Close the doors. It has leg room. It's deeper than you first think."

Nelson closed the doors and turned the handle.

"Try to get out," he whispered to the door. The door rattled, shook and bounced when Pez started hitting it with his fist. "Stop, stop, stop it." Nelson opened the door. Pez' face became red with frustration and a little panic. "See this rod. It locks the door when I turn the handle. Move it down if you need to get out." Pez nodded his head.

Nelson shut the door again and turned the handle. He crawled inside the second cabinet and was surprised when his legs unfurled to their full length. The air inside smelled of sulfur and rotten meat. The metal walls amplified every movement so that every scrape of a button or belt buckle sounded like a cannonade echoing across the barge. Nelson reached out slowly and closed the door. He groped for the rod in the dark and slipped it closed after several attempts. Suddenly, his breathing became a bellows feeding a blast furnace.

His thoughts were loud, overbearing, part static, part fear, part trying to find comfort in a coffin-sized metal cabinet, part unbelieving that they could have escaped so easily, and part suspecting Pez of being in league with the pack, because Pez had been the one to come up with the idea of the boat, had directed him to the river, and had so easily found these cabinets. What if he had led him to the phone company barge filled with captured souls being transported to some diabolical process?

His breathing slowed after an hour or so. The air inside became humid with his breath. The static in his mind had disappeared and the suspicious thoughts about Pez had receded, replaced by a blankness. He found that lying on his back with his hands under his head to be the most comfortable position with the least amount of pressure points. He also found that if he kept his eyes open and stared into the blackness his thoughts remained as black and featureless as his sight, but once he closed them something in the shutting of his lids triggered his subconscious into action and the foundation for paranoid constructions began to be rapidly laid. When the hydraulics swung the crane back on deck and footsteps passed the cabinet, Nelson pressed himself against the side, hoping that if a sailor opened the door they might not see him in the shadows. Footsteps passed several more times and then quiet returned. After another hour or two of stillness Nelson's eyes, dry and tired of trying to focus in the void, closed on their own. He slept through the arrival of the tug, the preparations for leaving, and a brief conversation between two crewman that took place outside the cabinet, during which one crewman expressed dismay that the barge would not be staying the night, because he had hoped to go to a specific bar where all the sailors hung out and talk to a woman who always perched at the corner of the bar and who would always be willing to spend some time talking, and if a sailor had enough conversational game she'd be willing to take them home and make them forget their lives on the water for a few hours and if she didn't make herself available, or if his conversation fell below her standard, then he wanted to go to a club where the strippers grew unruly thatches over their pussies. The other crewman, obviously older and tired of such harangues and recounted adventures filled with explicit and lurid detail told the younger crewman that he should be thankful for the tight schedule because it meant the mills cooked steel and steel meant money and money earned by sailing these beautiful, unpredictable lakes shouldn't be spent on whores and looking at pussy, not matter how unruly. The younger sailor responded that the older sailor had forgotten the torture of being young and full of cum and working on this miserable boat on these temperamental and gloomy lakes. Nelson slept through someone opening and closing the cabinet door, the barge floating away from the shore, the tug powering it down the river, releasing it past the break wall of the lake, and the barge firing up its own power and gliding across Lake Erie through a dense mist.

Under the Bell Tower, Waiting for His Voice

After saying goodbye to Koo Koo, Ellen Oglethorpe pushed the cotton balls deep into her ears. She slipped through the door and tested the protection of the cotton against the web of violation. Through the thin guard the ripping of the sky and the smashing of the air sounded just below a roar. Outside sounded quiet enough to concentrate on walking, but she couldn't risk thinking and opening her mind to marauding surfers. She walked under the shade of a Norway maple on legs covered in alligator skin. Years and frostbite had done her beauty in, but her legs had been especially ravaged as they were swollen and sagging. The Sisters of Divine Mercy had given her the dress she wore, a fourth or fifth-hand maid's uniform of powder blue with broad white pockets. Sister Bollo had told her she looked just like a little Amish girl ready to squeeze the milk from a cow's teat. Ellen thought the image too earthy and sensual for Sister Bollo to have said, but even nuns were susceptible to the lure of touching and groping. Ellen smiled to God once a day, because even though He tested her more than Job himself, she knew, she believed, as she passed a compact mirror before her face, that she had retained the complexion of a twenty year old. Not that having a smooth complexion helped fight off the marauders. The pink glow of her cheeks had never faded and she still resembled a peach on a tree. Mirror, mirror on the wall, who will rape me first of all? She dabbed powder under her left eye. No one she had ever met had the cruelty within them to tell her the peach she had been had fallen off the tree and now lay under forty blankets of rotting leaves. Her bright red jacket really brought out the gifts her face had to offer, she thought as she slipped the compact into the white pocket of her dress. She wanted to thank the man behind the counter in the Salvation Army store because his prices were so reasonable. She had bought a wool overcoat, obviously a few seasons out of fashion, for the paltry sum of two sticks of brittle Juicy Fruit and a light bulb with a burned-up filament. A sweet man with pleasant eyes and a melodious voice who turned the simplest phrases into song, a mask hiding the heart of a jackal. Lewdness and impurity rode his sweat down his handsome and tanned face. She could smell his appetites and even though she had been lonely for the longest time she could not submit. Even in her early womanhood she had tried to avoid the roving hands of males, but she had been tricked once or twice in the foul popcorn darkness, where the blue light from the screen licked her eyes, charged with ions and lust, where the actors spoke to her from their two-dimensional sets and beckoned to her to enjoy the world of her body and to give pleasure to the nearest man to her in the theater. But she had escaped mechanic hand greasy fingernail contamination. Under the shadow play of BUtterfield 8, a puppet show really of lusty, immoral demons, the hand slid up her thigh, under her skirt and just as he pulled the cotton aside, just as she had leaned her head back and let the ions fall upon her throat she heard His voice. Could He be standing in the back of the theater, a few rows away from her surrender or did He speak from the speakers of the theater or did He simply rise up from the teachings and her study of His words? Sweet Jesus, someone else's savior. Bittersweet Lord. She crossed herself. She knew her curses were the shouts of a fool. Her words were a hiccup in a howling wind.

"Oh, that my grief were fully weighed, and the calamity laid with it in the scales for then it would be heavier than the sand of the sea. Father why have I been afflicted? Why have you turned me out?" Ellen said to the cracks in the sidewalk.

Whenever she thought or spoke of God an image of her jaunty father followed a few paces behind. Sister Bollo had told her not to mention her biological father and God the Lord in the same breath, intimating Ellen might be on the cusp of sacrilege. Men cannot be God. No man is God, she said. Girls adore their fathers, she said. But Ellen dear, she said. You are a woman. You must know by now that men are weak, she said. You must know by now that men can be wicked and cruel and that God's grace is immense, his wisdom divine. Ellen dear, your father may have read the Bible to you, but Ellen, you poor dear, he didn't write it. Oh, Sister Bollo, Ellen said, once Poppa climbs into my head or raises his head inside my head because he's really never outside my head he becomes all and more. I carry him with me wherever I go and when he makes himself heard his voice becomes a chorus of voices. The National Aeronautic and Space Administration? Dreamer of moon shots and moon rocks and moon rovers, those little buggies the astronauts used to drive around the moon. Who else but an American would think of driving on the moon? Two men and then a highway, Poppa said, facing his rows and rows of books with cruel scratchings on the pages, the numbers and divisions and the multiplications and the terse and ultimately disappointed explanations because if I couldn't follow logic I should just close the book and pick up a romance or a picture book. I would sit on his knee, Sister Bollo, and I could smell the smoke in his beard. He tried to show me his books and help me understand, but my mind opened like a sieve through which he poured an ocean of knowledge that splashed to the floor. Poor papa, a genius cavorting among the apes, but in the end his arteries betrayed him, constricting enough to slowly kill his brain and make him a tyrant. First, the logic became muddled, then confused, then upside down, then he refused to wear pants and after a half dozen complaints of indecency he ended up in a home for people with ailing brains. Yes, Ellen, yes, Sister Bollo said, we all have our stories of loss. The body is frail and its decay is cruel. We all bury someone we love. Look to God, Ellen, look to Him. He is the only constant.

A piercing beep, sounding like the screech of an owl amplified a thousandfold, echoed through the neighborhood. A backhoe wobbled toward the house where Ellen Oglethorpe had lived. Her legs could not run to stop them. She reached out and placed a hand against the trunk of a tree. Oh, how her legs tormented her. Why hadn't she let the doctors take them? What had He in store for her? Sister Bollo always reminded her to remember that we shall indeed accept good from God, and shall not we accept adversity? Sister Bollo looked at her with a kind face and the gentlest of smiles, acting as if her words and countenance could turn off the spigot of torment so Ellen told her that the thing she greatly feared had come upon her and what she dreaded had happened to her. She had no rest, for trouble came and came and came. If her legs could have carried her she would have thrown herself on the porch and let the bucket of the backhoe cut her in half as it gouged at the wood. If her voice had been strong enough she would have shouted, ordering the machine into a humiliating retreat and commanded it to respect her memories and her fragile past. A wave of pain rolled through her belly. In the past few days the pain had been creeping higher and Ellen did not know how to push it back down to her legs. The backhoe pivoted and the claw rose high in the air, gathered strength, and gored the side of the house. The arm rose again and smashed the porch, where He read The Press and smoked a pungent Turkish blend of tobacco in his pipe and where she had played dolls with Caroline Ambassador, the flaxen-haired girl who lived down the street. When Ellen thought of Caroline she thought of her with a doll's face, big black eyes painted on porcelain with the softest yellow hair with the consistency of corn silk sprouting from the scalp. The claw smashed open the front door, the portal into and out of the golden wooden light, releasing air heavy with the scent of baking apples and slow cooking oatmeal. The air warmed by radiators escaping to the ozone. Radiators that never knocked or clanked because her father tended to the boiler like they were counting on it to fly to the moon and back. Mother standing in the kitchen gathering the meal with the same look of crazed concentration as her father had when he read his indecipherable books. The ingredients were all grouped in straight lines and neat piles and ordered either by the alphabet or the size of the container they were in. She remained neat through the most complicated or disastrous recipes without a speck of flour or leaf of parsley clinging to her dress or apron. How is it possible that debris would not stick to her or that she washed her clothes for form's sake because they never attracted enough dirt to warrant the use of water and detergent? The floor beneath her looks like a floor of a ballroom and her perfect feet look ready to float across the wood in a dazzling pattern. She smiles and places a hand under Ellen's chin. You look famished, she said, and cold. It started out so pleasant this morning, a fragment of summer, but by the looks of your cheeks winter has returned. And you've only worn that thin red jacket over that pretty blue dress with the white pockets. What kind of mother lets their child out wearing only a thin red jacket? She had tried to live with the raging tyrant, tried to protect him from the world without aim, but his vessels and arteries wrapped themselves around her neck like a spindly boa and choked the will out of her until one day he died in his bed, wearing stained pajamas and a horrible scowl, thrashing at the air. Nothing remained of her when he passed so she died with him, quietly and unexpectedly on the kitchen floor. Ellen found her on the floor holding the lid of a flour tin and sadly the contents, nearly a full pound of flour, coated her body from her knees to her chin, as if all the flour she had ever avoided had its final revenge. The supporting beams of the house were knocked askew and it folded in upon itself as the workmen sprayed thin reeds of water to keep the dust from spreading. Five other men, waiting for the house to settle, stood at the perimeter of the yard as the backhoe driver leaned back in his chair and reflected upon his work, now in a pile. Ellen would have liked to think of them as pallbearers and priests presiding over the internment of her memories, but hadn't she just witnessed the destruction by their own hands? Were they not butchers and surgeons hacking and sawing in the name of their own greed? I'm sure in the annals of human history many murderers served as pallbearers to their victims, but had family and friends obliged the ruse knowingly? What would Sister Bollo say about equating a killer with a priest? Oh, remember my life as a breath and my eye will never again see good. While your eyes are upon me, I shall no longer be. As the cloud of my house disappears and vanishes away, so does he who goes down to the grave and does not come up. I will never return to this house, nor shall this place know me anymore. When I say my bed will comfort me and my couch will ease the pain of these legs you scare me with dreams and terrify me with visions and the soundscape of hell's ninth circle, so that my soul chooses strangling and death rather than this broken body filled with pain. I loathe this life, father. I would not live forever. Leave me alone and climb out of my head once and for all. My days are but a breath blown away by the breeze. So, after hours of speculation and worry, this is how it ends, in a poisonous cloud surrounded by a brace of jackals as witnesses. Ellen pushed off the tree and hobbled down the sidewalk. She knew the tears in her eyes should wash the murder from her sight, but the fluid did nothing more than remind her how weak she had become in the face of this ripping torrent. If her legs would carry her she would make mass and pray again for Him to kill her body and to kill the jackals for pulverizing her soul in front of her eyes. She would ask Sister Bollo where one lives after their soul has been murdered.

Ellen took a step forward and the toe of her oversized shoe caught the seam of the sidewalk and she crumpled on the green grass of a neighbor's front lawn. Five people rushed to her aid: a man who was drinking milk in his living room and staring out his window, a woman walking her dog, a Nova Scotia Duck-Tolling Retriever, across the street, a mailman who had just paused to take off his hat and wipe the sweat from his forehead, and a young couple just back from a late breakfast of toast and jam and three pots of coffee as they struggled through individual alcohol-related hangovers induced by spending too much time together and disliking the other's personality, but who couldn't help but touch each other so they walked with a hand on each other's hip, and the rhythm of their steps reminded them to go home and fuck. They all ran to Ellen and asked in a rush what had happened, did anything hurt, can you sit up, can you remain lying down, has this happened before, is this related to your legs, can anybody on this street afford a maid, who's your owner, where do you live, are you coherent, is anything broken, is there someone we can call?

What explanation did she owe these random people? Agents, no doubt, of government departments growing in cellar offices of granite and brick buildings with imperturbable facades, called names like Department of Overt Suppression and Control and the Federal Bureau of Misanthropy and Logic. When she heard the man holding a half-full glass of milk say he thought they should call an ambulance she finally spoke.

"No ambulance please. They would just drive me to a furnace or a pit," she said as she pulled one of the cotton balls from her ears and held it in the palm of her hand. The shattered nature of her voice startled the group and they all drew closer to protect her.

"What can we do for you?" the woman with the dog asked. "Would you like something to drink?" The dog sat behind her on its haunches, gathering in the scene with sleepy eyes.

"Don't know what happened. I suppose the concussion of the house falling down must have knocked me down. I don't know what I was thinking really. Who could stand while your home is crushed before your very eyes, leaving you bereft and aggrieved. Who could remain upright against a force like that?"

No one could follow her words and they looked to each other for possible explanations. The circle slackened, maybe took a step back, and a ripple of anxiety forced the dog to its feet.

"Certainly you all heard and saw the house go down. Just a few minutes ago? Blown apart by priests and pallbearers."

They looked up and down the street, but all the houses stood and would stand for years to come. The neighborhood sat silent under the sun and no backhoe and no cloud of dust rolled over the yards. Her rescue party exchanged looks again and the man with the milk twirled a finger around his ear, indicating that he diagnosed Ellen with a scrambled brain.

"Where do you live?" the woman with the dog persisted, her voice rising an octave because she realized now she had become involved in a drama not of her liking.

"I was on my way to ask Sister Bollo that very question. Maybe it's an existential question at its root. Where does one ever live in righteousness before the Lord if He destroys every home you've ever known?"

"Do you have any family?"

"Oh, no, I have been cast away."

"Let's help you to your feet and see if you can stand," the mailman said, implying that once she was upright the responsibility of the group who witnessed her fall ended. If she held her feet they could go about their business. The other four in the group thought the mailman wise and they silently agreed with his morality forged by walking neighborhoods for twenty years and seeing tragedies big and small.

The man with the milk set down his glass and placed a hand underneath Ellen's arm and the mailman slipped a hand underneath her opposite arm. After a silent count of three they hoisted her from the ground. The young couple reached out hands to hold her back and steady her wobble. Fresh torment pulsed through her legs, but Ellen remained upright. The group released their hands and slowly drew away with open palms until they were convinced Ellen would remain on her feet. The woman asked one more time if she wanted to go to the emergency room because her elbow looked swollen and she could tell by Ellen's expression that she experienced discomfort. The other four groaned, thinking they may be drawn in again and would be unable to go about their business until the ambulance arrived and the police took statements from everyone, but Ellen waved her away and shook her head. The group happily returned to their lives and Ellen continued down the sidewalk.

She had no hope of making mass now, but she decided to walk to St. Ignatius and stand under the bell tower and listen to the bells like she had done a hundred times before. Ellen's brother and sister expected her to become a nun after the funeral of her mother. Since childhood she believed she would one day marry Jesus and take him into her heart. She shunned the games in the street and the muddy boys who would one day turn into filthy mechanics staring at her breasts and begging her to let them touch one of them. It doesn't even have to be a two-for-one deal, they would say. She would stand under the silhouette of the bell tower and wait for the bell to swing, wait for Jesus to shout his dominion over the neighborhood. She smiled haughtily, knowing the thunderous shout of Jesus silenced petty conversations about sex or money or both and hurtful gossip sharpened by bored women looking for something to slice. His love would pause baseball games even though a long fly ball still hung in the air and the winning run watched from second base to see if the ball would drop, would subdue the static and whipsaw prose of radio announcers driven to sell you soap and cornflakes, would make her father look up from a forest of triangles and equations that ebbed and flowed for pages to check his watch against the time of the bells because he knew that even though Father Mondo delivered heavily accented Latin and he never bothered to learn Aramaic he was punctual, having something of an obsession with timepieces, and would fight its way through the smoke and dust of the neighborhood factories to give hope to the workers or make them openly wonder if the day would ever end. For a minute the neighborhood listened to the only true voice the world has ever known before the sound wave of the bell died in a tangle of branches. Everyday at noon it was the same until one day Father Mondo pulled the rope and the bell responded with a clank. A crack had opened up along the top and the bell fell into disuse. Father Mondo moped around the church and wrote several entreaties to the bishop for money to replace the bell, but the bishop sent a letter describing the financial state of the church, and specifically Father Mondo's parish, instead of money. Several collections were started, but none ever raised enough money to cast a new bell and the donations were passed along to the bishop for disbursement and everyone forgot about the bell except for Ellen. She tried to make a case for the bell to the priests who followed Father Mondo, but not one of them saw the purpose of a new bell when more pressing concerns of maintenance threatened the building, especially when one considered that a leaky roof and a crumbling foundation topped the list. Charlie Doogan, a known drunk with an indentation on his forehead that traveled from his right eyebrow to above his hairline so that he looked like someone had either taken apart his skull and forgot how to put it back together or had tried to drive a mattock through his brain, the second version being closer to the truth than the first, had been paid to maintain the grounds. Like all drunks, his drinking took precedence over his life's duties, including maintaining the grounds of St. Ignatius, so he forgot to check the bolts of the bell for rust and signs of stress, so that in the bell's fiftieth year the moorings gave way and it tumbled out of the tower. It gave one more thunderous clang as it smashed against the sidewalk below and broke in two, with one part rolling under an untrimmed hedge and the other rolling into the street. The closest witnesses to its demise were a robber wearing a ski mask, holding up the gas station across the street, and the clerk who stared into the end of a pistol. The robber asked the terrified clerk what he thought the noise had been, like a kind of fucked up burglar alarm. The clerk sputtered and spit and shook his head to say he didn't know what could make that sound, but the robber, sufficiently spooked, left the station with a candy bar and forgot the pile of cash on the counter. Of course when the clerk told the story to his family and friends almost every single one of them said he had been witness to a miracle, that God had singled him out to save, not a small act given the soaring murder rate, and he should consider seriously how he could best spend his second gifted life. The only hold out amongst his friends, a misanthrope and crank, told him he could have just as easily been walking to his house on the sidewalk when the bell came down and the police would have had to wash his brains down the storm sewer grate to get the street clean of his life, otherwise known as the earth's ten billionth miracle.

Ellen still came and stood under the tower, waiting. What bell could now rise above the din? Jesus' voice had been reduced to a whisper. She replaced the cotton ball in her ear, because the raging wind could sense her exposure. She checked the snugness of the other ball and pushed it farther down the ear canal. Maybe he would come in silence since he couldn't surf the electronic riptide. His words often sparked and hummed through the air, shouted and spit with venom by a cavalcade of prancing serpents on the stage. A billboard rose from the top of a squat brick building that advertised a bank. The family in the advertisement looked like a family she had known fifty years before and she wondered how the photographer got them to smile so broadly as she remembered them as a morose family who thought only of the bad in people and who drew their blinds on Sundays when other families walked past their house on the way to church.

The bell had been the first sign of her love for Jesus and he guided her actions and told her to prepare to marry him. He kept her safe in the sex drenched theater and he kept her away from impregnation and contamination. All the girls could do nothing but talk about boys and when she tried to talk to them about real love and everlasting devotion they would arch their eyebrows at her, tell her the day wasn't Sunday and they had no obligation to sit through church, that she didn't wear a habit, and how about next time when you feel the urge to talk about Jesus keep it to yourself, because after high school she could enter a convent and talk about Jesus all she wanted. She pictured her room in the convent with white walls, a black iron bed, a wash basin, a black and leatherbound Bible next to the bed, and an oversized wooden crucifix hanging on the wall. She would pray and perform mundane tasks around the convent. Her home would be small but supremely quiet.

After high school she lived with her parents for a few years before they died, because her mother told her she needed help with the tyrant because he had become too much for one woman to handle and that entering the convent would be synonymous with acknowledging her father had the marital right to kill her mother. Ellen had been little help against him, and she came to see her inability as the very acknowledgment that her mother tried to leave unspoken, but as she rapidly declined she thought herself an accessory to uxoricide. When she had been freed to make a life for herself, the convent, where her heart had been set and where her life everlasting room lay waiting for her, burned down from an errant candle. God burned the sister who set the fire by breaking the rules and trying to read by candlelight in her room from scalp to toes, but he spared her a grueling rehabilitation by letting her die of smoke inhalation. The building turned to ash and charred wood. Even though Ellen's sister told her there were other convents and other orders that would gladly accept such an energetic devotee to Christ, Ellen believed that dreams burned for a reason. She tried to tell her sister that her room, the only room where she could be a nun, had burned down along with her leatherbound Bible and the wooden crucifix, and once the symbols of a future life had been consumed the life itself could never be lived. She could not tell her sister she suspected that she herself had set the fire. She had lit the candle in a dark nave and crept into the nun's room and watched her sleeping for awhile before setting the candle under the bed so she could be burned from underneath. She didn't understand the import of what she had done until she heard the poor creature's screams. She tried to get a look at the nun's face as she tried to climb out of the collapsing bed. She thought she may be looking at a mirror and a slightly older refection of her future self, but the skin of her face bubbled off before she could make positive identification. Even then God gave her the opportunity to douse the flames with water from the water basin. She backed out of the room and shunned the outstretched, pleading arms of the helpless nun. She shut the door and walked down the deserted hallway, through a small courtyard designed for meditation and reflection, and off the convent grounds. Because she failed to raise an alarm when the fire had still been small and controllable, she had doomed the convent. She waited behind a tree, clawing at its bark and peeking at the dark and silent building until flames became visible at the roof line. She knew she could never return again. She told her sister that she wouldn't go, couldn't go really, because she thought she loved Jesus, but it turned out that she hadn't been worthy of his love. Her sister could not be so easily convinced, so she lobbed argument after argument at her with her two main points being that if she didn't join the convent she would either have to find a job or a husband with the second point being that Ellen could not live with her as she had a husband and two small children with a third on the way. Ellen told her she wanted neither a job nor a husband and she wouldn't think of upsetting the domestic balance of her sister's household. She asked her sister if she could stay in their parents' home and her sister explained that mother had willed the house to her because she had a growing family but that Ellen would receive a small sum of money to get her life started and eventually she would have to find work because the inheritance wouldn't be enough to carry her through her life, she still being so young. She had lost both her past and future homes.

She found other homes. The first she could call her very own was an efficiency apartment nestled on the second floor above a butcher's shop on a busy commercial street. Her front window looked down upon an intersection and when she first moved in she liked to count the cars as they piled up behind the red light or the mass of people swarming on the sidewalk waiting to cross the street. She supplemented her inheritance with a part-time secretary job at the church. She handled correspondence for the priest, helped keep his calendar of duties straight, counted the collections and maintained a simple weekly ledger of accounts. At noon she sat back in her chair and listened to the bell. Sometimes if the weather turned nice she would walk outside and listen to the full sound as the bell challenged the traffic and the secular din. She bought a black iron bed, a leatherbound Bible, a wash basin, even though a bathroom with a sink and running water sat a few steps away from her bed, a pine dresser and a wooden crucifix. Her sister had offered her some of her parents' furniture, but Ellen thought it impossible to bring artifacts from the past into the present without paying a heavy toll. She didn't tell her sister this, but she explained instead that she expected no visitors so she would not need chairs. She preferred simplicity and as much open space as possible in her small apartment.

"You'll have visitors eventually. I'll keep the chairs until you want them. And take down that cross, Ellen. You'll scare away all the men. Did you have to buy one so big?"

"What men?" she asked.

Her sister shook her head and left the apartment without explaining what men she meant. Ellen found praying in her efficiency above the butcher shop to be difficult because the room always smelled like meat and the butcher laughed and cursed throughout the day until late evening when he went home after scrubbing his shop clean. His laugh expanded, echoed and filled a room and had the rhythm of a two-stroke engine, while his curses were a tailored string of invective whipsawed through the air that left stunned silence and a respectful awe in their wake. Ellen could only guess at their meaning, having never heard most of the words until she had moved into the apartment. She found herself listening to the curses like she would a sermon, gathering the meaning from the cadence and pulling the words apart like a cotton ball in her hand. She worried that some of the butcher's words would make it into her prayers and she would curse God without knowing.

Ellen had noticed the meat smell the moment she had walked into the apartment, but she pushed it aside as a minor concern and rented the room anyway. She thought at night the smell would dissipate but spilled blood and cut flesh could not be deterred so easily. Through most of the year she left one of the front windows open, hoping the fresh air and car exhaust would mask the shop's odor, but it never left the room. After the first few months she could discern by the scent of the work when the butcher sliced beef or ground hamburger compared to when he made sausage, bratwurst or kielbasa or dissected a whole chicken into parts. The odor also made her hungry whenever she sat or lay in the apartment, which included most of her waking and sleeping life, except for the fifteen hours a week she spent at the church, as if the scent set-off a silent alarm of hunger with every inhalation. Saliva collected at the corners of her mouth and her stomach rumbled like a distant thunderstorm even after she had just finished a meal. She became insatiable and she fought her desire to hold food in her hand or feel it touch her lips in anticipation of the first bite. She tried to pray, but the prayers were already muddled with curses and now to add a cardinal sin like gluttony would only lower His estimation of her to just above the level of a slug. What could be the point of prayer if it had the opposite effect than what she intended? Sometimes when the strain of keeping food out of her mouth became too great she would go for a walk, but the streets were jammed with streetcars, smoke and men, who caught the musk of meat on her clothes and hair and set off after her, ogling her form and salivating onto their chins. She thought her job at the church would give her respite, but she found herself sneaking a row of communion wafers into her desk and nibbling on them throughout the day. Her discipline became unhinged. She ate more. The portions of her meals doubled and she even took to eating breakfast. She gained weight at her hips and her bras became tight and uncomfortable. Men no longer stayed at a respectable distance but advanced with impunity. Sly looks became outright propositions and Ellen's cheeks and forehead flamed red in response. She tried fasting daily, but she could only last an hour or two before her will succumbed and she swallowed large mouthfuls with an inadequate number of chews. She told her sister she wanted to move, but her sister reminded her that she had signed a year's lease and that she would have to pay no matter what and she reminded her again that she had no room in her house to take Ellen in.

"But I'm going to end up fat by the end of the year."

"No, with a bottom like that you'll end up married."

The butcher had been watching her since she had moved into the apartment. He owned the building and considered it good business to make sure his tenants lived a respectable life. When she came into the shop to inquire about the apartment he couldn't have conjured a better representation of the type of tenant he wanted in his building. Her ghostly complexion and sad, round eyes, darkened by deep grief, reminded him of one of the saints. He couldn't remember the saint's name, the name of the painting she reminded him of or the artist who painted it, but he remembered liking the painting when he saw it and thinking people bear terrible burdens and suffer torments unspeakable in the name of faith. When he learned her parents had died he liked to think of her as an orphan, even though no one used the word in relation to adults. Every time he saw her he felt anxiety at the prospect of such a frail girl trying to live in a brutal world. He knew men and somebody would crush her under his thumb or abuse her terribly. He kept the best cuts of meat for her and charged what he would for a soup bone. He threw in sausages for free and always took time to explain to her how to cook a particular cut to guarantee maximum tenderness. They were a collection of small gestures meant only to express a smaller kindness and to assuage the guilt of the butcher should anything unseemly happen to Ellen. At the very least he could be assured she wouldn't starve above his shop.

As the months rolled by he noticed a gradual lessening of the anxiety he felt when she entered the shop to buy sirloin or pay her rent. The rent payment had always been a particular source of guilt because what kind of man takes money from a frail orphan who looks like a famous saint. He knew the rent helped him stay in business and he hadn't created the brutal world or the innocents who were smashed by its machinery, but nothing made him feel worse about himself than when he held out his hand and watched her count out the payment of carefully folded and saved bills into his palm. But six months into her tenancy she came into the shop on the first of the month, bringing with her a breath of humid air, and he noticed for the first time the complete lack of anxiety. In the void a muted desire took hold. The saintly white skin had blossomed pink and full. Her eyes, so morose and dark a few months before, now seemed to glint with winter light. Under her plain clothes moved a woman's body, no longer orphaned from the world, but someone and something now able to spin the world like a globe on an axle. His desire surged when she counted out the rent into his palm.

"You are looking well," he said.

"I am feeling well. Very hungry, though.'

"You look like your hunger is being satisfied."

"Never."

"Is there anything I need to fix in your apartment?"

"No, everything works fine. I am comfortable. Hungry, but comfortable."

"Sometimes the thermostat sticks and the place gets too hot."

"I haven't noticed a problem."

The butcher tried to think of a joke or something amusing to see what a smile could do for her appearance, but he could think of nothing that didn't include a curse or a scatological reference. His hand with the bills piled on the palm remained in the air.

"Is there something wrong? Isn't it all there?

"You counted fine. It's just that sometimes I find money amusing. I mean it is just paper after all. So much weight for something that weighs so little."

"I try to avoid contradictions and riddles."

Ellen slipped away, leaving the butcher standing in his shop with his hand hanging in the air.

Over the next few weeks the butcher changed his habits. He muted his curses and replaced his truly inventive scatology with phrases suitable for children and nuns. He changed his apron twice a day because how could a man hope to catch a saint with blood smeared on his chest and belly? When Ellen came by to buy hamburger or pork he would smile as broadly as his face would allow, stretching three cheek muscles to the point of discomfort, and throw her a gentle joke, but she always watched it sail past and clatter to the ground. When he asked her what plans she had for the weekend she said 'prayers.' When he asked again if anything had broken in the apartment she shook her head and ran out of the store. Her answers were always the same no matter what approach the butcher used. The next month's rent she paid with a bank check that she had placed in an envelope and left in the mailbox. The butcher just happened to see the white of the envelope sticking out of the box when he closed up the shop. The mailman always brought the mail to the counter to have the butcher set aside a parcel he picked up at the end of his route and to talk about what games to bet on, depending on the season. When the butcher opened the envelope and found the check made out to his business he wanted to rip it up into a thousand little pieces and throw it down the sewer grate, because after all his trying she either refused to use his name or didn't know it in the first place.

The next day he flicked curses from his tongue like watermelon seeds and passersby on the sidewalk were startled out of their strides. He took to wearing his aprons for two days straight so that by the end of the second day the customers began wondering if he hadn't killed one of them in the back cooler. When Ellen came into the shop he barely acknowledged her and hurriedly wrapped her parcels so that the paper hung loose and the tape was crookedly applied. He suffered an embarrassing loss of professional pride, but at least she left the store quickly. As she turned and walked away the butcher's heart skipped and he closed his eyes against the image of her backside to beat back the impulse to hurdle the counter and wrestle her to the ground.

One Friday night the butcher sat on a stool behind the counter of Mibby's Tobacco Shop, placing bets on the American League schedule. The games seemed a muddle: no obvious mismatches with three or four starting pitchers who had been inconsistent all year. One start the stud may hurl a shutout and the next the bum wouldn't be able to get out of the third inning. He would lose all his money tonight no matter what he did. Mibby clipped off the end of a huge Cuban and handed it to the butcher, who patiently lit the end an edge at a time. After he tasted five or six mouthfuls of silky smoke he looked at Mibby, who held the same kind of cigar and posture on a similar stool. The smoke furled around their heads and sent them into a meditative silence until the butcher said:

"Have you ever made time with a saint?"

"A saint by day or night?"

"All day, every day."

"Looking for guided instruction or digging a moat?"

"Moat's been dug. Drawbridge nailed shut and never used. The castle reminds me of something out of a magazine."

"Where is your leverage? Where's your ladder or pole?"

The butcher told Mibby the story of Ellen, turning from ghostly waif to a woman who could inadvertently torture with the sway of her hips, in a slow and thoughtful cadence because the cigars were thick and long and neither man had anywhere to go.

"That explains the clean shirts and the washing behind the ears. Only a woman can drive a butcher to that level of cleanliness. I'm glad to see you've returned to normal."

"That did nothing. She still doesn't even know my name."

"What is your purpose? Is this a raid or a sacking? Are you looking to breech the walls and carry her off?"

"I'll see once I get there."

"Many an army has been lost because the objective has been unclear or the object of their strategy turns out not worth the cost. Look at Napoleon's army in Moscow. After fighting their way across the vast Russian countryside they finally enter Moscow with the thought they will hunker down for the winter and use it as a base of future operations. But they find the city empty, barren, abandoned and once they try to settle in the locals burn it to the ground. The army has no choice but to retreat across that vast countryside and is routed during the retreat. This self-immolation teaches me something. A woman may think it's better to be ash than taken by another, even when she's clearly lost the battle. So, even if you are successful in broaching her she may very well set fire to herself, so to speak. Be clear of your purpose."

"That's not easy. She barely speaks. She may be studying to be a nun. She works at the parish office as Father Corrigan's secretary."

"You're not the first to talk about her. Seems she's the talk of the street amongst men of a certain age and domestic situation, either free, open or bored. You may not be the first. I know there are armies advancing from every direction. Know that the thousand ships have been launched and they're all racing toward her shore."

"I would be the first. She hasn't realized she's a woman yet."

"It's a serious turn taking a woman out of a convent. That comes with responsibility. You don't take that and leave it at the side of the road to be used by another. That's something that must be kept, if you have a bone of decency in you."

"She won't leave my mind."

"The first step is to turn off her water. She will ask for help. You will enter her apartment. You now have a private moment to act. This will be her chance to submit because no one will be watching and no one will be judging whether she is a good girl or not. Or, if in fact she is studying to be a nun, you'll come back to your shop with a Bible sticking out of your ass."

"I don't think it will work."

"She'll need water. It is a fact of human life. She'll have to speak to you. Your natural charm will have to take over from there. I hope she can control her repugnance long enough to let you in. I'm thinking, actually, the only hope you have is that she's been waiting for the right moment to act on her urges. Otherwise, you're screwed. If she has been thinking of you, you have a chance, because you aren't going to convince her otherwise. Your words are not your strong suit."

"I've got no other ideas. Turn on the game so I can listen to how much money I'm going to lose."

The next morning the butcher woke up early and walked to his shop before the sun had risen. He found the water shut-off valve in the storage closet in the back of the first floor and turned it closed. He laughed at the possibility of the plan working and busied himself with preparing for the Saturday crush of customers. He figured by the end of the day he would be in her apartment and he carried a small bottle of cologne in his pants pocket for when she asked for help.

He usually kept the shop open until noon on Saturdays because after the morning rush business dropped off to almost nothing in the afternoon, but on this day he stayed open until 5:00 PM with the hopes of her coming down. He cleaned his knives, slicers, counters and floors three times before he locked up and cursed in one long string all the way home. He stayed home on Sunday and cooked himself a large steak on a charcoal grill under a brutal sun, which gave him a headache that started at his shoulders. He listened to the last game on his betting sheet, a game between the Tigers and White Sox, on a radio station out of Detroit and the game was basically over by the fifth because the Chicago pitching could throw nothing but junk that hung over the plate like apples hanging from a tree. Betting on the White Sox had been stupid enough, but he had lost every bet he had placed on the weekend games so he snapped off the radio and sipped whiskey until he fell asleep in his chair.

When he opened his shop the next morning he found no note from Ellen. He made enough noise to let her know he had come in, but she did not come down. He checked the shut-off valve again and gave it an extra twist even though the knob had already been turned so tight it couldn't move. He saw her pass by the front window on her way to her job, but she didn't stop to complain nor did she even look in the direction of the window when she passed. At lunch he closed the shop and unlocked her apartment with a spare key. He saw the crucifix, the iron bed, the Bible and wash basin but no obvious signs of a lack of water. There were no dirty dishes in the sink, the toilet held clear water, and the wash basin cradled a pool of fresh, cool water. The butcher tried the faucets and tried to flush the toilet but no water came. He opened the door to the back stairs and found two buckets on the landing and he followed the drips down the stairs to an outside faucet still leaking from having been recently used. He went inside and found the shut-off for this pipe and also turned it closed. Then, he took a tour of the perimeter of the building looking for other faucets he had forgotten about. He also inspected neighboring buildings for other sources of water so she couldn't escape again. Two women waited at the door when he reopened the shop and he smiled broadly at them even though they muttered something about making customers wait and that there were other shops where they could spend their money.

The butcher visited Mibby's shop on the way home and told him of the progress of the plan.

"Survival is innate with this one."

"How so?"

"How many women, or men for that matter, would have looked for an outside faucet and procured buckets for transport? Most of this modern civilization would have fallen to the floor and cried until somebody helped them fix their problem. Also, I can surmise that she wants to avoid you at all costs, even if it takes humping water up the stairs even if she has to take a little pee."

"Why would she avoid me?"

"Two possibilities. Either she is repulsed beyond imagination or she feels her loins glowing and doesn't trust the feeling, wants to bury it deep under the shrouds of Jesus."

"I'm leaning toward repulsed."

"You're modest. Remember, I keep track of your victories. It's quite an impressive list for a man just hitting his prime. Some men sing and women swoon. Some men have physiques that drive dames wild. You, my butcher friend, have porterhouse and sirloin. If I would have been thinking of a steady procurement of women I would have went into meat instead of tobacco. I don't think a woman has been in this shop for two years."

"She's not easy to understand."

"All the more reason to tread cautiously. What is your objective? Estimates of Napoleon's losses in Russia hover around 300,000. No small cost for conquering an empty city."

"I'm thinking that she breaks tomorrow."

"Resolution is almost always preferred, no matter the outcome, over anticipation. At least with a resolution you'll sleep after a while, after the mulling over is done."

The next morning the butcher all but staggered to work. Mibby had started pouring bourbon and when they killed his bottle they migrated to a bar within walking distance. He woke up drunk and when he opened his shop his hair still burst from his head in clumps and his breath smelled like a pool of blood, vegetable juice and spilled milk that had lain rancid in the bottom of a refrigerator for a couple of months. Even the thought of toothpaste made him queasy, so he left his teeth unbrushed. Ellen came in shortly after he unlocked the door.

"I have no water in my apartment," she said in a burst.

"None?"

"For a few days."

"Why didn't you tell me sooner? I'm always here."

"I thought it would be a bother."

"I'll look at it this afternoon after I close the shop."

Ellen nodded and slipped out before the butcher could offer her water from his sink.

For the rest of the day the butcher concentrated on not cutting off his fingers or vomiting in the hamburger. In the afternoon he closed a half hour early and washed his face and torso using a rag and floor cleaner. He soaked his head under cold water in the slop sink and raked his hair with his fingers. He dabbed a spot of cologne behind either ear, a gift from one of his women customers who wanted to thank him for bedding her on a bi-monthly basis, just enough to keep insanity away, as she said. He knocked on her door and Ellen opened it quickly as if she had been standing near it all day waiting for him to knock. The butcher had half-expected her to change her clothes and maybe dab some make-up on her face to accentuate her best features, but she still wore the same formless and colorless dress that looked straight out of a gulag and she had pulled her hair back so tight in a ponytail her forehead and temples looked stretched. Even in that awful sack of a dress her hips shone through and the butcher began sweating. She blocked the doorway and stared at him. The butcher made to step forward but she didn't flinch.

"You said you had trouble with the plumbing."

"I do."

"I have to come in to check it. If I can't see it I won't know what's going on."

Ellen relented and stepped aside as the butcher walked past. He went to the middle of the room and took in her habitat with a 360 degree spin as he had done when he broke in during his lunch hour. The crucifix seemed larger than he remembered it and he wondered what size nail she had used to hang it or if she knew to find the stud to secure something that big to the wall. The Bible lay splayed on the bed. The butcher hoped she had been reading about wanton fucking and murder to prepare her for his advance. He could only hope luck stayed with him more than his American League bets. Nothing else betrayed the life she led, not a pair of dirty panties, a half-filled glass, the smell of coffee grounds in the trash, nothing. Even the smell of her own skin and farts were absent from the air. How had she managed that with only cold water from the outside faucet? the butcher thought.

"The sink is over here."

The butcher walked over to the sink and made a show of turning on the faucet and studying the absence of rushing water. He tried both hot and cold knobs, ran a finger around the rim of the spout and even brought a drip of water that had been clinging to the inside of the faucet to his lips as if the trouble could be determined through taste. He opened the cabinet door beneath the sink and jammed his washed torso into the space to inspect the pipe underneath. He rested his head on the bottom of the cabinet and closed his eyes. He moved his arms to mime work and thought of Ellen staring at his legs and wondering what she thought, if she could reconcile his ape form with her carefully controlled life. He wished he had smeared mud on the bottom of his shoes and tracked up the floor. Five minutes later he pulled himself out and got to his feet.

"Now I have to check the bathroom."

"Is that necessary?"

The butcher realized she may be embarrassed for him to see a product of elimination swimming in the bowl and almost skipped this part of the act but decided a small humiliation may work in his favor.

"Does the toilet work?"

"No."

"I have to check it then."

He entered the bathroom and pushed the handle of the toilet and when it didn't flush he lifted the seat and lid. A small coil of shit lay half submerged in a small circle of water with a thin layer of toilet paper covering it like a blanket. He opened the tank and found it dry. He turned on the sink faucet to delay his exit and he tapped on the shower head with a knuckle that carried a dab of cow's blood in its folds. When he finally left the bathroom he found Ellen standing in the middle of the floor staring absently out of the window. The color of her cheeks had deepened from pink to red.

"You have no water. You should have come to see me sooner."

"I managed."

"I know, but you need a working toilet for God's sake." The butcher winced at his choice of words, hoping he hadn't pushed the humiliation too far and for using God in any context other than a prayer while around her. He spun a funnel cloud of curses in his head but kept them from becoming audible. "I'll go downstairs and see if the problem is down there. Leave the door open because I will have to come back." He discovered the weak link in the plan, because once he left and restored the water she could very easily lock the doors and thank him behind the lock and his advantage would be lost.

Ellen nodded silently and walked him to the door. On the landing outside he heard the deadbolt click behind him. He walked down the stairs and opened his shop, where he found the morning edition of the newspaper lying folded on a shelf behind the counter where he had left it in the morning unread because his eyes couldn't come close to focusing on the small type. He pulled a chair to the back of the shop and leaned his back against the cooler, reading the paper front to back and reading the sports section a second time. He stretched, yawned, smelled his armpits to make sure his deodorant held, made his way back to the water valve and turned the water back on. He slammed the newspaper down, jumped the stairs three at a time and loudly knocked on her door. For a moment or two when he couldn't hear her footsteps or any sound at all coming from inside the apartment he thought the day had been lost. She had either snuck out the back door or had heard the toilet tank filling and knew the water had returned. The panic subsided as Ellen opened the door and stepped aside to let the butcher enter. He went to the sink and turned both faucets open. After sputtering and spitting rust, the water ran strong and clear. He turned on every faucet in the apartment and even flushed the toilet. Ellen had remained near the door and left it open so that when the butcher returned to the room the path to the exit remained unblocked and unmistakable.

"That ought to do it."

"I appreciate you fixing the problem."

"You're paying rent."

"Yes."

"Next time call me sooner."

"If this is going to be a recurring problem could you show me what you did so I could fix it myself without bothering you?"

"It was a broken valve. It'll last fifty years. Just bad luck it broke this week."

"You said next time. I don't plan on living here fifty years."

"I meant if anything else goes wrong, a burnt out light, heating problems, anything at all. Come to the shop and tell me."

"Yes."

"Yes you will? Or yes I understand what you are telling me, but I'll probably sit in the dark before I tell you I have a problem?"

Ellen's head tingled. The butcher had advanced and stood close enough that she could feel the heat pouring from him and she could smell the specks of blood on his skin. The mask of his cheap cologne had worn off. The smell of pork loins, filets, and strip streaks rode his sweat out of his pours and filled her room. She fingered a pocket of crackers hidden in the pocket of her dress and she wanted nothing more than to rip open the packet with her teeth and crush them against her lips. She resisted and in place of the crackers she gnawed at her lips, hoping to taste the salty crumbs. If he didn't leave soon, she would draw blood, she thought, and when he finally left she would fry a sausage and drench it with its own fat along with mashed potatoes from two massive potatoes lying on top of her refrigerator. She would eat slowly, rolling the food across her tongue and chewing all the taste away before swallowing. Forty chews per bite. She would make the plate last an hour. She pinched the crackers into powder between her thumb and forefinger.

"The room is so stuffy. Why don't you open the windows? It's a beautiful, warm night. How many of these do we get in a year?"

The butcher walked over to the windows and found most had been painted shut. He pulled and pounded, rattling the glass and threatening to smash the panes, until they finally came free.

"Could you open these?"

"Just one."

Noise from the boulevard gushed into the room: men shouting aimless stories, car horns honking, racing motors, the click of the stoplight as it changed, the shriek of gulls as they circled a spill in a parking lot, the rustle of paper spun by the wind, and the grind and hum of machines hidden behind walls and producing metal parts for larger machines. Along with noise came light from fading sun and a warm moist breeze. Ellen clenched her jaw against the invasion into her room. The butcher's large body and his scented skin, the shouts of the street, the wind carrying minor demons on its back who jumped off and crawled under her bed and sink and may have had something to do with the water problem, the thoughts of submitting, of following the butcher to a cold, dark room and pulling the dress over her head and feeling his thick, rough fingers pawing at her flesh, afraid to breathe because once she exhales she may find she had just released her last breath. She wished she would have used her time alone to craft a mask, something cast iron and thick like a skillet, that could deflect all the senseless static of the street and its dispossessed people and would have protected her from the butcher as he paced in front of her windows, hands in pockets, head bowed in thought and wading in the static like he cavorted in a pounding ocean surf. The butcher stopped and stared at her plain white bedspread and tapped the pages of her Bible with his knuckles.

"Shut the door, Ellen."

She felt thankful to be able to grab the knob because it rooted her to the world, however briefly, before the butcher asked her to join him by the side of the bed. He watched her as she walked toward him, humiliating her, forcing her to commit the act before they had even touched. She stopped in front of him out of arm's reach, a small rebellion that he quietly crushed when he stepped forward and took her in his arms. His kiss pushed her head back and he pulled her against him until she could only take shallow breaths. His hands groped for possession and even though her body had been trapped against his belly and he touched and felt her warmth, he felt like he held an exhalation, free of scent, purpose and desire. Her dress lay on the floor, followed by her bra and underwear. The butcher dropped his pants but kept on his button-down shirt and as he pushed against her the buttons scraped her belly. She let her hands fall back flat against the mattress and she wondered where she would be when the butcher had finished. She imagined him taking a small blue and green globe in his hands and violently shaking it in the air as a horrible grimace spread across his face, sending her sprawling across miniature continents to an unknown destination. In what room could she now live since this one had now been scorched beyond habitation, the walls blackened, the crucifix charred and the bed dancing in blue flame?

A month later the butcher married her at the courthouse and she moved into his house the same day. They left the dresser, iron bed and crucifix in the apartment because the butcher insisted they share a bedroom and a bed in this new life. Ellen told her sister she would be happy to have a room of her own, but her sister told her that acting so distant so soon in the newlywed years would surely push him into the arms of other women and that she could get used to his burping and farting throughout the night.

'It isn't that. It's his breathing and his thoughts. I've never been so close to someone dreaming. I can only liken it to a horse's hooves on a cobblestone street clattering in my ear. I simply can't sleep. And his dreams are very often dirty. I could never repeat what I've heard and seen. Most of them I don't even know what they mean, but he thinks mostly below the waist. I'm a little afraid of his thoughts."

"Consider it a gift," her sister said. "I would love to know the depths of my husband's depravity. At least I would know then how to join him."

Free from the burden of living above the butcher shop, Ellen lost her appetite and with it her flattering weight. The butcher brought home choice steaks, filets, roasts and briskets, sausages, kielbasa, beef patties and livers, but Ellen would only pick and nibble around the edges if she tasted them at all. She had lost the joy a mouthful of blood had once given her. He exhorted her to eat and veiled concern and anger under weak jokes about her weight and her shrinking and less desirable bottom. The color of her skin returned to saintly alabaster and revealed the sharp lines of her bones underneath. She stopped carrying crackers in the pockets of her dress and the butcher had to remind her to go to the grocery store, because if left to her own appetite she would let the refrigerator and cupboards go empty.

She enjoyed the mornings and afternoons when he worked. The house calmed. The noise fell to the settling of boards and brick into the ground. She thought of the house as a ship, drifting and creaking in a flat ocean. Dust fell through the shafts of sunlight slicing through the windows and Ellen could watch the lazy swirl for hours. Her taste in reading alternated between the Bible and romances where men and women experienced physical love but were punished or thwarted in ways surely outside the realm of God's love. She had quit her job at the church and she stopped going to mass on Sundays because the butcher wouldn't go and she agreed with him that spending Sunday morning in bed as the rain, snow or sunlight battered the roof felt more enjoyable than the vast echoing hall with its drafts and Latin turbulence. God had ebbed from her life and she couldn't find a path back to Him. As she read His word the meaning became opaque as the text did not incite contemplation as much as annoyance. She became annoyed because the same characters always made the same mistakes. Joseph always let his brothers trick him into slavery. Jerusalem fell every time. A woman, led to sin by Zedekiah, became vile and all who once honored her now despised her, because they saw her nakedness. She spread her legs and the enemy placed his hand on her pleasant things. Thrilling and instructive but never a variation. Who doesn't cry when the pillars of the temple are dismantled and taken to Babylon? The bronze of the bulls and pomegranates soaring in the air chopped apart by soldiers to be smelted into the graven images of the conquerors. But must Zedekiah forever be a fool and a sinner? Must we trace his mistakes again and again? She preferred the swirl of dust in the sunlight to the crying out to the King of Israel, the last in the line of the house of David, to protect Jerusalem from being ravaged and turned into a whore. She even began holding romances in higher esteem because the writers wrote the characters as whores and devils who had never attended church, knew not the word, and lived by rules and random accidents and judgments that were never heartbreaking. They worked as clerks and typists and burned for men. They had not been given the duty of protecting the holiest of cities, nor would they ever consider themselves capable of the task.

The butcher worried about her aloneness. One day he brought home a spaniel pup, but she made him take it back to the breeder after two days of barking and yapping and destroying the carefully constructed peace of the house.

"Besides," she said. "I don't trust a wolf inside my house. Next they will allow dogs in the cathedral. Then, where will people go for peace and sanctuary? We will forget the purity of our existence. We will all be individual Jerusalems, rotten in the core and ready to collapse."

The butcher sighed. He picked up the dog and cradled it in his arms.

"If they let dogs in the cathedral I might go to mass. I wonder what barking sounds like a under those high ceilings."

He carried the dog out of the house, enjoying the warmth of its body against his arms and chest.

Next, he came home with a kitten, thinking they were practically silent creatures that slept most of the day, but Ellen wouldn't let him in the house with it. He built a small bed out of scrap wood and an old blanket and set it on the porch. The cat would keep the mice from invading the house and might even scare off some of the larger rats. Ellen wouldn't set food and water on the porch and wouldn't respond to its demanding mewing. The butcher tried to keep it fed, but after a week of irregular meals the cat either had a better offer or thought there had to be something else better in the neighborhood and they never saw it again. So, the butcher took it upon himself to be her entertainment and link to the outside world, at least what he knew of it from his customers, Mibby, newspapers and radio. He created worlds of gossip and intrigue from the houses that surrounded them. He told her who drank to excess, who mistreated his wife, who ran around behind her husband's back, the whispers about the priest being seen in the company of a divorcee at a restaurant in the country and not wearing his collar but an opened collared shirt and tight pants, about who made money and who spent more than they had, who moved to a new suburb with big lawns and no sidewalks and no neighbors to speak of, and what children would very likely end up in prison or on the dole with scrambled brains and their hands out. She listened, laughed, feigned concern and sometimes worried about the butcher's dreams as he spoke. Why didn't he ever speak of his dreams? Didn't he know his thoughts were broadcast as he slept and the missteps of other peoples' lives compared favorably to his own depravity?

Ellen came to enjoy the butcher's mauling and pawing of her body. She did not desire sex the way the butcher did, but she found her sensitive being to be well-suited and predisposed to intercourse. Once he entered her body she became excited quickly and soon became lost in the warm ripples surging through her body. His violation, his intrusion, his rape sometimes blocked the white noise violating her ears if she closed her eyes and concentrated on the sensation radiating from below. She would remember herself as a girl and remember her girlish abhorrence of sex, wondering why this feeling hadn't come to her when she thought of Jesus. Some of the nuns must have felt it and only made shrouded references to their orgasms when they spoke of marrying Jesus and she wondered if God ever worked through the body or if He stayed only in a person's mind. Why create a sentient being and then refuse them the full range of their senses? Why wouldn't he send bolts of orgasm to his flock to make them heel and stay and live by his word? Could pleasure ever be given to Christ? Would he refuse her if she spread her legs? Would he turn away and call her a whore and tell her that her fall from grace had been final and no path back to his heart existed? Or would he be like the butcher and show no hesitation in his desire of her body even though she had thinned and her body had lost its audacious allure? Did Christ know that she would never refuse him like she never refused the butcher?

Twenty years slipped by. They never had children even though they never used birth control. She had been pregnant for two months early in their marriage and the butcher's perseverated over the rejected dog and the neglected cat and he began to fret over the fate of their child. Surely she would know the difference and instinctively pick up the child and nurse it and love it. But just as the idea of a child gained hold of their imaginations and the butcher's fretting became full blown worry, she lost it one morning while the butcher cut ribs in preparation for Fourth of July picnics. She put her fingers in the blood on her thigh and she knew that she had willed the baby to die. She had asked her sister about children once a few weeks before, right after she found out the butcher had impregnated her. Her sister told her that no greater blessing on God's earth existed, that when she had a child she would find herself thinking and acting like a mother the moment she saw the newborn's face. Ellen asked her about the noise and the mess and the obvious disruption of routine. Her sister fell silent on the other end of the line as she composed herself, apparently, with deep drawn-out breaths.

"Why, Ellen, does everything have to be selfish with you? You're bringing a baby into the world and you're worried about noise? I suppose you're worried about sleep too?"

Ellen didn't tell her sister that she always worried about noise, because if you didn't think about it, how could you protect yourself from it? She had experienced her sister's children, first with the crying and the shouting and the shrieking and then the trail of food and snot and blood on the floors, tables and smeared deeply into the fabric of their clothes. They shattered rooms as they ran through them and their horrified cries punished their parents as night. They considered her a strange pale bird who visited them twice a month and they refused to call her auntie, because she felt cold to the touch and they could not find a trace of sincere happiness in her voice. She may have asked God to relieve her of this burden and He granted her wish even though she had fallen from grace because He cast benevolence even on the wayward and His love knew no bounds. When she touched the blood on her thigh she was not unhappy with the meaning.

From that experience she learned to control her body during sex. As the butcher groaned and ejaculated Ellen would concentrate on her egg and stop its rotation and cast a thin but impenetrable membrane over its skin that repelled all comers. Sometimes she imagined it like a forcefield, the kind that always showed up in science fiction stories, but she worried where the energy might come from to electrify such a barrier and how that could affect her gallbladder and kidneys, so mostly she considered her protection to be a blanket, carefully woven on a glittering loom that had been gifted to her from merciful God.

Her uterus would be littered with dead and dazed sperm and she would lower the barrier only after she felt no more squirming or kicking from the invading army. She kept them childless and in peace until her eggs stopped rolling and his sperm preferred sleep to the arduous journey in search of a purpose.

Heartbroken by their sterility, the butcher took other women. He had always imagined himself with a brood at his feet, squalling as they wrestled for his attention, and even his foreboding about Ellen's ability to assume motherhood had not dulled his hope. As month after month passed by without another pregnancy he increased the frequency of the attempts and settled on a rote sequence that provided the shortest route to climax since Ellen's body no longer offered grips to hold or elicited the same desire. He could be asleep ten minutes after initiating the session if he concentrated on the sensation and the purpose for the coitus. Ellen seemed to enjoy herself no matter how short the duration, so he worked at paring down the time so as not ot interrupt his sleeping schedule. He looked to his customers to satiate his need for excitement or variety in body types or positions. Almost everyone of his customers were women and on any given day one of them would be lonely because her husband refused to talk about their lives in any meaningful way or they would be angry at the prospect of living a lifetime with an alcoholic, philandering, sports-obsessed, hygiene-confused lout or poor enough to suggest that some payment arrangement could be made if the butcher would be so kind as to wrap up some hamburger for her children. He never expected much of himself in the way of fidelity when he married Ellen, but the sterility of the marriage provided him with the pass he needed to chase every opportunity.

The butcher used the iron bed in the apartment for his liaisons. He had taken down the crucifix and stored it in a closet. He wanted to throw it away, but superstition got the better of him and he worried Ellen might some day ask for it. He never rented the apartment again. He created tenants for Ellen's sake and told funny stories about them, using scraps of narratives he had heard through his customers and friends of the goings-on of the neighborhood. She marveled at the butcher's ability to run the shop, keep her entertained in the evening and handle the string of miscreants who had rented the apartment. Mibby liked to ask the butcher about his conquests as men with hunched backs and warts on their jaw do with men who have success with women. Mibby knew their husbands from the tobacco shop and his bookie business and he liked knowing which ones were cuckolds and which ones were not because it gave him an advantage when they placed bets. He found a cuckold lost more than he won and could be tricked into sucker bets more often than not. He could keep his mouth shut and kept the knowledge to himself, because he could think of no advantage to passing along the butcher's secrets to anyone. He asked for specific details about the firmness of a woman's breast or the shape of her ass without layers of clothing binding it or how the different parts of her body smelled. The butcher obliged, weaving the scene with every word in his arsenal and knowing when to add a crude touch or a silence that would make Mibby's imagination soar. After he told his stories the butcher always placed a dumb bet on a crippled long shot horse or a football team with cheerleaders for defense and Mibby cleaned up. He liked spending the butcher's money, but when Mibby started to think the butcher believed in his own superiority a little too much or when Mibby felt low about himself because in front of him stood a man with an enormous pot belly who smelled like cow's blood and liver and who bedded women with the frequency most masturbated, while anything wearing lipstick shunned Mibby, he would ask after his wife. In fact, Mibby loved to tell the story of how the butcher met his wife because the butcher acted upon his idea. The ruse was the only secret of the butcher's that he passed along, because it ended in marriage and could be considered a parable on how lies and deviousness could be used for the sake of goodness. The crowd at the tobacco shop always liked hearing the story and it always ended with the punchline, "But, in fact, the butcher was a plumber!" The butcher would chuckle along with the story and light a cigar, thinking of the fever he had felt when he thought about Ellen before she had become his bride. When Mibby asked about her after one of the butcher's better stories about his escapades, his face would briefly go dark before he told Mibby her health seemed just fine.

At first he felt a tinge of guilt that he could make love to other women on his wife's iron bed without feeling remorse before or during the act, but the newness of their bodies and their willingness or insistence on trying variations of the act swamped his morality and his sense of fairness. With each successive woman the bed became less the vehicle that carried Ellen to her new home and away from the idea of becoming a nun to a dirty stable that housed a history of the butcher's carnal desire. Ellen had given herself to him on this iron bed as she wanted to give herself to Jesus as she waited under the bell tower. It had been unfortunate, the butcher thought, that Ellen had given herself to someone so unworthy of the gift. These other women spread their legs at the slightest provocation, but Ellen submitted to him alone and he let the gift fall through his hands just like some stone-handed shortstop muffing an easy double-play ball. When a woman named Mia shouted out during a rowdy fuck that "You're a better plumber than a butcher!" The butcher slapped her across the face and had to restrain himself from beating her bloody. She laughed, licked the blood from her lip and asked him to do it again.

By the end of his career the butcher could remember that Ellen had been the first woman he had had on the bed, but she became confused with the other one hundred and fourteen women he had fucked so the collection of sensations enhanced the memory beyond possibility. Ellen became everywoman, capable and willing to do anything, still perfectly hipped and heavy breasted and insatiable. He had worked away the remnants of his remorse long ago and came to view the iron bed with nostalgia and pride like a wizened and half-paralyzed boxer staring at a lighted ring with a tear in his eye.

The butcher died of a brain aneurysm while stuffing bratwurst. The two women customers who witnessed his death said one second he talked about the secret of a good sausage, if not in a salacious way then certainly suggesting a double meaning to his knowledge, and the next he threw his arms out to the side as his eyes rolled back in his head. He staggered away from the bench and a horrible gurgling sound came from the back of his throat, sounding like a man choking on his own blood or a drunk partygoer yucking it up by trying to speak through a mouthful of beer. He keeled over and the two women, one who had already been on the iron bed and the second who he had been close to convincing to give it a try, rushed to his side. They held his hands and they believed he smiled when they touched. Their friends asked if he said any last words, any wisdom or confessions. They shook their heads no. The smile said it all, the two women said.

At the funeral Mibby shook Ellen's hand, but refrained from kissing her cheek because of the warts along his jaw, and told her that he thought the butcher the best plumber he had ever known. Ellen said she had to agree because the butcher could fix almost any plumbing problem even when all seemed hopeless and out of kilter. He never seemed for a moment to be lost. She overheard two other conversations as they talked about the butcher's plumbing ability and wondered when he had time to practice the trade. She sat away from the crowd and most of the mourners forgot or didn't know she had been his wife or why she haunted the funeral. The perfume of flowers soaked the air. So many bouquets came in the funeral director had to place some in the hallway. The notes were cryptic or written in some kind of code and most were addressed to a plumber instead of the butcher. At one point Ellen considered she may have walked into the wrong funeral and mourned the life of a man she didn't know, but she thought it would be rude to leave in the middle of the ceremony. The crowd grew and soon more people and more flowers jammed the room. The director had run out of room in the hallway so he stacked some of the bouquets of top of each other. She thought of the butcher's powdered face, waxen in death, underneath the lid, silent, while the party raged around him. She knew she had disappointed him in some fundamental way, but she would have not been able to come up with the reason if asked. Her life, she supposed, had never been meant for the temporal world. She had fallen into disgrace with the butcher, burning churches whenever they had the chance. Even the last act of his life fell outside the church. The dead should be surrounded by high-arched stain glass and the mortal chill of a stone cathedral during the last few moments above ground. She could not bring herself to ask the priest for the butcher because she had abandoned the church so long ago, had quit her job, had stolen communion wafers and burned down the convent. Besides the butcher had not even set foot in the cathedral even as a child, so what relation did his body have to the stained glass and the beatific head of Christ contemplating the loss of his mortal coil? But why did she sit in a room made to look like a fancy parlor with pretty women slathered in make-up and wearing tight dresses? Why did wall-to-wall carpet soften her steps and a low ceiling suffocate her from above? Why hadn't the priest come in his white robes, holding the sacraments and leering at the parade of sinners before him? No one, except Lucifer himself, had fallen so far so quickly as she had, Ellen thought. She sent her husband to the jaws of a three-headed beast. The funeral home had no bell tower. Where sang the voice of Jesus? They did not celebrate the ascension of the butcher's soul to heaven. They gave him a final bacchanal before fire and agony.

She hired an agent to sell the butcher shop and the building and to settle the debt the butcher had accumulated over the years. After the reconciliation Ellen collected a small sum of money that would care for her for a decade or more. She had no practice or interest in spending money and she could think of nothing to buy other than food and shoes when they wore out, because she mistrusted most material things. Hadn't her iron bed, her crucifix, her wash basin and dresser betrayed her and led her into the arms of the butcher? She was surprised to find no tenants living above the shop, because the butcher had talked about them so often. She sometimes thought of them during the day when the butcher worked. She imagined them as plump, rosy people gnawing on blood and meat and swelling by the hour. The animal blood coursing through their veins gave them sordid dreams of devils and nudity. The apartment had obviously not been lived in for a very long time. Dust coated the window sills, the counter and the top of the dresser. The closet had been jammed with odds and ends from the shop: a broken slicer, three rolls of brown paper wrapping, a cleaver with a broken handle, a package of new aprons a size too small to fit around the butcher's belly, and the crucifix buried beneath it all. She closed the door quickly and prayed He didn't remember her fall from grace, even though He saw all and knew all and not even a whisper of a thought could escape him. In the cupboard above the kitchen sink she found a giant ledger filled with the butcher's meticulous handwriting. He had logged every shipment, cash deposit, payment, tax, equipment expense and credit from the first day he had been in business with a running total of profit running page to page. The numbers on the first page looked exactly like the numbers on the last, with the last entry recorded just two days before he died. How did the butcher find such constancy through the decades? Somewhere the turns of his life should have affected the slant of his numbers, the roundness of his eights, the fullness of his zeros, but Ellen could find no difference as she studied the pages for well over two hours. The butcher had been born from the core of the earth and spewed as magma to the surface where he changed into an igneous rock. She saw him standing in a field littered with other rock, never changing, never cringing under hail or the sun.

Tucked into the middle of the ledger were two envelopes that Ellen opened after she had finished contemplating the butcher's stolidity. The envelopes were sent by the same woman from two different addresses, one from an apartment in Las Vegas and the other from a military base in Guam. She opened the letter from Vegas and found a handwritten letter to the butcher recounting a sexual act they had performed together that she likened to two trapeze artists fucking on the high ropes above a gasping audience and a pool of boiling tar. She went on to say that the memory of the act made her moan audibly, sometimes in inappropriate situations, when she thought of it and she abused the butcher for wasting his talents on a mousy nun who could no more handle his ferocity than a rabbit could handle a jackal. With the letter came a photographic self-portrait of the woman's hairy crotch with a finger inserted into her vagina up to the second knuckle. The second letter consisted mostly of a description of married life on Guam, the bleakness of the base and detailed descriptions of the air force wives who did nothing but complain about being relocated into the middle of a vast ocean on an awful island where the wind never seemed to stop blowing or lay on the beach with all but their pussies exposed so that the husbands of the other wives could dream of their barely covered crevices. The woman then spent an entire page describing her husband's small penis and bitterly mocking her decision to choose the romance of the uniform and radar navigation over good old-fashioned American girth. The memory of sex with the butcher has obviously faded because she made no mention of it in the second letter and this time sent a picture of herself in a bikini and sunglasses sitting on a towel with two other women who looked very much like her in sunglasses in front of a dying palm.

Ellen put the envelopes back in the ledger and placed the ledger back in the cupboard above the sink. She sat down on the old iron bed that had begun rusting in spots. Ellen knew the appropriate reaction to the discovery would be to cry or pound her fist against the bed, emotions that her sister could wield like a sword with deadly accuracy, but she could conjure nothing up that contained heat or violence. The butcher had died, and if he carried on in a secret life that life too had died, and all those people from the funeral shared moments of his life, those women who sent flowers were driven to acknowledging his death by something they shared, the men had talked with him about parts of the world she didn't understand and bore no relation to her own existence, but how many of them had slept beside him at night and listened to his dreams and knew the rot on which his house had been built? She hoped she found no other clues to his secret life. She hated mysteries and thought being a detective one of the worst jobs a person could ever hope to have. What did they do but rip off masks or pull down the pants of victims so the world could humiliate them? What would have happened had a detective discovered she had burned the convent? Would they have stripped her naked and hanged her from a tree so the nuns and monks could have abused her corpse? Hadn't her own personal torment been enough? Shouldn't the marriage to the butcher and turning away from God be enough of a payment? Did she need a detective to lay bare her acts and debase her in the eyes of everyone? So what purpose would it serve to poke around the grave of a moldering corpse to find the breadth of his betrayal? She really couldn't call his secret life a betrayal, but she had no other word for it. Had she betrayed the nuns when she burned down the convent? No, they stood aside as she refused God. The butcher lived as a craven, fallen creature. She needed to step aside and let the butcher explain his life and actions to Him. Why would she expect fidelity from him? He would never again tell her stories about people who didn't exist. She would never again hear his dreams or feel his farts release against her leg. His bulk would no longer tear the fabric of the air around her. She lay back on her old and stained bedspread and nestled her head on the greasy pillow. She stared at the blank walls and the water-stained ceiling. She couldn't decide whether she had found a new home or simply returned home after a long absence.

Ellen paid two neighbor boys to move the bed and dresser to her house. She gave them the bed and the cherry dresser with intricate inlay filigree she and the butcher had shared and five dollars to pay for the job. The boys didn't exactly know what to do with the bed and dresser but took them because they figured they could sell them somewhere for a nice profit. She also asked that they take the stained mattress from the iron bed and discard it somewhere. They knew of an illegal dump by the river so they agreed to take it. She lay on the floor on a blanket until a new mattress and bedspread were delivered a week later. When she climbed in and slipped under the top sheet and new bedspread she wondered if she would ever rise again.

She stopped reading and stared out the window or at the ceiling most of the day and some of the night as she lay in bed. She could see a tree branch, a patch of street, and the southern wall of the house across the street. The sun rose and set. Neighbors drove their cars back and forth along the street. Birds visited the branch briefly, never restful, never in the mood for contemplation, before taking flight to another branch or trying to pluck gnats out of the air. When her mother had died and she and her sister had to clean the house, they found a black and gold trunk filled with a miscellany of keepsakes and retired knickknacks tied to a particular memory that had died with their mother. In the trunk she found crayon pictures she had drawn as a child. A turtle with a flower for a head tilted toward a smiling moon sun, a sun with craters or a burning, radiant moon. Next came a bird with orange feathers riding a train, chasing after a rabbit with umbrella feet. The body of the enormous bird hung over the side of the train and it looked like its feet might be dragging on the ground as the train raced in pursuit. The bird looked slovenly, pot-bellied, relying on a machine for its once keen prowess. How had she known about middle-age and why had she picked the most graceful and free of creatures to ruin with decay? She now imagined birds had no middle-age at all but fell from the sky dead once their powers began to fail or younger raptors killed them or prowling cats, looking to exterminate anything that moved, ate them. What thought, now gone or mutated with adult knowledge, had she tried to express as a child? What had concerned her about the birds? She tried to inhabit the child's mind who drew the pictures, the child who had captured an illusion. Do children think in dreams? Are they bombarded by incongruities and missing juxtapositions and do even inanimate objects look back at them with a face as the children's books and shows would lead you to believe? But after trying to unravel the years she knew these moments were now inaccessible and to chase them, like the fat bird chasing the umbrella rabbit, would lead her nowhere but the blank wall and the water-stained ceiling and the patch of road outside her window. But, she thought, were there other memories and dreams, strands and fragments of thought she could weave or piece together to create a world of her own experience? Could she brace herself, lose herself in only what she had previously seen, felt, heard, tasted, smelled or thought and stop new sensations from pouring in, stop the rising torrent, end the making of memory?

Her sister thought Ellen had been devastated by the death of the butcher and that depression kept her from rising from bed. She strung up a litany of mounting evidence for her hairdresser to see. Ellen dressed in the butcher's pajamas and kept the pants up with a belt from one of his robes. She lay in bed all day staring out the window and never answered the door when she knocked. She ate less than a cockroach, nibbling at the edges of the food her sister brought her. She refused to think or speak about the future because she could not maintain that home lying in bed and it would be only a matter of months before raccoons lived in the attic and rats in the basement. What conclusion could a person draw other than Ellen had broken with reality because her husband had died unexpectedly and she found out what a philandering lout he really had been?

"Don't I have enough with my own husband and kids?" her sister asked the hairdresser. "Now I have a crazy sister on my hands. What am I supposed to do? Just watch her waste away?"

Her sister had taken Ellen's keys one visit and made duplicates so that she could come in without knocking. When she came she dusted the furniture nobody used and threw out the food she had brought the last time she visited and replaced it with fresh food that also wouldn't be eaten. Sometimes she left without saying hello to Ellen or even checking to see if she still breathed.

The earliest remaining artifacts from her childhood were the crayon pictures, but nothing starts with a finished picture. How many pages of scribble had she produced before the shapes started resembling the actual forms of creatures and heavenly bodies? What is a bird and how does it fly? What are the sun and the moon and how and when did she know both rolled through the sky and represented the duality of life and death, warmth and coldness, and that she could not imagine one without the other? When did she understand that flowers stood under the sun drinking light and water and producing the colors of dreams? Not the kind of flowers that filled the room around the butcher's corpse; not sickly sweet and hand-grown and arranged in sprays of impossible color. Her flowers were small, wild and bowed with every wind. They danced around her bare feet and invited her to lie down among them.

She retrieved a pad of paper and a pencil from a drawer in the kitchen. The stairs formed a brutal ascent that made her stop and grab the handrail to regain her breath before reaching the summit. She tried to write down the impressions she imagined, but she labored over forming the letters no less than an Akkadian scribe chiseling out a cuneiform history and when she saw the words wrought from such an effort she considered them no more than ugly scratchings that bore no resemblance to the colors, wind and sunshine she felt passing over her face. A child's mind couldn't be chained to an adult vocabulary and to abandon the words and ideas she had accumulated throughout her life in order to achieve childish simplicity seemed dishonest at best. At worst the artifice wouldn't stand against the torrent and she would be swept away in her sleep when she thought she had found safety. Ellen turned away from words and tried to draw, but what's brilliant and untutored as a child looks strange, misshapen, and lacking technique as an adult. The ink flower looked like a naked man fully aroused and the sun moon wore a leer instead of an open natural smile. She tore her drawings to pieces and then tried to create a new image instead of aping her childhood memories, but every drawing she produced started promising but ended looking like a humiliating confession of mortal sin. She abandoned language and art as routes to the beginning before she understood the violence of the whipsaw world and slid the paper and pencil underneath her bed.

The bed remained her vehicle for calling forth memory, even though she abandoned hope of reaching her first thought. She shifted instead to bringing to the surface as many thoughts, images, smells and other traces of her sensate being and live within them as fully as she could. Her body continued a slow decline to atrophy as an impression of her bones formed in the mattress, on her back with arms and legs slightly spread, her palms downward, her head cocked toward the right in the direction of the window. She felt the rough, whiskered cheek of her father against her own cheek. As her lips approached his mottled skin he released a deep breath. The humid air rippled across her face and smelled of hickory, cherry and whiskey. Somewhere under the bed lay a bottle and pipe, both strictly forbidden by the doctor but a prohibition enforced by no one. Her lips felt chapped because she had just returned from a walk in the wind and snow. He looked old and dry and Ellen could tell death stalked him. He tried to clear his throat and a thick rumble of phlegm startled her.

"What is it you're doing?" he said to her.

"I kissed you hello."

"No, you know what I mean, Why are you disturbing the bones of the dead? *Old man Oglethorpe lies a-mold-ring in the grave, Old man Oglethorpe lies a-mold'ring in the grave, Old man Oglethorpe lies a-mold'ring in the grave, His soul goes marching on, Glory, Glory! Hallelujah! Glory, Glory! Hallelujah! Glory, Glory! Hallelujah! His soul is marching on.*"

"It was cold outside. There's snow up to my knees."

"Are you a collector? A keeper?"

"What do you mean?"

"Has this become your responsibility? To keep the flame flickering? To remember my wasted form, the shell of what I once was? After all strength has drained from my muscle and my mind is nothing but muddle?"

"I don't see it that way, papa. Where else can I live? All my other homes have been burned down or soiled."

"You can remember the dead. You can't live with them."

"Where would you have me go? Where should I live?"

"You mean what should you live for? What is your religion?"

"Yes, yes, what is my religion."

"I'm sorry you are a keeper, a collector."

"Why papa?"

"To live without purpose and hope. To believe there are no other possible homes. My baby is bereft and castaway."

"Is the situation so desperate?"

"Memory is not belief. It is the remnant of belief. Can you find nothing else to believe in, Ellen? Anything? Materialism, soap operas, gossiping, charity? How could you so quickly come to the end of possibility? My lungs are three-quarters filled with phlegm and I'm thinking of becoming a marathoner, a long distance swimmer, a juggler on a unicycle."

"It's not possible for me."

"I'll grieve for you until my bones are powder. And for God's sake don't cremate me. I'm supposed to lie a-mold'ring in the grave. Fire is in the end of possibilities."

"I'll be alright, papa. I've always found a home."

"Is this your attempt to make me feel better about your chances? You believe these memories protect you. They do for now. But, Ellen, home is the Jericho wall against time. Eventually you will be alone with bricks and broken glass around your feet. Can't you hear the current swirling against the outside walls. This house is a stone in a river. There is no other possible outcome but to be worn away to nothing. There is no protection from the current. Memories are useless, useless."

Ellen listened and she could hear the roar of the current buffeting the sides of the house and finding leaks around the windows and doors, sneaking across the floor and ripping at everything in its way.

"Don't think you'll be spared. You are alone. Cast out whatever memories you can, knickknacks, keepsakes, memorabilia, trinkets bought from roadside stands. Throw them in the river or better yet burn them so there's no chance of them ever being found, no chance of you changing your mind and diving to the bottom to retrieve them from the silt. Forget. Memories are a trap. They will swamp you and push your head under the surface until you live and breathe with them."

"Yes, yes, that's what I've been searching for. This bed can only carry me so far, I'm afraid. I want, papa, to be rid of the current and the torrent. I want to walk in memory so I can live it all over again."

"You can't live with a paper bag over your head. Memory is a shroud."

"What am I to do?"

"Throw your memory away. Live in this present second. There is no second before and there is no second after. Face the current. It belongs to this very second."

"I can't. Who will care for you?"

"That's not your responsibility."

"You're asking me to accept banishment. To wander in a strange land as a stranger. I don't have the strength."

"Because you've been lying on your back for years."

"I was home."

"Ellen, home can just as easily be inside your skin."

Ellen left her bed and roamed around the house, collecting all the artifacts that had memories attached to them. Small things. A piece of blown glass shaped as a buck with eight point antlers the butcher had bought when they drove to the ocean. The butcher had a small piece of toilet paper stuck to his chin to stop the bleeding of a razor cut when he bought the glass. Ellen watched the paper bounce up and down as the butcher chatted with the clerk behind the counter and she wondered when he would remember that it remained on his chin. She found a flower she had pressed between the pages of her old Bible. The first flower to bloom under her influence, a blood red tulip that pushed its shoot through a late snow and tilted its bloom toward the window of her bedroom. Silverware and china bought shortly after they were married and used for Thanksgiving and Christmas dinners during the span of their marriage. She threw it all in the basement. Anything she could carry. Piles of mail and magazines that had accumulated on the floor even though her sister tried to sort some of the junk mail and pay the utility bills, lamps, vases, wine bottles, coffee percolators, pots and pans and cast iron skillets. She found that everything she touched had a memory. For the cast iron skillet she remembered scorching a pile of scrambled eggs but serving them to the butcher anyway. He chewed without pleasure and bolted down the food without raising his head or speaking, cleaning his plate and leaving for work with a grimace of indigestion. She remembered a vase holding a spray of dead flowers for weeks. At the time she preferred the dried-up and brown stage of the bloom over the stage of color and pliancy. All of it went into the basement, even though her father had recommended burning. She thought of her sister who, after she divorced, threw most of her belongings on the tree lawn the night before trash pick-up in an act of self-immolation the neighbors on her street still remember. In the morning when she heard the grind and whine of the trash truck parked in front of her house she ran outside wearing nothing but an open robe and panties and tried to stop the men from chucking away her life. They wouldn't let her climb into the truck to find her treasures and the men stared at the trees and clouds as she sobbed and forgot her robe had flapped open with the wind. The workers drove to the next pile, wondering what she could have thrown away to make her act like that. Ellen thought this way of shedding skin may be a family trait or instinct. Her sister didn't find the coincidence to be enlightening and she succumbed to a full-throated wail when she saw Ellen's bare house.

"You never should have done it. You'll miss those things more than you know! You'll feel adrift. I threw myself overboard when I purged my house. I threw the baby out with the bathwater! You should have talked to me. I could have told you not to do it!" her sister said between sobs.

Ellen didn't tell her sister that after her conversation with her father her purpose had turned from reliving memories to erasing them. She would know she had achieved her end when she saw a white screen cast in fluorescent light before her eyes, accompanied by the hum of an air conditioner, when she tried to conjure the past. She didn't know who she could confide in about her new purpose, but she could not consider her sister.

Months slipped by and her sister's anxiety grew with each successive visit. One night her sister chatted with her ex-husband over the phone and she told him she had taken steps to probate Ellen, to become her legal guardian and commit her to an institution because she had nearly starved herself and teetered on a complete mental collapse. Her ex-husband responded with a few beats of silence and then confided he thought the action long overdue.

"She should have checked herself in the day after the butcher's funeral. He kept her afloat. He protected her," the sister's ex-husband said.

"It was the goddamn butcher and all those women that drove her insane."

"Nonsense, she was a kook when he married her. She would have been walking the streets years ago if it wasn't for the butcher."

"God, what's wrong with me? Why do I keep forgetting you're a Grade A asshole?"

One day two men wearing matching uniforms appeared in Ellen's room and told her they were going to take her on a trip. She tried to tell them that her bed served as her home and automobile, and, even though it may not look like it, her bed represented her Paris and Rome. Trips were unnecessary and wasteful. But when she tried to speak the words came out as a croak and they took hold of her arms before she could clear her throat to continue the protest. They had carried a stretcher up the stairs, but she waved it away and walked to the ambulance with their help. She couldn't replace one home with an indentation of her body so quickly with a rolling rock hard home attended by solicitous goons. The cars roared down the street faster than she remembered. A gale of wind filled with chatter sucked from the surrounding houses, the curses and grinding of dirty, industrious men and the groaning of thousands of souls in pain blew against her face and bore down her ear canals. Near the sidewalk she could no longer stand against it and she slumped against the goons. One of the men held her awkwardly under the armpits as the other retrieved the stretcher. She lay on the hard mattress so unlike her own and asked them not to talk so loud. When they banged her into the back of the ambulance she pleaded with them to be careful, to think of themselves as mice taking a nocturnal stroll, because the roar of the world could be giving her brain damage. She asked them to turn down the radio and wondered if anything could be done to further muffle the infernal roaring of the ambulance's motor. She asked if the car horns she heard were not, in fact, the screams of pregnant women being impaled. One of the men gave her two cotton balls and said he could think of no better protection from the torrent than simple cotton.

She shut her eyes against the world and pushed the cotton balls as deep as they could go. She folded her hands across her breasts in the position she remembered the butcher's corpse had been shaped and she tried to die. Her body, the ignorant beast, thumped away stupidly, ignoring her commands. Her organs threw themselves in open revolt against her wishes and believed more in their individual rights than the common good. The roar washed around her.

The goons dropped her off at a square building with small windows high on the walls staffed by a band of Nazis costumed like nurses. They delighted in jabbing her with needles and making sure her asshole stayed clean. They force-fed her lumpy brown meals and lukewarm milk and everyday they made her get on her feet to perform a series of tricks for their amusement. Ellen thought she might be too old to be sold to the circus, but she wondered why these grim women delighted in making her stand on one foot and lift brightly colored weights like a trained seal. She couldn't refuse them because they had big muscular bottoms and large breasts squeezed into their uniforms that made Ellen think of trapped anger.

When the Nazis had their fill of her humiliation they let her lie in a room with two other women, both older and more infirm than she. Mrs. McVicker, the woman to her right, rattled on all day in a morphine-laced mumble. Something large and incurable had grown within her and she waited for the first open hospice bed the staff could find. The woman on her left, Ida, preferred to watch television all day and held gossip magazines in her lap even though she had been unable to read for five years because the letters on the page liked to roam and create words and sentences of their own choosing. The Nazis showed a minor kindness and gave Ellen foam ear plugs that blocked more of the hiss and venom of the television. If she lay on her side and stared at the wall away from the glow she could convince herself the invention had never been created and patented, had never come to market and sold more units than could be imagined and had never enslaved the populace with its slow drip of inanity. She had no more than an hour or two of undisturbed peace throughout the day, because once they served her one of those disgusting meals they followed with a snack or physical therapy or Nazi bloodletting or a young intern with barrettes in her hair peered up her vagina or an arthritic podiatrist clipped and filed her toenails while repeatedly asking her about the last time she clipped them or visitors came to the bedsides of the two dying women, family members parading past their ruined bodies and trying to communicate their need for money or furniture through the drugs swirling in the women's brains that ripped the quiet asunder.

Ellen tried to alter her sleeping hours by trying to stay awake at night and sleeping through the chaos of the day. She thought the night would be calmer and could provide long stretches of time where she could continue to dismantle and discard every last memory clogging the efficiency of her mind. But in the night elderly men cried out for their fathers. Death rattles shook the floors above and below her. Nurses smoked cigarettes in the stairwells, exchanged curses about their patients, and made scatological references that neither the speaker or listener could follow. Ellen dreamed other patients' dreams. She saw Ida walk down an aisle through overgrown hedges, her belly distended from an overdue pregnancy, sheathed in a chiffon dress that billowed and swirled like smoke. She stepped onto a raised stage and stood behind a wooden podium with a microphone attached to a flexible stand. She recited a litany of grievances she held against the world and city government as the dress slowly rotted away until she stood naked and still pregnant in front of an unseen but audibly breathing audience watching from the shadows. When the grievances were exhausted a man escorted her off the stage and sodomized her. The next night Mrs. McVicker drove her hands into the black earth, clawing at the moist roots and clearing a hole. She dropped a light bulb into the ground and brushed dirt over it. She dug a second hole and placed a shoe in the dirt. She felt the sun warming her neck and back as she made a third hole and buried a rotten apple and a peach pit. She stood up and realized she had dug the holes in the middle of a freeway and cars and trucks bore down upon her with the intent to kill before relenting at the last moment. She looked at her garden and sprouts that looked like catheters breaking through the ground. The force of a collision threw her into the air, spinning head over heels with two mangled legs courtesy of a car that looked like a chisel on wheels. Ellen jumped off her bed, but Mrs. McVicker slept through the dream and her waxen face did not betray the hostilities within. Ellen returned to sleeping at night for the refuge of her own dreams.

One day she asked the Nazis if she could be dressed. The flimsy gown open at the back gave her a constant chill and limited her movements unless she wanted to expose her bottom to wheezing men leering from darkened rooms, strapped to machines that regulated their bodies. The Nazis expressed a weary sympathy but told her clothes were the responsibility of the family and to their knowledge no one had yet been by to visit her. They promised to pass her case to the hospital social worker, who came to Ellen's room one day looking like she too hadn't eaten in a year, preferring to reveal the sharp edges of her bones under her sallow skin to carrying an extra ounce of weight. The social worker told Ellen her sister had become distraught, unable to come to terms with the fact she had committed her only sister. Her sister had asked again and again after Ellen's health and explained she had been trying to work up the courage to come to the hospital. Everyone had told her she had done the right thing for Ellen, that she would get well and come out and be able to face life, handle her affairs, pay her bills and eat regularly, but she knew Ellen would greet her with condemning eyes, would turn her love and care into a betrayal.

"She said she would come. She would come. Tell Ellen to be patient. It's all for the best. You don't think your sister betrayed you, do you Ellen?" the social worker said in a high-pitched voice more appropriate for a children's show where a blue cow or an orange jackal teaches the child how to properly use the potty.

"I just want something to cover my bottom. I'm tired of lying naked in this room," Ellen told her, hoping the social worker would leave her room soon. "I'm not looking for news of my sister. I never knew she fell in league with the Nazis, but I appreciate you telling me."

The social worker pursed her lips, wrote the request on a clipboard and quickstepped it to the door. She stopped in the frame and turned, something on her mind.

"We're not Nazis, Ellen. We're here to help you. Make you better."

"How can you help me? By the sound of your voice your expertise must be in puppet shows. How will that dam the torrent? Why must you all see my bottom whenever you like?"

A few days later the social worker came back with a pair of cotton pajamas and an extraordinary dress recently donated to the charity wing of the hospital by a woman of extraordinary means. When Ellen tried on the dress, deep green velvet, ankle length, tapered waist, high collar and a full skirt she looked ready for a heart disease fundraiser or the Elizabethan royal court. The nurses cooed and fussed over her for much too long, applying make-up, washing her hair, plucking hairs from her brows and chin, filing her fingernails and applying clear polish. One nurse brought in a pair of green velvet high heels but this finishing touch had to be quickly abandoned after Ellen almost broke her ankle and confessed she had never worn heels before. The nurse settled on a pair of black boots more functional than stylish.

Ellen wore the dress every day as she roamed the hallways of the building trying to regain her strength. She made no friends because the noises coming from the rooms terrified her. Drugs dripped down clear tubes into bruised arms. Monitors charted the slowing beats of tired hearts. Ventilators breathed. Men and women sat in their communal rooms under the blare and flash on their television sets. She thought the hospital building might be a giant machine living off the energy of its patients, sucking them dry of their blood and bile until they were raisins and easier to burn. In the evening she would change into her pajamas and take a few moments to brush the wrinkles and noise from the dress, because if she had a complaint about the dress it was that the thick velvet collected the day in its fabric, so she had to clean it every night before it became too heavy to wear.

She left one morning before dawn. She had awakened to the screams of a cancer patient whose morphine drip had run empty. She decided to dress and make a circuit through the hospital before the other patients woke or died. As she passed the room of the screaming women she saw the two night nurses attending to her and she wondered if the screams were a result of the cancer or the administration of officially sanctioned torture. At the end of the hall an emergency door had been propped open with a plastic bucket. The alarm had been disabled weeks ago because the door provided the quickest route for the nurses to sneak a quick smoke during their shifts. Ellen slipped through the door and down a flight of stairs where another door had been propped open. She walked into the outside world where the wind carried a tapestry of screams. She pulled the cotton balls from a hidden pocket near the waistband of the dress. She plugged her ears and closed her eyes and hoped when the bell rang in the tower she would hear its annunciation that Jesus still held dominion over the flock. He alone could stop the chaos and tumult.

Ellen walked the hours of daylight and slept on benches or chairs of the bus station, shopping malls, the library, public gardens or food courts. She found that if she walked until she could barely stay upright she would sleep quickly and deeply even in the most vicious and stinging current. Security guards acted gentle and kind to her because she spoke to them with politeness and respect and because she looked like the ragged queen of the dispossessed in her green velvet dress. When she snored and security received a complaint from an uptight shopper or store manager the guards would jostle her tenderly, refraining from addressing her as 'my liege' but whispering apologetically in her ear that she would have to move along. She thanked them for the use of the chair or stone bench and continued her aimless trek.

She found food by asking people who had some control or access to it for meals or snacks when she became hungry. The host or hostess sat her in obscure corners near the swinging doors to the bathrooms, kitchens, or storage rooms. Hot dog vendors gave her sausages loaded with whatever nutrients they could find in their carts. Delivery drivers left her packages of outdated pastries sealed in plastic and fast food managers marked her meals as inventory waste or loss. When she found someone who smiled at her or asked after her health, someone like Koo Koo Beatrice, she tended to put them on a daily schedule until they stopped smiling or asking after her health. Koo Koo had never stopped smiling so she stayed on the schedule for years.

The Sisters of Charity allowed her to sleep on a small, hard cot in a cold hallway filled with filing cabinets and broken chairs and desks. They asked her to be gone by eight in the morning and not return until eight at night, no matter the weather. Ellen sensed Sister Bollo and the other nuns were breaking rules for her, but they couldn't withdraw their mercy. Sister Bollo begged Ellen to call her sister and ask for help because how long did she think an older woman could live on the streets without something horrible and final happening to her. When Ellen called her sister the line stayed quiet several moments before her sister broke out into wheezing sobs. She asked Ellen for forgiveness and repented for a life filled with awful decisions that led to blind alleys and heartache. Ellen listened to the apology but couldn't think of a reason for it. Her sister had conspired with the Nazis to incarcerate her briefly, but they had elected her their queen and given her a royal dress and boots, so an apology seemed superfluous. Her sister had acted in concert with her beliefs and thought she helped Ellen. She couldn't tell her sister that she had forgiven her because she, after the sobs had subsided, had launched into a story of recently becoming engaged with a man who would be retiring to Las Vegas and that more than likely they would be leaving for the desert within a month. She told Ellen how unlike her first husband this man lived and that after a long, sad road of loneliness and sometimes despair she had found happiness with another person. The fact that he happened to be a man seemed close to a miracle. She described the job from which he retired, supervisor of a postal facility, his thick Popeye forearms, his trim physique and his appetite for life. Just before her sister launched into a description of their sexual life together Ellen set the phone receiver down on Sister Bollo's desk without hanging up and walked back to her cot. Ten minutes passed before her sister realized she had been talking to no one.

"Ellen? Where are you? How have you been getting along? Ellen?" her sister repeated several times before she hung up the phone.

"What did she say?" Sister Bollo asked the next morning.

"She's very happy."

"Will she help you?"

"Sister, how could she help me?"

"She could make sure you are not killed or raped on the street."

"There's nothing to be done with me."

"Do you have any other brothers or sisters?"

"I had a brother fifty years ago."

"Did he die as a child?"

"No, my sister told me he's in Peru running a brothel and wallowing in his own corruption. He's disowned his past and created something new and vile. I envy his ability to cast away memory and attachment. I tried and failed. I walk the same streets I did as a child. I wait to hear the same bell. He doesn't call me sister anymore. He tells his women that he lived as an orphan and that the State of Ohio raised him until he was emancipated at age fourteen. From there he made his way, scratching and clawing, until he figured out how to pay off the Peruvian police and collect a flock around him. Papa left nothing in the will for him."

"Your sister told you all of this?"

"Not all of it. Sometimes I can hear him thinking, killing the last of his memories of me. I'm conjured and then slowly strangled by his hand and sometimes drowned in a claw foot bathtub with rust stains near the drain. It depends on my size and age in the memory. My brother is capable of infanticide. I've seen him through my own baby eyes."

Sister Bollo patted Ellen's hand, unsure what to do, but she made an effort to smile and made a note to remember to find a doctor to look at Ellen's legs.

Ellen found the thin defense of the cotton balls to be less and less effective as the intensity of the roar increased and its duration lengthened. The current acted like a downpour or blizzard that could follow her anywhere, even indoors, anytime day or night. She labored over the construction of a small cube located left of her heart, a shape no bigger than a cubic inch, where she could retreat when the force threatened to overwhelm. She used the strategy that routed armies used of retreating to a walled city after they had been crushed on the field. Her body may ache, get cold, swell, and shake in the grips of an invading infection or virus, defeated by the current and lashed by the howl, but the cube stood as a keep that could never be breeched. Only she could fit into the cube. Jesus swam in her illogic and held his breath for long stretches before breaking the surface. Sometimes she could hear him knocking, but she would have to leave the cube for him to fit so she left him outside. She thought he had abandoned his temporal self on the cross and wondered why he still had mass. The butcher rode the moon sun as his pants fell down around his ankles and an erection rose to the cheers of a female audience. Her sister stood atop a landfill digging for shreds and remnants of their family and then reburying them in a cemetery choked with sumac and mint. The air smelled like her father's breath. Sometimes the cube would remained closed, as if Ellen had forgotten the combination or her keys, and she would be left to survive amidst her senses and memory. She would frantically search for an egress. The cube would eventually relent and she would crawl inside. She could fall asleep inside the cube but wake up outside of it. On those days she knew her time would be spent fending off the ferocious attacks of the current, like hacking away at aggressive jungle tendrils trying to wrap around her neck and choke her to death.

The dogs began watching her soon after she left the hospital. A lone stray would follow her on the sidewalk, head down, as he followed the ribbon of scents on the ground. The dog would be relieved or joined by another in the pack and the surveillance would continue. Sometimes the second or a third dog would make a closer approach, get close enough to smell the disease in her legs or curl up next to her when she fell asleep on a cold bench. She was a curiosity, something so vulnerable and weak that she could be taken at any time but something also that ignited their pity and their desire to protect. At times a small pack of four or five dogs would encircle her and she would hold out a tentative hand. Human petting had become anathema to them, but they would indulge a pat on the head or a scratch behind the ears. When she had food she would always drop some on the ground. They wouldn't eat the offering if it came directly from her hand, because they had long ago swore off handouts as traps. They watched her grow sick as her legs swelled, discolored and gave off a pungent sweet smell that made them salivate. They watched the velvet dress turn to tatters and be replaced first with a herringbone pantsuit that became so worn it fell off in pieces and then the maid's uniform. They watched her purposeful gait crumble a little each day until it had been reduced to an excruciating hobble. Her wobbling and falling occurred with greater frequency and sometimes the dogs would lick her scrapes or nudge her to her feet or lay across her to keep her warm as she recuperated from a fall. Ellen lay on the ground longer each time she fell. She sensed in the coming weeks she would fall one last time and close her eyes to the world. She died a little more each day before the eyes of the dogs and the process fascinated them.

The echo of the screeching machine still echoed through the neighborhood. Ellen had regained her gait after the neighbors had helped her to her feet. She had turned a corner away from their sight and their concern when both knees collapsed, sending her sprawling to the tree lawn. She ended the roll on her back and when she opened her eyes the sky lay under a blanket of maple leaves. She could sense the cube open its door. She entered and slammed the door shut behind her. She saw the lines of the door dissolve and the wall turned smooth and inscrutable. She no longer felt the damp earth on her back and the noises had stopped quickly as if someone had turned a radio off. She hoped her body lay in the shade and that she could die unnoticed. Had she known, truly known, this would be the moment of her exit she would have crawled inside the tree, wrapped the bark around her and taken her last breath.

Ten dogs approached her from ten different directions and each took a mouthful of the uniform. They carried her through the backyards of the neighborhood. They moved quickly because of the lightness of her body. Ellen remained at peace in her small, carefully constructed home.

A House is a Womb

Jack's mouth tasted like ash and his throat felt raw from breathing in the smoke of the burning houses. He pried himself out of the chair and straightened his back against a knot of atrophy and pain. His first step sent another jolt through his spine, but he kept walking and by the time he had taken ten steps he had forgotten the pain even though it continued to tear through his body.

A gaping black hole had been burned through the roof of the house behind him. Black smears crept from the windows where the smoke had escaped. Black puddles choked with ash and debris lay on the ground and the air smelled wet and burnt. The front door had been hacked away by the firefighters and inside resembled a charred cave. The house looked to be a complete loss and after the inspectors came and saw the hole in the roof and the burnt structure they would request a demolition right down to the foundation. Jack scanned his memory to recall if he knew of anywhere he could get topsoil and sapling fruit trees. He would plant them in a small orchard in the footprint of the foundation, but he would have to think of a way to keep the mature fruit from being stolen by the neighborhood kids or men who wanted their wives to bake them a fresh pie. He imagined a stone wall, using sandstone culled from local quarries, with broken glass cemented into the top of the wall to discourage any trespassers, but he figured he would have to settle for a wooden fence as tall as the building code would allow.

Jack looked to his right and saw the unintended consequence of his arson. The second house had burned quicker, as if the whole structure had been dipped in kerosene, and had collapsed while the firefighters were still spraying water on the flames. Two walls had fallen inward, causing the second story and roof to fall onto the first floor. On the ground lay burnt and soggy clothes, a sofa, two wing-back chairs, half of a mattress, a photo album, a dog's leash, a vase tipped on its side but still holding a spray of flowers, a broken coffee pot and two dead cats. In the backyard a small vegetable garden ringed with aluminum pie plates had been trampled under the feet of the firefighters and a kissing, wooden Dutch boy and girl had been decapitated and their heads lay at the feet of their still erect bodies. Jack felt a prick of indecision and not a little remorse pass through him. What the fuck have I done? he thought. Am I that much of a crazy fucking lunatic that I burn an old woman out of her house to have my way? What is it I've burned? Am I going to stop kids from partying and fucking? Is that suddenly my responsibility? What goddamn seawall would I need to build to stop that tide? Might as well say I'm going to push the earth into the sun. Am I just too goddamn old and jealous of their sleek bodies and firm titties and their not giving a good goddamn about consequences or rules? Some crazy old man comes rushing at them out of the night, brandishing fire, with the intent to burn them, kill them, blot them out so something new will grow. Weren't their impulses once my masters, my drive, my altar on which I prayed and fucked and didn't give a good goddamn? What have I done? Will they run to the police and instead of living in a cathedral of my own making I'll be in a concrete cell with a couple of pudwhackers the rest of my days or at least long enough to file a blade sharp enough to saw through my own throat? Who had the woman been? What will become of her? A nursing home? The attic or converted garage of a son or daughter? I have a half torn apart house and a list of felonies the length of my arm to show for my grand project, the last great construct of Cactus Jack, my exit. I could abandon it, move on, leave it and let Anne Marie go back to Ben, let Glover and Estonia have their baby in California near family and friends because what hope is there for a child growing up with me? They'd be better off having the kid next to a dumpster in New York City or in an abandoned factory. I took my shot and I found out I have no talent, no aim, no purpose. Some people are meant to be flotsam. Who am I building for? This goddamn dirty street is hanging by its fingertips. Rembrandt could paint a mural on the outside wall of the Quickie Mart and the next day bums would be pissing on it. What am I doing? Where does this ego come from? My women have said it comes from my pecker or my balls. I should be content to live in a condominium with a patch of grass the size of my foot. Pass out of this world unnoticed, no monument, no elegy, no tears, no remnant of the work of my hands. I need to burn out an old woman to make the smallest mark, a shallow knick, a faint scratch on the face of the world? Carry flame, burn, burn my humanity, burn my impulses and my ego in front of a witless audience. I am a goddamn worthless fuck trying to scream in a hurricane.

Jack sat on the porch of the first house, his feet on the steps and his back to the carnage. Anne Marie walked around the corner and paused when she saw him brooding, his head in his hands.

"Did a bomb go off?" she asked.

"Something like that. Did you sleep through the fire?"

"I didn't hear a thing. I was dead to the world. I haven't worked like that in years."

"It was quite a sight. Two houses burning at once. You didn't hear the sirens?"

"I heard them I suppose, but you always hear sirens and planes and screeching tires. How did the fire start?"

"I had enough. I meant to burn the rats out of this house. The other one was an accident. It burned faster than I've ever seen anything burn."

"Is Mrs. Kolchakski alright?"

"I don't know. They carried her out on a stretcher."

"Jesus, Jack." She sat down beside him on the steps and stared at Mrs. Kolchakski's house. "That's arson, right?"

"I know. I don't know what the fuck I was thinking. I'm like a fucking maniac. I think I only killed a couple of cats, fortunately."

"Did anybody see you?"

"I fought some kids. I'm sure they could guess where I live."

"They won't go to the cops. They're probably high again already. You're not thinking of turning yourself in are you?"

"No, I might get caught, but I'm not likely to turn myself in."

"Good, because I'm not crawling back to Ben and I want to see our house finished."

Jack looked at Anne Marie and wondered what miracle had made her accept him and his craziness.

"This doesn't make any difference to you?"

"What? The houses?"

"Of course the houses!"

"I'm thinking you committed worse crimes in your life, no?" She waited for Jack to cede the point by narrowing his eyes. "So, let's call this creative destruction and be done with it. You'll feel better after a cup of coffee."

Anne Marie stood up and held out her hand. Jack lurched to his feet and Anne Marie insisted that he hold the hand she had offered. She led him around the house and back to their yard and away from his crimes. He sat down in the chair he had slept in as Anne Marie made the coffee.

"So what's the next step? What do we do today?"

Next step? Jack thought. His next step would be to run away to another state without the burden of his material accumulation. Maybe he would even leave his truck. Maybe he would start walking without a direction or destination in mind and where his body finally died is where he would be buried. A freeway with oily asphalt and a cluster of gas stations and fast food chains came to his mind. Behind the buildings and greasy dumpsters lay a freshly dug and refilled grave with his belt buckle stuck in the dirt for lack of a headstone.

"Do you know the next step?" Anne Marie had watched his blank look long enough to know he wasn't at all thinking about the next step for the house.

"We're going to retrieve the lumber for the garage tonight."

"Retrieve?"

"Something like that."

"This is turning into quite the criminal enterprise."

"Have you thought about going back to Ben?"

"Why would you ask that? Didn't I just tell you I won't be crawling back to him? Is that what you want? I made a choice Jack and I stick with my choices until my choices give me no other options than to make another choice. Besides if you're thinking of running away from me again I want you to know this time I'll track you down and cut your legs off at the knees."

The first time Jack had run out on her they were eighteen years old and they had made vague plans of getting married and Jack said maybe he would join the military and he could provide a tidy living for her and a family. The weather was very much like the weather on this day when he finished his shift of digging out basements in a new suburban sub-division. His partner had been talking all day about a trip to Florida he had taken and how he had gotten drunk in Key West, so drunk that he passed out on the sidewalk and an elderly couple with leather skin dragged him to their deck and let him sleep it off and even made him a breakfast of Bloody Marys and French toast and Jack thought it sounded like a place he should visit before he married and joined the military. So he left without telling Anne Marie, thinking he would only be gone a week or two, but the partying kept going and soon he began looking for work. After he found a job building a row of condos and had been gone from Ohio for over four months he rationalized that she had forgotten about him, but, in truth, he didn't want to face her wrath because he had bailed on their dreams before they had begun.

He worked his way across the country, with a couple of stints in Alaska as a worker on the oil pipeline and as winter caretaker for a shuttered resort, a job which mainly consisted of trying to not talk to yourself, avoiding compulsive masturbation and rationing the booze during the long blizzards, and three years in minor league baseball, quickly becoming a good defensive catcher with the ability to scare fey pitchers into throwing quality strikes, but with no stick and no prospect of ever developing one. After a decade he made it back to Cleveland and saw Anne Marie on the street not far from the house where she grew up. She had begun dating Ben by then, but she and Jack picked up right where they left off and they spent the next eight months fucking and the same vague talk of marriage and stability began. Anne Marie didn't bring up the subject or push the idea, as Jack first mentioned the possibility of marriage and even then talked about buying a house, a house beaten and cheap in one of the city's worst neighborhoods that they could fix up and live together in. Anne Marie stared him down, called him a liar and said she didn't need to hear lies to keep fucking him. She couldn't help herself, true, but she had made the mistake of thinking Jack capable of marriage ten years before and she wouldn't make the same mistake twice. He bought her a silver ring without a diamond and called it a promise ring.

"You mean you promise to shut the fuck up about marrying me. You're ruining my desire. You keep it up and I'll marry Ben."

A friend offered Jack the chance to sail on a rich guy's yacht, who made his money by padding defense contracts and producing cheap plastic toys of hit television shows, across the Atlantic and through the Mediterranean and he accepted before he thought of Anne Marie. This time he told her he would be leaving right after they had had sex and he barely collected his clothes and slipped on his underwear before she pushed him out of her apartment. As he walked on the sidewalk he heard the ting of the promise ring hitting the cement and rolling into the street where it fell through a sewer grate.

"I'll pick up some three-quarter inch plywood for the subfloor while I'm at it."

"And we need sheetrock for the walls."

"Right, but not this trip. I have only one truck. We'll have to be in and out ."

"You won't be able to carry a whole garage's worth of lumber on your truck."

"I figured I'll get what I can. If I get half of what I need then that's half I didn't have before."

"It seems like too good of an opportunity to waste. Why don't you borrow one of their flatbeds. I'm assuming your getting the shipment from a lumber yard."

"Right."

"Those flatbeds have massive suspension and cranes to unload, right? Borrow it for the night and ditch it in another part of town."

"Brilliance and beauty all in the same package. Damn, I'm a lucky man."

"I do what I can."

"I'm supposed to be there tonight. Glover and I will take a break today and be fresh. We have a two hour window at the yard. We have to haul ass."

"Use the tow motors. Don't try it by hand. You'll never make it."

Jack started choreographing the approach, what lumber to find first, the loading, how to keep Glover from running or killing himself and their exit. He decided to go to the lumberyard in the day to get a fresh view of the layout, where the gate would be and what possible obstacles may be in his way.

"Looks like there's someone to see you," Anne Marie said as she pointed a finger toward a spot behind Jack's back.

He thought of the police or an officious fire inspector or a health inspector come to check on the illegal shitter or Kaufman or Cavano come to collect on the debt before it had been accrued, but when he turned around he saw Al K-wood el standing in the yard. His left eye had been swollen shut by a baseball-sized knot and his lips had been beaten, bruised and split until his mouth had no clear distinction. His shirt held a history of bleeding, some dried, some fresh, in a spray and drip pattern starting at the collar. He carried a small toddler's backpack covered with the smiling face of Elmo. His Nikes were untied and the laces had turned gray. His pants were belted a half an inch above his cock.

"Wood, come over, sit down before you fall down."

Jack didn't rise but waved Wood to an empty chair across from the blackened and cold fire pit. Wood walked slowly over to the chair and immediately slouched once he sat.

"Looks like the pack has a new alpha."

"What?" Wood mumbled.

"What happened?"

"They jumped me before I could even get out the door. I can't go back unless I take out 365 Everyday."

"365 Everyday is a person?"

"Ya."

"The person who replaced you?"

"Ya."

"So 365 Everyday has control of your projects?"

"Ya."

"Is this house outside the territory?"

Wood looked left and then right as if trying to locate a blue line drawn on the earth to indicate the boundary of his banishment.

"This far enough."

"We have no ice for that eye," Anne Marie said as she looked with concern at Wood's mangled face. "I could go down to Mary Kelly's and see if she has ice."

"I feel alright."

"You don't look right, son. You look beaten and mangled. You look like you've been run over by a truck or your head is about to pop with unregulated pressure. And if you look like that you don't have many chances of feeling alright. I have a couple of cold packs in my truck glove compartment. They sometimes come in handy to douse the fire in my knees."

Jack hobbled to the truck and fetched the cold packs, the chemical kind that when squeezed a small pouch inside breaks and the resulting mixture of chemicals causes a reaction of cool relief. Jack gave the packs to Anne Marie who rolled them in her hands to break the pouch and strategically place them on the worst parts of Wood's face.

"That eye looks really bad."

"It do kinda feel bad."

"You think you'll be up for a job tonight?"

"Jack, look at his face," Anne Marie pleaded.

"His hands look alright. I need an extra pair of hands."

"I be alright. You should worry about 365 Everyday."

"Look, I think you should just move on. I know what this is going to sound like and I know the possibility of you listening to me is almost zero. But listen to me. Consider it a blessing or a signpost or a signal or a flashlight illuminating a direction and path you never knew existed. There are other possibilities in life. You don't really have to fight over a little patch of dirt in a rotten public project. You don't have to give a rat's ass about that little patch of dirt because ain't nothing ever going to grow on it, ain't nothing good ever going to come of it. What did 365 Everyday win? A little patch of dirt that grass won't even grow on anymore. He'll be dead within a year because somebody else is going to get it into their heads that they want the patch of dirt. Step out of the loop, Wood. Consider yourself lucky it ended with a beating and not a bullet. Life sometimes pukes up a second chance and the fools who don't take it, don't listen to the very obvious message laid at their feet, such as 'Little patches of dirt are bullshit when you consider the globe in its entirety.' You're bruised, you're beat up…" Jack trailed off because as he looked at Wood he stopped believing in his own speech. He knew the likelihood of Wood walking away from his past life hovered just north of nil and the likelihood of Wood challenging 365 Everyday and being killed in the attempt or killing 365 Everyday and resuming his brief reign as King of the Ghetto Dirt Patch all but certain. Jack would show him an alternative, but Wood would break his heart in the end.

"365 Everyday isn't going to be alive in a year. It'll be less than that."

"Right, but you don't have to be the one to do it."

"Who going to do it then?"

"The next unlucky fucker with a little ambition and no talent or skills who had nobody looking over their shoulder telling him that taking over that fucking barren dirt patch would probably be the stupidest fucking thing he could ever do if he has a desire to live past twenty years of age."

"365 Everyday ain't no he."

"What?"

"She a girl. She my sister. Not no more, but she used to be my sister. We use to take baths together and sleep in the same bed until she grew titties."

"No shit. I didn't expect that. That shows you how clueless I've become. Girls taking over dirt patches, Jesus. In my day they always had something better to do than that."

"She mean. Nobody ever been meaner. She can't get nobody to fuck her unless she force 'em to. Everybody afraid to say no to her 'cause she don't forget and she don't show mercy."

"Except for you, her brother. She should have killed you like someone will kill her. You don't leave a rival alive, right? But she has a mercy spot somewhere inside her because she's your sister, because she remembers your little pecker floating in the bath water, because she knows deep down you carry the same blood and she doesn't want to break the heart of your mama. Show her the same mercy, or help her step out of the loop too. Take her and your mama to some other piece of dirt that's not diseased and hopeless."

"That was her mistake. She fucked up keeping me alive."

"That was her mercy. Another sign right in front of you. Take her mercy, accept it and move along."

Jack's words caught in his throat. He wanted to tell Wood that people and places filled the world, far beyond the scope of his imagination, and the only way to know they existed and believe in them was to find them, live with them, and learn from them. He wanted to tell him to dance naked on a beach and waggle his cock at the setting sun, to dive into the country and its people and never surface, to climb weatherworn hills shaped like women's buttocks and sit on a rock at the summit and survey the curve of the earth and the heat shimmering off her skin and thinking that each drop of sweat pouring from your head could be a tear, a gift from a humble supplicant. But how could he express that without sounding completely addled with age and memory? He never wanted to act like a goddamn missionary, so thinking he could cobble together an ad hoc gospel in light of his recent transgressions seemed flat out hypocritical. Where in his vision of the roaming saint did arson fit? Or attempted murder? Or manslaughter if old woman Kolchakski died? The air and ground around him felt laden with his own failure, his own fight over a parcel of land, so could he determine any difference between Wood's aim and his own? Weren't they both chasing the same vision, both crazed by their own need to exist in full, to be something other than just another animal sucking oxygen and blowing carbon dioxide. Maybe Wood could be harnessed, could be pointed in a different direction, could be forced to take a step away from his humiliation, but if the little fucker thought anything like him the prospect of such a transformation bordered on ludicrous.

"If you want to stay here you have to work. Tonight we're fetching a shipment of lumber and you're part of the crew. Anne Marie will show you a room that will be yours as long as you work, deal?"

"Ya."

"You'll sleep on the floor until we find another bed. I have an extra sleeping bag I bought from a neurasthenic ranch hand a few years back. Do you have an extra shirt in your Elmo bag?"

"No."

"Take off the colors and keep them off. While you're here you don't belong to anything or anyone except this house. Once you put them back on you leave. You bring that gang shit to my doorstep and you'll be the first one I kill. What did you wear?"

"White bandana, back left pocket. They took it and gave it to 365 Everyday. The only way I get it back is I go to her."

"Well, don't bring the fight here. Once you're ready, keep it to the dirt patch."

Al K-wood el nodded his agreement because, of course, the fight would have to be back at the projects. He'd kill her on the very spot they jumped him, between Buildings A and B, where they beat him and took the bandana out of his pocket. Five of his crew held him down as 365 Everyday pulled down his pants, stuck one of her fingers up his asshole, told him he had become nothing more than a bitch and wiped the residue of shit on his cheek. They beat him again and then carried him to the street, pants still down around his ankles and threw him down on the asphalt. He lay there some time before he could get his arms to work. No one came to help him or even looked at his bare ass in the street. 365 Everyday had put the word out he had been deposed. His mother finally came a few hours later with the Elmo bag and dropped it near his head and left without saying anything to him or pulling up his pants. When he killed 365 Everyday he would have to consider killing his mother for her own meanness and for raising a daughter who had turned into one of the meanest people in the city. He crawled on his hands and knees to the tree lawn, a patch of dirt with neither tree nor lawn and pulled himself up using a fire hydrant. He pissed himself and worried they had broken something inside because he could hardly feel the piss coming out of him. He could feel his face distorting as he staggered away. They had beaten his limbs with their fists and their booted feet and he couldn't tell if all of his bones were broken or how long he could remain standing. He picked up the Elmo bag and clutched it to his chest as if it held a nuclear secret or that it kept his ribs from falling out of his body. He walked until he found an abandoned house and he curled up on the back porch and passed out. His last coherent thought rose, his belief and lack of concern of never regaining consciousness, before all went dark. His dreams became a rush and tangle of images, a mob of mouths shaped like assholes, of large tattooed titties slapping him in the face, of his mother pulling him from her vagina and pitching him over a rusty fence into a field choked with weeds and snakes. When he awoke he opened the Elmo bag, hoping his mother had packed something he could use to kill 365 Everyday or some kind of medicine to help with the pain, but he only found a half-filled tube of travel-sized toothpaste, a frayed toothbrush that hadn't been his, a pair of socks, a pair of underwear, toe nail clippers, hand lotion and the silver mirror the crazy fuck in the truck had dropped. That constituted the sum of his inheritance. The glass in the mirror had not been replaced, but Wood had bought silver polish and had buffed every nook in the handle and frame. The fact his mother packed the mirror in the bag either showed a small kindness or she believed that without the glass the mirror couldn't be worth much or she had miscalculated its worth and quickly stuffed it in the bag without thinking once she heard the coup had succeeded. Did she beg 365 Everyday for her son's life or had she counseled her to leave no rivals and never stop yourself from plunging the knife in to the hilt? The mirror did remind him of Jack and his offer of a roof for work and given the state of his prospects he needed a place to stay. His other option included crawling onto a porch of an abandoned house and dying alone. He woke up briefly, tired to unbuckle his pants before he pissed himself again but the operation proved unsuccessful, and he passed out again before the piss turned cold.

When he woke up the second time he could raise his head and straighten his legs. Pain came from every muscle and joint when he pushed himself to a sitting position. He suppressed a cough because had he let it go he knew a stream of blood and sputum would have issued from his mouth and his ribs would have snapped in two. He knew where Jack lived. He had gotten high and drunk in the house behind Jack's and in the house he owned. The party had moved from Jack's when a gang of skinheads claimed it as their own and sprayed swastikas everywhere to announce their ownership. The skinheads started with a group of eight skinny white boys and only three believed enough in their philosophy to shave their heads, but soon enough they all sported clean domes. They started carving Aryan symbols of their own imagination and craft on their necks and face and they agreed a methamphetamine lab could finance the white revolution. Something had to be done. That part of the neighborhood hadn't been under his control, but it would have been a matter of time before the two hungry empires crossed and their mutual dreams of dominance and cash ran against one another. They took them out one by one, beat them, cut them, took their cheap guns, and made them run without having to kill one of them. 365 Everyday had come to the notice of the gang as his likely successor when she had the skinhead ringleader tied to the ground and she made everyone watch her mount and fuck him as he lay spread-eagle on the floor. She even let the Nazi come inside her and then she told him he would have to think about his little white sperm swimming inside her black pussy, trying to fuck her black egg and maybe one of his little boy sperms would be successful and she would get pregnant with a white baby with a little dick and when he came out of her pussy she would strangle him in his sleep and send him piece by piece in the mail to their new Nazi house because they would not be staying on this block unless he wanted to fuck her every night or have her ram a bottle up his ass. As Wood watched his sister get the Nazi's dick hard against his will and make him come in spite of himself, he watched the faces of his crew as they wished they could trade places with the Nazi and let 365 Everyday fuck their dick and get pregnant with a mean and monstrous child who would be able to control vast territories with their meanness. He knew he had to keep her happy or he would be killed. He would give her jobs, more responsibility, make her think she would rise up the ranks. He couldn't keep her under control, because he could never match the depth of her hatred or her ability to commit violence and she had more innate intelligence than he could ever hope to have. Whenever she wanted to take control she would have it. The crew would follow. Wood knew he should kill her or have her beaten, but he didn't think the crew would believe in the idea or carry out his orders against her, so his fall seemed all but inevitable. When she dismounted the Nazi and pulled on her pants she told the crew to let him go.

"He's going to grow his hair long and chase after black pussy now. Black pussy loves that soft white boy hair they can twirl in their fingers. He going to say 'I don't know what I was saying and thinking being a fucking head.' I don't have it in me to hate black pussy no more. I'm happy 365 Everyday showed me the way.'"

Wood thought she may be right because her ass and pussy were beautiful and the Nazi watched her as she dressed and his dick took a long time to go limp. He didn't say anything when he left the house and they never saw him or his Nazi crew on the block again, but Wood always imagined him just as 365 Everyday said as a dude with shoulder length hair, smoking pot, with the tattoos on his neck blotted out with a scribble, and the smell of black pussy on his lips.

Wood leaned back and he could feel his blood and brains swirling and dripping into a swampy, soft spot in the middle of his head. Maybe Jack could drill a hole in his skull and drain the liquid, because if the swampy spot could be drained he'd begin to feel better.

"Maybe he needs a doctor," Anne Marie whispered even though she stood very near Wood's ear.

"I'll get Glover and we'll carry him up to a room. We'll prop him against a wall. He's got to have a concussion. I've always been told not to lie down when I've had a concussion. Of course, we probably picked that up from some fucking movie or TV show. I don't know what the fuck to do, but I don't see how we get him to a doctor."

"We could take him to the Metro emergency room."

"I'm not in much of a mood to answer questions why this boy got beat up since I'm between felonies. Those houses are still smoking."

"Let's see how he does today."

Jack left to fetch Glover and Anne Marie adjusted the cold packs on Wood's face and held his wrist to count his pulse and time it by her wristwatch. His young heart pumped like the body knew no distress and his brain hadn't turned into a swampy mess. Glover came down wearing nothing but gym shorts from his high school, blue with a white stripe down the outside of both legs with 'Drillers' printed in blue on one side and an oil derrick and "BHS" printed on the other. Anne Marie held back the impulse to ask him if he had graduated from Bakersfield High because she could reasonably guess the answer. Jack tried to wake up Wood by sprinkling water on his face and repeating his name over and over again, but the one eye Wood could open remained closed. Jack instructed Glover to grab his feet and Jack threaded his arms under Wood's pits and clasped hands on his chest. They lifted him and crabwalked him down the driveway, through the house and up the stairs to an empty room with a clean floor. Glover struggled by the time they reached the room, but Jack showed no strain. Glover dropped Wood's legs and they bounced on the floor as Jack dragged him to a corner nearest the window and propped him against the wall.

"Who's he?" Glover asked through wheezes.

"Your replacement."

"What?"

"Another set of hands."

"Did you beat him up to get him to come here?"

"No, he came to our door like that. He wants to be here." They walked to the landing and Jack shut the door behind them. "Hopefully he'll make it through the day. After the fire I don't need a corpse in the house. The cops will really start sniffing around here."

"What fire?"

"Jesus, you really slept through it too? Half the goddamn block burned down last night and you didn't hear any of it?"

"Seriously?"

"Jesus fucking Christ, Glover! You'd sleep through a holocaust."

"Are you thinking about Nazis? I don't think they're coming back unless they're the ones that burned down the block."

"Could you scale back the stupidity. Sometimes when you talk it feels like I got sand in my eyes or in my blood. Goddamn irritating."

"You brought up The Holocaust."

"Look, we're taking a day off. We have a job tonight. We're going to collect some building materials. I haven't asked you to do anything illegal up to this point, but I'm not going to lie to you. We're breaking into a lumberyard and stealing what we need or at least what we can get our hands on. This is known as a felony. Felonies often have jail time associated with them and I've never asked anyone to commit so much as public expectoration without first knowing the consequences. You and the girl can stay in the house even if you decide you don't want to do it. It's not a condition and I ain't going to force you. But you got to think about what it will mean if we get caught. Public defender. Most likely jail time. B and E on your record for goddamn ever which will narrow your prospects to jobs requiring buckets of sweat and strong knees."

"Save the speeches, Jack. Sounds like fun. So, if we're not working today, then I'm going back to sleep. Gotta save my energy."

Jack nodded his approval and Glover pulled off his shorts and walked into his bedroom. Jack caught a flash of Estonia's bare thigh and hip before the door closed. Jack wanted to ask Glover why he felt the need to show him his cock when he could have just as easily walked into the room, shut the door and then took off his shorts, but Jack decided not to say anything and instead filed it under three possibilities, Glover's comfort with his own body and his understanding that everyone more or less had the same equipment so what difference did it make if Jack saw him naked since he'd seen his own penis every day since he could remember or the beginning of a run of exhibitionism that could either lead to harmless nude strolls through the house or flashing victims on street corners and college campuses and running back to his car and jerking off to the thrill or a budding homosexuality finding expression in odd forms, like exposing oneself to an old man free of that predilection.

The prospect of an entire day without work weighed on Jack as soon as Glover shut the door. The dead space between two felonies could be brutal even when occupied in constructive behavior, Jack knew, but lying around and brooding on his own dark deeds just before another plunge into darkness felt confusing, counterproductive and could lead him to making a mistake at the lumberyard. A list formed to fill the void. 1) Visit the lumberyard to check out layout (even though he'd been there two dozen times and could probably walk through the yard blindfolded.) Pay attention for signs of guard dogs, security cameras, silent alarms, spotlights, guard towers, barbed wire, trap doors, etc; 2) Prep kitchen or what's left of kitchen. Check beams again to see if termites or rot have gotten into them or any of that Nazi spray paint dripped through the cracks. Treat it like cancer. Miss one goddamn cell and we'll have a goddamn tumor growing right under our feet as we wash dishes or cook on the stove; 3) Decide position and full purpose of the garage. This will help check impulses. Otherwise I'll end up with the Taj Garage. I'll build a fucking spire! To what end? Draw blueprints? At least a goddamn rough sketch, otherwise…; 4) Check on Wood. If he takes a turn for the worse decide whether to take him to a doctor. If he dies where will we dispose of the corpse? Throw it in the lumberyard to throw off the scent? Confuse the cops. Kaufman will throw a shit fit. The body becomes a complication. Raise the level of inspection of cops. River would be the best bet. Viking without fire. Immersion and disposal; 5) Check dining room wall. Could be termites. If so, consider abandoning house if damage is extensive. Decision before the lumberyard? Hasn't the arson already committed me? The only way out is forward. I've sunk the ships at the shoreline. Fight or die. Fucking bugs. Do they have specks of Nazi paint in their bellies from gnawing on the wood? Poison. Steal poison; 6) Fuck! I need cement block for the garage footer. That would have been a good trick. The great grand glorious garage sinking into the earth, swallowed by the dirt, considered hubris, an abomination. The yard will have block but that seems impossible to load that too; 7) Fuck Anne Marie. Relieve the tension, take my mind off the job for a while. Lick her pussy and asshole. Get lost in the folds and crevices and her musk. Keep going until my erection feels like its going to burst or I'm going to blow the load before I even get into her pussy. Fuck her balls deep; 8) Look at roof. Use asphalt shingles as a last resort. I want cedar shake. I get one shot at this. What is the vision? What do I want to accomplish? Anyone can build a house with asphalt shingles, sheetrock walls, plywood cabinets, two bushes in front and a deck in back. Where's the goddamn hubris? Where's biting off more than you can chew? What the hell's wrong with having eyes bigger than your stomach? Does the world really need another hack? Another shitty house that's no more than a warehouse, a temporary stop, a crate, an envelope to slip in and out of and discard once you've been delivered to death's door. Push against mediocrity. Be conscious of craft. Always steal the best materials; 9) Make sure Glover can drive a stick. He'll need to drive the truck back from the yard because I'll be driving the flatbed. Another major oversight. Too many strands to remember. Everyday there's a chance of collapse. What are the chances Glover knows how to drive a stick?

Jack pounded on the door of Glover and Estonia's room. Glover padded to the door and opened it a crack, obviously hiding an erection. At least he doesn't feel that open, Jack thought.

"What? I thought we had a day off?"

"Do you know how to drive a stick shift?"

"In a car?"

"A truck. My truck."

"Nope. Never drove a stick."

"Go back to sleep or whatever."

Glover closed the door and Jack tromped down the stairs, watching his feet because he didn't want to catch sight of another task to add to his list, but when he saw his shoes he added that he would need to get a new pair of boots to finish the job because the leather had begun to separate from the sole on the left boot.

Anne Marie had made scrambled eggs and coffee and she smiled when she saw Jack round the corner. His countenance would have lifted had she not been standing in front of the massive black hulk of the burned house.

"Such a face. You'll feel better after you eat something."

"I need you to drive tonight."

"Of course I'm driving the truck tonight. You thought I'd stay home and bite my fingernails, waiting to see if you got caught or not? Really, Jack, do you think I'm the type of woman who could watch Glover drive the truck, knowing for certain that he was going to ram it into a telephone pole given the chance? Really? Did you think I would be able to sleep while you were gone? I know what I've signed on for. Do you want me in or not? I'm not going to keep forcing my way in, Jack. Open the door. Invite me in. I'll do anything for you and I want the same from you."

Despite the weight pressing down on his brain, Jack smiled and it grew into a lusty grin by the time she had finished her lecture. He took her by the hand and led her to the basement. She pulled off her jeans and underwear and placed her hands palms downward on the fourth step. Jack stood behind her and dropped his jeans to the floor. He grabbed her hips and she guided his cock into her. As he pushed, she pushed back, grinding and writhing. Officially, textbooks describe the act in this variation, speed and intensity as rutting and neither of the participants would have argued the point. They both came and Jack almost toppled over in a heap before balancing himself using Anne Marie's hips. Jack stepped back and Anne Marie held her position for a moment before straightening her back. They dressed and Jack kissed her, but he became aware of an ashen taste in his mouth so he ended the kiss before he wanted.

"That made a bad morning better," Jack said.

"When we stop doing that send me on my way. You won't even hear me walk out the door."

"What happened to 'until felonies do us apart?'"

"There's felonies and there is joy. I'm too old and impatient to live another moment of misery."

"You are a wonder."

They walked back to the fire and ate cold eggs and scorched coffee and Jack told Anne Marie about his list. She pointed out that he had left out a few techniques in the basement and that he really shouldn't cut corners or rush through a job. Of the other items on the list she had a way of analyzing his thoughts, parsing the steps needed to complete the task, and simplifying the approach. He likened her ability to a shower after a particularly sweaty and filthy job. Cleanliness brought possibilities and hope. She scrubbed the muddle from his thoughts.

Jack checked the dining room wall and the damage turned out to have been made by a small colony of carpenter bees. Anne Marie and he visited the lumberyard during the day where he bought some poison to snuff out the invaders. The layout of the yard looked exactly as he had remembered it: a small store in the front that sold nails, screws and various hand tools and a huge yard in the back dissected in a grid. The piles of lumber and other building materials were housed under a corrugated aluminum roof held up with steel pillars. The structure had no walls, but an eight foot high chain link fence topped with five strands of barbed wire lined the perimeter. Workers loaded a delivery truck in the middle of the building. Tow motors raced through the grid spewing blue exhaust. A long hydraulic arm swung from the bed of the truck and a worker hooked a bundle of plywood five feet thick. The arm lifted the mass without strain and set it down on the bed with a slight thump. Jack memorized where the stacks of lumber lay that he would need. He even ordered the loading sequence and traced the shortest route from one pile to the next.

"What do you think?" Anne Marie asked on the way home.

"If Cavano gets the gate open and we really have two hours, I'd say pretty simple."

"What was the payment?"

"I don't know, but I set my parameters. No killing. No drugs."

"What's left?"

"Just about every other illegal activity."

"What happens if he calls you and tells you to kill someone or carry drugs somewhere?"

"I told him the parameters."

"I don't think he believes in parameters."

"Then we might have to abandon our little dream and get the fuck out of town. I wouldn't be able to keep them off of us."

"Or it would mean doing the job and being done with it, because that might be the easier of the two."

"I could do the job. It might be easier."

After Jack poisoned the carpenter bees, he spent the rest of the day preparing for the night. Glover, Jack and Anne Marie agreed that Estonia would stay behind, even though she protested a little and tried to explain that she could be a lookout or something until Jack and Anne Marie glared at her, in effect arguing with their eyes that the three of them knew why she could not be included and that she needed to show a little common sense. She accepted her exclusion from the job in return for Jack and Anne Marie dropping the knowledge of her pregnancy from their faces and returning to the planning of the theft. She had hesitated in telling Glover because she thought he would leave, leave her stuck with Jack, leave Ohio and his mistake, leave forever and never see the baby. If she could delay his decision another day it would be another day that he stayed with her, no longer the intimate best friend she told her every thought to, but at least someone breathing, talking, and taking her mind off the coming catastrophe. She thought about telling him right after he told her what Jack had planned for the night, because he should probably know one of his sperm had hit the mark, considering he might be killed or arrested and be in jail for a long time. But the excitement in his voice and his thrill of doing something, especially something wildly illegal, against the kind of people who owned companies and lumberyards and one hundred thousand dollar cars and sprawling hillside mansions daunted her resolve. She smiled at his glee and said something weak like, "Don't get use to it. I'm not Thelma, and you're not Louise." The reference came from an old movie they had watched on cable one night when she first thought she may love him enough to leave with him. She considered it a harmless comment, protective, caring, a comment that maybe hinted at a shining future without worrying if a surveillance camera had picked up enough of his face for a positive I.D. or some true believer cop emptying his gun into Glover's chest over a pile of wood. But Glover said something back like, "What the fuck is that suppose to mean?" Estonia thought he may be reacting to the obvious gender inaccuracies between themselves and the movie characters, but she couldn't think of a male-female robbing duo so she went with Thelma and Louise. Why are men so hung up on ever being confused with women? But he followed up his initial statement with, "Don't you think I can do this?" and Estonia stared at him, her lip trembling, anger ripping through her body.

"I just meant don't get use to it. Don't turn into a criminal. Don't always think that stealing is the way to go. I don't think Jack is teaching the right lessons."

"I'll do what the fuck I want. How about that? I don't give a fuck what you think I can and can't do. I can do this. I'm not going to get caught. And if I want to I'll do it again."

Glover stomped away and shut himself in the outhouse because he knew Estonia gagged every time she came near it. She drifted back to their room and lay down. She watched a wasp that had ventured into the room and tried to find the exit through which it came. It hovered near the ceiling and dropped precipitously as if all power had been cut off to its wings and its body had turned leaden. It caught itself before crashing to the floor and made a run at the light coming through the window. After it smashed its head against the glass the wasp would wail a complaint and bounce against the width of the window.

Finally, it backed off and rose to the ceiling again in concentric circles and regrouped in the air as it prepared for another futile assault. Estonia closed her eyes and transformed into a human-sized wasp with strong, transparent wings. She rose to the ceiling and swooped toward the window, splintering the glass with her thick wasp head. She hovered in the air until she caught the scent of shit and she flew to the outhouse where she kicked off the roof. She spied Glover sitting bare-assed with his hand on his cock. She raised her stinger and drove the spike into his neck. She withdrew it and the sight of his blood on her barb enraged her so she plunged another strike into his heart. She felt the thrill of release as the poison flowed from her body. Unlike a honeybee, she wouldn't die for her anger and have to leave behind the stinger in his flesh. She wouldn't rip herself apart. Her anger had no limit and found expression in the perfect stinger as it continued to plunge again and again into his lifeless body.

Estonia took off her clothes and lay naked on the mattress with her hands clasped over her belly. She must have drifted off to sleep because when she opened her eyes Glover stood above her and she had not heard him come in. She watched as he looked at her, not knowing for a few moments that she had awakened. She imagined Glover had returned from the dead to exact his revenge and she couldn't defend herself because her stinger had gone limp from exhaustion. Will he still look at me the same way once he knows we've made such a colossal mistake? she thought.

"Do you notice anything different about my body?" she asked as she closed her eyes again because if she pretended his body wasn't in the same room, like she spoke into a phone receiver, the news would be easier to deliver.

"You're fucking hot. I can't believe how hot you are. I can't believe you're naked right now in this room in front of me."

"My body is changing. I'm gaining weight. My belly is getting bigger."

"You barely eat and you seem to throw up what you do eat."

"Right."

Estonia waited for the combination to dial in its last number and click open, but Glover took too long and she couldn't hold it in any longer.

"Glover, Jesus, I'm pregnant."

She opened her eyes in time to see a look of horror pass across his face and his stance, previously that of a starving man staring at a plate of fried food, noticeably retreated like she had just told him she had contracted a communicable disease easily passed to anyone within fifteen feet of the affected.

"That's great. Fucking great!" Estonia said, being swept away by a rising anger.

"What do you want me to do about it?"

"Do? Do? Take it back! Crawl up my pussy and take it back! I didn't ask for it! I didn't want it! I want a recall! Signal the retreat. Control-Alt-

Delete, you fuck. Do? Do? Cut off your balls and tell me you're sorry. Tell me you thought you pulled out in time but you must have been mistaken. That you must have dribbled something in, maybe just a couple of goddamn sperm and they hit the mark! Tell me you don't run away from your mistakes."

Glover knew he had taken a misstep and said something stupid, but instead of falling on his knees and embracing her and saying he was sorry for being crass and stupid, whether he held unresolved anger from their previous argument or he actually blamed her for her condition because her egg had rolled a strike down the fallopian tube or because he had no experience on how to surrender before they officially declared war, he took another step away from her, this time toward the door.

"I don't have money for an abortion."

"We don't have money for a baby, asshole. I can't go back to California and I can't go forward. I'm stuck right here. Right here. Right now."

"I'm not stuck."

If Glover had wanted to craft a three word sentence with more import and doom he would have been hard pressed to think of one in six months of trying, succinctly reminding her that he, as the male in the equation, had not become pregnant. Every fear she had imagined coalesced and dropped out of Glover's mouth like so many turds and they tumbled onto her naked belly. She thought, given her past experiences with screaming arguments against her parents, that she would feel the familiar choke in the throat and the rush of words swirling in her head until they formed a blistering stream of invective. None of it happened. She turned icy and calculating. Her thoughts sharpened as she believed that she watched the scene happen to some other dumb girl and that she could lead the poor thing through the ordeal with precise advice. Looking back years later she sometimes championed her response as her first true maternal impulse and other times she thought she may have just grown tired of Glover's drifting and indecision.

"I'm going to have a baby. But I'm not stuck with you. You've done your job."

Glover started pacing like she had set his hair on fire. She thought if he didn't find the door in the next couple of seconds he very well may jump through the window, because a pair of broken legs would be preferable to staying in the room with her. He found the door before the window and he stomped down the stairs, leaving the door swinging on its hinges. She left the door open and she remained on the bed naked. If Jack or Anne Marie or that new boy they dragged into the house happened by and saw her thatch and tits what did it matter? They couldn't see inside her. She could sit in a chair on the street and spread her legs for every passing car and it wouldn't matter. What knowledge of her would the drivers gain? They could gawk at her skin and the folds of her pussy. They could have her shell. Inside her grew something, a secret, a crossword puzzle being slowly revealed, a Rubik's cube clicking into place, a radio station emerging from the static. Only she could feel it growing and only she knew the solution.

Estonia expected Glover to come back after his anger left him, but after hours of waiting and dozing she dressed and went downstairs. She considered having to look for him the latest in a series of spectacular defeats and another obvious clue that Glover had the capacity and intent to leave. She found Jack in the backyard raking ash out of the grass. He had sprayed a large orange rectangle around the footprint of the old garage. He told her that Glover had left hours ago saying he wanted to go for a walk.

"No," Jack said. "He took nothing with him." He stopped raking and stared into her face. "You told him."

"I did."

Jack leaned on his rake as his eyes drifted away from her in search of a neutral spot to stare and contemplate this latest news and he saw the lopsided outhouse with a crown of ash, the two burned houses behind and the concrete pad from the old garage. When it occurred to him the pad and footer of the old garage would have to be taken out before the new garage could be built, he forgot momentarily why his eyes had wandered over his palate of incompetence in the first place.

"Did he say anything else to you?" Estonia asked.

Jack looked back at her and waited for his memory to catch up with his eyes.

"No, he just said he was going for a walk. What did he say to you? Did he say he was leaving? Because if he did that's going to fuck me for tonight. That boy upstairs ain't fit to walk and I bet if you asked him ten times what his name was he would come up with ten different answers."

"Where did he come from?"

"I'm not explaining that right now. Do you think Glover is coming back?"

"I think he'll come back. He was really looking forward to busting into the lumberyard. I don't know how long he's going to stay after that."

She surprised herself by not crying, by not screaming in a high, shrill voice that she should have known he would eventually be an unreliable fuck when she met him in Bakersfield, because he hadn't even graduated high school and he couldn't hold a job longer than a month before he pissed off the manager or forgot to show up for his shift, and by not really caring if he ever came back from his walk. He had one opportunity to help her and his first impulse had been to step away. How could he ever undo that? How could she ever believe his sincerity going forward?

"What happened to those houses?" she asked.

"I'm not explaining that either. There's too much to do to look back."

Jack left her standing and staring at the burned houses as she worried the world had gone crazy while she slept or had been visited by another war that had just missed the room in which she slept. Maybe the injured boy had something to do with the unmooring of the world, she thought.

Glover returned after dark and stayed away from Estonia, because he had no intention of continuing the conversation from earlier in the day. He had decided that Estonia had unfairly sprung the news on him and he had been unprepared, so he had not been at his best. News like that had to be meditated on for at least a few days before a sensible answer could be given. Jack swooped in and spouted a long string of directions that described Glover's exact role in the theft, really, to act as a lookout since he had never driven a tow motor, couldn't find the specific kinds of lumber Jack needed, really didn't know the difference between a 2 x 4 and a 2 x 6, had never driven a stick or a truck with a double-clutch and couldn't be trusted to operate the hydraulic arm to lift the lumber onto the flatbed because he would want to play with it and possibly kill Anne Marie or damage the lumber with his playfulness. Basically, Glover's presence would free Anne Marie to perform all the tasks he should have been able to perform as he watched for cops, security guards and German shepherds or Dobermans running at them with a purpose. Anne Marie seemed comfortable with every task Jack described so he elevated her position to co-conspirator and Glover's dropped to nothing more than a helper, although Cavano would know nothing of her role.

They left the house close to midnight and drove in silence to the lumberyard. Anne Marie sat in the middle of the bench seat with her hands on her lap. Glover looked out the window at the gloomy neighborhoods that perfectly reflected his mood. Jack whistled a song through his moustache as tuneless and flat as the growl of the truck's engine. He parked the truck on a side street in front of a dark house, facing the back gate of the yard. A dim security light illuminated the gate and the chain and lock that kept it closed.

A few minutes after one o'clock a car crept down the street and paused in front of the gate. The red brake lights masked the interior until a figure jumped from the passenger seat with a pair of bolt cutters. He snapped the chain with two powerful bites and the figure crawled back into the car, which then moved unhurriedly away.

"Goddamn drama. I could have done that. Cavano could have just told me to snap the chain with some goddamn cutters. Everybody loves thinking of plans. He thinks we're goddamn Navy Seals."

Jack started the truck and eased toward the gate. Ten yards away Glover hopped out and sprinted toward the entrance, untangled the chain and lock and threw them to the ground. He swung both sections of the gate open. Jack pulled in and Glover shut the gate behind the truck. He parked near a shed that he saw the drivers walk in and out of during his reconnaissance mission and guessed the keys to the delivery trucks would be hanging on hooks in a small wooden cabinet decorated with either a beaver shot of a too skinny, too young, too brainless and too hairless bimbo or a bumper sticker or two asserting the right of Americans to hunt any species to extinction, hate homosexuals or drive in a manner that led other drivers to eat shit. After he smashed the lock and took two steps into the shed he spied such a cabinet covered with American flag stickers, yellow smiley faces, hands with perfectly extended middle fingers and a bumper sticker bemoaning the greed and liberalism of Congress. Jack pulled open the latch and found all four sets of truck keys hanging in a neat row. He grabbed all four and walked out of the shed as fast as he could. He hobbled across the expanse of the large gravel lot to where the trucks were parked. He picked the first truck he came to and tried the keys until he found the match. As he scrambled into the cab he heard a tow motor start, meaning that Anne Marie had begun to collect the wood. Jack started the truck and drove it to the loading area, making sure to point it at the unlocked gate should they have to leave in a hurry. Anne Marie zipped into the area with a pallet of 2 x 4s and they switched places, Jack on the tow motor and Anne Marie in the truck working the hydraulic arm. Jack had driven tow motors since his first job as a teenager in a vast cold storage warehouse and felt more comfortable driving one than he did his own truck. Anne Marie had picked a worn-in Caterpillar that pulled to the left on the straightaways when he let the motor out full throttle, but the forklift purred up and down and had unbelievable power.

Jack roared up and down the aisles, finding the wood he needed, plucking pallets off the shelves or off the ground and racing them to the loading area. Anne Marie hooked them as they came and stacked them neatly on the flatbed. Glover lurked in the shadows on a stack of wood and stared at the gate, the street and the houses beyond. One car had driven past at normal speed and the houses had stayed dark after the truck and tow motor had shattered the peaceful night. He watched the same spot for an hour and a half as Jack and Anne Marie filled the flatbed. He had all but decided to sneak into the stacks and masturbate to the image of Estonia's naked body lying in repose on their shared bed when he saw a silhouette of a person slip between the ends of the gate and walk directly across the gravel towards them, not bothering to skim the shadows or approach slowly. Glover had stared at the spot for so long he couldn't process that the scene had now changed, that new information had been introduced and that his role of lookout had suddenly been given purpose. As the figure walked closer Glover could see he headed in the direction of the truck and Anne Marie and that he held his right arm out parallel to the ground. He held a gun in front of him. Glover felt his body wanting to move to the left, to the right, to charge the approaching silhouette or retreat through the stacks of wood and hurdle the barbed wire with a single leap, but he stayed rooted to the spot unsure whether to shout warning to Jack and give away his position in the shadows or wait to see the scene unfold and decide how to act after the figure made his intentions clear. Because it took effort and a clear decisive act to shout warning, Glover stayed mute and watched the man advance, holding off a decision for at least another couple of minutes.

Anne Marie swung one of the last loads onto the flatbed when she saw the hand holding the gun and realized the gunman pointed it toward her neck. She followed the arm to the man behind the hand holding the gun. Young and doughy with dumb eyes half hidden by swollen lumps of flesh crowding them from above and below, the man wore a security guard's uniform, untucked and in bad need of ironing. Anne turned off the motor of the hydraulic arm and turned herself in the seat to face the gun.

"What do you want?" she asked with as much annoyance as she could muster given that she had a gun pointed toward her body.

"I know what you're doing. Where's the other two? I've been watching you!"

"Who are you?"

"Somebody who knows what you're doing. Where's the other two?"

"What two? What are you talking about?"

"You're going to pay me. I know the deal, but you're going to pay me. Tell me where the other two are."

Glover stepped from the shadows and walked toward the gun, unable to think of anything else to do. The man turned and pointed the gun at Glover as he approached.

"There's one. That's far enough."

Glover stopped about twenty feet away. The three of them heard the roar of the tow motor before they saw Jack careen around a corner of an aisle and head straight for the security guard. Jack's calculation that he could travel the distance between the corner and the guard before the man could aim the gun with any accuracy proved to be correct. Just as the guard thought he had a reasonable chance of mortally wounding Jack with a bullet and started to apply pressure to the trigger, the left fork on the tow motor gored him in the right knee. The tow motor shot past and carried the guard with it, ripping and tearing the leg. The gun clattered against the ground and slid against the tire of the flatbed. Jack slammed on the brakes and the man sailed off the fork and landed on his neck and head. He flopped against a stack of wood and blood poured out of the nearly severed leg. Jack jumped off the tow motor and ran to the mangled body, pointing at the gun as he passed.

"Pick that up, Glover. Anne Marie, is everything tied down?"

"Yes, except the last bit."

"You get in my truck and get out of here."

Anne Marie jumped off the flatbed and she and Glover sprinted to Jack's truck. Jack stooped over the dead man, trying to determine if he still breathed, standing in his blood. On the left chest of his uniform lay a patch that said Liberty Security and on his right chest hung a tin badge in the shape of a star with a screaming eagle bursting from its center. Who the fuck was this? What had happened? Didn't they get the goddamn memo out to stay the fuck away for two hours so Jack could take the lumber he needed for his Taj Garage? Jack tried to put an explanation together to know how to proceed. So, Cavano or one of his crew tells the security guard to go get a lap dance or get blown from the hours of one to three and not to worry about the reason and not to worry about losing an eight dollar an hour job because if Liberty Security sees fit to fire you Cavano can find you another job as long as you're willing to go the extra mile, as long as you don't refuse any job and you don't come up with parameters to limit your usefulness. The guard doesn't like lap dances or his penis emits an odor that he's embarrassed about so he won't let prostitutes touch their lips to it and he decides to watch what he isn't suppose to watch. Sometime during the robbery he gets the idea that these three thieves are hauling thousands of dollars worth of lumber out of the yard so one way of augmenting an eight dollar an hour job is to get paid by the thieves. They'll give him five hundred bucks so there's no trouble and no police, right? They'll be happy to pay it because they don't want witnesses or cops and if the one witness to the crime says all he wants is five hundred bucks and he'll go away and stay silent forever then everyone makes out, right? The thieves get their lumber and the guard gets paid, unless there's a crazy fuck on a tow motor who boils with rage when he sees Anne Marie threatened with a gun. What's a crazy fuck to do when he sees the only tether he has to this world about to be gunned down by a pudgy guard with retarded eyes who's unable to think through all the possible scenarios of a half-baked plan? Always include the possibility of a crazy fuck on a tow motor to blast apart your plans. It's called the chaos theory.

Jack knew that if he left the body, first Cavano, then Kaufman, would contract to have him killed. Once Cavano's men successfully assassinated him, Kaufman's men would follow and hack apart his body or shit in his corpse's mouth to add an exclamation point to his just extermination. He had to clean up the mess and risk being caught, but in all likelihood the person due back at three lay dead at his feet. So, he had some time to do it right. The night had returned to a dreadful quiet after all the engines had been turned off. Skunks, raccoons and opossums slunk in the shadows and rooted through garbage cans. He found a big blue tarp and laid it out on the concrete away from the pool of blood. Bloody footprints fouled the area, but Jack decided to leave cleaning them up for last.

He dragged and rolled the corpse on the tarp. The leg hung by a single tendon and threatened to fall off completely, but it stayed attached long enough for Jack to put the body in position, flat on its back, arms folded over the chest, with the leg fit into the space it should occupy. He wrapped the tarp around the body and tied the ends with rope. Jack threw a piece of plywood on the ground and dragged the corpse on to it. He jumped back on the tow motor and maneuvered the forks under the plywood and lifted the body. He drove over to the flatbed and raised the fork to the top of its height and deposited the body on the top of the lumber. Jack jumped off the tow motor and hauled himself up the flatbed and then the stack of wood. As he climbed up the wood he happened to look down and he saw the blood had seeped toward a drain and looked like a long-stemmed rose. For the first time he became aware of the buzz of the vapor light overhead that sounded like a hive of bees. He held the wood tight for a moment, thinking he might pass out, before he lashed the body to the lumber.

He jumped off the flatbed and the jolt against his knees almost knocked him over because the pain burst alive in shocking and severe waves. He caught his breath, limped to the tow motor and drove it back to its designated parking space. He wiped off the fork and checked the tire tread to make sure he hadn't driven through the blood. He ran to the shed where he had found the truck keys. He looked like a thoroughbred still running after it had shattered three of its legs. He rifled through the cabinets until he found chemical degreaser for concrete and a push broom. First, he pushed the blood toward the drain, causing a giant smear. Blood had splattered everywhere, on his shoes, pant legs, hands, on half the loading area it seemed. The broom made it worse and when he poured the chemical degreaser the reaction between blood and chemical created a pink foam that moved no easier toward the drain. He needed water. He searched the back of the building and found an outside spigot and made one more trip to the shed and found a coiled hose. At this point he thought there must be either sparks or blood shooting from his knees, but he stopped himself from looking. As he carried the hose across the lot he sensed that night waning and daybreak bearing down on him. A pulse had quickened. A few more cars wandered down the street. A few more phlegmy coughs signaled the end of REM and a few more alarms for the early risers signaled the end of sleep altogether.

Jack snaked the hose from the spigot through the lumber to the blood smear. The hose had a sprayer attached to its end with enough water pressure to produce a strong jet that blasted the blood off the concrete and to the drain. After spraying it clean he again poured the chemical on the concrete and on the tops of his shoes and hems of his pant legs. He sprayed the concrete, shoes and pants and repeated the process three times. He wouldn't beat a forensics examination, but he wanted to clean the area well enough to pass the notice of the yard workers who would no doubt be nursing hangovers from sex, pot, televised sports and booze. He enlarged the radius of his cleaning and poured the degreaser until he emptied the bottle. He wound up the hose and replaced it back in the shed and threw the broom on the flatbed since he had no time to clean it. He gave the area one last look. In the daylight the spots he had missed would probably be obvious, but under the vapor light everything looked clean and wet. He climbed into the cab and threw the empty bottle of degreaser on the floor.

Jack maneuvered the truck through the gate that Anne Marie and Glover had left partially open and crept down the street one mile per hour under the speed limit. He wouldn't have time to dump the body, unload the lumber and abandon the flatbed in some out of the way random place that would not lead the police back to his house. The body had to be separated from the truck and never be found because the more he thought about it the more he became convinced that if the murder didn't stir up the cops then it would stir up Cavano and Kaufman who would take a dim view of his sloppiness. All of them would link the disappearance of the guard with the robbery, but no one would know exactly what happened and the cops may even consider the poor doughy guard a suspect. Cavano and Kaufman didn't live under burdens of proof, evidence that would stand up under intense scrutiny, or whether a skilled and crafty lawyer had the ability to convince twelve dolts of innocence or guilt. They would know Jack had killed the guard, not really care about the circumstances since the guard had not followed instructions, but would care if Jack had left enough evidence in the yard to cause inquiries. Who could have imagined the guard would bleed so much that it would look like Jack had slaughtered an elephant? Jack looked at his hands holding the steering wheel without gloves and he thought of the door to the truck, the tow motor, the door knob of the shed, the stickered cabinet, all covered with perfect or partial fingerprints from his greasy hands. Of course his fingerprints were on file in six states, including Ohio, and one thumb print would be enough to identify him and bring his past to bear against him. He hoped the deal Kaufman set-up included a clause that there would be no investigation or that the cops would be slipped some money to write a vague report, detailed enough to pass through an insurance adjuster but containing no real information that could actually lead to an arrest.

Jack stopped in front of his house. Anne Marie had parked his truck in the grass so the driveway lay clear. He backed-up the flatbed without touching a blade of grass, so deftly did he steer. He continued backing until the back tire rolled over the remnants of the old garage. Anne Marie and Glover stood around a small circle of fire with their arms wrapped around their torsos even though the night had stayed pleasantly warm. Jack unlashed the body and used a hand signal for Glover and Anne Marie to stand back. He pushed the corpse off the truck and it landed as something ripe and soft would land, two hundred and twenty pounds of soft and ripe falling fifteen feet. Jack jumped down and joined them by the fire.

"What are we going to do with it?" Anne Marie whispered over the flames.

"I have an idea," Jack said as he pointed to the outhouse, but they couldn't pick up the direction he pointed or they may have thought he meant one of the burned houses, so he spoke instead. "The shitter. We put him in the shitter."

"You can't be serious, Jack," Anne Marie said as she put a hand to her mouth, thinking she could retch any second.

"Let's unload the lumber first. We have to drag the outhouse off the hole using chains and my truck, but I can't get back here until this flatbed's out of here."

"We can't put him in there, Jack. Does the word abomination mean anything to you?"

"Look, he can't never be found and I'm thinking he'll never be found in there. Besides, we haven't filled it up with much shit yet. We still got plenty of room."

"But on our property? Where we're going to live?"

"I'm not likely to forget killing him anyhow and this way we can keep an eye on him. I can pay my penance by tending to his grave. I'm not likely to feel better if he was floating in the river or buried behind some factory or burned in a fifty-five gallon drum. We'll plant something on top of him and with his flesh and all that shit it might grow taller than the house. What else can we do?"

"I don't see another option either. It's goddamn creepy burying a corpse in your yard."

"I'm stuck on the idea. I can't see another option either. Sometimes an idea can be dominant and just because its dominant it blots out all other possibilities that might be better but you just can't see them. So, unless the two of you can come up with a better option of disposing of the body it's going to be the shitter."

"I see what you mean. It makes sense, I guess."

Glover stayed silent as he stared at the lump underneath the tarp.

"I didn't want to kill him. He's a goddamn bleeder."

"I think his neck broke," Glover piped in with a thick voice.

"He wasn't supposed to be there.'

"It feels really late. We need to get this wood off the truck and get rid of the truck somewhere before we worry about the body." She looked up and hoped she didn't see the first streaks of dawn. She saw a patchwork of muted stars in a lightening sky.

Anne Marie climbed into the cab and found the control panel of the hydraulic arm as Jack hauled himself up the flatbed. He hooked the bundles and Anne Marie swung the arm so the bundles landed in the yard. Glover unhooked them when she set them down and she swung the arm back towards Jack. In this way they unloaded the truck in under an hour. They stacked the wood in perfect rows with an alley for his truck to drag the outhouse. Jack allowed himself a moment to watch Anne Marie in action as she swung the last pallet in place. He wondered what kind of mischief they could have conjured had they stayed together when they were young. There weren't many beautiful and thieving women in the world who could operate a hydraulic arm, drive a stick shift and so easily accept the slaughter of another human being with the aplomb Anne Marie had demonstrated. Yet, there she sat with sweat on her face and her heavy breasts, concentrating on the task at hand in a hurricane of chaos. He wanted to breathe the musk of her skin and consummate this horrible night with a quick fuck over the boy's corpse, demonstrating to the sad and mangled body that people who knew what they were doing and knew when to follow orders and when to freelance lived to fuck, while doughy idiots with half-baked plans got buried in a shitter unceremoniously. He jumped off the flatbed to clear his mind and barked at Anne Marie to stow the arm and follow him in his truck. He told Glover to stay back and guard the corpse to keep rats and stray dogs off it.

They snaked their way out of the neighborhood and entered a highway going south. As they picked up speed Jack constantly checked the rearview and side mirrors to make sure Anne Marie had stayed with him. They drove to an abandoned auto assembly plant twenty-five miles away. Jack thought leaving the truck in another county might confuse the police enough about the origin and residency of the perpetrators or cause enough of a bureaucratic snag between rival police departments that the matter of a simple and insured burglary would be dead-filed within a week. He had no unique understanding of police departments. He just wanted the flatbed out of his neighborhood. Every other thought he draped over his reasoning started out as nothing more than hopeful speculation.

Jack pulled the truck into a weedy asphalt lot through a broken gate and drove near the center of the black field big enough to hold 6,000 cars of workers who had been fired a decade before. Jack left the keys in the ignition and climbed into the passenger side seat of his truck. They drove in silence almost halfway back until Anne Marie gave Jack a sideways glance and Jack returned the look.

"I can't think of anyplace else to put the body. I think you're right about it being the best place," said Anne Marie.

"I don't like the idea any better than you do. I guess I'll get the chance to be the caretaker of my own murder."

"I wouldn't call it murder. It was like self-defense."

"I wouldn't do nothing different. I saw that boy pointing a gun at you and I could feel myself going crazy and there wasn't much I could do to stop myself. That boy was a goner the second he decided to point that gun at you. If I didn't have a tow motor I would have strangled him with my own hands."

Anne Marie placed her right hand over Jack's left even though the vibration of the truck on the highway made one-handed steering both frightening and thrilling. Her thoughts and feelings about the killing hadn't settled into a construct recognizable and firm, but Jack's motive meant quite a deal to her even though the doughy kid looked scared and confused and probably would have given up the gun willingly had he been asked. The ripping of his leg and the sickening sound the snapping of his neck made when he landed on the concrete would be memories she would carry with her until she died, and she had a hard time reconciling any motive, no matter how romantic, with that outcome. But what if the guard in his nervousness had pulled the trigger and the resulting bullet had torn through her neck, blasting away the carotid artery and trachea? She had to entertain every possibility before she contaminated her thinking with judgment or condemnation of Jack's anticipatory attack. Would he have thrown my body in the outhouse? She kept her questions to herself, not wanting to know the answer.

They pulled into the house and found Glover near the spot where they had left him, by the almost dead fire, staring at the body in the tarp. Jack pulled out a flashlight from his toolbox and ran downstairs to the basement. He came back with two thick chains and strode over to the outhouse. They had built the structure like a small house so he had to be clever and not rely on brute strength.

He inspected the structure and hobbled back to the basement and returned with a cordless drill and two thick eyelet hooks. He dropped to his knees in front of the outhouse, drilled the starter holes in the front floor beam and screwed the eyelets into the board until the shafts disappeared. He fed each chain through an eyelet and hooked the chain to itself. Anne Marie backed-up the truck and Jack looped the chains around the trailer hitch and motioned Anne Marie to inch forward. He stopped her when the chains were taut. Jack motioned again and she slowly pushed the accelerator to the floor. The floor joists of the outhouse had been nailed together in the same direction as the truck pulled so when a force capable of moving the structure was achieved the joists acted as skis and the outhouse jauntily bounced across the yard. Jack stopped her before she dragged it down the street. The three walked to the corpse and stood over it. They had to drag the body since if one of them accidently grabbed the leg it very well could have come off in their hands. Each took a handful of tarp near the head and pulled the doughy mass across the grass. Jack could have done it himself, but he thought the fact Anne Marie and Glover were willing to help meant they had fully accepted or were well on there way to accepting their culpability and their roles as accessories. At the edge of the hole they straightened their backs and tried to slow their breathing.

"Would it be worse if we said a few words?" Anne Marie asked.

"I suppose I could try. I mean it's not going to be any worse than what we've already done. It won't help us much, but it might help him some."

"Give it a try. If you get stuck or don't have anything to say I'll chime in."

"Son, you're dead and in a tarp and about to be buried in a pit of human waste, but don't think too bad about it because it's where we all end up one way or another. You left your house today with the thought of new possibilities, new money, a new scheme to lighten the load off of your back because the bills seem relentless and there's never enough money. It's sad to think that the money you tried to steal from us would have gone straight to a utility company, a liquor store, or some computer store for an armful of video games and there ain't nothing sadder than death, except maybe that point in some people's lives when they should be dead but their body just won't give up the ghost and they all sit around together like a field of dying weeds waiting for the end. But I don't imagine you thought of dying when you left your house. There's an old proverb from Africa, or the Indians who lived on this land before we come, that says the house is a womb and with each day we are born again into the world. It's something to think about and remember because each day is full of promise and you have the opportunity to straighten out all the crooked things you did the day before or at least to forgot enough of them to get out of bed and face a new world. Because if everyone is being born again then the world is new everyday. But one of those days is the day you die and you stop being able to create new worlds. That's where you are now by my hand, at least by my tow motor driving ability. You've seen your last new world. I wonder if it's the world you will take with you into the afterlife. Do you get to pick the world or is it the last one you experience? I'm sorry that your friends and family will forever wonder what became of you and they won't have a grave to weed when they feel like they are missing you, but I don't plan on spending the rest of my days in a cage. First of all, that's not much raw material to spin new worlds out of, seeing how it's a building full of men ass fucking and secondly, if a person takes the last world he created with him into the afterlife, I'm not particularly keen spending infinity in such a manner. It's a sad fact that for your bones they will lie unknown until some archeologist two thousand years from now unearths you and writes a paper on ceremonial shit burials on the late-twentieth and early twenty-first century's urban environments. Finally, whatever happens after death, face it down with courage and your head held high. It's not your fault you ran into a crazy fuck like me who loves a woman more than anything he's ever known. I know it don't mean much coming from a man like me. I've not led an exemplary life. I wear no collar or vestments. I have heard the chimes at midnight and the rooster crow. I've been mean and petty. I've been drunk and lost. I've committed violence with my hands. But let this temporal world go. Forget your video games and your pornography, forget the pain and shame of dying with a cut-off leg and a broken neck for a few shekels, some filthy lucre. Forget vengeance and pride and forget the possibility of more possibilities. Release your hatreds and prejudices and your ambitions. You've been reminded that you are part of an unseen universe. Your worries are rot. Take your place in the lap of God. Amen."

They all stared at the body wrapped in the tarp and considered briefly where their deaths would take place and who would bury them, if they were so lucky to be buried and not left on the ground to rot and be eaten by maggots and scavengers. On a sign from Jack they bent down and pushed the corpse into the hole where it landed on the soft bed of shit. Jack retrieved three shovels and they threw enough dirt in the hole to cover the body in six inches of clay. After brushing the dirt from their hands and jamming the shovel blades into the ground so they formed a small copse, Jack drove his truck to the back of the lot, over the remnants of the garage and through the rotten wooden fence lying on the perimeter of his yard. He and Anne Marie hooked the chains to the back of the outhouse and Jack pulled it back in place with the truck.

"Jack, I'm thinking I won't be shitting in there anymore," Glover said. "I mean we could probably put some plumbing in the house, right?"

"We have wood for the garage, but we don't have copper. The garage and the kitchen floor are first. I've got to figure out a way to get plumbing, so until then you'll have figure out where you're going to shit because this is the only option we have here."

"It's not right."

"Maybe, but right has nothing to do with it."

"Maybe you should have started with the plumbing. Maybe running water shouldn't be considered a luxury."

"It'll give you another reason to visit Mary Kelly."

Glover walked away, shaking his head and thinking he would never find a spot in the house or the yard or possibly the planet where people lived by some basic and normal rules and girls got pregnant when they wanted to and not at the worst possible moment and you weren't expected to kill people over lumber and you certainly weren't expected to take a dump on a human corpse every morning after coffee. How could he spend his time perched on the seat knowing what rotted under him? He imagined taking a crap on a grave in a fancy cemetery for rich people crowded with granite monoliths, pylons, Doric columns, and carved angels watching over the army of dead and he decided that even though it would serve them right considering they had stolen so much money in their lifetimes and somehow and somewhere impoverished whole cities of families like his own, he wouldn't be able to eliminate under those circumstances, so how could he crap on the poor security guard not much older than him and probably just as poor? Jack was right, he would talk to the lady down the street, Mary Kelly, and see if he could use her toilet. Maybe he'd start fucking her because at least she had running water and a toilet and had lived past the time of getting pregnant or knew how to prevent it.

The next two weeks were somber, quiet and productive. Jack and Glover smashed up the old concrete pad with sledgehammers and dug and poured a footer for the new structure. Once Jack put his hammer to the first nail he thought of nothing else but building the garage. He ate less, pushing the food around his plate in a preoccupied manner, slept half as many hours than before the construction began, but he still had sex with Anne Marie every night although he found himself lasting longer and longer because even though he had a naked woman in his arms who acted as a willing and able partner who had an array of tricks and techniques that would have made a stripper blush, he found himself thinking of the next day's work during coitus and sometimes forgot his dick remained inside her until she moved her hip a certain way or moaned so loudly it snapped him out of his reverie. Fortunately, he never gave voice to his plans and never asked her opinion about the garage during sex, successfully avoiding humiliating her.

So, the garage rose in a fury and kept rising until Jack had built a two story building with a loft above the space for two cars. The loft had high ceilings and a hole at either end where five foot long windows would be placed. He roughed in a spot for a bathroom, small kitchen and a closet where a small furnace could be hooked up. In an act of fancy he made the staircase to the loft spiral and placed it inside a narrow turret that bulged from the left front corner of the building and ended in a high and sharp peak. The turret could have been considered wasteful, a fantasy, especially on a garage, and where the wall of the turret met the roofline would cause nothing but problems in the freezing and thawing of winter, but once Jack had the image in his mind he poured all of his energy into its construction. He hadn't settled on the turret when he had made the material list for the theft so he ran short of wood. Peeling off some money from his dirty and worn roll of bills he went back to the lumberyard, gambling the place didn't have surveillance cameras he hadn't seen and that a grainy picture of his ugly mug didn't hang over the counter with a reward listed above or below his face. He chuckled audibly at his wild west conceit and wondered if he would ever be able to think without the crutch of clichés. If they caught him by a wanted poster or by some other means he expected he would have the courage to hang himself with a bed sheet before his life in a cage had truly begun.

Jack walked the yard and saw the blood stains he had missed under the dim vapor light, drops really, that had turned brown and gray from exposure to the air and being run over by tow motor tires loaded with wood. The place looked the same except for a new chain on the gate, a new door on the shed, and a new security guard prowling the yard and carrying a black revolver that seemed to hang past his knee. The guard was off-duty Oliver Brankowski, who, with his partner Hayes, had written the original burglary report for the lumberyard. The owner told them that his security guard had come up missing and that he worked at the yard only a couple of months and that he couldn't believe a retard like him could plan and pull a major theft costing in the thousands. They had turned it over to the detectives. Brankowski asked for a moonlighting job a couple of days after the report had been written. A persistent insomnia had taken hold of him and the job in the yard could make his sleeplessness pay.

A missing person's report came in from an old widow who hadn't seen her tenant in a month, which she thought very unlike him because he kept a regular schedule. Hayes moaned when the sergeant gave them the task of following-up on the report since the detectives didn't bother with such reports until the beat cops unearthed something. These calls usually ended with Brankowski and Hayes or any other cop on the sergeant's shit list entering some dirty and forgotten apartment and finding suicides with half a head blasted away or hanging blue-faced from a light fixture or covered in vomit and blood from lethal drug and alcohol cocktails or victims of massive heart attacks or aneurysms cut down in the middle of the most mundane tasks, cooking eggs, applying makeup, shitting, reading or sleeping. So, Hayes and Brankowski, knew they had been buried deep, probably at the very bottom, of the sergeant's list of most favored officers, and responded to the call at the end of their shift. They used the landlady's key to enter the second floor apartment, the top half of a double home. Even though they didn't find a corpse, they concluded the tenant must be dead somewhere. It looked like the homes of heart attack cases, everything in place, a load of food in the fridge, knickknacks and talismans lining the shelves, clothes neatly tucked into dresser drawers, a small pile of soiled clothes at the bottom of the closet, a note to remind himself of an errand now three weeks past, coins scattered on the kitchen counter, a dark computer when turned-on revealed a history of porno and dating sites and an aberrant interest in how to raise turnips, but nothing to suggest an interest in methods of suicide or research on how to dissect goats and prostitutes and how to mix and match their parts. They surmised he had planned to live his tucked away life and eat from the loaded fridge in a prolonged binge. They typed what they found without the speculation, because the detectives and the sergeant hated speculation and overly descriptive language, and forwarded the report on. Hayes told the landlady she might want to get someone to clean the apartment because, in his opinion, her tenant would not be back. When Brankowski started the job at the lumberyard he snooped around some and saw the bleached concrete and the brown blood stains Jack had missed, but he kept the information to himself. He had given up being promoted to detective a long time ago and the minute he forwarded information or evidence the detectives should have found themselves he would either be mocked for acting outside his pay grade or reprimanded for taking a job at an open crime scene and acting like some kind of half-assed undercover jerk in a security uniform. He decided to keep the job and use the money to buy the biggest flat screen his wall could hold.

Jack pulled the wood he needed, loaded it onto his truck and paid without being arrested. He drove home in higher spirits than he had felt in two weeks. Usually when he had to part with some of his fiercely saved money his stomach felt leaden and he thought of ways to show contrition just short of flagellation, but the slim possibility of not being punished for the murder overrode his anxiety concerning his slowly disappearing savings. Soon, they would have to find ways to make money, including jobs if necessary, or in the winter they would starve in their newly renovated home. He had heard the scrap yards were paying good prices for copper and Glover, Wood and he could strip a house of its plumbing in about an hour once the boys were trained. They could make enough on the harvesting without having to commit the best hours of the best days to creating somebody else's fortune. Wonders of the world, cathedrals, monuments of human achievement could not be squeezed into the hours after work or on weekends. Until finished, the house would be his purpose. The best his body still had to offer would be reserved for the house and work could wait until the last nail had been driven home in this rebirth.

The idea of buying or building a house had been in the back of his mind for decades. He had tried several times before when something would take root in him, a desire for permanency or an exhaustion from rolling through the country at one hundred miles per hour every day of every year. So, when this impulse budded and started growing he would begin to horde money, thinking the house would be a possibility after he had saved a certain amount of cash. He would eat nothing but a bowl of white rice and a shot of whiskey each day for a month or two or three straight and he would take as much overtime as his employer could give. He would siphon gas from his neighbor's tank and would give up his apartment and crash on the couches and floors of anyone who would have him. In these spells he usually resorted to frantic masturbation because it cost no money and remained under his control. Friends from work always told him he could just as easily find a working woman and use her money to pay the bills while he saved, but the thought smacked of dependency and deceit to him so he chose the path of the anchorite. Though, each time something would happen to derail his plans. A woman would kiss him on the ear and his resolve would waver and his disgust of himself for jerking off three or four times a day would roar to the surface and soon he would be blowing money in restaurants and bars and on clothes and shoes, throwing down a trail of money in the chase of flesh that mocked his thrift and sacrifice. Another time, after nearly six months of economy, a plank fell from a scaffolding and very nearly knocked the brains from his skull and caused him to lie in a hospital bed for a month with scrambled thoughts and a gruesome dent while the doctors zipped away to the countryside with his cash in their foreign make convertibles with their impossibly pretty wives. Or worst of all, after a prolonged period of fasting, self-abusing celibacy, and sleeping on a carpet thick with dust mites and animal hair, he would snap under the weight of his own impulses and binge on whatever his appetites demanded. His vision of his house would collapse into a blue dot like an old television tube going dark, and he would gamble, whore, and drink until the money had been spent, but the blue dot always stayed on the screen and never entirely extinguished. He began to think what he wanted could not be achieved in one lifetime. So, over the years he made and spent fortunes that could have paid for twenty modest houses but none of these possibilities matched this monument blooming in his imagination.

This attempt began on a lonesome and cold night in the desert as Jack held a dented silver flask in one hand and a can of coke in the other as he sat on a rock staring at a clump of Joshua trees. He alternated drinks from either hand and kept drinking until the rock on which he sat felt like an appropriate and enticing mattress. His life had unraveled again in a way his life always seemed to come undone. His boss had turned miserly and mean, taking to snarling and trying to short his crew's pay by deducting hours from their week arbitrarily and illegally. His girlfriend had taken up religion and spent her weekends praying and refusing points of entry that, until the Word had taken hold of her, had been willingly offered. He felt lonesome and drunk, aching to begin again but wondering if he had any more beginnings to begin. The familiar image of Anne Marie scissoring her way across a black field came to him. She made her way toward him and when she raised her white face to the sun and smiled broadly a terrible ripping pain shook his intestines. He rolled to his side, clutching his gut and crying against his pain and lonesomeness and believing he just might die on the baked hard dirt. He threw up whiskey, coke and blood and bile and crawled on his hands and knees toward his truck. If death had come then he would die fighting and struggling and clawing, at least moving toward something and not accept it passively on his back. He made it only a few feet before another spasm sent him to the ground clutching his flaming gut. The fifteen year old Anne Marie touched his burning forehead and stroked his cheek with the back of her hand, feeling like an ice cube had been drawn across a scorching griddle. She unbuttoned her shirt and exposed her perfect breasts. She pulled his head to her chest and the coolness of her flesh ratcheted down his fever a notch below burning. She cradled and rocked him until he calmed and abandoned the fight. He would welcome death with diginity and calm. She lay his head on a rock and stood up, walking toward a wooden porch with a screen door and two wooden chairs on either side of the front door. She beckoned him to follow but locomotion seemed absolutely impossible, so he stayed where he lay and sank into the sand.

Jack returned to consciousness in a hospital room as he recovered from a burst appendix. He would have died in the desert holding the trunk of a Joshua tree with his head on a stone pillow if it hadn't been for a carload of teenagers looking for a quiet place to get high and practice group sex. The driver thought of giving his friends a thrill by driving over Jack's body once he saw him sprawled out on the ground, but he stayed the impulse because he feared breaking his front axel on Jack's massive head. They called the police and gave the location of the body before speeding away, avoiding arrest for drunk driving, public intoxication, drug possession, driving without a license, expired tags, driving without wearing a seat beat, underage drinking, statutory rape, carrying a concealed weapon, driving with a busted headlight, receiving stolen property, possession of drug paraphernalia, probation violations, driving while engaged in sodomy and altering the intake flow of the car's catalytic converter.

Jack rolled his fever dream back and forth through his conscious thoughts until a permanent groove had been worn away in his thinking. He didn't often take to signs, mythologies or bringing dreams into the conscious world to be dissected and analyzed like they were maps to better understanding, but Anne Marie had sprung up again and this time refused to be budged until he properly acknowledged the import of her visitation. His girlfriend, who had gone by Nikki Wick before she found the Word and who now gave Jack vague mumbled answers when he asked about her identity like she had become a chrysalis being formed, came to the hospital room loaded on a pharmaceutical homebrew and laid hands on Jack, telling him once the poison of sin had been extracted from his flesh his spirit would recover. Then, she asked him for money and he told her he lost his cash in the desert or it had been stolen by the gang who found him when in truth he knew it lay curled in a coffee can nestled amidst the rest of his junk in a storage facility off the highway. She left and never returned and Jack lay in bed for five days waiting for the peritonitis to subside, thinking what every minute of his stay cost him, like a running total of dollars wasted accumulating on one of the screens behind his head. Since the doctors and nurses had told him he had very nearly died and that it took doses of antibiotics usually reserved for large farm animals to control the infection he thought he should stay put and figure out how to skip out on the bill later. And there, thinking of Anne Marie as a perfectly formed angel sent from his memory to guide him finally to a place of peace, he decided to give permanency, however brief it turned out to be, one more chance. He would leave his debts, take his money and his belongings and move back to Cleveland. Even though he had spent his adult life roaming around the country, mostly west of the Mississippi, he had been shaped by the smoky city by the lake more than he ever consciously acknowledged. Why not build his masterpiece in the place where he grew up and where his mother and father lay buried and moldering and complete the pattern begun when he crawled the same ground as a squalling infant? Anne Marie surely still lived there. What would she say when he knocked on her door?

Jack drove the wood home and over the next week he, Glover, and Anne Marie finished the garage and the subfloor of the kitchen. He decided to pour the concrete pad himself so he rented a machine that tamped the earth and he worried over every bump until the ground looked ready to be converted to a dance floor. Then he rented a small cement mixer and bought bags of powdered concrete and rebar. In a day he had mixed the cement, laid the rebar and poured the floor, brushing a delicate swirl on the surface resembling satellite photos of brewing hurricanes. After the cement set for a few days the four of them emptied the basement of Jack's possessions and stacked them in the garage as Jack separated and ordered the boxes into columns for eventual placement in the house. The stay in the damp basement hadn't ruined or damaged anything and Jack had to fight to keep from lingering over the boxes and flood his memory with how each item had been obtained and the purpose for carrying it forward in his life. Wood tried to help, but even though he had regained his feet and his injuries had retreated he fell victim to terrifying and debilitating vertigo and migraine headaches. So Jack made him sit and watch and hoped that when he healed Wood would have picked up on some technique and would understand how long and hard Jack expected him to work. But when Jack looked at Wood's face as he watched the construction, he held little hope that anything stuck in his damaged brain.

Jack hoped Wood would come around before Glover left, because it had become increasingly apparent to Jack that Glover would be leaving soon. While Glover and Estonia never talked about the pregnancy in front of Anne Marie and him, they rattled the house with screaming matches once they had retreated to their bedroom to presumably sleep. Glover took to hanging out and sometimes sleeping in the loft above the garage once it had been roughed in. They barely looked at each other when they were working together as fight after fight piled up between them with no satisfactory resolution. At dinner they stayed apart, both sullen and miserable, both hoping that the other would give ground or accept defeat or at least smile in their direction to begin to build on something positive and not related to the pregnancy. Neither would grant such a favor to the other. Jack and Anne Marie watched it all, but both were exhausted, frenzied, and thrilled as the house shook off its dead skin and enticed them along with its promise of providing exquisite space for their long delayed life, so they struggled with formulating advice to the young couple that would help bring them back together. Both tried pointing out the mistakes they themselves had made when they were young like Glover and Estonia, sometimes in a group at dinner and sometimes one-on-one as they worked separate from each other. Anne Marie rolled out the joy of birth and watching an infant take his first breath as they clenched their face against the light and cold. Jack tried a couple of solos on personal responsibility, sacrifice and the terror and thrill of rushing headlong down a path you neither wanted nor had prepared for, yet you understood it as the only reasonable path to take. Jack and Anne Marie each decided to act more affectionately toward one another than came naturally to model behavior, thinking neither had seen two people in love older than their mid-teens and seeing adults cooing and fussing over each other may dislodge some of the anger between them. Nothing worked, of course, because Glover hated Estonia for getting pregnant and refusing to consider abortion and Estonia hated Glover for not pulling out in time and flooding her vagina with hungry young sperm. They couldn't get past these grievances and they decided that anger could be just as valuable and satisfying as love. It could end one way once they had decided upon this course. Glover would stand down and leave the field. Estonia could go nowhere and Glover had nothing tying him to Cleveland other than Estonia and she actively and purposefully sawed through the rope.

Jack didn't know whether Estonia knew about the murder because neither he nor Anne Marie spoke to her about that night and Jack had a hard time believing Glover had spoken to her because of their shattered intimacy. The murder gave Glover another reason to flee and to consider this chapter of his life an ugly and horrifying branch that he should abandon with speed. Had Estonia known she probably would have relented some in her yelping about unfairness and stupid boys with cocks for brains as she could have placed her situation in the larger context of death, mayhem and prison for all. But Jack and Anne Marie would not tell her. She was young, pregnant, and distraught and they couldn't trust what flight of contrition and repentance might take hold of her that would make her run to the cops or blather on to a neighbor about a corpse in the shitter. Instead, Jack tried to keep an eye on Glover and look for signs that he prepared for his exit. So, when he saw Glover's backpack stowed in the loft, packed and strapped closed, after Glover had left to shower at Mary Kelly's after a brutal day of work, Jack decided to stay-up as long as his body would allow him that night and catch Glover trying to slink away in the dark.

Jack guessed Glover would leave through the backyard after he came out of the garage so Jack set up a chair near the outhouse with a view of the garage door. He liked Glover, but he really wanted him to stay because he had turned into a competent helper who didn't talk more than he worked. Jack had worked next to chattering fools and by the end of the day he had wanted to drive a nail through their heads to get them to shut up. Glover understood and respected Jack's need for quiet and they worked hours at a time in silence. He wouldn't be easy to replace given that Jack couldn't pay and some of the really hard work had yet to be done.

Around 3:00 am Jack witnessed a shadow slip from the side of the garage. Glover took a couple a purposeful strides towards the back of the property and Jack stood up and with his arms folded across his chest.

"Where you going Glover?"

Glover flinched and backpedaled, tottering wildly before he caught himself.

"Jesus Christ! What are you doing out here?"

"I was thinking about you. I was thinking about the packed rucksack hidden away in the loft. I was thinking that you think you and Estonia haven't exactly been seeing eye to eye. I was thinking that you think you have every reason to leave this wreckage and you think you can do whatever it is you want to do. So, since I can't sleep with all this thinking running through my head I thought I'd come down here and see if my hunches were correct. I thought if Glover does try to leave I'll be there to intercept him and convince him that he's about to make the biggest goddamn mistake of his life. That's pretty much what I'm doing out here. What about you? Why for christsakes are you out here in the wee of the morning?"

"I don't think that's your business."

"Goddamn right it's my business. We're about to start a complete roof tear off, right down to the goddamn rafters. The roof is steep and high and I'm too old to do it alone. My best worker has a rucksack on his back and is planning on slinking away without a goodbye and you're telling me it's not my business. My worker is about to leave his knocked-up girlfriend on my doorstep for me to care for, like I have nothing better to do. He's about to run out on his responsibility and it's not my business? I think, son, that I'm right in line behind Estonia knowing this is very much my business."

'I'm leaving Jack. I've made up my mind."

"Why would you do something stupid like that?"

"The plan was never to leave Bakersfield to run to Cleveland and have a baby. I could have done that back in California. That was the whole point. Get out of there before I got somebody pregnant and had to start working in one of the factories, living in a cardboard apartment with a ten year-old TV and a fat wife. I didn't leave there to come and do it here."

"But it's done."

"She won't get rid of it. It's like she's punishing me for fucking her. So, if she wants it she can have it and I don't have to be around since she's not going to listen to me anyway."

"Stay with her. The memory of your leaving is going to be far worse than you can imagine, worse than some puke on your shoulder and shit on your fingers, worse than sleep deprivation and staying in on Saturday night."

"I'm not doing it."

"Why?"

"Because I want to see stuff and I don't know if Estonia is the best I can find. How am I supposed to know? I've only lived in Bakersfield."

"I can stop you from leaving tonight, but I can't be looking over my shoulder all goddamn day wondering if you're going to be there. I'm telling you not to do this. When I see somebody about to create a regret the size of the Grand Tetons I have to step in for basic human decency. Stay with her. Do you need to be reminded just how stunningly beautiful and goddamn Basque she is?"

"I'd regret it more if I stayed."

"But you'd still have a beautiful girlfriend and a baby that's probably going to have your face and dick to bounce on your knee."

"That's not me."

"All I can tell you is that every single person in the country is thrown some shit, some worse than you're getting, some a little better, but it's not the shit that's important. Everybody gets it in the end, it all looks pretty much the same, there's nothing new under sun. The important thing is how you deal with it. What decision do you make once the shit storm starts? Do you run into the howling wind without clothes or direction or do you seek shelter and hunker down and wait for it to pass, all the while thinking what you can learn from the squall line. One bad decision can lead to a dozen more and soon you're walking on a path you had no intention of following. Most times it's in the wrong direction and let me tell you from experience it usually leads to some dusty collection of buildings populated with folks more dead than alive, trapped in closed circuits and so bored they don't even know they're not supposed to be bored. You're about to take your first step and make your first bad decision."

"By that logic I made my first bad decision when I left Bakersfield or when I thought I could pull out in time when I was fucking Estonia. Maybe I'm changing direction right now before I get further down the road to your zombie village, maybe I see the same thing you're talking about at the end of this road and I'm getting the fuck off before it gets any worse."

"You should trust me Glover. I hate to think I've lived through all that I have and learned all that I have and watch you not take advantage of the information. I know what I'm talking about here."

"I'm not you Jack. Nothing says I have to end up like that. Thanks for letting me sleep here, even though you worked me like a dog and beat the shit out of me. Never mind that other thing over there."

Glover shrugged toward the outhouse and held out a hand for Jack to shake and Jack took it reluctantly.

"Can't you just wait until the baby is born and see how you feel then?"

Glover dropped Jack's hand, turned and walked into the shadows. Jack followed the creaking of his rucksack and the swish of his shoes on the wet grass and then the scrape of concrete until Glover's presence exited from his realm. Jack had left women in the dead of night with no note of final parting and probably had a child or two in the world who carried a portion of his genetics who he'd never seen, but he didn't mine his own spotty record in conjuring up advice for Glover. His decisions had been his own regarding a specific set of circumstances and they couldn't be applied to Glover. Jack's love of women burned bright and fast, except for his love for Anne Marie, which had never stopped smoldering. He had to dig through his memory to find an equivalent story to match the one that had just unfolded in front of him, a story of a poor luckless and friendless wretch who turned away from love because turning away seemed as good an idea as staying with the only person in the world who would ever understand him. The story began on a timber farm rising on a damp and misty ridge. Jack had committed to a couple of years of migrant work and had already harvested oranges in Florida, soy in Arkansas, salmon in Alaska, apples in Washington and grapefruits and grapes in California when he signed on for a stint planting white pine. He slept in a tent in a small cluster of other tents around a damp fire pit and shared his own with a guy named Jeff who liked to be called Leroy or Roy because the name means 'the king' in French, but Roy never fully explained the reasons why he carried the titular office. Down the slope by a little creek, Mexican workers had created their own community and most of them only spoke emergency English. Jack had yet to pick up Spanish so even though he wanted to hear about their villages deep in Mexico and their long trek north he had to content himself with agreeable grunts and head nods as they worked shoulder to shoulder. Roy knew Spanish and conversed more easily and naturally in it than his first language, which by the time he had met Jack had devolved into an exhausted patois of old catch phrases gleaned from the vast and unrelenting American pop culture and nearly extinct bromides that all but suffocated the opportunity for real communication. Jack felt like he lived with a man who lived in the detritus of his culture, either because his limited curiosity had already exhausted all avenues of inquiry, or he never understood anything about where he lived or the neighbors who lived next to him so he retreated into a hoary common language that somebody somewhere in the nation had once liked and had used as a shortcut to developing their own personalities and humor. Unburdened from the references because the Mexicans had no idea what he talked about when he said, "Wham bam thank you ma'am'" when he jammed a sapling in a hole or sang "This is the story of a lovely lady" whenever one of the young Mexican girls passed by, he became lively, funny and original when he spoke to them in Spanish and soon made several good friends among the their crew. Soon, he brought the families and the chatter of birds conversing in a foreign tongue to their sad grouping of soggy tents and soon fresh tortillas and beans replaced their canned soup. Some of the miscreants in their village protested about bringing the Mexicans into their camp, but Jack made it be known that anyone who had a problem should come talk to him so the grievances faded away before they gained any momentum.

Jack watched Roy hold court over the ten or twelve Mexicans who frequented their camp and soon he had been given a tribute in the form of a girl barely sixteen and she and Roy began to take long strolls over the brown and soft carpet of pine needles and through the rows of foot high saplings. They made love under the canopy of old growth trees saved from the saw until the price of wood rose another notch or two and Jack started picking up snatches of marriage talk that seemed to be planned within the same planting season and that after the ceremony Roy would join them in their wandering. When Jack asked Roy about the plans he looked like he formulated a carefully constructed answer then came out with something like, "The worm has turned my friend. There's trouble in River City." Jack asked him what the fuck that meant and Roy returned with: "Love may be as soft as an easy chair since we are in an evergreen forest, but I need a plop, plop, fizz, fizz relief plan, son. I started out on my journey a horndog and now I got myself a bride waiting in the wings. Break a goddamn leg. Break a goddamn leg. A goddamn working world, Jackie, full of surprises. I'm goddamn flummoxed and befuzzled. She is a beauty though." Jack wondered what the Mexicans would think of him if Roy could muster the same pattern in Spanish, but it would be years before they understood enough English to understand the miscalculation they had made. In truth, he envied Roy because the girl's face and form stunned him, a natural beauty with glistening black hair and an arched eyebrow on which hung an encyclopedia of mischief. Her parents whispered thankful prayers that she would marry before tragedy struck her down or she became confused in her thinking and left for one of the American cities where she would become nothing but a trained monkey for men. Not that her parents thought that marrying a crazy migrant gringo represented the best path, but at least she would become a citizen and have a remote chance of not being broken, feeble and fat on her thirtieth birthday.

Everyone agreed to a small ceremony on top of a ridge on a Sunday morning because they felt too tired from working the other six days and the bosses might fire them all if they took off for something as superfluous as a wedding. The owner agreed to let them have the reception in an old barracks that hadn't been used since a worker had their throat slit in the night five years before. A Pentecostal preacher who had drifted up from West Virginia and who sometimes ministered to the Mexicans for the lack of a priest agreed to marry them. The women of the crew, both Mexican and American, cooked all Friday night, Saturday night and Sunday morning. They made a blend of country Mexican and country American, tortillas and fried chicken, black beans and pork and beans, flan and sponge cake, tequila and Pabst Blue Ribbon.

The only piece missing from the wedding turned out to be the groom. Jack had heard some rustling in the tent the night before and he thought Roy might be in the grips of marriage jitters, but when he awoke the next morning to the smell of cooking throughout the camp it because obvious that Roy had fled. Jack sought out the brother of the bride, who knew the most English of the family, and told him what he had found. The brother came back to the tent and stared at the trampled down spot where Roy had slept for weeks. Nothing of Roy remained except his cheap sleeping bag. Jack noticed the brother's white shirt for the first time, so white and starched he looked as if a man servant had dressed him. He fetched his father who came and stared at the abandoned spot in the tent and exchanged a rapid fire summation of the morning's discovery that included gesticulating wildly and talking over each other. The father too wore an impossibly clean white shirt that practically glowed next to his sun-baked skin. They looked to Jack for answers but he could only answer with a shrug, because even though he slept in the same tent as Roy he wanted to make it clear to the family that he had no insight into Roy's actions and wouldn't defend the idiot in any way. The father and son left the campsite, staring at their feet, intent on murder. The whole camp ate the wedding feast under the trees or leaning against the barracks or sitting around a few lopsided tables adorned with wildflowers and plastic tablecloths. Everyone kept on their best clothes even after they heard Roy had skipped out and there would be no wedding, including the bride who sat on the ground in her wedding dress eating hot tortillas and laughing with a group of men. Her parents worried about her fate and drank three times as much tequila as normal for them, argued briefly with the brother the best way to track Roy and whether or not to cut off his balls or slit his throat, and fell into a troubled sleep together in their tent with their legs lying outside the opening.

Jack came across Roy four years later in Carson City. Jack and a buddy had just gotten paid enormous overtime checks and they could think of nothing else better to do than take a blistering road trip through Nevada to go see his buddy's albino step-sister get married to a car salesman who never stopped talking about and touching the woman's skin. They rolled into a chain restaurant decorated to look vaguely like an American pub circa 1850-1894 with faux velocipedes hanging from the ceilings, old-timey sepia photos of families, houses, farms, cityscapes, and children with glorious ringlets brushing their shoulders, train schedules, boat schedules, newspaper reprints, watch fobs, spyglasses, box cameras, advertisements for liquor and face powder, copper spoons and ladles covered in patina, large portraits of Chester Arthur and Rutherford B. Hayes, a collection of corsets and bloomers, snuff boxes, a board with twenty varieties of pince-nez, top hats, riding crops, carriage wheels, and postcards of women in bathing suits once thought to be scandalous and meant to be carried in a pocket and shared in a smoky room with other men in love with women's bare ankles, adorned the walls and made the diners feel like they were securely squirreled away inside a past century where the people existed with charming and rudimentary tools while they wolfed down plates of factory food prepared six states away and reheated for their pleasure.

Jack and his buddy sat in a booth looking at the oversized menu made to look like aging parchment. The pictures of the selections looked satisfying and comfortable, like heaping plates of food a person could make at home, when they didn't eat out of a box or bag, with alternating bites of crispiness and creaminess, doused with butter and salt. Jack's alcohol-fueled hunger ground against him. Although the portions in the pictures looked mammoth, more like family platters than individual servings, Jack thought be might just order two or three entrees. Roy came to their table adorned with pince-nez on his nose, a tight fitting vest over his thick belly, a cheap pocket watch and fob hanging from the vest and two arm garters on his biceps over a white billowy shirt with enormous sleeves. His face and hands didn't look that much cleaner than when they shared the tent on the ridge.

"You missed a fine meal, Roy, there under the pine trees."

Roy stared at Jack who no doubt looked fatter or thinner, older or just out of context within the restaurant and the era that never had been. When he recognized Jack he smiled as if trying to keep the smile secret, like he had thought of a private joke or had an illicit thought.

"You know this little bunny had to keep going and going."

"To here? Jesus, Roy, this isn't much of a job?"

"Ya, I'd rather have bad knees, a bad back, a fat Mexican wife who lost her looks the day after I married her and a gaggle of Mexican kids pissing at my feet. That would have just been super-duper, chief-o."

Roy wrote down their orders and left to place them. Jack's buddy leaned across the table and talked from the side of his mouth.

"Did you ever get the urge to throw somebody down and rape their asshole until they passed out? The waiter might get something in the parking lot if he don't shut it."

Jack hoped the albino wedding would go off without a hitch so that they could drive home and he would never have to hang-out with this guy again. When Roy returned with their drinks Jack seized his arm and brought his ear close to his mouth.

"Listen pal-o. That was one of the most beautiful girls I've ever seen. When men start turning away from that we might as well all fuck our hands while we hold a mirror up to our faces. You just about killed all of us in that camp or made us into something less than men. We thought if that motherfucker could turn away from that then what in God's name were we capable of. There was no reason for it. You're supposed to take the prize once you've earned it. You don't run out on your luck. What the fuck was the matter with you?"

"Exit stage left. Know what I mean?"

No, I don't and stop talking like fucking idiot for once."

"It's all the same, her pussy and your plate of cheese fries. She loved me for a moment and I moved on. Some others have loved me and even more have hated me and put restraining orders in place. What do you care? I'm sure she would have blown you after I left if you could have asked her in Spanish? I left the light on for you and the door open. So why are you busting my gnads for it now?"

"I know it's pretty easy to embrace nihilism when you work in an environment like this but you are completely fucked in the head. She wasn't some frumpy girl at a bus stop. You were supposed to take it as far as it would go, you were supposed to run out the string, fucked until your heart exploded, fought until she clawed off your face or left you blind, worried about her leaving until your intestines were so goddamn twisted up you would think you'd never shit properly again. What the hell happened in your life you don't understand that?"

Jack's buddy winked at him and motioned with his head they should take Roy to the parking lot now and put his impulses into action. Jack avoided his eyes and thought about hitching back home and skipping the wedding. Roy stared over the heads of the diners to a spot near the far wall where a fake gaslight on a pole stood.

He began speaking as if waking from a dream. "Well, la-de-da. Words to live by kemosabe. I have tables to wait on. You have a wonderful life in the fields of the lord and don't forget that we live on tips."

Jack thought that someone so twisted up would eventually end up hanging from a noose, but he never saw or heard from Roy again so he never knew how he ended his days. But now Glover pushed aside Roy and assumed the prime spot of those he knew who blasted apart their lives because of a lack of imagination or wild animal fear of growing up and assuming the duties and responsibilities of a man.

Jack stayed awake until the sun came up, occupying himself with a flashlight and a century-old translation of *Don Quixote*. How much shit had he taken over the years for reading at night around a campfire or on break, eating a sandwich with one hand and holding a book with the other or carrying a newspaper under his arm high up scaffolding or ironwork? Jack never looked like a reader and books never looked right in his two massive paws. Also, his weathered face could not be contorted into a look of contemplation or focused intelligence any more than a chunk of granite could, so when he would break out a book a howl of protest would invariably rise, bashing him for his pretension and effeminacy. Sometimes the anger rose so fast a person would have thought he had pulled out a foot long dildo, greased it up and asked if anyone wanted to have a go. Usually as a retort he would begin to read aloud like a daddy to his sleepy children and no matter whose words he read Whitman, Rilke, Proust, Melville, Stendal, the words gained control and soothed the ignorant and confused and those filled with hate and envy. The reading didn't always work and once or twice he fought with his fists over Faulkner or Dostoevsky and once jammed a paperback of *The Idiot* in the mouth of a blowhard who called him a prancing faggot whose mouth moved when he read. He never much believed in evangelism and had very little interest in turning the cretins, clods and miscreants of his working life into readers of the finest writers in world history. He just wanted to be left alone for a few moments while he thought of lives and worlds outside of his own and maybe even pick up some philosophy or history that'd help him make sense of the tangle of the world. He sold his body and his strength to his bosses but his mind would remain his own.

Jack made a breakfast of pancakes, bacon and perfect coffee and when Estonia and Anne Marie shuffled down to the concrete pad through the smell of burning fat and saw Glover's empty chair they both knew he had gone. Jack silently practiced the cadence of his news several times before coming out with it.

"I couldn't get him to stay. He left around three in the morning."

Estonia nodded, acknowledging she understood the news but not betraying the rage and confusion brewing inside her.

"He may get a taste of life without you and come crawling back. I'm talking about on his hands and knees and begging forgiveness. Men sometimes have to act out the pantomime of freedom to realize it's not something they want anyway," Jack said to Anne Marie because Estonia wouldn't look up from her pancake.

"Maybe after forty years he'll come back. That'll be something to look forward to," Estonia snarled.

Anne Marie couldn't help but laugh and she put a hand over her mouth once she realized Estonia hadn't meant it as a joke and Jack hadn't taken it for one either.

"Keep to things you know, Stone."

"Don't call me that."

"What? I'm stuck calling you a four syllable name? It's exhausting."

"My dad used to call me that and let's say I don't need that particular memory right now. It's not exactly pleasant and if I have one more thing go wrong or I have to think of my fucked-up life anymore I'm going to start screaming and I don't think I'm going to be able to stop. So no fucking nicknames, ok?

"We're here for you, Estonia." Anne Marie patted her on the knee.

"I know. But I only met you a few weeks ago and you two are the only two left. That's so sad and lonely and I can't stop crying. I've got no one. I'm on my own and I don't know how or why it happened. Am I so horrible that everyone runs away?"

"Jack and I are here. We're not leaving, at least if we have anything to say about it in the end. We'll make a beautiful room for you and the baby. You're not alone."

Estonia started crying again but kept eating her pancakes even though the surging, roiling emotion had all but extinguished her hunger.

"Thank you. It means a lot. I don't know what I would have done or where I'd be right now if you had kicked us out. Glover would have left me in a ditch. Maybe even bashed my skull in just to cover his tracks and make sure a baby never came knocking on his door after he had married some other bitch and had other kids with her in a nice little bungalow and after he found something he liked to do and starting making real money and the baby told him that his mother was a stripper and his first memory from inside the womb was her belly rubbing up against a stripper pole and he always thought it was her hand petting him until he grew up and realized what she did for a living and understood that this whole time he loved the pole more than his own mother and he was hoping his father was normal and could help raise him outside the influence of his godawful mommy."

Jack waited for the torrent of words and sobs to subside and rolled his response around his mouth with his tongue before making it audible.

"You can always go back home. Grandchildren have a way of softening folks. The attention will stop being on you and it all turns toward the baby and they'll more often than not want what's best for the baby, even if that means helping you out some."

"The best for the baby would probably mean they would try to take him away from me because they think I'm the world's worst girl and that I can't do anything right. A lot of that had to do with Glover and my dad caught me a couple of times with boys and one time a cop caught me and a boy in the park while I was giving him a blowjob and the cop made a super big deal about it and dragged me home with smeared lipstick on my chin and told my parents all the gory details so my dad thinks I'm just a plain slut and if they have homes for sluts, I mean county-run warehouses next to or in the nuthouses they'll try to commit me and try to make everyone think I'm insane and they'll hold this big martyr party with our family and friends and I'll be paraded around like I should be in a cage and gawked at like I'm a living, breathing first class slut just caught from the wilds of America and stand back men, she'll suck your cock or grab your ass if you get too close to the cage. So now I'm going to go home with Glover's baby and no Glover? No way. Their anger wouldn't stop at small humiliations. They may just chain me naked in the front yard and make me miserable in every conceivable way. Besides, that place is no place to raise a baby. Look what they did to me."

Jack and Anne Marie looked at Estonia and saw no visible scars or traces of past abuse and were once again taken aback by her beauty and the radiance of her skin. The incongruity of her plea for help, her dark allusions to a tangled history of emotion created by insidious parents enthralled with torture could not be aligned with her stunning face and form, so Jack and Anne Marie took a shortcut and discounted most of everything she said, preferring to believe what they saw over what they heard. How bad could her life have been if she had come out of it looking like that? Once her hormones had settled into a more predictable pattern maybe they could make her see the sense of returning home and accepting a small amount of shame in return for a roof and food. That conversation could wait until after she had the baby and Estonia recognized the cold and brutal emptiness yawning before her and she realized she had to do everything to provide a future for the child. Anne Marie thought of two other possible scenarios. One, she and Jack being arrested and stuck in jail for killing and burying the doughy kid or two, once they held the infant in their arms and heard his gentle cooing they would never want Estonia to leave and would start to consider her the daughter they should have had together.

"I'm sorry 'Ston-i-a. I'm afraid the boy couldn't find his own asshole if asked." Jack kicked an ember back into the pit that had tumbled on to the grass.

Estonia felt the need to lash out at Jack for not giving Glover enough credit, but she remembered the empty chair and his cowardice and that made her even more mad, but she maintained enough reason to also remember he had some good qualities buried under the fear. They finished breakfast in silence and Wood walked into the backyard as they were finishing. He wore sweatpants with no shoes or shirt. He had deep blue tattoos up and down his arms that could barely be seen through the deep brown of his skin. Images had also been begun on his chest and back but looked abandoned, like sketchbook doodles working out a larger idea.

"My head feels better. It's morning, right?"

"Yes, Wood, it is late morning already. Past seven. We should be working by now, but we've been delayed some. You ready to work and earn your keep?"

"Ya, I think so."

"Anne Marie guessed at your size and went out and bought work boots and clothes. We wear clothes to work in and we don't let our peckers flap in the breeze."

Estonia looked back at her half-eaten pancake and curl of bacon because she, in fact, had been staring directly at Wood's penis behind the thin cotton and aching a little bit for Glover.

"I don't have to sleep in my work boots, right? I just woke up."

"He is feeling better. He's getting an edge to him. I was beginning to think something had been knocked out of your head permanently."

"Just some headaches and I couldn't see for shit."

"I know a way to clear the rest of the cobwebs out of there. Eat this plate of food on the run, get dressed and meet me back down here in ten minutes. The work clothes are in the corner of your room."

With no sleep Jack didn't have the energy and balance to climb on the roof so he decided to finish what he could in the kitchen. The subfloor had already been laid so he went out and bought some drywall and insulation and spent the next three days rewiring all the light switches and outlets, insulating and hanging drywall. Of all Jack's innate talents, hanging, taping and mudding drywall rose to the level of mastery. He filled the joint between two pieces faster than most and feathered the compound so perfectly he never left the hint of a seam. He knew he could support himself on this ability alone and always had entrée into a crew once they saw his work. If he had had less imagination he would have been able to stick as a hanger and would now have been collecting a fat pension, but such would not be his course. Wood tried to hang a few pieces and mangled the edges and screwed the screws too deeply, but Jack erased the mistakes with a few flicks of his blade. They decided to wait on the flooring and painting until they saw the color of the cabinets to match the color, so they had nothing left to do in the kitchen until Anne Marie's brother delivered them.

The roof came next. Jack inspected the sheathing and beams from the attic and found the whole western side to be discolored and spongy from leaks. He remembered seeing this on his initial inspection, but his excitement over buying the house at the time must have clouded his judgment about the extent of the damage. Everything would have to come off to the beams and even they may have to be replaced if the rot had spread to their core. The attic itself had a high ceiling and a crudely laid plank floor, but with a week's worth of work the space would be livable. Jack tried to keep the ideas at bay until he finished the roof, but an image of a high peaked room with gleaming white walls and sunlight slicing through the air pushed its way into his thoughts and he began to calculate how much drywall and insulation he would need and what kind of flooring would look best in the space. His choices altered wildly from a wide plank rustic and rough hewn board to narrow boards of oak or maple so finely polished they looked like they could have been part of a table holding a feast served with centuries old china and real silver.

When he climbed onto the roof he found four layers of shingles nailed on top of each other. The materials and workmanship devolved with each layer so that the top layer looked like it had been nailed down by an old rummy who had stolen mismatched shingles from other houses. They had taken three big bundles of cedar shake from the lumberyard and he didn't know if he had enough to cover the entire roof, but at most he would be only a few square feet short. It would be the only cedar roof on the street and probably in the entire neighborhood and Jack couldn't help but wonder if he had intercepted a shipment meant for some rich guy's house in the suburbs, because the regular contractors who used the yard hadn't nailed down cedar in their entire careers.

Wood turned out to be afraid of heights and every time he started up the ladder he froze near the middle and he couldn't reach out his useless alligator arms to the next rung and he started shaking. Jack had to admit he missed Glover. The kid would have scrambled up the ladder and performed cartwheels on the roof and would have eaten his lunch sitting cross-legged on the chimney without a taint of fear. Wood knew better and his body shut down when he tried to push himself past his own narrow experience. Glover's leaving did have one positive effect on Jack as he firmly recommitted to finishing the house. He had wavered in his commitment to the project and had considered running. Arson and murder could unnerve any man and cast a dim light on his ability to make sound decisions, but when he thought of Glover tramping through the night with his rucksack on, his face pointed towards new experience and his mind set on dismantling the past, Jack felt lucky to have dodged the urge to run like he had been unable to do so many times before. He imagined himself, his tired and beaten self and not himself as Glover's age and with his energy, sleeping on couches and floors, working whatever job he could find, and drinking to make it seem more like a party and less like drudgery. The urge had passed him forever and now what he felt about flight and new beginnings seemed like a shadow of an old habit, repeated a thousand times in the past but now broken and unable to be repeated even one more time. So, he flushed away thoughts of leaving and he would live in his crumbling house with a corpse in the backyard.

At rest he may have tipped his hat to Glover or credited him with a parcel of gratitude for clarifying his own path, but as they worked he cursed and abused him with every rung of the ladder and every nail pounded home. The tear-off went slow because Jack had to rip off all those layers of shingles and rotten boards. He drank two gallons of water a day and urinated off the side of the roof onto the neighbor's driveway so he didn't have to climb the ladder. Wood stayed on the ground and collected all the discarded shingles and wood and put them in the bed of the truck. He needed another dumpster, but he wouldn't call Kaufman or his man because nothing good could come of stirring up that hornet's nest right now.

Rebuilding the roof tortured Jack's old knees. He and Wood carried the sheathing inside to the attic once the roof had been completely taken off and the rafters exposed. Jack could have saved a portion of the sheathing of the old roof, but he imagined himself worrying about the old boards, and if it leaked in a few years, cursing himself for his shortcut rehabilitation, so he replaced three rafters and sheathed it all in new plywood. After the new sheathing had been nailed down Jack had to carry the cedar shake to the roof. He shouldered as much as he could until the agony of his knees made another trip impossible. Then, he nailed down the shingles he had managed to haul to the roof. This way he hoped his knees might stop screaming by the time all the shake had been nailed and he could attempt a few more trips. His knees swelled so much he half-expected the seams of his jeans to burst from the pressure. Wood tried twice to carry the shingles to the roof after Jack spewed a string of epithets at him that angered him so much he wanted to show Jack that he could carry the shingles without a problem, but when he reached the roof he flattened himself against the sheathing and panicked, both times. Jack talked to him in tones reserved for potential suicides perched on the edge of a bridge and eventually got him to put a foot on the first rung and slither down the ladder, shaking, sweating and barely holding onto consciousness.

After the second time Jack kept the curses to himself but thought of sending Wood back to 365 Everyday to be sodomized and humiliated, but instead he held out hope that he could find a talent in Wood that didn't involve heights and that he could become useful. Besides, the pain that wracked his body left him little energy to worry about Wood, so he focused on every rung as he climbed and every hammer swing as he methodically covered the roof with gleaming cedar shake. By the end of the job he popped ibuprofen by the handful, knowing this would be the last roof he ever put on.

The morning after he finished the roof he awoke from a troubled sleep and a particularly virulent nightmare. In it he had young legs and a strong back and he walked through room after room filled with diaphanous shrouds and the smell of polyurethane. Estonia handed him her baby, a little pink girl with a mischievous smile and eyes that bore right through him. Someone spoke through the shroud, convincing him the best way to help the child would be to shoot her in the head. He raised a gun and pulled the trigger and blood poured from the sweet little mouth. Jack howled. He had made a mistake. He placed his hands over the hole from where the blood poured, hoping to stop the flow and keep life contained and pumping. Who tricked him and whispered through the shroud? The little girl died in his arms and Jack became frantic and wild until crushing regret twisted the blood out of his heart and the air from his lungs. Estonia pulled apart her robe and revealed her beautiful pussy and told Jack they could have another baby now that he cleared the one last obstacle that stopped them from being together. She asked him over and over what he had done with Glover. Jack knew they could never replicate the shining perfect soul of the baby he had just killed. He couldn't imagine living in the world without the baby and the prospect of living filled with agony yawned before him. Jack knew he would have to carry the baby with him whenever he went and he could never wash the blood from his hands.

Jack thought he might be going crazy and he couldn't force his heart to calm. He wanted to wake Anne Marie and tell her his dream, including the part with Estonia, and admit to the endlessness of his depravity, of his ogling of the girl, of his thoughts of Mary Kelly, but she looked deep in sleep and what could she tell him other than dreams are not reality and no way would he ever think of hurting Estonia's baby. She would say the dream had been born from overwork and the anxiety of his having to complete the job alone. Jack crawled off the bed and pulled himself up using the windowsill and wall to get to his feet. He bent down to pick up his pants and a back spasm ripped down his spine so violently he thought he may never be able to straighten up again. Holding the pants with his left hand he used his right to push off against the sill and inch his back upright. The effort exhausted him and set off a chain of other intense spasms across his chest and thighs. Jack thought his muscles had finally gone into open revolt. He could not fill his lungs with air below his nipples and he leaned heavily against the wall. Slowly the riot subsided and he could lift a leg into his pants and then the other. Lifting his legs relieved some of the pressure on his spine so he raised his arms above his head and slowly twisted to determine the extent of the damage. He looked out the window through a temporary screen he had nailed over the broken pane. The mornings had grown cooler, hinting at the encroaching autumn and Jack had a long way to go to make the house snow and windproof. If he had to nail plywood over all the broken windows because, even though it would make the long and cold Cleveland winters that much more bleak, he didn't see he had much of a choice, especially now that his body had begun to betray him.

In the yard he saw movement, a scuttling, like a large dark lobster moving through the shadows. It circled a spot near the sidewalk, moved backward and forward, and suddenly broke apart. Ten or twelve dogs stepped back from a small body, took one last sniff or gave the body one last nudge of the nose, then scattered with a quick sprint. The body made a small smudge in the moonlight. Jack woke Anne Marie and asked her to bring a blanket to the front yard once she dressed. His spine and knees absorbed blow after blow as he descended the stars and he moved so slowly that Anne Marie caught up with him by the time he stepped off the final stair.

"What's this about?" Anne Marie stood with a blanket clutched to her chest and a halo of stray hairs framing her face.

"Another development. A waking dream, I think, or an hallucination dropped into my lap."

"I have no idea what you're talking about. You've been pushing yourself too hard."

"Look." He pointed to the spot where the body lay. They paused on the porch and Jack gathered his strength to walk down the porch steps. "I think it's a body of some sort. I saw it being dumped off."

They cautiously approached the body, which lay on its back with its face pointing toward the moon. Jack lowered himself to his knees. He knew at some point during the day his brain would get tired of all the pain sensors lighting up its matter and it would simply turn off the sensations and he would regain full range of motion, but until then every movement shocked him with fresh agony.

"It's an old woman. She's wearing a dress that looks like a maid's outfit."

Anne Marie crouched beside Jack and looked into the woman's face and held up her wrist to check for a pulse.

"This is Ellen Oglethorpe. She owned this house. Remember I told you she lived on the porch for a while. People tell me she always comes back. They don't know where she goes, but she always comes back. She's alive." Anne Marie tucked the blanket around Ellen. "Did you see who dropped her off?"

"No, it's dark. I could just see shadows."

"Did you see what kind of car they were driving?"

"They weren't driving."

"Weird. Who could do such a thing? Leave an old woman on the grass. That's beyond the beyond."

"I suppose we should bring her inside. We're running out of bedrooms."

"There's the small one in the back. Nobody's in there yet. I just can't leave her here. She'll die."

"The outhouse might end up being a mass grave."

Anne Marie didn't acknowledge the joke and moved around to Ellen's legs to help hoist her. "Can you carry her? You look a little slow this morning."

"I can't imagine that little body weighs more than a stack of shingles. I'll manage."

Jack picked up Ellen and slung her over his shoulder. He thought she weighed much less than a stack of shingles and noticed she smelled of dirt and worms. Anne Marie ran ahead and spread out blankets on the floor in the little bedroom that had a shallow closet and a window that looked over the turret of the garage. She balled up a sheet and tried to tuck the ends to create a pillow. They could keep Ellen warm and dry and that counted for something. She wouldn't have to sleep on the ground or a porch or be at the mercy of an unkind world. Anne Marie remembered the iron bed in the basement and she resolved to buy a mattress for it when the stores opened later in the morning. Ellen needed a doctor and some kind of treatment for her legs, but if they took her to the county hospital she would end up in the psych ward again and look what that cycle had done to her. Jack staggered in, audibly creaking and grinding like an old greasy machine that had run dry of oil and he set her down on the nest of blankets. Ellen had remained sleeping and when Anne Marie pulled a blanket over her body she curled around the wool and looked no bigger than a child.

Anne Marie told Jack about the bed in the basement and he thought about how to sand the rust from it and paint it, but Anne Marie told him not to worry about the bed lasting, because by the look of Ellen's legs the bed would only be in use for a short time.

"If she stays with us more than a couple of weeks you can worry about making it pretty. I just want to get her off the floor. She needs a doctor. Do you know anyone?"

"I wouldn't send her to the county hospital. They might just put her down to save the expense. I know someone that might come. I wouldn't call him for Wood, but he might come out for an old lady."

"Is he a doctor?"

"Used to be. He lost his license, but they didn't take away the knowledge in his head. He'll make her comfortable. Let me go down and look at the bed. I'm sure the bolts are lost or rusted through. I'll make some modifications," Jack said as he watched Anne Marie standing over Ellen, an analytical look locked on her face, hands on hips, a natural nurse with no tools other than a blanket and a floor.

"We have quite a family."

Anne Marie looked towards him as he stood in the doorway and flashed him a smile and said, "If this keeps going we're going to need a bigger house or an annex."

"There's plenty more vacant houses in the neighborhood. We'll own the whole goddamn block."

"Jack Cactus, it's a good thing we didn't marry when we were young. We'd have fifteen children and my old womb would be aching for more."

"That's the God's honest truth."

Jack hobbled down the stairs thinking he might paint the bed anyway. It would take only a few hours and the old woman would have something nice to die on. The doctor would confirm what he and Anne Marie already knew, that Ellen had a massive infection creeping close to her heart. He just couldn't see letting the old lady die on a rusty bed. There had to be some dignity left in the world.

A Liquid Breath

Nelson crawled out of the storage compartment, sliding on his torso until his hands touched the deck. He pulled until his legs came free of the edge. He couldn't remember falling asleep and he couldn't place the moment he became awake because he blinked against the pitch black of the compartment for some time until he recognized consciousness. He waited to leave until the sound of his breathing reverberating on the metal walls drove him to claustrophobia. Nelson stood up and closed the compartment door. A few dim lights high on the ship and weak moonlight illuminated the deck, but to Nelson's saucer-sized pupils it looked as if he had crawled into a day blazing with sun. The barge plowed through water, shimmering and flat except for the wake. Pez' door hung open and Nelson hissed his name into the black cavity. His own harsh whisper, loose and warbling as the sound waves lost force and broke down, came back to him. Pez had obviously left the compartment. Nelson formulated two theories for his departure: one, that he had to urinate so he found a secluded spot on deck and pissed through the railing and into the lake or two, he had to walk off the claustrophobia much like Nelson had to do, which seemed the least likely of the two since Pez had lived most of his adult life in a hole.

Nelson waited for his return and when several minutes passed he decided the explore the deck. He thought he would walk until full circulation returned to his body and the sound of his own breathing left his ears before he would return to the compartment. He walked along the railing, lightly rapping his fingers on the top rail as the water churned below. Pez could have slipped through the gaps and fallen to the black water with his pecker flapping, and his small smudge of a body could have sunk and disappeared with a few ill-timed breaths. His palms moistened as he looked at the possible path of descent and hoped Pez had the fortune of knocking his head against the side of the ship and drowning in an unconscious state and not thrashing about in wild animal terror until he exhausted his energy and sank to the bottom, conscious all the way down as water filled his lungs. Ever since Nelson had seen a television program on a basic cable channel that described the process of drowning, which explained with crude animation and ethereal music that the brain stayed alive and remained quite active many minutes after the lungs had filled with water, so the victim sat in a front row and conscious seat watching their own demise, he had altered his opinion of vast and black expanses of water and now veered away from the railing and stayed three feet from the edge.

He made two full circuits around the deck, avoiding the dim pools of light and keeping an eye on the black windows of the bridge. Small red and green lights illuminated the back of a chair, coat rack and a calendar three years out of date. At the stern of the ship he found a door that had been left ajar. It opened to a staircase down and saw the stairs emptied into a lighted hallway that led to the bowels of the ship. Pez could have set off exploring, Nelson thought, but that made as much sense as Pez feeling claustrophobic for the same reason that if a person lived in a hole the impulse to explore must not be particularly strong. He certainly wouldn't explore on his own volition, so either he had been caught sleeping in the compartment and dragged to the bottom of the barge for questioning or he now sat on the silt of the lake, blinking in the darkness, waiting for his brain to stop processing the horror around him. Nelson needed to find him or come up with a more positive scenario to relieve the panic brewing in his own psyche.

Nelson crept down the stairs, rehearsing possible answers to likely questions if a crewman on duty or in the grips of insomnia might lob his way once they startled each other in the hallway or around a blind corner. He tried to formulate something original and workable, but all the attempts ended with lame and obvious constructs, which could only result in an arrest or a beating administered by the crew. He settled on a victim narrative, hoary, creaky but still possible that went something like, "I was sitting at a bar talking to this knock-out, so damn beautiful that she made my toes ache and she was wearing this slinky dress that hung from her tits in just the right way and a subtle perfume, the smallest whiff, a delicate hint of neatly groomed pubic hair in the midst of which a tender pink vagina and a slightly engorged clitoris and labia were nestled securely but pulsed with anticipation. I bought her drinks, so many drinks of various colors and shades and made from of a shelf full of different varieties of liquors and she in turn bought me drinks of cheaper, harder stuff that pummeled my liver with violent blows and I kept looking into her eyes and she kept looking at the spot where my penis lay, eagerly hoping to see it rise like one of those fundraising thermometers that count the progress of a charity campaign and I have to admit those eyes drew it up like a fucking holy roller backwoods snake handler and it swelled to bursting and the glans swayed back and forth to the tones of her husky, smoky voice and the dénouement suddenly issued from her mouth and she invited me back to her place to finish the night fucking in any configuration I may desire and when I stood up I realized my head had been filled with bricks or wet bags of cement and I remember my forehead bouncing off the bar and as I crumpled I saw her face and she was laughing-I was just another conquest, helpless, incapacitated, a drunken Samson, enfeebled, and when I woke up I was in the storage compartment of this boat with my pockets turned out and no shoes."

If he sold the story with enough bewilderment and detail it might fend off further enquiry because why would anyone want to hitch a ride going to the ore fields anyway? As much as he hated to do it he would have to pitch his shoes overboard to keep the story consistent. He bent over to take his shoes off, but no shoes covered his feet. How had he walked twice around the deck without noticing the sensation of cold steel against his feet? Going back up the stairs and returning to the storage compartment, he expected to find his shoes, neatly placed side by side with a sock stuffed into each one. Maybe he took them off in his sleep to be more comfortable or maybe he had used them as a pillow. The shoes were not in the compartment or on the deck in front of the compartment and Nelson wanted to slam the aluminum door repeatedly until he felt rage and frustration no more. He began to think how he could have lost them, clinging to a hope that he had lost them, inadvertently dumping them over the side when....when? Had he been sleepwalking? Had the dogs penetrated so far into his mind that they could control his actions, commanding him in his sleep, setting him on a path of self-destruction without even being onboard? Had Pez played a practical joke and jumped overboard with them in hand? Did he have more sinister reasons for his actions? The man hated shoes. He may have been getting back at Nelson for the Shoe Horn ordeal or for dragging him out of the hole and onto the barge. Whatever the reason he happened to be barefoot again and now his feet felt cold and ached from standing flat-footed on the deeply cold steel.

Nelson made his way back to the open door, unaware that he pressed his head between two open palms and walked in a pattern that resembled an EKG of a rapidly pumping heart. He slammed into the side of the door frame and his elbow caught the brunt of the blow. Lowering his arms and rubbing the spot where bone is close to the skin, Nelson remembered that the barge crewman would have shoes and he could easily steal a pair while they slept if he could find their sleeping quarters. Down the stairs seemed like an obvious place to house the few crewman who tended the boat even though most of the hull would be used for cargo like coal or iron ore. They may also sleep above deck or under the bridge. Nelson again retraced his steps to the storage bin and looked across the deck that had been filled with black angular masses, except for a white pod that looked like it had been bolted down after construction of the barge. He crept over to it and one of the outer doors had been labeled a men's bathroom, but someone had drawn a huge phallus and a noose around the neck of the universal man symbol. He looked through a small plastic widow and saw a kitchenette stacked with dirty pots and plates. Around the other side of the pod he found and tried a door and the latch popped open. He heard snoring, wheezing and a phlegm rattle that sounded like oil bubbling from someone's throat. In the off chance the crew still maintained a form of domestic order, he bent down and searched the floor near the door for a pile of shoes. On his first attempt he came away with a leather work boot and an athletic shoe. He dumped them both and on his second try he came away with their missing twins. On the third try he kept ahold of the athletic shoe, found its mate, and then slithered back out of the door. He would put on the shoes, go back to the compartment, and, when he heard the engine stop and the and the boat stop moving, make a dash for the gangplank. He could make a life in a squalid village on the edge of a coal or iron field. He could slip away to another city with sun or a beach and find another woman like Jules who would stay with him awhile because of inertia or lack or ambition or because, when he had enough sleep and could successively fend off black moods, he could be an attentive and effective lover. He could find his friend Pez and spoon with him deep in a hole. He could decide to sleep the next three hundred years without hoping ever to regain consciousness.

Nelson walked back to the storage compartment holding the shoes in his hands and when he opened the door he paused. He still had not walked down the staircase and checked for Pez. If he did not would he always wonder what happened to him and would he always feel shame for not at least checking the most obvious spot on the barge? Didn't he owe Pez something for leading him out of the city and coming up with the barge idea? He would check to see where the staircase led, and if Pez didn't turn up below deck then Nelson could crawl back to his small dark spot with a clear conscience and definitively believe Pez to have been lost overboard and drown in the lake. He crept down the stairs less concerned about meeting a crewman, because now he had his story of how he came to be on the barge held in front of him like a shield, even though the story needed to be edited and the details tightened. At the bottom a hallway led to the right and left and the sound of the massive engine vibrated through the walls and floor. Nelson went to the right and found a locked door. Then, he went left and found another locked door. When he applied force from his shoulder the door popped open. He slid his hand up and down the wall to the left of the door to find the light switch.

An overhead bank of fluorescent lights burst on and Nelson recoiled. From across the room a figure lurched off a small foldaway cot and stood up, wearing baggy boxer shorts patterned with a hundred cackling heads of a cartoon character but no shirt. A tattoo wrapped around his torso much like an anaconda would if it had the intent of squeezing all the air from his lungs. The rest of the crewman consisted of bone and sinew and little hair on taut skin. Nelson hesitated, trapped in the doorway with his mind absent a plan. The hesitation allowed the crewman to awake fully and take a few steps toward Nelson and now he looked very agile and poised to rush at him and subdue him with a flurry of punches.

"You really need to tell me who the fuck you are," he said as he bounced on his toes and moved his arms to indicate that once Nelson gave an inadequate answer he would pay for awaking him out of a deep, deep sleep.

"I am...someone...who woke up on a barge," and he launched into his story of being drugged and rolled by a woman at a bar, forgetting a few details but getting the essence and moral of the story correct. The telling seemed effective enough to place it near the bottom rung of 'sailors being mugged or rolled or seduced at a port-o-call stories' except Nelson couldn't call himself a sailor and instead of being missing from a ship he had been dumped on a ship to be carried away from the scene of the crime. The crewman lowered his arms during the story and followed the words closely. "And so I woke up in a storage compartment in the middle of the night not knowing where the fuck I am and I start walking around the boat and I found this room, " Nelson ended.

"Two questions. One, was she a chick-with-dick? And two, why are you carrying a pair of shoes that look suspiciously like my boy Larry's? I know they're Larry's because I was at Shoe Horn when he bought them."

"I don't know if she had a dick. We didn't get that far."

"It's a better story if she has a dick. It makes your experience exotic, freaky, maybe even gives you a whiff of homosexuality or it makes the listener think about their own latent homosexuality and makes them think how far they would have gone with the pretty little he-she or what exactly happened when you were passed out. Did she pull down your drawers and give your wiener a little nibble or did she use the opportunity to have her way with your butthole? See, the possibilities just add to your embarrassment and the listener feels curiosity or disgust for you. She could have even left a perfect print of her lips on the helmet of your dick as a reminder. A present? An invitation to come back again to the fox in a brunette wig and a plunging neck line and mammoth hands? Have you checked your dick for lipstick?"

Nelson shook his head. "No, I didn't think to check. I didn't think we got that far."

"No? You might want to before going to the bridge and presenting this little story to the Captain and the rest of the crew. Now what about the second question? Why are you carrying Larry's shoes?"

Nelson looked at his hand and Larry's cross-trainers dangled from his hand. He couldn't remember why he hadn't put them on his feet.

"They took my shoes again. I needed a pair and I found these."

"Did you take them off Larry's feet? Because he's been talking about them ever since he bought them and really doesn't like to be without them. I got a pair of slippers with him at the 2-4-1."

"They were on the floor."

"That will not go well for you. Stealing shoes is...very egregious. That will be frowned upon, I'm sure."

"My feet were cold, they ached. I was confused and frightened to wake up on a barge. I didn't know where I was and really how I got here. I still don't know where I am."

"Your feet were so cold that you thought you'd carry the shoes around in your hand? So confused you didn't go to the most obvious place a drugged and rolled john would go if he really didn't know where he was or how he got here, namely the bridge? I'm sure you've seen *Star Trek* or fucking pirate movies or one or two movies set on ships at seas like *Midway* or *Mutiny on the Bounty* and let's not get into if you prefer Brando or Clark Gable because frankly I could not care less how your yearnings are expressed by the actor you choose to love, with the point being, the question really for you is where does the Captain stand in these stories? At the bridge, behind the ship's wheel, atop the lever, over a bank of glowing plastic buttons with navigation screens, radar, and radio at his fingertips. I'm thinking it's pretty much universal knowledge that the motherfucker in charge of a boat stands on the bridge and that the bridge is up, not down, and it's as high up as the boat goes and the Captain stands astride like a colossus, pitying the worms around his magnificent feet. Everybody knows the only things you'll find in the hold are rats and worms and cargo and these things don't command a boat and they won't answer your questions or clear your confusion if indeed you are confused. So why did you go down the stairs when you could have gone up?"

"I don't know. I saw an open door and I was looking for my friend and I came down."

"Whoa! Wait. What friend? There's no friend in your story. Are you calling the he-she your friend? Did you think she came along with you and the two of you were going to have a romantic little cruise on the lake?"

"I was with a little guy no more than five foot tall, very dirty, filthy exaggerated toenails and a strange little face."

"So, the chick-with-a-dick was angling for a threesome with you and a dirty little midget? Is this what I'm hearing now?"

"No, he was with me, but he wasn't talking to the girl."

"The alleged girl."

"The alleged girl, I guess."

"With a dick."

"We didn't get that far. I told you."

"I thought the matter was settled. You still don't know? You still haven't checked your dick for lipstick? You haven't analyzed your homosexual impulses that obviously would be ignited once presented with a beautiful faux woman, thus satisfying a female standard used as you whack off to lingerie catalogs and hardcore polaroids of some poor wife with their assholes spread...I'm twisted and wrapped around the curve of the breast from the side and the small of the back just above the crack, adolescent structures always desired and always chased...anyway, here you are sitting on a barstool knowing that this caricature of your masturbatory fantasies really is a man but you let yourself be tricked because how often can you let yourself explore an impulse without guilt?"

"I'm not sure this had anything to do with my situation."

"You're stupid. How do you think it's going to go with the Captain? These are softball questions lobbed up in the air for you to crush them, but you're so twisted with contradictions I'm not sure what happened to you or why it happened to you or really how it happened to you. I keep asking myself why are you on the boat? And I'm a fucking engine worm, a bilge rat, who lives most of his life in a fluorescent room under the deck with this engine roar in my ears. If you can't get past me then the Captain will eat your heart out while it's still pumping." The crewman found a pair of coveralls and slipped them on over his boxers and put on a pair of rubber slippers. "Let's go rouse the Captain and see if your story passes muster. We'll end up heaving you right over the side of the boat."

The crewman pushed Nelson out of the door and up the staircase and then stopped him with a hand on his shoulder in front of a locked door. The crewman had a string of keys the size of his fist tethered to his coveralls and he picked one cleanly from three dozen of its cousins. He unlocked the door and pointed up another staircase, this one illuminated by small red lights embedded in the wall so Nelson thought he could be entering a photographic darkroom but pushed the notion away as being impossible and anachronistic. The staircase rose, narrow, long and steep. Their footsteps echoed against the metallic steps and as Nelson walked closer to the top he could hear a rumble of voices coming from a room at the crest of the stairs. The crewman stopped him again at the top, so he could pass him and walk over to a small group of five men clustered around a green light on the other side of the room. The rumbling tones stopped when the crewman broke into the circle and whispered something that Nelson could not hear. They turned and looked at Nelson, who thought about running down the stairs, but to where? He imagined a comic chase around the finite limits of the boat, dodging crewmen and their stun guns, until he tripped and a rugby scrum landed on his back, a brief human crush, which reminded him of football games he played as a kid, before the electricity started flowing from the tips of their prods and guns. Two men stepped aside, revealing a massive, fleshy face seated behind the undulating green light, which cast curling and loopy waves over the man's thick, iron beard, his eyes, and a hairline that seemed to begin about a half-inch above his eyebrows. Even seated he commanded the men, the room and the barge and probably the lake and the fish swirling around the boat. With a slight wink of his right eye, he pulled Nelson forward and his eyes, heavy-lidded and glowing green, watched him with curiosity and mischief as Nelson covered the space between the top of the stairs and the group.

"Welcome to the U.S.S. Bilgewater," the Captain said in a voice that exploded like a shotgun in a closed room and dripped with hilarity.

"Is that really the name?" Nelson asked because he could think of nothing else to say.

"No, is this boy addled? Is he drunk? First of all, we're not in the service of the United States Navy and second, what idiot other than myself, trying to break the ice of a situation where my crewman has found a stowaway, a waif, a feral man hiding aboard my ship and who has come to me for a reckoning, who other than that would name this magnificent piece of steel something as humble and disgusting as bilgewater? I'm not in the habit of naming ships other than for broad comic purposes. You seem fragile, no, cracked I think, hairlines all over your surface, maybe unnoticeable at this point but nevertheless serious enough to have compromised the integrity of your structure. Far be it for me to be the one to make it all come down crashing down, creating a little pile of what looks like crematory waste where you once stood. Boys, I'm getting the image, a strong, pliable image of a pair of legs standing upright, solid, unmovable, wearing polyester slacks and bare feet. But low and behold look what is next to those bare feet. I imagine it once was a head, a torso, a face, but now it's a pile of dust that has a different form, a conical shape. It's perfectly formed and has the consistency of a ground-up coffee bean. You know you want to touch the perfect form but doing so will mar, possibly destroy, its beauty. But enough of my birdsong. The name of our humble boat, of course, is *The Red Laugh*. No one knows where it comes from or what it means even though it has certain poetic allusions dripping from it. The owners name the boats and one never suspects moneyed people with having senses of humor or souls deeper than their hordes of cash."

"Have you thought of Leonid Andreyev's novel of the same name?" Nelson asked.

"Prisoners, a group of trembling, terrified men. When they were led out of the train the crowd gave a roar-the roar of an enormous, sausage dog, whose chain is too short and not strong enough. The crowd gave a roar and was silent, breathing deeply, which they advanced in a compact group with their hands in their pockets, smiling with their white lips as if currying favor, and stepping out in such a manner as if somebody was just going to strike them with a long stick under the knees from behind."

Nelson briefly closed his eyes to imagine Andreyev's scene and feel kinship with his prisoners being marched before the crowd, and when he opened them again he saw that the captain had broken out is a massive grin, finding immense delight in his own erudition.

"Something enormous, red and bloody, was standing before me, laughing a toothless laugh. That is the red laugh. When the earth goes mad, it begins to laugh like that. You know, the earth has gone mad. There are no more flowers or songs on it; it has become round, smooth and red like a scalped head. Do you see it?" said Nelson as he strained to remember the text.

"Yes, I see it. It is laughing," the Captain returned.

"Look what its brain is like. It is red, like bloody porridge, and is muddled."

"It is crying out."

"It is in pain. It has no flowers or songs. And now- let me lie down with you."

"You are heavy and I am afraid."

"We, the dead, lie down on the living. Do you feel warm?

"Yes."

"Are you comfortable?"

"I am dying."

"Awake and cry out. Awake and cry out. I am going away…"

They stopped and looked at each other as if they had just broken off a duel with five foot long sabers and torches, satisfied with a draw.

"Well, well, well, well, no ordinary stowaway indeed. He knows a bit of Russian literature. Indeed not ordinary. So how is it that he comes to be on my boat in the middle of Lake Erie? Given his intelligence I want to consider him a gift from the bosses, but I'm not jumping to my judgment until I've sorted all the facts. Somebody start."

"He told me a hoary story about being rolled in a bar by a viper-like woman, but I gave him some pointers, which I hope he has taken and incorporated to make the story more believable and, should I say, more interesting," the crewman in coveralls piped in.

The Captain did not look the crewman's way while he spoke but watched Nelson's face for telltale twitches or ticks "I'm sure you told him to include a chick-with-a-dick somewhere in the narrative, no?"

"I suggested….yes, I did. Otherwise the story was too familiar, too common. The way he told it could have come right out of a sea shanty for God sakes. Robert Louis Stevenson and Melville both would have rejected it as clichéd. There was nothing believable in it."

"So, including a transvestite makes it more believable?"

"I don't think they are the same thing. True, both involve men wearing women's clothing but your classic chick-with-a-dick might take it a step further and seek homosexual sex with normally heterosexual men because she has fully assumed her role as a female and she looks only to pick up men, not homosexual men because they are not attracted to women, but heterosexual men because if she can fool them, lure them, bait them, then she has become a woman in her eyes and that's more than enough sexual gratification than she could ever want. And if it turns out that the heterosexual score happens to like dick once he finds out then all the better for the both of them."

"I know that perversions have swamped the mainstream, including chicks-with-dicks, citizens sexually cavorting in furry bunny suits, lesbian rite-of-passage ceremonies for college co-eds, and the like, I'm not completely unaware of their existence and their obvious lure, but it seems to me that adding these modern twists, these silly distractions that are momentarily titillating can make a story more believable because the listener, in their haste to hear something unique and perverted fails to notice obvious discrepancies, but perversions can also slide into cliché in a matter of hours and, oddly, such detail will be seen as entertaining and diversionary, but in the end it throws the whole narrative structure into question and the storyteller will be faced with a mob he has lost to falsehoods." The Captain stopped talking, but no one filled the silence until he continued. "So, in review, our engine man, our very own hairy ape with a bachelor's degree has found another stowaway. He does not have a ticket even for our steerage, but this is no immigrant, no illegal slipping across the border looking for food. He appears to be holding a pair of shoes swiped from one of the crew, because all of us know those pair of shoes, don't we? Haven't we been harangued and buttonholed enough by crewman Larry on the virtues on these very shoes? I hope he sleeps through this dialogue because he would want to rip our poor stow-a-way throw-away's heart out if he saw him touching his vaunted pair. Now, our poor throw-a-way is about to tell us how he ended up on the barge, and why he would ever want to sneak to Wisconsin on a boat when he just as easily could have stolen a car and driven. Unfortunately, the captain and his crew, which in cases such as this act as an ad hoc jury, take a dim view of stowaways and stowaways can turn into throw-a-ways with the tiniest misstep. Really, we're not morally against stealing a ride. The boat could take the whole city on its back if they felt ready to evacuate. No, really we are concerned with stowaways for purely legal reasons. Who can forget the brouhaha created by the bum aboard *The Butterfinger* who unknowingly crawled inside the cargo hold for a little nap to sleep off his Boone's Farm drunk and was buried under a thousand tons of coal and he was only found as he nearly tumbled into a furnace of a smelting plant and whose heirs, while they had written off the poor sodden fellow as a hopeless wastrel and latent pedophile reaped a few million dollars for their trouble, which led to a rash of bum suicides aboard cargo barges, the thinking of the victims being their subsequent deaths would be one last fuck you to their families who, every time they visited the vacation house or hopped into their impractical sports car or draped themselves in outrageously expensive clothes bought with the proceeds from the death of the blackest and meanest of sheep the family would ever know, would be forced to think of him and reassess his value and purpose on the earth. Well, you can imagine this rash, this influenza, really a pandemic of suicides nearly crippled the shipping industry. Two companies went belly-up under the weight of the lawsuits and our very own company, which I must confess has a taste for madness and hysteria, implemented new safety and security protocols. Stowaways, bums like yourself, were not to be tolerated. I'm speaking of zero tolerance in the company's manuals and memos written in overwrought prose, and they were to be dealt with using the exact process developed by corporate. So, if I were a man with a predilection for following orders we would now set in motion the following: Number One) Discovery-ascertain the purpose of the violator's intent following the profiling techniques outlined in Addendum A, being sure to recognize pertinent facts such as age, gender, ethnicity, nationality, clothing, extent of inebriation, cleanliness, godliness, athleticism, degree of myopia, state of shoes (if barefoot go directly to Addendum B protocol), size of penis, depth of education, degree of hair loss on head and coverage on the balance of body, recent job history, political party affiliation, State residency, degree of dirtiness, lung capacity, state of teeth and evidence of recent dental work, number of tattoos, piercings, scars, open wounds, etc.); Number Two) Verify- after collecting preliminary data follow questioning protocol again. This second line of inquiry is to be accompanied with the forms of flesh and mind torture as described and demonstrated in the Enhanced Interrogation Techniques section of Attachment Nine. Repeat as many times as necessary. However, inquisitor should be cognizant of the capacity for cruelty he or she possesses (refer back to psychological profile developed by company assessment) and always maintain sessions within acceptable bounds. Note: Legality of accepted techniques is negotiable and ever-changing so do not be restrained by your own inadequate concept of the law, i.e. acting like a shithouse lawyer. If you have a question immediately contact the central office, using the reference system outlined in the Version Six Codex; Number Three) Humiliation- once guilt has been established the captain is in position to set in motion the two-step punishment phase. The first, humiliation, is essential to the fulfillment of the second, sanctions. In the humiliation phase the offender should be, to use a metaphor for the construction-minded, torn down brick-by-brick until both he and the captain and the crew believe his punishment is apt, overdue and a natural terminus for his faulty judgments. Begin with nudity and keep offender naked throughout the duration of the humiliation phase. If it is determined offender holds exhibitionist tendencies then concentrate on violating anal cavity or genital region. Our research has shown the majority of possible offenders (Note: All men, women and children are in sequential stages of offense, think egg, larva, pupa and butterfly) can be shamed by the state of their teeth. Exploit this whenever possible. Mocking of body in general is an efficient tool in the humiliation phase, but it should be understood that humiliation is more art than science, making the Discovery and Verification stages essential to a successful judgment and termination. The captain must use what he or she has learned during the previous stages in the humiliation stage (i.e. Offender is divorced because his wife committed adultery. Captain has a range of options at his disposal, including tales of famous cuckolds, DVDs of husbands watching their wives have sex with groups of men, re-enactment if ship has female crew member or a man who is willing and able play the part of the wife, exploitation of reasons for divorce including sexual inadequacy, lack of intimacy, job loss, hair loss, child-rearing disagreements, disease, disenchantment, mental illness and inertia, phone call to wife with prepared questions designed for prompting self-flagellation (headquarters has several actresses on retainer to perform role of wife, if needed) and forcing offender to publicly masturbate to the image of his wife having sex with another man. Captain may opt out of watching this, but remember ejaculation must be witnessed to be humiliating. The company understands that most, if not all, of possible offenders have experienced a string of abuses, humiliations and degradations or they wouldn't be attempting to stowaway on a boat sailing between industrial port cities and coal and iron ranges. Humiliation may be hard, if not impossible, to achieve with offender, so it is important that offender is seen as less than human by crew. Given the rash of these offenses the crew may see a number of trials during a single run between destinations, so the company has trademarked the term "shitrats" to describe all offenders and the captain and crew are encouraged to use this term whenever possible. It is highly improbable that the captain will find a crewman who has an affinity for both shit and rats (a Lipton and Wise survey commissioned by the company has found that current crewman give shit a 3% favorable rating and rats a 7% favorable and crewman responding favorably to both shit and rats was below 2%, but less than .25% responded favorably to the term shitrat). The crew must be made to feel dominant, superior, engaged in the assignation of guilt, outraged at the violation and absolutely committed to retribution when enacting the humiliation and sanction phases. In order to protect the company from discovery by so-called legal entities the captain must tend to the hearts and minds of the crew, otherwise the captain will be a gun with no bullets, a tree trunk with no branches, a driver with no car. When the captain has determined the shitrat has been sufficiently humiliated or has determined that said shitrat is impossible to humiliate or the shitrat enjoys the humiliation protocols then immediately proceed to the sanction phase. Remember, company research shows that a majority of shitrats are more than likely waiting for punishment, an appropriate sentence to fit their offenses of squandered lives, mismanaged opportunities, of letting natural advantages lie fallow; Number Four) sanctions- the captain has an array of possible sanctions within the sentencing guidelines, but…ah…shouldn't we wait on this one? We can discuss it once we are there. No need to get too ahead of ourselves in our little journey. You can see, however, the company in all of its raging and beautiful madness has given us an assortment of tools to handle any offense. Now, let's begin at the beginning. I'm a big fan of linear thought and explanation. In school I drew timelines as doodles. I'm a veritable slave to chronology. So tell us your story succinctly. Detail cannot mask a wobbly plot in this case, but really we're looking at plot only. Do not use the chick-with-a-dick structure. It will not come as a surprise and I don't personally find, as I have said, that variety of perversion all that interesting. First there is discovery, then verification. I prefer to skip verification if at all possible because it can become very tedious and quite long. Tell me the truth and I will know it. As for humiliation I can tell even with your erudition you are far past humiliation, maybe. What would be the proper form? The company's standard nudity protocol never works. How many men have we seen flapping their dicks at us like we were schoolgirls? I imagine I could spank you in knowledge of the arts. Your Andreyev recitation makes me think there's a pocket of ego and pride tucked away under your miserable shell. I could root it out and flay it. You wouldn't know what I was talking about but I made this video game whore at the Gallstone Bar and Grille show me her titties just last week. The bartender said only one person had ever gotten farther with the quiz. God knows I'll dump in a truckload of quarters in that machine to see her pussy."

"She took off her panties for me. I am the one."

"You're the one who cracked the code?"

"She has auburn hair. Her smile squeezes the blood from your heart. The most beautiful woman I've ever seen. How did she end up offering herself up like that? At least she made it a challenge."

"What is the name of the preacher in *Moby Dick*?"

"Father Mapple"

"I refused to look it up. I have to honor her by winning fair and square."

"As she has receded into the past I have begun to think she was an angel trapped behind the glass."

"Jesus, you really are the one! You really are the one who cracked the code, who pulled those dainty panties down her thighs. I must say I'm honored and a little humbled. I've not shown you the proper hospitality! Put on those shoes. I'll make Larry understand who you are. Pull up a chair. You saw her bush, tender and beautiful. Oh, sir, you are a wizard! I am the Captain, but I know when I'm in the presence of greatness. I feel like a schoolgirl. My goddamn groin is getting moist. You are the one. Fucking hell, what a lucky find. Imagine how close we were to the sanction phase and casting off a genius. If I hadn't mentioned her we would have never known."

"I'm sure I could do it again if you want to see her. I'm sure there will be a different set of questions, but I know I could nail them."

"Ah! What? He has her at his command? It's like an angel has descended from heaven and found the scab in the middle of my back that I could never reach and with delicate, tender fingers has assuaged the itch from my skin. I'm not one for impulse, but I'm prepared to offer you a job aboard this barge. There's time for reading. The boat runs itself, basically. It's been eons since I've met an individual I felt I could learn from. Christ, if you show me her soft auburn snatch I'll consider making you my number two. You'll be on your way to becoming a captain. It's a beautiful lake, tempestuous and wicked. She knows my desires and I've given her everything I've ever thought, known or felt. In the quiet she understands."

The crewman who had discovered Nelson leaned over and whispered in the Captain's ear for a minute or two. The Captain stared straight ahead, his countenance darkening the longer the whisper lasted. Finally, the crewman broke from his ear and the Captain turned his eyes to his hands folded in his lap and let the silence hang as he thought through his response.

"My engineer has informed me that I am on the cusp of violating company protocol and for the best interest of the boat and the crew he has invoked an anticipatory appeal on two points. One, you are technically a stowaway, a shitrat, and the stowaway protocol must be followed even if it ends in exoneration and the offering of a crew position. Order and organization must be maintained. We must think of the barge first, individual desires second. My excitement in finding "the one" carried me beyond the protocol, so I apologize to the crew and the ship for my error. I wish to thank our crewman Honeycrisp for his judicial acumen. The second point that Mr. Honeycrisp has elucidated is that our stowaway happens to have no shoes and, to bring further emphasis to this point, happens to be holding a pair of shoes purchased and adored by another crewman, Mr. Larry Chancellor. This observation intuits that our friend slipped onto the barge with no shoes, meaning that we should proceed directly to the Addendum K protocol otherwise known as The Shoeless Shitrat Elimination and Decontamination Protocol. The company gives us some flexibility in this regard, so before dispatching the discovery and verification phases and setting Addendum K in motion I am going to ask the standard questions and give our stowaway a chance to explain himself. Agreed?" The Captain looked at his crewmen who nodded their reluctant acceptance of the altered protocol. The Captain could tell he still had firm control, but he would have to do something generous in the days to come to guarantee their full acceptance. "Fine, so I am going to ask you a series of questions and you are to answer them as truthfully and fully as you are able. Sometimes the truth can be elusive or it is processed through a filter known as you. We understand, so maybe I should say I am interested in your truthful perspective. Understand?"

Nelson nodded that he understood even though he tried desperately to come up with a statement that would be an untruth from his perspective. The Captain caught his look and let out an exaggerated sigh and rolled his eyes to the ceiling.

"Wash chicks-with-dicks from your mind. Honeycrisp, while a stickler for rules, has a way of mucking up the proceedings with his fetishes."

"Right."

"Good. What is your name?"

"Nelson Munroe."

"Occupation?"

"Unemployed."

"Previous occupation."

"Actuary."

"Where do you live?"

"I'm searching for a place to live. I'm between cities."

"Last known address?"

"Tampa Bay, Florida."

"Purpose for being in Cleveland."

"I ran a shipment of cocaine up from Tampa and tried to deliver it to Montenegro," Nelson blurted. His confidence in the fairness and impartiality of the Captain made him cling to the truth and ride it like a sled down an icy hill, racing to his doom.

"Previous occupation?"

"Drug mule."

The Captain scratched out the first answer and wrote the second next to the blot.

"Height?"

"Six foot and two inches, more or less."

"Weight?"

"180 pounds."

"Ah, nicely trim and fit. Shoe size?"

"Ten and a half."

"Chest measurement. The size of your suit jackets."

"Forty-two."

"Arm length?"

"Thirty-six."

"Head circumference?"

"Twenty-five inches."

"Penis length when flaccid?"

"I don't know."

The Captain waited, a look of infinite patience on his face.

"Five inches."

"Length when fully engorged?"

"Seven inches."

"Girth when fully engorged?"

"Three and a quarter inches."

"Date of last dental check-up?"

"Two years ago."

"Are you on any prescriptions?"

"No."

"Are you an alcoholic or habitual drug user?"

"What does habitual mean?"

"For the sake of argument, let's say every day."

"Every day? No."

"What is your standing with Montenegro?"

"Fugitive."

"Why did you attempt an unauthorized boarding of *The Red Laugh*?"

"I am sneaking out of the city. I feared the airport would be watched. My car has been disabled. I don't like busses. I'm tired and weak. I couldn't walk back to Florida. My friend Pez suggested we take the barge. He said it had the best chance for success. No one would be watching."

"Did you board the barge with shoes on?"

"Yes, I had shoes. They were taken from me while I slept in the storage compartment."

"Did you board the barge with a friend?'

"Yes."

"We have found no sign of him."

"He may have jumped or fallen overboard."

"Why?"

"I don't think he could handle wide open spaces. He lived underground for years."

"When you say underground, you don't mean 'apart from the mainstream' do you? I'm not even sensing a Dostoevsky allusion. I sense a different meaning here."

"I mean underground in a hole."

The Captain leaned back in his chair and bit the knuckle of his thumb, looking like a reluctant boxer hesitating before throwing a final and fatal punch.

"Who put him in the hole?"

"Dogs. Some kind of wild hellhound. A pack."

"Why are you a fugitive from Montenegro?"

"I lost the shipment. I took it to the drop-off location, but I was too late and I was late because ever since I've been in Cleveland I've been hounded by the pack. There's a pack of some sort roaming through town. They are relentless. They can't be stopped, because it's impossible to know how many there are, where they are, when they are watching. They buried me a hole. They've taken my shoes. They stopped the delivery. They must have taken Pez off the boat or pushed him and made the lake his last hole. He wouldn't have jumped I don't think. I came aboard with shoes and now I don't have them. Who else would take them? Did you take them? Did I throw them overboard in a fit of sleepwalking self-destruction? Pez wouldn't take them. He would never include the shoes in a practical joke. He knows what they cost and what they mean. Who else? It started, I think, with that video game. I stripped her, that auburn beauty, and met a man named Joshua, no, Jack, something like that and he took me to a party where dogs were dancing and I've been in a cycle of torture ever since."

The Captain patted Honeycrisp's back, the man who had stopped him from departing from the protocol and, as it turned out, from endangering the boat.

"Men you can see how often we skirt disaster. My best intensions, my over-eagerness to connect with a man...should I say it?...who is my equal could have led us to ruin. Even though I am the Captain I too am propelled by irrational thought, desire, loneliness, greed and ego. These insidious impulses batter and pummel my defenses and the one who stands before you slipped in and infected my reason. He shows that every trick is at their disposal; they know all the ways you can be brought down. Engineer Honeycrisp has performed a great service to me personally and to the institution that is this boat and for that reason I will be considering elevating him to number two, or at least promote him from the bottom rung he now inhabits. Men, proceed to the emergency protocol as outlined in Addendum K."

The five crewman rushed Nelson and seized him before he had a chance to run or even drop the shoes, and he put up both hands to protect himself. His clothes were yanked off of him and the cross-trainers were pried out of his hand. Within a minute Nelson stood in his underwear, held by a crewman on either side, facing the Captain, who sauntered toward him. He had turned the expression on his face into an oval of inscrutable slate.

"Open your mouth."

Nelson complied and the Captain produced a small and bright pen light and gave Nelson's teeth and tongue a thorough examination. The Captain walked behind Nelson and the guards, touched Nelson's spine between the shoulder blades and walked his fingers down the vertebrae to the tail bone. The Captain's hand felt abnormally hot as if he had just pulled it out of an oven mitt or a sink filled with scalding water. He leaned toward Nelson's ear.

"Did you really solve her?"

"I did."

The Captain sighed and leaned back away from Nelson's ear.

"Tis a pity. Take him to isolation."

"What happened to Pez? What did you do with Pez? He finally made it out and you threw him in the lake."

The crewman pulled at Nelson and half-dragged him down the stairs, onto the deck, down the length of the boat to the bow, down another short flight of steps under the deck, to a hallway lighted with buzzing and flickering fluorescence and finally to a steel door with massive rivets lining its perimeter so that it looked like it could never be opened again. Honeycrisp used a combination of keys in a predetermined order and the door swung open on hidden hinges. The crewmen pushed Nelson across the threshold into darkness. The door slammed shut behind him and he listened to the reverse sequence of keys locking in him. After a moment of total darkness a small light, recessed in the ceiling, flickered alive. The room may have been ten feet by ten feet and the walls, floor and ceiling had all been painted the same deep gray. He could find no light switch on the wall so one of the crewmen, in a show of small mercy, must have turned the light on from the outside. The room lay barren of detail except for a drain in the middle of the floor. The floor slightly sloped from all four corners to this center point. Nelson thought of ritual slaughter, his blood draining lazily from one of the remote corners to the center drain, the paint dark enough to mask stray splatter and viscera. He sat on the floor. His underwear held several strata of filth, like he had worn it for weeks straight with no relief or washing. He thought about taking it off, but the soiled cotton gave him some comfort. He thought about masturbating to pass the time, but he determined the crew might take a dim view of semen on their drain or he thought they might have a hidden camera somewhere in the walls or ceiling and masturbating for the entertainment of a group of men gave him no pleasure. He lay back and stared at the ceiling, the gray walls, and the dim light and remained on his back for hours. His thoughts became turgid and half-formed. He even found it difficult to rouse a worry and he thought he may have reached a terminus, a place where his thoughts and energy would subside even if he continued breathing. After what could have been days a small slot opened in the ceiling and an oversized capsule tumbled through the air and landed a few feet from Nelson's head. The force of the landing on the steel floor caused a wall between two chemical reservoirs in the capsule to rupture and a thick white vapor boiled out of the capsule where the chemicals kissed. He turned his face toward the vapor, breathed deeply and passed out.

Hands jostled, shook, slapped and dragged Nelson to the deck of the barge. The Captain's face loomed above him or in front of him. The night air felt cold against his thighs. Honeycrisp threw water in his face and another slap stung his cheek. He remembered stowing away on the barge and the room with the oversized capsule. Behind the Captain's head looked like the skyline of Cleveland.

"There's focus in his eyes. Throw him over," the Captain commanded.

Nelson tumbled though the air, a smear of images that included a black river, illuminated buildings, the side of the barge, a patch of black sky and five or six heads peering over the railing watching his descent, tumbled past him. The first part of his body to enter the water was his shoulder, followed quickly by his ribs, hip, face and legs. The impact forced the air from his lungs and he shot toward the bottom of the river. His feet touched the thick, slimy slit and the cold began to suffocate him. Above him and around him black water swirled as the barge pulled away. He touched the bottom with his hands and kept his eyes closed because he thought if he opened his eyes he might see a drowned Pez, eyeless and bloated from weeks in the water. His lungs were burning and a knot had begun to form in his throat. He dampened his panic by trying to convince himself he sat in a familiar, well-worn dirt hole. He just needed to take a breath and comfort would flow inside and through him. One breath or two and the muddy river water would fill his lungs past the knot in his throat and he could die. The crude animation of the basic cable show about drowning flashed through his mind, showing a very alive brain conscious of its own death, and he suddenly kicked against the river bottom and clawed his way to the surface. When he broke the surface he gulped air and hacked it back out with painful coughs. He spotted the dark outlines of weeds and floated and pulled himself through the water until he touched the steel bulkhead. He held on to the top of the wall until his breathing returned to more or less a normal rate. He began shivering so he pulled himself out of the water enough to use his belly as a fulcrum on the top of the wall. He jackknifed his body, grabbed two handfuls of thick weeds, and pulled until his legs flopped onto the bank. He staggered to his feet and began a herky-jerky dance as he tried to stay warm while trying to shake the remaining water from his body.

Nelson lurched through a narrow wedge of weeds until he found a cracked and pitted road, where he turned left and proceeded in a shambling march. Surely once the sun rose and the world awoke the police would find him by the side of the road, barefoot and wearing only dirty underwear, and they would whisk him off the street for being indecent and lock him in a foul smelling room that also felt strangely comfortable, something akin to a diseased fetus crawling into another mother's filthy womb. He walked past vaguely familiar landmarks and felt he had a better understanding of the tangle of streets and warehouses now that he navigated them for the third time. He found a road leading out of the valley and he ascended it with his head down, watching for the jagged edges of debris that could slice his foot open. The sun had broken the horizon and cast the city in a soft pink light. As he reached the summit of the hill he heard a distant putter of exhaust from below and behind him. Nelson turned and saw a small, dented car with streaks of rust along the doors and on the hood. The engine wheezed and grinded against the strain of the hill and it sounded like a tailpipe scraped and bounced along the asphalt. As the car reached the crest Nelson jumped into the middle of the street. The startled driver slammed on the brakes and stalled the car in a wild scramble of hands and feet. The car started rolling backwards as the driver tried to restart the engine, which she checked by pulling the emergency brake. A wail of fear shot from the window.

"I'll run you down. I swear I'll run you down," Koo Koo Beatrice shouted.

Nelson spread his arms from his side as if welcoming the car's grill and bumper. Koo Koo started the car, ground the gears until she found first and tried to dart around him, but Nelson jumped in the car's path again. She slammed on the brakes, but this time the bumper clipped Nelson's leg and sent him sprawling to the ground. Koo Koo came out of the car holding a long kitchen knife and when she stood over him pointed it at his face.

"Why did you do that? Are you hurt? Are you going to do that again because next time I won't stop and I'll just run over you," came out in a rush.

"Why don't you call the police? I don't mind." Nelson propped himself up on his elbows and looked into her face and recognized her from the diner.

"Why should I call the police? Have you done something?" She lowered the knife but still kept a strong grip on it.

"It might be the simplest solution. I'm sure they have a process for people like me."

"You came in my diner about a week ago." Koo Koo furrowed her forehead with concentration, trying to connect her memory with the present in something resembling a linear construct.

"A week? No, I think it was two days ago, maybe yesterday."

"No, at least a week. You had no shoes on and you forgot your wallet. I serve my regulars so strangers tend to stick out."

"As you can see my fortunes have taken a turn for the worse."

"That's the dirtiest pair of underwear I've ever seen."

They each took a moment to appreciate the amount of filth ground into the cotton.

"As you can see they have taken nearly everything. My only possession is this ragged pair of underwear."

"Who robbed you? The people at Shoe Horn? I wouldn't be surprised because that place has the creepiest look and all kind of stories are coming out of there. A friend of mine said it looks like a cross between a spaceship and a gulag."

"No, it wasn't Shoe Horn. I don't know who they were."

"It looks like you got rolled in a bar. I heard a lot of that is happening now, especially with men impersonating women, which, if you ask me, is about as creepy as you can get."

"I don't know where to go from here. Do you have any ideas?"

"Look, you made me late for work so you can start by getting out of the road," she said as she looked at Nelson's prone, nearly naked body and felt pity and concern. "I'm taking it that you have no one to call who will help you out?" Nelson slowly shook his head and Koo Koo thought of her regulars Brankowski and Hayes who could arrest Nelson if he turned out to be more insane than he had already exhibited. She held out a hand and helped him to his feet. "Why don't you get in the car and I'll take you to work. I think there's an old pair of coveralls in the backroom from the last cook. They should fit. I don't think he left shoes, though. You could always go back to Shoe Horn to get a pair."

"I'm not going back there. I stole the last pair and I don't think they would welcome me back."

"Look, I'm about to let you into my car, even though you're practically naked and now you're telling me you're a thief. What else are you? Did you really get mugged or are you just a garden variety freak who likes to show himself in his underwear to unsuspecting women? I need to know what to expect before you get in the car."

"I would have answered a different way a couple of days ago, but now I'm thinking there's something wrong with me."

"Like what? A specific pattern of behavior would be helpful."

"If you're asking whether or not I cling to fantasies of chopping up women or abusing them in nefarious ways the answer is no. My imagination on that front goes no further than the Marquis de Sade. My fetish seems to involve the obtaining and losing of shoes. My struggle to leave this city has buried me deeper than I thought I could go. So, even though you are a very beautiful woman I feel no violent impulses toward you. I am only grateful that you stopped, but it also would have been acceptable to have run me over and left me broken by the side of the road, just like it would now be acceptable for you to retract your offer of a ride and drive away to your diner."

"How did you lose your clothes?"

"The losing of my clothes either involved a devious but gorgeous transvestite or a captain of a barge who had committed most of the world's literature to memory. I'm not sure which is true, but the result is the same. They left me a pair of underwear that might not even be mine. I think they may be a pair left by my girlfriend's lover that accidently ended up in our wash. They don't fit right and I don't think I've ever bought this brand, so in all likelihood all that I have left is a pair or borrowed underwear."

"Her lover's underwear? I'd say that's pretty low."

"Rock bottom."

"Get in the car. God, I'm late. There's got to be a crowd at the door already. They all love routine. If I take a day off I pay for it with snide comments and hurt feelings for a week."

They climbed into her old Volkswagen. The seats, the dash and the carpet had been sun-bleached and held the memory of 35,000 entrances and exits and the cabin smelled like tobacco ash and hairspray. The back seat lay under a pile of debris, everything from utility bills to romance novels with no covers on them to empty lipstick tubes to napkins and empty bottles and cans of juice and tea. Koo Koo quickly cleared the passenger seat before Nelson sat down. She accelerated and the car shimmied, squeaked and wobbled around them as if the integrity of the car's architecture had been comprised or the rivets had all but given way. She flipped him a glamour magazine that sported a large painted head of a woman so drugged and beautiful she had ceased to exist in the conscious realm and had been doomed to flit from magazine cover to magazine cover looking for her lost humanity.

"Cover yourself. It's the dirt that bothers me more than anything else."

Nelson opened the magazine in half and placed in on his lap. The woman stared back at him, unconcerned about her sudden proximity to his cock and silently signaling for help to escape her plastic and painted world or like a Siren tried to entice Nelson to join her in her studio and forget all that he had known. Nelson placed a hand over her face, thus blocking her entreaties.

Koo Koo squinted at the road. Even if she hadn't accidently sat on her glasses a week before she probably would have not have been wearing them for the sake of vanity. The road held large objects and bright signs and she did not need much sharp detail or clear sight while driving. She lit a cigarette and smiled from the corner of her mouth closest to the cracked side window. Nowadays even a dirty bum had the potential of being offended by cigarette smoke and some of her craziest customers were more worried about cancer than where their next meal would be coming from. She kept Nelson in her periphery, watching for any quick movements directed toward her, even though he seemed docile and beaten. She wondered what her friend Maggie might say if she saw her driving down the road with a dirty and naked bum with a glam magazine splayed across his lap like he hid an inopportune erection. Maggie always scolded her for her lack of awareness or judgment when it came to situations involving men. She said Koo Koo only saw the hurt and pain in their eyes and always missed the violence and capacity for torture in their hearts. She had a point. Her empathy extended to women, of course, but men carried around their smashed manhood and disappointments with humor and a determination that bordered on lunacy. How could she help but be attracted to the condemned dancing on the platform of the gallows? Only a few men she had met had turned into bitches after a spectacular run of misfortune and even they could laugh at their own ruin after a few drinks or they summoned the energy for a rally because they thought they could have some success with her. Maggie rolled her eyes demonstratively at her cockeyed worldview, reminding Koo Koo that men committed ninety-five percent of violence and the other five percent was committed by women responding to the violence of men and these little broken boys she took so fondly under her wing, into her nest, were all monsters in waiting, more than capable of hurting the one person who had held out their hand to help. Is it any wonder that Dr. Jekyll and Mr. Hyde or the Wolfman or any other story in which a timid and nerdy soul turns into an uncontrollable monster is about a man? Don't you think these tales are warnings to women that every man carries the blackness within him, is ready to succumb to it and can't be responsible for the devastation his monster wreaks? One night, in a fit of frustration, Koo Koo called Maggie a bitter old hag and Maggie scowled back and said to mark her words that Koo Koo Beatrice would one day collect the wrong stray and she would wake up dead. They didn't speak for months after that and when they finally did begin talking again they never mentioned that particular exchange.

"Have you decided who took your pants?" Koo Koo asked through a breath of smoke.

Nelson shook his head. The transvestite story sounded more plausible, but he didn't want to commit quite yet. Koo Koo pulled to the curb in front of the diner. X-Ray and Checkers leaned against the building staring at their shoes. Gaby paced in front of them, yakking an unbroken string of words in the cadence of an electric mixer. Her thoughts centered on her worry that Koo Koo had been abducted or hurt in a traffic accident, so her details included every half-remembered murder, traffic fatality, rape, and medical malpractice suit she had seen on television or had read in the paper. Checkers tried to stop the flow a few times, but he knew in the end that once she had taken flight nothing could stop her except the need for oxygen and when that happened the words would slow to a drizzle between gulping breaths and only then would he have a chance to redirect her. They all three turned when they heard Koo Koo's signature engine putter and Gaby sighed dramatically, enveloping both her relief and anger at Koo Koo for making her worry.

"It's a man. A man made her late. That shouldn't be surprising. And it's a man who's not wearing a shirt. That is surprising. Koo Koo doesn't often let her affairs spill into the public realm, but a man with no shirt is an absolute scandal!" Gaby wobbled over to the passenger side of the car as Koo Koo exited the driver's side. "A man with no pants either! Koo Koo has embraced scandal with both hands! Who's in the car Koo Koo?"

"I found him in the middle of the road."

"Had he shed his clothes or was this a service you provided?"

"Goodness Gaby. You want me to gossip about myself?" she said in mock indignation. "Alas, I found him in his underwear."

"And you still picked him up? One day someone will nominate you for saint, of course, you'll have to perform a miracle or two before you'll receive consideration but you're still young."

"Maybe you can cure my bladder from bursting at the seams," Checkers called to them.

"Shut up! Koo Koo has a man!" She turned back to Koo Koo and lowered her voice. "Checkers is so sad when he walks around the house in his underwear. His droopy testicles and his gray and holey pair of briefs make me want to cry. I buy him robes, but he won't wear them. His old man's body and his sex covered in rags, the sadness of the sight gnaws at my intestines."

Koo Koo walked to the front of the diner with Gaby in her wake.

"Our Koo Koo has found herself a stud. Once a woman finds her man she forgets about everything else. What chance do we stand X-Ray? She won't be slinging hash much longer," Checkers brooded.

"Checkers! It's just a naked bum she picked up off the street. He's in no position to support her and take her away from us," Gaby had stopped and spoke directly into Checkers' face.

"A naked bum is as good as any, or at least as good as Koo Koo has ever had. She'll be distracted. Her mind will not stay on the eggs. It's the first day of the romance and already she's late."

X-Ray inched closer to the car and raised his glasses. He inspected Nelson from head to toe through the blue and red lenses. He lowered the glasses and walked directly to the side of the car where he cupped his hand to the glass to block glare and pressed his nose against the window. Nelson looked away from the crushed nose against the glass. X-Ray raised his glasses, scanned Nelson's body, lingering over his head, before turning on his heel and scurrying into the diner.

Koo Koo had already taken her place behind the counter, had fired up the griddles and now prepared a pot of strong black coffee that her customers preferred.

"Where did you find him?" X-Ray asked as he slid on his regular stool.

"In the street, for God's sake," Gaby roared. "How many times does she have to repeat it?"

"Mmmm, yes…yes…he's a jumble…been turned inside out by the looks of it …not everything is in the place it's supposed to be…I don't suppose it will have a lingering effect….but…well….to put it delicately he may have trouble functioning below decks…there will definitely be trouble in that area…form is function…his skin still looks elastic so there's some hope…there's always hope…at least that's what some people subscribe to…I've never been much of a believer in that bromide."

"I forgot to get him those overalls. Let me get him dressed then I'll cook your breakfasts." They moaned in protest and Checkers slammed his palm against the table.

"We had a nice arrangement here. Our needs were met. We had a capable and beautiful servant willing to dance for a pocketful of change. Once you introduce a bantam rooster into the proceedings it all gets blasted apart. He's turned her head. I don't want to lose Koo Koo, but it all seems so inevitable. Why do we always chose our own pleasure over service to mankind? What's wrong with a life of service behind a griddle?"

"Sometimes a girl needs to have a little fun. She's not here to be your nun. I take plenty good care of you."

"You're joking, right? You haven't cooked a breakfast in five years, for God's sake. Koo Koo has the calling."

Koo Koo came out of the backroom holding a pair of dusty coveralls and she walked outside to the car. Nelson had leaned the seat back and closed his eyes, but he hadn't fallen asleep yet even though his body felt leaden. Koo Koo knocked on the glass and held up the coveralls for him to see once he opened his eyes. He pushed open the door and she dropped the coveralls in his lap and when she saw the underwear again she decided that it would be a shame to put clean clothes over them.

"Take those off. I'll block you." She turned her back, putting her small frame between Nelson and one or two possible lines of sight out of fifty that a passing car or pedestrian would have into the car. No one passed by on the street anyway to see Nelson peel off the underwear and throw them in the storm drain under Koo Koo's car. Then, he slipped on the coveralls up to his waist. The previous cook had been several inches shorter than Nelson so when he pulled them over his hips the pant legs stopped well above his ankles. He stumbled out of the car and turned in circles as he tried to find the sleeve. Koo Koo stopped the spin, untwisted the coveralls and held the sleeve so Nelson could slip his arm through. When he finally managed to inch the zipper up its track his body felt compressed, except for his ankles and wrists which felt oddly exposed.

"You might as well owe me two breakfasts," said Koo Koo.

The seam of the coveralls sliced into the underside of his scrotum and worked itself deep into the crack of his ass so when he walked into the diner he looked as if he had been on the receiving end of a rough colonoscopy. He found a corner, put his head on the table and fell sound asleep before Koo Koo could come back with a cup of fresh coffee.

"You're wearing him out, Koo Koo my dear," Checkers pointed a thumb at Nelson's head. "And looks like you're ripping his hair out by the roots." Checkers referred to the patch of scalp exposed by the dogs.

X-Ray lifted his glasses from under the counter and examined Nelson again, after first sneaking a peek at Koo Koo's lacy thong. The scan confirmed his first examination. Nelson's organs were on the move.

"I think he might have been handsome once. Too bad you didn't meet him years ago," Gaby whispered over the counter to Koo Koo. "He must have been something before his troubles."

"He's not that bad. Just a little worn, a little beaten. Looks mostly like surface scratches."

"I've seen his look before. This is a downward spiral. There's no coming back for him."

"I found him in the road in his underwear. I have nothing invested in him."

"There's something amiss in his architecture...a collapsing...an imbalance..." X-Ray said to the counter.

"I'm just saying. A woman might get ideas. This one is beyond saving. He's one of them. There's nothing to be done but to stay away. It's always sad to see the handsome ones go. They look like they have more potential, but it the end..."

Business remained light most of the morning and Koo Koo decided to close shortly after noon when the lunchtime rush never materialized. She cleaned the griddles and sent X-Ray off to the Cooty Bar a few blocks away where he would spend the rest of the day nursing beers with rodent-like sips, always aware of his daily budget and how much time he would spend at every place. Koo Koo woke Nelson who jumped at her touch. He looked wild-eyed around the room until he locked onto his feet and tears began streaming from his eyes.

"I don't have any goddamn shoes. I need some goddamn shoes." A wave of emotion quivered through his words.

"There's the Shoe Horn," Koo Koo offered. "You can get almost anything for fifteen bucks. You could give me your size and I could go in and get a pair."

A sob burst from Nelson, catching them both by surprise.

"It's hard being without shoes, huh?"

Nelson nodded and covered his hands with his face. The prospect of hunting for shoes, of having to break in another pair of inflexible soles, of witnessing their hideous glare in the sun, of waking in the morning to bare feet, all of it pushed down on him and combined with the constriction of the too small coveralls and nearly suffocated him on the spot.

Maggie's face flashed into Koo Koo's mind. She scowled as she theatrically threw a black rose on the lid of a coffin being lowered into the ground. "Are you happy now, Koo Koo? Have you finally found the dénouement you have been seeking?" Koo Koo couldn't answer because she had forgotten the meaning of happy, but she thought she probably would not want to be dead.

"Look, at my apartment I have a pile of clothes an old boyfriend left. They probably would fit better than those coveralls. I think there's a pair of shoes. I could take you there. You slept through breakfast, so I could make you lunch."

"You don't really want to take me there. If you want the coveralls back I can give them back to you now."

"No, I don't want them back and I can't let you walk out of here with no shoes and no prospect of finding shoes. I don't need that guilt raining down on my head."

"When did he leave?"

"That gets right to the point, but no harm in an answer, I guess. Months ago. Vanished. Why did you think he did the leaving? I could have kicked him out. I could have been the one who left."

"People who take off always leave a few possessions, like it's a point of entry back, a hedging of bets. When you get kicked out you want every possession. You'll fight over a used toothbrush, or a package of roach traps."

"Have experience with this do you?"

"I think quite a bit of experience."

"He's not coming back. It was flight, more like fleeing a natural disaster than hedging a bet."

"I've done that too, I think."

"And left your shoes?"

The lightness Nelson had begun to feel collapsed. He looked at his feet and noticed his toenails needed clipping.

"I'm sorry. I forgot that's a sore spot. What's your name anyway?"

Nelson opened his mouth as if he knew the answer then stopped to think about how to form the syllables of his name. Just as he shaped the sound it became garbled in multiple layers of echo. When the echo died, his mind had been cleared of an answer. "That's an interesting question."

"C'mon. You're telling me you can't remember your name? Or do you just not want to tell me? Is whatever you've done to get where you are that bad? Is the law involved?"

"It's none of that. I remember. I'm blocked right now. I'm having difficulty with recall. I'm pretty sure I know my name."

"Did the transvestite hit you on the head?"

"I think the transvestite took my clothes and the Captain may have violated me in some way."

"What way? In a gay kind of way?'

"No, he disrupted something deep in my head. He reached down and scrambled my thoughts and altered everything so now its like I'm playing a chess match with crackers and string, know what I mean?"

"Not exactly. Wasn't there a little guy with you? The first time you came in the diner?"

"He didn't make it. I lost him en route."

Apprehension seeped though Koo Koo. She had picked up a man who couldn't say his name, who couldn't make up a name, who wouldn't create a comfortable fiction to make her feel at ease, who now owned only a pair of ridiculous coveralls, as open a wound as she would likely find walking on two bare feet, and who now had cryptically confessed to something dark happening to his sidekick. She ushered him to her car and wondered how many wild chances she had left in her life.

"Look, if you don't want to take me to your apartment you can let me out here. I'll be fine."

"I think you have proven you definitely will not be fine. If you have any more weird revelations just keep them to yourself. We might be able to get through this if you keep quiet."

They drove the rest of the way to Koo Koo's apartment in silence. The outside door of the apartment building had been smashed off its hinges and the steel mail box that had a compartment for each of the apartments had been battered by a crowbar or baseball bat and had been spray-painted with dripping nonsensical graffiti. She retrieved her mail from one of the unlocked flaps and shuffled through a collection of bills as she led Nelson up the stairs to the second floor. The stairs were covered in a deep green carpet patterned with brown lozenges. Plumes of dust rose from their feet as they walked. The walls were scarred from the constant flow of itinerant renters banging their meager belongings up and down the stairs. The hallway smelled like burnt cooking oil and rotten fruit. Engrossed in the reckoning that had come in the mail, Koo Koo held open her apartment door for him and forgot her apprehension. The suffocation of her bills prodded her to become even more reckless.

Before him sprawled two enormous and open rooms. The floors had been sanded blonde and now blazed in the afternoon sun. They had walked into the living room, which held a sofa, two overstuffed chairs, a coffee table, a small bookcase jammed with paperbacks, two end tables and a fireplace with a wrought iron gate and the room still seemed spacious. A floor to ceiling painting hung on the wall behind the sofa and its width almost stretched the entire length of the wall as well.

"Why don't you take a bath first? You need a thorough soaking and cleaning. My shower is broken or I'd tell you to stand under it until the hot water gave out."

Nelson, absorbed in the painting, didn't answer Koo Koo. "OK, I'll go run the bath now." She walked through the dining room, past a long table with a full set of six chairs grouped around its perimeter and disappeared down a long hallway.

Nelson stepped closer to the painting, which had been executed in the manner of Hieronymus Bosch or Pieter Bruegel the Elder. The massive canvas held dozens of small tableaus painted in precise brushstrokes. Nelson's eye first caught the figure of a pale and frightened man, his mouth twisted with thoughts of torture and humiliation. Naked, he covered his genitals with his hands. He had let a beard grow and his hair sprouted in all directions. He stood slightly stooped, looking down, because he balanced himself on a tall column of rock and his toes hung over the edge because the perch was too small. Below him writhed an angry mass of people, some holding torches, others stones or clubs, their palpable hatred shining through on their faces. Their bodies were covered in dirt and tattered clothes. Nelson projected that the man on the column had been their leader and had betrayed them in some fundamental and irreversible way. Around the man and his judges rose other columns of flattened cars stacked like crushed aluminum cans, skyscrapers tilting from the earth like a collection of thrown darts. Figures, men and women, all naked and thin and pale clung to the columns as if escaping the raging torrent of a flood, looked to the ground with frightened eyes. A couple stood under an umbrella with only the exposed spines for protection, waiting for the coming storm. Men with dog heads and disproportionately large phalluses chased naked women and boys in circles, up barren trees, through streams and across meadows strewn with wild flowers and old tires. A few had caught their quarry but had the tables turned on them as groups of women ravaged the dog men, satisfying themselves by riding the phalluses and slicing the men's throats or eviscerating them. One woman, straddling her dog man, had a dog head as well. Nelson walked around the sofa to look at the bottom edge of the painting. In the lower left corner a small group of men had killed a dog and had thoroughly dissected it. Blood dripped from its chest cavity and onto a makeshift gurney made out of sawhorses, a wood front entrance door and lawnmower wheels bolted onto the legs of the horses to make it mobile. One scientist placed the dog's brain in an old fashioned scale and he used his own brain as a counterweight as the top of his skull had been sawn off and an empty cavity revealed. The discarded skull cap lay at his feet with hair still attached. The dog's brain was obviously heavier. Other scientists held the dog's entrails up to the light and another held the dog's heart to his mouth, chewing on the left ventricle. In another tableau a group of naked men and women were choking a dog to death. Slobber dripped from the dog's lips and teeth and its eyes revealed the end to be very near. Around the group of men and women a larger group of dogs had encircled them and approached their exposed assholes as they bent over to kill the dog. Several of the dogs already had erections and the intimation loomed that a group violation would be taking place soon. Surrounding this scene were ten or so other groupings of men and women losing individual battles with dogs. In one a couple huddled together as dogs leapt over them with unabashed joy. In another, a dog had a mouthful of a man's genitals as five other dogs rolled on the ground panting and laughing. Next to that, a man shimmied up a greased pole as dogs with long spears pricked him in the thighs and back. In another a woman hung upside down from a tree. A rope had been tied around her ankles but her hands and been left free. Her long red hair hung nearly to the ground. Dogs perched on the branches like grackles, watching her swing. One dog had ventured from his perch and clung to rope and hung upside down as well. Its long tongue had curled from his mouth and performed satisfying cunnilingus. Above that scene a line of men and women walked with their hands up as a guard of shepherds watched them. The prisoners were heading toward a grotesque meat grinder, cast iron and ornate but covered in viscera and blood. Three figures were trying to climb from the mouth of the grinder as their lower halves were consumed, and at the bottom ribbons of ground meat coiled on the grass. A pack of dogs sat along the edges of the pile happily eating. Men fucked dogs, but other dogs used the opportunity to chew the men's scrotums from behind as they thrust. Women danced with abandon with dogs on two legs. A small group of men and women sat in a circle watching television with a dog head on the screen as a pack advanced on them from behind in low hunting postures and raised back fur. Men and women tried to escape by swimming across a swift river, but dogs stood on a bridge and cut them down with precise sniper fire and hurled bricks. Women were trapped in oversized bird cages and were suspended over a scene of canine tranquility, sleeping in dog piles, puppies playing, and chasing rabbits through gardens and hedges. A family of four sat around a Christmas tree unwrapping their presents. Torn paper lay on the floor and each held an open box on their lap. The father's own head lay in his box. The mother's box contained her gravestone and the dates of her death, just a few months in the future, had already been chiseled into the stone. One child, a girl, held a box of human entrails and the second, a boy, held a box full of dog shit. A crowd of people emaciated and in the grips of starvation clung to a raised platform on which official and stern looking dogs paced back and forth, guarding an elegant dining table set with white china, gleaming silverware and crisp linen napkins. On a nearby buffet table sat a collection of silver serving bowls and plates. On the plates and bowls lay a rotting seven course meal with a cloud of flies hovering in the stench and covering the rims. Near the top of the canvas a young man took the skeleton ride. Fifteen dogs, each with a mouthful of skin, carried the prone man over a barren patch of land. His skin stretched tight over his bones and seemed in danger of tearing off his body and his teeth had been bared in a perpetual smile as if the body had been left in the desert for a month or two. His eyes were alive and he looked to the sky in a combination of exultation and fear. In the sky above all the scenes dogs hovered, kept aloft with large fly wings as they scanned the landscape looking to complete deadly sorties.

"I see you found the painting," said Koo Koo over Nelson's shoulder. "It's pretty mesmerizing. I usually sit with my back to it so I don't end up staring at it all night."

"Who did this?"

"That would be my ex."

"He was a painter?"

"If one painting makes you a painter, then he was a painter. In all the time he lived here he never worked on anything else. If you look at the bottom left hand corner you'll see he didn't quite finish it. There's a dime-sized spot of blank canvas. He almost painted it five or six times that I saw. Probably more times than that. He couldn't let it go. Couldn't finish."

"You really can't see it. I wouldn't have noticed it."

"But once you know it's there it becomes the focal point of the painting. One more flick of the brush and it's done, but he turned away. Believe me, I've spent enough hours staring at that thing to know what I'm talking about."

"Did he paint it here?"

Koo Koo rolled her eyes at the memory of a heavy burden. "He took over the second bedroom in the back. That was his studio while he was here.

He basically lived in there. He wouldn't come out for weeks at a time, at least when I was home. I had never been around somebody who was in the process of going insane until I met him. There was no helping him. I have no doubt he figured out a way to commit suicide where his body would be hard to find. He didn't come out on the other side, if you know what I mean? The bath is ready and I found some clothes that should fit. I put them in the bathroom. Follow me."

She led Nelson to a large bathroom with an intricate mosaic in the middle of the floor of a fruit bearing tree and swirling sky and earth. The walls were covered in a veneer of marble and the toilet and sink were so massive and stolid they looked like they had been carved of the same stone as the walls. Dragon head sconces hung on either side of a thick mirror that had lost half of its reflectivity.

"This is more ornate than I expected." Nelson's eye had caught a ribbon of inlaid glass tile that ringed the room at eye level.

"I'm the third or fourth generation after swank. Let's just say the rich moved on to better climes and took their capital with them. I've been only left traces. I can't believe the derelicts who lived here before me didn't try to chop that mosaic out of the floor and sell it for a bottle. Somehow it survived."

Nelson took a closer look at the tree, which held a spider web of cracks. The grout had yellowed with mildew and some of the branches had been chipped away.

"I'll make you lunch, but take your time. It's obviously been awhile since you touched clean water." Koo Koo left the bathroom, closing the door behind her.

Nelson looked at himself in the half-reflective mirror. He recognized the shape of his eyes, but they looked trapped inside a foreign mask. A wooly growth of beard covered his jaw and his skin looked like taut leather stretched over bone. His hair had dried plastered to his skull and had netted a handful of silt that clung to the strands. He turned away, sure that he would never have picked himself up had he been driving Koo Koo's car. He unzipped the coveralls and stepped out of them with not a little effort. His body held a collection of wounds and violations and when he lowered himself in the hot water all of the wounds collectively protested to his brain that any rise above an ambient temperature, even a degree or two, felt like a branding fresh from a bed of hot coals. Nelson pushed himself down and leaned back. He slid down until his shoulders were submerged. The tub extended long enough for him to lie down full length. At the time the tub had been dragged up the stairs and put in place it could have fit a family of four gnarled little immigrants, stunted for generations by bad nutrition and weak sunlight who suddenly were cavorting together in a pool-sized tub in a faux Roman bath. The last image Nelson held in his consciousness before he fell asleep consisted of a heavy breasted woman with thick black eyebrows and long black hair scrubbing the faces of two pink children with blotchy skin from stewing in the hot water as a swarthy little man with an enormous nose leaned back against the inside of the tub and watched his family as he smoked a thick cigar, considering the cost of the cigar used to be his month's wages in the country from which it came.

When he awoke Koo Koo stood over him, nudging his shoulder. He slowly sat up.

"Jesus, I thought you might have drowned," she said as she straightened her back as Nelson rose.

"The water is cold."

"Because you've been in here two hours and you're hair isn't even washed. Dunk your head."

Nelson slid back down and slipped his head under the water. He felt Koo Koo's fingers flit through his hair, trying to dislodge some of the sand. He broke the surface when his lungs began to ache and sat up again. She squirted a gob of shampoo on his scalp and worked it efficiently like she scrubbed a kitchen sink, avoiding the bald patch.

"What happened to you here?" She carefully touched the exposed, pink skin on his scalp.

"My hair?"

"Your absence of hair. Did the same person who took your clothes do this to you?"

"In a manner of speaking."

"Wash your face." She handed him a soapy washcloth. "You don't want to talk about it. I get it. Scrub. You have dirt under dirt."

Nelson scrubbed his face and dunked his head, fanning out his hair and releasing the shampoo. When he sat back up he began an attempt to explain himself, but Koo Koo had left the room. He climbed out and dried himself. When he pulled on the clothes she had left him, he found they fit perfectly. Her ex had the same waist width and leg length and the shirt hung neither too tight nor too loose. Even the shoes were his size and so familiar to an old pair he had worn out that a pulse of disorientation ran through him. Could he or objects associated with him travel backwards and forwards on the circuit? Could these objects be brought forward and play a role in the present? Were people and things constantly shifting back and forth, trying to find relevancy in time? Would he walk in the next room and see that Koo Koo had transformed into Jules and neither would remember having lived in Tampa or Jules' infidelity with Otter? Had all of his favorite shoes lined up in a row like they do in an organized closet and had they been waiting for him to conjure them when he found himself shoeless?

He drifted into the dining room and Koo Koo had heated up tomato soup and made a grilled cheese sandwich. An opened bottle of beer with condensation rolling down the glass stood next to both. Nelson fell into a creaking chair and attacked the food. He drank the beer first in three attempts and tipped the bowl of almost too cool soup down his throat. He finished the sandwich in four bites, chewing like he gnawed through a rope. He looked up only after he had finished all three.

"Would you like some more?"

"I could eat."

Koo Koo left the kitchen and he resisted the impulse to walk over to the painting and pick out more detail. In particular, he would look for a van and two rock-n-rollers, a gathering of hopping dogs and a dirty little man emerging from a hole in the ground. She came back with another round of beer, soup and sandwich and he bolted it down almost as quickly as the first time and pushed himself away from the table and rested his hands on his full belly to signal that his hunger had been quelled.

"So where do you go from here?"

"Back to Tampa, I guess. That was the first plan. Don't think I'll stay, but I'll collect a few things, close the bank accounts if there's anything left in them and find a new spot to move to."

"That's not much of a plan, if you ask me."

"I'm all out of plans."

"How are you getting back?"

Confusion flooded his thoughts as he remembered how the circuit had been blasted apart and that he had no idea how he would get back to Tampa or why he would go back there. Without Pez the possibility of coming up with a plan that had the chance of being successful seemed remote. He stared at his hands that lay over the knot in his belly. He couldn't have lifted his head at that moment had he wanted to with the weight of his circumstances raining down upon him.

"So your things are still at a girlfriend's or wife's apartment or house?

"Yes, there was a girlfriend."

"Do you remember her number?"

Nelson leaned back and jammed his hands in his front pockets and when he came up empty he leaned forward and searched the back.

"Those aren't your pants, remember?"

"I remember a number." Nelson resumed a slouched sitting position. "May I use your phone?"

Koo Koo retrieved a cordless and Nelson dialed 566-1799. Koo Koo recognized that the series of numbers as four short if Nelson really wanted to call Florida, but she didn't want to say anything to see how far he would take the ruse. The phone rang twice before a deep voice answered with a mumble from the back of his throat.

"Who is this?" Nelson asked.

"Who has called?"

"Is this Otter?"

"An Otter? What kind of question is that?"

"No, is your name Otter?"

"That's a ridiculous name!"

"I don't disagree. Is Jules there?"

"You have not answered my question. Who is calling?"

"Her boyfriend. Her ex-boyfriend, I mean."

"I'm sure Jules has many boyfriends. Which one are you?'

"Nelson."

A long silence followed as if the caller on the other line had taken another call or engaged in a conversation while cupping his hand over the mouthpiece.

"Where are you, Nelson? We've been looking for you. We're hoping for a chance to finally meet."

"Who's looking for me?"

"Tell me you cannot recall from your memory a person or organization that may be looking for you, that might have considerable interest in your whereabouts and your intentions."

"Zune? Gutterman?"

Another long silence followed.

"What do you know of them?" The voice broke the silence like a report from a rifle. "They've been eliminated many years ago. Why would you bring those ghosts up? They're looking for nothing but their own heads."

"Who is this?"

"Really, Nelson, you don't know why you called? Are you ready to end it? Turn yourself in and try your hand at my mercy?"

Nelson clicked off the phone and slowly set it down on the table.

"How many numbers did I dial?"

"I don't know. Check the dialed calls list." Koo Koo reached over and checked it herself. "You called a local number, 566-1799."

The phone rang in her hand and she pushed a button to answer it.

"Hello?"

"Is this Nelson's girlfriend? I thought he was trying to find an old girlfriend? Very brave to call an old girlfriend while the new one is sitting right next to you."

"I'm not his girlfriend. I found him in the street and I'm trying to help him get home."

"He's not somebody who can be helped, I'm afraid. He's past all that. So, be careful with that one. You sound like you could be reasonable. Your voice is sexy, so I'm thinking you're attractive, but a little worn and weary. Look for nothing in him. He's as good as dead. He should be dead by now, by anyone's accounting. It's a matter of luck that's gotten him this far, but sooner or later the piper has to be paid, no?"

"Would you like to speak to him?"

"No, not especially. I find your voice to be more pleasing. I am imagining you as quite the beauty in your day. Maybe you're ten years past your prime, but lately I find myself cultivating a fetish for things worn, outdated and weary from the number of days they have lived. My house is now filled with antiques. I drive vintage cars. I've begun shopping at Goodwill. The blinding flash of the new leaves me cold. My desire has turned toward experience and disappointment, suffocating disappointment. That's why I feel a strong attraction to you. Your voice holds all that I hold dear."

"Are you sure you don't want to speak to him?"

"No, I don't think I'll speak to him directly again. He equated me with two little rats that I dispatched years ago and for that I don't believe I can forgive him. I would like to ask you a favor though. Will you grant me a favor?"

"What it is? Tell me and I'll see if I can do it."

"Even faded beauties have conditions. It's simple. Ask him to say my name. Tell him to say my name loud enough for me to hear. Could you do that for me please?"

Koo Koo lowered the phone from her ear and pointed the microphone towards Nelson.

"He wants you to say his name." She shrugged her shoulders as she said it. She clicked on the speakerphone function.

Nelson stared at the phone and imagined Montenegro sitting in the dark warehouse on a stool in the middle of the floor like an actor who has staged his own life, waiting to hear Nelson mumble his name, listening to his own breathing, anticipating the syllables rattling through his ear, wanting to hear validation, a polite smattering of embarrassed applause meant to appease him because he wouldn't leave the stage until he got it.

"Montenegro," Nelson said in a conversational volume.

"I'll only ask you to do it once more. Just a little louder, taking into account you are transmitting over a cheap phone with a weak, tinny speaker and your mouth is some distance away. Just once more."

Nelson cleared his throat. "Montenegro," he said louder and as he said it a second time it occurred to him that very likely the name had been made-up, a stage name meant to mask a humble beginning or an ethnicity that would be easier to track and rooted out by the various bureaus and police departments whose livelihoods depend on drug arrests.

"Thank you, Nelson. I know a man in your circumstances can forget the small courtesies, but it's my belief that we should always be aware of offense and extend graciousness whenever possible. So, in this little bubble in which I live those who are speaking to me don't hang up the phone and don't pretend to not know my name. In my mind my name is never thrown in the hopper with the names of dirty scum like Zune or Gutterman. I'm sure you never met them and you have no idea the extent of the offense you have committed, but isn't it better to keep your fucking mouth shut instead of blurting out inadvertently offensive salvos? So, the insult issued from your lips can only exacerbate the consequences to come. One must always be aware of the words one is using, yes?"

The phone radiated silence. Koo Koo and Nelson stared at it, waiting for the lecture to continue and unable to answer his question as they feared whatever they said would send him off on another direction. After a minute or two it became obvious that Montenegro still waited for an answer to his question and was not going hang up until one of them said something.

"Yes, one always should be careful with the words they use," said Koo Koo.

"I want to hear him say it."

"I will carefully choose my words from now on."

"Good to hear. You will find your life to be more pleasant. Well spoken and carefully chosen words are the grease of society. Now, when are we going to meet. Nelson? There's this fact of you losing a shipment that hangs between us. It simply won't go away. I've tried very hard to root out incompetence from my organization. It's not easy nowadays. The kids are getting stupider by the day and the cops are more greedy. They aren't satisfied with a little grease to make their bills easier to pay. No, they want big cash for big ticket items. Boats, giant flat screens so they can pretend to be on the football field, giant trucks big enough to haul all their loot. So, into my struggle you stumble in, all but leaving a trail of cocaine for anyone to follow right to my doorstep. And to be taken by those two worms in a band? Do you have any sense, any ability at all? Did you hear their music? No, Nelson, your incompetence is stage five cancer. I have an oncologist on staff at all times and you need to come in for treatment. I aggressively pursue all malformed cells. I'll find you, sooner or later."

Montenegro clicked off and Koo Koo swept the phone off the table and into her lap.

"I think you dialed the wrong number."

"That would seem to be the case."

"Do you remember your girlfriend's number?"

Nelson told her the number and Koo Koo dialed it while keeping the phone in her lap, as if the sight of it would send Nelson into a tailspin of fear and paranoia. Once it started ringing she handed the phone to him. A phone company recording rasped into his ear that the number had been disconnected and no further information would ever be available. He handed the phone back to her.

"She's gone."

"What do you mean?" Koo Koo put the phone to her ear and after she heard the recording for herself she turned it off. "Did you give me the right number? Your memory seems a little shaky." She read the number back to him and when she confirmed she had dialed his old number she set the phone on the table. "Look, you can sleep in the studio. I haven't cleaned it since my ex left, but there's some kind of nasty cot in there he dragged from God knows where and just so you know I sleep with a gun so if you promise there's going to be no bullshit you can stay here until you figure out a way to get back to Tampa."

"You shouldn't do this. You heard him on the phone. You should probably take his advice since he makes a habit of killing people. If they find me they'll kill me right here and probably you too for helping me."

"First, they'll never find you here. You have to admit you ended up in a pretty random place. I should throw you out for lying to me, but I probably would have lied too if I was mixed up with that guy and I was a drug dealer. Somewhere you made a really bad decision."

"Drug mule. Nothing but a pack animal and you could never dream how bad of a decision I made or for that matter how many bad decisions it took to end in this spot. Once you get on a role it can be hard to stop."

"Alright, mule, I'll show you your stable. It's not pretty, but it's probably better than being followed by that guy. My second point was that you've seen this neighborhood, right? Pretty sketchy, right? So, sometimes inviting in the devil is better than waiting for him to come and visit, know what I mean? A known demon is better than an unknown demon, isn't that the saying?"

Nelson followed her to the back of the apartment. She stopped in front of the last door in a long hallway next to the backdoor. A padlock had been sloppily screwed into the door and frame. Koo Koo slipped out a key from her pants and unlocked it.

"It's habit more than anything else. He always kept it locked whenever he left and sometimes he would ask me to lock him in because he felt his creativity might be on a roll and he didn't want to ruin it by turning on a football game or eating a sandwich."

The studio had been organized around the production of the huge canvas. One wall held the negative space where the painting had been created with makeshift braces fashioned out of scrap wood lining the footprint of the canvas. On the floor in front of the wall sat a pile of paint cans and tubes, opened and dried, empty, kicked-over, all the paint squeezed out and the shuck left in a crumpled ball. One red pool and another brown had hardened on the floor. The remaining three walls were covered with sketches of the various scenes in the painting and some that never made it in on the final version. Most had been sketched in pencil, some in slashing brushstrokes. Nelson spotted three versions of the meat grinder, a more gruesome version of the holiday banquet table, a series of studies on skeletons, and even a fully designed sketch of the entire painting in which the dogs fought skeletons instead of flesh and blood human beings. Taped and pinned in the gaps between the sketches were Polaroid photos of a naked man miming the various poses of human figures in the painting.

"So all the figures in the painting are really him?" asked Nelson as he inspected a photo in which the model hung upside down from a tree, a thick rope around his ankles. "And you must have taken all these."

"They're all him. If you look closely at the women in the painting they don't look quite like women. Not enough hip, too lean and muscular. Their breasts look uncomfortable or out of place on their bodies. Kind of like Michelangelo. I mean, did he ever really paint or sculpt women or did he just paint men and stick boobs on them?"

"Why didn't he use you as a model?"

"I asked him that once. He screamed at me for about an hour saying over and over again what would I know about all this and who the fuck was I to say I knew something about all of this and how could I possibly get the poses right since I still thought dogs were cute and acceptable to have living in your house. I never asked him again. I just helped him set up the photos and left him alone from there."

"How long did it take for him to finish it?"

"Well, it's not finished, remember? And there were three other versions he burned, slashed or destroyed. One I think I liked better than this last one, less gruesome. He painted a small seed of hope in the one I liked and it made the violence and brutality seem even more foreign and weird. But I'd say on and off he worked on it for five years. He started on it the week after he moved in and worked on it slowly while he was here. He'd disappear for a few days now and again, sometimes a week, but he'd always come back and pick up right where he left off. That's the cot." She pointed to the back corner where the fold away bent under the weight of a pile of long overdue and presumed lost library books filled with photos of dogs and text describing their traits and trainability. "I have to run a few errands, so I'm assuming you are staying?"

"I'll stay. I have nowhere to go and no way to get there."

"You probably need to stop saying things like that because you're not filling me with confidence."

"I didn't know you needed confidence."

Koo Koo shook her head and walked out the door. "Remember, I sleep with a gun and no bullshit and we'll be fine." She closed the door behind her. She sauntered down the hall, wondering how she could cover her lie. She had no errands, but the moment she had said it she had an overwhelming desire to be away from Nelson. Seeing him in her ex's old clothes, standing amidst the sketches, looking at the world from an identical pair of hollow eyes gave her the creeps and she needed to be away from her own bad decision awhile to understand the possible consequences.

She gathered her keys and purse and walked to her car. She would give Nelson a few hours to settle, steal her blind or leave and when she returned she would live with the outcome of her decision. It sounded so pathetic and weak to her, the fact that she already subordinated her life to a man she had picked up from the street in his underwear. Clearly, a sociopath chased him and his pursuer sounded like he would never give up. He had agreed to carry drugs across state lines and he had lost his little sidekick, but yet here she fled her apartment, disrupting her routine for him, waiting for his decision after she had bathed and fed him. She could look forward to nothing but suffering and humiliation ahead. Maggie had chortled victory when she told her that her ex had fled. The world had warned her of his vagrancy and the world had been right, again. Now, she had picked up another homeless vagrant, a criminal vagrant, dressed him up in her vanished ex's clothes and offered him his old room. She decided she must despise herself deeply to create another pantomime in order to receive a fresh wound.

The sun had baked the inside of her car, so when she started it she turned on the air conditioner, even though it had stopped working years ago. The fan screamed and a strong smell of exhaust rolled up the windshield. She jammed the stick in reverse, whipped backwards, and sped out of the lot. Circumstantial evidence and pieces of stray gossip revealed that her ex had not killed himself, had not found some lonely branch in a seldom visited woods and hanged himself and now, as he hung undiscovered through summer his flesh had begun to bloat and drop from his body so that now, by all likelihood, a hiker would find a skeleton at the end of the rope. No, the more reasonable story had him running off to North Carolina with a devil named Chandra who squeezed her ample self into clothes two sizes too small and whose essence, if a person's spirit and purpose could ever be distilled into a scent, a perfume, reeked of intercourse and booze. Both had disappeared around the same time and they had run together years before in what her ex referred to as his dog years and everyone who knew them assumed, except Koo Koo because she had witnessed his inexorable disintegration and she looked at his painting everyday and knew there could be no new beginning with that tramp after wrenching that painting out of himself, they had reconnected the old circuit and fucked in the parking lots of truck shops and Shoney's and in the bathrooms of Waffle Houses on their way south.

She drove to a park that sat high on a bluff overlooking the lake. Ten or twelve solitary men sat in their cars, looking straight ahead, and watched for a signal from a man in another car or for a tender hustler to come sauntering into the park looking for cash to grease the night's party in exchange for some old man to suck his dick. Sometimes when Koo Koo came to the park a confused husband would get out of his car and approach her, more for appearance's sake than to actually pick her up, and they would chat for a few minutes and the husband would try to convince her that he didn't come to the park often. Where else could you find a cooling lake breeze other than this perfect bluff? More often than not they were strangely beautiful and just a little sad as they tried to summon up a lost heterosexuality in a park full of queers. This evening the men felt particularly feverish and desperate and had no time for appearances, so Koo Koo was able to leave her car and sit at a picnic table without anyone speaking to her. A barge skimmed across the water close to the horizon. The sun still hung oppressively in the sky, swelling throughout the day and threatening to lick the earth with tongues of flame. The water looked like it had been spread with a trowel and had all but hardened in place.

She had spent many evenings in the summer at this same table, watching the sail boats and motor boats float in circles. Tanned men stood at the wheel or the tiller, displaying their prowess at accumulating money and learning useless skills. How long would it be before he sat on the bluff waiting for another man to take his penis in his mouth? In fact, wouldn't they all chuck the pomp and circumstance, the boats, the suits, the new model cars, the rambling suburban houses with crisp lawns in exchange for a desperate man with a feverish forehead in their lap? Weren't all the toys just artifacts of deep misogyny? Bitterness can fill the void and it waits on the periphery for an opening. Koo Koo closed her eyes and leaned back. The sun glowed orange through her eyelids. Maggie would let her stay at her apartment for a few days until the man who couldn't remember his name had disappeared. She figured once the food in the apartment had been eaten he would move on, looking for another source. But could she really take the scolding, the lecture, the withering and superior looks from her friend when she told her why she couldn't go back to her apartment for a few days? When would she begin to feel less lost? Her string of unmoored and broken men had finally dragged her down. She had no energy or interest in untangling this new man from his own snares. If he stayed in the back room and they avoided entanglements and refused to develop anything beyond the relationship of man in need and a woman with more heart than brains his presence might have a calming effect on her life. He could block any other man from entering the picture and when she felt tempted she could just drop the line, "No, I can't go to my place. I'm living with a guy. No, not in the car either. He'll be expecting me. Jealous type, you know?" So, maybe he could be useful and safe. She couldn't take another wound like her ex, not this soon. He had crawled into her heart and seeped through her veins until she existed as nothing but a host for him and his cruelty.

She met him at a birthday party at the house of a woman named Jen, who used to work at the diner when business stayed more consistent because a couple of factories down the street were still open. Jen had something like five kids and a disabled husband who winced every time he moved his back or came down from a pot high. The party was for her youngest kid who either had a perpetual sneer on his lips or he consistently lost fights to his older siblings and learned to live life with swollen downturned lips from the beatings he took. Their house, a little vinyl-sided bungalow, sat in vast field of other bungalows that when seen from a passing plane might very well look like a military cemetery with rows and rows of matching headstones. Jen had inherited the tidy house from her parents and she had done everything in her power to blot out the memory of their pride, cleanliness and attention to maintenance of the home. A "Happy Birthday" sign in glittery letters had been tacked on a wall in the dining room and a clump of cupcakes on the kitchen counter with canned frosting smeared unevenly over the tops suggested a birthday party to be in progress, but other than that a visitor dropped into the middle of the melee would have never guessed the theme. Next to the cupcakes stood a copse of liquor bottles ranging from whiskey to peach schnapps to Jägermeister. No other children expect Jen's five in the backyard had come and they chased each other with switches ripped from trees and whipped at each other with intent. Women revealing a couple of inches of cleavage and their loose bellies and men in black or blue t-shirts and creative facial hair jammed the house. All were roaring drunk and the party seemed on the verge of turning into a riot or an orgy, depending on whether a boyfriend took offense to another man touching his girl and fists started flying or a women decided to undress and give free lap dances whereupon a host of zippers would come down. Classic rock, Molly Hatchet, Slade, and Lynyrd Skynyrd bludgeoned the crowd, but nobody moved to turn it down. Koo Koo had worn a shirt that she felt accentuated her breasts but kept them fully covered so she felt like a chaperone or a referee of some lewd sport. She set her present for the kid down on what she thought should be a clean part of the dining room table but she ended up placing it in a pool of spilled vodka and soda. She saw her ex for the first time at that moment. She looked out the back window and saw him watching the children attack each other and coaching the smallest one on how to flick the switch with wrist action instead of using his elbow and shoulder. He wore clothes a size too big for him and even then a disturbance brewed behind his eyes. Koo Koo walked up to him and flashed a smile, a smile she could wield like a broadsword when she wanted to, and asked him if he enjoyed whipping children. He looked at the switch in his hand and then at the older four who had knocked the youngest down and were pummeling him with slaps and tickles.

"Somebody has to keep them in line."

Koo Koo looked at the scrum. "I see you're doing a great job."

"I think it would be a riot to have a couple of them. I don't know what Jen and Lock were thinking having five, but if they all survive they're going to be tough and mean."

Suddenly, he teamed up with the youngest and started wildly switching the four bullies until he had them cowering under the violence of his blows. The youngest joined in and paid back all the whacks he had received. His drunken musing proved to be enough for Koo Koo to launch into a relationship and spend the next five years trying to rediscover this desire for paternity in him, even though they never spoke of having children and she religiously maintained a birth control regimen. The spark, the hope, lay buried under torrents of despair, and the possibility of children faded until it seemed impossible, something akin to designing a skyscraper with no architectural education or draining Lake Erie with a hand pump. Koo Koo forgot she could stop taking the pill and let her eggs roll unencumbered and more than likely she would have a baby, that currently the world had six or seven billion impossibilities walking and breathing. Sometimes her ex made lifting his head feel like a miracle.

Koo Koo realized shortly after he moved in that he all but swam in his clothes, which spoke less to fashion and more to illness.

"I've lost some weight," he told her.

She slowly started swapping his clothes for smaller sizes at a consignment shop, but she couldn't keep ahead of his shrinking. After a few months the new clothes practically fell off of him, even though he didn't lack for energy or violence and his appetite seemed intact. Koo Koo never saw him sleep and after they would have sex and the rush in her would finally subside and she would begin to feel drowsy he would still be pacing the apartment. Sometimes he would go on three or four hour walks in the middle of the night. Sometimes he would come back with mud on his face and hands or with a black and swollen eye or scrapes on his elbows and knees or bleeding from his lips, and he would shrug off any questions Koo Koo lobbed at him when she wanted to know what had happened. One day he left and hours later came back with a giant canvas and a couple of buckets of paint and began work on the painting. He sometimes still walked at night but as the concept of the painting grew he really couldn't be away from the canvas for more than an hour before an impulse drove him back to the studio. He became positively skeletal, but she did get him to drink a concoction loaded with vitamins and protein supplements that kept him from completely wasting away. She gave up trying to find new clothes for him because the sizes he needed had been made for teenage boys and she winced at the thought of his haunted frame wrapped in trendy, disposable styles.

With his self-absorption and active demons he wouldn't have been an obvious candidate to be a good lover, but oddly he stood out as the most attentive and thorough lover she had ever had. He learned her body and her moods and knew when to take a slow, teasing approach and when to throw her on her belly and be quick and hard. She looked forward to his touch during the day when she worked at the diner and felt disappointment on the nights when the painting or his roaming took precedence over sex.

Sex bound them together with the thinnest of threads. His language had deteriorated to the point where he could only string together a few syllables before he either became exhausted or lost the momentum of his meaning. When she talked to him about her customers and the craziness of the public in general, because, the truth be told, she had yet to serve a customer who functioned above the level of fundamentally nuts, he couldn't even muster the appropriate affirmative nods and agreeing noises or phrases to make her feel like she had an ally in the house. She would have thought he had forgotten her completely, if not for the sex. He might keep to his room, he might be unable to converse or socialize or sleep or work or live like a normal human being, but the sex told her he remained aware of her and he understood what she felt and when. What more could she ask for, really? Maggie pounded and pounded her to dump him, but Maggie had never felt her body under his touch. If she could have managed her jealousy she would have loaned him to Maggie for a night or two so she would see what she meant, so Maggie would stop her relentless screed against his attributes. Koo Koo knew no woman would so easily dump him, even though all the warnings flew high on the pole for all to see.

Soon they became entrenched in a predictable pattern. She would work all morning into the early afternoon and when she would come home she would fix him breakfast while she drank a glass of iced tea. She always ate at the diner to save money. She would talk for awhile to clear the debris from her head as he stared at her mouth or breasts. Then, they would have sex in the middle of the afternoon. After cooling off he would return to his studio and she would have the rest of the day free, which she filled with errands, talking on the phone to Maggie, sitting by the lake and television. She didn't live a bad life, she remembered thinking to herself. What more could be expected? He even drew her closer when the painting began to take shape and they began the series of photo studies. He took to searching tree lawns, rubbish piles, evictions, and dumpsters to find the props for each scene. He found the old Polaroid camera in a junk shop that came with a bag of old film cartridges and he badgered the owner until he relented and gave him both for future considerations that he expected would never be paid. He began with the buffet and dining room table scene, taking a couple of weeks to find all the silverware, serving dishes, and a rickety table with six chairs and a broken buffet he propped up with a cinder block. He pushed all of Koo Koo's living room furniture to the wall and set up the scene in the middle of the room. He set and reset the table and buffet and soaked rags in paint to stand in for rotting food. He shouted for Koo Koo to take a series of nude photos of him as he mimed the starving crowd. When he got what he thought he wanted, all of the junk ended up on the tree lawn, discarded for a second time.

So, a new pattern in their lives had begun. Now, when she came home from work he would not sit with her and eat lunch, but he wanted her immediately to come into his studio where the day's scene would be set up from what he had procured that morning or the night before. For scenes that involved trees or streams they traveled to a nearby river valley park where they walked deep in the woods, away from the bike paths and bridle trails, and he would enact the scene in a secluded spot. When he hanged himself upside down she thought he might die because they had an impossible time trying to get him back down. He had climbed onto a large horizontal branch, naked already, and tied a thick, course rope around the branch and his ankles. He first hung by his legs, his knees bent over the branch, and Koo Koo helped lower him by holding his hands and then his shoulders as he swung lower. The photos were disturbing and hilarious, a cross between bondage and a lynching. She liked the way his penis and testicles flopped against his belly and she laughed throughout the seven or eight shots. His face grew increasingly red and after she set the photos on the ground to develop and dry she tried to help him back on the branch. He had made the length of the rope too short because when she pushed his shoulders he could not grab a branch and she couldn't touch his ankles let alone untie them. After the first attempt both of them thought the proper technique would have been either to bring a ladder or to make the rope long enough that he hung close to the ground so that Koo Koo could have lifted him enough to create slack in the rope and untie his ankles. At that moment neither solved the problem of how she would hold him and untie his ankles at the same time. He tried to jackknife his body and take a hold of the rope and pull himself up, but he either needed to be a contortionist or much stronger than his current weakened state to pull off the maneuver. The rope cut into his ankles and he complained of a headache. Koo Koo climbed the tree, but she couldn't untie the knot because his weight had made it too tight. He started to scream and curse at her that he thought he was going to die and that she better think of some way to get him down. She thought it a ridiculous reaction from someone so vulnerable and so dependent on her ability and creativity to get him free. She thought for a moment of calling the fire department and completing his humiliation, but she wouldn't be able to tell them where they where exactly, so deep in the woods. He began to thrash his arms wildly around his head, trying to grab the ground but missing by a good two feet. His movement created a sway and this gave Koo Koo an idea. She calmed him down as best she could and tried to explain the plan. She would swing him like a pendulum until the arc of the swing brought him close enough to the trunk of the tree so he could grab a lower branch. If he could snag a branch he could pull himself up enough to slacken the rope and she could untie his ankles. He nodded that he understood the plan, barely keeping a lid on a full-blown, hysterical panic. She pushed against his butt and released to get a little momentum, then pushed harder and released three more times before he used his body to keep the arc going. He missed a branch three times before finally snagging it. He clung to it like a flood threatened to sweep him away until he caught his breath and some of the blood drained from his head. He pulled himself up to the next highest branch, then the next higher still, and he swung his legs over yet another branch and created some slack in the rope. Koo Koo climbed back up the tree and wedged herself between the trunk and branch and had to lean over him to untie his ankles. Her face was very close to his penis and she thought it would be a hoot to take it in her mouth because she had never given a blow job in a tree, but he shook and hadn't conquered his fear and almost pushed her out of the tree when she began.

"Are you a fucking maniac?" he yelled.

"Just bored."

Koo Koo loosened the knot and his ankles were badly rope-burned and bloody, but he managed to kick them free. With one last vindictive kick of the rope he lost his grip on the branch and tumbled to the ground, landing awkwardly on a root at the base of the tree. He rolled over onto his stomach and held his ribs, moaning. Koo Koo could have gone to his side and confronted him and asked him where it hurt and whether or not he thought anything had broken or burst. Instead, she climbed down and stood in the shade, reloading the scene in her mind. The pile of clothes on the ground with his discolored underwear on top like a disgusting whipped cream, the rope with a smear of skin and blood on a small swath, her naked boyfriend lying in the dirt, seven Polaroids lying in a row documenting his encroaching insanity, the sun filtering through the leaves and a weak breeze stirring the tops of the trees. Maggie had told her that given her track record with men she should have taken up nursing as a profession.

"You might as well get paid for all your misplaced empathy and compassion," Maggie told her.

Koo Koo knew herself better than Maggie, of course, and she knew she didn't feel so much empathy and compassion as plain curiosity, which is why she had always avoided the idea of becoming a nurse. She imagined herself withholding treatment or interventions for sick people because of her curiosity about the process of dying. She never felt capable of stopping disaster, but she wanted to be close enough to watch the destruction. She picked up his clothes and walked them over to him and dropped them on the ground.

"It's time to go," she told him. "Before you frighten some cub scout troop and get arrested for indecency."

After that he became more dependent on her and with his dependency came his anger. Knowing that she embodied his last tether to normalcy made him want to snap the line altogether and he could achieve his goal by making Koo Koo go away or she kicking him out. His outbursts could last hours, usually repeating the same stock phrases and themes that she cheated on him, that she smothered him, that she wanted nothing more than control of him, that she shrieked and bitched incessantly, that he could do better if he picked up a prostitute from some city corner and thank God they had never procreated and passed along all of their bruised and warped genes to a next generation. His sexual variations became more course, more predictable and less frequent. Her body became less of a violin and more of a drum, a single bass drum pounded on by two wooly mallets. He snapped at her as she lay obviously unsatisfied next to him, semen growing cold on her thigh, saying that she owned some responsibility for their withering connection. She told him maybe his artistry had moved onto another project, that her body should be framed and hung in a gallery as proof to his talent, but that it had ceased to be his muse. He almost smiled at her compliment before retreating back to his studio.

The photos continued until he had enough material to begin his big canvas and he worked out three times the number of scenes he eventually used in the final painting. In the first version he crammed the canvas with figures, pouring in everything from his imagination so that from a distance the painting looked like a writhing Celtic knot. Koo Koo caught a glimpse before he slashed it to pieces with a switchblade and burned the pieces in the fireplace, because, he said, if he kept the pieces he would be tempted to copy them and his next attempt would be ruined. The second version had been Koo Koo's favorite. He had chosen once scene and made it the entire painting, and he never repeated the scene in another version. In it a figure of a man had been tied to a tree, his back against the trunk. The leaves had fallen from the branches and lay rotting and brown on the ground. The rope that bound him looked gray and weathered and cut into his flesh. His clothes had been torn or had rotted off of him, except for a small loin cloth that covered a majority of his genitals and a button down collar and tie with the rest of the shirt missing. The sky behind him had been painted holocaust gray and the tree pitch black, so the man's pale flesh looked luminescent and tender. A solitary dog sat in the leaves to the left. The breed was elusive, indistinct, but the dog looked powerful even at rest. It looked away from the man, off canvas, as if it had heard the first footfall of something to come. Her ex had misgivings about the painting about half way through its completion, but he pushed forward until it had been fully executed. Koo Koo had walked into the unlocked room and stopped behind his shoulder as he analyzed it.

"Motherfucking saint redundancy. I thought I flushed that shit out of my head a long time ago. Christ hero warrior. Pathos and pabulum. Motherfucking saint icon bullshit falsehood. Prop-a-fucking-ganda trust in the truth and die in its service. Martyrdom goddamn! I'm locked into a martyr lie. Fuck! Why paint bullshit? This is pap. I might as well be on TV doping the masses with images with no context and words with no meaning."

"I like it better than the last one," Koo Koo ventured.

"Of course you do. Everyone would LIKE it better. It's a banality, a comfort, a goddamn broken-in shoe. Individual spirit facing down collective evil or certain doom, knowing the price will be his life but standing firm in his convictions, knowing the torture of his bodily flesh will never push him under or alter him from his course. This is just plain dreadful. I can't believe this still came out of my head. This is the water from the brainwash. All those hours sitting in a pew being conditioned. It's so deep in my head I might as well be an automaton. This had nothing to do with me. This is not my experience. I can't even figure out the purpose of the saints other than to tell peasants that it's possible to be perfect. I was always glad someone else was hacked apart by butcher knives or killed with a thousand arrows or boiled alive in the name of Jesus because I wouldn't have to do it. The saints were like product testers, making my soul safe and sound. Of course you like it better. You understand it immediately. It gives you continuity and activates all those synapses gummed up with sermons and all those longings that one day you will be perfect too, if only you could be tested and tortured like the saints."

Koo Koo realized that this speech had been the most words he had strung together in her presence since they had been living together and it represented probably more words than he had spoken in the previous two months. She didn't want him to retreat again, but she had to make an observation.

"Is this what you meant to do?"

"Fuck no, don't you get it? I'm leaning on that old saw, that crutch, because I can't think for myself. I only have other people's versions of life in my head. I can't drill down to my own experience no matter how hard I try."

"Well, he doesn't look like much of a saint to me other than the luminescence. Look at his face. He looks terrified. He knows that he's not dying for God. He has no beatific understanding that he has conquered death through his belief. His terror is temporal and real and it is happening to him now and there is no hope for redemption. He looks more like an animal caught in a snare. Something worse is coming. Something beyond our imagination. The dog knows it, senses it, welcomes it. He's one of your hellhounds, projecting threat. The landscape is barren and dead. Where's the entrance to heaven? Where's the escape route? By the looks of the old rope I'd say there is none. I'd say he's been bound to the tree for a long time and now he is preparing for the final indignity. I don't see a saint or a martyr. I feel horrible for him because he thinks there are ropes around him, that he doesn't know that he could walk away and dress and shave his cheeks and pretend that something mattered, that he just as easily could go over and pet the dog and not imagine him as a sentry or a scout of his undoing. I'd say you drilled right down to where you live and executed a brilliant expression if it, know what I mean?"

"I see only Hollywood and the Pope."

He retreated and his words stopped breaking the surface. After a couple of minutes of silence Koo Koo turned her back and as she exited the door she could hear him slashing and ripping the canvas, but she couldn't turn around and watch the destruction. A few hours later he came out spotted with dry flecks of paint and stood over her as she lay on the couch reading a mystery novel with an obvious solution. He dropped to his knees, looking wild in the eyes, and pinned both of her arms against her sides. Caught off guard she had been trapped and the more she pushed against his grip the more strength he used against her. He flipped her over and ripped at her skin and clothes. He became impatient with her thrashing and he punched her in the back and neck a few times. He had never punched her that hard. She relaxed because she didn't want to die at his hands and she let him enter her anus. He had fucked her there before but it had always come as a crescendo in a perfectly tuned symphony as his penis, heavily oiled, slid in and responded gently to the constriction. But now he raped and he pushed hard and raw against the sphincter and as she cried out in pain she worried he may be ripping something inside her. Mercifully, the rape ended as quickly as it had begun as he came in rapid-fire spurts. The semen burned against a fissure and she cried out when he withdrew. He stood up and sobbed. He looked at the trickle of blood and semen running out of her asshole and down her thigh and he tore at his face with his nails, scraping red swaths down his cheeks. Koo Koo rolled back on the couch, holding her stomach because she suddenly felt filled with bile, churning violently. He threw his head against the plaster and lathe wall and left a small imprint of his forehead. He staggered backwards and fled out the back door, wearing boxer shorts and a t-shirt, but no shoes, slapping his head like a swarm of mosquitoes, bees or Furies had been released against him.

Koo Koo made several decisions in the next hour that prolonged the end of their relationship. When she went to the emergency room to be stitched up she declined to say how it had happened for fear the hospital staff would call the police. She decided not to call the police herself and she did not call Maggie, who upon hearing the story would not have rested until a manhunt had been organized and he was eviscerated and castrated upon his capture. When she came home from the hospital she crawled into bed without checking if he had come back and didn't bother to slide the deadbolts in place. She relied on a belief that he had done his worst and she would be safe now. She tried taking the painkillers the doctor had prescribed, but each time she took one she vomited within five minutes. She twisted the bed sheets around her belly and through her legs and fell to sleep thinking her run of mistakes would never end.

In the morning he still hadn't come back and she thought the fear of arrest might have driven him away for good, but two weeks after the rape she heard him scuffling and banging in his room. She opened the door and there he stood in the middle of the floor wearing lime green shoes and knickers with a bare torso. His skin looked camouflaged with mud and shit. The scratches on his face had faded to soft pink. She wanted to tell him of her recovery, of the throbbing pain, of having work be close to torture, of not eating for fear of shitting, of her first shit when she screamed because she thought she had ruptured the wound, of the turd capped in blood, of her decision not to call the police because she didn't want an official and public record of her bad decisions, of biting her tongue when she talked to Maggie because she couldn't bear condemnation and ridicule on top of a busted asshole, but she found she couldn't talk to him dressed in knickers and awful shoes. Where had he found them in his size? Once he acknowledged her, he went back to his work of stretching a new canvas several times larger than the first two attempts

"So that's it? You can come back here without an apology? Without an explanation? I don't even think an apology covers enough territory, but at least it would be a start. A little penance at least would get the ball rolling in the right direction," she said from the doorway.

He looked at her like he no idea what she jabbered about as he walked toward her. Fear radiated through her body, but her feet felt rooted to the floor. She wouldn't be caught and dragged down from behind. At least she would look him in the face as he killed her. He closed the door in her face and locked it from the inside without a word. She had to take a step back to avoid the door hitting her in the nose.

"Fuck you, right? I could still call the police, you fucker."

That night he crept into her room. She had nearly fallen asleep and she could smell him before she could feel him. When his lips touched her hand she nearly jumped out of bed, but he held her and kissed her two or three more times and convinced her he wanted to find his old mastery of her body. His stench suffocated her and burned the back of her throat and she tried to breathe through her mouth to avoid nausea. He flitted over her body like a spider and she swore his fingers rode the heat of her skin. He turned her over, which sent a spike of fear through her, but he gently licked her asshole and she thought she might never stop coming. Then, she mounted him and he followed her rhythm as she pounded against him. He came only after she had exhausted herself, and they fell asleep in each other's arms.

He launched into the third version of the painting, filling the canvas with quick, sloppy brushstrokes. The figures had little detail except for their twisted mouths and fearful eyes, looking like they all had been caught in the middle of a frightened shriek. A chorus of dogs all had red eyes and black fur and looked more like hellhounds than in the other versions. The scenes were more redundant and obviously sexual. The dogs had an anal fetish and the whole sense of the painting came close to crumbling into pornography. Erect penises popped out of the murky background, semen trails were splattered in random designs, breasts and vaginas glowed pink and red and the dogs all wore leering expressions. Dog satyrs had stumbled upon a nunnery and the painting caught them in the throes of their feast. The few men who had once had the task of guarding the virgins lay dead with their eyes plucked out and their penises cut off. Dogs carried both eyeballs and flaccid dicks aloft. The women ran, wilted, lay prone and willing, and battled to the death with their hands and teeth. The dogs chased, awkwardly standing on their hind legs and supporting huge phalluses with their front paws. The painting disappeared as quickly as it appeared, burned one night in the fireplace.

He began the final version the next day. When Koo Koo saw the size of the stretched canvas propped against the wall and a rickety step ladder he had found on a tree lawn that he would use to reach the canvas' upper limit, she rolled her eyes at his misguided ambition. He would not be able to execute a painting so large, she thought, not because he lacked the will or talent to complete it but his relentless self-criticism would never allow him to see the end. How could he keep his ego together through the hours of solitary creation where he would be sitting on a ledge in a howling winter storm? But he kept his head in each tableau and didn't let the enormity of the canvas swamp his ambition. Each scene emerged a chapter and he painted and repainted, spending hours on a solitary figure's teeth or fingernails, until he simply couldn't paint or think about the scene anymore. He covered the finished scenes with bed sheets so as not to be distracted as he painted a new tableau. He worried that if he had to look at what he had painted he would want to change it, blot it out entirely and start again, or that the new scene would be influenced by the old, as if he would try to work a solution in the new scene he couldn't find in the old. So, over the years it took to complete the final version Koo Koo caught only glimpses of individual tableaus and saw the entire painting only after he had left.

He left early one morning in mid-February. She woke up to a cold draft blowing across her face. When she exhaled she could see her breath. She pulled the covers over her head and stayed that way until she processed the fact that she lay inside an apartment and that the air should be warm enough so that she should not be able see her breath. She wrapped a blanket around her shoulders and padded to the backdoor, which stood wide open with a steady wind of arctic air blowing in. The door to the studio had been left open also and Koo Koo thought at first of burglary but realized her ex's instability would be a more likely answer. Nothing in the studio had been disturbed and the painting still leaned against the wall entirely covered in bed sheets and rags. He had made his bed for the first time in years. His few clothes remained hanging in the closet. She walked the entire apartment. Nothing came up missing, except him. She closed the backdoor and turned the heat up a few degrees. He had disappeared so many times she found it difficult to summon worry, although he had never left the backdoor open before. Even after he raped her and had blood running down his cheeks and forehead he had locked and closed the door. After a month she finally took the shroud off the painting and gasped at the complexity and brilliance of its execution. When she noticed the dime-sized spot of blank canvas she sensed that he would never return. To return would be to complete the painting and close a door on five years of his life, on her. Too good to destroy and too good to finish because finishing meant stasis and stasis meant atrophy and atrophy led directly to death faster than a person could fall out of a tree, the painting would remain alive and he would be able to carry it with him wherever he went. She eventually moved the painting to the living room and locked the studio door. She couldn't bring herself to clean it, because she didn't need the room. She had the right to clean the room and reclaim it for her own, but she loved the painting and she liked having the studio where it had been created. Even though the person who had created it had vacated the space the remnants of his musings remained and Koo Koo liked knowing there had been something in her life that didn't smell like fried eggs or hash browns and aimed a little higher than filling already fat bellies. She never had the nerve to go back to the spot in the woods where the rope hung to see if he had tied his neck to the other end of it.

Now she had let this other man take up residence. She knew she created nothing more than a puppet show that aped her previous life with her ex. He seemed so hollowed out and lifeless that his capabilities extended as far as responding to her commands and dancing at the end of her hand. She sensed no violence in him; some battle had already been lost. But why invite him in? Had she been fooling herself that much? Did she miss her ex, even after a year, so much that she would take in a reasonable facsimile and pretend their time together had never been broken? Did she expect him to take up the brushes and create something beautiful and strange? Did she want meaning back in her life? What were the chances of meeting two men with the ability and passion to create something like that?

A man sat down on the other end of the picnic table and leaned his head back to catch the weak evening sun. His face glowed with an impossible tan, which made his blonde hair look almost white. He wore a loose sleeveless shirt and running shorts and shoes. If he had been running he had not broken a sweat. He looked in Koo Koo's direction and held the look a long time, until Koo Koo felt discomfort.

"You're not going to bother me, are you?"

"No, unless you want to be bothered?" His voice sounded rich and deep. She had been expecting an effeminate lilt.

"I don't want to be bothered. I'm watching the lake."

"Fascinating. A giant lake. Water. Can't even see a ripple this evening. Makes me think of a bowl with milk and the milk is no longer cold. Let's say it's room temperature."

"Gray milk?"

"It's not the color. Something about the absence of movement. I imagine a giant spoon thundering from the sky and all those little boats are Cheerios. The godhead has awakened and he's ready for breakfast."

"I'm not getting that. A bathtub maybe. A calm ocean. I can imagine I'm on a Caribbean island and that ice cream stand over there sells Mai Tais for like fifty cents."

"And there are brown boys with cocks that look like thick ropes hanging between their thighs. I've been on that beach."

Koo Koo collapsed into herself and turned her head away from him. Maggie had told her or she had read somewhere some pop psychology snippet that men thought about sex something like once every five seconds. She never believed it and passed it off as some titillating attention grabber until she started paying attention and realized the study had grossly underestimated the frequency of the occurrences.

"I'm sorry. That was inappropriate. I'm just an old queen who forgot his manners a long time ago."

Koo Koo turned her head toward him. "You don't look old."

"Being gay is like being a football player. The window of physical grace is very small. You spend the rest of your life pining over the few years you were beautiful, thinking it should be the norm, but the sad truth is that beauty in your life is the anomaly. I'm crumbling. So I fantasize about my lost youth and beautiful boys make me angry with desire. So I blurt out inappropriate comments to unsuspecting women."

"I've heard worse, I guess."

"Still, just because I can be compared favorably to knuckle-dragging Neanderthals and their rudimentary command of aggressive sexual language is not much of an excuse for me. My lack of manners is turning into Tourette's, for God's sake. It's painful to hear."

"I was just about to leave anyway. I have to check on a friend."

"Is he sick, this friend?"

"No, I would say he's more disturbed than sick. I'm not yet sure what he's capable of."

"Have you known him long? Friends, especially old friends, can be such a burden. Always cashing in on old times. Always thinking of how you were and not how you are now. Maybe they're angry that you've moved on. I try to keep my number of friends low. They all want time and I have no time. They all want cash and I tell them I have none, even though they know I'm loaded. So, he's an old friend mooching your food and living in the past?"

"I've known him a day. I found him in the road."

"Oh, you really don't know what he's capable of."

"I know just about everything men are capable of and I've known it for a number of years."

"It shows around your hips and eyes."

"Was that the Tourette's again? Because that was a little rude."

"I'm unmerciful. I use the same knife on myself if it makes you feel better. Besides, you embody all that I hold dear. Lately, I find myself cultivating a fetish for things worn, outdated or weary from the number of days they have lived. My house is filled with antiques. My desire has turned toward experience and disappointment, suffocating disappointment. I feel a strong attraction to you; you must sense it. I would like nothing more than to spend a few hours alone with you."

Koo Koo felt herself sinking under waves of fear. She wondered if all the other men in the cars were Montenegro's henchmen and what she thought to be a public spot had suddenly turned private and sinister.

"What do you want?"

He looked at her with a quizzical look. "Want? Haven't I just said I wanted to spend a few hours alone with you? Isn't that enough? Aren't we spending a pleasant evening at the lake chatting about desire and picking up men along the side of the road?"

"This doesn't feel pleasant. The conversation is not pleasant."

"No? I said the evening is pleasant. I said nothing about being pleasant myself and speaking of pleasant things. I haven't been pleasant in a decade at least, but I can still recognize the pleasantness of a lake breeze rolling off the lake and the temperature being perfectly ambient on your skin and the perfect light from a sun about to sink into the water. What's not pleasant about that? Now, if I were to project my unspoken thoughts onto the canvas I see before me the scene would change into a lake of tar with all kinds of beasts trapped in the viscosity and slowly they sink until the tar suffocates their screams. Not so pleasant. So you can see why I would worry about the development of Tourette's Syndrome, because unleashing such images in public will lesson my chances of getting laid by someone who isn't attracted to the money, certainly, and probably I'll run out of friends to speak to because no one can listen too long to such darkness."

"You probably would be alone."

"I'm alone now and I always have been. Obviously you share the same state. Why else would you bring a stray into your apartment? That seems a little risky, maybe even a little rash. Why don't you help out at a homeless shelter and ladle out soup to the drunks and psychotics if you have some charity fetish to work through? Donate your favorite clothes. The homeless also have the most odious shoes. Give some money, a lot of money, a big chunk of your paycheck so you can hardly pay your bills. That should take care of the impulse and might even make you angry because you had to sacrifice something in order for the bums to live another day. You'll feel you've done something for bruised humanity and you'll stop putting your life in danger. Unless danger is the fetish and not charity."

"Really? Did you compare notes with my friend Maggie?" As soon as she said her name she regretted it, not knowing how large a circle of slaughter Montenegro planned. "You're one to talk about risk? Why do you come to this park and pick-up anonymous men? Isn't that a bit risky?"

"There are mostly heavy regulars and once-a-monthers here tonight. Let's call them semi-anonymous. We've all probably been with each other a dozen times, but I don't know any of their names. The once-a-monthers are in a lighter rotation, obviously. I come here when I want to have my cock sucked by someone different than my current boyfriend or girlfriend. Oh, there I go again with my manners. Nothing to be done once the genie is out of the bottle. But that's the reason and yes there is an element of risk, but these men are so warped and gentle the risk is minimal. The only time I see them get excited is when some new boy comes strolling through. All the cars start bouncing in unison. Sometimes it's comforting to know that I am the worst demon in the park. I really have nothing to fear."

"But how is it different than picking up a man wearing underwear from the street?"

"Oh, he was only wearing underwear? You left that detail out. That changes the sense of the situation somewhat. I can't decide if it makes him pathetically vulnerable or dirty and creepy. Either you are a saintly nursemaid or completely out of your skull for letting him into the car. Were they tidy-whiteys?"

"Well, they were more gray than white. Disgusting, but they were briefs."

"Bedraggled, an orphan of the storm. Was it less charity and more curiosity? How does a man end up on the road in his underwear?"

"It was either a captain or a transvestite who rolled him?"

"Why would a captain roll someone? Why would he risk his position? It's no small title to achieve. The shipping companies are risking their name and goods to his stewardship. It's kind of a bizarre notion that a captain would take interest and then take the poor man's pants, but logically the motive isn't there. Captains have bigger concerns. I'd bet on the evil fucking transvestites. I lived with one a few years back when I was trying to keep up appearances. She was very pretty and even had small enough hands to make her transformation complete. Talk about your lying, thieving psychos. My God, that one stole everything I owned except the pants I was wearing, but I was in love and I overlooked the big things and small things until one day I woke up and saw myself as an old fool, chasing beauty again, clinging to my last shred of heterosexual attraction. I wouldn't be surprised if she's moved on to stealing pants men ARE wearing."

"I should get back and see what he's doing." Koo Koo knew she couldn't leave because Montenegro would follow her and find Nelson and she would betray him.

"If he's going to root through your panty drawer, he's already done that."

"I know. I'm worried, though."

"More worried than sitting at this picnic table with me?"

"That's my problem. I don't worry about myself. I never worry about myself. Demons and fools never worry about themselves."

"Spend a few hours with me Koo Koo Beatrice."

"How do you know my name?"

"Surprisingly, I do have a service for caller identification and unbelievably you don't have a restricted phone number. Once you have a phone number an address is not so hard to find. I was so happy that it turned out to be you. I've seen you here before, you know. All the queens talk about you, make up histories of you, pretend to be able to read your moods and graft fresh arguments or joys onto your expressions. There's something about your tragically worn demeanor that we can relate to. We see us in you, except you are far prettier and far more tragic. You are sometimes the only entertainment we have as we sit in our cars, staring at each other through our windshields. So, imagine my delight when you walked out of the apartment building and drove away in that deathtrap you call a car and came to the park. How could I not follow? As soon as you left I knew where you were going."

"Why were you at my apartment?"

"To take Nelson away."

"Will he be gone when I get back?"

"Do you want to save your dirty man?"

"What does that mean?"

"It means a choice now confronts you Koo Koo Beatrice. I have a car with two goons sitting in front of your apartment building right now. They are awaiting a call from me whether to proceed up the stairs and seize Mr. Munroe and bring him to me at a previously agreed upon location or to leave and get a bite to eat, probably something greasy and tainted if I know my help. So the question is how far does your charity extend? What price are you willing to pay for a man you barely know? Who would blame you if you said that you owe him nothing, that he still should be on the side of the road, naked and alone, that why would you think of putting yourself in harm's way for someone you've known only hours? But come with me. Spend the evening with me."

"To what purpose."

"Consider it a date, if that helps."

"I don't think you'll harm me. I helped him before I knew he was wanted. I don't know him and I wasn't involved in the transaction he screwed up. Unless you're an ordinary serial killer I can't see how the blame falls on me. This is where the fool part of my personality kicks in. Bullets are flying over my head and mortars are falling next to me and I walk oblivious into the valley of the shadow of death."

"I can't say I'm not flattered by the poetry, but are you always this paranoid about a date?"

"Really? I'm suppose to act like this is an ordinary pickup?"

"I would like you to."

"Except that a man's life hangs in the balance based on my decision, that you've granted me the power of life and death over someone I don't know."

"I didn't say the ante hadn't been upped."

"Sure, what plans do you have in store?"

"This is a yes?"

"Sure."

"I would like you to get into my car right now. I'll take you to dinner and we'll chat. I want to know everything about you and I want to see the faces of all these old queens as you get into my car. I will be known as a giant among men, with a silver tongue and a light touch. I will have snared the most elusive quarry of Blowjob Park."

"I'm honored. Does the title come with a sash and tiara?"

"Oh, if I thought it would have helped I would have given you one long ago."

They walked over to his car, a 1973 orange DeTomaso Pantera that he had restored meticulously over the previous five years. The interior smelled of new leather seats and spearmint gum. Koo Koo felt as if she had slipped into the cockpit of a rocket.

"5.7 inch Cleveland V-8, 4-barrel carburetor with 310 horse. They built this engine right over in Brookpark. It's a goddamn monster in this car."

"I have no idea what you're talking about."

"Right, I forgot what you drove. The best thing that could happen to you is your car roll into the lake and never be seen again. Really, Koo Koo, you'd be better off with a mule and a wagon."

Her ex had also criticized her car every time he saw or had to sit in it, citing traffic fatality statistics, the safety advances of the last decade, the sheer awfulness of being publicly mangled in a car, the possibility of carbon monoxide poisoning, and the long term effects of the rattling and shrieking engine on her hearing. She listened until she could take no more and then asked him if they could take his car instead. Since he hadn't owned a car in at least seven years the jab usually kept him quiet long enough for them to get where they were going.

Montenegro took her to one of his warehouses deep in a gloomy neighborhood of double houses and abandoned brick factories, closed gas stations, and storefront grocery stores and hair salons with hand painted signs of dubious graphic quality. A garage door opened electronically and he pulled the Pantera inside.

"Are you taking me to the fucking bat cave?" She meant for it to sound like a joke, but the cadence of the sentence betrayed fear and anxiety simmering near hysteria. All of her talk of the blessed fool walking through war zones without a scratch had abandoned her and she was left with a very deep animal fear of death at the hands of Montenegro.

"Dear, I have some dresses stored on the second floor. I can't take you to dinner dressed in shorts and flipflops. I have a roomful of shoes too, still in the box. Unless you fear indigestion, you might as well relax. I had an idea for a clothing store at one time that I abandoned. My little tranny was going to manage it. I thought it would keep her out of trouble, but she wasn't capable and I was left with a store full of clothes.The styles may be a few seasons out of date, but I doubt that matters much to you. The idea would have worked. Word would have spread that a tranny was managing the store. We would have cornered the transvestite market, both the actives and the men who squirrel away their secret clothes in the back of their SUVs or behind their gun cabinets. We would have attracted women who get tired of having to deal with catty bitches while trying on clothes. Even though she could be wicked and critical, she gave women a wide berth and felt kinship. Then, you can't forget the freak factor and all the gawkers and gay curious shoppers who would have come in. Retail as entertainment, as a wild ride to the dark recesses of your own mind."

They walked up a metal staircase bolted to a brick wall and Montenegro led her to a space that had been constructed as a prototype of the store. Racks and mannequins, some with men bodies and women heads, modeled the clothes, which were tasteful and well-designed, much to Koo Koo's surprise. Several color schemes had been tested on the walls. Five different kinds of light fixtures hung from the ceiling, from spare and functional industrial to Victorian glass and fuss. A cashier stand had been built of plywood in the middle of the floor and only a bird's eye view would reveal the shape to be an erect penis, as if she told herself a private joke or she had built a talisman to help her get through the boring or hectic days of managing a retail store. Fortunately, the motif had not been repeated elsewhere, but she had convinced herself the counter would make men and women empty their pockets, paying a ceremonial tithe at the exact center of the universe.

"You look like a six, no?" Montenegro asked as he held up one of his favorite dresses, made of creamy silk with thin shoulder straps and a hemline that stopped mid-thigh. "The problem is going to be the bust. Our would-be customers all have implants so we had to order lots of room up top. That doesn't look like a concern for you."

"Jesus, I feel like I'm at a store. Enough of the comments. I'm trying to keep my composure and you're not helping much."

"Noted. You look like a 34B, yes? No tranny gets B implants. Those fuckers like the flash and dash of display." He sorted through the clothes and pulled out a simple black dress that shimmered slightly under a Victorian light bulb shaped like a gas jet. "Here, this will probably work. Might be a little tight in the butt. Sorry, I forgot. Shoes are stacked along that wall. Black is to the right, the last five columns. The dressing room is right over there."

He left the store through a doorway behind the cashier counter and Koo Koo stood still, holding the dress and amazed at the expense of the abandoned clothes hanging on the racks and draped over the mannequins. The dress actually felt tight across her bottom, but otherwise it fit well. She found a pair of black pumps and looked through the racks of clothes until Montenegro came back. He appeared through the same doorway wearing a cream silk suit with a radiant tie and a matching handkerchief. His shoes flashed in the light and looked like they may be shooting sparks as he walked toward her.

"No hose?"

Koo Koo looked at her legs. Fortunately she had shaved them the day before so she didn't mind them bare. "It's summer. You can get away without wearing hose in the summer."

"You can get away with everything, dear. The point is to know what looks good and not to show your poor breeding."

"Are we really going to have an argument about pantyhose?"

"Not if you put them on."

His voice held enough of a threat that Koo Koo walked over to the hose display, shaped as two large hands palms up, offering the world manna in the form of pantyhose.

She slipped back into the dressing room and as she slipped the dress off she heard his footsteps stop outside the door.

"Take your panties off. I want you to just wear the hose under the dress."

"I'm conservative. I wear panties under my hose."

"I don't want to argue every point. You can suffer a little discomfort knowing that you are making me happy, no?"

"Can you tell me again why it's my job to make you happy?"

He answered her question with silence. Koo Koo thought of just putting the hose over her underwear anyway, but he would need verification and she didn't have an extra pair of panties to show him she had followed his command. So, she took the panties off and kicked them through the gap at the bottom of the door.

"Oh, how pleasant. A little cotton trap of secretions." He kicked the underwear back under the door. Koo Koo picked them up and put them back on and dressed quickly so as not to arouse any suspicion. When she stepped out of the dressing room she stopped in front of him and awaited another criticism. Montenegro stepped back and raised a hand to his chin, striking a mock pose of concentration.

"You've lost your ragged edge. You are too beautiful, somehow. I should have had you keep your rags on and we could have gone to a hot dog stand or got a bag of fries. I can't explain it, but you're less appealing to me now. I would never pick you out of a crowd now. You would never be our queen dressed like that. I don't see what was lost anymore. I see only what is left."

"It's been a long time since I've had a conversation with a man in which he's not trying to get me to bed. If all men talked like you the world's population problem would be solved."

"At least I'm not telling you that you look fine. I know what is anathema to most women. You'd rather hear blunt honesty than a tepid lie or worse yet, a disinterested lie."

"No, I'd rather hear a crafty lie, an I-can't-tell-how-he-did-it sleight of hand that fills me with confidence and a little braggadocio. Blunt honesty I got by the truckloads."

"You look nice. You look fine."

"And you are a goddamn dickhead."

Montenegro bowed with a smile on his lips, then offered his hand and led her down the staircase, back to the Pantera. They drove through the city, now dark. Koo Koo had lived all her life in Cleveland so she knew most of the city, except parts of the eastside that had collapsed under poverty and crime, and unless you were looking for drugs or prostitutes on the last rung of humanity you had no reason to visit these neighborhoods, so she acted surprised when he turned away from downtown where the most expensive and fanciest restaurants served and turned toward a part of town known as the poorest and most desperate, where the cops had turned over law enforcement to teenage gangs, although the laws they enforced were mercurial and arbitrary.

They stopped in front of a dark house with a dim porch light. Montenegro opened the door for Koo Koo and held her hand as they walked toward the front door. As they got closer she could hear the muffled lilt of Miles Davis' *In a Silent Way.* On each side of the door lay a dog, black with massive Labrador heads, so still they could have been mistaken for cheesy statues, aping the stone sentinels of grander places. Their eyes followed the couple as they entered the door, but otherwise they did not move.

Inside they were greeted by a man who gave Montenegro a deferential bow as he shook his hand, holding on two beats too long. Completely bald with an oversized and obviously dyed moustache, the man wore black silk pajamas and silk slippers.

"It is always a pleasure to see you, Mr. M."

"Is the chef in tonight?"

"Yes, but very cranky. He's been hung over all day and taking it out on the skillets and me. He made an absolutely dreadful soufflé for brunch. Tasted like he baked it with gravel and sand and he's been trying his hand at lamb chops all evening. God, to think those poor little beasts sacrificed themselves so they could be fussed and mussed with until you don't know whether you're eating lamb or rat. I just want to tell him to give it a rest, sleep it off, and come back tomorrow when he can think straight. The man has talent, no question, but there's no control. He has a ninety-five mile per hour fastball, but he has no idea where the ball is going once it leaves his hand."

"Tell him I'm here and I'm craving red pepper gnocchi."

"But sir, really, he's not himself. I'm afraid you'll be disappointed and you'll take a dim view of our establishment. Days like these kill reputations. We rely on your recommendations and patronage. The man can't fry an egg right now."

"Indulge me."

The man left and returned quickly. "We have a problem. He's passed out on the floor. He's breathing, I think. There's a pulse. He must have continued drinking all day and I didn't know it. Sometimes his demons get the better of him."

"Let's have a look." Montenegro said. He walked through a swinging door into a gleaming silver commercial kitchen which held a tapestry of scents, from freshly peeled potatoes to scorched tomato sauce to a heavy swirl of boiled pasta. On the floor in front of the stove lay the chef, looking more portly and misshapen lying down than he ever did when he was on his feet. He still held a slotted spoon and looked like he had been stuck down in a field of battle as if, having had his armor torn from him, he used the spoon to protect his heart.

"Did he say anything before he went down or did you find him like this?"

"I found him like this."

"He has that drunken sprawl, you know what I mean? He doesn't look in pain," Koo Koo said as she thought of the hundred or so times she had witnessed the same prone position from her string of boyfriends. "You could throw water on him, but then you'll just have an awake drunk and who really wants to listen to that. It's better to let him sleep it off. We'll be spared his brilliance."

"A woman of profound experience and grace," the man in pajamas said as he grabbed her hand and kissed her knuckles. "There should be a ring on this finger. Men have turned away from the obvious and the good."

"Let's get him out of the way and I'll cook us something." Koo Koo tried to get her hand back, but the man held on.

"You'll ruin the dress."

"I'll put on an apron. I know what I'm doing."

"He really is a gifted chef. He obviously has his problems. That's why he's not working in one of the downtown spots. By now everyone in town knows and he's on his way down. He's worth about a month of brilliance before this starts happening."

"I'll cook my specialty."

"Which is?"

"Go sit down and I'll bring it out. It won't take more than fifteen minutes."

"I can't wait," Montenegro said in all seriousness.

They dragged the chef to the farthest corner and propped his back up against the wall. Koo Koo shooed the man in pajamas and Montenegro out of the kitchen and set to work. She knew her range did not extend much beyond eggs and all the possibilities for their presentation, so she decided on omelets with a side of hash browns, which she knew sounded lowly and common, but so few people actually had had good omelets and fewer still good hash browns that she thought she could impress him. She skirted the line between delivering a swamp of tastes battling each other for supremacy and finding an extraordinary combination of flavors that sequenced perfectly as the food traveled along the tongue. She threw flecks of fresh parsley on top as if holding the last note of a brilliant and troubled symphony that had threatened to careen out of control but the conductor had kept together through force of will.

When she set the plate in front of Montenegro he started laughing and began a mocking screed with "What did I expect from a woman like you?" But he took a bite before he ended his thought and the lure of balanced tastes stopped him short. When he tried the hash browns his concentration locked onto the plate and he didn't look up until he had eaten it clean. "Sweet Jesus, Koo Koo, where did you learn to cook like that?"

"I have a diner."

"Really? You must give me the address? You aren't eating?"

She had made herself an omelet, but she left it in the kitchen. She began to think of how many eggs she cracked a day, every day, for years and her appetite had subsided. "I thought I was hungry, but when you cook sometimes food is ruined."

"What else has been ruined?"

"What do you mean?"

"What else has been ruined by repetition? By you knowing the outcome before you even start? By knowing all the pieces and the parts so thoroughly that the alchemic process no longer delights and mystifies? By believing the metaphysical is no longer possible and nothing exists past our fingertips?"

"Do you have to ask? Wouldn't the answer be obvious?"

"The facts of the answer are obvious, but your view of them is unique. I still cling to my belief in the power of the individual to delight and surprise. For instance, would I have thought we would be having dinner in this restaurant tonight, that you would have concocted the best omelet I've ever tasted." The man in pajamas set down two glasses of grappa on the table and disappeared. "That so many talents are hidden from view and that it's almost impossible to know the full range of a single human brain."

"OK, big deal, you want to know my ruin? I can scare up the whole sad history without much trouble."

"I would like nothing better."

"Oh, but the list is so long, I think."

"Consider it your life's work."

"Oh, God, I'm the Rosa Luxemberg of men."

"I'm stunned by that citation. You are full of surprises, Koo Koo. Just when I think you are faded and past your prime you put on that black dress and douse the raging years. Just when I'm about to laugh at being served an omelet at my favorite restaurant, where I was once served bat's head soup and deep-fried grub, I taste perfection on the end of a fork, and now this, Rosa Luxemberg, my lord."

Koo Koo smirked at her victories, because she knew over time they would mean nothing.

"So, I had my first boyfriend at the age of thirteen. His name was Bradley Dunneford and I liked the way his hair curled over his forehead and the shape of his hands and the fact he had his mother's eyes, which were almost black and more beautiful than any marble I'd ever seen. We didn't get much past handholding and kissing before he moved across country because his dad was sick of factory work and winter and he wanted to go to Orlando and work in a car dealership. For the longest time I expected Bradley to show up in movies, tragic and pouty, with long hair and I thought I would buy posters to these movies and watch him from my bed and I would collect all the posters of all the movies he would be in and I would tragically pine after him day after day. Sadly, his movie career was a figment of my desire and I never heard of him again. Bradley was followed by Steve Ony and everybody figured that he must have Asian blood because of his name and a slight stretching of his eyes and poor Steve didn't have a full range of social skills. He may have had a friend or two, but when I showed him some kindness by letting him copy my homework or letting him sit next to me in study hall he tried to crawl inside my skin and see the world through my eyes and think my thoughts, which, he hoped, were all about him and his talents. He would wait for me on the sidewalk outside my house even though he lived blocks away and my house was nowhere close to his way to school and he would call me when he thought my parents might be asleep. He switched lockers to be next to mine. So, I found a boy named Walt Evans, who wore black concert t-shirts and had really long hair and who had older brothers who had let him try pot and beat him until he was tough and who I pretended to like so that Steve would stop bothering me, but Steve wouldn't stop and didn't stop even after Walt beat him up outside of my house before school one morning. He didn't stop after Walt and his buddies locked him in his locker. When I changed classes I could hear him breathing and whimpering, but I never told anyone and he wasn't let out until the boy on the other side let a hall monitor know. He didn't stop when Walt and his friends ripped off his baseball pants after a game and made him walk home in his underwear. Steve only stopped after I agreed to touch his penis in exchange for peace and quiet. I knew Walt would never stop because he liked torture. So, in the basement of my house in front of our washer and dryer he pulled down his pants and I touched my first penis, as frightening a memory as a girl can ever have, by the way. He kind of shrieked and moaned and jumped backwards like he had been shocked. For a few months I had the notion that all penis' were that sensitive and I listened for the shrieks of boys as they pulled them out and urinated in the bathroom and I sometimes wondered how they could stand the chafing of tight jeans as they walked down the school hallway. Anyway, then, he pulled up his pants and moved his locker back to his original spot and never showed up on my sidewalk again. Walt broke up with me because it was no longer fun without Steve, so I went a few months before I started going out with Chan, whose last name I can't remember, and I can't imagine how we really ended up together because he still liked model cars and model monsters and had a line of werewolves, Draculas, and Frankensteins on his shelf in his bedroom, but somehow a few hormones broke through all those childhood fascinations and he convinced me to let him finger me, but I never saw or touched his penis, which, frankly I was glad to not have the pleasure, because I really didn't want to hear that boy shriek again so soon. It also occurred to me that I could have been the reason for the shrieking and I began to worry that electrical charges pulsed through my fingers and I would be unable to touch any boy no matter my lust or desire because I had been cursed. I also remember Chan being a really good kisser, like he had practiced with his sisters, but he never told me if he had. After Chan the intensity turned up a notch. The first girl to get pregnant in our class announced her due date and all the blood rushed from our heads and to our wombs and vaginas as we knew the game had begun. We suspected up until that point that other girls might be having sex, but the pregnancy was proof positive that it was happening so everybody hopped on the train. I continued my string of losers and misfits and joined the flock of the deflowered with a boy named Stuart, whose face was covered in acne and who had a thumb for a penis. My big moment came and I could feel nothing and I kept asking if he was sure he was inside, quite a feat when exploring unexplored, barely touched, virgin territory. He played soccer so he had a slim boy body that was worth giving more chances, but after an entire spring of being come on without a flicker of sensation I dumped him. I was also really tired of hearing about soccer and I needed to see what else was on the horizon. I couldn't figure out all the fuss about it, if it felt no better than that. By then my dad had left and my mom was working a hundred hours a week at the hospital to keep the family going. I had my first bottle of beer with Stuart and, you know, it wasn't long before boys and alcohol became inextricably linked. So a group of twenty or thirty of us formed, sometimes larger when guests were brought in and sometimes down to the core of the group, which, I guess if I think about it, was no more than ten. Anyway the party moved from house to warehouse to abandoned houses to fields to boats tethered to the docks and I think the whole point of the group was to be a group that discouraged coupling for more than a night or two. Somebody would bring pot or really nasty grind-your-teeth acid and everybody would drink until they were stupid and I ended up having sex with all the boys as did all the girl members. They were Kevin, Dave, Eugene, Ken, Tim, Larry, another Steve and two Jeffs, probably they were the main core. I liked Larry the best because looking back he was obviously gay and he did his best to fake heterosexual sex by being extremely attentive to my body, every inch, every hair and mole. Sometimes I told him I thought I was under dissection in the biology lab. How he kept it together without being repulsed is beyond me. The others showed me that dicks come in different sizes, which put poor Stuart in his proper place on the scale, and they gave me the first inkling of what was to come because after I made the rounds, after I gave myself to everyone and the other four girls gave themselves up they started calling us whores and started asking if we'd do other guys and hinting at entries that looked unnatural and painful. I hated all of them, even the girls. We had plunged into the abyss with the bravery of kamikazes, but we bitched and gossiped and tried to ruin each other before we ever reached our target, which, looking back, had to be some kind of tragic early death or what we thought death was. I was the first to leave and by then my studies were in such a tangle that I dropped out. I didn't tell my mom for six months. I didn't tell her that I hung out in the downtown library instead of going to school. I never told her that I read six, seven hours a day and that I was through with talking to boys. That old group came around the house every now and again, but I wouldn't go with them. I thought if they were capable of asking me for sex, then demeaning me for agreeing, I didn't know what they could be capable of. One time only Larry came to my house, drunk to the point of staggering, and wept on my shoulder, telling me he missed me even though he thought I was a disgusting skank with a weird woman's body. I let him cry until he passed out, then my sister and I dragged him across the street to a vacant lot that a neighbor was using as a vegetable garden and let him sleep it off under the tomato plants. Anyway, so when I told my mom I had stopped attending school and that I had let a string of boys inside me she started weeping and saying I was making the same mistakes she made, and I was following the same path that she had walked that led her to being a single mom with swollen ankles and a tricky back that sometimes pushed all the air from her lungs. I couldn't disagree. So I got a job in a factory where I couldn't see across the floor because of all the smoke and I lasted a month, because every time I'd walk by the men at their machines they would hoot and salivate and stutter step in place, except the ones who really hated their wives who just scowled or threw bolts at me with my back turned. So, if you imagine my life as a stone ball rolling down a hill this would be the point where momentum has gathered and the ball has picked up speed and everything is a blur and I have no idea where I'm headed, but I know I'm getting there faster and faster. So, I'm seventeen at this point, right, a dropout with no prospects, but I have some attributes. Now it feels like I've spent the past twenty-five years without a break in boyfriends until this past year. I stopped drinking and putting my ass in the air and I feel pretty good about it. I met Olin, the first guy I thought I was going to marry. He was set to go to college to become a chemical engineer. His family had enough money to understand what an engineer does and how to get the skills to become one. My mom knew a little about doctors and nurses, but she was basically clueless how our world was created or how people earned livings other than most people made a hell of lot more than her in her hundred hours at the hospital. Olin was also the smartest and most serious guy I had ever met and we couldn't keep our hands off of each other until I got pregnant. I think I knew when the sperm hit the egg because it felt like an asteroid burying itself in the crust of the moon, or at least how I imagine that would feel. Olin, of course, wanted no part of a baby before college so he borrowed some abortion money and told me to call him after I had the procedure. I had to go to the clinic alone, because I didn't have any close friends at the time and I thought the news would just about kill my poor mother. Memories of those few weeks are a blur, but I have a sense memory of sobbing, vomiting and being unable to twist my torso because my ribs hurt so bad from all the wailing and retching. I also started thinking about families who had money and families that didn't and the wildly different paths the two of us were on. It wasn't that I didn't think it was fair, but I realized people like Olin maybe would never have to grow up while people like me, if I made the same mistakes, would be nothing more than roadkill in a weedy ditch. Of course I never called him again, but I saw him twice around town and ended up fucking him out of spite or self-abuse or maybe to try to get pregnant again so this time he would want the baby. That plan didn't work out so well, but Olin had a friend by the name of Sonny who waited for Olin to leave for college and made his move. Sonny had no ambitions or much intelligence. He talked a lot about football and really liked to get drunk on the weekends and hangout with his friends. He waited a while to introduce me to the group because they all knew Olin and when he did there was some protest and one fistfight, but Sonny told them the story of the abortion and how Olin wouldn't even go down to the clinic with me so the sympathy swung to me and they agreed they wouldn't ask the fucking college boy over when he was on Christmas break. It's never good to start out as the victim, of course, and have everyone know that you've had an abortion. I was happy for Sonny's idiocy. I got to like football a little bit and the screaming at the television and the deep depression on Sunday nights and Monday mornings after a loss. It was nice to pretend to care about something that didn't matter in the least, to throw all of your emotion and pride into a bunch of guys knocking another bunch of guys to the ground. Every once in while Sonny would get nosebleed tickets to a game and we would tailgate in a parking lot along the lake that was part summer barbeque and part arctic camping with the wind ripping across the lake. I don't think Sonny could believe I had dropped into his lap and he had me slated as the mother of his children who would create her Sunday specialty for the games and I would cook it year after year until we were fat and too old to take the lake wind. I couldn't see it so I cheated on him a few times with a married guy I worked with at a photo store. His name was Dan and he had young children and a wife, who was panicking because she saw where their deficit spending would lead them. I was a diversion, at least I thought I was a diversion from his horrible finances and he was a diversion from ten hours of football on both Saturdays and Sundays and another four on Monday nights, but after a few weeks of sex in the photo storeroom or in his Toyota or when we could both lie and say we had to work and we could sneak to my apartment to perform something more than a quasi-public quickie, he shows up on my doorstep with a suitcase with an explanation that he had told his wife everything about us and that he was ready to start a new life. I think I said something like, 'Start a new life, debt free.' And I could see his face collapse, the very definition of crestfallen. So, he limped back to his wife with apologies and humility and I dumped Sonny the next week and I thought that at long last I was boyfriend-free, but a day after I told Sonny that I, in fact, hated football and didn't know the difference between a flanker screen and a sweep, a dark and handsome man came into the photo shop dressed in a perfectly pressed suit and shirt like he had just stepped from a dressing room equipped with attendants skilled at fitting and ironing. His name was Geronimo and he dropped off negatives of Europe and group shots of an equally beautiful family and by the time he returned to pick up his photos I was in love with the possibility of him. I flirted with him and held the package of photos in my hand until he asked me out while Dan fumbled at the cash register, red in the face and a pretty obvious erection tenting his pants. So life began with Geronimo who had closets full of perfectly pressed clothes and polished shoes and an apartment with new leather furniture and actual books of literature, but who had, unfortunately, the dick of a baby. Smaller than Stuart's. Smaller than small. I thought I had begun with the smallest model and was working my way up through the ranks but this came as a serious blow. I had started at the beginning again. I worked at it and worked at it, but I swear I could get it to grow no bigger than a pen cap. When I blew him it felt no bigger than a Tootsie Roll and his full extension made it nowhere close to the bitter taste buds on the back on my tongue. He jetted all over the world as a consultant for the automotive industry and he took me to Japan and Brazil, because for a while I was determined not to throw him away over his undersized anatomy. How superficial, right? How unfair, no? He could speak four languages fluently, for God's sake. He had no pimples or moles or birthmarks on his skin at all. His teeth were perfectly straight and his breath always smelled like ginger and anise. Amazingly, he belonged to a gym and showered in public and once took me to a nude beach in San Diego and took off his shorts and walked around with nothing to show. I don't know if he didn't know or whether he hoped everyone would think he stepped out of the icy ocean or if he just wanted to humiliate himself because he knew we was not worth the money he made in his consultancy, but there he was, not on display, and I wanted to slink into the ocean and swim to the next beach and take up with someone of normal size right there on the spot. So, in this frame of mind is it any wonder I leaped without thinking? So, next up was a neb who bagged groceries and who always looked at me moon-eyed when I was in the checkout line. It was at an organic health food store so I convinced myself he was bagging groceries for a higher cause, that he was a bohemian or a punk who rejected corporate foods and agribusiness and genetically modified vegetables that look too bright, that are too big, and taste like Styrofoam or silly string. The truth was he had reached the summit of his responsibilities that his abilities could handle, but he had no issues with his endowments and he worshipped me. If I would have let him capture my farts in mason jars he would have had a collection that filled a room. Part of his devotion came from my voracious appetite for sex once I felt him inside me. The sluice gates opened and my little neb, Pat, was in for an education. I poured everything into him because I had just spent two years with an elegant eunuch. I honed his skills until he became a great lover. He had nothing else in his mind other than my body and my moods. Our conversations were inane, mostly about the people who came through the grocery store, but Pat couldn't help but mock the anorexics, the pierced, the tattooed, the women with middle-age spreads looking to regain their form, the hippies with beards, the runners with sinewy thighs, the paranoids who were convinced that cancer was a government invention to thin the herd, and the neurotics who tasted poison in everything they ate. I tried to tell him that these people were interesting because they had fallen out of the mainstream, that they probably knew more than you would at first suspect, that anybody who thought about what they ate was probably somebody worth talking to, but Pat couldn't see past their masks and public personas, because, like I said, he was the dimmest of bulbs. But, worship can be seductive and for a while I didn't mind being an altar and floating in a cloud of frankincense and myrrh and having daily sacrifices performed for me in the guise of going to the grocery store or giving me a pedicure or washing my clothes or cooking for me or spending an hour trimming my bush while I talked on the phone to my friends. Gods must get bored after a while. All the sacrifice becomes rote and loses the power to impress, so you start throwing down harder tasks. You become more demanding. You lose your patience more quickly when the task isn't completed in the time and manner you wanted it completed. I made poor Pat spend his measly check on a pair of fancy shoes I desired. I told him to lose weight, cut his hair, get his ear pierced, wear more interesting clothing, brush his teeth twice a day, trim his nose hairs, to stop talking to his idiot friends, and to think of me first, always. I asked him what books he planned to read, even though I knew he struggled with words and had barely graduated high school. I tried to make him cry once a week for fun, because he wouldn't fight back. He wouldn't fight against his object of worship, I found. He took my punishment and tried to understand what he did to deserve such harsh treatment, he humbled himself, he threw himself on the ground and rolled in mud and threw dust on his head and wailed to God to make him a better person. I, like everyone before me, failed the test of power. Instead of a benevolent leader I turned into a despot. I was Pol Pot with a pedicure and a trimmed bush. I was Robert Mugabe with boobs. I couldn't stand what I had become, so I set him free one winter morning after he scraped the ice off of my windshield and shoveled the drive. Of course, true believers don't go away so quickly and Pat howled outside my doorstep for months, begging to be let back in. He sent crates of flowers, no doubt stolen from the health food store. He called incessantly and when he heard my voice he began sobbing into the receiver. He danced naked and drunk on my front lawn until a neighbor called the cops and he was arrested for public indecency and public intoxication. He wrote me notes that could have been scrawled by an ape for as much sense as they made. He showed up at work, by now I had started at the diner, and ordered coffee and sat in a corner table and stared at me all day. I think he must have lost his job for all the attention he was paying me. I let it go on for six weeks because his stares were based in worship and humiliation and sometimes it's hard for a goddess to step off the throne even if her neb had turned into a stalker. I put an end to it by buying a bottle of Mighty Cleanse Colon Cleaner and mixing it in his coffee. I knew he used about six tablespoons of sugar per cup so he wasn't going to taste it. I have to give him credit. He lasted about a week. Every day you could see the magic start to happen. First his face would get red, then he would start to sweat and then he would begin to hold his stomach and put his forehead on the table. Poor little neb. Then, he'd duck walk with a puckered sphincter to the bathroom and spend the next hour releasing his toxins. See what power does? I had no qualms about torturing him. He was a dumb worm and I wanted to be rid of him. Finally, he figured out that the diner coffee didn't agree with him. He might have given up coffee altogether. Maybe he has a story about the week in his life when coffee turned on him, I don't know. But after all that he faded away and I never heard from him again. But of course I was far from through. Next up was a chemical engineer named Griffin. Ah, Olin revisited, right? A return to what could have been before the abortion. But Griffin was different. He was gentle and kind. He talked in a soft voice and wore a fluffy beard and small smarty glasses. He was lean and when he walked he looked like a pair of scissors walking. He earned a lot of money, which, of course, he saved judiciously in certificates of deposit, selecting one after researching every bank in the region. He wanted to fix me. Eliminate all the residue of my short stint as an object of desire and worship. He balanced my checkbook, bought a GED study guide and researched the times and places where the test was given. He inflated my tires to the proper pressure and changed the oil in the car, which he said looked like molasses and he turned red in the face when I asked if that was what it was supposed to look like. He negotiated with my landlord for a new furnace and the replacement of a few broken windows. He showed me some great hiking trails in West Virginia and I even went camping for the first time. The problem, you ask? It's a theme, I guess, of my story, the sex tripped us up. Like I said he was very gentle and he liked to softly kiss me on the lips first, for what seemed like an hour, then he would tentatively put his hand on breast and stroke my nipple and cradle them in his hands like he was trying to determine the cup size. This also would go on for an hour. Then, maybe he would finger me, maybe not. If he did it would be another hour. All the while he would keep his dick out of range of my hand because he was worried about premature ejaculation, which actually was a big risk with him. Anyway, then I would have to lie on my back and he would make love to me slowly and gently with measured thrusts, calculated for the perfect depth with a micrometer, no doubt. I sometimes believed I was being measured while I slept. Anyway, we always made love and we never fucked. You should have seen his face when I would waggle my ass in the air and tell him to fuck me. You would have thought I told him I changed the oil in my car every fifteen thousand miles or that I preferred creation myths over the theory of evolution. The poor man was aghast at my need to sometimes be fucked hard and fast, to be taken, have my butt slapped, and be thrown to the side. Believe me, a steady diet of that can get old real fast, but you have to have your man act like a selfish beast who can't control himself at the site of your naked form every once in a while. He didn't understand. I tried to put it into terms he could understand. I would say something like didn't we bring forward some of the wild beast that no doubt Australopithecus afarensis was, that do you think they worried about gentleness and process? I, one time, early in our relationship, said something like that but said the word Neanderthal and I got a lecture on how Neanderthals were not our ancestors and very probably human beings forced them into extinction through expansion into their hunting grounds and possibly disease brought up from Africa that the Neanderthals had no immunity against, think Europeans and the Native Americans. Needless to say, none of this talk led anywhere close to fucking, so I backtracked to Pat for a few weeks, who was, of course, leery, but ultimately he obliged. After Pat reminded me how incredibly dumb he was and how good of a lover he was I went back to Griffin for a while, but eventually that all ended when his company moved him to Alabama. He asked me to go, but I just couldn't imagine continuing life with all that respect and tentativeness. So Phil followed Griffin, and Phil was a roaring drunk who ran through a series of sales jobs and our time together was riddled with titanic drunken fights, dishes thrown loaded with food, a lot of time spent in dark corners and shadows, and Phil talking about his two or three therapy sessions per week and how one therapist had a lisp and another who had mastered the art of sleeping with his eyes open. The relationship ran too hot and it burned up quickly. I could do nothing with his rage. His daddy had whipped him and screamed at him for his first eighteen years and that cast the die of his life. No amount of talk and alcohol was going to change that. Next was Dave who liked to ride his bike a lot. He even bought me a bike so I could ride with him and I'm not talking little trips around the neighborhood. Thirty miles was the shortest ride he would go and I got the sense he was riding away from demons or trying to burn through his own rage, but he had chosen a bike instead of alcohol. I never really understood what he did for a living, something to do with unions and political hand-to-hand combat. I considered him a labyrinth or a hall of mirrors, I could never really settle on the appropriate metaphor. A union knee-buster who read Sartre and Proust. A Neanderthal with a master's degree in English. A working class kid with an encyclopedic knowledge of classical music. A freak who could drink a case of beer at night and wake up and ride a blistering fifty mile bike ride in the morning. I suspected him of being crippled in some fundamental way, but I never found it. He was a guy who had the same job for ten years, but who sometimes disappeared for a week or two at a time and sometimes drank as much as Phil but somehow managed to keep it all together. Everything was fine and then it wasn't, and he left me with a bike, a really tight butt and a bunch of bike clothes I would never wear again. That one hurt because it was the most normal relationship I would ever have and it seemed like that was how adults were supposed to live, active, not a lot of screaming, sex that wasn't frightening, riddled with kink or flat out boring. But that wasn't to be my life. So, batter up! Ivan Drostev, an impotent little creep, whose only fall back was licking my pussy with his lizard tongue. Strike three! Pauly, an overweight auditor with Crone's disease, who unfortunately died three years after I stopped seeing him. Inning over! Greg, a moody architect who had squirreled himself away in a house in the woods in the far, far ex-burbs, you know, one of those guys you're afraid to talk politics with or talk about people in general for fear he was going to come out with some rant based in militia doctrine. Popout to the short stop! Then there was a car salesman named Chip who talked me into buying that VW I still have and somehow he slipped a date into the fine print of the sales agreement. I went with him for awhile and his bi-polar life of living high off the hog when the sales were rolling, expensive bottles of wine, great restaurants, ridiculously expensive clothes and shoes and then Raman noodles, ketchup sandwiches, thrift stores and hand-me-downs when sales died for a week or two every couple of months. I started to see credit like the tide of an ocean, always on the move, never constant, with high tides and low tides, sometimes covering up all the bad decisions and pain people were living with and sometimes laying it bare in the sun, leaving all of us crabs with nothing to do but scramble for cover. Chip never understood the cycles or the odds. When he was on fire the good times would never end and when he had gone cold the spiral downward would never stop. And then my ex, the loner, the painter, the rapist. I could go on for about an hour on that one, but I'm a little tired. I've given you only the highlights. There are some minor characters lurking in the shadows, but if I included them we would be here all night and my narrative would swell into an unwieldy mass. And now this next one is in my house and I can already see the pattern developing. I can already see life with him and without him."

Montenegro let silence hang as he waited for the echo of her words to die. He leaned back deliberately and folded his hands on the table.

"Do you feel a part of you belongs to me now?"

"Old stories, old boyfriends. Stories of my ruin."

"No, you've gifted me part of you. Thank you. I know more about you now than I ever did about my previous ten lovers combined."

"Like I said, it's not particularly hard to remember these stories. None of them have faded or sunk below the surface. They're all bubbling right on top waiting for recall."

"You are my Salome."

"Meaning?"

"I give you back the head of your dirty man in underwear. You've danced expertly enough to keep him alive. Of course, he will never acknowledge or appreciate what you've done for him. He will never pay the debt down nor even make much of an attempt. But it would seem cruel to take him away from you now. You have to act in your little pantomime and boo hoo when he leaves and rip out your hair and ask yourself again and again why and how you get yourselves in these messes, knowing without messes you really wouldn't know how to live. There are reasons we pick dirty men wearing underwear, sitting on the side of the road with a price on their head."

"I'm fully aware of my culpability. But Salome was served a decapitated head. I'm not sure your metaphor holds together."

"So, allow me to be presumptuous. You will play out whatever script is left with your dirty man, but a new man has already broken the horizon. It's like having two suns in the sky at the same time, but one is obviously setting and the other is definitely rising. And this new man will come to your diner for your fluffy omelets and to be able to watch you as you cook and he will develop the romance as if he's soldering a microchip by hand. The courtship will be excruciatingly slow and deliberate and by the time he first touches you, your skin will feel as if it burns under his touch. He will be the worst and best of your decisions. You'll question your good fortune, because how could somebody mired in the worst of our desires be so attentive, respectful and generous. You'll fret about AIDS and every other known pathogen transmitted through sexual contact because you'll come to know he has placed no limits or barriers in his way of gratification and who wants to be the recipient of a past due bill not of your own spending? You'll also come to know that he has his blood analyzed incessantly and he always has a bandage on one of his fingertips or in the crux of his arm. His skewed ethical system contains the clause that should he have the misfortune of contracting herpes, gonorrhea, syphilis, HIV, chlamydia, HPV, a yeast infection or crabs he does not want to pass it along. A dealer yes, a carrier no. Skewed, I know. And since there seemed to be a theme to your misfortunes you'll also come to know that he has practiced and become a journeyman in all forms of sex and knows the purpose is getting off. So, you will see he knows how to employ his fingers, tongue, lips and cock, which is healthy and thick and that has never failed to delight the recipient of its attention. But you'll feel like you are walking a tight rope over a pool of lava and the sweat from your toes is steaming off your skin as you step. Somedays the air will be thick with paranoia and your man's moods can be black since everyone has been trying to tear him down since time began. But he never turns his moods on you as he sees you as safe harbor in the chaos he is surfing. When you feel a tingle of love you will ask him to take his money, his loads and loads of money, and retire before the life catches him and he'll say that he can no more retire than she can stop making bad choices in men, so you'll have to accept the fact that he will be killed or die from being eaten alive by the stress. You'll always think the end could come in a hail of bullets as you and he step into a car, but that's strictly Hollywood or Ciudad Jaurez or Mogadishu. In Cleveland we prefer knives and dismemberment with a healthy dose of torture, must be the clouds and the moody lake that drives us away from the quick fix into contemplative and excruciatingly premeditated violence. Anyway, it will be a life like no other, and it awaits you when your loose strings are tied or cut. Everything has an order, a slotting, and the dirty man in his underwear appears to be next, since he owes his life to you. The man on the horizon can wait until your saintliness is abjectly rejected again."

Koo Koo found she had a hard time breathing because her lungs felt like they had constricted to the size of her fists. She simultaneously wanted to run and take his cock into her mouth, so she remained paralyzed and breathed the shallow breaths of a rabbit.

"Let me drive you back to your car. Cabs don't come into this neighborhood. You can keep the dress for another occasion. I'll keep your clothes for when you need them after you spend the night with me and you want to lounge comfortably in my apartment."

"Do you live in that warehouse?"

"I sometimes sleep there. There's a very nice suite behind the model store that I had custom built, but I've been known to sleep most anywhere. I have fourteen places I call my own. Some I haven't been to in a year, but wherever I am there I am. I try to follow no set routine."

He rose and held out a hand for her, which she accepted even though she felt more than capable of rising from her chair by her own power, and he kept hold of her hand until they reached the passenger door of the Pantera. He also opened the car door for her and bowed a little when she slipped in. The courtship had begun.

They drove back to her car in silence, Koo Koo listening to the purr of the engine and Montenegro listening for any creaks or groans in the body or suspension that he wanted to catch before they became a larger problem. When they came to the park Koo Koo's car stood alone with a ticket under its wiper. All the men had either made a catch, had settled for something known and uninspiring, had gone home alone to their wives and families or to watch porn on their computers. Montenegro scrambled out, opened her door and pecked her on the cheek with dry lips that smelled faintly of the fresh oregano she had chopped into the omelet.

She drove to her apartment in a daze. She didn't know what she would do if she found upon her return that Nelson had left. She knew she couldn't possibly be ready for life with Montenegro to begin. She had no doubt that it would develop exactly the way he had described it, but the idea needed time to gestate before it became a reality and Nelson stood as a necessary breakwall to Montenegro's influence.

She found him sitting on the edge of the cot in the studio. He had barely made a wrinkle in the blanket stretched across the cot and if he left the apartment at that moment it would have been the only evidence of his presence. Koo Koo looked at him and felt annoyance and relief, both stemming from the fact that he had not left. She knew it would take some time to untangle all of these contradictory thoughts and the longer they stayed tangled the longer she could keep Montenegro at bay. Had she really saved him from death or was that just bravado from Montenegro? Had she even meant to?

"You can stay. I might want you to sleep on the couch. It's a little strange for me to have someone else sleeping in this room."

"I won't disturb anything. I'll live like a spider."

"Do you want to call your girlfriend again?"

"She's gone. The line was dead. I have nowhere else to go."

"Last stop, Koo Koo Beatrice."

So their life together began. Koo Koo went to her diner as always and when she came home she made Nelson a small lunch. She sometimes chatted about the antics of her clientele or relayed a new theory of conspiracy agreed upon by their collective consciousness. She told them when one of them died, like X-Ray, who passed away from a beating delivered by an ex-marine who took offense to his ongoing examinations and prognosis of testicular cancer and impotence. She told him when one of them disappeared, like Ellen Oglethorpe, who had never returned to the diner and none of the other patrons had ever seen her on the streets. Koo Koo had even inquired at the Sisters of Charity, but the nuns were mean and uncommunicative and they told Koo Koo that Ellen had been blessed and walked in the shadow of God, and Koo Koo received a glare over half moon glasses in return for her inquiry. She asked if walking in the shadow of God meant that Ellen had died. She felt the word catch in her throat and it came out half-pronounced and hushed. The nun escorted her to the door and closed it in her face without an answer. That ended her detective work, but sometimes she thought of Ellen when she saw a flattened soda can on the road or an old woman staggering down the sidewalk toward the cathedral or on a forgotten errand.

Koo Koo knew that most of her stories were repetitive and boring after the curiosity wore off and she gave Nelson some credit for patiently listening to her and even asking questions to aid the stories along. What could be done with the fractured logic of the diner and the same crowd mouthing the same paranoia every day? The cops Hayes and Brankowski were sometimes good for gossip and stories of dumb and desperate criminals and their ridiculous ideas of the perfect crime, but they mostly talked about murders, even though they were just beat cops and had no chance of ever being able to transfer into the homicide department. The stories of murders drove Nelson deep within himself as he no doubt thought about his own death sentence and the imminence of his own execution. Koo Koo never told him about her new customer who came in every other day and ordered a grapefruit half, coffee and rye toast, who sat in the corner and read a newspaper and watched her over the top edge of the newsprint, who sometimes engaged in the diner conversations, following the lines of irrationality and adding his own perspective, steeped in paranoia and mistrust. On the days he did not come she caught herself looking at his spot and aching for his presence. On the days when he walked through the door she could feel the weight on her bones and her mood lighten. Koo Koo knew she acted selfishly by not telling Nelson she had danced away his death sentence, because she thought the day she told him he would walk out of the apartment and never return. He could return the favor she had granted him when she scraped him off the road, even though he performed the task unwittingly.

So after she had come home and made Nelson lunch and told the stories from the day he would walk back to the studio and lie on the cot, staring at the ceiling or falling into a doze. He would come out again at dinner. In the early evening they would share another small meal and eat in silence because most often nothing had happened since lunch worth talking about, especially on Nelson's part. The pattern developed and repeated itself over months until a dusting of snow swirled over the ground and the radiators in the apartment knocked and clicked as the steam ran through them. Koo Koo changed the course one day as she listened to Nelson take a shower. She waited until he had turned off the water, took off her clothes and walked into the bathroom. Nelson blotted his face dry with a towel and when he lowered it she stepped to him and took a firm and oddly formal grasp of his penis. She pulled him into the bedroom and they had sex like residents of a refugee camp, desperate, awkward, meaningless and necessary. When it ended, Nelson crawled off the bed and left the bedroom. He dressed in the studio, concerned with this new development. He spent the previous months in the studio thinking, sleeping and practicing for the Captain. He had an idea that everything he had ever read had been stored somewhere in his brain and if he could unlock the information he would be able to recite whole novels and books of non-fiction whenever he wanted to recall them. Certainly, if he showed up at the barge and recited *The Brothers Karamazov* from memory the Captain would have no choice but to accept him on the crew. Nelson would ride the strange lake with his brethren and the concerns from shore would be forgotten. He had not gotten far in the project as he could only recite ten pages of Tolstoy, a section deep within *Anna Karenina,* and the entire collection of Curious George books his parents had found at the library for him. The Captain would not be impressed and he had no chance of ever leaving shore if he didn't make more significant progress.

He had no impulse to create. He sometimes looked at the paints drying in their buckets or tubes and thought they may as well be the remnants of a dismantled internal combustion engine deconstructed to its smallest part, because in either case, whether paint or a machine part, he had no chance of doing something useful with them. He considered writing, but his thoughts were too random and dark and he feared, given the literature project, he would only be regurgitating all those half remembered novels in a mutilated form and that didn't seem worth the effort. He decided not to manipulate his environment, to not try to create form from chaos, to make something, even a stick figure on a napkin, from nothing, to not pretend he could form any attachment with anyone or any discipline long enough to produce significant results. If he could have realistically and thoroughly considered himself a plant he would have happily turned his consciousness to the notion and stood in the corner of the studio waiting for water and a beam of sun.

Now, after months of moving neither forward nor backward they had now conjoined and set in motion the machinery of doom. He couldn't understand why she had come to him as he couldn't detect anything desirable about his person or demeanor, but she obviously wanted movement, development, something to grow and fret over and ultimately reject. So they lurched into a relationship that looked very much like the boarding arrangement they had before except that soon after dinner on most days they engaged in perfunctory sex. Both were intrigued they could fuck so consistently night after night with no passion and the least interest in the other person. Koo Koo fought the urge to talk about their predicament because she realized words would do nothing to change the situation and that the arrangement would only last until she believed herself ready for Montenegro, who she began to think of as Zeus transformed into a bull, snorting and frothing at the mouth, waiting in a nearby pen for her to don her costume so they could create a new monstrosity and Nelson, for his part, considered the sex a step above masturbation so he continued to stay engaged. They would kiss briefly and Koo Koo would turn to jacking off Nelson, her strokes coming in the same rhythm and mechanical form as if she pumped up a bicycle tire, and blowing him if his erection proved to be lackluster and he would try to deftly touch her clitoris and labia, but he really never could get in tune and he usually ended up pawing her too hard until she grabbed his hand to stop him. Once they became aroused Koo Koo decided the position; her favorite being on top, facing away from him, known as the reverse cowgirl. This position worked best for his size of penis and provided the most anonymity and least intimacy that she could think of. She controlled the tempo, the depth, and she did not have to look in his face so she could imagine anyone underneath her. The face and body more often than not now took on the appearance and feel of Montenegro so the time spent passed tolerably. She would orgasm more often than not, nothing uncontrolled or sweeping, but efficient and shallow, feeling like she had driven the last rivet of her assembly line day.

When they finished she would dismount and immediately walk to the bathroom to clean herself off and she would return wrapped in a bathrobe, no matter the temperature of the room. She would fuss with the covers, smooth out her pillow and sit on the edge of the bed, collapsing on herself, anxious for Nelson to leave the room and let her move on to her next task. Nelson sometimes lounged or dozed, legs splayed, as she flitted about the room all but shooing him off the bed with a broom. In these moments they disliked each other, she, because Nelson seemed to desire a kind of post-coital intimacy they could never achieve and he, because, he hated having to disrupt his post-coital nap that always felt so satisfying and free of the swirling neurosis. He would relent before he fell asleep and stagger off to his cot and his scratchy sheets and thin wool blanket.

He began to read again. If he couldn't dazzle the Captain with his powers of memory he would impress him with his depth of knowledge. He tore through Koo Koo's small collection of mass market paperbacks and asked her to pick up books from the library on her way home from work. He reconstructed his foundation of world literature from the beginning. He remembered he could read some Latin and Greek and had Koo Koo special order the Greek texts of Homer, Plato, and the playwrights and the Latin versions of Virgil, Sappho, Ovid and Julius Caesar. They were all familiar texts, but it had been years since he had read them and all had greater resonance and power because he had life experience, because of the grinding of the passing days seemed to be getting harder and faster, because he had a fading memory of the briefest moments of joy on which to draw. The fact that these masterpieces had ever been created out of chaos and raging emotion, poverty, political intrigue, disease, unease, and hunger stood as testament to the power of chance and the near impossibility of meaningful creation. From there he skipped to the Russians then the French, got hung up for awhile on Norse and Germanic heroic tales and spent some time with Asian literature, all the while devouring huge swaths of history, philosophy and entertainment. He slept less, ate less, and had his nose in a book whenever he wasn't sleeping or fucking Koo Koo. Unlike his younger days, he could feel the words slipping from his mind as soon as he read them. He sometimes had to read a page ten times before he understood its meaning and even after he struggled in this way he would immediately forget what he had learned. Greek had come back to him with a little practice, but Latin proved more difficult and he progressed torturously slow through those texts. He could no longer commit whole passages to memory although the texts he had memorized when he had been younger remained intact.

Nelson and Koo Koo never ventured out in public together. They never went to movies or dinner and he never met her best friend Maggie or anyone else in her life. He never returned to the diner and the most he ever traveled consisted of a short circuit around the block when the sun reached its brightest and highest point. He didn't know if the dogs or Montenegro moved by day, but all of his experiences with both had been associated with night so he never left the apartment after dusk. Koo Koo hoped she would meet someone else in the interim while Nelson satisfied base desires and Montenegro waited in the wings. Maggie always questioned her about the man in her apartment, but Koo Koo passed him off as a boarder who worked in a machine shop and kept mostly to himself. She talked about the drop-off of business at the diner and her inability to meet her obligations, although Maggie had noticed a new wardrobe forming with new accessories that were a step above tin and glass. Koo Koo hated lying to her best friend and she would have loved to talk through her situation down to the last scrap of minutiae, but Nelson remained inexplicable and Montenegro probably even more so and Maggie would have pounced on her and gnawed away until she admitted that she truly had no concept on how to live her life, that she had no recognizable and pursuable goals, and that her self-esteem had dropped so low it would not register on any valid or objective meter.

How long did their lives together last in this form? Months? Years? Nelson couldn't be sure. One day passed exactly like the other, except that different readings of literature colored the meaning and mood. He fought the realization that his studies had no point or aim, because he would never be able to trot out his acumen at a party or gallery opening or find anyone, man or woman, who cared much that he spent his days interpreting the traces of human thought that had accumulated on library shelves for the past eight thousand years. This made the loss of the Captain all the more bitter. Surely their common interest superseded company rules. When two men like themselves find each other amongst the mob of philistines and poseurs rules should be ignored and circumvented whenever possible. He would have stayed on the ship tending to his small job until the day he died. He believed in the Captain as a shield and a guiding light. The dogs would have never come aboard. They would have understood they had been tricked out of existence. He would have forgotten the mystery of poor Pez and the circumstantial evidence that the dogs had indeed come aboard and had either learned to row and had taken him back to his hole or all had committed suicide by drowning. Company rules had obviously not included a provision for a course of appeal, but the rejection stung too harshly and the prospect for contentment too great for Nelson to give up entirely. He thought of finding the dock where *The Red Laugh* had moored and waiting for the Captain to come ashore and throw himself at his feet if falling prostrate would lead to acceptance. Beg him to be merciful and bring him into the fold. He could even agree to forego the job if regular communication could be established so that his studies would not seem so purposeless. He could surprise him, stun him with his depth. He would take on the role of guru and show the Captain the path to enlightenment, and he, Nelson Munroe, would act as his personal guide. Surely with such an opportunity for fellowship the Captain would find a way to break the rules that kept his crew in good order. Nelson feared being shunned by the Captain again because a second refusal would be final and all hope would vanish, and Koo Koo would never take an interest in his studies. She would never understand the acquisition of knowledge as important and interesting as painting something flashy and overbearing as a wall-sized canvas of your personal demons. Had she at least picked up one of the books he offered her and merely thumbed through it, maybe changed the shape of her uneducated eyes to indicate a reasonable interest, he might have been able to quell the impulse to visit the Captain and seek a lasting friendship. When he pushed a massive critical edition of *The Brothers Karamazov* toward her or offered her *Journey to the End of Night* as bedtime reading, she never reached out a hand to even touch one of the books. She never acknowledged its existence or believed it worth reading or believed she could read one of them, enjoy it, and not believe that he offered the books as a form of communion and not to remind her he thought her unlearned and stupid. Nelson asked her not to be offended because he had not meant to comment on her complete lack of interest in the best stories and commentary on the human condition that ever existed, but he actually just wanted another human being to share a small amount of his experience so they could talk about something other than food and his deconstruction.

He asked to borrow her car and made her draw a very large and clear map from her apartment to the docks. Koo Koo offered to drive him, being a little taken aback that he wanted to leave the block, but Nelson refused and told her he had a personal matter that didn't involve illegal activity or another woman. Koo Koo laughed to herself at the thought of Nelson cheating on her. She imagined there might be more messed up women in the world than herself, but she couldn't imagine what they might look like, why they would choose Nelson, or how they would have met him, unless on his walks around the block he had decided to sit in the road in his underwear and wait for another ditz to pick him up because the sad and exposed droop of his briefs made them ache with pity. She gave him the keys and half of her hoped she would never see him or her smoky, rattling car again.

Nelson had Koo Koo call the shipping company and after talking to four people she was transferred to the fifth, an intern who sat sitting in the antechamber of a senior manager's office while the senior manager used her lunch hour to get acupuncture for her increasingly balky back. The intern broke company policy first by answering the phone in a reasonably cheery voice, second, by giving his full name, third, by not immediately transferring the call once he had established that the person on the other end of the line represented neither a cargo client, vendor nor employee, fourth, by researching and answering the question, in this case "when was the barge *The Red Laugh* due back in Cleveland?" by reading off the proprietary and confidential shipping schedule, and fifth, by flirting with Koo Koo because she had a husky voice that reminded him of one of his favorite bartenders, sixth, by asking for her number and procuring it with little effort and seventh, by locking himself in the senior manager's bathroom and masturbating into a clump of toilet paper while looking at a photo of the senior manager in a tight ski outfit he had taken from her desk while playing Koo Koo's voice over in his head. While he would not be caught for these seven infractions this time, the intern did display a complete lack of awareness of and respect for an agreed upon set of procedures and policies that would eventually lead to him being terminated before the end of his placement.

Koo Koo found out that *The Red Laugh* would sail back to Cleveland two days from the day of the call at five o'clock in the morning, barring inclement weather or a terrorist plot to bomb a load of iron ore. The intern called her the next day looking for a date, but Koo Koo came to her senses and declined because she didn't need yet another complication to confuse the situation. Nelson tripled the rate of his studying as if cramming for a final that would decide if he could graduate. Even though he hoped a friendship with the Captain could lead to a placement aboard the ship, he couldn't let on that the purpose of the visit was strictly mercenary. He needed to suppress his desperation and put the Captain at ease. Maybe he could win another visit, scheduled this time, when they could share a coffee or a beer and talk through the night. He certainly would make a better impression than the last time he saw him. The color had returned to his skin, he had slept regularly for months, the bald patch on his scalp had grown back in, he wore reasonably clean underwear because he had access to a washer and dryer in the basement of the building, and his thoughts, while turgid, had calmed and were no longer scrambled and paranoid. Maybe the Captain would see Nelson as capable of assuming the role of peer, and if not a peer in the Captain's eyes, then maybe he would consider him a solid candidate for a spot on the crew. Healthy, clean, his demons put to rest, with a roiling stew of literary allusions at his command.

He drove to the dock in the shadow of the mill two hours before the barge had been scheduled to dock, following Koo Koo's carefully drawn directions. He parked the car on the side of a road with broken and cracked asphalt, half on a bank of gray weeds and half on the gravel berm littered with cigarette butts and crushed beer cans, and waited. He kept the windows rolled up and the doors locked even though he knew the dogs would find a way in if they wanted to. The seats smelled of Koo Koo's hairspray and perfume as these scents had managed to mask the odors of burnt oil and scalded transmission fluid and Nelson became a little disgusted and melancholy at the thought of her spraying lacquer on her hair in the car. How could she perform a masquerade every single day? Why did she still wear make-up? Would the inmates at the diner even notice? He always tasted the residue of the spray on his toothbrush or felt it on his soap or on the floor around the sink and on the sink and faucets as well. The idea of asphyxiating herself by spraying the can in the tiny cabin of the car irritated him and he wished he could push out a fart to smell something natural and foul.

The barge came to a stop at exactly five, at least according to the cheap digital watch Nelson wore that also belonged to the painter. He had no doubt the Captain would get the ship to the dock on time. When would the Captain leave the ship? Did he ever set foot on dry land or had he committed himself to a life on water? Nelson had prepared himself to sneak aboard a second time should that be necessary in order for him to see the Captain. The conveyer belts began unloading the iron ore and would continue for a few hours as he watched the stairs for the Captain's shape, but the Captain had been sitting down when Nelson saw him and his memory had been corrupted by the fear of the trial and the humiliation of his banishment so he had to admit to himself that he really had no idea what shape he had to look for. So when all but a few stray nuggets had been spit to shore and Nelson had been waiting in the car for over four hours he finally jumped out and walked with some resolve toward the barge. A few men stood on the dock monitoring the unloading and they turned their attention to his approaching figure as he covered the ground between them. By the time he had reached them their arms were folded in a solid defensive manner and their heads were cocked to the side with a 'what the fuck could you possibly want' tilt.

"I'm here to see the Captain," said Nelson when he was twenty-five feet away from the men and he kept repeating the phrase until he stood in front of them. He summoned all his confidence and repeated it one more time.

"The Captain doesn't see people. The Captain stays in his cabin," said the first crew member who had a black shadow of whiskers from under his nose to a line just above the collar of his shirt.

"People he does not see," said the second crewman, balding and paunchy, with a green tint to his skin. Nelson thought he recognized his shoes as the pair he had stolen, but he couldn't be sure because they were nearly black with grime and frayed along the sole.

"He'll see me or I'll wait until he comes off the boat."

"The Captain does not leave the boat. On shore he is not a captain. On the boat he is our leader and sage. He takes his responsibilities very seriously."

"Practically chained to the deck, that one is."

"Look, he offered me a job once and I want to take him up on his offer."

"Technically, the Captain does not hire the crew. Corporate takes care of that."

"He's a big believer in the HR process."

"My God, the battery of tests you have to take. They almost drummed me out because I made a joke asking if I was being hired to be a barge rat or an astronaut."

"They look in every orifice, if you know what I mean."

"Seriously, it was just a couple of months ago. Maybe a year or two. I don't know. Not that long, maybe, but he said he wanted me for his crew."

"A year or two?"

"A year is like a decade in the shipping industry."

"Slow boats and mercurial time."

"What does it matter?" Nelson began to look back and forth between their faces, trying to get advance warning of the blow to come. "I'm sure he will remember me."

"I mean this is a whole new crew with a new captain. We started sailing together just last month."

"A new captain with a new way of doing things."

"What happened to the old captain?"

"If you believe the rumors his career ended in the most ugly way."

"If you want to believe rumors. The official story is different, but you can never believe the official story, right?"

"Why would you believe stories conjured up by public relations flaks and dewy-eyed interns. Most of their stuff is absolute dreck."

"True. There's never any flesh and blood in those narratives."

"People say the last captain ran off with a tranny he met at a bar."

"A chick with a dick."

"They say the last captain was also not one to leave the ship much. He tended to the barge like it was a fair, sick child, touching the rivets, scouting for oil drips, keeping his eye on rust and decay, checking and rechecking the electrical and navigation systems day after day. One night the crew convinced him to go ashore and share a drink with them. They had just successfully completed their two-hundredth voyage together and they were in a mood to celebrate. Well, unfortunately they went to a bar known to be frequented by sailors, pirates, out-of-work schoolteachers, and transsexuals, and the Captain took a shine to a devious little he-she who turned his head away from the ship, until he only thought of him-her. What until that moment seemed unimaginable became reality. The Captain left the ship in the hands of the crew while he followed his muse. The scuttlebutt around the company is the crew went on quite a ramble once the Captain left them."

"As much of a ramble as you can go on in a barge."

"Still, they found them in Baie Comeau drunk out of their minds, shoeless, and with conflicting stories as to the whereabouts of the Captain. They let the barge drift down the seaway and they came ashore in the lifeboats. It was all the company could do to save The *Red Laugh* because she experienced extensive hull damage. The board of directors argued about changing her name to start fresh and to bury this embarrassing incident deep in the bowels of company history. They had a lot of explaining and bribing to do to both the Canadian and American governments to keep their licenses intact, but they prevailed on the strength of strippers, paid junkets to warmer climes, cases of wine and partnerships in sketchy land deals. But the name stayed because the originator of it who was still on the board, blind now, nearly deaf and crazy as a shithouse rat threatened to filibuster in the form of taking a dump on the board room table if they continued to consider a name change. At the end of the day he won, of course, leaving no room for compromise as he was on record with that foul threat."

"That crew sure went on a toot."

"So, corporate tried to find the most miserable, the most buttoned-up and straight-laced sonofabitch in the fleet to take over the helm of the barge. The rumor is that they've instituted a new assessment test for the captain position to determine how tight an applicant's sphincter is. They say our Captain scored in the ninety-ninth percentile and his asshole is so tight his turds come out looking like straws."

"Captain O' Captain. Our stinking captain."

"The ship has weathered every rack, the prize we sought is won
The part is near, the bells I hear, the people all exulting
While follow eyes the steady lead, the vessel grim and daring
But o heart! Heart! Heart!
O the bloody drops of red
While on the deck our Captain lies,

Fallen cold and dead," Nelson recited in a reverent tone.

"I wouldn't talk about our Captain being dead. It's not a fucking joke. You can't imagine the number of assassins sent to kill them."

"Corporate takes this kind of talk very seriously. They won't fuck around."

"No, a threat enacts the Healthy Limb Healthy Head Security Protocol. I haven't seen it in person, but they say once you've seen it you really won't believe the efficiency and brutality of its design."

"It's a poem. Have you heard of Walt Whitman?" Nelson hoped some of the Captain's acumen had trickled down through the ranks.

"No, no time for any of that."

"The new captain deloused the boat the first thing he came aboard. We chucked crate after crate of books into the middle of the lake. It's like we made a temporary paper reef there were so many volumes."

"We figured if these books led to the Captain running off with a chick-with-a-dick then, well, who really needs that influence in your life, you know what I mean?"

"It was a very cleansing experience."

"The first couple of books were hard because you felt like you were pitching little pieces of art into the water, but I just kept thinking of lying next to a woman with a cock and that kept my mind straight."

"Is there any word where the previous captain went? Any word at all?" Nelson asked.

"Where can you go after an incident like that?"

"Squirrel away in a city I suppose."

"A big city. A mammoth city with every variation and perversion on display."

"Anyway, you could try to call corporate. They probably have his last address because they had to send his last check somewhere, right? But, the probability of them giving you the information is pretty slim. I don't think they give up addresses of employees, former and current, even to creditors or the FBI. The libertarian streak runs deep in this place."

"Right next to the fascist streak."

"And both are mottled with bureaucracy."

Nelson could think of no other questions and nodded his head in acquiescence. He mumbled a thank you and walked back to his car. When they heard the engine start and saw the trail of blue smoke weaving down the road the crewmen looked at each other and began laughing, holding their sides as if they were about to burst.

"He takes out Whitman like he's holding a knife."

"It's a poem. Have you heard of Walt Whitman?" the second crewman said in his best imitation of Nelson's voice and inflection.

"Jesus, next I thought he was going to recite some Rimbaud or Eliot. Rimbaud is a poet too. Have your heard of him?

"So you think that was him?"

"Definitely."

"It's a little weird meeting someone who's worn your shoes."

"Should we tell the Captain?"

"He said he wanted to know if he ever came around. He told me to tell him right away."

"That fucker is going to be thinking about those crates of books sinking to the bottom of the lake for the rest of his life."

"That was a great image. Had you thought of that or was it strictly improvisation?"

"I thought about the image of destroyed books. Up until I opened my mouth I thought it would be moldering crates sitting on some dock though the spring and winter, but even that image leaves some hope of discovery and rescue. The lake imagery surprised me, but I can't say I'm unhappy with the outcome."

"No, very final. A waterlogged book is worse than fire I think. Especially when they swell and bloat. I think the word 'delouse' was a nice touch. Something exquisitely fascist about it."

"I've always wanted to use that word in some context. But I have a question. Why doesn't the Captain want to see him? He seems like someone who could fit in. We made fun of him for his Whitman but think how many other applicants could actually do that during an interview. What did you know before you came aboard?"

"I know. I feel a little bad for him. Where else is he going to go with all that swirling in his head. I doubt he'd last very long working at the Shoe Horn. But the Captain calls him a cancer and an earwig. He fears him you can tell. I think he knows he would be vulnerable to his diseases. Think of us as Native Americans and he as a disease-ridden European come to our shores. We have no natural immunity against him. We'd run the ship aground within a month if he came onboard."

"You're not giving us much credit. We've fought off a number of diseases."

"It's the Captain's call. He's kept us safe up until this point. I'm willing to give him the benefit of the doubt."

"Let's not tell the engineer that we used his chick-with-dick narrative."

"God no, that would only encourage him. He was right. Given the right circumstances the story can work, but if he doesn't stop refining and retelling it soon I'm going to smother him in his sleep."

"I think that's why he lives below deck. I think he knows that's our intent."

"Why do you think it took so long for that guy to come back?"

"I don't know, but I hope he comes tomorrow and whenever we come to port because that was the most fun I've had in a while."

"You're a sick fuck. That could be you out there. Don't start thinking you're superior just because you're working the barge."

"True. True."

They bounded up the steps to tell the Captain their story, hoping to amuse him and be rewarded for following his directions so closely after these many months. The first crewman felt a tremor of trepidation, hoping Nelson didn't follow through with the suggestion of calling corporate and inquiring into the whereabouts of the Captain. Even though he could easily be passed off as a drunk or a crank and he had no chance of receiving an answer, the company recorded every inquiry and even rants from drunks and cranks could end up being a blot on the Captain's record. His duty as a crewman meant he kept the Captain's record clean, not dim his prospects. The crewman saw himself in Nelson's shoes and hoped his transgressions never led to him being cast from the barge. In the future he would keep his mouth shut and not sympathize with the plight of a man on shore.

Nelson squeezed the steering wheel until his knuckles ached. If the Captain had succumbed what hope could there be for him? The stolid mass of the Captain's body and the features of his face that looked like they had been crudely chiseled out of stone came to his mind and he could not place him anywhere except on the bridge piloting the barge in the unearthly green light of the instrument panel. Is he pushing a mop or washing dishes? How far had he fallen and how had he kept from disintegrating during the fall? Where were the dogs? Why hadn't they come for him so he could be done with the struggle? How much longer could he keep the charade going of living with Koo Koo? How many more times would it take for him to watch her move mechanically into position to accept his penis before he wanted to strangle her? He had reached the end of this arrangement.

He set Koo Koo's keys on the dining room table and retreated to his room. He locked his door, then thought better of it and unlocked it again. He also unlocked the back door and pulled it open slightly as an invitation. After a few nights he resumed his routine with Koo Koo, even though he could tell his anger toward her grew. He closed his eyes so as not to witness the complete lack of passion in their lovemaking and his killing impulses subsided. Koo Koo felt a difference in his force and rhythm and hoped this meant they were beginning a new phase that would include a bit of thrashing and a releasing of worry and self-consciousness. Nelson unlocked the door each night. He waited for the dogs to come. He waited through the rest of summer, through another fall and winter. His reading continued but at a slower meandering pace, because he had lost his goal and he often couldn't come up with a logical reason for all the studying. Koo Koo began to respect the seriousness of his studies and the volume of pages he ripped through week after week. Something other than charity crept into her thoughts about him and she found herself wanting to ask about his reading, how the books related to each other and how far on the arc of human thought did he think he had traveled so far? But she kept her questions to herself because she resisted getting closer to him, falling more under his sway, and making his concerns her own. She lost little pieces of herself during sex and their fractured conversations, so to speed up the process with questions and conversations based on his interests seemed imprudent if she wanted him to leave eventually. But no matter how much she resisted she started to feel something other than rote kindness and superficial charity. A something that bordered on warmth and worry that would have seemed impossible for her to feel just a few weeks before.

By spring Nelson had given up hope the dogs would ever come again. He began to think of them as hallucinations, even though to his knowledge hallucinations don't bite your clothes and carry you away to remote holes in the earth. They were obviously not going to rescue him from his monotony. They couldn't be summoned, he guessed, because these dogs were not like a trained pet. They didn't perform tricks, they found their own food, they preferred to sleep out at night, and they never came when called. Would they stop him from leaving the city? Did they care at all anymore? His battle to leave seemed remote and unreal. Now, where would he go anyway? What did it matter? Even if he had enough energy and will to leave where would he go? He couldn't think of one appealing destination worth the fight to find. So, he used his time to improve his Latin enough to be able to think and write in it without hesitation. Greek had come back to him in huge chunks and he understood a level of Homer that he never would have understood in English. But to what end? Koo Koo had started to show some interest, but her knowledge was so rudimentary he could find no point of entry to a meaningful dialogue. He needed scholars who had walked the same path to show him the blind alleys, the fruitless searches and the groves of golden apples. He needed someone to slice apart his developing thesis, free of jealousy and sexual contact. He needed the Captain. Even though the Captain's embrace of bureaucracy reminded him of college professors, his vitality and force resisted putrefaction and irrelevance. But how could he explain his act of going insane with a chick-with-a-dick in tow? Maybe he presented for the world, in fact, the last act of a great mind. Why not accumulate the world's knowledge, the generations of thought, the hours of craft and sweat embodied in perfectly wrought sentences and chuck it all for the love of a he-she? The act itself would be sung for generations to come. Somewhere in the underworld the shade of Odysseus is grinning at the prospect, he thought.

One evening as he crept to the back door to unlock it, he decided to step onto the back landing and breathe the still warm air. The view consisted of a collection of backyards filled with broken cars, dog pens, rusting swing sets, concrete blocks, clothes lines, cheap charcoal grills abused by many winters, and a soaked and moldering mattress leaning against a house. No dogs were out in their yards, and, Nelson suspected, they would not have noticed had they been. They had given up on him or had broken him. They knew where he lived and they didn't care. In the small backyard of the apartment building stood a garage and an unused patch of mud and grass that the owners mowed two or three times a year. Leaning up against the garage a stood shovel with a slick wooden handle and a rusty spade. Nelson did not remember seeing it before, but he also couldn't remember standing on the back landing long enough to remember the view. No matter how long the shovel had stood there or whether Nelson had ever recognized its existence the fact remained that there it stood. From around the corner of the garage walked a chocolate lab and shepherd mix. It sat near the spade of the shovel and raised its eyes to where Nelson stood. The face looked neither kind nor menacing and neither invited Nelson to pick up the shovel nor warned him against its use. The dog presented the shovel as an option. Nelson felt a rush of conflicting emotions and plans of action. He had checked his first impulse to jump inside the apartment and lock and barricade the doors, because the return of a single dog, something he had worried over and wished for, gave him little comfort. He also wanted to walk toward the dog and pet its head, if the dog would allow it, and grab the big thick neck in an embrace and ask the dog what his next step should be. No doubt the dog had answers and had come for a reason. After so many months, possibly years, their return exhilarated him. Why had he ever feared them? He remembered with nausea killing a few on the highway and wondered where that bit of electricity now lay, dormant or extinguished, that had made him commit such a foul act.

He took a tentative step down the stairs to see if the dog would run, because it could have been just a stray looking for a meal or a new name, depending on its ambition. The dog did not flinch and did not take its eyes off of Nelson. It kept a steady, thoughtful and patient stare, because it knew the outcome of this encounter long before Nelson would. Nelson took another step and another and the dog did not move. Nelson jumped down the steps two and three at a time in wild joy. He had been delivered from his monotony. He wanted to jump off the staircase and somersault through the air, but he managed to keep his hand on the banister as he jumped and ran. He bolted to the dog and grabbed its jowls and nuzzled his face against its wet nose. Unperturbed, the dog shook him off and rose to all fours. Nelson jumped from side to side, then back, slapping the dog on the ears each time. Nelson jumped forward and belted the dog under the chin and twisted an ear hard. The dog sprang on him and slammed him to the ground, first pinning his neck to the grass with its paws, then seizing Nelson's neck in its mouth. Its hot breath smelled like garbage and vomit. Nelson writhed and tried to pry the jaws off of his throat but the more he moved the farther the dog sank its teeth into his neck. When he stopped moving the dog slackened its grip, then released him altogether but not before licking the saliva off of Nelson's chin. The dog returned to its spot next to the shovel. Subdued, Nelson stood up and brushed the dirt from his pants. He walked slowly over to the dog and offered his hand. The dog stared at the hand and then at Nelson's eyes and then back to the hand. It had no reason or inclination to smell the offered hand because all the information it needed had been gathered when he had Nelson pinned in its jaws. It knew

Nelson and considered him neither a friend nor an enemy and understood his fear and ultimate surrender. Nelson withdrew his hand and waited for the rest of the pack to attack, to carry him away, to bury him with Pez, if Pez were still alive, and guard him and force him to live underground.

Nelson looked over his shoulder but saw only muddy grass and Koo Koo's rusting car. He picked up the shovel and measured its weight and balance in his hand as the dog slipped out of range should Nelson decided to wield it as a weapon. The shovel had been made to last and it felt heavy in his hand, so he cocked it against his shoulder and began walking. He had hoped the dog would give him direction, but as he walked the dog stayed eight feet behind him and kept that distance no matter if Nelson sped up or slowed down. He walked down the driveway, turned left and continued randomly turning right and left as he came to cross streets, conscious of not making a huge circle and ending up at Koo Koo's apartment with nothing but sore feet and a sore shoulder to show for his effort. He walked until dark. Porch lights popped on and when a stray car passed by the headlights felt harsh enough to tear the fabric of the air. Eventually he came to an open field that once held a brewery, which had enjoyed fifty years of success until one day a drunken crew accidently bottled poisonous cleaning fluid with a batch of beer, killing five and sickening dozens of old drunks who favored the brew. After the machinery and assets were sold at auction to satisfy the lawsuits the building fell abandoned and the government eventually tore it down a decade after the incident. Nelson walked through the high grass and trash the grass had snared. The dog disappeared, but Nelson could hear it breathing and the rustling of its paws as it walked.

Near the middle of the field Nelson stopped and slammed the shovel into the ground. He threw a clump of dirt to the side. He hacked, clawed and chopped at the ground, wasting energy with little progress. He settled down, took measure of the task at hand, and developed a steady technique that brought the right amount of dirt from the hole with each gouge. Soon, he stood in a hole up to his shins, then his thighs, and then his chest. He imagined the dogs in the weeds watching him, making sure he dug the hole deep enough, wide enough and dry enough to live. He saw the Captain's face, the engineer and the rest of the crew. Pez sat on a pile of bricks, the last remnant of the old brewery, picking his teeth and whistling *Mood Indigo*. Jules and Koo Koo stood with arms crossed, glaring at him and commiserating about the moment when luck had abandoned them for good. Zune and Gutterman smiled oily smiles from the shadows. The shade of Montenegro with a dozen henchmen walked through the weeds wielding clubs and axes, looking more like a medieval gang than contemporary thugs. They scattered the rest of the onlookers, even the dogs, and formed a tight circle around the ever deepening hole. By now Nelson stood up to his neck in the hole and he stopped and looked at the leering face of Montenegro. Nelson expected his eyes to glow red, but no light came forth.

"Why are you following me?"

"We're not following you. The field is public. We, the people in the form of government, own this field. Somebody had to clean it up once the brewers abandoned the spot."

"I think I'm digging through chemicals. That can't be good for my lungs."

"No, making beer was a dirty business. They dumped everything in the ground. This is nothing but a field of poison. Your lungs will probably burn up like a moth's wing in fire."

"I'm not convinced I can live in here."

"Shouldn't you be digging?"

"But how far should I go. Pez had such a long and perfect tunnel. The sides were smooth and the angle sheltered us from the rain. I'm afraid I'm making the hole too up and down. How will I get out once I get in? What happens if there is a big rain storm and the hole starts filling up with water? I'll drown like a rat in a well."

"Start your angle. You need to dig at least another ten feet. Fill this bucket and yank the rope when its filled. My men will pull it to the surface for you." Montenegro said as he dropped a bucket with a rope tied around its handle into the hole.

"Are you going to hound me forever?"

"I'm not hounding you. I'm supervising. I have an interest that this job is done right."

"What is your interest?"

"I'd rather not say."

"This seems like a strange punishment for losing a shipment of cocaine."

"This is not a punishment, my friend."

"What is your interest?"

"Sir, the nature of this conversation will take an indelicate turn should we continue down this line of inquiry. Let sleeping dogs lie."

"You're going to drive me mad."

"Keep digging. Dawn comes early for a man with a shovel."

Nelson continued digging throughout the night.

Copper and Steam

A crack in the plaster crooked its way from the corner of the window to the ceiling where it sprayed into a web of smaller cracks. Voices slipped from the fissure and slid down the wall to the floor, duck-walking toward her ear and infecting the room with waves of violence and fear. The Nazis were rounding up the Jews, the homosexuals, the Jehovah Witnesses, the disabled, the brown-eyed, the old and decrepit, the bald and the insane. Babies were thrown in trash compacters and the streets ran with the blood of innocents. Corpses rotted in doorways were they had fallen. Flesh dripped and dropped from bone. A stained bed sheet hung over the window, blocking the sun from entering the room. The pattern of the stain had been crudely fashioned into a symbol. A Star of David or a smear of Passover blood? Who could step forward as a benefactor in the end of times? The sad and pretty lady Koo Koo had held out her hand, but she had been lost in the maelstrom and Ellen would never be able to find her again. She hoped Koo Koo hadn't been killed on the streets or that she hadn't been violated by the roving bands of thugs and sergeants. Sister Bollo threw lightening from her eyes and twisted off the heads of squirrels and cats. She rose up, her skirt blown agape by a sharp wind, a terrifying saint. Her love proved fierce and awful and her state of grace could be worse than Ellen's state of sin. She could only blame herself for the world spun out of control, since her mind, once it had been entrapped by the voices and noises, could be turned inside out and all of her bad and evil thoughts would come true and she could make those around her dance and jerk like marionettes. She had made Sister Bollo mean and she had unleashed those armies who had ravaged the city and killed Koo Koo with their attentions. But she could not control the demons who kept her locked in this room. She had seen three of them: a lady with a kind face and hands that looked like they could strangle cattle, a man hidden behind a large mustache with the interstate highway system etched on his face, and a pretty girl with hypnotizing ears, pregnant from one of the roving jackals, a tormenter who had the head of a goat and a coal black nature whose eyes looked like planets of a distant solar system as they swirled with blue and terra cotta as fierce storms raged across their landscapes. They had told her she lay in her room, had always been in her room and they had rescued it and her and had made it her room again. She wondered about the intent of such a ruse. She had seen one or two stage plays and she remembered how the crews and designers could make the audience think the actors were in a living room or pier when all the while they stood on a wooden stage. Had she been reduced to an entertainment for these devils? Had they killed the young and able-bodied and now settled for easier prey?

A knock sounded on the door and Ellen sank further into her mattress. The state of her legs had trapped her in the bed but that didn't calm her desire to run. In walked the kind-faced lady and another man she had never seen before. His face looked beautiful and chiseled but also yellow and unshaven. His thick hair had a streak of chalk white down the center. His teeth were stained and his fingernails unclipped. The lady said the man was a doctor, but he held up a protesting hand and told her that he had some training and he would look at her but that he could no longer be considered a doctor. What purpose this honesty? Ellen felt more trust in him because he would not identify himself with the class of professionals who call themselves doctors when everyone who knew anything knew that they were nothing more than latent necrophiliacs. Doctors spoke in pigeon Latin that sounded like the result of a child's language game made up on the spot on a rainy day when electricity had stopped surging through the walls. This man who did not identify himself as a doctor took her temperature, felt her pulse, placed an icy stethoscope between her breasts and her back and spent most of the visit inspecting her legs. He didn't mask his diagnosis with a cheery smile. His face hardened at the sight and smell of death creeping up from her ankles and even if he had kept his license to practice medicine there would have been very little that could have been done to save her. He pulled her nightgown up to the top of her thighs and ran a hand through his gray streaked hair. He looked awfully handsome, but his beauty must have been a curse because the moment when he looked at her legs one last time he looked like a man who had been chased by the Furies across the world and back. He bowed to her, which she thought a little strange even from a beautiful man, and left the room too quickly to acknowledge Ellen's return smile. It had been a long time since she had smiled and the act cost her great effort and her face felt a new warmth that worried her as the disease in her legs might have traveled to her face. The smile receded when she remembered that Sister Bollo had told her that people smiled too much and usually, probably ninety percent of the time, used the smile to mask sin or invite sin or to remember sin, but that God never asked for a smile or a laugh because hilarity, joy and devotion were not necessarily compatible. She smiled, no doubt, at the handsome man who was not a doctor because he touched her thighs and hips and saw everything below her waist. Devils are relentless. Sister Bollo relentlessly spoke of their nature and how, even when a person is sick in bed and made ugly by disease, they will come into their room and spy on their privates and touch their thighs and put that person in the clutch of thrill. She pulled the covers to her chin even though the room felt dense with heat and humidity.

The man who was not a doctor closed the door behind him and found Jack and Anne Marie in the backyard sitting in lawn chairs drinking soda. Jack's shirt had been entirely soaked in sweat and swaths of grime slowly washed down this cheeks and neck. He told them that even though he no longer held a medical license, he could still tell the presence of gangrene when he saw it and he reckoned the infection had already traveled past her hips. If they took her to the hospital the doctors would probably amputate to her hips and pump her full of antibiotics, but even such a radical intervention would not save her. She would be dead in a matter of days, if not hours, and they could do little more than make her comfortable in the last moments of her life. He wrote out a prescription for morphine on one of his old prescription pads that he carried around in his pocket when asked to make calls such as these. He told them what pharmacy would fill the prescription, a friend from the old days who still believed in his ability and who refused to acknowledge his lack of a valid medical license. He washed the scrips through other orders and charged double the price on all such orders. Obviously, whoever went to the man who was no longer a doctor didn't want to access the formal health care system or any legal complication that may go along with such a visit, so a price had to be paid for the pharmacist's risk and silence. Mostly, he treated gunshot and knife wounds from the ongoing street wars and had watched many young men and women die under his hands. He asked if either Jack or Anne Marie had experience giving injections and both nodded. Anne Marie's mother had been diabetic and she had given her hundreds of shots. Jack had dabbled in heroin for a few months and lived with a woman who had made it a way of life and always asked Jack to perform the injection because he had a knack of hitting a vein the first time. He never forgot the technique. Really of all the things a person could learn, the technique of shooting a drug into a vein was the least likely to be forgotten, given the consequences should the attempt be bungled.

Jack paid the man fifty dollars for his trouble and watched as the man whisked the damp cash into his pocket without counting it or thoroughly acknowledging it had touched his palm. The man made a slight bow and Jack couldn't tell if he meant to mock him or earnestly thank him, but he didn't like it. Why confuse a simple parting with an ostentatious move like that? Why risk being slapped or beaten by acknowledging the superior rank of the person you are leaving, especially when Jack stood soaked in sweat and felt grime working under his clothes and obviously held no rank superior to any man, even one who had fumbled away his golden medical license? Jack passed the prescription to Anne Marie and bowed deeply back, popping up ready for a fight if the doctor gave him any backtalk. The doctor smiled and walked away to a beat up Audi that he had bought after he had finished his residency and that represented for a few weeks the tangible reward for all his work and study until more valuable and impressive possessions, like a sprawling house on four acres of woods and an Oxford educated wife who bewitched their circle of friends and made him the envy of onlookers and gawkers, eclipsed the machine. Now, wire held up the bumpers of the Audi and arrhythmia had taken up residence in the pistons.

"We'll make her comfortable. It's a damn shame," said Jack as Anne Marie took his hand.

"How could she walk on those legs? How could nobody notice?"

Jack retrieved the morphine from the pharmacy the man who was not a doctor recommended. The place sat on a corner of two busy streets across from a closed down peep show and adult theater and next to a hubcap reseller. They sold drugs in the back and processed foods and cigarettes in the front, and because they were one of the few independent pharmacies left in the city they had to adapt some of the business practices of the national chains to modestly compete. The pharmacist smiled at the prescription and charged Jack a fortune for the morphine, so he bought a coke, a bag of chips and a candy bar to lessen the blow. Sometimes Jack wondered why there were laws at all. People were going to do what they wanted no matter the potential consequence. Jack had been on the wrong side of the law all of his life and he felt none the worse for wear. The thought of going to jail for buying morphine for a dying old lady made him a little angry. He checked himself from going into a rant about the fortunes of rich and poor and the inherent injustice bred into America because who really, besides the dashboard of his truck, would listen? Even if he had a crowd before him holding signs and wearing buttons displaying his face and he had stuffed himself into a suit and tie and carefully prepared his speech with facts and rhetorical flourishes neither the rich nor the poor would want to hear what he had to say. The poor lived the inequities everyday and already knew them to be true or they were so delusional they thought they lived like everybody else, that everybody lived in trailers on cement blocks, or that everybody lost their teeth to rot or lived in swaths of country where no jobs ever existed. The rich, of course, skulked around the edges and buried themselves behind walls and institutions and lush enclaves and vacationed on islands and lived amongst their brethren in remote neighborhoods. They knew they feasted on the inequities and having some wildman tell them so would be amusing and quaint. In the end, both rich and poor would hate him and kill him if they could, each for their own reasons.

Jack had no place to bury Ellen once she died. They could ask the county to dispose of her corpse but that might lead to an investigation or an autopsy. What would happen if the coroner told detectives that massive amounts of illegal morphine pooled in her veins? What would happen if they started digging a little more and they found the body in the shitter and then they asked for a receipt for all that new wood used to build the garage and they suddenly remembered the arson fire adjacent to the backyard of this already suspicious wild man? He didn't mind a cage for a few days but rotting in one until his death held no appeal and, even worse, the thought of the state injecting him with a cocktail aimed squarely at stopping his heart closed the options for Ellen's body. He favored a spot in the backyard between the garage and the shitter. He would chisel a stone that in some way reminded the living of her life without using her name or dates, because he couldn't abide another gravestone in the backyard. Gravestones begat other gravestones and soon he would have a field of the dead behind his house, which would be sure to tip off housing inspectors that he had not followed the proper codes. He'd find a simple poem and carve it into rock. Something appropriate to its purpose. Something about love and tragedy and the lonesomeness of existence. Something also appropriate to the house, which, in the short time he had owned it, had become laden with burden. He felt like the world's sorrow had come rushing in to fill the void once he had opened the doors. He never considered he might be building a refuge or a sanctuary. Hadn't he brought the sorrow with him like a breeze wrapped around his neck? Hadn't he been the author of most of the violence and pain, except for impregnating Estonia, which escaped his responsibility only because Glover had gotten to her first? Estonia's full breasts and bulging stomach came to his mind and made him smile. The house would be mostly done by the time the baby arrived. The dust would be out of the air and the smell of paint would be dissipated and they would have a squalling baby amongst them, something to counterbalance the sorrow and death and give him a reason to want to see the next year and the year after that.

The house had taught him, a willful and ignorant student, that he was old and dying. Not dying like Ellen Oglethorpe in the bed on the second floor in the room with warped floorboards and cracked walls, but certainly deep within a phase of physical limitation and spiritual lamentation as he became increasingly aware his body could not perform the tasks he asked it to do. The roof had nearly finished him off and now when he looked at it from the street the raw pain in his knees and back tempered the beauty of the cedar shingles alight in the sun. After he finished the roof he had two more months of reasonably good weather and the house needed most of its siding replaced, as well as insulated and painted. He would have liked to buy new windows before the cold winds started, but the house had thirty-three of them and a quick run of the numbers in his head verified the budget as impossible. The windows were odd sizes and would have to be specially ordered. He could think of several ways to steal them that involved false identities and stolen credit cards, but Jack had run up against his tolerance for more theft after the debacle in the lumberyard. He hadn't bought the house with the idea of stealing all the materials, but since he had no budget for them, what alternative did he leave himself? A new window had its allure, but was another crime really necessary? He already had to find a way to replenish his cash reserves because feeding four people, four working people, burned through his cash faster than he ever imagined. He would keep the old windows. So, Jack glazed and repaired each one, which required the window to be taken out and carried to his workshop in the garage where he sanded eight or nine layers of latex and lead paint off the frame, replaced any damaged lattice or section of frame hit with rot, sized and cut new glass, and glazed the glass in place. On the inside he sanded the tough hardwood until it looked new and carefully brushed on polyurethane over the surface until the wood gleamed. He then replaced the cords and found and reconnected the weights that had fallen into the walls. He replaced the trim and sills where necessary. Each window took a full twelve hours to complete and after thirty-three repetitions over a month of good weather had been used up.

Ellen Oglethorpe remained living through the month. The man who was not a doctor had been mistaken concerning the veracity of the infection and Anne Marie began to feel guilty about not taking her to the hospital a month before, where men and women who still could call themselves doctors would have had a chance to treat her back to health. After each day passed they felt it too late to change their decision and the disease that probably had no relation to gangrene slowly advanced. Jack and Wood moved her out of her room by each lifting an end of the old iron bed and walking it across the hall to Jack and Anne Marie's room, so Jack could recondition the windows without hearing Ellen's deep morphine wheeze while he worked. Jack and Anne Marie endured two restless nights on the floor of the room and both attributed their sleeplessness to Ellen's lingering and sorrowful presence.

As Jack worked on the windows during day he gave Wood the task of mapping all the vacant houses in the vicinity, writing down their addresses and nearest cross streets in a pocket-sized spiral notebook. Ordered to use his own judgment, which represented a gamble considering his fractured thought processes, Wood had been ordered to kick open a basement window and determine if the copper pipes still hung in the house. Jack instructed him how to find the copper in a basement and how to write a C next to each address where the pipes remained. Wood entered every vacant house he could find and a couple that looked vacant but ended up having families living behind the plywood sheets over the windows and doors. In these cases he excused himself the best he could, saying he he had been looking for a place to stay for the night because his momma had kicked him out of her house and each time mothers with small babies hanging off their legs ordered him out without sympathy or much anger, since they squatted on the property as well. Wood's survey uncovered a small treasure of copper as most of the homes had recently been vacated and the salvage yards had not yet sent their crews into the neighborhood to strip the houses. Jack had thought that given the state of his own house's plumbing the neighborhood would have already been stripped clean, so when Wood told him what he found and showed him his notebook with the addresses and C's written in a child's scrip, Jack organized his business. One afternoon he visited three salvage yards and inquired about the price of copper. At the first stop the man in the office straightened his neck and had a hard time swallowing a wad of ham and bread after Jack asked the question. He told Jack he didn't accept copper pipe or gutters ever since the time he inadvertently scrapped the copper downspouts of St. Basil's, which a crackhead had brought to him after he had ripped them off the walls. The second and third yards were both crooked and told Jack they would take as much copper as he could bring them because the Chinese had an insatiable appetite for all metals and the prices for scrap were going through the roof and both said he could expect about a hundred dollars per house if he stripped it clean. Jack picked the second scrap yard as his partner because the man seemed more crooked than the third because the innate ugliness of his face and the multitude of tattoos inked over his body, including a red lipstick print and a gothic lettered "FUCK YOU" on his neck that told Jack the man had abandoned society and its laws a long time ago. They had seventy-five to eighty houses on Wood's list and they could easily strip two houses a night. The money would keep them alive until they completed the house.

During the time Jack finished the windows and began work on the siding and insulation, he would sleep a few hours between dusk and midnight, rouse himself, prepare the night's route and drive to the first house around two in the morning. Wood would slide into the basement window and open the back door. Jack carried a pair of bolt cutters that sliced copper pipe with a flick of his wrists and he went to work on the basement where the pipe hung almost always exposed. Jack left nothing. He could strip a house in an hour and became expert in yanking it out of the walls. Wood helped by carrying the pipe to the truck and carefully setting it down in the truck bed. For light Jack used a flashlight he had duct-taped onto a construction helmet, fashioning a miner's light which left both hands free to cut. By four in the morning they were usually finished with a two hundred dollar haul in the bed of his truck. Jack stored the pipe in the backyard next to the garage, on the very spot where Ellen should have been buried by then. After a week's accumulation he would take the pipe to the scrap yard. He sifted and sorted through the pipe and kept the best pieces to plumb his own house and after the first month he had accumulated enough pipe to complete the job. They tore through Wood's first list and Jack made him go to other neighborhoods to scout more houses. Jack didn't think they could ever get to the end of all the abandoned houses.

"Here comes the King of Copper." The owner of the scrap yard beamed as Jack entered this small and dirty office which was really just a 10 x 10 shack set down in the middle of soaring piles of tangled and gnarled metals.

"That's not a name I want."

"But it's one you've earned. The cops have been snooping around here. Like they give a shit. The only reason why they came is 'cuz they got complaints. That councilman called the news channel. Those assholes who called themselves the Newshounds or some bullshit. I hope that one motherfucker with the pinched face and big nose comes snooping around here. I'll ship little bits of him to China and India with one of my loads."

"A councilman?"

"Oh, that little bunghole who wears his pants up the crack of his ass. Real choirboy. Mr Scripture with a double chin."

"I don't know him."

"You'd know him if you saw him. He's a real crusader. Remember when he and his wife took pictures of guys coming into the neighborhood to get blown by whores. Remember all those pictures on the net with guys leaning back, mouths open, and you could just see the tops of the whores' frizzy hair? The dynamic duo even published the dudes' license plate numbers and make and model of their cars just so there would be no mistake. So, he's a real saint."

"I never see the news."

"You are the news this week! The King of Copper!"

"This isn't good."

"No, a lot of snoops. A lot of saints. Watch out for the saints. The cops don't give a fuck about copper. They get pressure from the saints and they have to come out and ask me some questions. I give them some baseball tickets or a bottle of fucking booze, sometimes they hold out for more, but shit, the cost of doing business, right? Like they're going to worry about copper when they've got a goddamn street war going on. You ever look in the paper and see how many motherfuckers get shot everyday?"

"Are you saying I should cool it for awhile?"

"I don't tell the King what to do. The Chinese are animals for metals. Beasts. I don't know what's happening over there, but it's like a frenzy. They don't even negotiate. My broker takes it for whatever price I have the balls to ask for because he knows he's going to get double whatever I say. Course, all this publicity about the mysterious King of Copper has brought out the rats too. You're going to have lots of competition now. The Newshounds have given everybody an idea on how to make an extra buck. I had a couple of kids come in here today on bicycles carrying copper pipe, for fuck's sake."

"Of course, all this money from the Chinese you aren't kicking down to me."

"We all got our risks. You don't think I have to give my shit to some crooked shipper who knows all about where the harvest comes from? You don't think I have to pay him for his service? If they could trace that pile of copper back to a specific house I'm just as fucked as you."

When he drove out of the yard Jack looked for the councilman with the pants up his ass and a camera around his neck, taking pictures of the license plates of trucks entering and exiting the scrap yard. He imagined his wife with pimples on her chin and straight dirty blonde hair pulled back into a pony tail, thick in the hips, maybe little glasses on her nose, waiting for the saint councilman to notice her quiet devotion to the cause and her desire to fuck until dawn. He reconsidered and washed the image from his mind because picking on the wife, while somehow satisfying, brought him no closer to a solution.

He suspended the operation and when he counted his money he found he had accumulated over eight thousand dollars in a little over six weeks' worth of work. The money would probably not get them through winter but by then he would have to come up with another scheme to make money. The house would be close to completion and Jack could find a job on which to survive if need be.

One day as Jack stood on a ladder, nailing new lengths of siding on the house and priming the bare wood with paint, a black sedan with dark windows and muscular design stopped in front of his house and idled. Jack watched the car without moving his head in its direction and would have let it idle until it burned through its gas before he climbed down the ladder and asked the driver what business he had in the neighborhood. The window slipped down and Kaufman's familiar screech ripped through the air. Jack climbed down the ladder and brushed off sawdust from his hands and arms and wiped sweat from his face with a faded bandana as he approached the car. The electronic locks popped open and they sounded like a pneumatic nail gun trying to blast through the door. Jack could smell Kaufman's cigar halfway across the yard and now stood in its exhaust as he leaned in the window.

"Get the fuck in, Jack. I don't like someone leaning on my car. That goddamn belt buckle of yours is going to scratch my finish. Are you going to pay my body man to buff out the scratch, honest to God." Kaufman, the cigar jammed in the corner of his mouth, used an index finger to motion for Jack to open the door and sit next to him. Jack looked down and saw that an enormous semi-automatic handgun already occupied the seat.

"Two problems with that. One, I'm filthy and I'd feel ashamed to soil that leather and sit in such tight quarters of a car with the stink coming off my skin and two, I guess you expect me to sit on that piece of military hardware lying on the seat?" Jack said as he pointed to the gun.

"Christ, throw that in the back seat. Fuck, here I'll get it." Kaufman grabbed the gun and flipped it to the back seat and Jack couldn't help but wince when it landed, half expecting a bullet to come tearing through the door or window. "You can never be too prepared for bullshit in this goddamn neighborhood."

Jack opened the door and slid into the seat. His stench smelled worse than he expected, but at least Kaufman's cigar masked most of it.

"Really, Jack, this is where you live? I've seen some shitholes, but Jesus, what the hell were you thinking dropping anchor here? This street could be in the slums of Jakarta for God's sake."

Kaufman sped away and drove too fast for the narrow streets, but he managed, through skill or luck, not to smash any of the cars parked along the street or people wandering off the curb who misjudged the speed of the roaring black sedan.

"There's a development." Kaufman worked the cigar back to life and a thin stream of smoke escaped from his mouth as he spoke. "A shitstorm, probably. A kid is missing from the lumberyard. Nobody knows nothing. No, that's not right. I mean that everybody knows something. The fact is nobody knows where the kid is. Everybody says he was a little pudsucker and a sniveling little creep voted most likely to cut up girls and fuck their raw stumps, know what I mean? But everybody's got a momma or a neighbor and now the lumberyard hired a cop who's snooping around and asking questions. The lumberyard doesn't give a shit, but they have to keep up appearances, right? Or the suspicion starts pointing to them and the last thing the owner, Zig Method, needs is people snooping around his business. He's so goddamn crooked his great-grandchildren will have to complete his jail time. Anyway, no one liked the little pudsucker anyway, but he disappeared on the night of your little adventure. A big fucking haul of beautiful wood and this little pudsucker was a security guard, so it looks like he's in on the deal, that he took his cut and went into hiding. Not bad. Case closed. Only a crazy fuck who lives in these neighborhoods could come up with something so beautifully crooked and neat. The story might be good for paperwork and an insurance claim, but guys like us, Jack, crazy fucks ourselves, know better, right, Jack? I mean Cavano is right up my ass, Jack. What could I say? Nothing. I told him I didn't know about the little pudsucker and his whereabouts. Told him I wasn't going to ask. The sonofabitch brought it up right before we were teeing off on Number 1 at Pine Hills, like tinkering with my head was going to make me play worse. I had to hear that bullshit all eighteen Jack, but I drilled putts, even though I played the short game like I had Parkinson's."

"I told Cavano I had a debt. I'm not backing out of that."

"The interest rate just tripled, my friend."

"I'll have to live with it."

"Jesus, Jack, you had the world by the balls, in your own way. You never could figure out how to make money the easy way, but damn, you had broads by the bucket, you lived where you wanted to live, you never took up fucking golf, which is the worst, most ass-violating game ever invented. If you ever want to see what it feels like to have a pussy take up fucking golf, honest to God. And now what are you doing? I hope we don't get strong winds this winter or Jackie's house is going to fall on his little piggy head. And look what you've got on your hands. The blood of a pudsucker. Jesus, Jack, you don't kill the little snivelers. Point them in the direction of a juicy asshole and they'll be fine."

Jack opened his mouth and Kaufman thought an explanation or confession may be coming so he held up a hand and stopped Jack from speaking.

"I don't want to know. I don't need to know. I know too much already. They could lock me up for four hundred years on my thoughts alone. When I walk through my office and see the girls in their cubes, because you've seen the broads I hire, I get thoughts, Jackie. I'm telling you, those images alone could send me to the can. So, I don't want to know the details of your troubles. The last thing I need to know is your troubles. I'm sure you had a good reason to off the little pudsucker but just so you know you've introduced chaos into our arrangement. I've got anger and paranoia to try to keep a lid on."

"Where are we going?"

"You need a shvitz. Look at you Jack. You're losing weight. Looks like you can barely move. You stink worse than my cigar. I was on my way over there. You might as well come too. I'll buy you a steak in the bargain even though I'm so fucking pissed at you I could run you over with my car."

"Sometimes there are complications, fuck-ups."

"Ya, well, file this one under ass fuck-up because you could have brought us all down. They're keeping an eye on the cop. He won't get too far. They've planted all kind of bullshit to twist his head, plus he doesn't seem all that bright to begin with. My word was the only thing that kept you alive. If I would have been silent they would have come after you hard. There would have been no question. You should know that. Every night you live after today you should blow a kiss in the direction of my cock before you go to sleep and say a prayer and use your dick as rosary beads, chanting my name."

They pulled up to a squat brick building with a gravel lot and a high cyclone fence around the perimeter of the yard. Late model foreign sedans and luxury SUVs filled the lot and an attendant with an oversized torso and holding a shotgun rose from his stool as Kaufman's car entered. Kaufman lowered the window and nodded and the attendant returned the nod and lowered the gun. The buildings clustered around the lot had fallen vacant and had been boarded-up or housed nail salons and resale shops that sold the cheap and broken detritus of the poor on the first floor and dark apartments on the second. Across the street stood a small cemetery crowded on all sides by a gas station with oily pumps and a broken sign, a church that had been connected to the cemetery but had changed denominations a dozen times and now the parishioners had no relation to the corpses buried in the ground, and a row of frame houses that had weathered two decades of misfortune and inattention.

Kaufman and Jack entered the building and were met by another attendant. Kaufman gave his name and the attendant looked in a large book the size of a photo album and found Kaufman's name written in a florid script. He used an archaic system of symbols to record their visit as Kaufman rattled off a list of services they would be needing, bath steam, message, steaks and laundry for Jack's soiled clothes. Kaufman led Jack up a flight of dimly lit stairs to a locker room crammed with cots side by side. They edged around the cots and found two empty lockers. They took off their clothes and an old hunchback gathered Jack's soiled pile and hobbled off. They each took a towel from a counter and walked out of the door to a concrete tomb with a small pool cut in the middle of the floor and filled with murky water. Random shower heads hung from the wall. A man who looked boiled and skinned came from behind a wooden door and plunged into the pool, gasping as he broke the surface. Jack stood under and shower head and turned on the water. A swirl of black water pooled at his feet and he stayed under the spray his skin felt like it had lost its elasticity. He tried to scrub the stains off his hands and forearms with little luck. Kaufman had taken a quick rinse and gone ahead into a steam room behind the wooden door. When Jack entered he was met by twenty or so naked men sitting on risers, facing a giant black oven belching steam. Torrents of conversations echoed through the room as if Jack had just walked into an antechamber of the Senate as they argued policy, goaded each other with personal taunts, emphasized points by slapping their hands on the bench beside them and laughing at the inanity of trying to pass any bill the anesthetized American public would fully understand. Kaufman had climbed to the top riser where the steam curled thick and opaque and he already had beads of sweat on his forehead. He had engaged in a conversation with two elderly men sitting close together and the men looked like they had heard Kaufman's stories a hundred times before as they patiently listened without changing their expressions. Jack climbed the risers and took a place next to Kaufman. He never felt more like a beast with his thick frame, scrapes, scars, bruises, a big and hard belly, coarse hair covering his body and the raw burn of the sun on his arms and neck next to the supple pale bodies of accountants, businessmen, dentists, lawyers, judges, doctors and scientists who filled the benches. Jack could smell the softness rising from their bodies even though the crowd looked trim and fit, something like fresh dough when it's first placed into an oven. They had small hands, trimmed hair and delicate feet, the natural adaptation of human beings who sat behind desks under florescent light in climate-controlled offices. Jack could have been a bear Kaufman had snared on a trip to the wilderness and brought back for protection and as a curiosity. The heat felt a little like what he experienced on top of the roof with the sun full bore, except he didn't need to concentrate all his powers just to stay alive and not end up in a crumpled heap, broken and bleeding, on the grass. He didn't see the purpose of sweating more than he already had this month and he wondered if he had any water left in his body to squeeze out, but in a few moments his pores opened and sweat dripped from his face and fingertips.

"Jack, I want you to come back to work for me. You've made yourself a clusterfuck of a mess on your own. You need structure, Jack. You need to work on something other than that fucking hovel you call a house. You need steady money, steady assignments, a string of broads like a haul of caught fish and a shvitz and steak every now and again and you'll stay out of trouble. No little pudsuckers will come up missing. Neighborhoods won't burn down. Houses won't be turned into scrap and the King of Copper can retire."

"I need to finish the house. I've got to do plumbing, electrical, sheetrock, paint and gut the bathrooms and put in the kitchen."

"What the fuck do I care about your shithole? Drill a fucking glory hole in every wall and have a broad on her knees in every room waiting for manna to come poking through for all I care. What does that have to do with my offer? Are you a numbskull, Jackie?"

"I have to finish the job before I do anything else. Then, I'll worry about my debt to Cavano and I'll think about your offer."

"You dumb ape. What do you think I'm talking about? I'll take the Cavano bullshit off of you, but you have to come work for me. You handle jobs like no one else I've had. What's with the fucking house? I tell you I want to give you a job and rescue your ape asshole and you start rattling on about plumbing. Fuck, Jackie, honest to God, if you didn't have so much talent I'd let those Cavano goons have at it."

"You're looking at someone who hasn't finished a goddamn thing in his life. I've done this about three dozen times before. Just about when I get ready to finish I get distracted or I run or something gets fucked up and I'm on to the next thing. If I take my eye off the house we won't have plumbing until the baby starts school."

"Baby? You finally knock some broad up? You're going to be a daddy?"

"A granddaddy of sorts. Just a kid I found living in the house. Boyfriend took off."

"So just you and this knocked-up little girl living in that shithole, honest to God. You better find a chaperone or there will be baby girls running around with that Jack Cactus mustache and baby boys swinging their dicks that look like elephant trunks just like their pappy."

Jack told him the story of his family, including Ellen Oglethorpe who may have been dropped off in his front yard by a pack of dogs, as they walked to the cold pool. They took a plunge and walked back into the steam to start the process over again. They sat on the lowest bench and Kaufman let him unravel the story and kept quiet longer than usual. They jumped into the cold water again and showered. Kaufman led him to the massage tables where they lay next to each other and two balding masseuses, brothers born less than a year apart, began to work their muscles.

"OK, Jackie, I'm just your humble private. You're the generalissimo. You have your ideas and your circumstances, but you still have a mess to clean up. I can keep Cavano off your back a little while. All he needs is a backrub and a little ball tickle every now and again, but after a while he gets impatient and rash. I need a commitment from you Jackie. Without a commitment I can do nothing for you."

"I'll go to work for you once I get the house done."

"I'll give you three months."

"Alright. That's fair. I can't complain about that."

"That's my Jackie. Now don't let that bald fuck touch your pecker. He gets ideas. And don't think about all those broads you've had. The last thing anyone needs to see is that thing at full attention. You'll make us feel like little boys, honest to God."

The masseuse worked hard on Jack's knotted muscles and made him wince more than once as he struck an old injury or one of the fifty or so fresh violations to his skin. Afterwards, parts of Jack felt relaxed and loose, but other parts throbbed with pain as if the masseuse had done other damage. Kaufman insisted they complete another cycle of steam, plunge, and shower before they dressed. Jack's clothes had been laundered, an unadvertised special service Kaufman had paid for, and when Jack slipped them on he frowned at the crease in his blue jeans and the starch in his t-shirt. Kaufman led him to the dining room where they had a massive meal of steak, pierogies, roasted asparagus, clam chowder, salad, bread, applesauce and oversized Czech beers that were a favorite brand of the cook.

Kaufman harangued Jack to tell him about his sexual experiences, in detail, making him stop, repeat certain descriptions, slow down, include details he had not thought important like the shape of her neck, how far apart her breasts hung, how they hung when she crawled on all fours, the softness of her hair, the timbre of her voice, and the imperfections, the moles, the scars, the freckles, the hairs and the signs of age on her skin. For Kaufman, the details were the story. He cared little for plot or the complicated and conflicting emotions raging in the heads of Jack and his partners as they conjoined and experimented. He wanted to know how a woman's asshole smelled and tasted, the shape of her sphincter, how close the clump of pubic hair grew to the opening, her commitment to cleanliness, how long Jack lasted, down to the second, once he entered the hole, the techniques he used to avoid damage, the brand of lubrication, the sound of anal orgasm, the sound of the sphincter closing around his cock, as well as the shape of her ass, the length of her legs, the width of her hips, and whether a gap existed between the tops of her thighs when she stood and whether the sight of the small of her back made him want to come, but Kaufman definitely did not want to know the back story that she had sworn off vaginal sex because of her fear of pregnancy that had seized her because of an abortion, a miscarriage and a severely deformed baby who had lived just a few hours outside the womb. Her fear had swamped any possible enjoyment tied to vaginal stimulation so she became an expert in all things oral and anal and always remained a popular date among her circle of men and women, and Kaufman also did not want to know that she and Jack had lived together for a few months until his craving for pussy grew too large for him to control and he ended their relationship by fucking her friends without bothering to conceal his conquests.

Jack waited until the end of dinner to tell the story of the tattoo, a story Kaufman always enjoyed hearing and had waited all afternoon to hear the telling, but he wouldn't ask Jack to jump ahead for fear of ruining his anticipation. The encounter happened in a time when the only women who had tattoos were indigenous Matses of the Amazon river basin, the Maori of New Zealand, the remnants of other indigenous cultures who practice ceremonial body art, and whores bored by their frequent visits to jail who wanted to inflict pain on their arms or legs or needed a ready canvas for deeply suppressed artistic tendencies. Jack met her walking her dog, part Rhodesian Ridgeback, part bear, and he chatted her up with the snarling, drooling beast sitting near her leg and waiting for enough slack in the leash to rip the windpipe out of Jack's throat and bury him under a tree for later gnawing. He convinced her to lock the dog up in a cage and come out for a drink with him. His success surprised him because she wore clothes that did not accentuate her body with a high collar and a high waist that followed no natural curve so that her head looked like a soft fruit poking out of a burlap sack, which did not advertise interest or availability, but Jack had a hunch that something special lie underneath. Also, he felt fortunate that she could hear his rap above the snarling dog and could concentrate long enough to return some interest in him. She didn't seem the type to date a ragged monster like Jack, but she drank with him for hours and turned the conversation more lurid and explicit as more and more empties were whisked away. She passed Jack peyote and he swallowed it with a shot of whiskey. Soon they were back at her apartment, pawing each other on her couch. The dog began to whine and bark. The bark sounded like a shotgun fired in the next room and the force broke their concentration a couple of times, so she wrapped a chain that looked better suited for locking a factory gate around its neck and took the dog out to crap and piss. Jack leaned his head back and the peyote began to weave through his thoughts like a vine, overly aggressive, relentless, bent on choking all rivals and spreading through his brain and forming a clump that could not be killed. She returned, but the dog had been left tied outside and its howls sounded like spirits buffeting the house. Soon they were naked, kneeling, and facing each other on a mattress on the floor. She had worn her sack dress for purely defensive purposes. Her body shone perfectly proportioned and Jack felt himself involuntarily leaning toward her, wanting to taste every inch of her skin. On the sheet in the half light of a lamp, properly displayed, her body compelled men to write poetry and crash their cars into groves of trees and concrete barriers. They kissed and balls of electricity flew from their mouths and Jack thought he may have bitten into the wire connecting the lamp to the wall socket. Her skull became translucent and returned to an opaque state only after they broke their embrace. She turned her body and first Jack thought he had found another woman dependent on ass fucking, but the tattoo on her back blotted out all thoughts of the past or future. From her neck to her waist, the whole expanse of her long torso, ink filled the space. A thousand designs wove together in a tapestry, a Celtic tangle of fish with legs, elongated heads twisting around flowering fruit trees, flaming hands, women with exposed breasts standing waist deep in vats of lava, sleek murderous panthers stalked along her shoulder blades, rats looking like bespectacled old men gnawed on leather-bound books, tombstone carved with the names of every person who had meant something to her and who had, unfortunately, died, their skeletons lying under stones above the dirt, chickens with their heads cut off, badgers with blood dripping from their teeth, peasants bowed under the weight of discarded car tires and drums of used motor oil, cats sat on thrones of dead mice, plucking lyres or shaking tambourines and belting out full throated songs, planes dragged banners crying out her love for her children and her parents, elephants bugled under a new moon and a lioness smashed her head into the ground in the throes of a frenzy, booted feet walked through quicksand, strawberries, ripe and heavy, hung on a twisted wine, corpulent hearts dripped tears of blood, saints stared with large, compassionate doe eyes, arms open and welcoming all who wished to enter. Jack did, bypassing her asshole, and her back twitched and writhed and the thousand characters began dancing and twirling. They danced to the rhythm of his thrusts and drooled like a thousand demons caught in a fever dream. They egged Jack on and pleaded with him to make the music last. He fought against ejaculation and concentrated on a toe-tapping goat until the danger passed. They fucked until a flood covered her thighs and sweat poured from his head and dripped onto the tattoos. The demons greeted the rain with ecstasy and terror. She beat the bed with her fists and chewed her pillow until her mouth filled with feathers. Jack slipped a finger into her asshole because the way it had puckered it surely had something on its mind, and he thought he would like to hear its thoughts. When Jack came he thought a bomb had gone off in the adjoining apartment and debris from the explosion and the waves of heat and the horrifying ripping sound of pulverized concrete and brick hurtling toward him had blasted him off of his mount. His skin rippled with heat as his blood boiled and poured into his penis, stretching it to its very limit of available material, creating a personal record for length and girth that would never be beaten, and the cells from his scalp and his toes shuddered with the sudden loss of heat and oxygen. The force of the ejaculate blew him backwards like the recoil of a large caliber rifle and he sprayed semen on her ass checks and the back of her thighs. Her back and the chorus jerked off the mattress, looking exactly like she had been shot. They shared a scream and both finally stopped writhing in different parts of the room. Jack had his back up against the wall, the cord of the table lamp wrapped around his leg, the lamp lying next to his thigh, without its shade with the shattered hot bulb sprinkled across his belly and chest and the flagstaff of his penis refusing to relent. She ended up entangled with a potted plant and an alarm clock that gave weather bulletins whenever the National Weather Service issued a warning. The shrill alarm from the clock pulsed. A dusting of dirt covered most of her hair, her face and left breast. She fumbled with the alarm until she found the off switch and she let her head fall back in the crumpled leaves of the plant. They tried to shower, but the water felt like razor blades against their engorged skin, so they settled on a blistering hot bath. Jack told the same joke three times about making fuck soup and three times she laughed harder than the previous time until the third time he said it she had to gasp for breath to keep from choking.

The water managed to douse some of the fire for a brief moment, but after they toweled each other off and the blood began to pool again in Jack's penis it started all over again, more measured and tired at first, but once her lips touched his belly and then enclosed on the knob of his cock they were both lost once again. The second time she mounted him and kept the tattoos out of

366

sight, which should have produced a hallucinatory fuck, but her characters, knowing they were hidden began to sing in a ragged chorus, mixing church hymnals, pop songs, and rock anthems in their set. They started with *A Poor Wayfaring Man of Grief* to *Mine Eyes Have Seen the Glory of the Coming of the Lord* to *Surrender* by Cheap Trick and *I Drove All Night* by Roy Orbison and *I Just Want to Celebrate* by Rare Earth. In each song the chorus either tried to project a grave seriousness for the hymnals or tried to imitate the singers of the rock songs with little success. They tried *Fair Wave the Golden Corn* and *Resurrection Morn So Fair*, *Alison* by Elvis Costello and *Dear Mr. Fantasy* by Traffic. Then they moved to Cole Porter and ripped through a set that included: *Cherry Pie Ought to Be You, Ace in the Hole, Silk Stockings, Goodbye, Little Dream, Goodbye, Night and Day, Begin the Beguine, Wouldn't it be Fine, My Heart belongs to Daddy, Wow-Ooh-Wolf, I Get a Kick Out of You, Zombie Dance, When Black Sallie Sings Pagliacci, Under the Press,* and *Make a Date with a Psychoanalyst.* They added a small section of Kurt Weill, *Alabama Song, Balla de von der Sexuella,* and *Dance of the Golden Calf* before the voices fell silent and Jack thought he would be able to finish, but the pause was brief and soon the first quavering notes of *Das Rheingold* began. Their renditions of popular songs may have been ragged, imitative and lacking an innate understanding of the music, but their opera exploded from their throats assured and perfect and filled the room to the corners with violence and mystery. Jack floated on the chords and lay suspended above the mattress as she pounded away with her hips. He released fear and rational constructs such as knowing the day of the week, how much money was in his wallet, how could he get her to go on another date, what did work have in store for him in the morning, his worry that the peyote would subside in time for him to run the bulldozer he worked, his sudden hunger and the steps he would have to take to satisfy the urge, who was playing the instruments to accompany the angelic voices coming from her back, what had happened to his car keys, had she told him whether or not she had taken a birth control pill or had she erected some other barrier against his sperm and would he ever be able to live a moderately straight life again after this plunge into the realm of demons and angels. He erased it all and drifted on the waves of the music with the music being an ocean filling the room and Jack being content to drift until the ocean evaporated and returned to the earth as random notes of rain.

The chorus never took a break between acts and they staggered tired and spent to the end as Jack came on the final note. She shrieked and punched him with intent twice in the face. As blood seeped across his teeth, Jack gasped and felt as if his heart had been wrung entirely of blood from its chambers. She collapsed to the mattress and passed out within minutes. Jack fought the tide, remembering the angry dog and not wanting to fall asleep exposed and defenseless, but he succumbed quickly. They shared a dream in which they both worked in an office, one cube next to the other, but the panel separating the cubes had a tunnel carved through it so they could pass back and forth without being detected. She and Jack had obviously made the tunnel because they held broken ball point pens in their hands, ink stains on their knuckles and palms, and scraps of torn cloth and metal shavings on their clothes and at their feet. Between typing and answering the phone they fucked until they decided to become one person so they could fuck unnoticed whenever they wanted just by conjuring up the desire. The merging led to a thousand orgasms a day, unemployment, hunger and eventual starvation, but even after the carcass had rotted down to the bone the intensity of their pleasure looped again and again.

They woke up famished and moderately sober. They ate at a diner and made plans to spend at least a week naked and on peyote. Her brother owned a cabin in the mountains they could use. She would find the dealer who had sold her the peyote and she would buy enough to keep them high for a week. They had to wait for over a month for the shipment to come in, but they had continued having sex as they waited, maintaining a glimmer of transcendence each time but they were obviously losing power with each session. When they were finally able to get away they found the cabin to be small, filthy, freezing from no insulation and large fissures in the walls and when they turned on the small heater, the cabin filled with kerosene fumes. They gobbled the peyote freely and tried every position either one of them had ever heard of. Jack's thoughts resembled a lost transmission of a shortwave radio, even though there were soaring moments of beauty, but he thought of them as nothing more than teases, mocking reminders, and nothing more. They had not brought much food and by the end of the week they were exhausted and sore, their throats were raw and they carried around massive headaches from breathing kerosene fumes. Hunger descended upon them so powerfully they felt like they were being consumed from the inside. They decided together that the memory of their first night would be more important to their lives than trying to recreate it. They could only diminish the experience. They needed to cut off the frustration before they were driven insane. So they never fucked again even though they sometimes saw each other around and edged toward temptation. Jack stopped taking peyote and she stopped adding tattoos and wearing high neck collars. She tried to wear open back tops whenever she could so that some man might find the place Jack had, but mostly she elicited fear and derision, but she persisted out of spite and desperation.

Kaufman had stopped eating and had left half of the slab of steak on his plate.

"Honest to God, Jack. Good thing you didn't tell me that story in the sauna. I would have had a hard time explaining my boner to that den of thieves, which I'm proud to say I have right now. I would have had to ask one of those pudsucker attorneys for some relief. They'll do any goddamn thing for a buck, my God."

"I'm happy I could entertain, I guess."

"Goddamn, fucking Nazi music. It's like you lived one of my dreams. I can't get a broad to fuck to Nazi music let alone have her back sing it to me."

"It only happened once."

"Of course it happened once. That's a once in a lifetime event. Honest to fucking God. You were right to end it, though. You would have ended up smacking her around or killing her out of frustration. That'll drive a man crazy trying to get that back. You know, I don't think this boner is going to go down. I think it's bigger. Every time I think of the Nazi music it gets a little bigger. That's what would have happened to you, walking around with a boner, and I'm not sure you can even walk when that cock of yours gets hard, screaming at her back to start singing again."

"There was no way we could have stayed together."

"Tell me again about the part when her asshole almost started speaking."

Jack repeated the parts of the story Kaufman wanted as they finished dinner and the encores lasted until Kaufman pulled up in front if Jack's house and let him out.

"It's not that bad of a house, Jackie. I can't figure out why you want to live around these animals, but you obviously have your own problems. Where the hell else is a murdering arsonist thief going to live except in my neighborhood? But you can't afford to buy onto my street. Keep fit, Jackie, because I have lots for you to do. Stay strong. Stay strong."

Kaufman tore down the road, leaving Jack in a small storm of dust. Anne Marie met Jack at the front door by kissing and hugging him, then pushing him away so she could get a better look at him.

"You leave in a black car and come back laundered and pressed. You're full of surprises, Jack."

"There's more to come."

"I have a surprise of my own. You've got to see this."

"Glover come back?"

"No," Anne Marie said as she gave Jack a dismissive shake of the head. "Follow me."

Anne Marie led him to Ellen's room. As they approached the door Jack felt disappointed and a little dread, figuring no good surprise could come from the old woman. Anne Marie rapped on the door with her knuckles and they entered after hearing muffled permission to enter the room. Ellen sat up in bed, drinking from an oversized mug. He hair had been combed and pulled back into a neat ponytail. Estonia sat on a small stool, her back against the wall, wearing a t-shirt and sweatpants and resting a similar mug on her distended belly and watching steam rise over the edge. The shirt looked four sizes too small as it revealed the knot of her belly button and the top half of her breasts. They hadn't shopped for maternity clothes yet. Anne Marie had given her some castoffs from her closet, she being nearly twice the size of Estonia, but the pants or sweatpants always fell off her hips and she would only wear the dresses when she wanted to feel old and miserable and on the cusp of insignificance.

"This is my room," Ellen said to Anne Marie and Jack after they had stopped walking. Her eyes looked clear of morphine and Estonia had smeared lip balm over her cracked lips. "I lived in this room many years after my husband died."

"This isn't the master bedroom," Jack interjected.

"I watched a crack form at the corner of the ceiling and make its way all the way to the floor. The solid old house kept most of the sounds out, the electrical storm. They tried every day. They pried that crack open, but they couldn't squeeze through. But they tried every day. I see you've patched it. The wall is so smooth."

"What happened?" Jack whispered in the direction of Anne Marie, but everyone in the room heard.

"I came here to give her a drink and I started talking to her like I always do, but this time she responded and started telling me her life with a butcher and her friend, Sister Bollo, and she seems better, suddenly. I don't know is this is the last of her reason before she…"

"Sister Bollo is no friend. She may be many things, a master, a redeemer, a demon, a whore, a punisher, a jester. She has many faces she had never revealed to me, I think. But she had told me to my face that she is not a friend. It may have been a warning or a statement of fact. I've settled on that it probably was both a warning and a declarative statement, but it's no more than an educated guess."

"Better is a relative term, I suppose," said Anne Marie.

"Sister Bollo said she has a weakness and the devil exploits weakness wherever he can find it. She said no matter how many good works she performed she wouldn't be able to work off her weakness for fucking."

Hearing the curse come out of Ellen's mouth, the three frowned at the thought of the old lady even knowing the word. Anne Marie and Jack lamented that the coarseness of the world had slithered into every corner and affected everything it touched, leaving nothing of value in its wake. They also had assumed Sister Bollo to be a nun, but given the revelation they became a little confused as to who she was or what position she might hold. For her part, Estonia thought it gross and unfunny and feared what else might come out of the old lady's mouth.

"I never asked her who her partners were. I imagined they were demons who came to her at night."

Jack could think of nothing to say so he sprinted from the room. He had already lost most of the day to Kaufman and the thought of losing the rest to a babbling old woman drove him to his work. Anne Marie followed him and stopped him halfway down the first flight of stairs.

"So what should we do?" Anne Marie asked.

"What do you mean? Let her stay. Where's she going to go? She's not out of the woods yet, anyway. Make her comfortable and stop giving her morphine. That fucking doctor. I could have done better than him. They must cover gangrene the first week in medical school because that's all he learned before he got kicked out."

"The story is that he almost made it through his residency or was in his first full year as a doctor and something happened."

"Ya, he poisoned an entire wing of a hospital."

"Something like that."

"Have you seen Wood?"

"He worked without you. He asked me what to do so I got him to clean the backyard and the garage."

"Jesus, and he did it?"

Anne Marie nodded and made a face that expressed she couldn't believe it either but that the sequence actually happened as she said. Jack found him in the backyard sorting the good plumbing into orderly stacks, organizing the pipe into similar lengths and gathering all valves and corner pieces into separate stacks. The yard and workshop had been cleared of debris and Wood had loaded it on the truck bed. He had even swept the driveway and stacked extra siding along the side of the house underneath the ladder where Jack had been working. Wood gave Jack a brief look out of the corner of his eye but otherwise didn't acknowledge his presence and kept to his organizing.

"Wood, what the hell got into you? The place looks great."

"I can't stand to be bored. There ain't nothing to do around here but work."

Jack released him for the day and told him to go have fun. Wood mulled over the word 'fun' and screwed up his face in an exaggerated squint to tell Jack that fun no longer played a part in his life. Fun meant hanging out with his friends playing basketball or getting high or fucking until his balls ached. All that ended when 365 Everyday fucked him in the ass and threw him out of his world. Everyone who witnessed it would never forget what had happened even if he did come back and shoot the bitch in the head. Even if he shot every last fucker who had witnessed his humiliation, he knew they had told everybody they knew about what 365 Everyday had done to him, so he would never find the end of the tree. He could never get back what he had. Instead of being the man who held the estates, he turned into the boy who got fucked in the ass in the street in front of all of his friends by his sister. She lived evil and thought brilliantly and knew how to crush someone without killing them.

Wood walked to a gas station twenty blocks away that sat just outside of 365 Everyday's territory. The place sold booze, cigarettes and lottery tickets and sometimes he or one of the boys would go there when the owner had stolen cigarettes under cost of legal packs or if they wanted to pawn food stamps they had stolen from the old ladies in the projects. He slid around the corner of the building and stood next to a dumpster, which gave him a clear view of the pumps and parking lot and who came in and out of the building. He saw mostly losers in dirty jeans with greasy hair and pot bellies and their fat girlfriends or common law wives with their distended faces and asses and gray and faded drunks with a bottle in one hand and a string of lottery tickets in the other. They paid no attention to Wood lurking by the dumpster even though he stood in the most suspicious spot if he planned to jump the drunks and steal their lottery tickets or slap around their fat girlfriends or stick a gun in the faces of the greasy hillbillies who looked like younger versions of Jack and who smelled just as bad and who worked like idiots until their bodies collapsed and they took to drinking and ended up addicted to scratching off little boxes from government-issued cards in hopes of raking in millions so they could buy a better grade of booze from a fancier store in a better neighborhood.

Wood had been coming here every day for a month and he had only seen a kid they called Little Keys, the younger brother of Keystone, who had been shot through the ear by a cop when he refused to get to the ground to be handcuffed because he wore a new pair of pants for the first time and didn't want to get them dirty. He hadn't talked to Little Keys, because the kid hardly knew Wood, so he let him pass when he walked by holding three cartons of cigarettes that were 365 Everyday's brand. Wood hoped that one day 365 Everyday would come walking across the parking lot alone and distracted and she would turn her back to him and he would have a clean shot of plunging a knife through her neck and she would fall dead without knowing what had happened, but he knew she would never be alone or vulnerable and if she ever walked her fat ass to the store there would be four of the boys beside and behind her. Today, Blizzard walked across the lot and disappeared inside. Blizzard was the same age as Wood and sometimes they had included him in the selling. His mother sent Blizzard to Alabama every year for months at a time because she thought the country would keep him out of trouble, but the boys in Alabama gave him the name Blizzard and taught him a different kind of trouble that included alcohol that tasted like gasoline and how to find hidden pot fields. He never rose in rank because Wood never knew when he would leave or for how long he would be gone, but when he came back to town he kept the party going with his homemade brew that drove everybody crazy for a few days. Blizzard walked out of the store holding a bottle of liquor wrapped with a brown bag. Wood stepped from the corner and whistled a loud blast by jamming a finger on either side of his mouth, a trick his uncle had taught him that no one else could do. Blizzard turned, lucky to have held onto the bottle and ready for a fight, but when he saw Wood walking toward him a trace of a smile appeared on his lips.

"How's 365 Everyday doing?"

"She's alright, you know, same as always. Why do you care?"

"What are you going to do? Stick with her?"

"Are there options?"

"I'm coming back. That bitch doesn't get the last word."

"Naw, you ain't coming back, Wood, that's for sure."

"I'm not going down that easy."

"You've been taken down, far as I can see."

"Don't mean I have to stay down."

"Yes it do. You down. Stay down. There's nothing left for you there. That's nothing but history for you."

"You tell DNA, Goldfish, Nine Points and Sim Sim to meet me here tomorrow at the same time." They were his top lieutenants under his organization.

"You can call them. Why do I want to get involved in your bullshit?"

"All you have to do is tell them to meet me here. That's not much. Besides, if you want to stay at your momma's place after I come back you'll do this thing. It ain't much I'm asking."

"I don't think they'll come. Goldfish is fucking 365 and she's taken care of the rest of them. They have more money in their pockets and get more pussy than when you were around. I don't see them moving on her."

"Cut the fucking analysis. You going to give me the play-by-play next? Just tell them to be here. Skip Goldfish."

"Awright." Blizzard walked away without looking back and after a few strides looked like he had never stopped.

Wood didn't have a plan. Like when he ran the projects, he acted on impulse. The idea of rallying his lieutenants came to him as he whistled and now he had set the coup in motion. His mistake had been not recognizing that his sister had grown up a demon with an evil mind. He had used her for his purposes, like telling her to pick up the shits, the men who drove too new cars and who weren't the regular customers rolling in the neighborhood like migratory birds every week, but who slowly cruised the street looking for drugs or pussy so that he and the boys could rob them, sometimes taking the too new car to a chop shop the same day and having a couple thousand dollars in their pockets that same night, but he had failed to recognize how powerful she had grown and how quick she understood every scam and how she would never be satisfied with her role as bait. He still didn't know how she had turned everyone against him, but now that they had a taste of her rule they had to know they had made a mistake. They had followed the wrong bitch and they would be looking for a change. Tonight he would devise a plan and lay it out for them. He would expand their roles, raise their pay, pick a successor the right way so that the most competent motherfucker would work to keep Wood in power until his time came. Maybe he would enforce more discipline this time. He would stop them from getting high, at least before noon, and demand they chase pussy less. Make them pick girlfriends so that they always wouldn't be looking or changing and swapping and talking about nothing else. He'd come up with a schedule for work like the number of hours per day and the number of hours per week and they would stick to it. He would give everyone specific tasks and they would have to repeat them until they mastered it before moving on. His mistake had been that he thought of himself as the leader of a rolling mass like an ocean or a stream or lava and he content himself with being drowned or burned alive when he should have concentrated his strength and abilities on changing the nature of the mass itself. Made it manageable, turned it from a river of lava into a kiddy pool filled with warm and dirty water, something he could stomp through when he pleased or he could lay back his head and close his eyes and maybe accept a blowjob and not worry about the water growing hands and pulling him under. He hadn't thought of what he would do with 365 Everyday, but it would have to be some kind of permanent mutilation that would stop her from ever trying her bullshit again, like cutting off her hands or lips and maybe her ears. He felt suddenly sick to his stomach like he had just bolted down a bottle of the cheapest wine and a fistful of hamburger. He would have to tell them what he planned to do with 365 Everyday. If he started babbling on about cutting off her lips, they would know he acted on fantasy and he didn't really have the necessary evil to keep them focused and together. Maybe that ultimately had been his mistake, maybe he was too soft and they had traded him in for a deeper and more efficient evil. Would they ever return, knowing the efficiency of true evil?

He received his answer the next day when he waited at the gas station for five hours until midnight and no one showed up. He pulled his phone from his pocket, but the service had been turned off a month ago for non-payment since his bills went to his old address and he couldn't retrieve them. He had carried the dead phone around like a talisman that would carry him back to his old life when it rang every few minutes with requests and questions. He smashed the phone on the street and the battery skittered across the pavement and into a storm sewer. He stood by an old weathered pay phone and he started to dial DNA's number. He easily remembered it because he had dialed it every day for years. He stopped before he dialed the last two numbers because he couldn't think of what he would say to him when he answered. DNA had left him, held him on the ground while 365 Everyday sodomized him and now he had not shown up when he had been asked, so what really could be said between them? The others had participated or stood by when it happened, so how could they be trusted? Maybe he'd find a gun and kill 365 Everyday himself just to get some of his pride back, just to show the likes of Goldfish and DNA, Nine Points and Sim Sim that when he told them to meet him they should out of fear and respect and not treat him like some forgotten bitch. He sprinted back to Jack's house, trying to quell the rage within him, saving it until he would need it.

Glover stood on a rock jutting from the top of a cliff as a wind from the Atlantic Ocean whistled past his ears. Below him on the damp sand a couple of friends threw a waterlogged football back and forth as a third friend mauled a girl on a blanket behind a pile of rocks.

"Hey you fuckers!" he yelled, but the Atlantic and the wind tossed his words like grains of sand and blew them over his head, throwing them into the weeds unheard.

They had dared him to scale the cliff but halfway up the ascent they became bored with charting his slow progress and stopped watching and two found the football and the other the blanket. He and the girl would have been stripped by now if the wind hadn't been freezing. Glover waved his arms and tried to yell again, but he had no luck in gaining their attention. He walked away from the edge and explored the flat top, littered with massive stones and thin brown weeds that looked like a remnant of a fence. He found a small pile of beer cans, a blackened circle with charred pieces of woods, a shoe with a missing tongue and a discolored piece of Tupperware in the weeds. He found himself thinking about the person who had lost a shoe and the group who built the fire and huddled around the weak flames, drinking beer and talking about cars or movies or the ocean you couldn't touch because it felt like ice even when the sun blazed. He saw the fire play on Estonia's face as she looked down on an infant. Jack, or someone who looked identical to Jack, dozed in the shadows and he rested his feet so close to the fire the soles of his shoes steamed. Faces unseen in the firelight laughed as Jack's snores rose and entwined with the steam from his shoes. Estonia's baby looked exactly like her with a thatch of Glover's hair. He fell to his knees and vomited a pint of cheap wine and a bag of salt and vinegar potato chips and between retches he sobbed wildly. The fact that his body had been paralyzed momentarily as his stomach purged the offensive brew stopped him from sprinting toward the cliff and diving headlong onto the rocks below. Jack woke up from his doze and stared at Glover through the fire.

"I told you the memory of leaving would be worse than anything a baby could spit up or shit out. How's it feel to have a burden?" Jack said through his mustache even though he couldn't see his lips move.

"Fuck off, Jack. You planted this shit in my head."

"No, I just told you it would be there. So, what have you run away to?"

After Glover had left Jack standing in his driveway he walked to Mary Kelly's house and pounded on the door until she answered. She came to the door in silk shorts and a t-shirt with no bra and when she recognized Glover pounding on her door she transitioned from fear and suspicion to anger within a few breaths. Glover asked her if he could stay at her house for a few days, and when she said no he asked if he could sleep with her that night before he left town. She asked if he didn't have a pregnant girlfriend, and when he asked her how she knew she told him she knew everything that happened on the street, even why the two houses burned, because she kept her eyes open and paid attention to changes. Glover asked what Estonia had to do with sleeping with him and she slammed the door in his face. He pounded on the door again until she opened it, but this time she held a large carving knife by her side. Glover asked her why she held the knife.

"Emphasis," she said.

He asked her what she knew about the burned houses and she said:

"Jack burned them down so he could plant an orchard and a vegetable garden."

Glover corrected her by retelling the story Jack had told him that a party had gotten out of control and someone had kicked over a kerosene lamp and both house burned. Mary Kelly asked him if he believed everything Jack told him and Glover became flush in the face and reiterated the story and assured her that the story happened to be true because he had been there and why would he have any reason to protect Jack now that he had decided to leave town.

"I can see how Jack can be pretty convincing. I don't think he told you the truth."

Glover again asked her to sleep with him and she told him that she had a son a few years older than him and that he should go back to his pregnant girlfriend if he wanted to do something worth doing. He touched her face and neck and she pulled him into the kitchen and they fucked on the floor underneath the sink where it smelled of cleanser and mildew. Even though she remained quiet so as not to wake up her son, Mary Kelly moved with such precision and grace that Glover knew if he could convince her to let him stay for a few days he could learn something valuable from her. Afterwards as they whispered in the dark and she held his dick in her hand he asked again if he could stay for a few days. He could tell she thought over the request carefully, but then she asked him if he could live in a house on the same street as his pregnant girlfriend or whether that maniac Jack would ever let the arrangement stand. She told him if he went for a run he had to go further than five doors. Glover asked if she had slept with Jack and she laughed at his jealousy, forgetting for a moment about waking her son.

"I won't tell you I didn't think about it, but I like Anne Marie too much and Jack might be ten years past being worth it."

Glover liked that line and repeated it often throughout the rest of his flight. He wished he could see Jack's face when Mary Kelly turned him down and his balls shriveled up to a size no bigger than blueberries, because he knew the old horn dog had his sights set upon her. She made him erect again and mounted him. Glover closed his eyes, held onto her hips and let her do all the work to find a tempo best suited to her mood. The kitchen light burst on and her son stood in the doorway looking down at them in flagrante delicto, yawning. She rolled off of Glover, exposing herself even more to her son, before she found her shorts and slipped them on. Her son's eyes had not followed her but stayed on Glover as he lay on the floor with an erect penis still wet from his mother. Glover didn't know if the guy wanted to kick him in the balls for fucking his mother or lick her lubrication off the helmet of his dick. Her son stared too long without acting and both Glover and Mary Kelly understood the reason, and he didn't stop staring even after he knew he had been caught. His fingers played with his zipper and started to draw it down. Glover turned his back and started to dress.

"Stop that," Mary Kelly said as she pulled on her shirt and pushed her son out of the kitchen.

"You're the one who brought a naked boy into the house. It's not my fault."

"Another reason you can't stay. This one is starting to find himself." The argument continued in the next room and up the stairs, where a door slammed two or three times before quiet returned to the house.

Mary Kelly returned to the kitchen and searched the floor for a lost earring and to make sure nothing of the act or of Glover's had been left behind. She handed him his backpack and told him she sometimes wished she could fit all of her possessions into a backpack or purse and run away, but she always came up against the facts that she had grown too old, had too many responsibilities and liked her possessions too much to let those kind of fantasies destroy her. Glover toyed with the idea of asking her to come with him, but he resisted because one, she would laugh at him, two, she would probably tell him clearly that he would never be worth the hardship and three, having dragged Estonia almost the entire width of the country, he looked forward to time alone when he didn't have to consult, argue, whine or flat out beg just to have something done the way he wanted it done. Mary Kelly kissed him on the forehead and handed him an orange for the road. She ushered him out the door and before he left he asked how he could find E. 55th. She told him to walk east but didn't ask why he wanted to go there. She obviously wanted him out of her sight and wanted to put their coupling behind her as quickly as possible. He didn't tell Mary Kelly that Cleveland had one last chance to keep him and he pulled out the Cleveland Press article about Dr. Thompson's Mystic Cult that he had sealed in a sandwich bag. He found the address listed in the article and memorized the sequence of numbers.

Glover walked out of the neighborhood and found a main road. He turned toward a gray horizon, figuring that way to be east. He crossed a bridge with massive stone giants flanking the roadway. One held an early model of an automobile and the other held a steam engine. The faces of the giants were kindly and serene like they were deeply contented at being employed holding up the bridge. He walked for an half an hour, past a dark baseball stadium and low brick buildings surrounded by barbed wire. The first employees unlocked a McDonald's. A balding man sat behind a desk staring into a computer. Glover watched him briefly as he passed through the glass block windows of the building as he passed, watching the blue face as it stared at the images on the screen, and he wondered why someone would have to stare into a computer even before the sun rose. The numbers of the streets crept higher. A few homeless shadows slept behind corners or shuffled through the gray light with no destination in mind. He found E. 55th and first turned left and walked a few blocks before he noticed the numbers went down and that he walked away from the address of Dr. Thompson's cult. He retraced his steps and passed the same warehouses and concrete bunkers and the avenue he had walked down. He ignored the fact the events in the article happened eighty years ago and that eighty years in the United States might as well be a million given cities could rise, fall, and rise again and turn to dust in that time.Glover did not have a good grasp of time, even though both Jack and Estonia told him that nothing remained after eighty years, he couldn't quite believe it or understand why that would be so.

By the looks of the street this part of Cleveland had been evacuated after a deadly toxic spill or a mysterious and fatal strain of influenza had ripped through the populace, killing nine out of every ten persons. Glover found the spot where the building should have stood, now the terminus of a freeway that linked the neighborhood to larger interstates a few miles away. He never did believe much in superstitions or the metaphysical, but he believed less in coincidence or chance so when unexplained events happened his thoughts skewed toward the fantastic. So, when he tore open the wall and found the newspaper with the story of Dr. Thompson's Mystic Cult he thought there must be a reason for him finding it. If not a direct invitation to join the cult, a place that seemed much to his liking given the sacraments of cocaine and women, then somewhere embedded in the words there had to be a clue. Maybe if he went to the spot where the cult existed there may be a sign to point him in a direction. Estonia's news had blown apart the investigation and he forgot about the article until he began packing to leave. Not only did he find it when packing, but it fluttered out of his shirt and landed at his feet, face up and intact, even though the paper was so fragile he feared breathing on it. Sometimes the world throws you a clue so obvious that it's impossible to miss or ignore. If you miss it purposely or ignore the import of its placement, you do so at your own peril, because why would the world take the trouble to spit up a clue and have it land at your feet if it didn't want you to respond to its missive?

Initially, Glover felt disappointed to find that the cult had been torn down and paved over and that the semi-trucks and commuters had no clue of the history they drove over, even though, he admitted, most people wouldn't find Dr. Thompson's cult all that interesting other than the sensationalism and sordidness of the story. Somewhere in the very back of his thoughts resided the hope that he would find an organization actively recruiting members and that he would join and sleep in the cult that very night and assume the role of acolyte. But the article had a much more obvious clue in mind, something simple and straight-forward that even Glover couldn't miss. He stood in front of an open freeway, leading to undiscovered country, back to vagrancy and hunger, back to happenstance shelter and the kindness of strangers. Everything pointed away from Estonia. He put the article in his backpack and started walking the side of the highway, intent on hitchhiking somewhere not here.

An old, retired man picked him up within a few minutes. The man insisted that Glover looked tired and hungry and that he should come home with him for a bite to eat and a soft bed on which to rest. He said his wife made the best soup in the neighborhood and that she would make him feel right at home, just like he had come to visit his granny. Glover replied he had only been up for a few hours and he had eaten before he left the last place where he slept so he needed neither a bed nor food. The man repeated his observation as if he still wanted to convince Glover, but he could come up with nothing else in the way of an argument, so he restated that Glover looked famished, nearly dead from starvation and that he, the driver, should not have even have picked him up, because, at first, he thought Glover might be one of the lost ones walking the road, stumbling, disoriented, wild-eyed and that could only mean two things, exhaustion and hunger. Glover could not argue the fact that he felt both tired and hungry. The man would hear nothing to the contrary. The man had left the highway and weaved through narrow neighborhood streets. He stopped in front of a worker cottage nestled in a dozen blocks of identical homes and when he started walking toward the house Glover picked a direction randomly away from the house and began sprinting. The man bade him farewell with a line of muted curses that sounded like a voice from a fading radio station.

"My wife will be sorely disappointed!" the man shouted after him.

From there Glover stole a moped in front of a convenience store after he passed by it several times to make sure it hadn't been locked. Directionless, he rode in circles and even once passed the convenience store again before he found his way out of the city's tangled streets. The owner of the moped had either not yet known his moped had been stolen or the chase and had been stymied by Glover's serpentine escape route. The moped could reach the top speed of thirty-two miles per hour and it groaned and whined as it crested a long hill along the eastern border of the city. The rich had obviously seized the high ground as Glover passed brick estates with long green lawns and gleaming concrete driveways under a canopy of massive oak, maple and walnut trees that turned the rays of the sun into a pleasant dappling of warm light. Glover imagined that should things get out of hand like a riot or even some more organized violence the rich could easily defend the hill behind hastily built ramparts and stop the mob from taking what they had accumulated.

He rode for another hour before the moped ran out of gas, so he pushed it into a weed choked ditch by the side of the road and began walking. He had no money so he could not keep the moped running. Every penny he scraped off the street would have to go towards food and he didn't want to have to make a choice between gas and oil for the two stroke engine or satiating his hunger. He could have sold it, but that would have taken planning and luck and the idea seemed more trouble than the money he could make. No one picked him up the rest of the day and he ended up sleeping in a cemetery under a big broad tree. By then he felt hungry and thirsty since his body had gotten use to the regular meals Jack had served them. He comforted himself with the knowledge that in a few days his stomach would shrink to the size of a peanut and his hunger would dull into an ache he could live with. He had done it before.

When he woke up at sunrise he had to piss and he tried not to piss where he thought a body might be lying. He felt stiff and cold and the urine came out like a rope. Touching his cock gave him the idea to masturbate, so he leaned against the tree and stood over the field of headstones as he thought of Estonia and the dozens of positions and poses he had seen her perfect body assume. He remembered the taste of her skin from head to toe because his lips had traveled across every square inch of her. He settled on the way she had of turning over and biting the edge of a pillow as she raised her hips and spread her legs when she wanted him from behind. He could never last long when she did that and this morning in the cemetery, even through memory, she had the same affect on him.He came into the air, but some of the ejaculation clung to his fingers so he wiped them against a nearby headstone of a man named Harvey Broome b. 1853 d. 1899. Glover took off his pants and underwear and lay on Mr. Broome's grave in the dewy grass so he could feel the air against his balls and as a protection against turning and walking back to Cleveland to live with Estonia, Anne Marie and Jack. When the impulse had passed and the image of Estonia had dissolved back to memory he dressed and continued walking east, trying not to think of the troublesome brew his hunger kicked up in his stomach.

No one picked him up for two days, so he walked about fourteen hours each day. Several Amish buggies passed him with frothing horses in the lead. The drivers never said hello, but one of them cracked his whip a foot over Glover's head as they passed and when Glover looked up he saw the insane and grinning face of a dumb Abraham Lincoln wearing suspenders and a black, broad-brimmed hat. Glover picked up a rock, cocked his arm and had the driver's back squarely in his sights as he rode in an open buggy, but he turned around and whistled the rock at a speed limit sign. It smacked the target with a clang, but either the clatter of the wheels drowned out the bull's-eye or the driver feigned indifference because he never turned back to look at him. Glover didn't know whether or not the driver would fight, but he would not be easy to tangle with given his broad back and thick arms strengthened by farm work and jobs at the local factories and no doubt his black clad clan lurked in the fields around him, ready to assist should trouble start, so Glover let him clatter away without further incident.

In the evening of the second day of walking he came to a little town with a central square that none of the residents seemed to use much anymore. A Civil War cannon had been welded to an iron slab with its mouth pointing toward a real estate office. A weathered gazebo wrapped in faded bunting stood near the cannon and sprinkled across the vast lawn were granite or bronze markers commemorating a town father, the war dead, or a previous generation who wanted to remind future generations they had the foresight to plant a row of towering sycamores at the far eastern edge of the square because they believed in the restorative powers of nature and healthy civic volunteerism. Glover stole a melted candy bar off the front seat of a car through an open window. The chocolate and caramel made him sick and he threw up in an alleyway between a diner and a gun shop. The windows of the gun shop had been covered with posters of women with guns: a dirty blonde in faded jeans

380

and sleeveless top unzipped between her breasts as she held a Barrett 98Bravo .338 lapua mag rifle as she asked the question "How big is your gun?"; another with a side shot of a raven-haired model pushing down a school girl plaid skirt with a Baretta Px4 Storm subcompact, revealing the top of a black lacy thong and a lizard tattoo, apeing a good little school girl addicted to guns and the men who love them, and a third poster twice as large as the other two of two oiled models wearing micro bikinis, very small cloth triangles covering their nipples and drastically pruned thatches, touching their asses together as they both held Colt M4 Commando machine guns, projecting a macho lesbianism that had seemingly been nurtured at an ocean side shooting range and commando training center.

Glover steadied himself against the side of the building and dry-heaved until the convulsions finally subsided. He spotted a dumpster behind the diner and figured he would find at least some stale bread if not something better in it. He walked slowly to the back of the building, holding his stomach for fear of making the convulsions return, and opened the lid. The dumpster had recently been emptied so the level of garbage had fallen out of reach, so he used his stomach as a fulcrum and jack-knifed his torso into the interior. He found a bag of rolls, a half brick of cheddar cheese and two thoroughly bruised apples, enough food to last him three days. When he pulled himself out and landed on the gravel surrounding the dumpster, he heard a cough behind him. Glover turned and saw the backdoor of the gun shop now open and a tall, thin figure blocking the path between the buildings. A pistol hung loosely in his left hand.

"Don't little rats from the city understand the concept of private property?"

Glover looked at the cheese and bread in one hand and the apples in the other and wondered if he should drop them at his feet or throw the apples at the man with the gun, maybe get lucky enough to hit him in the balls and drop him so he could run by.

"I got them from the dumpster."

"Also private property. Garbage isn't public until the city boys take it away. Give the city what is the city's."

"You want me to put it back?"

"That would be the right move and then you can take your little rat ass and walk away from my alley and never think of returning."

Glover turned, opened the dumpster, all the while feeling his back breakout in itches where the bullets could possibly enter, placed the food inside and closed the lid. He faced the man for a few moments. They both stood looking at each other, Glover afraid to approach or pass him without some signal of release and the man content to make Glover squirm until he asked permission to leave.

"May I leave?" Glover finally asked and as an answer the man holstered his pistol by his hip.

As Glover walked by the man sneered something else about how city rats should stay where they belong with the other rats. Glover couldn't let the comment go by without a response, so he turned his head as he kept walking and told him he came from Bakersfield, California and he had set out to see the country and maybe find a place to land and he had met some really good people and some bad people, but no one had ever pulled a gun on him until now, and while he did have the right, he guessed, to watch out for his property and his neighbor's property he couldn't understand why he cared if he took garbage from the dumpster, food that would be obviously going straight to the landfill to rot. By the end of the speech he had made the corner of the building and once out of the man's line of sight he took off in a sprint. He couldn't be sure if he had actually articulated the speech or had thought it through silently in his head, but in either case it gave him some satisfaction to tell the guy not everyone pulled a gun at the first sign of trouble and, other than being attacked by Jack while he banged Estonia, which very well could have been the moment of conception since he had been distracted by the crazed old man staggering toward them just as he came and he may have never pulled out at all until his brain registered the need to fight and not fuck, no one had given him much trouble. The sprint didn't last very long as his ribs ached from vomiting and the energy he used to run one hundred yards drained his body differently than the energy used to walk one hundred yards, so he felt wobbly and winded and had to stop. He remembered the poor loser with the mangled leg who Jack and he had buried under the outhouse and he thought about going back to the guy with the gun and asking him if he had ever killed anyone or had ever buried a bloody corpse in a grave of piss and shit. The guy would probably shoot him, but at least he would know that Glover wouldn't act like a pussy, that he could be an accessory to manslaughter as well as anyone and that abusing a corpse came to him like second nature. He could find no effective salve to heal the wound of having to drop perfectly good food and run with his tail between his legs.

Glover could hear a car engine approaching from behind and he ignored it until a voice called out to him. He expected to turn and face a shotgun and see a flash and die with the roar of the powder in his ears, but instead the man sat behind the wheel of an old pickup and motioned him to the open passenger side window.

"I owe you a dinner. Get in." He didn't smile, but at that moment he didn't seem very imposing either with his length folded up into the cab of the truck and without a gun in his hand. Glover opened the door and hopped in.

They drove down a hill from the summit of the square and wound around a road that led away from a small cluster of homes to large tracts with fields loaded with corn and beans, all the while listening to a Kate Bush CD in the truck's modified stereo system. The man mouthed the words like someone who had heard the music a hundred times and in some places let out a shriek as he tried to follow some of the higher notes. Glover had never heard of Kate

Bush before and he found her singing a little unsettling given its intensity and because the man beside him seemed determined to sing every word in the wrong pitch. To distract himself, he watched the passing corn fields and reflected on how many acres of farms he had seen on his trek across the country. Could he think of anything more lonesome than walking through endless wheat fields in the gloom of twilight as the bats take wing, knowing you'll be sleeping in the chill with the field mice? Estonia and he hadn't expected to feel terror in the country and neither spoke much about their thoughts, but in the unpopulated green swaths of rolling land they experienced something close to quaking fear as they lay awake in each other arms in the fields of rasping wheat. They tried to make their ideas into a movie script where two young people walk into the country to a cabin in an open field at the top of a sweeping hill to drink and fuck and when they return to their normal lives all the people had vanished. They've not been killed in a nuclear exchange or a massive epidemic, but somehow a scientist had inadvertently opened a window or door, possibly torn a large and irreparable hole, in the dimensional fabric of the universe, and, much like a hole being blown in a pressurized cabin of an airplane all the people of the planet, except the couple, who have been saved because they accidently lay in the one spot void of suction on the planet, have been sucked into another dimension where they live lives that resemble their old lives except they have lost all of their body warmth and they hate to touch each other. Another plot involved the same scientist who accidently tells his housekeeper of his discovery of a gateway between dimensions because he's lonely and all of his old friends and family have long ago dropped him because they think he is a crackpot trying to find doorways in the air. The scientist recognizes the housekeeper as quite beautiful, even in the maid's uniform with her hair pinned back and cleanser coating her arms up to her elbows, and he dreams of making her his wife, once he can drum up the courage to ask her, but the housekeeper has other plans because although she is beautiful with an almost perfect figure (a critic might linger on the formation of her toes as a concern), she has grown a kernel of bitterness toward society because she, with obvious talents, still has to clean up the dirt of other people to put food on her table. So, she sells the discovery to a rival scientist for a pittance given the significance of the gateway. The rival scientist in turn sells it to the world with the promise of a better dimension, a perfect dimension without disease, famine or hatred as the website and TV commercials say that are developed by a leading public relations firm out of New York. After the worldwide advertizing campaign takes hold and a couple of wars start and a series of earthquakes, hurricanes and floods pummel the planet the masses line up for the gateway thinking the end of days has finally come. The scientist even develops a sliding scale for payment so the poor sign-up en mass. But, unfortunately, the population jumps headlong into their doom, because once someone jumps through the gate she can't come back and the people find the new dimension to be made of paper mache and wax covering concrete and asphalt and once the too hot sun rises the mask is burned off and the people realize they will all die of starvation because all the arable land has been paved over. The heroes emerge from their seclusion and find the first scientist sitting in his lab littered with broken computers and beakers. He is the last person besides the couple in the old dimension. He holds a picture of the housekeeper and wails over the cruelty of the human heart. He browbeats them with a long speech about how they are the last hope of humanity and how they will be the new Adam and Eve and how they must keep the seed alive and produce as many babies as possible. He, the scientist, will plunge headlong through the gateway and find his beloved and the doorway back to this dimension, which according to his calculations should be near Balchik, a seaside resort on a small bay on the Black Sea, 31 km north of Varna and 37 km southeast of Dobrich and 500 km east of Sofia. They watch him dive into the gateway and the scene switches to the new dimension as he steps out. He is immediately attacked by a mob wielding chunks of concrete, including the housekeeper who is now ugly, emaciated, and mad with grief over her betrayal. Only too late does she realize they've just killed scientist and their last, best hope for survival. She is seized by a new paroxysm of grief, but she does find the blood-stained directions to the return door and she drifts away from the mob in the direction of Balchik. The couple renames themselves A and E and sets about trying to repopulate the world and they die from old age with fourteen children and twenty-seven grandchildren, issue of brother-sister matches, but the soft focus and sweeping orchestral music glosses over this inconvenient and troubling fact. The story always ends with the couple dying together in the same bed in the White House as they hold hands with their children and grandchildren. They take their last breath and together they are the first deaths of New Earth. For Glover and Estonia the stories helped keep fear and loneliness at bay until their imaginations waned and they were back in the open fields in the black night with the brushstrokes of stars overhead and the miles of wheat around them. At that moment they could not have been closer.

The man pulled down a dirt and gravel road and then a driveway that didn't look much different than the road to a sprawling ranch with a new oversized garage looming in the backyard. Towering oaks and maples surrounded the lawn, a small open patch that stayed cool and damp. He led Glover inside the house, where every inch of visible space had been decorated in cowboys and sepia. Old portraits of cowboys with weathered, maniacal faces, men who had seen slaughter, insanity and the void, filled the walls. Glover thought he could recognize the fear of emptiness in their eyes even though their skin looked tough enough to be turned into shoe leather. Other shots showed cowboys standing over fallen buffalo or Native Americans astride muscular horses covered in a sheen of sweat, dressed in full headgear and posing with long bows. On an antique roll top desk a series of snapshots had been laid out in a grid, more images of pioneer life strangely absent of women. The furniture, massive, leather and brown, dominated the room. The rugs, thick and woven with bold Mexican patterns of black, red and white, protected the hardwood floor, which had been buffed to a gleam. Near the kitchen a western saddle rested on a display stand and the stirrups had been polished constantly. Above the saddle on the wall hung a pair of antique spurs with intricate designs or stars in the leather. The man went to fetch two beers from the refrigerator as Glover sat down on the couch. Before him on the coffee table, a chunk of a walnut tree sanded and polished into a low table, a spray of literary journals, hunting magazines, gun catalogs and four copies of a guns and girls calendar called *Second Amendment Foxes* lay in perfect order. Glover opened one of the calendars and saw that the photo for May matched one of the posters in the gun shop window. The man paused at the threshold, holding the beers in between his fingers on one hand, and watched Glover leaf through the calendar. After Glover noticed him watching, he continued on into the room.

"Those girls are local. Every last one. A man can dig up some whores when he needs to," he said as he handed Glover a beer. "I printed that last year and it paid for an Elk hunting trip in Alaska. Not a bad trade. Of course, if the Puritans of this town had their way I would have dressed the girls in flour sacks and not let them put makeup on and not let them comb their hair, but who would want to buy a calendar like that? A red-blooded man needs to see some skin. The Puritans don't believe in red-blooded men or erections, for God's sake. Did you hear about the bullshit that happened last month?"

"No, I've been on the road for awhile and I don't think I've seen a television in about a year."

"Ah, on a Kerouac tramp?"

Glover shook his head and leaned back because the couple of sips of beer he had taken had already scrambled his attention. He hoped that food would be following soon.

"The city elders tried to tell me I couldn't display the Second Amendment Foxes in my shop window. They tried to slap an obscenity charge and a disturbing the peace charge and an I-don't-like-vagina charge and I told them that all the parts that need to be covered are covered and shouldn't we celebrate a country that can produce such women who have ass and love guns to help keep the Gestapo from entering the gates. The Puritans rose in anger and told me my exploitive display was not consistent with the historic nature of the town square and when tourists from around the world descend on our perfect little hamlet for the annual bacchanal known as the Pancake Flip and Syrup Festival the eyes of their children, the gentle ladies and the faggot men will be burned to their retinas at the site of a beautiful whore in a thong, toting some hardware that could stop an army. The goddamn TV news descended on me like a flock of crows and I was on all four stations locally. There was talk of CNN doing a story and a couple of friends told me they talked to a couple of stringers doing background, but nothing came of it. I couldn't believe the shitstorm caused by the town nannies and the Puritans. You've got to see this. You would have thought I hung up a dead faggot in the window." The man practically ran out of the room to a connecting hallway. Glover turned over the calendar and looked at the back cover, reading the photography had been shot by Strom Williams, and he thought the man might never have gotten around to telling him his name.

Williams called to him from down the hallway and Glover walked to a small bedroom that had been converted to an office. Oversized black and white portraits of Hemingway, Faulkner, Melville and Twain dominated the walls. Books were piled up in intricate towers around an antique desk with a matching wood chair on which the latest and fastest Mac with a monitor as large as Hemingway's head rested. Williams had fired up the computer and had loaded a video of his stint on the news. An overwrought intro read by a blonde reporter with exaggerated television features, large head, expressive eyes, full lips and straight, white teeth that looked implanted made Glover think of a children's puppet show, except with slow evocative phrasing that bordered on an invitation, a come on. The interview took place in front of the store with the posters serving as a background. The editors had distorted the one poster with the models touching their asses so the viewers could fill in a more salacious and illegal image like a double-headed dildo protruding from both their viginas. Williams tried to explain his position, but he mooned over the reporter and he couldn't help himself from making suggestive eye movements as he lost the thread of his first and second amendment argument. The other stations hadn't the foresight to send a woman to a sexist fight, so the men reporters threw up easy questions to Williams who frothed and steamed as he unwrapped his screed. He gave them an hour's worth of material to edit down to a twenty second blast and they left satiated and with a calendar to pass around the newsroom. Williams then rifled through his desk and showed Glover a dossier of print articles, editorials and internet stories about his poster display.

"And I don't show one nipple or stray pube in this calendar. Next year I'm doing a nude shoot and I'm going to make posters twice as big. Real, artistic black and whites and maybe a couple of full beavers. I mean I'm going to find models with pink and robust labias and I'm going to use electrical tape to cover the offensive parts and those fucking posters are going to hang in my shop until the sun burns the paper into confetti. I live amongst Puritans and nannies, but where else can I go? Live in the city with the rats? Where can you go where you can do what you want, when you want, without the nattering gossips tsk-tsking you and the government behemoth stomping on your neck?"

Glover didn't know if Williams expected an answer. His speech sounded rehearsed and Glover thought he may have been recruited as an audience and nothing more. In fact, Williams, whenever asked about the dispute or whenever he felt it necessary to relate the story from beginning to end on a virgin listener, did lift entire sections of the speeches he gave the television stations and print reporters, honing the message and sharpening the articulation of the villains with each telling.

"There's no place left. Goddamn government will sniff you out even if you're living in Death Valley or among the crags of the Grand Tetons. They don't want you thinking for yourself and most of all they don't want you thinking about pussy, because a government of faggots and nannies wants you to turn into a faggot yourself and you better pile up the insurance policies and pay an army of dickless insurance agents because you can't fart without thinking of the consequences for you and your family. Goddamn, my gas may be offensive, but it's mine. My Christian friends think it is the end of times. I tell them it may be more likely that it's the end of living and once the end of living comes the citizens of our once great nation will beg for the end of time."

"I don't know anything about that."

"No, you wouldn't know anything about that. Here's a white boy digging in the garbage for his supper. He looks lean and mean, but he doesn't work and he doesn't have an address, or even a home for a day. He has no land and no tether. He lives off the castaways of decent folk. He's content being a leech and a bottom feeder."

"That food was fine. It just couldn't be sold no more."

"Unrepentant trash. But you don't know any better. I don't fault you. You're just another clueless victim of the government. They've taken away your balls and you don't even know it. You're a beggar. They've thrown you away and given you no chance. They couldn't educate you or didn't want to educate you. They thought they'd throw you on a factory line until they thought of a better idea of having all the yellows and browns work the line. What the fuck are they going to do with you? You are extra capacity. Hands with no work or purpose. An undeveloped brain given no task to improve. All they want to do know is wait for you to fuck up and then they can throw you in jail. You don't even know your fate has already been inputted into a database and you're a statistic waiting to flower. You don't read and you half-believe what they threw at you at school. Most likely you went to a government school and you never thought about the fact that a government school might not actually give the truth about itself, might not introduce some ideas that would cause the whole repressive state to collapse in on itself, ideas that might lead to an armed rebellion or at least cause the cops to hunker down in their bunkers and watch on their video monitors as the great struggle for survival ensues. The end of nannies and taxes. You want another beer?"

"Do you have food?"

"You were willing to eat out of a dumpster and now you're demanding food?" Williams said as his eyes flared and he half-rose from his chair. He cocked his arm like he was going to sail a punch at Glover's head then broke into a laugh. "I'm just fucking with you. How long has it been since you've eaten?"

When Glover told him it had only been a couple of days Williams raised an eyebrow and seemed disappointed. "I thought it would have been a week at least. Digging through the garbage after only two days doesn't bode well for you. You're easily desperate."

Williams made Glover a turkey sandwich and watched him eat before an idea struck him and he disappeared to another part of the house. Glover chewed slowly and forced the sandwich down. After the first couple of bites he felt full, but he forced himself to burp and continue eating until he finished. He turned and flinched as he saw Williams striding toward him with a pistol in his right hand and a pistol and book in his left hand.

"Jesus, you're a little jumpy. If I wanted you dead I would have put a bullet in your brain from the doorway."

"That's comforting."

"At least it would have been quick. You never would have known you we're dead. So, after you're done we'll go out back and shoot targets before it gets dark." He set the pistols on the table and cradled the book in his hands. "I know you said you weren't a reader. Sometimes I wonder how or why I kept reading myself, but I have a curious mind and I can't help myself. I have to know what's behind the curtain. I want to see the rivers of thought running through the heads of titans. Of course, among the many other things I do, I'm a writer, so it's natural that I read, I guess. You haven't had much of a chance, but you can start now. You can start anytime but why let the mysteries of the world wait? This book started me out. It's the one that I remember set my thoughts ablaze. I wasn't unlike you, all cock and stupidity, and it was like I stumbled on the poetry of the universe or a new Rosetta stone, know what I mean? Here, I have something like ten copies of it. I try to give it out when I think it will do some good. I can afford to give you one in the hopes it will turn you away from eating garbage."

Williams held out the book to Glover, who expected to see a copy of the Bible or *On the Road* or *The Book of Law* by Aleister Crowley because the people who he had known who had sworn to the life-changing properties of a book usually offered one of the three. Instead, Williams offered him *Atlas Shrugged* and Glover at first thought the cover looked homosexual with a nude art deco titan holding up the earth, and when he flipped it over and saw a picture of a severe looking woman lesbian on the back cover, so he didn't know what to think.

"This unlocks the first door. I could give you a list of others."

Glover set the book down on the edge of the counter and took another sip of beer. Williams looked disapprovingly at him as if he expected Glover to begin reading immediately and report on the sudden improvement in the structures of his thinking. They stared at each other until Glover acquiesced by stuffing the book into his backpack, thinking the pages might be good to start a fire once he got back on the road. Williams began a rambling dissertation on Objectivism and the value of the individual and the fact that laissez-faire capitalism had become the purest form of human existence because it awarded achievement and innovation and that great innovations eventually benefited everyone, such as a numbskull with a 50 IQ who now has access to penicillin, blood transfusions and latex dildos and all the things his addled brain would never have been able to invent and these men and women, free from the shackles of government and nannyism, invented these beneficial innovations, so we would all be better off if the government and the nannies would just get out of the way of the innovators and let them create and let their intelligence and drive improve the world. Williams then constructed a bridge between individual rights and the value, indeed, the necessity of doing whatever one pleases at all times and his dispute with the town nannies over his poster display. His summation included a frenzied and breathless call for the action steps that: 1) all Americans should be required to read *Atlas Shrugged* and *The Fountainhead* and critical essays on their literary merits should be required before any kid is given a high school diploma, and 2) if he desired to show a six foot by nine foot photo of a pierced labia or an aroused clitoris he should be given the freedom to do so because the connection between sex and guns could not, in fact, be denied. A man with a boner was a man who would be leaving his store with a brand new firearm. He then trailed off as he explained the difficulty in explaining this connection to the town nannies and the looks of disgust and condemnation on their faces as he sat in front of the zoning board.

He picked up a gun in each hand and told Glover to follow him. They left the house through the back door and walked past the oversized garage and a dog kennel that held three bloodhounds that followed them with their eyes but otherwise did not move. Williams had created a firing range in a small clearing surrounded by dark and damp woods. He had tacked paper bull's-eye targets on cleverly built stands made of scrap lumber. The lumber had been torn apart by bullets and looked ready to collapse from a compromised structure. Starting at the targets he counted off twenty-five paces in his head, turned and readied himself to shoot by loosening his arms and stretching his back. With a jerk he leveled the gun and squeezed off seven quick shots. All the shots had no more than a six inch variance in the entry point in the target. He gave Glover some instruction, told him to think of the gun as an extension of his arm, to remain loose but in control, stay focused on the target and aim using the site. Williams reminded him he held Beretta 84 FS Cheetah .380, which had a sensitive trigger, and asked him to try to hit the target and to point it nowhere else, because, frankly, he didn't want to have to dig a bullet out of his leg or his jaw. Glover fired off ten rounds and hit the target with six, enough to garner an appreciative nod from Williams. Over the next hour they fired hundreds of rounds and stopped only when darkness had fallen and they could no longer see the targets. They went back inside and Glover rubbed the soreness out of his arm, thinking he never saw Williams miss the target even once. The moss of the clearing had been replaced by a carpet of casings, a testament to Williams' practice schedule. Glover ate two more sandwiches and they both drank more beer. Williams told Glover about an oriental massage parlor he frequented in Warren and that he could drive there in less than a half hour. Glover told him he had no money to eat let alone spend on whores, but Williams waved away the concern, saying and he had money because he had embraced and understood capitalism and individual responsibility and he would, not out of charity, but out of a desire to keep the night rolling, pick up the cost of the massage as long as Glover could be satisfied with nothing more than a handjob.

"Everything is reasonable at that place, except for pussy. Their price structure is a little out of whack."

So they drove through dark rolling hills and forests until they came to the first signs of sprawl away from the center of a dying city, a cluster of flimsy houses built around a cul-de-sac with no trees taller than a sapling and all the yards, both front and back, brightly illuminated with banks of spotlights. Next came gas stations and a bar that looked like an original roadhouse placed away from the town for discreet trysts and homemade booze. Then they passed a massive expanse of big box stores with a still bustling parking lot aglow with a thousand lights so that it looked like a sterile oasis or an airport with a confusing jumble of crisscrossing runways. They passed fast food joints, oil change garages and small and dirty aluminum clad ranch houses with the road as their front yard and with a line of electrical towers cutting through their back yards. Glover thought someone should set fire to the houses as an act of mercy.

Williams pulled into an old strip mall where the majority of store fronts had been boarded up, casualties of the cheaper prices and convenience of the big boxes, but a barbershop, a pizza carryout, a state licensed liquor store, a Christian book and biblical supply store, a Chinese restaurant and the massage parlor managed to thrive. The cars in the lot were weighted toward the pizza carryout and the massage parlor at this time of night. They went in and Williams and the front desk clerk greeted each other without smiles. A look of stress passed across her face and she asked in half language and half pantomime whether they would be together or separate. Williams asked her when he ever gave the inclination that he may play for the other side and she stared at his lips as he spoke, but she could not decipher what he said. He exaggerated disgust and told her they would be separate and to never ask him that again unless he brought a whore from the outside with him. The clerk smiled and bowed her head, responding in a pleasant way that she had no idea what Williams might be talking about. Williams whispered to Glover that fresh girls came off the boat every week and sometimes they were confused about the business they had been sold to and sometimes they cried when they got you off, but you would think the geniuses who owned the place would put a whore at the desk who knew a little more English than a nod and a wink.

They were led down a narrow hall that had been painted blood red and had been decorated with Chinese kitsch, a painted hand fan, a paper lantern, a New Year's dragon in cardboard with movable limbs, a scroll with peace and harmony written in Chinese characters framing a painting of a spring-fed lake with pandas and butterflies quenching their thirst at water's edge, and three opera masks arranged in such a way that made them look like they were having a conversation with each other though their expressions never changed, all bought no doubt at a novelty store for under two dollars apiece. The clerk opened the first door they came to and motioned for Glover to enter. The room had been painted ochre and a single naked incandescent bulb hung from the ceiling and made the space look like a construction site or an interrogation room. It smelled of oil and disinfectant and the cot in the middle of the floor had been stripped of its sheets, so the striped mattress added a military or prison touch to the decorating. A girl of no more than twelve came in with sheets under her arms and made the cot without looking at Glover directly, but she kept him in her periphery and knew where he stood at all times. She rushed out of the room and quietly shut the door as if the latch had been fashioned out of heirloom crystal and she had been given the job to protect its value and craftsmanship. An old woman, her gray hair pulled back in a bun and wearing a silken robe the same color as the hallway, strode in and ordered Glover to take off his clothes and to hang them on a hook by the door. She had only a few teeth remaining in her jaws and her skin reminded Glover of a crinkled brown paper bag. Before he undressed he considered running, but even though he really didn't want her to touch him he could figure no way out without being rude as sometimes this ingrained politeness paralyzed him and made him endure experiences he otherwise would have avoided. Besides, running might cause the whore to yell and he imagined Williams chasing him across the parking lot and forcing him to come back and get his money's worth of all that hard-earned capital. Naked, he lay on the cot and she told him to turn over on his stomach. She produced a bottle of massage oil from the pocket of her robe, spread it across her hands and very nearly pounced on his back. The cot skidded some and creaked under their combined weight. Her bony fingers were incredibly strong and they bore into his muscles and popped ligaments and within minutes he had forgotten where he lay. His mouth fell open and a small swirl of drool escaped his lips. She had him turn back over and worked briefly on his face and chest before expertly touching his balls and perineum until he became fully erect. He kept his eyes closed tight and tried to think of Estonia or Mary Kelly and settled on a combination of both, but the woman's tough, strong hands felt like neither of them so the images died. She understood the physiology of a cock so well he felt deep sensation and Glover opened his eyes and watched her work. Her expression looked like she could have been stirring soup, dicing vegetables, or solving an incredibly complicated jigsaw puzzle. Her complete lack of emotion did not dampen his enthusiasm and somehow heightened the sensation so much that his cock felt separate from him like she had unscrewed it, taken it to the corner of the room and stroked it to a frenzy while he watched from the cot. She knew when he was ready to come, produced a damp rag from another part of her robe and snagged the semen mid-air as he released. She wiped the head of his cock and ten seconds later nothing remained of the transaction except his shrinking erection and a spot of semen clogging his urinary meatus. The woman exited with the stride of an uptight quality control expert before Glover even sat up. It occurred to him that Williams would be occupied a few minutes longer given he had paid for more complicated services and that this moment would be a great opportunity to leave his company since Williams had driven him that much closer to the east coast, and he asked himself what good ending could come after a night of guns, beer and whores. He dressed and found his way to the exit. Williams had locked the truck and Glover had left the backpack inside. He couldn't repay Williams' hospitality by smashing a window to retrieve the backpack so he decided to leave it and the dirty, ragged clothes it held. The loss of the article about Dr. Thompson's Mystic Cult disappointed him, because he still had a strong feeling that a person should hold onto the signposts of his life, not for purely nostalgic reasons, but every clue might be a part of a larger clue that could be unveiled years later.

He ran across the parking lot and the street and hid behind a sickly hedge. He watched the truck for an hour before Williams came out, scanned the parking lot for a few moments, and then drove away. He figured Williams wouldn't give up so easily and he was proved right when he saw Williams slowly rolling down the street from the opposite direction he had left. Glover flattened himself in the shadow and held his breath as the truck and his backpack drove by. He hoped Williams would throw the pack out in anger or disgust, but he must have remembered his book being inside so he held on to it. Glover thought of going back into the parlor and chatting up the clerk, because he needed something to balance his growing revulsion from the handjob, but he imagined unseen bouncers with guns who would take a dim view of him hanging around their lobby and fresh merchandise.

Mistakenly, he started walking west, eventually saw a directional sign that told him he walked westward, turned, retraced his steps and continued walking through the night. The commercial strip turned into denser and more distressed development, dirty houses crammed into yards filled with tires, broken toys and rusting motors, one story brick buildings built in rectangles with no windows and no exterior features that could have functioned as a crematorium, a bingo hall, or a plumbing supply warehouse, and a dozen or so makeshift churches and old Catholic structures long abandoned by the flock. The town gave way to black countryside and woods and after a couple of hours the traffic stopped completely. Glover watched the ground and mulled over again and again that just a few days into this flight his possessions had been reduced to a pair of work boots, a pair of ratty socks, a pair of jeans weakening at the knees and frayed along the bottom hem, a pair of underwear rapidly disintegrating and a t-shirt, a souvenir from a BMX race two years old. The night air had turned crisp and his arms felt cold, and he knew he would not be able to sleep or even rest enough to make stopping worth the effort, so he listened to the sound of his boots crunching on the gravel and the rustle and flap of night creatures as they bore witness to his journey.

He walked until noon the next day when he came to a truck stop, no more than an old restaurant with a giant parking lot. The owner let the truckers sleep in his lot and gave them discounted prices on food because the Turnpike Commission had built service centers along the side of the turnpike a few miles to the south and killed most of his business because the truckers, the vacationers, and the businessmen had no reason to leave that closed circuit and venture to his store. More than one trucker confided in him to let whores patrol the lot and his business would pick up, but he lived a pleasant life with his wife and two daughters and thought he might get a job serving food at the state prison or a desk job with the county before allowing that kind of activity on his lot. The owner gave Glover a glass of water and allowed him to use the restroom. Glover avoided the mirror, but washed his face and the back of his neck. The humid and close smell of frying food nauseated him, but he did plan on hanging around the lot until the restaurant closed and rifling through the dumpster for dinner. The place looked so sad and poor he didn't think he could ask the owner outright for charity because he looked like he needed some himself. A trucker, who had just loaded up on mashed potatoes and gravy with hot turkey slices, coffee and two slices of cherry pie and who refused to eat or shit at the state sanctioned service centers because they reminded him too much of socialism, altered Glover's plans when he asked him if he needed a ride. Glover told him he wanted to go as far as the east coast and the trucker said he was driving to Delaware. When Glover asked if Delaware lay close to the coast the trucker produced a sarcastic leer and asked how Glover could ever get to his destination if he didn't know where his destination happened to be. Glover shrugged his shoulders and wanted to know how close Delaware would be to New York, but he really didn't want to endure another smile like that, a smile that reminded him he was a dumb fucker with no plan in a world full of people with plans, education and purpose.

It turned out to be a good ride, though, as the trucker stayed mostly quiet and after a while started listening to an audio book about how to structure a stock portfolio and the drone of words put Glover to sleep for a few hours. When he woke up he found the trucker in the exact same position behind the wheel and even though the book had advanced it sounded like the same chapter to Glover. The trucker gave him snacks, coke, corn chips and a few cookies and when the book finally ended they rode in silence, as the trucker contemplated his next move in the financial markets.

The trucker dropped Glover off at the outskirts of a town called Lewes, Delaware and as he walked closer to the center of the city he could smell the ocean and hear the faint rumble of breakers. The sun balanced on the horizon like a gymnast on a beam as families drove past, having left the beach with sunburns, jellyfish stings and sand in their suits. He passed a house party that had spilled onto the front lawn of a house and the sidewalk. Rich kids in bikinis and surfer wear huddled around a keg with reggae helping to slide them into oblivion and each other's bed where they would share contagions of crabs. Glover remembered parties in Bakersfield that looked the same except the kids wore jeans and t-shirts and where he knew everybody and he talked about nothing all night and day until he convinced a girl to come with him to a dark room of the house. He thought of trying to join the party, but the kids looked uptight and violent, because even the reggae and beachwear couldn't mask their agendas, plans, purpose and expensive educations in how to get theirs and take yours. This had to be a party of assholes and schemers, fraternity and sorority creeps prone to forming packs and hating strangers. He hoped they would leave the keg in the yard overnight with something left in the bottom so he could siphon off a couple of foamy drafts. The air smelled of fried clams and lobster boil from a nearby restaurant. He began to think dimly of a half-remembered myth about a man presented with banquet tables filled with food, the finest wines from the most select grapes and women perfectly sculpted and wanton throughout eternity, but the man does not have the power to eat, drink or touch so he goes through time with hunger gnawing his gut, his lips cracked and bleeding from thirst, and the worst case of blue balls in recorded history and the dark recesses of myth. He couldn't remember what the myth meant exactly or what the man had done to deserve such cruel punishment at the hands of his sinister gods, but it approximated the torture he had begun to feel. He found the beach and walked to the water's edge still wearing his work boots. He spotted a grove of low, twisted trees to the right where he figured he could sleep that night if he could stand the sand fleas. A weathered hotel stood to the left, on the edge of a broad expanse of sand and rolling ocean waves slowly moving toward the shore. He wanted to take off his clothes and jump in the water as some kind of prize for having successfully crossed the country using his own wits, but he thought he might drown in the undertow from exhaustion and get arrested for indecency, so he fell down in the sand and fell quickly to sleep. He awoke after a few hours, waited until the restaurant closed and picked two fistfuls of fried scraps and lobster pieces from the dumpster and walked to the twisted grove where he found a place to eat and sleep, somewhat protected from the ocean wind. As he began to get use to the itch of fleas and mites chewing his skin, closing in again on a light sleep, a loud, drunken conversation erupted from a nearby camp that Glover had not noticed.

Three guys had returned from a bar or party and talked over each other as they spouted observations about bikinis and the smell of salt in a girl's hair and the futility of drinking if it just led to sleeping in the sand with a couple of other smelly dudes, punctuated with howls of laughter and more drinking. Eventually the conversation turned to a collective plan of driving up to Maine to work the blueberry fields, pocket a load of cash and take the party to Amsterdam or Prague. Glover could just make out that they planned to leave in the morning and that one of them would contact the field supervisor who always looked for a crew. The voices eventually trailed off as one by one they passed out.

In the morning Glover woke up feeling like he had been a Thanksgiving feast for the colony of insects and chilled to his core from sleeping near the ocean in a T-shirt. He walked through the scrub and found the camp and all three were still asleep in their tents, so he walked on the beach for an hour collecting sand dollars and sea glass before dumping the collection back in the ocean and returning to the camp. By this time all three had awoken and were breaking down their tents and rolling their sleeping bags. They didn't acknowledge Glover as he stood at the edge of the camp, so he asked them if they were going to the blueberry fields in Maine and whether they could give him a ride. The tallest and strongest looking kid told him they had no room, but one of them, Shel Hamilton, saw the BMX shirt and asked Glover if he had raced. Glover told him he did, as he had spent five years, ages 11 to 16, thinking of nothing but BMX and entering races whenever his mom could scrape up the entrance fees and felt like hauling him and his bike to the track, until he realized he had reached his peak and that his peak fell far short of the top rider. He quit because he felt sick of being embarrassed on the track and hadn't even looked at a bike since. Shel had a similar story except that he, around the age of fifteen, took a header off his bike and broke vertebrae C-4 and C-5 and just by lucky chance the break hadn't severed his spinal nerves, so other than giving up BMX and being immobilized for two months, the fall had no lasting effect.

Shel lobbied the others, Drew and Peter, to let Glover come even though he had no gear or money. Shel eventually won the argument because the other two couldn't think of a compelling reason for excluding Glover. As payment, Glover entertained them with his newly acquired stories on the way up the coast. He told them about Williams and the Asian whorehouse, Jack and the lumberyard theft (leaving out the parts about the murder and the subsequent burial in the shitter), about the beautiful Estonia (leaving out the part about her pregnancy and his sneaking away in the night without even a goodbye), about Mary Kelly and her idiot son catching them fucking and the kid looking at his dick like it had become filet mignon, about the trek across the states from Bakersfield and how, if he could take an educated guess, the entire country had gone crazy and he thought that we would one day realize it and that he didn't know what would happen when the realization occurred, but it wouldn't be good because, as far as he could tell, everybody thought they were doing the right thing and that everybody else had gone crazy and had become bent on ruining the country.

"Just so you know," the three said. "We are fucking crazy and we know it." They laughed until they cried and for his stories Glover shared their meals, beer and pot. They were skeptical about Glover's stories and a little in awe because no matter how many times they took trips or tramped about nothing ever really seemed to happen except drinking and hangovers, sometimes a fight, or sometimes favors were coaxed from drunken girls.Glover told them to strip their lives down to the clothes on their back and all kinds of shit would start happening, because they would no longer have protection and their ability to influence circumstances will become greatly reduced.

"Throw away your debit card and you'll see how fucked up the world really is."

They thought about it awhile and decided they liked having money because it increased their chances of getting laid on a regular basis.Glover could have those other experiences and tell them about it.

They made it to Maine and set up camp on the shore of a spring fed lake at the edge of the vast blueberry fields. Glover shared Shel's tent and used an extra blanket he had brought for a sleeping bag. They were hired onto a crew and worked twelve hour days, bending over and raking the berries of the low bushes with a tool that looked like a dustpan with teeth like a comb. The worker held it by a handle and raked the long teeth through the bush. The teeth were set far enough apart to let the branches go through, but they plucked the berries and some leaves and the berries rolled to the pan at the back of the tool. They dumped a full rake into a five gallon bucket. Once they filled two five gallon buckets they carried them down to the end of the row where the supervisor Big Jim Gouda stood next to a winnowing machine. They poured the berries and leaves down a chute and it shook and blew air across the surface of the pile as it rolled down the chute, separating and blowing the leaves to the ground. The cleaned berries fell down another chute into stained and weathered wooden boxes. Each five gallon bucket of berries produced three boxes and they earned $2.50 per box, so each bucket made them $7.50. Every day they could pick 50 boxes or 17 five gallon buckets, which meant over a hundred dollars for the day. By the end of the harvest they could accumulate a couple of thousand dollars minus expenses for food and beer. Sometimes the field grew into scrub with few berries on the bushes and they complained to Big Jim Gouda, but he didn't acknowledge their complaints and told them they could only work what the company gave them. He kept track of their harvest on a clipboard and watched to see who busted ass in the scrub and who acted like a whiny bitch, so he knew who to throw into the choicest parts of the fields that looked like a giant hand had thrown down a massive purple blanket, or so Big Jim thought in his more poetic moments. At the end of the week Big Jim paid by checks and told them which bank in the town of Cherryfield would cash them with a one dollar fee. The crew pushed Big Jim to work on Saturdays because they wanted to make money and two days off in a row would be nothing but trouble, since they would all have over five hundred dollars in their pockets with nothing to do but drink, eat candy bars and drive around looking for girls in an unpopulated land. So, they worked Saturdays and only had one night to drink to excess and one morning of waking up feeling so terrible all they soaked their heads in the lake and did not start moving with purpose until well after noon.

Shel befriended a family of Seventh Day Adventists who also camped at the lake. The father had hollow, dark eyes that looked like he had stared at fire or unspeakable wartime violence for too long and the mother was fat and smiling, but the smile looked vacant and haunted because her husband's terror had blanched the joy from her life. The couple had two daughters, the real reason for Shel's reconnaissance, both in their teens and who had acquired the best features from both parents even though the mix blended differently. The older daughter sported large breasts and a heavy, earthy build while the younger one looked lithe and athletic, laughed without the haunted edge of the family that the older one had acquired as well. The mother took pity on the four boys because their dinners usually consisted of cold sandwiches of tuna or peanut butter and jelly or peanut butter and honey, so after a few conversations with Shel she invited them to dinner. As long as they didn't drink in the family's camp they could enjoy stews and casseroles made in her Dutch oven and they were able to watch the color rise on the girl's necks as they talked to them. The meals made work the next day easier and the presence of the girls within walking distance of their camp made them feel less lonesome even though they had no chance of getting either of them since the father kept a close eye on both because he knew what could happen to beautiful girls no matter their upbringing and belief in the great savior.

Drew ruined the relationship between the two camps. He came from more money than the rest of them put together and he would begin his third year at Brown University after the harvest, where he glided through a political science degree in preparation for Harvard Law. He knew he would end up in New York with a knockout wife addicted to yoga and a good job in corporate law. He also knew he had the brains and the connections through his father to make it happen, but before his life began in earnest he had decided to seek out experiences unknown to corporate lawyers in Manhattan, like blueberry picking in Maine under a high, blistering sun or squatting for a summer in an abandoned tenement in the South Bronx. While his more industrious classmates interned at law offices and talent agencies and his more reckless classmates partied on the beaches of Ibiza or Miami, he had chosen experiences not aligned with his career trajectory. His father worried silently that some kind of blue collar or poverty romance had infected him, because while he approved of Prince Hal fucking and drinking with wastrels before he assumed his birthright, the idea of squatting and slumming with no obvious enjoyment gave him restless nights and caused a wedge between father and son that never existed before. But Drew knew he played in worlds he would never see again, worlds that held no romance for him other than it caused discomfort to his classmates and his father. His classmates thought he had gone crazy or that he had thought of a new angle to beef up his résumé or wondered if partying in the South Bronx amongst the crackheads and gunfire in an abandoned tenement could be better than partying at Ibiza, and his father wondered, according to Drew, that he might turn his back on law and do something tragic like study social services or till in the field of ineffective government interventions aimed at the poor. So, Drew, like most tourists, never really followed the rules of the worlds where he slummed. At the tenement he sometimes ordered takeout or had sparsely attended parties of his wealthy friends on one of the abandoned floors, and in Maine, after Shel had befriended the Seventh Day Adventist family who cooked for them and opened their hearts to the boys, Drew decided that skinny dipping would be an appropriate act after Shel had invited the family over for a swim in the hopes of seeing the older daughter in a bathing suit. Shel had gotten the family in the water and even though the girls were in suits that practically started at their throats and ended at their knees, their figures could not be hidden once the suits got wet. Drew stood on the bank, dropped his shorts and let out a whoop so all eyes involuntarily turned toward him. He took big strides and splashed into the water toward the family. Everybody shrieked, the girls, their parents, and even Shel, Peter and Glover because they knew the relationship with the family and those hearty casseroles and those tender and fresh daughters had ended with one flap of Drew's cock. The mother and father hustled the girls out of the water with shouts or horror and remonstrance. Shel climbed out of the water and pounded the dirt of the bank muttering "stupid motherfucker" over and over again. Glover and Peter dried off and started making peanut butter and honey sandwiches for dinner. They stayed mad at Drew for a few days, but he owned the car, which would take them out of the blueberry fields and transported them to beer, so they softened toward him and started to make jokes that his cock made the world shriek. Drew bought them a better brand of beer and even sprung for a meal at a diner in Cherryfield.

Shel tried to smooth it over with the family by apologizing for Drew, but the girls wouldn't look at him and started blushing as soon as he entered their camp and Shel not only felt like he had been the one to expose himself but that he tried to apologize with his cock hanging through his zipper. The mother and father acted hurt and betrayed and no amount of apologizing would ever get them to break bread again with such dirty boys. Shel told them he understood and with one last effort added that he would pray for Drew and hope he saw his way clear to decency. They nodded their approval but otherwise were unmoved in their hardness toward him.

They continued to work in the fields until the season wound down and for a celebration they bought a trunk full of beer, liquor and food they could cook over a fire on the beach. Drew chatted with the bank clerk who waited on them every payday and convinced her to come along and asked if she had any friends who would want to party as well. She agreed because she could tell that Drew acted like no ordinary migrant with blueberry stained jeans and hands, even though he had both, because he had a serious looking novel sticking out of his back pocket and his accent sounded soft and sweet. She could get none of her friends to agree to come because they didn't feel like rewarding boys they had never met before, but the clerk followed them in her car and ended up fucking Drew on the found blanket near the rocks. She became so drunk she wouldn't have minded if all of them had taken a turn, but she didn't ask and they didn't think of it.

Glover drank, watched the ocean and climbed the cliff with his head spinning under the influence of the cheapest and most foul liquor he had ever tasted. Jack came at him like fire as he vomited at his feet. He had a decision to make. Peter and Shel were taking off a semester of their haphazard studies at the University of Massachusetts and planning to see how far across Europe they could get on their blueberry money. They had invited Glover to replace Drew, who, of course, would be returning to Brown on schedule. Glover told them about his plan to go to New York and they laughed and told him his blueberry money would last barely a month unless he wanted to squat like Drew had done, but, they warned, that he should remember that Drew never gave up his cell phone or ATM card. He could expect a brutal and frightening experience given that he only had his tiny bankroll to protect him. He heard the Seventh Day Adventists were traveling on to California to the next harvest season and he would have liked to join them, not because of the girls, but because they seemed whole and grounded even though they lived on the edge of terror and hysteria.

Glover wiped his mouth, dried his eyes and staggered along the top of the cliff until he found a dirt path heading down. He told Peter and Shel he had made it to the top and that they were bastards for not watching and making sure he hadn't fallen to his death. Shel told him he knew he had it all the way and what good would it have been to watch him fall because he would have been dead either way. They waited for Drew to fuck the bank clerk a second time and then gathered up their unfinished liquor and trudged back to the car. The bank clerk had become too drunk to stand on her own, let alone drive, so they nominated Glover to drive her car because if he could scale a cliff he could drive a car with no problem. They threw the girl in the back seat of her car where she threw up on herself, the floor, the widows and the seat. Glover drove with the windows down but no amount of rushing air could carry away the smell of rotten liquor and stomach acid. When they got back to Cherryfield, Drew pulled into the back parking lot of the bank where she worked. He told Glover to leave her in the car and to come with them, but Glover told him he thought it would be a fucked-up thank you for a night of fucking because somebody would find her, most likely the cops, and they would have to report the discovery to the bank president that one of his employees had been found covered in vomit and semen, drunk and incoherent.

"How many jobs do you think are in this fucking town? We can't do that to her."

"Fuck off, if you want to fuck that pussy after I came all over it be my fucking guest. I don't give a shit if that cunt loses her job."

Glover jumped out of the car and Drew jumped out to meet him, but Glover launched himself in the air and punched Drew in the right eye before he could set himself. Drew staggered back until he finally fell against his car where he lost consciousness. Pain reverberated through Glover's arm and he thought he may have broken his hand or wrist. Shel and Peter jumped out of the car and opened their arms, miming 'whatthefuckdude' as if a prelude to more fighting, but the three of them knew they had nothing against each other than divided loyalties to Drew.

"That fucker had it coming since he showed his dick to those sweet girls. You know it."

They agreed, but they now had to worry about a concussion or a cracked skull or a fucking hemorrhage. Shel straightened out Drew's neck, but stood up quickly as he realized he could have done more damage. Glover said maybe next time Drew would think twice before shitting on a girl nice enough to let him into her pants and they said if he didn't turn out to be brain damaged they doubted very much it would make any difference. Glover always carried his blueberry money with him in the front pocket of his jeans so he didn't have to go back to camp. He told them he would take care of the girl and that they should find a hospital to get Drew's skull checked because he probably broke his hand with the punch. They dragged and pushed Drew into the back seat, looking pissed, and spun out of the bank lot in the opposite direction of the camp.

Glover turned the girl over, trying to avoid the vomit and found her driver's license in the back pocket of her jeans. He read the address and drove around for an hour trying to find the street name. Even though the town was small and there weren't that many streets, the streets they did have were not well marked or lighted so he could have been driving on the floor of the ocean for all he knew. Finally, he saw a sign that pointed him toward a state highway which connected to an interstate and soon he drove 75 MPH away from the address. At first he had no clear plan what to do, but after an hour of highway the bank clerk still showed no signs of waking, so when Glover saw a sign for motel rooms for $39.99 per night he pulled off.

He paid cash. Fortunately, the clerk didn't ask for identification. He drove the car to the door of the room, unlocked it and propped it open by stuffing a phone book beneath the edge because it had been equipped with a spring-loaded closer. He waited to make sure no one crossed the lot or left their rooms. After a few minutes of no discernible movement in the vicinity, he opened the door, grabbed the clerk and dragged her into the room. She barely roused as her heels scraped along the parking lot, the concrete of the sidewalk and then the carpet of the room. He pulled her onto the bed and left her on her back. He found a pen in the car glove compartment and wrote a note on the back of a flyer advertising a traveling carnival with a wrestling bear and midget clog dance extravaganza and complete midget village. He wrote that he felt sorry for taking her car, but he needed wheels and she practically offered the use of them, because she should really be careful who she partied with, because she'll never know their intent unless she can witness them over time and that not everyone believes in the golden rule though he had a dim recollection of what that meant exactly. He also wrote the part about Drew wanting to leave her in the bank parking lot and how he punched him and how he tried to find her home but these country roads are not well marked or lighted. He set the note by the table lamp and gave the bank clerk one last look before he left, deciding to take her clothes with him. He stripped her down to her skin, rolling her back and forth to release the clothing trapped underneath her. She mumbled a few times but otherwise stayed unconscious. Glover rolled them into a sodden ball and threw them into the trunk on top of a pile of children's board books from the local library and a Winnie the Pooh pull toy boat that began *Row, Row, Row Your Boat* when the clothes jostled it. Glover slammed the trunk lid to muffle the song and to fight the realization that he had to be six ways a bastard for leaving the clerk in such a predicament. He walked back to the room and gathered all the bath towels, blankets and ripped the phone out of the wall with two violent jerks. He passed her prone and naked body again on his way out. He needed to escape the state, in case Drew died or had been seriously hurt or if someone had now begun wondering why the bank clerk had not returned, so he had to make it as hard as possible for her to get help. She may have a hard time explaining to her mother or friends how she ended up in a motel room without her car or clothes and her kid would probably be worried sick that she had never come home, but at least she wouldn't lose her job. He picked up the note and jammed it in his pocket, thinking better of leaving any clues for the police to follow should they be called in.

He drove out of the lot and continued down a commercial strip until he found an all night drugstore where he asked the clerk for the best cleanser for getting vomit out of a carpet. Not surprisingly, she had fielded similar requests several times this week during her graveyard shift.

The clerk, a middle-aged lady who had lost her job two summers before when the glass factory closed and who didn't want to hear any more details of Glover's lost night, showed him two products, a vomit absorbent that would take care of anything not already soaked into the carpet and a hand held carpet cleaner with a built-in brush head that had been designed with cars in mind. She paused and also suggested that he may need an air freshener given the distinctive and foul smell of fresh vomit and some hand wipes because its dirty business cleaning up someone's vomit and by the smell of his hands he had already begun the job.

He paid $32.16 for the products and couldn't help thinking of the price in terms of boxes of blueberries and the four hours it had taken him to earn this amount bent over in the sun. The fact that he had already spent over seventy dollars in less than an hour worried him, because money could evaporate by buying bullshit and he now had less than two thousand dollars in his pocket. Although, the seventy dollars had netted him a car. Even though he had never sold a stolen car he figured he could make more than seventy dollars on it. Jack would know how to sell the car and what price he should get, so he had to find someone like Jack to help him through the transaction. He drove further down the strip to the last building before the land turned back into countryside. The building had the vague shape of the defunct Red Barn fast food chain, but it had been modified several times as local restaurateurs tried their luck at their own themes and cuisines, but everyone found the place to be located too far away from the highway exit and that hungry travelers always rolled into some other place before reaching the last building on the strip.

Glover spread the absorbent on the carpet and seat and waited seven minutes as instructed by the directions on the can. He picked up the vomit/absorbent mixture with a bath towel and threw the sodden cloth into the parking lot. He followed with the carpet cleaner and brushed down the whole area twice before wiping up the foam with another bath towel. He sprayed most of the can of freshener throughout the interior and stood outside while the scented fog settled onto the fibers of the seats, the steering wheel and dash. She had given him lilac and Glover thought he might prefer the smell of vomit over the chemical approximation of the flower. He picked up the towels and threw them into the trunk on top of the bank clerk's clothes and he saw the children's books again. He considered his options as guilt made the air in his lungs feel leaden and made his stomach churn. He could leave the car in the parking space outside the room where she lay and hitch out of town. He could take her with him. He could leave by the highway and thank her for her generosity or her inability to hold alcohol. She, in turn, would thank him for not being a pervert who could have taken advantage of her disabled state. Glover could come up with no supporting evidence for any of the options other than he had become a bastard six ways, and he did briefly wonder if he could sneak back to her room and have sex with her without her waking up. He would take the car, knowing he had checked an impulse for a far worse crime. The vomit and lilac smell, alongside the idea of Drew's sperm already swimming inside her, doused any ideas of rape that might have been percolating in his thoughts. Also, if he started fucking her he could have expected a visitation from Jack, who would be sorely pissed he had resorted to the a base act of rape and old Jack might beat him off the girl from rage and righteousness.

He entered the highway and drove south on I-95. He drove past Portland and skirted New Hampshire as circumstances had obviously pushed him toward New York because the road signs told him where the road led. He drove through the night with the semi-trailers and drunks and came to the I-95 and I-90 interchange. He let his hands fall off the wheel and he waited for the car to decide whether he would go west through Massachusetts, New York, Pennsylvania and back to Ohio on the shores of Lake Erie, or south through a slice of Massachusetts, Rhode Island, Connecticut to New York City, which had been the original plan he and Estonia had concocted the night they left Bakersfield as they sat in a Denny's and shared a hamburger and held hands across the table and both were conscious of how corny and ordinary they must have looked, but none of the fat families and zombie waitresses could hear the story of their future together away from a shithole city in the middle of nowhere or they would have understood that nothing could be corny about holding hands in a Denny's when you're about to jump into the abyss together. The steering wheel vibrated as the car drifted to the left. Glover let the drift continue until the wheels hit the rumble strips at the side of road. The car had decided on New York, because I-95 spun off to the left and the car, even though it may have been influenced by the slant of the road and the less than perfect wheel alignment, had obviously pulled to the left.

He felt let down by the car because he had begun to fantasize about driving back to Ohio, pulling into Jack's driveway with a roll of cash in his pocket and proving to the three of them that he could take care of himself, that he could contribute to the house and at least pay his way or pay some for the baby and all the clothes and diapers he would need. He would let Jack sell the car for cash and that would also help with expenses or they would keep it so they didn't have to drive around in Jack's rotting truck. And somewhere in this fantasy he drove Estonia to the hospital as she panted and sweated, but Glover kept cool and calmly drove through the winding city streets. But the car had smashed the fantasy and he drove the remaining miles in the dark, arriving at the outskirts of the city near dawn. He had been to Los Angeles several times so he had seen a big city before and he could drive in heavy traffic, but nothing prepared him for the height of the city or the sense that he could be killed at any moment with no one noticing or much caring. He exited on Henry Hudson parkway because he couldn't move over a lane as the traffic had become thick and no one acknowledged his blinker to merge. He summoned the necessary rage and focus to compete with thousands of snarling engines and yanked the car effectively through the streets, but he had no destination in mind and he drove aimlessly through Manhattan and after a few hours came three observations: if he wanted to see more than bumpers and brake lights he had to park the car somewhere, he wished for nothing more than for Estonia to be sitting next to him so he could have watched her face as she realized they had really gotten out of crappy Bakersfield, and the impossibility of finding a gas station in Manhattan if you didn't know where to look.

Glover parked the car in an expensive deck and didn't check the prices before he turned the keys over to the valet. He noticed for the first time that the keys were connected to a plastic heart with a picture of two toddlers inserted on a bed of glitter. The valet noticed the picture first and his reaction caused Glover to look and the valet knew Glover had stolen the car and he gave the car a quick look to make sure it was worth the parking fees should the company need to sell it to earn back the money for the spot it would occupy.

"Nice looking kids," the valet said

"Ya, beauties. We're just visiting my cousin's sister and they asked me to park the car."

The valet arched his eyebrow and gave Glover a ticket. He took the ticket and walked out of the garage and into the city. The buildings loomed above him and he thought they might be alive. He could feel their moist breath on his neck. He felt part of the surging crowds walking with purpose and he tried to approximate the crowd's stride and their grim masks. Even though every kind of person passed him, as far as he could tell he stood out as the only one with blueberry stained clothes from collar to shoes and the only one with blueberry stained hands and hair that hadn't been washed in hot water for about two months. He passed by a couple of hundred clothing stores, but he thought he should shower before trying to buy new clothes. The clerks would take a dim view of him touching their merchandise in his state. He knew enough about hotels to walk away from the granite and marble buildings and wide avenues and he found streets with dingy brick and long shadows, but none of the hotels would rent him a room because he had no identification and no credit card. He kicked himself for not stealing the bank clerk's purse or Drew's ATM card for backup. So, he kept walking and he made an entire loop of Manhattan that first day and when he became exhausted he slept briefly on a bench in Tompkins Square Park until a couple of pit bulls began licking his face and when he woke up a man stood over him unlacing his work boots. When he realized Glover had awakened he asked him if he wanted his dick sucked. When Glover declined the man asked wistfully where all the faggots had gone. Glover told him he didn't know and the man walked away, but the pit bulls stayed. They sat at the end of the bench and stood up when Glover rose. They followed him for a few blocks, looking expectantly at him for a treat or a head scratch, until they realized Glover possessed no treats and acted a little leery of putting his hand near their mouths. He walked another hour and the dogs followed, sometimes veering off or turning down an alleyway and Glover would think he had lost them, but they would turn up again on the corner ahead of him with open friendly mouths and drool hanging from their lips to the sidewalk. They sometimes fell behind him with a half a block between them and sometimes they would close ranks and one would walk closely in front and the other closely behind in a kind escort. A couple of people yelled at Glover to keep his dogs leashed because they feared the dogs, but everyone on the sidewalk gave him a wide berth to pass and said nothing. The crowds thinned and the streetlights seemed to grow dimmer and more of them had burned out and not been replaced. The buildings looked like they had been painted with black, fetid paint. Glover saw a hotel sign and entered the lobby through a wobbly revolving door and the dogs followed a section behind and Glover thought of trapping them inside between revolutions and leaving by a swinging door on the left, but the plan hadn't formed quickly enough and they pushed their way into the building and stood beside him. The clerk accepted cash and asked for no identification. Glover tried to tell him that $120.00 was too much for a night and the clerk looked at the dogs and Glover's clothes and told him he looked in no position to negotiate and asked him if he remembered that they stood in New York City. The clerk dangled the key to a fifth floor room at the end of his fingers. Glover paid and the clerk slipped the key into his hand. He and the dogs rode the elevator up and found the room at the end of a long dank hall. The air of the room smelled like it had been trapped inside for five years and carried traces of human secretions and every product produced and sold to mask the odor of these secretions. The dogs jumped on the bed and began playing by trying to eat each other's face or locking on the throat of its friend and growling in mock anger. Glover locked himself in the bathroom and sat on the toilet, carefully unlacing his boots and pulling them off because his feet were throbbing and blistered along the rise of each heel. The boots were a size too big and they tended to slip when he walked and eighteen hours of walking in Manhattan after the blueberry fields had destroyed his socks. The blisters had popped and begun to grow again through the blood and shredded skin. He stripped off his clothes and stepped into the bathtub and pulled the shower curtain closed. He stood under a trickle of water and tried to scrub the blueberry stains off of his hands and arms. The shower needed to be hotter with a stronger stream, but be felt cleaner after he scraped the hotel soap, which smelled like a cross between a chemical designed to dissolve hair and a bowl of oatmeal, across his skin. He washed his hair, stepped out of the shower and hoped the dogs had gone, but as he toweled himself off he could hear them whimpering and scratching at the door. When he opened the door two eager faces greeted him and they tried to lick the drops of water off his shins. Glover closed the drain of the tub and filled it a few inches so the dogs could drink. They growled as they drank but were grateful for his kindness. He couldn't bring himself to wear the soiled blueberry clothes over his clean skin so he lay on the bed and turned on the television. After so many months of not watching the shows felt like an invasion of flashing patterns and puppet heads shouting in an incomprehensible language as if they were transmissions from a country submerged under the ocean, but the drone made his drowsy. The dogs jumped on the bed and found the negative space around Glover's body and curled up to sleep. One rested his head under Glover's outstretched arm and the other nuzzled against his knee. They all began to breathe heavily and they all drifted off to sleep.

Glover looked down the length of his legs. He wiggled his toes. It seemed like his toes were the only part of his body he could still move. His bare feet pointed toward the ceiling. Somebody had stolen his shoes and socks. He wore his blueberry pants, only now the stains had turned black and slick. A naked boy crawled across the floor and burrowed between his legs. He unbuttoned and unzipped Glover's pants. He tugged and stroked Glover's cock but couldn't get it to rise. He used his mouth and Glover wanted to push him off, but his arms had been weighed down by lead weights or had been paralyzed and even keeping his eyelids open to watch the boy's determination took tremendous effort. Beside him a girl wearing ripped jeans and a white bra that had turned gray from disinterest lay curled. She may have been sucking her thumb, but Glover couldn't move his head the inch he needed to confirm it. The naked boy held Glover's scrotum in his hand and considered his limp dick like he had come across an extremely difficult puzzle beyond his understanding or patience. He crawled away with his ass in the air, an invitation of sorts for those with enough energy or life to give it a try.

Glover lay on the floor of a long warehouse. The tall and arched windows were boarded up except for one, where the wood had been peeled away to let in a weak shaft of sunlight. A squatter had tapped into the electricity of the building next door, a forgotten warehouse for rotary dial telephone parts still part of the massive land holdings of the phone company, so a few naked bulbs hung from the ceiling. Thirteen people, all under twenty, lay on the floor or sat on unclaimed chairs or tried to fuck on beaten mattresses that looked like they had been military cots for World War II. Glover wore a hooded sweatshirt that covered the bruises on his arm were a needle had been repeatedly jabbed. The blueberry money had long been spent and now he had lost his shoes. The money for drugs now came from raids on the local warehouses of businesses, sometimes a straight-up mugging or beating on the street. They could always find something to steal and sell. He couldn't remember the name of the girl lying next to him and she didn't know how to fuck very well, but something about her ears reminded him of Estonia. The thought of Estonia still made him smile. He still hadn't met anyone as beautiful or sweet and he often thought they should have stayed in Bakersfield. He hoped the baby didn't look too much like him so that she wouldn't be reminded every day that he had left, but the squalling and the shitting reminded her enough, he guessed. He thought he might like to fuck the thumbsucker next to him and focus on her ears so that he could pretend he had gone back with Estonia and they had never quarreled and he had never hardened against her, but his body responded to no impulse or command. The naked boy had left Glover's fly open and his cock exposed to the air, an invitation to anyone who wanted a suck, but he couldn't lift his arms to put it away. And anyway, sometimes a rich faggot wanted to see what a young cock looked like again and they paid him money, not a lot, but enough and sometimes he came and sometimes he didn't and they would get pissy when he didn't, but really, if they saw what he saw, bald, fat faggots who had turned half-woman could they come? He thought he felt a sensation through his fingertips, but it passed and his hand lay limp. The thumbsucker in the dirty bra stirred and opened her eyes momentarily. She either asked him if he felt alright or if he knew whether or not all the heroin had been used. He couldn't be sure because the words sounded like they had been spoken underwater, and since he couldn't move his jaw to work out a response the question didn't much matter. She sat up and looked at his exposed cock and started laughing. She flicked it with a forefinger and it jumped.

"I think this one might be dead," she said to no one in particular because no one was listening.

Glover lost consciousness as the girl's ear floated briefly before him and then faded to black.

Jack finished replacing the rotting siding and primed it with four different half cans of mediocre primer that he had carried in the back of his truck for over a year. Anne Marie and he couldn't agree on a color and wouldn't agree through the winter and halfway through the next summer when Jack finally prevailed, when he painted the house a color closest to the color of a field of wheat stretching past the horizon and he painted the trim a color that looked something like a steaming heap of compost. So, once the primer had been applied he knew they would stay at loggerheads for the foreseeable future. Jack turned his attention to the plumbing. He sorted through the pile of pipe he had stolen from the neighborhood houses, reordering the work Wood had done, and, working from the basement, erected lines up to the kitchen and the bathrooms on the first and second floors. Originally, he had planned to convert the small bedroom where Ellen lay into a large bathroom with a Jacuzzi and walk-in shower erected in tile, but since she had been gaining weight and her color had improved and she had begun talking about taking a walk around the block as long as there were no dogs on the loose, he figured the bedroom would be occupied for the time being, and he wouldn't get caught up in another flight of fancy, like the turret, when so many other basic repairs needed to be done.

He finished the plumbing in two days and it would have been quicker had Wood been of use. He had slid back to daydreaming and loafing as he obviously thought about everything except the here and now. Jack would bark an order to him that would sail past his ears, bounce off a wall and come back to Jack unheard and therefore not acted upon. Jack felt the anger build inside of him and he wanted to tear into Wood for his stupidity and inattention, but he checked himself and picked up the tool or the length of pipe himself. Screaming at Wood would throw off his concentration and delay the work. Arguing with Wood seemed useless because the boy had slipped too far for training and he would probably never be employable in an honest vocation. Jack felt a little sheepish that the plumbing had only taken two days with just him working, because he had made Anne Marie and a pregnant Estonia trudge out to the shitter and defecate on top of a corpse, not to mention making them carry bedpans that Ellen filled on a regular basis down the stairs and through the house and yard. Incredibly, they had been able to keep the project moving forward given his obvious lack of sense and proper planning, let alone his lack of understanding that the difference between sacrificing creature comforts for the good of all and downright insensitivity to discomfort. If they ever wondered how long he would make them shit on a corpse they didn't ask, much to their enduring credit, but shame on him for not thinking of the question first. Of course, the mock guilt glossed over the fact that when he completed the plumbing, when their showers worked, there would be no reason for him to see Mary Kelly and that may have been a contributing factor in how he had scheduled the work.

Jack followed the plumbing with rebuilding both bathrooms. The upstairs bathroom was too small for a Jacuzzi and the old iron claw foot tub had held up under extreme conditions that included urine, several winters, rodent nests, vomit, 30,000 baths, and diesel fuel. He had Wood scrub the tub for two days as he hung drywall, taped and mudded the walls, and sanded and feathered on a topcoat. He let Anne Marie pick the paint color with no resistance to make up for their disagreement on the exterior color and she picked a deep lavender that immediately lent a feminine touch to the house. After painting he set a new floor with slate tiles he had found one day sitting next to a dumpster behind a strip mall. Whoever put them there knew they were too expensive to throw away so they put them next to the dumpster in hopes someone could use them. He set the toilet and sink and connected the plumbing. Then, he retrieved a long metal pole with a claw on the end that he had carried with him for decades and located the water shut off valve in his front yard. He turned on the water by plunging the pole into the ground, ramming it down a narrow pipe until the claw caught the valve ten feet below ground. He gave it four turns and water rushed toward the house. The water first ran black, then brown, then red, then yellow, then finally clear. He connected his hot water tank, but they still had no hot water because he had not yet had the natural gas turned back on. The house had been heated with steam, but the boiler had been dissected and the movable parts sold for scrap even before the Nazis took up residence. Fortunately, most of the radiators had been left. Jack hadn't come up with a plan on how to replace the nonfunctioning boiler because it would have to be new or reconditioned and set in place by a crew who he would have to pay because stealing something that large and humping it down the stairs with just Wood could not be done. A new boiler would cost him at least five thousand dollars, maybe three thousand for a reconditioned one, and he didn't have enough cash even with the copper money, unless he wanted to spend everything except the loose change in his pocket, which would have been fine unless somebody wanted dinner the following evening after the boiler had been purchased. Jack would have survived the winter by burning scrap wood in the fireplace and shutting off all but the essential rooms until the cold broke, but with Ellen and Estonia and a baby coming he had to adjust his thinking again. He said to Wood that he didn't know how they would have heat in the winter and that winter could start any day given the fickleness of Ohio weather. Wood asked him what he talked about and Jack explained that a crew of salvagers had hit the house before he bought it and had ripped out the essential parts of the boiler and they needed a boiler to create steam. Wood asked how much a new one cost and shrugged his shoulders when Jack told him the figure. He expected the price to be much more and said that five thousand could be easily found. Jack expected he knew where Wood would look and he shook him off saying that he wouldn't get in involved in that sector of the economy.

"I'm not talking about selling Jack. I'm talking about taking. It won't be copper prices either."

Jack shook his head and said he wouldn't steal from a drug dealer for a boiler and he wouldn't ask Wood to either. He may be crazy, but nowhere in his craziness lay a death wish, so they could just drop this idea before speaking more about it, Jack told Wood. Wood dropped the conversation, but he had been given an idea on how to fuck up 365 Everyday's operation that she had taken from him. No one individual saw five thousand except her and she held the money only briefly before she turned it over to Hare, who acted as one of Montenegro's lieutenants and who had personally recruited Wood into the organization. Wood figured several levels existed between Hare and Montenegro, but he could never guess who they were or how many levels there might be. Hare had a dead eye that had never been replaced with glass and it stared with a dime-size pupil and a cloudy iris. Wood swore that even though the eye never moved that Hare could see out of it, like a smaller eye hiding behind the dead one. If he killed Hare, and he questioned if he could take him out successfully even with a gun because the eye could be mesmerizing and the small eye probably saw more and had sharper focus than a regular eye, he might set in motion punishment from the top directed at 365 Everyday for not securing her territory the way the organization expected. He knew if Hare saw him first he would attempt to kill him on the spot, because he knew the story of 365 Everyday's coup and Wood's humiliation, so Wood no longer had standing and could only be trying to start a shitstorm by approaching his recruiter and ex-supervisor. So, Wood planned an ambush and he decided against using a gun because if he pointed it at Hare he would have to use it. He had never killed or even shot anyone before and he didn't think he would be able to look into that dead eye and pull the trigger. He settled on an iron pipe he found among Jack's possessions, small enough to carry and heavy enough to crack open a skull. He guessed he could approach Hare from behind and smack him on the head before the eye had a chance to paralyze him. Hare always carried rolls of cash and a Glock 22 and in his apartment there would be more cash, weapons and product. Hare had let Wood come in one time and stand at the threshold while he sorted through Wood's delivery and Wood remembered a flat screen TV the size of a small movie screen, a woman in hot pants snorting coke off of a kitchen counter, and a dead cactus sitting in the corner that had deflated and lay down over the edges of the pot. Hare told him to stay by the door and disappeared into an unseen room. The woman never acknowledged Wood and after she had plowed through a thick line she grabbed the counter and leaned heavily forward. Wood thought she might topple over, but she held on and began to mangle a song in a guttural voice that sounded like an engine of a backhoe. Hare returned and gave Wood a bag of crack made up of three hundred individual bags each containing a rock and told him again never to show up at his apartment. Hare would find him when he needed him and not the other way around. He sounded too paranoid not to be sitting on a huge stash of something, so Wood filed away the information and recalled it when Jack told him about the boiler. The old man had saved his life and knew nothing of what 365 Everyday had done to him, so he deserved something in return like a fistful of drug money or a cache of rifles he could pawn or trade for a boiler.

Wood used the skills he learned stealing copper and kicked in a basement window of the house where Hare lived. He lived on the second floor of an up and down double. Wood hoped there would be an internal staircase from the basement to the second floor, but both apartments shared the basement and the staircase leading to both ended in a locked door. Wood returned to the basement, but found nothing down there except rat traps with a residue of peanut butter the rats had all but licked off without springing the traps closed, a ten-speed bicycle with two flat tires and a washer and dryer. Hare dressed in ironed and creased clothes that always looked uncomfortable, but Wood couldn't see him washing his own clothes or, if he did his own laundry, how long it would be before he came to the basement to wash a load since Wood had never seen Hare wear the same thing twice. He couldn't wait down in the basement with the rats for a week in the hope that Hare needed clean underwear, so he walked up the stairs and tried Hare's back door again. Hare had replaced the old wooden door with a steel security door, the jambs had been reinforced with steel plating and a thick deadbolt had been set, so the entrance to get in would be to hack a hole in the wall and bypass the deadbolt altogether.

Sometimes, though, luck plays a much greater role than planning, because as Wood inspected the door and prepared to retreat back to Jack's house, the back door opened and Hare took a step out, looking at his keys in his hand and carrying a messenger bag over his shoulder. Wood jumped back and Hare looked up because of the scrape of Wood's shoe and the disturbance of air around him. Wood raised the pipe over his head and brought it down hard. The pipe grazed Hare's head, catching the top flap of his ear and bending it double on its way to landing against his collarbone. Hare lurched forward and dropped the bag at his feet and Wood followed with a blow across the bleeding ear and his cheek. Hare raised his arms in front of him, but Wood stood in the periphery of the dead eye and Hare never saw the third blow that caught him across the forehead. He crumpled to the landing. Wood dragged him into the apartment and closed the door behind him. He searched the bag and found a laptop, cell phone and a handful of bills with stamps neatly placed in the corners of the envelopes. The Glock 22 rested inside his jacket pocket and Wood pulled it out and stuffed it into the bag next to the laptop. He searched the apartment and found two more handguns, a Beretta 9mm and a Smith and Wesson Model 29 .44 magnum, a pile of cash the size of two bricks in the freezer inside a box for a family-sized fried chicken frozen dinner, a few hundred rocks of crack inside a lunchbox with a *Transformers* theme with the shipment date written in marker on the outside, a kind of expiration date for all the health-minded crackheads, and a new cactus sitting in the same position where the old one had died. Wood tried to feel Hare's pulse, but he had no idea what a pulse should feel like and he never found anything resembling a steady beat. He then held up his fingers to Hare's mouth and thought he could feel faint breath sliding across his fingertips. He imagined the dead eye opening and hypnotizing him, ordering him to turn over so Hare could jam the Glock up his asshole and fire a bullet through his intestines. He retrieved the Glock and fired two bullets into Hare's head and if he could tell anything by the way the body jerked he had certainly been alive before the bullets tore through his brain. Wood picked up the messenger bag and left the apartment before seeing the blood really start pouring and cursed himself when he realized he had forgotten the keys to Hare's one year old Jeep Grand Cherokee sitting in the driveway of the house. He slung the bag, loaded with the guns, drugs and money, over his shoulder and made his way back to Jack's house. He went to his room, ignoring a shout from Jack to come help him, and shut the door. He counted the money and the little rocks of crack and tallied that he had taken $12,794 and 192 rocks. The money probably all came from 365 Everday and her crew and the drugs were probably going back to her.

He gave all the money to Jack, handing him the brick of cash as he grouted the bathroom tile.

"Where'd you get this?"

"From a little bunny."

"Bunny as in whore? They don't carry this kind of cash."

"This bunny he owed me. He ain't no whore no more."

Jack stared at the cash in his hand and knew that it had been taken from somewhere in the drug distribution network that plagued the neighborhood so deeply he sometimes wondered if neighbors sold to each other just to keep the same cash passing from hand to hand. Jack peeled off $6,000 to cover the boiler and Wood's room and board and gave the rest back to him.

"If you give it to me it'll just go into this goddamn house. You might need it for something else if someone comes looking for this." Jack shook the bills in the air. "Those motherfuckers aren't going to be happy to see their money converted into a boiler. I'd like to see them try to carry one of those fuckers out of here. I'd like to see them try to walk over me to get to it. I appreciate the effort Wood, I sincerely do, but I don't believe this is over by a long shot."

"He ain't coming. Nobody coming here for the money."

Wood kept the drugs and that night he sat in the dark backyard after everyone had gone to sleep and smoked a rock under a sky with no stars and no moon. As he blew the last of the smoke he had convinced himself that he wouldn't find peace until he had taken back what had been his and that meant killing 365 Everyday. Killing Hare had been easier than he thought and maybe he had been a quiz to get prepared for the real test. She had taken something from him more valuable than his life. She knew he wouldn't be able to tolerate the laughing, the banishment and the disrespect. She knew he would come back someday because what other reason did she have to keep him alive? He couldn't return the favor, because raping 365 Everyday, even in the ass, even with 36 guys, even with a bottle or a broomstick would be futile because the holes of devils are forever enticing and ever expanding and they couldn't be harmed or ripped. Once he started fucking her she would set off a powerful magnetic pull and he would be sucked into her cunt or her asshole inch by inch until darkness enveloped him. He would live inside her with her other victims and every time some new stud decided to challenge the devil the trapped and imprisoned would run for cover as a dick burst over their heads, thrusting and pounding until the horrible whirring of the magnetic pull began and they would watch her cunt walls close around the quarry and soon the dick would shrink and shrivel and a small confused man, naked or with his pants down by his ankles, would fall to the cunt floor and take his place among the other victims. He would kill her instead, shoot her in the head using the lightweight Glock and with a couple of squeezes of the trigger he would release all of the victims from her cunt, a thousand men and probably a few women, shrunken and moist with sensitive eyes from having lived in deep twilight since their ensnarement. They would be his new army, loyal to him because he saved them from the devil's cunt.

He slept in the next morning and dressed leisurely, knowing that 365 Everyday and her crew would have slept late too. Before he left he knocked on Estonia's door and she told him to go away so he knocked again and kept knocking until she said whoever the fuck knocked on the door could come the fuck in. She still lay in bed, on her side with a pillow between her knees. She wore a bra and panties that looked like they had shrunk six sizes in relation to her swollen body. She lifted a hand from her eyes and saw Wood standing in the doorway and half-apologized, saying she thought Jack had been trying to get her up to work. Wood asked her if she felt alright and Estonia told him she felt good five minutes out of every hour, which had improved from the early days of the pregnancy. It took Wood a few moments to do the math and when he finished the calculation he understood her sarcasm. He chuckled too late, so late that Estonia cast a glance toward him and wondered if he was making a joke of her body. He dropped the smile when he noticed her reaction, confused about whether she had meant the math to be a joke. Hesitantly, he held out Jack's silver mirror he had found in the road when he first met him and told Estonia that he would like her to have it. She fingered a small dent along the top ridge and ran her hand over the whole of the mirror. Even though the glass had been broken, the mirror looked beautiful and heavy and the designs so delicate she felt like she held a mirror wrapped in silver lace. He gave her the remaining cash he had stolen from Hare, $6,794. She laid down the mirror beside her thigh and held the cash cupped in both hands like Wood had ladled two large scoops of melting ice cream into her palms.

"Jack wouldn't take it. He think only about himself and this goddamn house. He didn't think about taking it for you or the baby."

"Why are you giving me this? Are you leaving?"

"I have some unfinished business that I got to do. If it works I won't be coming back and if it don't work then I'm definitely not coming back."

Estonia asked the obvious question hanging between both possibilities, whether Wood could see a scenario where he came back to the house or just stayed at the house and forgot his unfinished business.

"No, I ain't letting that go. I got to go do it. There ain't no choice." Wood thought about telling Estonia the story of his humiliation to make her understand his motives, but he couldn't humiliate himself again in front of a pretty girl.

"I think it's better just to forget the past, especially when it's all fucked up. There's plenty of people out there that don't know anything about your unfinished business, like me or Jack."

"I'm not letting it go, no way."

"Then why didn't you just say you're leaving the house and you're saying goodbye?" She turned over and dropped the cash to the floor. She pulled off her panties and positioned herself on her hands and knees. "Since you're leaving the least you can do is give me a nice slow fuck because God knows when the next time I might have the opportunity."

"I don't usually fuck sick, pregnant girls."

"I'm not that sick, anymore. I can still fuck and I guess the best thing is that I can't get pregnant."

So, Wood fucked her from behind until she ground her face into her pillow and came. He lasted longer than usual because he worried his dick thrust too close to the baby's head or much like the trapped men inside 365 Everyday's cunt the baby had opened his eyes and watched his thrusting dick with a mixture of fear and revulsion. He started to pull out when he felt himself about to come, but he remembered the baby so he came inside her. He wondered if he had given the poor baby a shower. The baby would remember and loathe him when she came into the light. She would search her attendants for the bastard who came in her face and made her lose her innocence before she had a chance to take her first breath. They broke apart and Estonia pulled on her panties.

"We should have done more of that," Estonia said through a half-smile.

"You were puking most of the time."

Estonia admitted that might be a turn-off, more than her puffed up body, more than the acne of her chin, more than her belly button that now actually looked like a button holding her stomach together, more than her swollen breasts that now resembled pendulums, more than her brittle hair that sometimes fell out at her touch, more than her foul smelling burps that sometimes erupted without warning and burned her esophagus all day and more than her crippling depression that had driven her to bed and made her feel like someone slowly crushed her throat as someone else sat on her chest to ensure that any air that had been able to pass her constricted throat could not enter her lungs. She gave Wood's penis one last squeeze and told him good luck with his business, essentially telling him to get lost so she could get back to her sickness and sleep. She put the money and the mirror in a pile near the edge of the mattress, put the pillow back between her knees and closed her eyes to Wood's exit. Wood pulled on his pants and left the room with a stray thought that it had been unfortunate Glover had impregnated her before he had a chance to come inside because he liked the idea of a piece of him being passed along and growing long after he died.

He took the Glock and the Beretta 9mm because they were more compact and lighter than the Smith and Wesson .44 magnum, which felt akin to a cannon. Hare probably bought the .44 as an homage to all those Dirty Harry movies he watched on his flatscreen, because he liked to think of himself as extraordinary and in control. He stuck the guns in the pockets of his jacket and held the handles as he walked so they wouldn't fall out. He walked down Jack's street, turned left, right and then again left and he found the road to the projects. The sun blanched the sky of color. Light came from everywhere and eliminated shadows. Wood glowed as his skin shone with a thousand tiny reflections, blazing with heatless fire. Somebody would probably recognize him and call 365 Everyday and tell her that her assassin had come for her. Once he stepped on the project lawn he would shoot anyone he saw because either they had been sent to stop him or they were too stupid to understand why he had come back and they needed to be shot for exhibiting willful ignorance. No one was out, not even kids. Most of the air conditioners in the apartments had broken long ago so everyone should be out trying to find shade on the treeless lawn. Wood thought of the old people too frail or too afraid to leave their apartments, silently sweltering in their fetid ovens. He stood against the building where he had been raised and thought about going to see his mother, but she had sided with 365 Everyday and had accepted his expulsion and never came looking for him or cared whether he had lived or died. What Wood couldn't have known was that his mother had called the morgue and asked if an unidentified young man had been brought in, and when she had been told they currently had two such dead young men yet unclaimed from the week's violence she took a bus to University Circle to the coroner's office, riding the whole way with her heart in her throat, and she viewed two beauties in their refrigerated compartments and thankfully neither one of them she recognized as Wood, although the violence had made the identification hard to decipher. She lied to Sheila (365 Everyday) and told her she had a job interview at one of the hospitals and Sheila asked why she wanted to work when they had all the money they would need. Their mother sighed in response because she couldn't tell Sheila that she would be the queen for no more than six months when some kid who she thinks can't keep his hands off his pecker long enough to wipe his nose will come up behind her and shoot her in the skull. She couldn't tell Sheila this very obvious fact gleaned from three decades of close observation of the projects, because her sweet daughter had gone insane from knowing nothing but drugs and violence. Delonte (Wood) had retained a certain sweetness to him even when he became a thug.

Wood figured he would have time after he killed 365 Everyday to reconcile with his mother or extract a price for her turning her back on him and aligning with 365 Everyday. He crept around the corner of the building and spied a barren courtyard trapped inside the looming hulks of three other buildings. In the opposite corner 365 Everyday sat on a folding lawn chair. Beside her smoked a flimsy charcoal grill and even from across the courtyard Wood could smell charred hamburger. Goldfish and DNA boxed each other with their shirts off and Nine Points and Little Keys played basketball without a hoop, a game where Nine Points dribbled the ball on the uneven sidewalk and Little Keys tried to play defense and steal it. Nine Points had huge hands, quick reflexes and stood a foot taller than Little Keys so he could back him down at will. A couple of girls, whores who 365 Everyday let hang around to keep the boys happy because as a general rule she hated females who she wasn't fucking, sat against the wall of the nearest building with Blizzard, out of Wood's direct view. Nobody seemed to be tending the meat as it burned on the grill. Wood could have crept around the perimeter of the buildings and had a chance to come up behind and fire before they knew what hit them, but that tactic wouldn't help him regain his territory and dignity. He'd be known as the sneak who got off a lucky shot and nobody would follow him because nobody follows sneaks. Instead, he held both guns in his pockets and walked across the courtyard towards the group. 365 Everyday saw him first when he was twenty yards away and recognized him at twelve, just as he pulled the Glock out of his pocket and aimed it at her as he continued to walk straight toward her. The first shot tore off her index and middle fingers of her right hand as she held it up to signal to Wood to stop walking towards her and to get the fuck off the property. The second shot split her right ear and she would have placed her right hand over the dangling and burning cartilage had the pain allowed her to lift her hand. Wood fired the Beretta at will, but aiming and shooting with his left hand resulted in eight wild shots or various angles and heights. Only one bullet found a home in the ear of DNA who collapsed with a scream. The rest of the group dove to the ground and shouted, except Blizzard who had a hand down the pants and up the shirt of one of the whores and who had just decided to take both of them back to his mother's apartment and fuck them both because his mother was at work as a nurse's assistant at one of the downtown hospitals and he needed a good fuck to keep his mind clear of wanting 365 Everyday, which everyone knew not to do. Blizzard's position against the wall in the shadow and behind the whores shielded him from Wood as he walked closer, so Wood never saw Blizzard scramble to his knees, pick up his Smith and Wesson Model 10 Military and Police Revolver, an old service revolver once worn but never shot outside the firing range in a twenty-five year career of a suburban cop, aim and fire a shot at his head. The bullet entered his neck just below the chin and splintered his C-2 vertebrae after passing through the esophagus. Woods staggered backwards and died on his back in the dirt. His third shot from his right hand from the Glock blasted away one of the legs of the charcoal grill, sending it toppling over and spilling meat and coals onto the ground. The group scattered, the whores ran as fast as their impractically heeled shoes could take them, Goldfish crouched over DNA and pressed his fingers over the wound but the blood poured to the ground as he gagged and choked. Goldfish wept and could think of nothing else to do. Nine Points and Little Keys found their basketball and ran back to their apartments. Blizzard found and picked up 365 Everyday's fingers, the two larger pieces he could find and held them in his hand the whole way to the hospital as he drove the truck his uncle in Alabama had given him as a way to secure some honest work. 365 Everyday held her hand against her belly and forgot that her ear could fall off onto the truck seat at any moment because she realized then who her next challenger would be as word spread of Blizzard's shot with a hand that smelled like a whore's cunt, that he carried her ruined fingers in the palm of his hand all the way to the hospital without flinching or puking, and that as she sat frozen as her brother shot her up he killed Wood with a gun he thought to keep close. They also wouldn't forget that she had kept Wood alive and her own stupidity had cost her two fingers and an ear. Blizzard was soft and loyal to a fault and he could be dispatched without much trouble or fight. She figured his uncle in Alabama would want his truck back once she has finished with Blizzard, bloodstains and all.

Estonia sat on the edge of the mattress and wished Wood had stayed so he could fuck her again. She had pushed sex out of her mind for months because of her nausea, her grief over the loss of her tight girl's body, and her black, bottomless anger towards Glover, but Wood's dick had cracked the dam so that on top of all of her other troubles she craved another fuck with no boy in sight, at least until she deflated and her acne cleared up. She dressed as she stared out of the window. Anne Marie had collected a suitcase full of maternity clothes from various sources without much acknowledgement to fashion, trends, or the decade in which they now lived, but at least the clothes hung loose and expanded with her. She picked up the money and the mirror and thought about giving the money to Jack or Anne Marie, but Wood said Jack had refused it and Anne Marie would turn around and try to give it to Jack as well, so she decided to keep it until Wood returned and give it back to him or she would keep it for the baby and buy some new clothes, not hand-me-downs, and a new crib where she could sleep, and new toys probably, once she figured out what toys she would like. She started to cry over Wood's generosity and she would have given him a blow job had he been there. Maybe his generosity could have been the start of something between them. Maybe he could have filled a gaping hole in her life and given her some comfort and company, company other than that provided by the three ancients, the term she used for Jack, Anne Marie and the crazy lady. She walked out of the room and down the stairs and Jack almost ran her down as he came up the stairs with a bucket filled with fresh grout.

"You get any bigger and I'll either have to put in another staircase or I'll install an elevator," Jack said as he squeezed past her.

She told him to fuck off and became flushed in the face when he told her to watch her mouth. She felt a pulse of black anger surge through her limbs and she told him to expect far worse to come out of her mouth if he continued commenting on the state of her once perfect body. Jack backed down and apologized for the comment, but Estonia's anger wouldn't subside so quickly, so when Jack asked her if she had seen Wood she told him the story about the mirror and the money and that Wood acted like he would not be coming back to the house. She had planned not to tell Jack about the money, because he had already refused it and because she needed it for the baby or the mirror because Wood had told her it had fallen off the back of Jack's truck and Wood had saved it and given it to her. The story came out like a scolding lecture with no lesson. Jack set the bucket down and asked to see the mirror. He followed Estonia into her room.

"This used to be my mother's. There was a matching comb and brush, but those have been lost over the years. I think this was the last of the things I had from her. You lose them over time until there is nothing. Then you pass along your stuff that will be lost over the years until there is nothing left of you and even the last people who hold your memory will be gone. I maybe have another ninety years on the planet. Maybe that baby of yours will remember me, maybe he'll have some ancient hammer or saw and think how it used to be old Jack's and how Jack used to play with him when he was a little boy. I dropped it on the street? The comb, the brush and the mirror all sat in a row on my mother's dressing table, which had this thick oval mirror and she would sit in front of it and brush her hair for what seemed like hours to a kid. Sometimes I would sit next to her, far enough away to watch her elbows move, and watch her in the big oval mirror. She was very pretty, probably as pretty as you without the Basque coloring, and she only wore make-up once or twice as I can remember to go to a wedding of a rich cousin's kid or to go to an anniversary dinner at the best restaurant in town. She would hold this mirror close to her face and inspect her skin. She was merciless about her appearance, but I think she marveled at her skin's elasticity and its ability to hold up to the pressure of gravity. She remained pretty throughout her life and she used this mirror even when she went into a nursing home for the last year. I can imagine her face and what she would have said to me had she known I dropped it into the street."

"You can have it back."

"No, I'll fix it properly. I'll take the dent out of it and get a glass that fits and isn't taped on. It's yours. It belongs in the realm of pretty women. I don't look at my skin. She'd like to know that it's getting use, especially by someone as pretty as you, even though you're getting bigger than this fucking house."

"Do I have to tell you to fuck off twice in the same conversation?"

"I think you just did."

"And just when I thought you had this sweet, gooey center and you might be a human being after all."

"You wouldn't be the first to make that mistake. Did Wood say where he was going?"

"That he had business, that's all."

Jack washed his hands and forearms slowly and methodically. He walked to his truck and knew that the bucket of grout would be ruined by the time he got back, but sometimes circumstances presented themselves that demanded he act in a human fashion. He hadn't much hope of stopping Wood from acting out his foolishness, but if there may be a chance at an intervention he had to give it a try. He drove to the projects and arrived moments after the ambulances. He considered rolling by, seeing what he could see from the truck, and returning home, but he couldn't see anything past the first buildings by the street. So he parked and walked down the broken sidewalk between two buildings and into the courtyard. Two paramedics with a stretcher, three cops and an elderly lady stood over Wood's body. Another grouping stood over DNA. No one else had come out of the apartments. The cops watched Jack approach as the paramedics pulled the sheet over Wood's face. By the time he hobbled to the body all six people were watching him.

"You must be lost," a cop said with his arms folded across his chest.

"No, not lost," Jack mumbled.

"Did you lose this?" The cop pointed to the body.

"Let me see."

The paramedics each took a corner and folded down the sheet, exposing Wood's face and shredded neck.

"His name is Wood, don't know what his real name is. He lives in the projects here. He was doing some remodeling work for me and he didn't show up today, which was unlike him, so I came to see if anything happened."

"Something happened," the first cop said and Jack figured he must outrank the others or he had the biggest mouth. "As you can see."

They asked him forty questions and wouldn't let him leave for over an hour, because he had become their only lead and the only person they could find willing to talk. The elderly lady happened to be returning from working at her church when she saw the flashing lights and the police and she stopped to ask them what had happened. Everyone else in the apartments facing the courtyard either were not at home or feigned a late afternoon somnambulance when questioned if they had heard or seen anything of the murder. Jack ended by giving his name and address and the paramedics asked him if he would claim the body if no one else came forward. Jack said he would if no one came forward. 365 Everyday had already called Goldfish with her intact hand and told him to spread the word that Wood's body had to be left to rot on the ground, but 365 Everyday didn't know about DNA lying dead on the ground too and that somebody had panicked and called 911 before her command had spread. Not even his mother would be likely to bury the corpse or have it cremated.

Anne Marie made arrangements to have the body taken to a crematorium and she paid for the cremation out of her own money. In a couple of weeks they received a package in the mail that contained Wood's ashes. The remains rested inside a thick plastic bag inside a cardboard box with a mailing label on the outside. Estonia picked it up from the porch and when she realized what she held in her hand she almost dropped it on the floor. She started laughing with a trace of hysteria and fear as she imagined the afterlife run by the post office. She saw family members writing the addresses where they wanted to send the deceased and waving goodbye to them as men in blue shirts and pith helmets came to fetch them. Those families bearing a grudge could write 'hell' on the package or if the deceased hated the cold they could send them to the Yukon Territory or the top of K-2. The dead who led exemplary lives and spread love and peace could be sent to bleach in the sun of a beach or they could lie on the roadways of Provence or Florence. Poor Wood never made it out of the city of his birth, living in the residue of once smoky skies.

Jack went back to the projects and found Wood's mother. She talked to him through a half-opened door and kept asking Jack to lower his voice. He told her he had her son's ashes and he showed her the box. She began to weep and told Jack through the sobs that she didn't have a son and that she only had a daughter. She repeated several times that she only had a daughter. Jack asked her if Wood had liked the water, either the lake or river, and she told him she couldn't remember him ever talking about water and that he may have never been to the beach. Jack held out the box one more time in hopes that she would take it and stand up to whoever blocked her from acknowledging the boy, but she started to cry again and kissed the box so that both tears and ruby red lipstick imprinted on the cardboard. Jack thought of burying the box in the courtyard of the projects since Wood had died fighting over control of its dirt and weeds, but the government kept mulling over the idea of ripping down the buildings and replacing them with new apartments that weren't infused with lead paint and asbestos and didn't resemble prison blocks. The new designs at least reflected the new prison architecture with contrasting brick inlay and mansard roofs with faux patina and not 70s era brutalism that made the residents feel like they were living inside a rote math equation. Jack didn't want to plant Wood just to have him dug up and carted to a landfill or crushed underneath the wheels of a backhoe.

He returned home with the box and Estonia, Anne Marie and he squeezed into the truck and drove to the edge of the river. Jack peeled back a chain link fence and they followed a narrow path through the weeds to a rusty bulkhead. They stood on the edge for a moment and watched the churning water cut past the skyscrapers on the other side. Jack felt the weight of the box in his hand and calculated how far he could throw it into the river so that the current might have a chance to sweep it into the lake and Wood wouldn't end up bobbing in the scum on the river's edge. Anne Marie said it would be more fitting if they emptied the ashes into the water and not have Wood be inside a plastic bag for all eternity or until the bag burst which very likely could be another millennium or so. Jack had envisioned the box floating, but Anne Marie had been right, since bone chips and very little air filled the box, it would sink straight to the bottom and lay in silt and heavy metals poured into the river over the last two hundred years. So Jack ripped off the cardboard and unwound the top of the bag. It had been tightly closed with a twisty and his swollen and sore fingers no longer had the dexterity to unwrap the ends so he handed it over to Anne Marie. She untied it carefully and handed the bag back to Jack with the top open. She asked Jack to say a few words and Jack could think of nothing to say but that he felt sorry, sorry that Wood had died fighting over a scrap of grass poisoned for decades by toxic rain and the footprints of drug dealers, sorry that his mother would not be at the river to say goodbye to his bagful of remains, sorry that he hadn't shown Wood the path out of the ghetto, out of prison, out of an early, stupid death, out of the limited constructs that had trapped his mind and had given him no other alternatives, and finally sorry that the three of them didn't know whether or not he liked the water or if preferred a small hole under a broad, leafy oak that overlooked a small valley or a pasture or if he would have preferred to have been poured down the throat of his killer so that he could choke him and rip him from the inside out.

Jack leaned over the river and poured the bone chips and ash into the water. Some landed on the bulkhead and on Jack's shoes, but the majority made it to the water. Jack assured Wood that the river emptied into Lake Erie and that the lake poured into Lake Ontario and that he would have a choice of floating through the Welland Canal, a man-made shipping lane or floating down the Niagara River and going over the falls except he wouldn't need a barrel or a life preserver and the roar of the water wouldn't frighten him and the cold wouldn't make him shiver. Given the chance he should choose the Niagara because the chance of picking up oil and gasoline in the Welland seemed pretty great given the industrial nature of the canal. Then, he would be on to Ontario and the St. Lawrence Seaway and eventually the Atlantic Ocean where he would become part of the brine and he could forget his little patch of toxic grass and consider himself a citizen of the world. Or he could go the other way and drift into Michigan, Huron and Superior and float for an eternity, and even though he wouldn't become brine he could become the silt on the bottom of the lake floors which contained the entire history of man's walk on the earth since the glaciers had melted. Either way the ashes floated would be an improvement over the projects, of that Jack could be sure.

White Witch

Sterling Hayes knocked on the door of a duplex and thought he recognized the house but couldn't think why he would remember it. Brankowski thumped down the stairs and unlocked the door. He held an open beer and handed it to Hayes even before he crossed the threshold. Out of uniform, Brankowski looked stronger and more intimidating, as an observer expected the toughness in the uniform, but out of it his strength seemed misplaced and out of proportion to everyday life. Hayes took the beer and asked why he already recognized Brankowski's new apartment. Brankowski laughed his 'figure it out yourself, fucker' laugh and bounded up the stairs in a linebacker lurch. When Hayes stepped on the top landing and saw a sticker for an obscure rock band on the door and a "Don't come a knocking if the house is a rocking" sign hung on a nail below the sticker, he remembered the apartment as belonging to the kid who had disappeared from the lumberyard. Brankowski and he had come over to the house to interview the landlady who called in the missing persons' report. They had turned over the report to the detectives who promptly filed it away and forgot about the lack of leads and the lack of any relative pushing for answers. They guessed the little pudwhacker had skipped on his rent and now lived in a new city with another crappy job.

Inside the apartment, very little had changed. The rooms were filled with cheap, beaten furniture, stacks of books and magazines aligned in Doric columns against every free wall, and a dim, brown light as if all who came inside teetered on the edge of sleep or death. Brankowski had added a 54 inch flat screen TV which rose above the books and magazines like a monolith placed there for domination and surveillance and a relatively new laptop, that purred on the dusty couch.

"I'm going to start with an obvious observation, because I have been trained, I've honed my observation skills to the finest point. I've got eyes of a goddamn eagle. Yes, I'm going to start by asking if you've completely lost your mind? I'm talking full blown hallucinatory worlds with chorus lines of Jimmy Carters flapping their junk to an audience of jackals and hermaphrodites kind of crazy. Then I'm going to ask you why you so desperately want to get fired from your job as an officer of the law- a job you've performed, adequately performed, for the past sixteen years, sometimes slogging through, sometimes performing in such a manner as to make your superiors mildly pleased- because taking the kid's job at the lumberyard is one thing, a bizarre thing, but in the end just one thing, but moving into his apartment and assuming control of his possessions will, even in your carefully staged hallucinatory world, no doubt set in motion a process of discipline which very well could lead to a public flogging and a humiliating end to a sixteen year career, four short years away from a full pension and full-time pussy chasing and checker playing on a street corner of your choice. Then I'm going to finish this inquiry with the question 'what did you do with your own shit, the leather couches, the walnut bar, the pedestrian and hokey, albeit well-executed artwork of snow-capped mountains and trout streams?'"

Throughout Hayes' speech Brankowski's grin grew wider and his eyes looked like they might be filling with tears of hilarity. When Hayes had finished he stared at Brankowski as he drank half of the beer with one swig and gently set the bottle down on an end table that looked like it had caught a disease that made it shed its paint in uneven patches.

"Let me pull out the clichéd but useful phrase repeated ad nauseam by perpetrators caught and facing lengthy and violent prison terms, 'Let me explain.' Let me, Hayes, before you start believing that my insanity has been made manifest. Let me explain to you that ideas creep up on you sometimes and you're doing a thing before you even realize it."

"Which may be another definition of insanity."

"I didn't interrupt you, brother. I let you unravel the thread, so extend the same courtesy to me as well." Hayes nodded his apologies. "So, it bothered me to distraction that we answered the call to the lumberyard, gathered a fistful of clues that pointed directly to foul play- the blood on the loading dock, the missing lumber, the pudwhacker's disappearance, the missing security tape, the fingerprints on the tow motor-in blood no less- it bothered me that we turned over this bevy of leads to our crack detectives in a nicely typed report, who promptly shoved it up their asses and forgot about it. So, I get the job at night in the lumberyard to see what I could see. I found more splatter, brown and flaking by the time I found it and even though the spot had been run over a thousand times by the wheels of tow motors I could picture where our boy died in a lake of his own blood. There's other stuff too. A calendar in the shed that displays a fetish for camel toe and erect nipples behind gauzy swimsuit material where he kept his schedule and stray thoughts and the man had plans for the next two months, sad plans, plans of an undereducated cretin lurking in the shadows of society, but they were no doubt plans: a dentist appointment for a dead tooth, an oil change, a ranking of the hottest women news anchors and the times they came on television, a concert of a death metal trio, with the crowning event being a two day trip to Mountaineer Casino in West Virginia to lose the little money he had on slots or blackjack, where he would stammer his way through negotiations with a sad whore. The West Virginia trip bore no association with a plan of flight after a big heist, unless he carried the lumber or somehow figured out how to sell the load on the street for a few hundred bucks. Besides, he had to wait another four months to go."

"Have you seen the price of lumber lately? He could have got good money for it. Goddamn hurricanes and tornadoes are ripping up the country. We can't rebuild fast enough. Pretty soon they're going to take toothpicks off the shelf and rebuild houses with them."

"I've asked you not to interrupt. No doubt the price of lumber would be an interesting tangent, however, the story is already bogging down from too much exposition and not enough suspense. You throw another tangent in there and the teller and the listener are both fucked."

"Pardon. Occupational hazard."

"Hayes, sheath your clichés, you're better than that. Fuck, next you're going to work in 'the thin blue line' somewhere and I'm going to have to vomit on your shoes. Anyway, I was working there a month or so and his landlady calls. I had given her my card. She said she lost yours, but I don't remember you giving her one in the first place. The man is always conveniently out of cards."

"If you want me to keep my mouth shut you best not go on the offensive. I'm not likely to stay quiet and just take it."

"Noted. Anyway, she said her tenant hadn't returned and she needed the rent for the apartment and what did I suggest she do with all his left behind stuff. I visited her and looked over the apartment again and kind of on a whim and kind of in a lightning flash of genius I told her I would rent the apartment because I had grown uncomfortable in my old place."

"Because you fucked your next door neighbor and found out that one, she was ten years older than she said she was, two, was a jealous, raving bitch who thought her pussy had magical powers and once you touched it she could dictate your thoughts and actions and three, completely disregarding my advice about fucking neighbors you bore ahead, jumped into the flames, dove headlong into the boiling stew and had to resort to sneaking in and out of your apartment after you broke off the affair."

"Hayes, really, now my mind is on her screeching face, of her punching my door or playing Salsa music at an unbearable level when she thought I had brought home a woman, of her leaving written rants under my windshield wiper, of her showing up sobbing and naked at my door, hoping that I would confuse pity and lust or the combination of both would push me back into the stew. I've completely lost the thread of our dear little pudwhacker."

"I wanted to remind you that shit gets fucked up when you don't listen to my advice or take me into your counsel. For instance, had you called me the instant you thought of renting this apartment I could have talked you off the ledge. I could have elucidated the folly of such a course of action."

"Ok, I withdraw the complaint. I am rightfully chastised, but, of course, you haven't heard the entire story and you have no idea why I have summoned you here tonight, so once again your ADHD is clouding and obscuring your judgment, so how could you really know whether my impulsive and probably self-destructive behavior has in fact opened a line of inquiry not known or explored? In essence, I sit here bearing fruit."

"Continue"

"So, I move in. I sell my other stuff. I don't call you to see if you want the walnut bar because I know you will disapprove and I'm trying to save that bloated and yellow liver of yours. The crazy neighbor buys my water bed, if you can believe that, saying she hopes I can see her fucking men on the bed and the thoughts drive me crazy. I tell her she bought a bed, not a crystal ball, not a telepathy enhancer and decoder, not even a piece of my life because as soon as her cash touched my hand- I insisted on my price and she insisted on paying- the bed was hers and not mine and I hoped she herself participated with a throng of men on her newly acquired bed. She told me she might start using it for voodoo and she would stick a knife where she thought my dick had rested and I said if my pee started burning or the flow was cut off I would give her a call because you don't just throw away women who can control that sort of thing. Funny thing is Hayes, I've had some very explicit dreams involving her and men of every race and shape. You can't imagine what she does or for how long. The variations on a theme are staggering."

"I can imagine," Hayes interjected.

"I sold the other stuff for a fraction of what I bought it for and moved in here and started inhabiting the little pudwhacker's life. That column of magazines over there is a tree of porn. He had an interest in dominant women, craven men, maybe a little torture and a healthy dose of humiliation. He had a collection of a magazine devoted to showing fully clothed women pointing and laughing at men with little dicks. He also has a major vein of traditional ass in the air porn, buttholes exposed, nicely illuminated, toes curled. That stack over there is classic sci-fi: Bradbury, Clarke, Herbert, LeGuin, Pohl, Asimov, Clement, all in pocket paperback versions, yellowed and brittle. The smell of rotting paper was one of the first things I noticed when I started living here. Musty but comfortable, like the cells of a body slowly deteriorating. I can't tell if he read them, but he owned them for some reason. That stack is nothing but baseball, a couple of biographies but mostly statistics and player profiles dating back in the early 1900s. That stack is all about mechanical engineering, that stack is birds of the world, that stack is more porn but shot in black and white with less rigid posing, meaning these women don't show their assholes and the photographer is dickless for not knowing the most interesting parts of a woman, and over there is a stack of catalogs for old toys-mostly pre-internet publications kept for God knows what reason."

"I'm sure there's a point to this cataloging of interests." Hayes tried to drink from his beer but realized he had finished it, so he rooted through Brankowski's refrigerator for another. He found the beer easily, since the only other items sharing the shelves with an opened case of beer were an unopened and outdated jar of mayonnaise, an empty milk carton and a jar of peanut butter, which of course, didn't need to be refrigerated. "Did you find anything else besides the books, which, I'm sorry to tell you Brank isn't the sharpest detective work I've seen."

"So, besides the books, which, I have to disagree, do show a certain engagement with society. There were parts he connected with. He loved to whack his pud. He obsessed over the on-base percentage of every leadoff hitter from 1930 onward, so he had his tethers to the world."

"Oh, Brank, back away from the psychology. You know not what you do."

"We know more about human behavior than any psychologist, no?" Hayes conceded the point with a bow of his head. "Anyway, downtown brought back his computer and I happened to be at home and it's a good thing I looked through the peep hole before I opened the door because two runners were standing outside."

"Did you recognize them?"

"I've seen them before. I avoided an awkward moment and possible discovery."

"Why would they bring back a computer to an apartment of a missing person?"

"Bureaucratic inefficiencies have clogged the arteries my friend. The heart suffers in silence."

"Now I have to put up with aphorisms?"

"So the computer shows up formatted, wiped clean. Those apes downtown destroyed anything that might be on it. Then, I find an old address book in his sock drawer. He obviously hadn't kept it up because there were only a few addresses penciled in and they all looked like they had been entered at the same time, like on the day he bought the book he had the intention of ordering his life and the few contacts he had and preparing for the scores of friends to come. Who knows whether he could have ever acquired friends, friends maybe who liked illuminated buttholes and who know who Ben Chapman was and what his career on-base percentage was. I did find a man, a brother, with the same last name who lives in Tucson. I called him and some foxy sounding lady answered and brought him to the phone. I wanted to ask him if he had a ten inch cock and if that was why his wife sounded like an orgasm come to life, but I asked him instead if he was related to our missing boy, presumably now a victim. He answered that, in fact, he was his brother and asked what the cocksucking faggot had done now. We weren't off to a good start. The man shared his blood, the blood that had been sprayed all over the concrete and dirt, turning black underneath the tires of tow motors. I told him who I was, why I was calling and I told him by the evidence that I had collected his brother was not a homosexual and, in fact, may have dedicated too much of his imagination to the female form, given the quantities of porn that didn't even have a dick in the composition, even as a frame of reference or to remind the consumer of the image that the reason for the model to raise her ass in the air was to invite her imaginary partner to slam her balls deep. He said that I didn't sound like a cop and I followed that up with the obvious retort 'What are cops suppose to sound like exactly?' His only answer was silence, so we let that vein of conversation drop away. Then he asked what the fuck I wanted and I told him that his dear brother was missing, that foul play may be involved, that I was doing everything I could do but a little familial pressure on the department might dislodge some resources and a more thorough official inquiry. The brother said the little faggot probably went to a gay colony to get slammed up the ass and he sounded like he had every intention of slamming down the phone, but I stopped him and asked, 'What exactly is a gay colony?' He stammered and stuttered and if he hadn't been conditioned to show some respect to cops he probably would have told me that I was the governor of the gay colony, but he decided, instead, to slam down the phone. Other than that I got nothing. All the other numbers are disconnected and there was nothing else in this goddamn apartment that points to any other entanglement or complication."

"You rip up your life, sell your shit, run away to this shithole and that's all you have?"

"Yep, the poor little fucker will be forgotten in another week. The brother is obsessed with his latent homosexuality, of which there is none that I can see. The landlady is now getting rent from me at least for the next year. The lumberyard has a new night watchman, which also happens to be me, but I'll be leaving soon and they'll hire another neb. I'll sell his porn collection or maybe I'll donate it to a library book sale, maybe I'll dump it into the collection box. Ah, I don't like that joke much. I don't want to inflict those perfectly lighted buttholes on some poor librarian trying to hold the line against chaos."

"I can't say I think much of your police work, Brank. You got nothing."

"But I didn't know that when I began."

They lapsed into silence and drank their beers, each staring at a different stack of books.

"Oh, I did find this." Brankowski walked over to the artistic porn stack and picked up a DVD in a jewel case off the top of the tower. "It was in an envelope addressed to the lumberyard owner. Our little pudwhacker must have snitched it from his office or the mail pile. He either never got a chance to look at it, forgot about it or realized he had jumped into a bottomless pool of shit by stealing the boss' mail because the unopened envelope was hidden behind the refrigerator. Actually, it was duct-taped to the back so it wouldn't slip down or show a corner. At first I thought it might be drugs, you know, why the fuck else would it be taped behind a refrigerator, but all that was inside was the DVD and a note saying, shit, I have it here." Brankowski pulled out his wallet and produced a slip a paper folded twice, either to fit inside his wallet or the jewel case. "The note just says, 'Problem solved' and when you see the DVD you'll understand of what problem the writer of the note speaks."

"Should I get another beer before we start this?" Hayes asked.

"Ya, probably…uh…nevermind, I'll let it come at you like it came at me."

Hayes walked to the kitchen and returned. He twisted off the cap and flicked it into an open mouth trash can already half-filled with beer bottles and caps. He kept hold of the bottle in his right hand. It would not stay filled for long, so why even put it down? Brankowski blew dust from the surface of the DVD and placed it in the player, returning to the couch with the remote in his hand. He aimed the remote like he would his service revolver and the screen turned blue. Both settled in on opposite ends of the musty couch.

A jagged white line starts from the bottom of the screen and dances its way to the top….blue screen, white static, blue….the hum of a motor… swirling blue streams left to right…the light is low and the picture reveals its pixels almost to the level of pointillism…the frame holds mostly steady… with a normal tremor…focus…blur…focus…asphalt glows green and yellow…squat black buildings melt around the frame…a screeching blast of noise spikes the microphone and a blot of distortion fills the room…volume is lowered and then off…a dashboard littered with crumpled cigarette packs, fast food wrappers and maps…the view swings to the left, smearing of images… closing to darkness…the light comes back up…the frame holds on a sunken-eyed boy with long black hair…he leans over the wheel and snorts coke off the webbing between this thumb and forefinger…he shakes his head…his hair flies…the boy's bony shoulder and arm…the frame bounces…traces of light create concentric circles…faded and ripped jeans…a dirt path through knee-high weeds… a chorus of birds slip by overhead…the huff of the lungs from the camera holder…a house…a cabin set off in the woods…half-heartedly maintained…a maze of rusted junk on the lawn…tires…washing machines…a crushed mailbox…a door…an abrupt edit…a flash of blue screen…a mass of tangled brown hair…the top of a head working up and down…clumsy zoom in, out…zoom in, slow, labored focus…thick soft curls…focus…abrupt manual zoom out…fleshtones…a bare belly, maybe…a smudge of a penis appearing and disappearing into the tangle of curls…eyes…stoned…girl with a thin smooth face..either she has no blemishes on her pearly skin or the cheap camera has kindly made her radiant…erect dick grazes chin… a hand shoots in from the left and smothers the lens…a painted white door…chipped and peeling…a foot rises from the bottom of the frame and kicks the door…the door bursts open…the concussion peaks the microphone…naked boy sitting on the toilet with his hand jammed between his legs like he's worried about an uncontrollable spray…he sees camera and starts laughing wildly…a large turd…coiled and half-submerged in the water…a product of gorging on fast food…zoom in until the lens catches the texture under the harsh bathroom light…montage of heads cut out of magazines lying in toilet water and being flushed...Martha Stewart...George Bush...anorexic models...senators...princes...dictators of African countries...actors and actresses...yellow walls and a brown carpet... a naked woman flops and spins in a parody of a dance... parts of her body have gone soft and have distended...too much make-up covers too much life...blue eye shadow makes her look insane or in disguise...off camera an electric guitar whines...a spoon on a trash can lid keeps the beat... the beat stops...the boy from the toilet dances in from the left...he spins her around to face him...he paws at her breasts...pours cocaine on her nipples and much of it falls to the floor...he snorts and licks off the remaining powder... he pushes her against a yellow wall...his pants fall to the floor...her legs wrap around his hips...his buttocks clench and unclench...she rises off the floor as she slides up the wall...she looks bored and preoccupied...the frame moves steadily across the room to the sunken-eyed boy couching and playing his guitar plugged into a brand new amp.

Brankowski clicked the pause button.

"I know what you are thinking, Oliver," Hayes said as he stared at the image of the frozen guitar player mid-strum.

"What am I thinking?"

"If libido number one is ramrodding the whore and this guy is providing the soundtrack then who just panned the camera?"

"A nice and steady pan too. No shake. No tremor."

"Tripod, no?"

"Noted and filed."

...the guitar player completes the downward stroke...his head jerks up and he arches his eyebrows and looks directly at the camera...he shrugs his shoulders visibly and looks back to the strings...the camera pans back to the naked couple...they bounce against the wall until it shudders...they bounce against the wall until a painting of a kitten with a ball of string falls off its hook and the frame splits apart on the floor...the couple falls to the floor...the boy is laughing...the boy reaches off camera and his hand returns holding a small bag of cocaine...the boy snorts cocaine off of her ass...the women looks tired and annoyed...he offers the woman some and she takes a furtive snort as if she knows she is opening a door that will lead to the next level of hell and she is about to ask the camera operator how many levels of hell exists or could a person keep on creating strata after strata as their humanity is completely stripped away and could these acts of destruction and creation continue ad infinitum...on the floor upside down the boy looks at the camera...he lurches up and has a hard time remaining on all fours as he squints into the camera... "Log, Log, Log"....Log finally looks up and towards Treg..."Look who is running the fucking camera"...Log comes closer...the guitar hangs from his shoulder and bounces against his hip...without betraying his intention Log slings the guitar in the air...most of the flight is off camera as it spins though the air and takes out the legs of the tripod..the frame jerks forward and spins... the camera bounces against the ground...when it stops moving it faces an

428

electrical outlet, part of a baseboard and a dirty section of wall…the broken microphone emits a deep electric tone…

The two watched the electrical outlet for five minutes before Hayes broke the meditation

"How much longer does this go on for?"

"I don't know. Another ten minutes maybe. It might be a good time to take a piss or get another beer. I find the pause useful. It lets my mind absorb some of the images that passed before. It gives me time to think what is happening off camera. Who's the cameraman? How did he react to having a guitar thrown at him? Sometimes I think movies should include segments in the narrative where the viewer is supposed to doze or meditate. What better way to entertain than to turn the audience's dreams against them?"

"I think the pudwhacker has gotten to you."

"Not enough dreams or fantasies in our lives. Just lots of people doing fucked-up shit to one another outside the realm of reason."

"Wait, don't you think most of it starts as dreams or fantasies. Stray sparks outside the reason of the law?"

"I suppose dreams include greed and stupidity."

"Christ, I have a turtlehead poking out of my sphincter. Where's the john?"

Brankowski pointed down the hall and Hayes lurched off the couch and ambled out of the room. He shut the bathroom door and sat on the toilet. The tiny room had been made smaller by having been painted black. Hayes wondered if someone at some point had used the room as a darkroom, long before the advent of immediate digital images, and he immediately conjured up images of the hardest of hardcore pornography involving animals, children and small electrical appliances. At least he had the awareness that he could think of no pictures within the realm of normalcy and that, he thought, might be where he and Brankowski differed. Hayes knew worlds existed outside the murders, accidents, drunken fights, suicides and paranoia that roared through his days like a fever dream. The counterpoint to insanity was normalcy, blandness, an electrical outlet. Brankowski had been right about the outlet. Sometimes you had to look at something and not expect it to burst into flames or shoot lightening from its slots and fry a group of partygoers until the tops of their heads smoked and their eyes burst into flames. Hayes knew these worlds existed, even though his last contact with them had been long ago, so that even though the doors to these worlds may have closed for good at least he knew the rooms still existed. Brankowki had come to believe that nothing existed beyond mayhem and all of the families who moved away to big lawns and treeless streets had escaped the torrent by dumb luck and that every one of them carried a seed with them, so that no matter where they were they remained savage and unrepentant. To Brankowski the normal world had not so much been obscured or closed as it had been laid bare and hope and belief looked like artifice and hypocrisy no matter from what angle they were viewed. Either the schism between them would grow until they couldn't function as partners or Hayes would join Brankowski and forget the worlds behind the doors ever existed, because it had become obvious to Hayes that Brankowski had no intention of returning. Suddenly his breathing became labored, difficult, and he splashed water on his face and the back of his neck. He stared into the mirror to remind his conscious mind to stay tethered to the world. He flushed the toilet for cover and slowly felt able to go back to the room.

Brankowski sat still with a steady blue light illuminating his face. Hayes fetched another beer and sat down heavily on the couch. The screen held the same shot of the electrical outlet and the same electric tone hummed.

"Can you at least hit mute? That noise feels like a worm in my brain trying to eat its way through to the other side."

"It's almost over."

"How many times have you watched this?"

"Every day since I found it."

"Which was when?"

"I might watch this every day for the rest of my life."

...the screen flickers...goes black...static rises from the bottom... daylight deep yellow seeps from the corners...brilliant greens and blues sharpen...a blonde girl with shoulder length hair in a white sundress and a big straw hat pirouettes on a gentle slope covered in a carpet of thick grass...there is something of a parody about her...you wish she existed...you wish girls still dressed like this on brilliant summer days...she spins and smiles...she is extraordinarily beautiful...you think you recognize her from a magazine... many magazines...she is so familiar, yet she is too beautiful to have been a part of your life...she turns her audience into trolls when they gaze upon her...she spins and smiles...her arms stretched toward the sun...she kicks off her shoes and, of course, her toes are delicate and white, so tender and supple it is impossible not imagine yourself kissing the half moons on her cuticles and them tasting like fresh, sweet earth...she dances in circles until she is dizzy...she wobbles and tumbles over...laughing...you fret over the grass stain on her hip...the stain feels like a tragedy...you want the scene replayed, but this time you'll be there to catch her before her hip grinds into the grass... your troll-like visage will break the spell she has cast so there is no possibility of you replaying the scene, of you ever entering the scene...she notices the camera or you and the smile fades from her face...an intrusion...a voyeur... you feel dirty and ashamed for spying on her in an unguarded moment...she had never invited you into her life...she wanted a moment alone in her pretty dress on a day when the sky revealed infinity...she jumps to her feet and runs toward the camera eye...teeth bared...her hair is suddenly wild, untamed, like white fire pouring out of her scalp...you're paralyzed as she draws near... you can smell her perfume and the closeness of her skin makes you dizzy... she is running at you to strangle you, truly and thoroughly suffocate you until you are lifeless...you are a troll and you are a voyeur living in the cool, damp shadow…away from her sun..the camera tilts and rolls…a flash of cheek and a white tooth…the blue sky…a blue eye…the green grass…the camera remains on the ground…her bare foot enters from the left and then the right and the feet walk across the screen…you feel lifeless and rejected…probably dead…you want to stand up and rush after her…watch her bare and perfect form until she disappears over the horizon or behind a copse of trees…you can't move…you are the camera…you'll have to be content with your last image of your life's collection of images being her bare heel walking away…fade to black…pink flesh tone fills the screen and a slow, excruciatingly slow zoom reveals you were watching her forehead…it is the same girl…maybe older…or wiser… or angry…you are not the same person she left lying on the ground…you are someone all together different…you want her face to lighten up… to beam…to catch joy from the air…but the light is different…diffused…gray…brown… you still feel ugly and estranged from her even though she has changed… she locks onto your eyes…defiance…she seems unable to comprehend the situation she finds herself in…she stands in the middle of a pool of mud… there are animal tracks along the muddy edge…deep tracks from cows and horses…the water is almost viscous…her legs are dirty up to her knees…mud drips from her head and her hair is no longer blonde…she looks feral with her hair matted against her skull even though the dress remains perfectly white… dazzlingly white against the brown of the mud…there is a thick hemp rope tied around her neck…the end disappears into the mud, presumably tied to a concrete block or some other kind of anchor…her jaw is set against you… even though the rope has to be uncomfortable, if not painful, against the tender skin of her neck she is not going to show her discomfort…because, after all, you are a troll… a handful of mud sails through the air and hits her in the belly…did you throw it?…the mud stains the folds of her dress and you feel something akin to exaltation seeing the pristine dress ruined…it's something different than the grass stain…the grass stain was an unfortunate blemish… an accident…the mud is of your own making…destruction…another handful flies from the right and hits her in the arm…she will not acknowledge the attacks so you step up the aggression and mud explodes from all directions until the dress is gray and soaked…hanging heavily from her shoulders…she may be taken down by the weight…you suddenly smell shit and you realize some of the missiles carried dung as the payload…her face remains clean and it looks like it is hovering unconnected to the neck or body because the rest of her blends so perfectly with the pool of mud…she unbuttons a line of buttons down the front of her dress…titillation races through you and pools in your groin…a part of you, maybe a simple majority of you doesn't want to see her nude because it seems like coercion given that she has a rope around her neck and she is anchored in a pool of mud…but why not?…when will you ever get the chance to see someone so perfect, so ideal without clothes?…women like her do not exist in the street, in grocery stores, in bowling alleys…they don't eat in restaurants…they don't drive cars…they live in hidden rooms on inaccessible continents because the flight service is limited to charters and private jets only and you have access to neither...somehow you've trapped one and since she thinks you are a troll you are free to be true to your nature... no matter how you get a glimpse of her perfect flesh it will be in line with your troll beliefs...she peels off her dress, which is no small task because it is heavy and wet...she reveals a brown, mud-colored dress underneath the once white dress...same style and fit...the same color as her filthy arms and legs...her body looks to have the same build even though she was wearing at least two layers of dress...you think she may be an onion or an artichoke...layer after the same layer...she laughs at you, of course, because she knows what you had expected, maybe a little hidden skin, and she delights in smashing your expectations...it seems to you...if she is like an onion she will continue to take off layers she will eventually vanish...you'll be left with a pile of dresses... the substance is in the layers...you decide to leave her tied to the block in the pool of manure and mud...the camera moves slowly and jerkily away from her...you are leaving...her smile wanes as she grows smaller and smaller until she and the mud pool is a tiny dot in the upper right corner of the screen...fade to black...

Brankowski hit the pause button. Hayes tore his eyes away from the screen and looked at Brankowski, who still stared at the black square.

"What the fuck was that?" asked Hayes. His skin felt alive with a colony of red ants.

"At first I thought the two jackoffs taped over a movie, but did you notice it was the same cheap digital look...same available light...same homemade feel, except instead of documenting turds they went for high concept. High goddamn concept."

"I might have preferred the electrical outlet."

"That's what I'm telling you Hayes. The shit that's in your own head just needs a vehicle to release it."

"Brank, man, I don't want your dreams on the loose. That would be like releasing a golem or a flock of vampire bats. The world is not ready for your mind, at least not in physical form."

"There wouldn't be girls in white dresses."

"No, I imagine not. Not only do I see revenge fantasies, but I'm thinking there might be buckets of gore."

"What do you know? Are you the same patrolman who questioned my police work? Yes? My technique, while unorthodox, has turned up this evidence a squad of detectives couldn't find. I'm not sure you know what's in my mind."

"I think I owe you an apology on that one."

"Apologies between us are unnecessary. You've seen the first two acts. Was the second act an explanation, a comment, a reason to show that unbelievably beautiful woman on the screen? Filler? Meandering? Are we supposed to say, 'What the fuck was that?' or 'Was that absolutely fucking necessary?' It has been edited in and it comes after fifteen minutes of an electrical plug and an electric hum. Was she a dream? A result of the meditation? Or are we supposed to be asleep and are we to let that woman in the white dress run through our dreams, influence and manipulate the images in our subconscious, meaning the electrical outlet puts you to sleep and once you're asleep the woman in the white dress comes along and plants some seed so deep in your mind it might not bloom until a week, a month, or a year later. You may think about her in the conscious world without knowing why or how she got there. You may think your actions are rational and controlled by an alert and conscious mind, but the whole time this lady is pulling the levers and strings like a puppet master and you respond to every tug and pull like it's actually you doing the thinking. Once the groundwork has been laid. Once the exposition has been developed then…we know the two kids are on a cocaine binge without much luck in attracting women…a whore and one stoned girl…but secretions are on the move in your body…you feel titillation, arousal of some sort, your blood has broken its torpor and it is prepared to take you were you think you want to go; it has made you ready and receptive to influence, but your defenses, your reason, your realism needs to be neutered, so up pops the electrical plug and you drowse, you sleep, your reason crumbles because how better to attack reason than through dreams. Call her a witch, a shaman. In any case, this DVD isn't so much about entertainment or about passing along knowledge, even with its obvious documentary techniques, this is about rewiring your brain and the witch is the electrician."

"As your partner, I need to know if you are insane."

"No, I think the witch is all about efficiency and innovation. She's repairing the crossed wires and the short circuits. You took a shit during the outlet sequence or you'd better understand."

Hayes thought of the grueling process of requesting and breaking-in a new partner, a request that would require at least four typed forms, to interviews as to the reason for the request during which Hayes would have to elucidate the irreconcilable differences, because the schism had become complete and irreconcilable, without revealing that Brankowski had lost control of his faculties, babbled on about white witches, moved into a victim's apartment, sold his belongings, took a job at an active crime scene and thereby jeopardized his job and a pension just four short years away, and killed the chances of ever getting convictions because he had stolen evidence and prejudiced possible witnesses. A new partner could have their own problems. They could be someone who may eat fast food and have gastrointestinal problems, someone who would reject the kindly attention of Koo Koo Beatrice, some crewcut marine who thinks he's patrolling the streets of Fallujah, or some racist fuck who can't stand patrolling a city of dark people and can't believe he has to share a car with one of them, or someone, instead of benignly crumbling and succumbing to the realm of the white witch is consumed by the rage of the job and shoots some stupid teenager in the face, because the kid doesn't respond fast enough, like a teenager ever would anyhow, and his first bullet sets off a hail of other bullets from other cops because they don't know who fired first, but they do know they are pissed at the sullen teenager in front of them and they all fire for ten seconds and dark blood seeps from at least thirty-two holes in the now dead teenager's body. He trailed two years behind Brankowski and he would have to break someone in eventually, because teaming with Brank meant no hope of promotion, no detective job, nothing on the desk or in the jail, not so much because the powers-that-be hated them or thought of them at all other than they knew Brankowski came from Polish peasant stock and Hayes came from slave lineage and they had a place where their dull minds could thrive and they patroled for twenty years in a labyrinth where the exits had been bricked up once they had entered.

"I don't believe the pudwhacker stole the mail and stumbled upon this. I think it was given to him to rewire his brain and set him on a course in direct opposition to his nature and his pattern. Call it crude chaos theory. We can't find him because he has been rewired and acts and thinks like a completely different person who no one knows, who has not yet developed his own pattern yet, who probably has lost weight and cleared up his persistent acne, who has stopped the habitual whacking of his pud over asshole buds, who got a haircut, who's thinking of returning to school to learn a trade, who is plotting revenge on his hateful brother, who has his eye on a girl with wide hips who works at a coffee shop, who swears off sci-fi and movies and reads only newspapers and periodicals to become a man of his age with statistics, trends and fads roaring through his head, who thinks in charts and surveys and understands all problems have edges and ends and nothing stretches to infinity so everything is solvable and decipherable given time, who is utterly powerless to disrupt his own soaring arc to enlightenment or at least material success. If he walked in here we would be astonished, maybe he would be wearing some fine threads from a swank shop and his milky clear skin would give us pause. His own mother would take him for a stranger and once he told her his name she would melt with pride and her decades of misery and shame for her pathetic attempt at raising a misfit child would he shed and her soul lightened. She would also, in her heart or hearts, be terrified of this new person and his obvious power. As to the purpose of all this I am still clueless, but I know a new bird has taken wing."

"Proceed to the dénouncemént," Hayes interrupted.

"I've uncovered a major brainwash, a blessed mindfuck and all you want to do is get to the end?"

"Hit play goddamnit."

…the eye of the white witch returns…it fills the screen…each blink is like an earthquake…a shuttering of the world…pan out…Treg and Log sit in upholstered high back chairs…both are painted fire red from their hairlines to their toe nails…at first you can't tell they are naked because each body part blends with the other, but as the camera stays the details grow..their penises have been meticulously painted as have their eyelids...their armpits are shaved...their chests and groins are shaved...the whites if their eyes couldn't be painted or stained so they pop from the red like radiant raccoon eyes in a black forest...minstrel eyes on a darkened stage...there's a microphone between them that looks like an adder head sheathed in a tube sock to trim the peaks of sounds...three old video cameras sit on tripods around them...a ragged paparazzi...who abandoned their equipment in boredom or hunger... Treg and Log have been left to tell their story to an empty room...a forgotten news conference...they don't try to move...they don't lean forward...their backs are glued to the chairs...sometimes they disappear when they close their eyes or blink...they are a fading reception...wind is blowing and bending an antennae and their images are all but lost in a blanket of static...the light grows dim then brightness again like a cloud passed between them and the light... but they are inside...a banner hangs behind them advertizing a Thai martial arts movie...a foot sails across a wheat background...a dislocated jaw barely hangs on its hinges...a woman empathizes and has gone wet in the crotch watching the dissection of the foot's enemies...would she marry the foot?... or at least grant a session or two of victory sex...have the foot's children?... an army of boys trained in a mysterious martial arts discipline until they could enter the service of a corrupt and syphilitic emperor...one can imagine the big toe...highly trained, finely tuned, with strength beyond imagining entering her pussy as she writhes in an ecstasy born of volcanoes and hurricanes... the big toe has opened the crease for the second and a third...soon they are joined by the fourth and fifth and as each toe is added her pleasure deepens... they are not five separate, serpent toes...they act as one with the big toe as the conductor, wielding the orchestra of four...they have a stratagem for attacking her pussy...for finding every spot wired for pleasure and they morph from an orchestra to a jazz band..more suitable to their numbers and temperaments...a tight jazz band willing to subsume their egos to their genius leader and play off his riffs, support his rhythms, create the sonic space to let his solos warp the room and her pussy...she beats the mattress...she beats the pillow...she bares her teeth and seems on the verge of descending into a grand mal seizure with foam at the corners of her mouth when the big toe pauses...lets the vibrations settle and her white hot nerves cool ever so slightly...the toe is rewarded with an orgasm rushing down its nail, down the crevasse between itself and the second toe and it lets all the toes dance in the rain and celebrate their success... then they withdraw...the first to leave a great party...they walk across the fallen streamers, spilled alcohol, popped balloons, confetti...on the way they kick more ass...dislocate more jaws...living a mercenary's life...the white witch returns...she walks solemnly in from the left...her posture is perfect, regal...she reminds you of a bird...she steps between the chairs, behind them, facing the camera...the searing white of her dress blots out Treg and Log... they are impotent demons, craven and afraid of her majesty...she kisses each on the ear closest to her...the right ear of Treg, the left ear of Log..."Please be sure our guests are comfortable.."

Brankowski hits the pause button…rewinds…plays the voice again.

"Who does that sound like?"

"I know who you're thinking of. Can't think of the name. I almost see his face."

"Guy on TV?"

"No. Why would a guy on TV be in this no cost video? No, I'm thinking of that train wreck, used to be a boxer, the guy did time…beat his girlfriend nearly to death, hangs out on Quincy."

"Purdy McKee?"

"Right."

"No, it's not him. Remember, they found him with a knife in his throat over on St. Clair. It was New Year's Day, fucking cold. The perp left the knife lodged between the esophagus and the spine. Left it with bloody fingerprints. He might as well have left a business card and a map right to his house."

"How did I miss that? How come you know that and I don't?"

"You don't pay attention."

"Shit. I know this city like the veins of my dick."

"You know too much about the veins of your dick and not enough about the city."

"You scare me about the parts you do know."

"You knew about Purdy. You were there the night Zicko told the story. That night we were drinking like fiends, like a nasty hot virus called to be quenched, but no matter how much we put in our guts the damn thing grew more angry."

"Was that at the Drink and Wink?"

"Fuck no. You go to that place?"

"I've been known to go there."

"That's some hardcore shit in there, my friend. I'm not sure I feel comfortable with you cataloging my eccentricities when you are a patron of that dirty cunt hole of a place."

"Was it at the Tardy Boy over on Clark?"

"That's turned into a he-she hangout."

"Bailey Wick?

"Nope."

"The Egg Crater?"

"We would never go there. A confused theme with confused clientele."

"The Blasted Midget?"

"I can't stay there for more than a few drinks. Why do I want to look at photos and paintings of drunken dwarves and little people when I drink."

"The Blood and Snout?"

"Seriously."

"The Byte and Pye?

"Right. That's where we were."

"We were shooting pool and you were already pissed about the strip trivia video game because you couldn't get past the first question."

"Uh-huh."

"And as I seem to remember you almost beat a guy to death for spilling beer on your back and down the crack of your ass."

"He knew I was a cop and he did that on purpose."

"I saw that guy last month at Hot Dawg."

"You eat at that place? That's like eating rat hair on a bun."

"He still walks with a limp. I think you shortened his right leg."

"That goddamn beer was cold going down the crack of my ass."

"The night you beat the guy Zicko sat at the bar and told us the story of Purdy McKee. Zicko happened to be there the night Purdy was killed and he even talked to Purdy about his daughter who won a scholarship to a university somewhere in the fucking desert about ten minutes before this guy Purdy didn't even know comes up and sticks the knife in his throat. Blood shoots across the bar and Purdy started making gasping sounds as the knife had cut off his air supply, but somehow the tough sonofabitch manages to get off a kick to the guy's balls which sends him to the ground and then Purdy kicks the guy in the head a couple of times before he staggers out the door and dies on the frozen sidewalk with an arctic wind howling over him. Turns out to be a case of mistaken identity. The guy thought Purdy was the bus driver who had molested his daughter a decade before. Turns out he had been tracking him for days trying to build up the nerve, but once he was drunk enough he figured out how to use the knife. The guy hanged himself in his cell when he found out he had killed the wrong guy. He tried to bribe the guard to keep his belt, but the guard reminded him that he had no money and because they had taken it from him and he wouldn't take checks. The guard told him the sheets worked just as well and that's how he did it."

"I'm losing the thread of why we are talking about this."

"The point is that the voice on the DVD can't be Purdy McKee because he's been dead over a year. Besides, how would he be involved in a production like this? No way. You know his daughter never came back from the desert to the funeral. She had no time to look back and bury the bones of her papa."

"But wasn't Purdy a molester himself?"

"He was. The city entered no great morning period when he passed. He was a mutant with a crossed wire. He prayed on the innocent. The boxing probably scrambled his brains. Just another fucking guy waiting to go off."

"So maybe he did molest the guy's daughter."

"Well, there may have been a clerical error on the county's part. The files or pictures of another molester were mixed on the internet site and even though the guy sat in the courtroom every hour of the trial and gave tearful testimony about the innocence that had been taken from his beautiful daughter and even though he knew the guy's name who committed the heinous deed, and even though he thought he memorized the perp's face, the back of his skull, the veins on his hand, the untrimmed fingernails, the thinning hair on the temples and the crown, the sclerotic spine, the humped shoulders, the slightly misshapen nose, the intervening decade had been hard on the poor sap of a father. First, his business failed. He had a computer store that was ground to dust by the national chains and global trade, he had to watch his daughter's increasing promiscuity with horror and helplessness, and he could trace her undoing back to that day on the bus. His wife got sick of his cock because a cock destroyed her daughter for no good reason and her husband had a cock and that very same cock drove him to fantasies of revenge most of his waking life and infected a good portion of his dreams, if he could be believed. She didn't want another women to lick her pussy and the thought of licking someone else's made her sick to her stomach, so she fell into a torpor fueled by high fat foods, television and despair. She knew her daughter was hurtling toward disaster, but she lived in twilight, a half-sleep that precluded any intervention. So you can imagine with all this swirling in your head, looming poverty, forced celibacy, wanton promiscuity, his brain could get in a muddle and he could stick the knife in the throat of the wrong guy."

"I don't understand. With the internet error. Was he following the right name with the wrong picture or the right picture with the wrong name?"

"I think the right name with the wrong picture."

"But how would he find him in the first place?"

"Remember, it took days."

"Not impossible, I suppose, but fantastical. This is skating on the edge of legend."

"But back to the point of Purdy McKee. The guy on the DVD sounds like somebody on TV. Some announcer from the He-She Channel or the Snooker Channel. Some fucking voice that's planted an egg deep within my brain and that little egg is just about to turn into a maggot and eat its way out. In other words it's driving me fucking nuts. It has a familiar unfamiliarity to it. It is the sound of my father's voice shouting to me while I'm underwater or trying to talk to me through the waves of high fever and cold sweats. It's the voice of a broken apostle whose master is dead and who could not remain true to his teachings after he has passed on. It's my voice as I talk into the black pool of a coffee cup, trying to find reason in the chaos of foam clinging to the edges. It's the voice of an airport announcer reciting the Tibetan Book of the Dead through a megaphone."

"Play it again."

Brankowski played it again and they once more looked at each other. Hayes shrugged and Brankowski grabbed his head in a vise grip between his two massive hands. He let the DVD play.

…Log motions to the white witch and she leans over, offering her ear to his mouth…he whispers…she straightens and poses in mock contemplation and then walks off camera…she returns with a small notebook and pen…once in his hands he starts scribbling and all else falls away as he concentrates on the small lined paper...muffled chuckling...gallows humor...laughing at disease and mayhem and tragedy and sudden, violent thrashings of the earth as fragile human beings, soft tropical creatures, run for inadequate cover...wind rips through grass huts...forty feet of salt water suddenly over your head...still the laughter...the lazy chuckle...Log bends over the paper as his concentration deepens...the scratching of his pen is the only sound...the white witch appears behind him and peers over his shoulder...the lens zooms in on her face...she flutters her eyelids and winks mischievously...she flirts with your heart and your scrotum...you can feel both tightening...she brings you into her confidence...you are partners in crime...either be the joke or be in on the joke...you don't want to be laughed at...especially by her...you don't want to be shunned...please play with my heart a little more, you think...will she flick her tongue along the seam of my sac, you pathetically hope...you are different... you will convince the white witch to touch a troll...she leans over and whispers in Log's ear...gorgeous, long shot of cleavage and tender white skin...he leans closer to the paper...his nose is an inch away from the notebook...the pen claws at the paper...the white witch taps him on the shoulder and whispers again into his ear...he violently elbows her in the belly...she shrieks and crumples below the frame...moaning and retching...triumph and rage race through you...you sit up in your chair to see below the edge of the screen... you want the bitch to suffer and you want to kill Log for delivering the blow... you hope she is not carrying your seed...your heir...only she can bring it forth in this world...you will hate the baby because he can possess her and you cannot...he came from inside her pussy and carries half of her with him...he is not an emissary or diplomat of yours...he is your rival and usurper even though you never held the title...more retching...Treg's mouth hangs open... you notice...you are unmoved not because you fail to see his horror, his conscious understanding that he is a participant in a ceremony of murder and mutilation, not because it isn't fascinating to watch someone not being able to breathe because of a wave, a torrent, of anxiety and fear has stricken them, not because his eyes have acquired a glint of madness as if his brain, unable to accept his demise, unable to accept the responsibility of leading the body into a hideous trap, has decided to scramble his thoughts and throw in stray images, incongruous scenes of families at dinner and puppies with unicorn horns to mask its own dreadful incompetence...no...Treg's drama is interesting and fascinating but your attention is off screen...focused on the floor slick with vomit...the acid burn in the back of your throat...the bruised and spasming diaphragm...several deep breaths...each one slower than the preceding one... Log has returned to writing...then he pauses...thinking of a word or an image... his body seems on the edge of defeat or sleep...the process has pummeled him backwards...his chin rises from the paper...his eyes are disoriented... unfocused...a tentative stroke of the pen on the paper...then a flick...a furious scribble...a white hand grabs the back of Log's chair...connected to a thin, pale arm...the top of her blonde head comes into view...then her face...her face looks stricken…the eyes are red and watering…the nose is slightly running and a glint of snot hangs on her upper lip…her forehead is creased with worry lines and her temples are damp with sweat…she is a monument soiled…a church shit upon…a cradle used to catch the streams of semen exploding from a circle jerk…she wipes the residue of stomach acid and snot from her lips with the back of her free hand…she pulls herself to her feet…she exhales suddenly and dramatically and you think she may pitch whatever is left in her stomach onto Log's head, but she controls the spasm…a loud, heavy and distorted music fills the room…Treg manages a smile after a few chords and an indecipherable stanza…he recognizes it as his own voice as it is the recording his band made before they dissolved on the road and it makes him cry to think about how one van tour can begin with enthusiasm and a little hope for adventure and end this way…and he manages to concoct a prayer that includes the hope that he will get the chance to slink back to his warehouse job, forget about music, begin a routine of drinking beer the moment he leaves work, preferably in the car before it's even started, and not stopping until bedtime, never listen to another chord of music, and sell his guitars and amps for a flat screen and watch football until he passes out…but your only concern is for the ears of the white witch…she looks distressed at the noise…you see the chords traveling through the air…bullies among the molecules, plowing, punching and kicking the quiet away…supercharged and amplified…on an amphetamine high…flying with purpose…they blast into the delicate pinna hanging on either side of her head…the curves and ridges catch the torrent and the sound floods the auditory canal like a gallon of water poured into a Dixie cup…What's on the bottom of the cup?...you worry…taut, fresh tympanic membranes and as the sound vibrates through them like a cheap kazoo…the discomfort becomes more visible on her face…you demand someone cut off the music, but you sense it is the soundtrack to coming dread…the noise tears through the malleus, incus, and staples ossicles right to the basilar membrane of the cochlea and the basilar membrane gets about as hot as a car seat on a July afternoon…they push the sound forward or inward to the vestibulocochlear nerve which is like railroad tracks to her brain…you suddenly feel the music as well…you are in a muddle because you have been worrying about her and her ears…you cannot process what you hear…you feel assaulted and you roll the sound back and forth like you've taken too big of a bite of food except now more sound pours in after the first assault and more after that until your brain feels hot, stressed and stricken…the ache begins…she has raised her hands to her ears as a buffer…the last line of defense…she can't follow the undependable beat…the guitar sounds like machinery run with no oil…the voice is a howl but not powerful enough to command the instruments, so it is lost to wallow among reverberation and feedback…Treg bobs his head…he can't help himself…he has learned to follow the inconsistent drumming…he has never had a drummer who could keep a steady beat…the white witch notices the movement of his head…she balls up her hand and punches him in the ear…

hard enough to send pain through her hand and arm and hard enough to knock Treg out of the frame...the punch has knocked him out of the chair...she shakes the pain out of her arm and hand...Treg pulls himself off the floor and rises from the bottom of the screen...he may have the first stirrings of an erection...it is so hard to tell with the red paint...the white witch pretends not to notice...Treg keeps the witch in his periphery...he doesn't want to be surprised again...the music is lowered...an obvious turn or push of the volume control because the structure of the song showed no signs of abating...she has an idea...she sneaks behind Log...she is looking very closely at his red penis... you think she may be having a sexual moment...maybe not a fantasy, but a flitting desire...Log may have earned his name through his appendage... instead, she snatches the writing pad from his hands with a flash of her hand and white arm...she holds the pad above her head...Treg looks worried...he tries to throw a hand over Log's forearm to keep him from jumping from the seat, but Log jumps anyway and topples over the chair...the witch dances away off screen...Log stumbles after her...Treg slumps in his chair and covers his eyes with his hands...she screams...there's muffled shouting...a high-pitched shriek...a wail...a moan...silence...the screen stays the same for several minutes...Treg collapsed upon himself...a red smear...an empty chair knocked over...screen time is eternity...a second seems like an hour...you feel like squirming and finding the remote and fast-forwarding past this statis, but the echo of the shriek is in your ears and something may happen any second...you don't want to forward past it...past...because rewinding, stopping and playing again ruins the continuity...the white witch walks back on screen from the opposite direction from where she left...there is a blood splatter on her dress...an upward splatter...she rights the chair, making sure it is in its original position on the floor...you wonder if there are tape marks to guide the placement...there is some planning in this tableau...she walks off screen again...she returns holding Log's head against her belly...the way people sometimes hold an excessively large watermelon...a new streak of blood runs down the skirt of her dress...you can't believe it...you don't want to believe it...you have been numbed by years of horror movies produced by small budget producers looking for notoriety for putting the bloodiest, goriest, least socially redeeming pieces of trash on the screen...everyone has tried decapitation scenes with very little success...too awful...the proportions of the head never seem right...the lips and ears always look too waxen...there's nothing in your memory to compare it to except other horror films trying to employ the same ultimate horror and you never stop thinking of it as a special effect...but it is Log's head...no question...the white witch dumps it on the chair and grabs it by the ears so that it sits up on the flat cut...the instrument must have been very sharp because the cut looks very clean...the eyelids have drawn open...the jaw has slackened and the mouth has fallen open...the chin almost touches the cushion of the seat...you start sweating and your stomach starts brewing acid...this is the first real decapitated head you've seen...you know you could have gone through life without seeing this...but now you've seen it and you will always have a point of reference...cheesy movie special effects have been routed from your memory...you've reached the bottom of human depravity...evisceration, the lopping off of limbs, rape, skull smashing don't compare with this finality...there is no chance for hope or even gory thrills...irrevocable...this word comes to your mind and you smile at its flaccid inadequacy in describing what you see...you fall into a state of despair...the white witch...the neck of her dress has been torn, showing a patch of lacy bra underneath...she produces the notebook from a fold in her dress...a secret pocket to keep her lipstick, vials of drugs and knives...she clears her throat to read...how has she kept her humor after carrying his head?...how has she become so monstrous...you still want to fuck her...even more...her beautiful façade hides the heart of a troll...even though you know your time on top would be brief and any encounter would end with you splayed on the covers and she ramming something large and inadequately greased up your asshole... she stands with a conscious posture...unbelievably, she commands the frame even with a decapitated head staring at you... Treg, red and deconstructing... how the fuck is there a head on the chair?...yes, it is a head and you wonder what her cunt looks and smells like...she smiles at you...it is a sly smile...has she read your thoughts?...is she flattered or has she included you in the atrocity?...ensnaring you in the conspiracy with a wink...she focuses on the notebook and begins reading:

> "I made a deal with a dog,
> really just a cur.
> He told me to wish upon a star
> Sirius, Alpha Canus Majorus, the Dog Star
> of course.
>
> It wasn't so much his breeding
> that led me astray.
> His slinky gait told me
> he couldn't be trusted, but I trusted,
> I placed my hand in his paw
>
> Maybe it was his affable way
> of smelling his own ass
> That convinced me to raise my eyes
> to the white dwarf.
> To believe my fate would be carried
> on his breath.
>
> I really can't abide
> a two-timing dog.

Here I sit with my head
in my hands.
Waiting for his…"

…she looks up from the page and hunches her shoulders…she looks through the remaining pages but she can't find the end of the thought…she lowers the notebook…her voice is younger than you expect…she sounds barely twenty…maybe a crease near her eye betrays her…cracks in the veneer…the tableau is exhausted…it seems ready to collapse…if it was film it would melt over the projector bulb…it if were tape it would now wrap around the audio-video heads…with the DVD the best you can hope for is a deep scratch and a freeze frame…a locking-up…an imprisonment that catches the image and won't let it move…the scene really needs to end…your nerves are frayed and have started flapping like broken power lines in a storm…the white witch will not release you…she stares into the lens…Log stares into the lens… has his tongue crept out of his mouth?…Treg lowers his hands and you see again the whites of his eyes…the witch has remembered him…slowly her head turns in his direction as a smile seeps across her face…the camera holds another thirty seconds…another eternity…another universe after you've reach the edge of our own…you feel like you may convulse or vomit…you hope they don't show the beheading this time…if it happens let it happen off screen… you whisper a plea pathetically to the screen as if the white witch would listen to your entreaties…the image dissolves to a moment of blackness…did someone walk in front of the camera?…the light rises again…the frame is all but empty and brilliantly lit…a light purer than fluorescence…no sickly green tint…in the center of the screen are two sticks leaning away from each other… one at 40 degrees and the other at 105 degrees…the camera begins a slow and steady march toward the sticks…a tracking shot…somehow wheels are involved…maybe a tripod nestled atop a wheelchair…the approach is smooth…it's not long before you recognize the sticks as legs and you discern a small dark patch hovering between the two angles…is it her?…would she bestow such a gift?…she lies on a table…a white sheet is draped over her top and cascading down to the floor…you believe it might be an operating room or some other medical environment, but there is no other indication that this is the case…given what you've just seen, white should no longer connote sterility, cleanliness and science, but your brain has vast and deep grooves where information pools in stagnant, foul-smelling ponds and the white witch hasn't had the time to clean all the channels…the lens is drawing closer…her cunt is visible and you feel yourself inching closer to the screen…she has cropped and shaped the hair but not shaven herself completely…of that you are thankful… the hair traps scent and tastes bitter on your tongue and provides comfort and reason in the chaos…the moment of clarity will be brief because when you lick the labia, clitoris or the shuttered eye of her asshole you will be lost and comfort and reason will be torn away…the lens is bearing down on her…her cunt is as beautiful as her face...tinted with blood racing under the skin and swollen from feeling your hot breath sliding across its surface only to be trapped in the coils of her hair...your breath is now part of her scent...your dick feels as hard as a broomstick and raging with sensitivity...her cunt fills the screen and the base of her thighs frame it on either side...the camera has stopped its forward progress and lingers, contemplates... the assurance of its approach has broken down into confusion and hesitancy...unsure how to proceed...you have no choice but to pull out your cock and masturbate...the spider's touch of your fingers make your cock quiver...it is less like a broomstick than a handle of a blazing hot cast iron skillet...without any effort you have ejaculated on the floor...luckily you've ripped up the carpet and refinished the hardwood floors long ago so clean-up will be easy...you wish you could have waited and prolonged the experience because now you have a picture of a beautiful cunt sizzling on your television screen and it has lost 75 percent of its power and appeal...the camera senses your ejaculation and your anxiety over your eagerness or knows from experience that anyone will have climaxed at this point in the presentation so we move on...he moves forward...her labia, minora and majora, fill the screen...the vaginal opening hangs in the middle draped with a pink fold...small stubble on the area below...the camera continues forward until the image is smeared and you think she is being fucked by the camera except there is no in-out, just one long in...the flesh smears into darkness and a cheesy, wind-blowing-through-a-tunnel sound effect begins... there are echoes...footsteps clicking on a long, barren hallway...low grinding white noise rising in volume...flecks of pink and red pulsing at the edges...the effects make it seem like you are hurtling through a tunnel...fast...the black deepens...the colors grow more saturated...the white noise sounds like a dying machine...dry pistons covered in sand...a burning van flashes on the screen... flames swirling through the broken windows...back to the tunnel...the colors are flying faster...they are smears of faces and trees, of dogs, houses and stoplights...they are telephone poles and candles, toilet seats and bare feet... the same van again, flames extinguished or exhausted...a small trail of smoke from a pool of melted plastic...the paint scorched...behind the hulk the river churns...back in the tunnel...the noise now sounds like a thousand violins shrieking...as if violins were made from the wood of slave ships...the strings made from the guts of eviscerated prisoners and the thighbones of rabid goats used for bows...there's a vortex in the middle of the screen, growing smaller... the tunnel spirals...again your head moves forward...Treg on the floor, trapped by many sets of hands...the sound abruptly stops...his screams are silent...a sharpened and gleaming knife...the kind used in slaughterhouses by dull, mute men who spend their working lives ankle deep in blood and entrails...presses down on Treg's throat...there is at first a ribbon of blood...his eyes hold bottomless terror...the noise explodes...the tunnel is spinning...the entrance or exit into the next room is now a pinprick slightly above the dead center of the screen...you are dizzy and nauseous...the sound clicks off...the knife is halfway through the neck and by the amount of gushing blood the superficial cervical artery, the internal jugular vein and the external carotid artery have all been severed...the knife seems snagged on the esophagus or trachea...maybe a vertebrae...the tunnel is a spinning disk...no longer a tunnel it seems...the noise now sounds like a giant machine crushing stone, skulls and the mantel of the earth with a pair of claws bigger than most cities...the disk spins for a few minutes...if you haven't vomited yet the queasy motion is designed to put you over the edge...Treg's head hangs on by a few threads of sinew...the terrorized cast of his eyes has faded...he stares blankly off screen...the butcher's hands cut the remaining ligaments and the impossible gap between head and body opens... someone grabs the feet of the body and drags it away...leaving a smear of blood and the head...you can feel your last defense...something akin to moral outrage, but more likely it's the scream of a terrified animal understanding the fragility of his own neck...an instinct has been laid bare or rendered useless...you can't tell...you burst through the exit...the screen stops spinning...the noise belches one last time...she's there again...the white witch...dressed in a new gown...showered...hair falling gently on her shoulders...she lies down on a luxuriant couch...drowsy from heat and sleep... on the ground in front of the couch sit the heads of Treg and Log...she closes her eyes...you are convinced she will dream a gentle dream...slow dissolve... hulking steel mill in the background...two small figures carry a body to the river and after a few swings to gain momentum they release their grip and it sails into the water...they drag another and replicate the movements, the same steps...the second body joins the first...a slow zoom out until the mill looks small on the screen...a van of indistinguishable make snakes its way across the bottom of the screen and disappears past the right edge...the scene is held for a moment...fade to black.

Hayes closed his eyes and used his middle fingers to slide over the curve of his eyeballs under the lids.

"Brank, I'm in your army. That bitch scrambled my brains."

Brankowski turned toward Hayes, still under the witch's spell and nodded inaccurately in his direction. He noticed his penis hanging out of his pants, half-erect, with a dollop of semen gumming up the hole. During the last few showings he had taken to masturbating, but he had no memory of the act this time. He stood up and stuffed his penis back in his pants and asked Hayes if he wanted another beer. Hayes asked if he had an aspirin or some kind of pill that would erase his memory and cleanse his eyes.

"The first time is harsh. The viewing is all about shock and fear. That's what she uses to blast apart your brain. That's the demolition. Next, she'll start to lay the bed for the new circuit and then she'll lay the conduit and then pull wire through it and then she'll flip the switch, turning on your brand new brain. I think she's pulling the wire in my head as we speak."

"Are you going to make a copy of it for me?"

"Can't copy it. There's some kind of encryption on it. When I try to copy it the copied DVD just shows a building with a green door, static shot. I've tried about thirty times and it's always the same building, same door."

"When are you going to turn it into the department?"

"Our department? The police? Once her work is done or I might keep it."

"Decapitation is illegal in all fifty states and most of Mexico. And it shouldn't be hard to find the woman. There aren't many faces like that in town."

"She can't go to jail. Give her time with you. She becomes clear after you allow her to do her work. Her voice rises above the din."

"It's pretty clear she's one sick bitch."

Brankowski became quiet and walked into the kitchen, fetching two beers. He handed one to Hayes, who forgot to ask Brankowski if he had washed his hands before to touched the beer can, because he was unsettled by how abruptly quiet had descended on his partner. He wished at that moment that he had brought his gun because Brankowski had his and had obviously slipped past reason. Hayes took the beer and twisted off the cap.

"We are cops, Brank, and that is one fucked-up crime."

"But she can't go to jail. Thinking of her in jail would drive me more nuts than I already am. You need to watch it again. It's important that you understand. There's no one else, Hayes, but you. If you don't understand then I have nowhere else to go. I can't bear the burden alone. It's too much. The department will scan the DVD for clues, post her face on the internet, visit the buildings and landmarks they recognize. They will see it only as a crime. We have the opportunity for a whole new wiring. This is her poem to the world and a set of instructions. How do you turn your back on evolution? How do you forgot a change in the hardwiring? It's really important for you to understand. I'm not strong enough to carry it alone. I'll admit it. I have no problem telling you she's more powerful than me."

Hayes noticed the spray of semen on the floor and the dark blot on Brankowki's pants where the dollop from his penis had seeped. How in God's name had he not noticed Brankowski jerking off on the couch beside him? He closed his eyes and again caressed his hot eyelids.

"What do you want me to do?"

"I want you to watch it again."

"How many times?"

"However many times it takes to finish the job. I feel like I'm almost there. I'll be your guide. I'll hold your hand. I'll lead you to the light. It's right here in our grasp. We're not talking about crime. These two corpses are superfluous. She's found the new level, the next level, the other level. This is an invitation to join. The pudwhacker must have been successful. Maybe he just dissolved and he now lives at her feet. Maybe his job is to trim her toenails, a small job admittedly, but when you are asked to serve you kill your own ego and you serve. There is a greater good. This is about casting off our skins."

"You know, you could just take up Jesus."

"Fuck, Hayes. This landed in my lap. This is a found object, the last talisman, a holy relic, the shinbone of Ganesha. This is the spilled seed of Odin and the egg of Frigg. You walk through the door. You grab the knob and walk through the door."

"Or you turn it in as evidence of a crime."

"Haven't we cleared that up?"

"Not to my satisfaction."

"Hayes, you are a devil on whose nature nurture can never stick."

"OK, turn it on. Let me see what she can do."

"Brankowski slumped back on the couch, pleased and smiling. He pointed the remote at the TV.

A jagged white line starts from the bottom of the screen and dances its way to the top….blue screen, white static, blue….the hum of a motor…

The Moon is a Demon

The world lay before him as a collection of scents. The ground entombed histories, narratives of putrefaction and birth. The inexorable turning of worms released smells trapped for a thousand years, a native's urine, the burst gl and of a skunk, lilacs and corpses, ash and broken eggs. Subterranean fragrances, fear, anger, lust and hunger. Always hunger. Hunger as an engine providing the propulsion forward. The invisible hand, pushed on the back, roused us from dangerous, luxuriant sleep, caused us to consider war when the sun parched the earth and baked our crops to withered stalks. The moon smelled of fear and cold, white fire. The moon hung as an unblinking eye, guarding a lost brethren in the throes of impulse and instinct.

Nelson moved his head and a metallic clank emanated from his neck. He looked out through a rectangular opening with a shredded cloth flap hanging from a nail onto a swampy yard. Rain came down in sheets and drummed against a roof a foot above his head. In places, the rain found a crack and dripped through. A puddle outside the opening threatened to gain volume and pour through the doorway. Far from washing or masking the smell of the earth, the rain released a thick musk so filled with narratives of the animals, plants and elements that had passed before that it all became indecipherable, a muddle. Nelson leaned his head toward the opening and a metallic ripple followed. At his feet lay a section of coiled chain. One end of the chain ran out the door and the other end ran up his leg and chest. He grabbed and followed it to his neck where it ended at a thick leather collar spiked with heavy studs. He found the terminus of the chain, but it didn't end with an easily manipulated fastener. The last link seemed welded closed around a ring fastened to the collar. The collar itself had no buckle his hands could find. The leather felt smooth and snug around his neck and no matter how many times his hand passed over the circuit they ended at the beginning with no success. He grabbed the other end of the chain and pulled it into the shelter until it became taut. He had fifteen feet of wet and muddy chain coiled at his feet when he finished pulling, but the chain had been tied to something heavy or a stake in the ground because it wouldn't give no matter how hard he pulled. To investigate would have meant walking out into the driving rain and he felt comfortable and warm, so the mystery could wait until the rain slackened. He didn't recognize the clothing he wore and he didn't think it odd his feet were bare and black with dirt and grime. His head bobbed with sleep and just as he curled up in the driest corner he felt the chain uncoiling and disappearing through the doorway until it became taut. The first pull did not bring him to full consciousness, but a second, harder tug and the rumble of a voice muffled by the rain sent panic through him. A third tug came and another attempt at communication from the voice through the rain. The words sounded as if delivered by a female voice, high and soft, easily drowned by the downpour. Steady pressure pulled at Nelson's neck.

"Champ! Champ?" the voice shouted. "Do you want to come inside?"

The question felt seductive. Nelson imagined curling up next to a steaming radiator or a forced-air vent and sleeping through the afternoon, a distant drumbeat of rain on the roof and windows. Something reminded him that he probably wouldn't be invited in once the voice saw that he in no way resembled Champ. He looked at his hands and feet to confirm his suspicions and saw his skin reddened by the cold and dampness. The chain jerked impatiently and he decided to make a run for it. He crawled through the opening and a horrified shriek met him. He looked wildly around the yard to find his bearings. He saw a woman wearing a bright red raincoat backing away, tripping and falling backwards into the mud, cataloged a fence, a tree, a garage, a parked car, a muddy patch where Champ must have done most of his digging, and a scattering of faded and broken toys that could have been taken for debris after a tornado. He sprinted toward the picket fence that only stood four foot high and Nelson thought he may be able to hurdle it without breaking stride, since he began the sprint with a burst of power and speed. Just as his thigh tensed for the jump, a perfect jump that would allow his trailing shin to kiss the blunt point of a picket and his foot to fold up just in time to miss the collision, a jump that would carry him away from Champ's frightened owner, the chain snapped taut and stopped the momentum of his neck and head. His legs took one more stride before flying in the air and for a moment his body hung parallel to the ground as his eyes bulged out from the sudden strangulation. The flight lasted briefly and looked ungainly as Nelson landed on the ground flat on his back. He looked up at an old oak tree spreading out above him and wondered if the chain had enough length to throw over one of the branches and hang himself. Once he regained his breath and tired of lying in the grass he stood up and followed the chain to its source. He became aware that the shrieking hadn't stopped even though the woman had disappeared back in the house. Nelson found the terminus of the chain fastened to a steel eyelet, which looked like it had once been used to pull ore boats, sunk into a cylinder of cement buried in the ground. After a few pulls he gave up and started pulling at his neck and still could not find a buckle or any way of unfastening the chain. He pulled until his neck felt raw and scratched and then he slunk back to the doghouse to get out of the rain. He curled in the damp straw and after the remnants of panic subsided he fell into a light sleep.

A minute or an hour later Officer Sterling Hayes tapped on the roof with his billy and Nelson jerked awake. When he looked through the opening he saw two pairs of blue legs splattered with mud, but the rain had eased into a light drizzle. Hayes knocked again.

"Champ? Is that you Champ? Why don't you come out so we can give you a pet?" Hayes said.

Nelson obeyed and crawled out of the opening, head bent, cowering. Hayes and Brankowski both stepped back and once Nelson had completely extricated himself from the doghouse they exchanged a look of exhausted hilarity. They had spent another night watching the film and had begun to question where the demarcation between dreams and reality lay. Brankowski looked at the old oak and fully expected the white witch to step from behind the trunk and send a message through pantomime. Hayes contemplated Nelson gravely in the mud and wondered what type of language he could use to describe this offense. Trespassing and animal cruelty seemed woefully inadequate. He wanted to channel something sinister and filled to the brim with bathos. He and Brankowski had walked away from official language, categories, known criminal offenses and readable reports weeks before.

"Are you going to arrest him?" the husband of the frightened woman piped in from over Hayes' shoulder.

"Ask him what he did with Champ," the wife added.

"Ask him why he's chained in our yard."

"Ask him why he's such a freak."

"Ask him if he gets his jollies scaring women."

"Ask him if this is some kind of stupid stunt, like they make people do on the radio so they can win tickets or free chicken."

Brankowski turned to the couple and raised his hands, palms outward, to make them stop. To his amazement they did stop even though he could tell they had more directions they were itching to cast.

"OK, Champ. It's time for you to start talking," Hayes said to Nelson's back.

"I wish he wouldn't call him that," the woman whispered to her husband. "It's disrespectful. We still don't know what happened to Champ and I feel he's making light of it. I wish he'd call him anything but Champ."

"You still might have a chance to talk yourself out of this."

Nelson raised his head and surveyed the four people looking at him and expecting some kind of explanation to his behavior, but he had no explanation or memory of how he came to be chained in the yard. He did decide to at least mitigate some of the impatience, annoyance and possible outright dislike building against him.

"I am Monrovia. I am Samuel Doe on the throne, casting babies into the fire and hacking through the city with a machete in one hand and a Bible in the other. I am a debauching Cyclops, squatting on my haunches, sniffing for a female Cyclops, dizzy from drink, begging for a whiff of vagina…" Nelson stopped when he recognized confusion on the four faces. The construction of his thought collapsed like a building blown apart by a bomb, and he stood as the victim, covered in dust, bleeding from the head, stumbling aimlessly through the rubble.

"Drugs, Brank?"

"No, I'm thinking Schizo Americano. Probably a garden variety found on most street corners, schools and homesteads."

"I am Uncle Tom U.F.O., I kiss your toe nails and seek obsequiousness. I am a seeker of socks. They won't stay on my feet. I am a full Nelson, a huckleberry, a favorite among bears. I grow in damp, acidic soil. I am your huckleberry, Mr. Montenegro. My scoat is snug."

"Well, well, well, did any particular word stand on its head in Huckleberry's soliloquy?"

"Hmmm, let me guess…I got it…huckleberry? No…no…no…damn I guess I'd have to say evil incarnate, a devil who has departed the realm of decency. The rotted core, the unchecked impulse, the river of nihilism, the font of despair, the fountainhead himself, J. Montenegro."

"You are both observant and eloquent. It seems we have stumbled on more wreckage."

"He's no black box."

"God no, he's a worm, a worker bee, a castoff, another failure washed ashore, bleached and half-dead."

"They keep coming. One after the other."

"What would the white witch say?"

"She would say come to my bosom and cry your cold tears. I can't explain your lost humanity or the lost throne where once you sat. I can no longer dance and clap for your silly songs and I won't kiss away your bruises, but I will show you that pain is optional and to cling to the past is like clinging to smoke, steam or confetti. Embrace the new and forget what you once were. I'm paraphrasing, of course. She's more eloquent with a shifting of her eyelids than I'll ever be with a million words. Her words would be like daggers into our hearts."

Nelson gathered himself, breathed evenly, and attempted a narrative that would allow him to walk away from the police, the doghouse, and the increasingly panicked couple who had begun to fear the worst for their pet of five years.

"I began as a spark, a pulse, shot through a well worn path, carrying a burden of my own making. I am a tangled branch, a disgruntled root, forever pushing through soil littered with chalk and granite. Circuitry is deceiving and confusing. I am no engineer, no scientist. I was a pulse outside of a circuit board. I traveled through no wire. I am an arc, static, St. Elmo's fire. I am a free agent. It begins with a single follicle, a gray bristle connected to a globule of slimy fat on the maxilla. I thought it was an itch and with a dry phalange I try to scrape it away, but others sprout like a rash, a roaring disease, on the mandible and the skull. A subcutaneous sheen crept up the metatarsals of the feet, the tibia, patella, fibula and femur. Soon, all the dry bones radiate with living tissue. The dermis flows in streams from the eye sockets. The epidermis is a fleshy plastic, stretched tight. I opened my eyelids and looked through coursing blood. Electricity had taken form and I was no longer just a pulse. I could no longer say I was just a huckleberry or a Cyclops for that matter. I ran. I ran after the silver moon."

"Brank, you're going to have to write the report on this one. What can be said?"

"Hayes, you're passing up an opportunity. How often do we get a chance to describe chaos? Mostly we deal with wife-beating and drunken stupidity. On the ground before you is a man in fragments, so shattered an accounting of the sum of his parts is pert near impossible. Don't shy away from the possibility of greatness. This report could be talked about for generations."

"Are you going to try to find Champ? He was like a son to us," the woman said with a catch in her throat.

Hayes pulled out a pearl-handled knife from his pocket and flipped it open. He told Nelson not to move and cut the collar from his neck. Before Nelson could stand up or think about standing up Hayes slapped handcuffs on his wrists and hoisted him to his feet.

"We'll take Mr. Huckleberry in for questioning. We've got smart people down there that can figure out what to charge him with, but short of a confession that he dined on your puppy the chances of finding out what happened to Champ are slim to none."

"Are you completely out of your mind?" the man asked. "Are you seriously suggesting to my wife that he may have eaten the dog?"

"No, I said that short of some confession of barbarism we have very little to go on, very little to charge him with. We've got trespassing so far, maybe public intoxication, maybe pubic insanity and disturbing the peace, who knows, I'll let them figure it out downtown."

"Isn't it fucking obvious what's going on here?" the man seethed.

Hayes and Brankowski shared a look and then burst out laughing. They escorted Nelson to the cruiser, pulled away and didn't stop laughing until they were halfway to the station, leaving the couple with an empty doghouse and grief.

After a short drive to the Fourth District station and a very short processing, because Nelson had no other belongings other than the clothes he wore and he couldn't remember or couldn't say his name, previous address or social security number, Hayes and Brankowski sat him down in a small white room where the wall had been scuffed and chipped by the backs of chairs and the occasional wrestling match between an officer and the accused. On the wall nearest where Nelson sat a collection of dried snot splotches hung displayed as if each successive arrestee had been spurred on to make a contribution as a futile stand against the wheels of justice or rage against being denied a proper tissue. The room smelled of sweat, alcohol and stale tobacco smoke, because apparently the cops still allowed the arrestees to smoke if it meant a quicker confession. A small white table sat between Nelson and Brankowski and Hayes. Each sat on hard plastic chairs that were easy to wipe down with disinfectant.

"Tell us about Montenegro," Hayes began.

"It's the only way out of this little white box."

After the doghouse the interrogation room seemed like a cathedral. Nelson had no confidence that he had the energy or capability to make himself understood.

"Tell us about Montenegro," Brankowski added.

Nelson tried to tell them about the circuit, about the woman in the video game who beckoned him to the shore where that crazy fuck lived, about the boozing and the dogs, Pez, the theft of his shoes, and, of course, the Captain and everything else he could remember since he had driven into town, but he simply couldn't get his thoughts to match his speech. His rational self, alive and functioning well, had been driven back, had shrunk to the size of a golf ball in a remote part of the brain where it sat radiating pure, sensible thought, while the rest of the brain cooked in the heat of an intense fever. The golf ball sent out a detailed confession only to watch it get caught in the eddies and waves of nonsense until its momentum had been arrested and the confession died in a stagnant pool on the edge of an unused part of the brain. The golf ball likened it to sending a carrier pigeon into the teeth of a hurricane. So, when Brankowski repeatedly asked about Montenegro and Nelson wanted to tell them of the kindness of Koo Koo and accidently calling Montenegro after his phone number had once been disconnected, he could only manage to say, "Eviscerated Zune walks from the sea, guts in hands, the sting of salt on his lips and eyes. Where has he left his blanket, his keys, his needle and thread?" Hayes and Brankowski knew of Zune, knew him to be a dead rival of Montenegro, who had been blown up in a car bomb after visiting the dentist, the same dentist who helped identify the body because the blast had not destroyed Zune's new bridgework. The fact that Nelson knew his name intensified their interest in him and lengthened the interrogation far past normal operating procedures. As quickly as the name came, it washed back into the tide, so when they traveled a line of inquiry about Zune they followed a lopsided circle to nowhere. After a few hours they left him in the room and went and had lunch from a fast food Chinese place that made their stomachs feel leaden and their foreheads and palms greasy. They came back to the room slower and less interested in what they could find out and just wanted to finish the process and send Nelson on his way to the next step in the system.

"We're going to give this one last try Huckleberry. There's only one way out of this little white box and all the other boxes and cages that will follow. Outside of this little white box is a blue-green planet, an orbiting rock battered and bruised by evil and decay, by hidden agendas and the pursuit of one's own tail. The inhabitants roam the rock with fear in their hearts and minds filled with burden and chaos. They consider men like Montenegro and Zune to be outcasts, but they have been cast out of their own hearts, their own minds. They have made manifest the stomping golems, Frankenstein monsters, the proverbial other that is within and without."

"Anytime you want to abridge is okie dokie with me," Hayes interrupted.

"My apologies, most humble and sincere." Brankowski followed with a slight bow of the head. "Listen, Huckleberry, the entire force, at least the cops not on his payroll, has been trying to catch Montenegro for over two years now. He is the best of the worst. A known quantity, indefinable. He brings a number one, killerdiller, kickass, ballsoff, uncut, unlaced, motherfuck monkey's paw powder into our humble community, knocking the turds right out of our youth, our businessmen, our sports stars, our housefraus, our hairdressers and teachers of our fair city. We've seen them in the river, lying in ditches and streams, encased in the mangled carcass of a too fast car, sitting in their own excretions. A mystic would call it a reckoning, but even without committing to hysterical language I feel comfortable calling it a plague upon our people. The first stirrings of doomsday? Maybe, but whatever the ultimate end, we know, I know, we are in the midst of a disease, an affliction. So imagine our position, a couple of guys given the task of controlling this rising sea, and we find a very confused and shattered man babbling on about Zune and the fiend, the butcher boy, Jack Black himself, J. Montenegro. If, again, you are capable of imagining our position you'll understand why we need an explanation from you, Huckleberry."

Nelson thought about the moon. It was a dream. Its silver light brushed against the grass like silk against a woman's breast. He ran. He could feel blood wash against his teeth. His stomach felt leaden the more he drank. His paws tore at the dirt and his tongue lolled from his dark lips. The moon was a demon to be driven below the horizon, to be blotted from his dreams, so its light couldn't dictate his actions and wash his thoughts away. He looked at Brankowski, then Hayes.

"Silver spoons lined up on a table, glinting in the early morning light. Little spoons, maybe for a baby or a miniature tea set with small tea cups with handles so small an adult finger could never hope to hold. The spoons are perfect for a monkey's lips or for tapping a small beat on the table, a tiny drummer amidst the roar of the world."

Brankowski slapped Nelson across the face, smacking a good portion of his nose.

"Fuck you. Turn off the tape," he yelled to the ceiling. "Stop fucking with us. I feel like punching you until you're dead or both my hands fall off, whichever comes first."

"I am a whispering vulva! Dancing in the swamp gasses! I am a black rook! I am a sacrifice. Hold out my fucking heart! I want to see my fucking heart! My diseased blood will corrode your stone alter and bring disrepute to your temple. I will clog the path to Tlazolteotl. Even she cannot cleanse my blood. I bring her a carcass of filth and disease and even she looks away in disgust. No one will be cleansed after me. I have brought horror to the world. I am the pandemic. I am pleading for quarantine! I am the great leveler!"

"So, do you think they took out his brain?" Hayes said as he leaned back in his chair until the front legs came off the ground.

"No, just fucked up the one he has."

The moon always rises. No matter how long he runs to push it below the horizon or how long he concentrates, whenever he loses concentration the moon will bob to the surface and reflect its ghastly light over the grass and through the trees. The moon is a demon, unshakeable, always rising, mute and smug as it lords over the night and watches the life that scurries and slinks through the dark, the lost battalions searching for light. He can't stop running and battling to smother the moon.

In a beige courtroom that felt like it might be four stories underground or on a submarine, when, in fact, it sat on the eighth story of a tower called the Justice Center. Nelson sat next to his court appointed public defender who scrolled through his email on his phone with Nelson's unopened case file lying on the table in front of him. Nelson surveyed the room with heavy lids hanging just above his pupils. His soiled clothes had been replaced with an orange jumpsuit and his bare feet had been shod in orange foam slippers. The bailiff told the assembled to rise and Judge Margaret McGonagle, stooped with arthritis, walked in. She paused beside her chair and her gaze swept over the heads of her motley congregation and she made them stand an instant more than they expected to garner a drop of respect, a flick of the whip from a hunched old lady, who had seen, or heard about, every variation of human behavior and didn't like much of it. She grabbed the edge of the desk in front of her and eased herself down in the chair. The chair had caused a minor controversy when it had been purchased because it had been designed with orthopedic properties to her exact bodily proportions to relieve the pain in her spine as she presided over the courtroom and the subsequent cost of a handmade chair pushed the court over its budget. The newspaper ran three stories and an editorial about taxpayer waste with Judge McGonagle as the latest and most egregious example, but the paper backed-off and even had to run an editorial retraction about the importance of the elderly in the workplace once a steady stream of complaints poured in calling the editors insensitive, anti-elderly, and purveyors of distortions and stereotypes, which caused concerns that their circulation numbers would plunge even lower than they were now showing. In her chair, behind her desk, elevated on a dais, in her robe, the judge felt physically intimidating, even though she barely brushed five feet tall, and she liked to loll and plod through her day deliberately, fully in control of the machine, obviously the boss and in no hurry to step back into the world of impossibly tall men and women with their beaming countenances and their ignorant disrespect of her position.

The bailiff recited Nelson's case number into the record as the judge read the file. The charges against him were trespassing, resisting arrest, animal cruelty, vandalism, public indecency (a trumped-up charge stemming from his lack of footwear), and stalking. A public intoxication charge had been dropped when the blood test showed a low level of iron but free of illicit drugs and alcohol. The judge read the charges aloud and asked Nelson how he answered the charges, guilty, not guilty or no contest. Everyone, prosecutor, defense attorney and judge were irritated that a plea deal hadn't yet been reached and this case mucked up the schedule of more ghastly trials. Nelson opened his mouth, paused, concentrated as hard as he could muster, or at least exhibited an effort that could have been taken for concentration, and let fly his answer.

"The umbrellas of cyborg…yammering snap…pistol love."

The judge looked over to the public defender.

"I don't know, your honor, he's been uncommunicative since the arrest, according to the report."

The judge looked over to the assistant prosecutor who looked at the tips of her scuffed shoes as she bounced on the balls of her feet so that she wouldn't feel bolted to the floor.

"Has a psych eval been performed on him yet?" She addressed the assistant prosecutor, but the question had been offered generally to the courtroom, to the inefficient bureaucracy on the floors below her, to the conspirators in the system who wanted to clog up her courtroom with irrelevancy and their own willful incompetence so that she retired and opened up a judgeship for the next generation of newly minted lawyers with Irish surnames. "Really?" she continued as no one responded and the assistant prosecutor didn't lift her head.

"I scream like a drooling egg! The world is without aimed! Bring me the head of Alfredo Tostada!"

"How could you possibly bring charges against an imbecile with syrup for brains? I need to see how nuts he is before we proceed, unless the prosecutor wants to drop the charges?"

"No, your honor, we will not drop the charges."

The judge wanted to release him because this type of petty grandstanding from the prosecutor irked her. The prosecutor had developed an everlasting hard-on against the homeless, nameless, and mentally ill since a deranged bum had been caught defecating on the courtroom steps. The terms animals, vermin, dirty maggots, fucking losers, cocksucking leeches, goddamn worthless shitheads, crazy dickheads, and schizo pissants had crept into the prosecutor's language so his staff pursued offenses committed by persons resembling the homeless and insane with abandon and, in some cases, zeal.

"Let's see if the psychiatrist can find a basic competence in there somewhere and then we'll worry about these charges," the judge concluded.

She avoided the trap of releasing Nelson, because, God forbid, if he committed some act, heinous and violent, after his release. The prosecutor would gather the cameras and reporters on the steps of the courthouse on the spot where the bum had deposited his turd and decry his position as the lone soldier against the tide of cruelty and menace and the victim's relatives of Nelson's potential heinous act would be trotted out and would condemn the ever-shrinking judge with the weak spine and the expensive chair.

"I lost my keys in the quarry. Shadow of eels wrap around my ankles. My head falls under the surface of a tide of gasoline. Only burning left," said Nelson, but no one really listened any more.

Two uniformed guards led him from the courtroom, back to his cell he shared with five other men. Bear, a name he collected as he gained girth and hair, had beaten his wife unconscious after arguing over a few hours he couldn't account for that he had used to sleep with his wife's ex-best friend, who had the finest shape he had ever seen. Daron Flowers and Delonte Richards had been picked up in separate arrests with almost identical scenarios and charges. A minor traffic violation, a dead headlight or a broken taillight, maybe an expired tag, leads to the stop. The cop comes to the window with his blood pressure screaming in his ears and his heart in his throat and smells pot or crack or burnt formaldehyde and melted plastic and asks the driver to step out of the car, which leads to a heated argument as to the purpose of the stop or the need for the driver to step out onto the asphalt. The anger rises and the cop asks for back-up. All the passengers are spilled onto the sidewalk and a search of the car produces guns with no permits, small quantities of drugs, maybe a couple of opened beers and given a quick background check that reveals both Delonte and Daron have similar offenses on their record and both are on probation, they are taken straight to jail where they can be assured they will remain for some time. The fourth cellmate, Spider, stabbed a friend in the gut after they argued over a debt of under a hundred dollars. Spider knew he owed the money, but he got sick of getting reminded every time his friend saw him and he had the bad luck of asking him for the fortieth time just after he lost big on a boxing match, Garcia v. Smithers, that ended in a bullshit TKO of Smithers who still stood with his mouthpiece in his mouth, and, as far as he could tell, still swinging, so Spider lost his money on some bullshit and not a minute later that stupid fuck comes in and asks for that old debt. The knife sliced his belly before he reached the end of the question. The fifth, a quiet guy that looked more like an engineer than a criminal, and who almost everyone in the jail assumed to be a john swept up in the prosecutor's other pet project of stamping out prostitution on a few well known streets that had served pimps, prostitutes and johns as a neutral meeting place for over a decade, Dan Evans, turned out to be more sinister than a geek looking to get blown by a tawdry and spent whore. Dan had been accused of stealing his mother's estate and blowing it on gambling and insane scams like layered mortgages and minor Ponzi schemes. His brother found the deceit too late to save his mother's house or her savings, too late to stop Dan from driving her deep into debt and ruining any plans he or his sisters had for the money. His brother called everyone he knew until he found a friend with high connections to the courts and had Dan arrested and thrown in jail with an exorbitant bail, when normally this brand of non-violent thievery would not warrant a single night in custody. His brother spread the word through the family not to help Dan make bail, but he didn't have to worry about that because Dan had borrowed and stolen from everyone he knew over the past five years so no one would rush forward and free him any time soon.

Nelson walked past them and settled in a corner smelling strongly of fresh piss. His cellmates left him alone, because early on when Spider watched him hour after hour pace in the exact same spot using the exact same movements to complete the circuit and finally asked him what he had done to land himself in this cage, and Nelson, without stopping his route, howled, "Mother's junction box hangs on the wall! I slid my hand in and felt the fuses. Who is the baby wizard?! Who brings communion to my shores?" they collectively considered him not worth the trouble of a conversation. Delonte now strode over to the corner and stood over Nelson who had collapsed into a ball with his head resting on his bent knees. He felt Delonte's breath and smelled his sour skin coated with old sweat and the recycled dust and bacteria of the cell.

"What happened to you? In the court. What they'd do?"

Nelson opened an eye and once he realized Delonte had directed his questions at him he raised his head.

"Witch doctor," Nelson said and he acted surprised the word almost matched the missive sent from his walnut-sized rational brain, so he tried to follow it up with something closer to the true meaning. "Shrunken head doctor. Shrinkeys. Send me to the shrink. I'm hoping the air won't be moist. They are sending me to a shrink- a psychiatrist." Nelson smiled and thought about a ray of sunshine slipping through the clouds and bouncing through eighteen layers of brick, mortar and steel by reflecting off watch faces, spoons, zippers, shoe eyelets, glasses until a weak flicker danced across his cheekbones.

"They need a doctor to tell them you're a crazy fuck?"

"Apparently so." Nelson felt emboldened. He had nailed the words on the first attempt.

"Are you from Florida?"

Jules returned to Nelson's mind briefly, but this Jules didn't have eyes and her left breast had become dramatically smaller than the right which hinted at cancer and a mastectomy. Her mouth smelled of tooth decay. She turned her back and faded away. He failed to catch the incongruity of Delonte's question. Nelson's tan had long ago faded to paleness and nothing in his orange jumpsuit indicated Florida's climate, but the misshapen Jules had distracted him so he answered with a nod, that he remembered living in Florida near or in Tampa and that he came to Cleveland for a business reason, a reason that now escaped his memory. Delonte and Daron exchanged looks and Delonte went back to his cot and lay down. He stared at the ceiling and chewed a soggy toothpick. Davon sat on the floor and put his head on his knees. Dan thought of masturbating, feeling the unexpected and growing warmth in his penis, and looked for an appropriate spot in the cage to perform the task. He decided to face the cage door away from his cellmates, but when he pulled out his dick and started working it Spider noticed and told him if he didn't put his dick back in his pants he would personally rip it off and stuff it in his mouth. Dan jammed the erection back in his pants and figured he would try again when everyone fell asleep, if everyone could ever fall asleep at the same time in this timeless, sunless, nightless room. Spider and the rest figured that Dan's story about his stealing from his family was just air and if he could jack off for no reason then he had to have been caught with a whore's head in his lap.

Nelson could smell fear trailing from the animal's haunches. His lungs work hard against the bitter air. Small blasts of steam shoot from his mouth and the mouths of the pack around him. They are at full sprint across an open field. They chase a shadow that smells like fear. Two dogs stand at a small rise ahead of them and the animal sees them, pauses, and darts to the right, but the going is slower in that direction as it claws against the soggy ground and through dense thickets. It has lost its way, its purpose, other than survival. The barbs tear at its flesh and the smell of fresh blood whips the pack forward through the swamp and they snap at pockets of rot and terror as they roll through the air. There is animal heat around his jowls. Thrashing. A panicked scream. He bites and his teeth sink through course, musky fur into sinew and blood. He can feel the breath rushing from the animal as it struggles against the snapping jaws. Soon it dies and they eat. Never enough food. Always on the edge of hunger and desperation. Always running toward the demon moon.

Dr. Mel Joonce sat crouched over a small green steno pad. He scratched out his thoughts in crisp black lines that looked like they had been forged from ten gauge wire. Dusk glowed purple through a small square window near the ceiling of his office. He had been known to stand on his desk to see out the window when the psychosis of the prisoners shook his own sanity. If he craned his neck he could see a slice of the lake between two warehouses and through the gaps in the trusses of a bridge. Sometimes sun would creep through the window frame and brighten a patch on his wall. He always tried to get his face in the rays because even the tepid warmth of the sun trying to come through the double panes of treated and tinted glass helped vary the climate controlled atmosphere and felt like a break in the relentless monotony of his job. Eighty percent of the jail population suffered from some kind of mental illness, from garden variety depression (and who wouldn't be a little depressed having been locked in a cage with the prospect of an endless string of days yawning before them?) to full-blown, living in the hallucinatory world, paranoid schizophrenics who struggled and wrestled with Nazis, warlocks, Beelzebub, or Ronald Reagan, and they couldn't be bothered with treatment or medication, because the meds made them weak and ineffectual in the death struggle, not to mention the devastation the drugs caused their livers and kidneys, so Dr. Joonce must be in collusion with the devils because why else would he want to weaken them and make victory that much easier? He had already been working twelve hours, but a court request from Judge McGonagle for a psych eval had come late in the day. If he didn't complete the evaluation quickly and return the report within the accepted time frame established in the judge's head, the phone calls would begin, first from her bailiff every hour on the hour after the unspoken deadline had passed, and if he ignored these calls or still didn't complete the report between the first call and the fifth call, then the judge herself would get on the line and demand the report. He sometimes enjoyed the calls from the judge because her whipsaw voice sounded so unlike his own and her bristling and fierce intelligence gave him small confidence that not everything in the world had gone to shit, even though she herself suffered from exhaustion and paranoia. He entertained himself with thoughts of starting up an affair with the judge, including a sequence where she barked orders at him while they had sex, but he never asked her on a date because he imagined his fantasy superior to an awful reality.

Dr. Joonce had requested the prisoner H.H. Huckleberry be brought to his office an hour before, so when someone knocked on the door he knew he had been delivered. He let Nelson in and nodded to the guard, an especially broad Cro-Magnon who looked like thinking made him physically ill. He pointed Nelson to a chair and closed the door in the guard's blank face. When he turned back around, Dr. Joonce saw that Nelson had not sat down and looked at his diplomas on the wall, the B.S. in Microbiology, Indiana University, Bloomington, IN, the M.S. in Molecular Biology, University of Wisconsin, Madison, WI, the M.D., University of Rochester, NY, the Residency in General Psychiatry, University of Michigan, Ann Arbor, MI and the M.A. in History from the University of Cincinnati he earned when he had a job near the campus when he thought it easier to go to classes than his lonely and stark apartment, and the M.A. in Philosophy from the University of Montana when for a brief few years he thought his shortness of breath and his alarming weight gain had as their source the unhealthy pattern of living in mediocre cities, so he committed to Montana and to a job as an adolescent psychiatrist, but even long hikes in Big Sky country, which he admittedly undertook infrequently, could not abate his expanding waistline, so he returned east. A majority of the inmates liked to inspect the diplomas to verify his credentials or to give themselves comfort that they were now in the hands of one of the educated elite who, because of years of study and training, would be able to untangle the mess of their misspent lives with a wave not unlike a magic spell shooting from the tip of his wand.

He pointed again to the chair and Nelson finally sat down. Dr. Joonce noted that Nelson smelled of stale urine and looked generally unkempt. His hair hung in a tangled mess and he had grown a thick mass of beard that sprouted in all directions. His fingernails were long and filthy. Dr. Joonce looked at the small window near the ceiling and cursed the architect again for specifying windows that couldn't be opened or looked through because what his office needed at that moment was a blast of cool air from over the lake to carry away the urine stench. It would also have been the perfect opportunity to stare out the window at the dark waves and contemplate the series of events that led him to be sitting in this coffin-sized office interviewing raving lunatics who smelled of urine, but since he had no window to speak of and standing on the desk would have been awkward with an inmate sitting at his feet, he launched into the interview.

"Do you have a history of drug use?"

Nelson stared back at him but made no attempt to answer the question, so Dr. Joonce repeated it. Nelson bit his lip shut. Dr. Joonce moved on.

"Are you currently taking any prescribed medications?"

Nelson knew better than to answer, because even after his modest success answering Delonte's questions he knew better than to trust his ability to speak. His cognitive ability seemed intact. The psychiatrist had asked him about prescribed medications and illegal drug use and Nelson had answers ready, but he feared these answers, yes to the first and no to the second, would never make it to his lips and giving incoherent answers to a psychiatrist seemed an unwise path to follow. Other questions followed. Is there a history of mental illness in your family? Have you recently been in an accident or have you recently suffered a head injury? Have you been diagnosed or treated in the previous year for cancer, heart disease, kidney failure, gallstones, impotence, lung disease, hamstring injuries, leukemia, hair loss, hearing loss or acid reflux? Have you recently lost a job, wife, child or children, your confidence, your hair, your house, your mother, your father, your cat, your dog, your parakeet, your faith, or your interest in sex? Are you heterosexual, homosexual, bisexual or do you have interest in forms of deviant sexual behavior, whether illegal or not? Do you consider yourself a Christian, Muslim, Jew, Buddhist, Baha'i, Hindu, Shinto, Taoist, Sikh, Confucian, Jainist, Hare Krishna, Unitarian, Saterian, Gnostic, Druze, Caodaist, Scientologist, or Romani? Do you believe that Elian Gonzalez is the new messiah? Are you Neo-Pagan, atheist, Rastafarian or Zoroastrian? Do you have fear of water, coffee, edges, animals, open spaces, spiders, trivets, garden trolls, tables, wind, snow, rain, flooding, illness, tooth decay, uncooked meat, spoiled milk, telephones, bare floors, babies, women, women with open-toed shoes, open doors, newspapers, cages, mouthwash, carrots, vegetables in general, oceans, ocean liners, crustaceans, electricity, plumbing, defecating in public restrooms, aprons, dirty dishes, sand in your bed, keys, shampoo, bath water, spoons or automobiles? How often do you think of suicide, patricide, infanticide, matricide, or non-specific homicide?

What emotion dominates your day: happiness, sadness, anger, elation, joy, contentment, worry, grumpiness, futility, apathy, disillusionment, feeling overwhelmed, boredom, sadism, or masochism? Would you describe your circle of friends as wide, small or non-existent? When was the last time you engaged in sexual intercourse? Was the sex mutual, paid for, forcibly taken or otherwise coerced? If coercion was involved, were you the perpetrator or the victim? Have you experienced any sudden weight loss or weight gain in the past six months? What is your total net worth in monetary value? What is your income? What is your debt? How did you accumulate your largest debt? What are the reasons for the debt? Have you been married? Do you have any children? If so, what are their ages? Do they live in your household? Do you pay child support? How would you describe your relationship with them- happy, intimate, troubled, distant, or ambivalent? How do you feel about your role as a parent? Can you provide material goods to them? Do they go hungry? Do they have adequate clothing and shelter? Are they on public assistance? Describe your influence on their minds and emotional well-being. What is your current occupation? How long have you been at your current job? Rate your level of job satisfaction on a 1 to 10 scale. Does your occupation align with your personal beliefs, goals, needs and wants? Have you thought or dreamed of doing other work? What barriers do you foresee to finding new employment? Rate your level of loyalty to your employer on a 1-10 scale. How long do you think the company will be in business? Describe what the company thinks of you. What have you saved for retirement? What is your projected retirement age? With your current savings how many years will you be able to be comfortably retired, given that social security will have been abolished by then? What is your level of faith in the stock market? In banks? What is your faith in anyone who counts money, invests money, tricks someone else out of money, flaunts money, worships at the cult of money, has faith in money? How would you describe your reading habits? Do you subscribe to any newspapers, magazines, book-of-the-month clubs or trade periodicals? What was the last book you read? What made you want to read it? Was it satisfying, maddening, opaque, devious, pretentious, awkward, inaccurate, depressing, humorous, bizarre, redundant, too long, too short, derivative, modern, post-modern, fractured, cohesive, boring, obvious, enlightening, well-crafted, plotless, masturbatory, frightening, cinematic, esoteric, persuasive, ridiculous, ponderous, or a sloppy mess of random scenes stitched together with the thinnest thread of logic? How many hours of television do you watch a day? A week? What are your favorite shows? What in the content appeals to you? How many hours a day do you stare at a computer? What do you do on the computer? Do you mask your interests, weaknesses and perversions by calling your computer time "work?" Do you participate in any extreme sports, such as rock climbing, skateboarding, surfing, parachuting, hang gliding, waterskiing, slalom skiing, scuba diving, long distance running, competitive cycling, ocean swimming, kayaking, rollerblading, ice skating, ice hockey or windsurfing?

How would you describe your relationship with your parents? Have you ever had sex with your mother or father? Have you directed any overt violence towards your parents? Have they directed any violence towards you? Do you have any siblings? Have you ever had sex with your siblings? Have you ever directed violence towards one of your siblings? Have any of your siblings directed violence at you? Do you regard any object with awe or believe that it is imbued with a metaphysical spirit or magical potency? Do you exhibit such worship or belief in regards to a particular part of man's and woman's body? How would you define your relationship with animals? Have you ever had sex with an animal? Have you ever euthanized an animal? For any reason other than you believed it should be dead? Have you ever abandoned an animal? If so, what do you think happened to that animal? Tell me about your diet. What do you consider a normal daily intake of food and drink? What is your typical breakfast, lunch, and dinner? How often do you snack? Do you drink regular or diet soda? How many servings of fruit do you eat in a day? Vegetables? How many servings of meat? Do you harbor any political or moral beliefs against the consuming of meat? What's the first thing that comes into your mind when I say chitterlings? Watermelon? Haggis? Bagels and lox? Chicken soup? Tomato soup? Pierogies? Stuffed cabbage? Chicken fried rice? Lo mein? Hummus? Falafel? Beef tenderloins? Hamburgers? Describe your interests or hobbies. Do you participate in Civil War reenactments? Are you part of a Renaissance Faire juggling troupe? Do you know the difference between a Ford 428/429 Cobra Jet and a Chevrolet 454 LSG? Do you prefer sun or shade? What kind of soil, acidic or alkaline? Clay or loam? What is the bloom season for the perennial Soapwort? Do you know its Latin name? Does if prefer sun or shade? What kind of soil does Soapwort prefer? Answer the same questions about Goat's Beard. Where is the habitat of the black-chinned hummingbird (Archilochus alexandri, Colibrí barba negra, Colibri à gorge noire, Koliberek czarnobrody)? True or False. The barn swallow (Hirundo rustica) eats only flying insects? What small shorebirds are known mainly for their reversed sex-role mating system in which females compete for mates and often breed with several partners while the male's primary function is to raise the young? What is the difference between a circular saw and a jig saw? Wall studs are typically placed how many inches apart? Writer Alfred Döblin was said to have rewritten his masterpiece *Berlin Alexanderplatz* after reading what author? Samuel Beckett was awarded the Nobel Prize for Literature in what year? What movement is Emil Nolde associated with? Who painted The Dog (c. 1820) on the wall of his own home, Qunita del Sordo? Are you attracted to women wearing plaster casts? Women who dress up in furry bunny costumes with fixed goofy smiles and large dead eyes? Do you like to be nude around clothed women? When was the last time you tasted a woman's asshole? Do you like shaved, trimmed or unruly thatches the size of a New York pizza slice? Have you engaged in voyeurism or exhibitionism? Are you particularly attracted to women on the spectrum of a human genome variation other than your own?

Latina, Asian, African, Native American, Arab, Tongan or other Pacific Islander, Indian or Persian? Are you attracted to women sweating or working out, hair tied back, a moist neck exposed except for the wisps of hair stuck to her hot, wet skin? Do you find your eyes tracking a woman's ass or breasts when you observe her? Have you ever made a girlfriend dress in a school girl skirt? Have you ever masturbated in public upon seeing an attractive female? Have you ever been chained to a floor, wall or ceiling by a woman? Have you ever submitted control to a dominate female archetype? Have you ever let a woman fuck you in the ass with a dildo? Do you prefer small or large breasted women? Has a woman ever laughed at or otherwise commented on the size of your penis? Describe your relationship with your penis. Is it a source of pride, shame or frustration? Are you attracted to women with tattoos, piercings, dyed hair, surgically altered, overly painted and plucked, with shaved or wooly armpits, with natural eye color or radiant, android-inspired contact lenses, with painted fingernails encrusted with rhinestones or Chinese characters meaning "goose fat" or "stagnant water" painted on the thumbnail or the nail of the forefinger or painted toenails that look like she may have stubbed all ten toes simultaneously, which caused bleeding underneath the nails and which will take months to grow out? Are you attracted to women wearing cornrows, dreadlocks, shaved scalps, swirled and sprayed hair that could pass for sculpture in flea markets and roadside stands proclaiming "Reel Amish Crafts?" Do you prefer painted lips, powdered cheeks, and glittering eyes or the natural look that reveals every crack and blemish that reminds you this creature is an animal of the earth and deserving of desires, impulses and urges? Have you ever been sexually gratified while thinking of a woman wearing a leather tool belt or discussing the differences in torque and horsepower between a Ford 428/429 Cobra Jet and a Chevrolet 454 LS6? Do you like g-strings and thongs, granny panties or pajamas riding up the crack of her ass? Have you ever been attracted to the sourness of morning breath or ejaculate hardened on her thigh from the previous night's session of lovemaking? How extensively have you traveled? How many of the fifty states have you visited? List the states you have visited. Have you traveled to Haiti or Cuba? What oceans have you swum in? Have you been at an elevation over 13,000 feet other than an airplane flight? What is the longest flight you have taken? What continents have you visited? Does travel interest you in any way? How many photographs with your visage somewhere in the frame do you think exist? How many Super 8mm or 8mm films of you exist? How many videotapes or recording in a digital format of you do you think exist? Are there any audio recordings of your voice? Have you ever kept a journal or diary? Have you ever written a short story, novel, play, screenplay, or poem based on the events of your life? What made the event so noteworthy it had to be recorded in written form? Have you ever heard the phrase "it was just like in a movie" to describe an event, thought, coincidence or ironic twist? What made the incident movie-like? How often do you use colloquialisms in your speech? What do the following colloquialisms mean? 1. The worm had turned. 2. We are going to have a come to Jesus meeting. 3. You're the one fucking the chicken, I'm just holding its wings. 4. Time to piss on the fire and call the dogs. How would you describe the breadth and depth of your vocabulary? Are you curious about what words mean and what their etymology is? Are you curious about how machines work? The history of an idea or invention? The origin of the species? Have you ever dreamed of Neanderthals? Have you ever considered the first meeting between Neanderthals and Homo Sapiens? Have you ever owned or frequently used a telescope or a microscope? Can you name over five constellations? Explain in simple terms the concept of dark matter? How many sexual partners have you had in your life? How often you do masturbate? Do you drink coffee, tea or hot cocoa? What is you favorite color? Do you have any known allergies? Have you suffered from abnormal discomfort from a bee sting, breathing dust, eating chocolate or drinking orange juice? Have your hands ever swelled after being licked by a dog? What noise do you find to be the most irritating? Do you prefer mornings or evenings? Are you a morning person or a night owl? Given a choice would you prefer a 95° F degree day with over 90% humidity or a 10° F day with an arctic wind carrying snowflakes the size of your fist? What do you think brought you to this point in your life? Why are you in jail talking to a jail psychiatrist in this air-conditioned room with a window that cannot open (even though it's understandable that the architect would design the building so that the inmates couldn't jump out the window and escape, if one wanted to be charitable to his lack of understanding of basic human needs, because this office happens to be on the 12th floor so anyone willing to jump from the window would surely fall to their deaths and the county administration would have had to erect narrow spikes made of U.S. steel to catch the falling bodies and limit the splatter on the sidewalks)? Why are you here? What led you to this predicament? Could you have made different choices which would have led to a different outcome? What path are you currently hurtling down? Is it a well-worn path or are you blazing a trail of your very own? You can answer any of these questions at any time. We have all night.

    Nelson had sent answers to his lips, but none made it to their destination and his head began to ache because of the cacophonous clatter of his thoughts. Dr. Mel Joonce watched him open his mouth as if trying to speak only to close it again before formulating words. He leaned back in his chair and drummed his fingertips together as he rested his hands on his belly. The judge would not accept a report filled with "did not answer" to every question because H.H. Huckleberry did not present obvious catatonia nor obvious physical limitations that would impede his speech. She would also cast aspersions at Dr. Joonce, fuming that he lacked the discipline and patience with the most pathological inmates, that she would call him next time she needed someone to potty train an inmate or blow his nose free of mucous. He thought for a moment, flipping through the alternative approaches that he could use and settled on the Semantic Interpretation and Psychological Profile Assessment test, Series

4 (SIPP-v4). The test consisted of a series of twenty cards with ambiguous scenes drawn in a strangely dated style somewhere between Norman Rockwell and pulp magazine tableaus, created by tracing an original image and looking completely derivative and original at the same time.

Dr. Joonce rose from his chair and found the cards stacked loosely on a bottom shelf of a cabinet pushed into the corner of his room. He would show the twenty ambiguous scenes to the patient and have him interpret the scene, describing what he sees, giving his view of what had happened and projecting into the future lives of the ambiguous players. He hoped an image or two would rattle H. H. Huckleberry's mind and shake loose his thoughts and words so he could write something down on the report for the judge and she could look a little kindly on him in the future. The cards were 8 x 10 and made of thick cardboard, dog-eared at the corners from being shuffled around over the years. Dr. Joonce set them on his desk and pulled a small recorder from a drawer in the desk. He checked the battery life, the amount of tape left and fiddled with the angle of the tiny microphone so that it pointed unobstructed towards Nelson's mouth. It seemed like too much preparation for a man who had not spoken, but D. Joone couldn't really trust his note taking because he tended to write impressions rather than transcription and several lawyers pounded him on the stand when his answers drifted towards poetry and vagueness. He explained to Nelson the purpose of the test, that, of course, there were no wrong answers, that he should just talk without premeditation, tell Dr. Joonce a story, to confront what was on the card, to imagine the scene in real life, to let fly his interpretation, his subjective, personal interpretation. Nothing more, nothing less.

Dr. Joonce presented the first card to Nelson by placing it down on the desk in front of him. Nelson blinked at it. It depicted a boy about eight years old sitting in a chair. The view is a profile. In front of him resting on a low table is a cello. The boy holds the bow in his hand. His face holds a contemplative look. There is a shadow of a lamp behind him, possibly connoting a family household. Dr. Joonce put his hands on his belly again, leaned back in the chair and waited. He waited a full five minutes before leaning forward and clicking off the recorder. He looked at his watch, feeling impatient but knowing he had no plans after work, that he had nowhere to go, no one to call, no television to turn on, no current book that had grabbed his interest, no dog to feed and even no dinner to cook because he had begun to diet again to eliminate his growing paunch.

"Ok, how about pen and paper? You get one last shot before I ask Charon to take you back across the river," Dr. Joonce said as he found an old ballpoint and a few sheets of copy paper in the middle drawer of his desk.

Nelson took the pen from Dr. Joonce and flipped it in circles using his thumb, forefinger and middle finger. It felt like it had been years since he had used his fine motor skills. His fingers were stiff and clumsy, but the movement of the three fingers made him want to loosen up both hands and wrists so he began flexing his fingers and rotating his wrists.

"Could you attempt to answer the question as posed?" A hint of a stare crept into Dr. Joonce's eyes. He couldn't yet tell if H. H. Huckleberry played a game with him, but if he didn't attempt an honest effort with these cards he may just tell the judge that, based on Dr. Joonce's education, degrees and years of observation and experience, Huckleberry had faked insanity and that he was obviously competent to stand trial and be released to the general jail population, figuring this would be the exact opposite of what Huckleberry tried to achieve with his obvious recalcitrance.

Nelson touched the pen to the paper and after the first few wavering marks the words began to flow. He answered the question.

I see a boy sitting alone in a living room. It's probably a nice day and all he wants to do is ride his bike to the school playground and play basketball. But at some point in the past he either told his parents that he wanted to play the cello or they picked the instrument for him because he is too clumsy for the violin, too weak to blow the trumpet, too confused for the clarinet or saxophone. Now he is being forced to practice to either justify the expense of renting the cello and buying private lessons or as a form of torture to instill discipline deep within the psyche of the child. Sitting before him in the guise of the cello sits an opportunity for achievement, success, a chance to stand out in the crowd and turn the shriek and scream of misplayed notes into soaring songs if only he would pick up the fucking instrument. Pick up the instrument, fucker! All you have to do is practice a little. Give of yourself and you will succeed. He is afraid of himself. He will never pick up the cello. He will slink back to the corner, back to the shadow.

Dr. Joonce replaced the first card with a second. This card showed a young girl in the foreground holding a book. From the side a frumpy looking pregnant woman with wisps of hair covering her eyes looks about to speak to the girl. In the background a man hunches over a broken machine, maybe a farm implement, maybe the engine to something else. His arms are covered with grease to his elbows and his big toe on his right shoe is sticking through the worn leather. He's wearing overalls. Nelson studied it for several minutes then began writing.

I smell oil and sweat. The girl is all thumbs, unfit for the physical life. She has discovered books as a portal to another life. She believes, even as a child, that these books she has discovered will lead her to a better life filled with men in soft suits and undershirts, with trimmed beards and deodorant slicking their armpits. She does not know she'll more than likely end up a clerk, a cashier or a receptionist for a machine parts company where the salesmen and factory workers will always try to look down her shirt.Now, she can fantasize about lakeside cottages and foods imported from around the globe. Her mother, heavy with more spawn, looks at her with pride and confusion. Whose book it that? Who gave it to her? What would impel a child to read something other than the Word? She has turned into "the other" right before their eyes, a stranger in the household, mulling over a burgeoning set of very different values. She is rejecting the family's life, but the mother has some secret pride that at least she provided the environment for this girl to be able to change. The father, poor sap, is a desperate worker who likes fucking his wife, but he has been told and he has internalized that contraception is an affront to God, who created all those playful little sperm devils not to be delivered into one's own hand or on the thigh of your wife and certainly not into a bag of plastic or a cloud of sperm killing foam. So, the old man wears away his fingers and life with punishing work, trying to keep clothes on the backs and food in the bellies of the brood. He's seen his daughter read and sometimes chuckles at the idea of the little wisp breaking away from the iron constructs that have kept the family desperate since their last name began, that the child thinks maybe she will finish high school and go to college, when most likely one of the boy children from an equally desperate family will impregnate her at fourteen or fifteen and seal their fate. He knows he should support her more, help keep those hungry peckers away from her, give her a chance to get the hell out of his misery, but these goddamn machines keep breaking and they need the machines to feed the family. Her fancies will kill them. Without the machines there is only starvation.

Nelson felt thrilled that a small and steady flow of words in logical form had found a way through the confusion. He turned over the second card face down to indicate he had completed his interpretation and that he wanted another card to analyze. The new card showed a boy sitting in front of a rotting clapboard-sided house. The glass in a window to the right has been replaced by sections of discarded cardboard. The wood of the house has not been painted in decades. The boy is dirty and wears no shoes. No one else is on the picture. He sits in the front door opening. No door is visible yet there seem to be hinges.

The boy sits at the front of his house after an economic cataclysm or pandemic. His parents have died from starvation or disease and their rotting corpses lie in the backyard on the edge of a fetid pond. He only goes back there when he wants to ask one of them a question about hunger or his chances for survival. His sisters have left. The twins followed a troupe of thieves disguised as jugglers, fire-eaters, and handymen on their way through a landscape of devastation, a post-consumer, post-apocalyptic, post-government, post-radio, post-television world of Medieval hamlets. The second sister married a tinker in a made-up ceremony on the highest hill in town under two diseased apple trees. The couple conjured up a baroque language that included words like fidelity and heartstrings and honor-bound and exchanged trinkets crudely made of tin to look like a frog for the groom and a swan for the bride. All the clergy had left town in mass migration, some people walking with children and rucksacks on their backs, others riding their bikes as long as the inner tubes lasted, and still others driving their cars until the gasoline ran out. They sing tired songs as they go, still believing the whole world had not yet collapsed and that somewhere there is a place, a country, a city-state still functioning and caring for its people. The sisters each thought the other would take the boy, but he has been left to survive on his own. He has burned the front door for warmth on a particularly bitter and snowy January day. How long will he last given he makes decisions with a child's understanding? He has eaten his shoes and he has been surviving off the rotted windfall apples from the autumn before and the rain he can collect as it drips off the roof.

Nelson leaned back and shook his writing hand. He had been gripping the pen too tight and trying to keep up with his thoughts. Dr. Joonce swept up the card and replaced it with a fourth. This card showed a woman standing outside a doorway. She is holding her face in her hand and is weeping into her palm. She is wearing a robe and a negligee underneath. Through the doorway she sees a young man sprawled out on the bed. He is still wearing a suit and tie, although the tie has been loosened and the shirt is rumpled and stained. His hair is obviously disheveled and he is obviously unconscious. His mouth has dropped open. Nelson began to write.

They are a young married couple, maybe under two years since the wedding, or they've decided to live together to test their compatibility. She, against her better judgment and the warnings of family and friends, has fallen in love with him. She had active fantasies of creating a house around him and having his children and taking family vacations and cooking his favorite meals so she can see a boyish delight creep across his face and performing fellatio for him whenever he desires it and working hand-in-hand to build a future. Unfortunately, what she didn't know before they were married or before they decided to move in together or before she had fallen so deeply in love with this flawed man in that he loved vodka and whores above all else in life. He tells her this is the way he will move up in the company. It is the corporate culture he tells her. The CEO and his cronies are the biggest collection of degenerates this side of the Rockies and at least three times a week they demand late work and inevitably the late work migrates to a private bar packed with men and women from the company who are determined to move up in the company no matter the cost to their personal pride, even if it means engaging in this drunken, whoring puppet show for the bosses. The woman has a hard time arguing with her young husband or lover because the paychecks have been getting larger and his titles are getting longer and less understandable, moving from Sales Representative to Regional Manager to Assistant Director of Regional Strategy and Development to Director of Regional Strategy and Development to Senior Director and Vice President of Acquiring, Dismantling, and Disposing, but this does not make her feel less miserable or less trapped or less of a fool when she smells another woman's perfume stinking up her bed. When he finally passes out she smells his fingertips to track where they have been. Most nights she is confronted with olfactory evidence that his fingers have explored creases and orifices outside the marriage contract or outside their understanding when they decided to move in together. She is weeping into the smell of another woman that had rubbed off on the palm of her hand from his fingertips. She wonders how a marriage with so much promise could sour so quickly. Her love has been abused and battered.

A knock sounded on the door and Dr. Joonce told the person to come in. The guard poked his head in and asked how much longer the session would take. Dr. Joonce looked at the pile of unviewed cards and told the guard it would probably take another couple of hours. The guard motioned Dr. Joonce into the hallway. He followed the guard's direction and shut the door behind him.

"My shift ends in a half hour, Doc. They won't approve no overtime."

"What do you want me to do about it?"

"I'm just saying that I have to leave in a half hour, so when you come out here and there's another guard sitting there you'll know why."

"Thank you. You're right. I probably would have wondered what happened to you."

"I didn't want you to worry or think I took off or something."

"That's very conscientious of you."

"I believe in communication."

Dr. Joonce looked at his watch. He may very well be here until midnight by the time he completed the interview and wrote the report for the judge. He made a promise to not sleep in his chair and to at least go home and take a shower and lie in his bed for an hour or two, just to give his back a rest. He thanked the guard again and turned to go back to his office.

"Hey, Doc. Do you have any pets?"

"I find I work too many hours to have a pet."

"You should get yourself a dog, something big and slobbery."

"Like I said, when you work as many hours as I do it would be unfair to the poor beast."

"Doc, sometimes you have to look after yourself. Maybe a dog would get you out of the office. Maybe you need something to get home to."

Dr. Joonce looked into the big, dumb face of the guard, who smiled back at him, and tried to find the sarcasm, the edge of the knife, the whiff of bullshit at his expense.

"That's good advice. But even if I could get a dog I wouldn't get something big and slobbery."

"C'mon, Doc, you're not telling me you'd get something like a pug or a French bulldog, some little old lady dog that never leaves your side?"

"My mother had corgis. The family loved those dogs."

"Jesus, Doc. Dogs are like cars. They are outward expressions of what we believe we are inside. I never thought of you as a corgi man. I thought for sure you'd go the foxhound route. To each his own, right, Doc?"

Dr. Joonce paused, nodded his head because answering the question would have led to further conversation, and returned to his office. The guard tried to say something else before the door fully closed, but Dr. Joonce had stopped listening. Nelson hadn't moved since Dr. Joonce had left. Even though he had stopped writing he still stared at the card on the desk, either completing the story in his head or creating an alternate version outside his first attempt. Dr. Joonce started to apologize for the interruption, but he checked himself since the interruption merely delayed Nelson's return to the jail cell, so the delay would be not much of an inconvenience at all and certainly not worth the apology. Dr. Joonce returned to his chair and gave Nelson another card.

The fifth card showed a young woman trying to read to a child seated on the floor. The child has turned away and is not looking at the woman. She is holding a stuffed bunny on her lap. In the far background a man stands with his hands on his hips, looking toward the woman and child.

This is a scene of a family relationship. The mother is trying to read to her daughter who is refusing to listen. She has been playing with her bunny. She has set up an elaborate tea party with a host of stuffed animals, a skunk, a badger, a fluffy dog, a puffin sitting around a small table with plastic cups and a plastic tea pot. The skunk had just been telling his stories about his adventures in Rio de Janeiro when the mother has the idea to read to the child. She offers a picture book far under the ability of the child. The girl looks at her like she is crazy. She has begun to despise her mother in great surges of hate since daddy crept away in the night and started a new family with his former administrative assistant. This new man, this man in the background, the man on the periphery of their lives smells like man deodorant and whiskey. He laughs too hard at his own unfunny jokes. He always teases her, pokes her in the ribs, and has no clue of how to talk to her. He's always grabbing her mother's ass and kissing her on the back of the neck when she is cooking. He always wears thin dress pants that show his near constant erection. The frustrated mother has pulled down *The Brothers Karamazov* to read. "If the little bitch doesn't like picture books anymore I'll give her something to read." It's only a matter of time before the two of them are screaming at each other, probably simultaneously, a screeching family chorus for all the neighborhood to hear, until the man retreats to the basement to watch football. The child may end up hating literature if it is used as weapon and punishment, but she understands the religious fervor of Alyosha Karamazov more than she will tell her mother, who thinks Dostoevsky is the perfect punishment for a high-minded, arrogant child who has dismissed her picture books too soon, and the book becomes a topic of heated debate amongst the tea party after her mother leaves.

Dr. Joonce pulled the card away and several sheets of paper crowded with Nelson's small, cramped script. On each of the pages he wrote the date and H.H. Huckleberry. He placed another card in front of him. Two women dressed in lab coats stand near a counter. One woman, hair down, is stirring liquid in a beaker. There are several other beakers on the table and all are empty except a few in which the liquid looks unstable. The second woman stands a little distant with her hands clasped behind her back. She is older than the first woman but still quite beautiful. Her lab coat is unbuttoned, revealing heavy breasts. There may be a hint of cleavage poking from the top of the shirt.

Nelson's hand hovered over the blank sheet of paper before attacking the white space.

The older woman is a supervisor or holds a senior position in the laboratory. She has come to supervise the technique and efficiency of the younger woman. She has left her lab coat unbuttoned and she is showing off her breasts not because she has latent homosexual desires, but she wants to remind the younger woman that she too is a woman brimming with sexual power and that she can still make her male colleagues snap to attention by wearing a form-fitting blouse. The supervisor likes the potential of the younger woman, thinks she may make a good lab tech after she is thoroughly trained, but doesn't know if she will recommend the company keep her based on her observed work. The younger woman has buttoned up her lab coat to her throat because she believes the older woman would like to have sex with her but is too repressed to ask for it. The younger woman believes she is desirable, believes she gives off a pleasant erotic scent. She knows she has inadvertently enticed men and women by just being natural and relaxed. Friends have told her that her core is sexy, but she has to cover up this aspect of her being because being desirable in the eyes of the bosses can lead to trouble, as it has in the past, and she really needs this job. She needs this job because she has accumulated credit card debt and her car had been shaking and shimmying to the right for months. She needs this job because she believes she is a natural chemist, a savant, a mystic alchemist, who will discover anti-aging creams what will iron out any wrinkle in two applications. She will construct salves that dissolve herpes sores and stop bleeding no matter how large the wound. She has conveniently overlooked the fact that her job consists of testing urine and blood for illegal narcotics and high concentrations of alcohol for a major worldwide corporate behemoth where the majority of jobs require the aid of mind-killing drugs for the worker to make it through the day. The directors of the behemoth have come to understand the jobs with their company kill the minds of their workers, but instead of changing the nature of the jobs they have implemented a company-wide, indeed, a world-wide drug testing sweep. They end up not firing anyone because they discover 62% of their workforce, from the retail end to corporate management, has tainted urine. Firing those 62% of workers would bring the company and national economy to its knees, maybe even cause a global depression because the company has grown so incredibly bloated, so the marketing department has worked overtime in creating anti-drug and anti-alcohol pamphlets to be placed on the employee lunchrooms and executive toilets around the globe. The older woman wonders if the younger woman tastes as good as she smells. Of course, the older woman does not yet know the younger woman thinks the tainted piss and blood will unlock a fundamental understanding of the human condition and have a marketable application.

Dr. Joonce quickly replaces the cards when Nelson paused long enough for him to think he had finished. The next card showed a fully dressed man standing over a naked woman who lies in bed. The covers are tangled around her feet. She is asleep or has closed her eyes against the light. The man seems distraught. He has put his hands over his face and the hunch of his back makes him look like he might be ready to fall to his knees. There are a couple of books on the nightstand. The woman does not shave or otherwise trim her pubic hair.

The man is faced with the object of his desire, a woman who he has tried to bed for three years. This is a woman he has taken to dinner, sent emails to once a day at noon when his lunch break begins, has taken to the sea and ogled her firm breasts and round ass in a bikini, who has detailed her history of previous relationships that includes paranoia, debauchery, forced lesbianism, kidnapping, torture and gunplay, a woman who he had thought about when he has fallen asleep, continued the thought in very detailed and lurid dreams, and woke up six hours later with the thought still processing through his mind, a woman who knows he has madly loved her for the past three years but has chosen to dangle the bait in front of him, string him along, play with his heart like a balled up sock made into a chew toy for a dog. The man is happy for the torture, because he is delighted a woman pays attention to him, that a woman believes he is worthy of her flirtations, and if he does not have the opportunity to touch her skin or make her orgasm then he can provide pleasure to her through his agony. But on this night he has drunk one shot of bourbon and one beer too many and has decided to drive to her house and tell her that either she starts fucking him or she could just stop telling him about her criminal boyfriends and their fetishes because if he had to visualize one of those monsters pawing her skin one more time then he may run her and the boyfriend down with car. But when he arrives at the house he stays in his car for an hour watching the dark windows, hoping a light would come on or hoping to see her weaving into her driveway, drunk, with makeup smeared down her chin and her dress askew, looking out of control and abused, so her spell on him could be broken. But no light ever comes on in the house and when he checks he sees her car already in the garage. He walks through the unlocked back door. It makes him think that she is expecting him. Luckily, she owns two cats and no dogs and the cats run to the basement when they see his shadow and hear his footsteps. He walks through the kitchen and up the stairs and into her bedroom. There she lays naked. It is a hot night and the old house does not have central air. The window unit leaks and makes the room too cold so when she leaves it on she always awakes with sore shoulders, erect nipples and frozen sinuses. She has taken to sleeping naked with no covers. She knows he is in the room. She is waiting for him to decide his next move, but she is frozen in fear. He will either masturbate and ejaculate on her belly or he will rape her. She will continue to feign slumber should he choose the more passive route and she will let her dreams careen to a dark place. If he chooses violence she will pretend to wake on the second or third thrust and plead with him to stop, even though she knows he will not stop. He has his quarry he has long chased. Her pet has turned on her and she feels sick with shame. She has driven an otherwise decent and sad man to rape her, but she thinks she may have also performed a service for him. She has shown him the limit of his patience, the edges of his hate and selfishness, and the end of his love. After three miserable years he has decided to take what he wants and needs with the aid of a gallon of alcohol. He chooses rape and she does not stop him and she continues to feigh sleep. The man stands up, puts on his pants and realizes he has destroyed the possibility of love freely given, of desire elicited through charm, wit and self-assurance. After he stops weeping he won't give a damn. He will think of the semen inside her and smile to himself. The spell has been broken. He is not curious whether or not she will press charges, because he is happy to be free of her and her horrible allure. He will wallow in his new found freedom and will gladly tell his story to the authorities should they ask and will plead guilty to whatever charge they can conjure, because he is giddy with freedom and not taking the longer view of possible consequences.

Dr. Joonce placed the eighth card in front of Nelson. He stifled a yawn and looked at the clock. He thought he may sleep on the floor of his office tonight, even though he had made it a point to promise himself he would not do that very thing. He had a change of underwear and socks tucked away in the filing cabinet and a toothbrush in a desk drawer next to a travel-sized tube of toothpaste. Nelson had stopped writing. Dr. Joonce noticed he had placed the card face-side down so that Nelson only saw a company logo of the test manufacturer and a trademark symbol. He apologized and flipped it over. The picture showed a young boy standing on a ledge or a ladder or a box. He is elevated and he is holding a rifle. He is pointing it up in the air. Below him two men work on a third man. They are some distance away. His belly has been sliced open and their hands are encased inside the opening in his flesh. The man's eyes are open and his mouth looks about to gape open, possibly to let out a scream or to instruct the men to move their hands a little to the left if they are to find what they are looking for.

This is the time after the corporations have stolen everyone's money through marketing schemes, indecipherable loans, fake checking and savings accounts, and all the stock exchanges in the world that zeroed out on the same day and the bosses have converted all that money into hand-built motor vehicles with armor plating and turrets, marble palaces built on the shores of oceans or mountain crevasses and bushels and bushels of cocaine. All the money has been siphoned away from the hands of workers and clerks, farmers and pensioners. The people have turned to weapons and robbery as anarchy replaces representative democracy and the republic turns into a fading and quaint memory. The boy is in the employ of the two men who are attacking the third. The boy's job is to stand on the box or ladder or cliff and snipe passing travelers, preferably not killing them outright but disabling them. He is the best shot most people have ever seen and in better times he would have joined the military or a police force or had a shelf full of trophies and ribbons from shooting competitions, but as it is he blows apart the hamstrings or hips of travelers passing by on bicycles or walking or riding in stitched together cars kept running on the parts of abandoned cars by men and women who know how to convert the engines to burn something other than gasoline. The sequence is always the same. The boy sits near his gun thumbing through his collection of well-worn, dog-eared comic books that haven't yet been burned for heat until he is warned that a traveler is coming down the path. It's usually his father who tells him with a bark, but sometimes his uncle will be the one to deliver the command. The boy will lie down on a dirt patch the size of his body and will aim his rifle towards the path, finding the traveler in his scope. He follows them for a while, especially if they are walking or slowly pedaling a bicycle. The angle of the perch allows him to have a clean shot for several hundred yards. He watches them until he knows them, learns their rhythm, their gait, their mood and their level of exhaustion. He is very calm. He would like to know where these people are going. What makes them think there are money, jobs, and a functioning society down this path? He will alternate between the hip and lower down just above the knee. His father and uncle are sometimes mad at him and not a little afraid when they see him cleanly shoot out a hip joint of a passerby. They know his talent is beyond them and when he gets older they will have nothing to offer him to keep him, even though they are the only family he has ever known. He will leave in search of a girl and he will be able to kill his way until he finds one, but for now his father and uncle are beneficiaries of his talent. Once he has disabled the traveler, or two travelers or three travelers if they have tried to keep their families together, they will wait until they can determine if the wounded have guns of their own and if they do he will shoot them through the palm and make them drop the weapon. His father and uncle will bolt out of their hiding places, two shallow holes dug out with empty tuna cans and covered with dead brush, wielding knives. They harvest the bodies. They fight over the livers and kidneys. The boy survives on flesh and is never given delicacies. By the looks of the men's expressions the slimy organs must taste better roasted than the seared cubes of meat, skin and fat he has to eat. The men are correct in their fears and their predictions. The boy stores up all of their indifference and selfishness and one night will channel it all into a blind, white hot rage and he will shoot them both in the head as they sleep and before he leaves camp, before he walks into a unknown and chaotic world a new orphan, a chaos that has not abated but had grown exponentially over the decade he had been culling the travelers, he will slice open their bellies and harvest their livers and kidneys. He will eat one liver before he goes, roasting it on a slow spit that he will crank himself, looking at the surprised, dead eyes of his family as he chews. He is an expert in dissection, even though it is the first time he had performed one, because he has closely watched his father and uncle harvest over the years. Sometimes his uncle called his father Doc, referring to the previous life of sanity, education, good works, and his honed skill of working on a body. The boy will salt the other organs and slip them into a worn canvas rucksack. He will leave the bodies to rot or be eaten by scavengers because he knows their flesh will be bitter and tough.

Nelson leaned back in the chair, yawned and stretched his back. His writing hand throbbed. Dr. Joonce looked through him with piercing eyes.

"Do you want to continue or are you too tired?"

"I'll write as much as you want me to if it means that I don't have to go back in that cell."

Nelson's voice startled both of them. Dr. Joonce made a note that even though it sounded halting and raspy, the voice held a certain intelligence and proper diction. The voice also made Dr. Joonce uncomfortable and a little fear pricked his skin, because he had just spent a couple of hours in his office listening to a monologue of his own familiar, nasally, slightly whining voice, whether spoken aloud or running through his head in an unhinged scat, as the only sound. Dr. Joonce had forgotten the guard, had dismissed his words and concern, but Nelson's croaking sentence had snapped him out of his mulling and reminded the good doctor that the inmate in front of him had abused a household pet, had tried to resist arrest, had tried to injure a policeman and had displayed disturbing anti-social behaviors, such as sitting in a urine-stained corner, since he had been arrested. Could the doctor be strangled before the guard knew he had been attacked? Dr. Joonce set another card in front of him.

A magnificent tower rises from an ocean cliff. A large veranda sweeps around the base of the tower and the roof line of the house juts off at an odd and impossible angle as if the artist rushed through the drawing and missed a logical perspective. A woman, tiny against the massive structure, looks over the edge to the ocean beyond and the tumbled down rocks below. Amongst the rocks near the ocean's edge a line of workers in hats carry rocks or bags of mortar on their hunched backs.

We see one of the nation's raiders standing amidst their spoils. She and her husband, a highly placed executive in a company that produces weapon systems and automobile parts, have had this ocean-side retreat built to their specifications. They have used the hands of thousands of itinerant workers to build the palace stone by stone. Guards with automatic weapons, produced by her husband's company, are always within shouting distance should one of the workers forget who they are and try to steal something or kidnap her. Her husband insisted they be hired for around the clock surveillance. Each spring, after the hard winter tide, they have the cliff face reinforced with mortar and stone. In the old days this would have been so outrageously expensive they could not have afforded it even with the husband's executive salary. Now, with so many men and women out of work and desperate the husband and wife and people of their economic stratus can indulge in almost any fantasy or whim. They had the internationally famous architect Boten Darling design the house and tower and the residence has already shown up in early surveys of late decade oceanfront architecture and even graced the cover of Oceanfront Building Materials Digest, which the husband had framed and is now hanging in their bedroom. Her husband is fit and tan, with styled hair and a trace of a continental accent. She has maintained a figure worthy of the retreat and their mid-tower condo in the city. He is a scientist turned engineer, who had promise as a researcher and had a gift for teaching, who decided to cash in his research for gobs of money and his oceanfront retreat, who rose to Vice President of Product Development, really the most important and sought after position in the company right after CEO, because he successfully brought to production a drone laser orb that has the ability to shoot a laser through the pupil of a target and sear their frontal lobe without a drop of blood or an entry wound other than a small dark spot floating on the eye and a bomb that once detonated propelled titanium shrapnel in a halo around the impact site no more than six inches off the ground. The bomb severs the feet of the target close to impact and shreds the Achilles tendons of the targets standing in the outer halo of the blast. The husband had the foresight to imagine the bomb being converted for domestic use to quell riots and strikes and he ordered that several halo sizes be developed. His hunch proved correct. As the country collapsed, riots became an everyday nuisance and more than once some workers got it into their head to stop working and to demand better wages or better food and liquor on the shelves. The company's largest customers as a type were the remaining public police forces and most all the private security forces. The company made money hand over fist and its stock shot upward to ridiculous heights, when the stock market existed. The woman had been something of a track star in her youth and narrowly missed being on the Olympic team in the 400m and 800m. She studied anthropology without any real interest, slept with a few scruffy boys, and tramped around the globe for a couple of years before choosing the engineer. His dullness and hypochondria were a small price to pay for this retreat and the view of the city from their condo. They could have moved higher in the tower, but the CEO of the company lived on the floor above them and stubbornly refused to move up and they could not live on a floor higher than the CEO so they stayed put. She sometimes wonders if the dirty workers want to touch her and she sometimes wears shear clothing as she strolls around the pool that looks like a large pond, trying to distract the workers from their dirty work. The workers, for their part, are happy for the spring work and know they will eat regular meals for the ten weeks it will take to finish shoring up the cliff, but each one, fifteen in all, think they would rather slice the lady of the manner's throat before they would have sex with her. They wonder at her ignorance of what hunger, disease, sorrow, burials, separations, and punishing physical labor can do to a man's libido. When she walks around in her see-through clothes she is mocking them, reminding them that they use to be young and their lovers could have hung wet towels or pots and pans on their arrow-straight erections. They all think of murder, but they keep their thoughts to themselves because they know better than to trust a hungry worker.

Should they speak a conspiracy would be born and the lady's throat would be cut until her head hung from her body by nothing but a few frayed tendons and the body would be dumped over the cliff to smash against the newly set mortar and rocks. She is unaware she is walking on the edge of a razor blade because she believes her money inoculates her from the violence and ignorance of the poor. They must be violent and ignorant or they wouldn't be poor. She doesn't understand these men were once autoworkers, teachers, certified public accountants, machinists, steelworkers, ironworkers, mathematicians and butchers and they believed their bloodline had been moving up in the world through hard work and sacrifice, and if not their children then their grandchildren would float across marble verandas and stare at the crashing waves in their spare moments and be grateful to their grandfather for killing himself with work. They believed all this before it all fell apart and they had to abandon their children and wives in desolate small towns because women with children had an easier time getting charity than if the family stayed intact. The missionaries and do-gooders would look at his strong back and thick forearms and tell the family that at least the man could earn some money through labor and maybe they would refer him to the cliff mansions for stone and mortar work, and even though he would tell them the wages the rich paid could barely feed him let alone a starving family, they would not give up the charity food. Maybe the missionaries would think to themselves that the man and woman should have considered their capacity for raising and providing for children before they started birthing them. They knew to keep their thoughts to themselves lest they unleash a wicked violence.

Dr. Joonce closed his eyes. He hadn't been aware that his eyeballs felt hot and swollen until his lids sheathed them. He would sleep well sitting in the chair or lying on the floor next to his desk where the rough husk of carpet would wear a small strawberry abrasion on his cheek as he squirmed to find comfort. He felt himself drifting and his own snort, a kind of bugle call of sleep, woke him enough for him to remember where he sat and that he still had a report to write that night. He probably had enough material to cook up a report. H.H. Huckleberry had been writing furiously. Dr. Joonce would have liked to start reading the pages and writing the report, but he found if he started reading with the inmate in the room they peppered him with questions about his reaction and became so distracted that they stopped concentrating on the card in front of them, effectively ending the exercise. So, he slid another card in front of Nelson that showed a middle-aged woman looking through a doorway into a dining room. The dining room table is empty except for a vase of flowers and no one sites in any of the chairs. Her expression reveals that she is looking at someone or something. She could be looking at the viewer or the card and thereby ruining the illusion of the pantomime, deconstructing the test and the players, or at someone or something just outside the frame of the picture. She is wearing a matronly dress.

She was once the mother of a teeming brood and the table holds the memories through a collection of nicks, burns, stains, paint and ink splotches, and the places where the finish has been worn off by the scuffing of plates and serving dishes. She had six children in all, the oldest three boys, the twin girls and the baby girl who held the whole family in the palm of her hand. The twins left at the age of fourteen even though they were seven years younger than the oldest, because they had prodigious musical talent and no teacher in town could teach them much after the age of twelve. Mother and father secured a full scholarship to an out-of-state musical academy and boarding school and when the twins left they didn't shed a tear for their sisters, brothers or parents, but assured them they would remember their love each day. They developed an act for two pianos during which they would play the same piece identically note for note, dressed to accentuate their identicalness. They even practiced their walk onstage and offstage and their thank you bow at the end of the performance. Audiences said the music sounded like the same person playing both pianos and the telepathy of the twins forged in the womb and reinforced through music made for great entertainment even though they were in the middle of the pack in terms of technique and repertoire at the academy. The oldest boy would not have left on his own. With each successive sibling he grew weaker and more wan and by the time he had five brothers and sisters he could barely make it through the day without napping in the basement or, if the weather turned nice, somewhere in the sprawling yard away from the brood. His father finally forced him out and secured a job on the county payroll, an exchange for campaign and fundraising help he had lent to a commissioner, and there he stayed for the next thirty-five years, only being promoted when everyone else in the department had either retired or died and serving in all capacities with no distinction. He retired with a full pension and spent his retirement in the dark rooms of his small aluminum-clad bungalow. He always came to reunions and family events but he had little to say. He sometimes had girlfriends, but they always faded away before a marriage could happen. The second and third oldest boys were close and hated the oldest boy for his weakness and irresolute life. They threw themselves into their studies and honed their sarcasm at the oldest brother's expense. They thought of trying their hand at comedy writing, but both ending up studying medicine and becoming doctors. Even as they grew older they talked everyday and emailed jokes back and forth using the same genre of jokes, usually starring a weak, imbecilic protagonist, having some variation of their brother's name. They talked incessantly about their twin sisters to their colleagues, who had seen the women perform on late night television numerous times and thought, like most critics thought, that they brought an interesting visual to the stage while playing ordinary and perhaps uninspired music, but they knew better than to level any criticism at the duo because their brother's unmerciful humor could make a person miserable. The youngest and by far the most beautiful of the lot glided through life so easily she often wondered why anyone should ever cry or contort their faces in a displeased frown or pout. Protected by her siblings she ran the house. The oldest loved her more than anyone he had ever known and would tell himself he felt stronger and more in tune with the world when he held her on his lap or played dolls with her or helped her build block towers so she could smash them to the ground. The doctors never turned their wit on her and helped her with her studies when they were home. They told her if they could take her tests for her they would and she laughed at their devotion and always gave them strong hugs in return. The twins loved to play for her because she would dance by the legs of the baby grand and make up nonsense songs to the tune they played. They would have loved to include her in the act, but the truth was her musical talent was limited, if not downright awful. Her inventiveness and energy delighted everyone who heard it, but not enough that someone would want to pay to see it. She found expression in running and over the years grew sleeker and faster and probably would have made the Olympic team had she not run against three women willing to inject their bodies with undetectable enhancements that gave them chin stubble, ear hair and voices that sounded like late night disc jockeys after smoking a pack of cigarettes. The injections cost her two hundredths of a second that separated her from third and fourth. She married a brilliant engineer turned businessman and she split her time between the city and her ocean retreat, where she oversees itinerant workers and flaunts her body in front of the collection of cripples and losers. Every Thanksgiving she hosts the family at the retreat. She sends the company helicopters to pick them all up. They all come because the youngest is the draw. They tell gentle stories of their dead father and they eat a handsome meal prepared by a French chef and served by a team of servers, the itinerant women who can clean up enough to be allowed entry into the house. Her husband is patient with the politics of the family and tries to ignore the thrusts and parries from the doctors who would like nothing more than to draw him into a full blown argument about the course of the world and the imminent destruction of all because of iniquity and nefarious weapon systems. So, the mother looks at her scarred table in her empty house and sometimes cries over the few brief years everyone had been together as they worked on their school projects at the table and the twins provided a constant soundtrack of scales, sonatas, and popular songs. She wonders why life has to be like smoke, obfuscating and choking a person, then rising and dissipating, leaving only the faintest traces that it had ever been. All of this history passes through her mind in the moment she pauses at the doorway and looks at the arranged flowers on the dining room table.

Nelson leaned back and stretched again. He violently shook his hand because he had gripped the pen so hard his hand had gone numb. He wondered if the words would be legible as they were now flowing out of his pen to the point his penmanship must have begun suffering. Dr. Joonce took the pages filled with writing too quickly for Nelson to be able to review for spelling, grammar and mistakes made because the pen couldn't pause long enough to make the proper letter. Dr. Joonce switched the cards. On the next card a group of men are sleeping on the ground, using each other for pillows. One man's head rests on another man's thigh, who uses the belly of another to rest his head. They all wear hats drawn over their eyes so the viewer cannot see their faces. Their clothes may be tattered or excessively wrinkled from lying on the ground. The perspective of the drawing is from an angle of someone standing over the men as they sleep.

Maybe these are the men we have seen before shoring up the cliff face for the still beautiful sister and almost Olympic runner. They are exhausted and all have fallen at the first comfortable spot they have seen and all are asleep within minutes of the falling. Maybe they dream of the curve of the woman's ass seen though gauzy material or the wisp of pubic hair between her thighs, but more than likely they don't dream at all. The sleep comes so hard and so fast the men may have thought they were dying and their brains are so confused about the state of their stricken bodies they abandon dreams and take inventory of the vital processes, making sure that nothing has shut down unexpectedly. They could also be dreaming of a brother or friend who had been shot in the hip or hamstring and his organs had been eaten while he still lived. They were held at bay by a child with a long and accurate rifle. They stayed until he stopped screaming, then they continued down the dusty path, pulling out the hair from the sides of their heads and punching their palms with impotent jabs, wailing that there is no justice or peace in this awful world. The jobs that they held and the houses where they lived and the new leased cars they traded in every three years and the wives who would iron their work clothes in the nude in the family room while watching a morning news show or who would stumble out of bed at 3:00 am to breast feed an infant and rock them back to sleep: all of it is a dream, a haunting that remains lodged in their memories as something that happened in their lives but could have existed in another dimension on a planet in a distant solar system, because that is how far and wide the schism between their old lives and their new lives has become. They openly wonder, but they never speak about why a body continues to live when there really is no purpose to life other than shoring up a sea wall that will have to be rebuilt the next spring anyway. They do speak of rumors they have heard, that the boy with the gun has moved to the road between two sparsely populated towns and the word is he's looking for a woman brave enough to be the sidekick to an assassin and cannibal or that a final famine is a few weeks away because the farmers have abandoned the fields and everyone else has forgotten how to grow crops or from the optimists who pass along the rumor that a new government has been formed and they have reconstituted the military, are training a police force, and have an ambitious plan of opening a congress and laying out a five year plan to establish order and security back in the land. If the group can manage a laugh this is when they usually do, because they have heard the optimistic rumors countless times before and in the past they sometimes allowed themselves to hope it could be true, but now they expect the optimists to tell them also that that government will be run by elves, the cabinet will be made up of the finest wizards and witches the president can find, and the five year plan includes rolling back the clock to a time before the cataclysm when their wives ironed clothes in the nude.

Dr. Joonce retrieved the card and replaced it with another. He knew he could have stopped, but H.H. Huckleberry seemed to be enjoying himself or at least he looked focused and concentrated and had lost the blank and dead stare he had when he walked into the room. This card showed a young woman sitting on the sidewalk or a narrow alleyway. She looks down at the cement. She is leaning to the side, the weight of her torso resting on her arm. It may be twilight. She is half in shadow cast from a looming brick building to her right. She's wearing hot pants and a loose blouse with a strangely formal and stiff collar. In the far background there is a smudge that looks like four legs.

She is an outcast, a pariah, a sacrifice. In her honor hidden drummers play a somber beat behind closed doors and windows, but she can hear the strike of the sticks through the thick walls of brick and mortar. It is now common that packs of dogs roam the streets, but no one can control when they come or why they come or for whom they come. Ceremonies have arisen to appease them or to fend them off, and, in some radical cases, to hunt them. The hunting parties never turn out well because the dogs are better hunters and they enjoy the sport, so always fewer hunters return than had left. This clan has chosen this young woman to face them. They have dressed her up like a prostitute and thrown her down on the pavement. They have not let her shower, bathe or even wash her face for a week. The prevailing wisdom is that scent has something to do with who is chosen and they have tried bathing all of their sacrifices and scenting them with odors that dogs are known to like: meat, urine, feces, and squirrel. The practice has met with little success, so they have tired a different tactic, natural human body odor. The clothing is nothing but perversity shown by the elders of the clan, because this woman is pure of heart and cannot imagine exchanging her body for cash under any circumstances, even though she has recently begun to think that she will have to pay for the services of a man who can achieve an erection, because all the men she as met for the past year remain flaccid and dispirited no matter what tricks she tries. She hopes the dogs will come. She wants to see where they will take her. She knows the dogs will not kill her and will not harm her if she does not struggle. People have returned after they have been taken. They are changed and the clan makes them sleep in separate quarters. For a time the clan offered the people who had already been taken as sacrifices, but the dogs would never take them when they were offered. The sacrifices eventually disappear but never at a time of a ceremony. So, the clan has taken to offering someone they thought most likely to be taken anyway. The woman's transgression is that she tried to sleep with two different men in the same week with no luck. In better times the story would have elicited a chuckle from a few co-workers over coffee, who would refer back to the bawdy story of the limp dicks for the balance of the day, but these were not those times, so the story becomes a parable of a lascivious woman who cannot be satiated because all the men she touches lose desire. Maybe the story borrows freely from King Midas or King Erysichthon, but no one remembers because all the old stories are being lost. This is not the first time she has been sent out into the street and it won't be the last. The dogs never come for her. Once as she dozed against a building, her skirt hiked up to her hips, three or four dogs came and licked her face and nuzzled her hands and feet. When she awoke to their entreaties a thrill ran through her, because she believed for a moment that they would take her away from this clan to a new life or show her a new understanding of life, but the encounter ended in disappointment when it became apparent they just wanted to wake her and get a few pets before trundling down the street. A lookout sitting behind a closed window on a high stool reported what he saw to the ruling elders. They puzzle over her power and probably each one then wished they could achieve at a least a half-erection, just enough stiffness to gain entry. In these times they had lowered their expectations and could not hope for anything more, like an arrow-straight erection and mutual orgasms, and they know even their tepid dreams are unrealistic. One asked if she had become a friend of the dogs. Another said they should consider a lifetime banishment given that she shared a bond with the beasts. What is she bringing into our homes? The women elders denounced her as a whore. Just look at how she dresses? Is it not unwise to harbor a slut in this era of flaccidity? She has shown no proclivity towards vagina so we ask you what is her purpose? Is she a personal demon? Is she a ravenous and filthy harpy come sailing from the heavens to laugh at your infirmities? The elders will listen to their reasoning and will agree to a permanent banishment, thus ensuring their extinction because she is the last of the fertile women of the clan and someday some man after a good night's sleep or torrid sexual dreams would have rallied enough to achieve a half-mast staff and managed to impregnate her. The birth would have signaled the beginning of a new golden age. The introduction of the baby in the clan would have drawn it closer, given it purpose, made the men seriously hunt for the golden grail of erectile dysfunction pills or direct some effort to eating more substantial meals and even turning to cannibalism and the women could have dusted off their collective wisdom of child-rearing and become a multi-headed grandmother. When she finds that the doors remain locked, the woman understands she has been cast out. Maybe the dogs will help her find a home. Maybe she will find the sniper and become his wife. She will learn to harvest and they will have a happy and healthy brood.

Dr. Joonce quickly replaced the cards and stifled a yawn. Even though he had a several cards left, he decided this would be his last one, thinking he had enough of H.H. Huckleberry's thoughts to make a diagnosis, at least one sound enough to pass by the public defender. On this card a man is climbing a hemp rope, the kind that hung from the ceilings of school gymnasiums a generation or two ago. He is naked but discreetly turned away from the viewer to spare her the sight of his penis or because the artist, unpracticed in drawing penises chose a pose to avoid drawing one. The viewer does not see where the rope terminates and cannot see how much farther the man has to climb if he wants to make it to the top. The viewer cannot see if the rope is frayed or leads to a small isolated perch or stretches for miles into the air. Below him a pack of dogs sit on their haunches and watches his progress. They look like they are waiting for dinner. Nelson counted the heads of the dogs and found there to be ten. He dropped the pen and leaned back in the chair. An angry glare settled in his eyes.

"Fetid chin. Broken armies melting in the rain! The mud holds the contagion of desire! Are you fucking with me, sir?" he said to the doctor.

The doctor noted the anger in his notebook by using a symbol that looked like a dead fish inside a long neck bottle. Dr. Joonce sometimes used his own set of symbols to denote his observations in case the patient snatched the notebook away to read his thoughts. Once, a patient took the notebook and leveled a terrible accusation at him, that he had been merely doodling and not paying attention. On that occasion an anorexic, bulimic and horribly neurotic college student peeked at his notebook while he looked for a book on a shelf to loan her. She wailed that not even her psychiatrist would listen to her and he doodled why while she talked. At that point to eliminate the possibility of further damage he told her that he had developed a system of symbols to help him write his notes. He used the remaining time of the session trying to calm her, and at the end she asked if the doctor would like to fuck her, right then on the carpet behind his desk, underneath the bookshelf, on the chair, using her asshole, her mouth, it did not matter how or why. He politely refused, whereupon she started wailing again, lamenting the fact that now no one even wanted to use her body. Dr. Joonce began doodling in earnest, a large breasted woman watching a television that had been plugged into her vagina.

"Mr. Huckleberry, why do you think I have an agenda against you?"

"This picture melts my cheese. Gives me heebies when I should have the jeebies."

"Copyrighted like all the rest. Part of a series that cost the taxpayers of the county a tidy sum."

"You picked the apple just for me, because they say I am a brute to dogs. I live in the underscore sea! I am a rational font."

Dr. Joonce leaned over the card to make sure he remembered which one he had used. He saw the naked man climbing the rope. In his experience, this card always elicited a wide range of responses from both men and women. From women, the responses ranged from those who had feared exposure as she climbed a rope in gym class to those who wished that all men lived naked in the trees and one could come pick one when she needed him to those who cast themselves as the pursuer off scene, holding a knife or gun to avenge any number of male transgressions from football addiction to a catalogue of mundane perversities. The men talked of rising in a company, but always feeling exposed no matter how high they climbed to fantasies of being naked in front of a crowd of clothed women to one man who confessed that he walked naked through ten acres of woods he owned almost every night in all kinds of weather. In winter he would stay out each night a little longer, hoping, he said, for a passive suicide, a cold and clean closure to his tangled and boiling thoughts. Something always drove him back to the warmth of the house. Dr. Joonce didn't remember the pack of dogs in the image. He looked closer and the pack had been drawn by a different artist using a different pen. The dogs looked a little crude and hurriedly drawn. He decided to let the modification pass because admitting the card had been compromised would have thrown the validity of the whole test into question.

"You should write the narrative based on what you observe and interpret. Don't try to guess my motives and don't write what you think I want to read. You will never be able to guess since there is no right answer and your narrative will not be your own. This is the last card and you've already written quite a lot. If this last card causes you distress we can stop here. You may have written enough already."

Nelson picked up the pen. The dogs were still there. He still believed that Dr. Joonce manipulated him and tried to open his skull to see if he had a deep hatred of dogs, to find some motive for his trumped-up charge. The faces of the dogs looked inscrutable, almost passive but for a glint of hungry intent.

The rope is tied to a branch of a tree. Think of the pack as vigilantes, a lynch mob. They have tracked the man for many years, so many years that the man does not consider himself on the run. The chase is his life. He does not remember a time before the dogs were on his trail. For a time they bayed and ran full tilt through the forests and over the streams and through the dirty streets of villages and cities. But their noise and exuberance always gave away their position and the man would pack up and run before they found his apartment or his garret or the garage where he slept on a bed of worn tires and foam ripped out of an old car seat. For a time he traveled with an outcast, beautiful and scarred by rejection and they had sex whenever and wherever they stopped. She nearly convinced him that they were destined for each other when he confessed that the dogs hounded him. She told him her story of banishment and that the purpose of her being cast out had been to save him from his fears and teach him how the dogs, while maybe not exactly benign, could at least be used to a person's advantage, that there was nothing particularly evil about them either, if you could even still use that word in this ruined world. They could be channeled and directed. That, she thought, existed as their duty and responsibility, to await your direction and carry out the order with all speed. So, she continued, he should think of their actions as really just a matter of control and nothing to do with morality, unless, of course, he wanted to make it about morality, if that gave him comfort. The dogs could become avenging angels or relentless devils, whatever you may need to make sense of the shattered world. Her teachings didn't stick. He snuck away from her on a clear day in the middle of the afternoon. He told her he would fill up the canteens at a reasonably clear stream he had seen over a hill. She said she would come with him, but he assured her he wouldn't be a minute and that when he returned they would have sex on the grass. The stream did exist and the water looked clear enough, but he could never be sure what poison might be invisibly lurking, but the man wrote a note with a nub of a pencil and the last full sheet of paper he had instead of retrieving water. The note did not measure up to the betrayal, as he wrote, "I'm sorry. See you around." He placed a rock on either end so that it would not blow away and walked through the stream and over a couple of more hills and out of her life. He forgot to leave her money, but he couldn't remember if anyone still used currency, so he fought the urge to go back and kept the bills in his pocket as a souvenir from another time. The dogs knew of the betrayal immediately and howled for over a week as they drew closer. The man barely slept and walked or jogged as fast as he could go when not sleeping. The faster he ran and the more he tried to forget, the closer they came. He peeled off articles of clothing and hid them in trees or in a thicket, hoping to delay or confuse the pack long enough for him to become lost. Nothing worked, of course. The dogs knew every trick their nose could play on them, so none of his diversions made any difference and the amount of time they were delayed amounted to a matter of minutes. They came for him, relentlessly. They tore at his clothes at night until he walked naked, except for his shoes and the low branches and brambles lashed at his thighs, belly and arms. At night he froze and tried to cover himself with wet leaves and mud and when the mud dried it helped insulate him from the cold, but the leaves did not help at all. The dogs finally found him as he lay in a marshy meadow full of shadow and dense air. He woke up and they sit around him in a circle. One holds the end of a coiled rope and when he is fully awake he takes it from the dog's mouth. They walk for miles through the forest, looking for a low branch. The trees are tall and thin and densely packed. All the low branches have died and have become brittle, not nearly strong enough to hold his weight. The dogs walks close and each take turns nuzzling his asshole to smell his thoughts as well as his diet. Finally, they come to another meadow that had once been used as a vegetable garden. The stone foundation of a farmhouse rises two feet in the air, but the rest of the house has rotted into the soil. A stately maple, probably planted by the farmers for shade and a windshield, stands near the foundation and spreads its branches over the footprint of the old house. The man throws the rope over a thick branch, thick enough to hold his weight and high enough to hang him without his toes scraping the grass. He kicks off his shoes and thinks of his corpse moldering in the wind, crows eating his flesh, the offal falling to the ground that will sink into the soil like the house before. When would another traveler pass by this forgotten homestead? They will find a skeleton hanging from a tree. Would the skeleton stay intact long enough to be found hanging by the rope or would it clatter to the ground once the ligaments rotted away? The traveler will incorrectly assume the skeleton hanging from the tree belongs to the owner of the ruined house and will concoct a satisfying story of failed crops, famine and the murder-suicide of the family and its patriarch. Where had he buried the bodies? Did he forget to save a bullet for himself? How long had the skeleton been swaying in the breeze, holding together by cured sinew? After the man ties the rope to the branch he looks for something to serve as gallows, something easily kicked over but high enough to provide swinging clearance from the ground. He searches the meadow, but everything associated with the farm has turned to dust and all the fallen trees in the forest are too big to drag. The dogs, sensing his frustration, create a step with their bodies. He ties a noose and as he stands on the structurally sound dog step and as he is about to slip the noose over his head and tighten it under his chin he experiences a flash of fear or panic or hope and he climbs up the rope and settles in one of the tall branches. The artist has chosen to depict the flight at the middle point of the ascent, showing neither the noose nor the tree branch. But what are the dogs sitting on if not the ground? I'm not willing to introduce levitating dogs in the story, so when the man kicks and pulls his way up the rope the noose loosened and fell apart. The dogs watch him climb to the highest branch and wedge himself in a crook and think that given his nudity the man must be quite uncomfortable and that he should be careful not to catch his scrotum on any branches. After a while the man stops looking down at the dogs, choosing instead to look in the distance over the forest ceiling. The dogs begin to feel drowsy and circle the trunk before falling asleep in a ragged ring around the tree. They will wait for him, until he decides to stick his head through another noose or until he dies in the branches.

Nelson held his face in his hands. He suddenly felt very weak and his arms braced the full weight of his head, keeping it from descending to the desk. Dr. Joonce looked at his clock and saw the time had crept past midnight, but his office looked the same noon, dawn or dusk. The window above him had turned black but this did not change the character of the room or the nature of the light buzzing from the fluorescent tubes. Dr. Joonce stayed a welling diatribe by remembering that human beings across the globe survived on less than subsistence wages and diets by breaking rocks into gravel with hand-held hammers, or digging mines with pick axes and shovels or sorting parts in a vast factory for 12 to 14 hours at a stretch, pissing where they stand because the line can never stop, so the fact that he didn't have a window either to open or look out, a window that would change the feel of the office as the day progresses and finally exhausts itself, a window that would make him a little more in tune with the earth's rotation, certainly no big deal in the grand scheme of human suffering and work, but that did not mean he could not feel irritated and oppressed by modernist architecture that trended toward blotting out human needs. The style of the building no doubt fit squarely in the category of brutalism and some architectural surveys used the jail and administration building as prime examples of buildings as fortresses, built in riot-pocked war zones and able to withstand a frenzied citizenry that has lost faith in their government, their jobs, the institutions of church, marriage and parenthood, and their inability to cope in an increasingly chaotic society (some reports indicated these roving mobs preferred violence and looting over sex or, possibly, the mob participants confused the two) and when these forces brewed the only thing left to do is build office buildings with no windows, no easily discernable or welcoming front door, crafted out of poured concrete and barbed wire. The architects couldn't design away the world's troubles, but they inadvertently added frenzy and panic to the mix. Some longed for a new classicism, true pillared temples exuding the hope and belief in our collective futures, but they could only ape the Greeks and Romans with faux pillars, holding up nothing, or friezes dedicated to commerce and business instead of benevolent and wrathful gods, so they too gave up and knew that producing anything in the faux classical mode, while immediately satisfying and comforting would be smashed and torn apart brick by brick hours after the building's dedication. So what's left but fascism? Intimidation? Prisons and walled fortresses? The government, faced with an unruly mob, did not mean to exude hope and appeal to the best angels of our nature, but instead wanted to show control and a concrete and barbed wire fist pounding on the street, ready to strike and crush rebellion.

Nelson's head slipped from his hand and lay on the desk. His right leg twitched as if he ran in his dreams. Dr. Joonce stretched and rose from his chair. His back felt knotted and deeply sore, a pain nestled in his discs, an inflammation, the first stirrings of meningitis. He walked out of the office and expected to see a guard sitting on a chair in the hallway talking on his cell phone to his girlfriend who would probably be sexy in an overweight, trailer park stuffed-into-two-sizes-too-small-jeans-with-belly-pudge-overhang kind of way jabbering about a horror film they had watched the night before that included kidney dissections with a paring knife and six decapitations or some other low brow nonsense like upcoming boxing-karate-wrestling-eye-gouging-brain-beating-brain-damaging fights that were all the rage with barely educated young men working mindless jobs that were all their minds could effectively handle. The chair sat empty and the bank of lights had been turned off so that the sea of cubicles slept under a brown half-light. Dr. Joonce thought the guard might be taking a bathroom or cigarette break so he waited for him for ten minutes by pacing the hallway between the cubicles and the outer offices. Dr. Joonce couldn't fathom working in the cubicles with no window at all, so he kept his mind off further random tirades by inspecting the personal affects the inhabitants had accumulated over the years. In the first cube, Alcoholic Anonymous stickers had been plastered over the filing cabinet and any surface, minus the desktop, that a sticker could adhere to, so that from any position from his chair he could look and be reminded that if he took another drink if would be a matter of days if not hours before he woke up in his own piss and vomit with unknown men passed out in his bed or his bathroom. Dr. Joonce counseled him briefly and diagnosed a repressed rage connected to his homosexuality and his family's complete rejection of him, but Dr. Joonce thought alcohol counseling would at least keep him alive long enough to confront his other scars, so he referred him to a friend who specialized in it. The second cubicle belonged to a woman who had the largest ass he had ever seen. Her torso looked normal, but right at her hips her figure swelled to fertility goddess proportions. She lived in a lily-white suburb of moderately successful people and her fey husband didn't look capable of handling that ass. She always complained black men whistled at her and four of five times exposed themselves to her as they cooed at her ass. Dr. Joonce asked her to consider it a compliment. While in some segments of society her proportions would be considered cartoonish, freakish and the object of ridicule, in other parts of society she is exalted, an example of the finest form that a woman can achieve. You are a fetish, a statue to be carried on a man's back to bring him luck or to be set beside a lovemaking couple to increase their chances of conception. Her form is perfection, and men, who often have sex bristling just beneath their skin, can do nothing but shout and touch themselves as an offering. So she led him into a trap. "But Doctor, what you think of it? Do you think I belong in a freak show?" Dr. Joonce's fingertips tingled at the memory of the response. He looked at her through an uncomfortable silence, then said, "I have often masturbated at the thought of your ass. That gene you carry, possibly a mutation, has driven men wild for millennia. I imagine Calypso with as ass like yours, driving Odysseus into forgetful comfort, casting a seven year spell over his wits. I imagine a woman looking like you leading the first group of homo sapiens out of Africa, the men searching for new hunting grounds to serve and preserve her shape. I think of the gene intimidating the Neanderthals into capitulation and eventual extinction. I believe it has saved us from our own extinction. What man, faced with famine, disease and death of everyone he loves, the disregard of an uncaring god or gods, what man wracked with pain and boils and in the clutches of fever and hallucinations could resist the siren call of that ass? He would fight through a death rattle to feel his member slide between those buns one last time, to plant his seed in such fertile soil. The men and women who hold you up to ridicule want to negate your power, believing your song can be made silent by a couple of punch lines and childish nattering. They fear your presence inside these walls with no useful windows. You are the primal urge. If a man touches that ass his education melts away, his position becomes moot, his standing in the community looks like a puppet show, his marriage is annulled, his children become bastards and he will spend at least the next seven years in your thrall." She stared at him, making sure he wasn't perpetuating some elaborate hoax that he had recorded for the sake of their co-workers, and left his office, unconvinced that she should appreciate men who masturbated for her in public. She did tell the doctor later that after their talk she bought a thong and showed her husband, who bemoaned that her ass had been a quarter of its current size, maybe even a full sixth, when they had married and asked her never to wear that goddamn piece of string again. She waited for the doctor to spin another appreciatory speech, but he could only conjure, "Ah, his loss, I am afraid," as a note of condolence.

Dr. Joonce scanned a line of photos she had tacked to a shelf, all vacation shots of she and her husband at different American sites, but no matter where they were, Yosemite, the Everglades, Lake Superior, the Carolina coast, the Mohave desert, Mt. Rainer, her ass dominated the frame, that and her husband's dissipated soul. He touched one of the pictures, a shot from behind as she ascended a forest path. He didn't think she ever understood that his speech acted as his way of touching himself and cooing after her. He threw out an invitation, a request, a goddamn straight forward come-on that she never acknowledged or spoke of again. He thought she might have taken to wearing tighter pants or bending over more in his presence, but he couldn't read her and he dropped the pursuit, thinking she might be too stupid to understand his likening her to Calypso as the highest of compliments and the affair would not have much chance of blooming. He used her phone to call the jail, but it rang and rang with no answer. He swore under his breath and walked back to his office. He roused Nelson by shaking him by the shoulder.

"Mr. Huckleberry, please. I am going to take you back now.'

As he leaned over Nelson, Dr. Joonce noticed that several of the handwritten sheets had been knocked to the floor, so he bent down to collect them. He looked at them closely to determine their order but found he couldn't read the writing. He adjusted his glasses to the edge of his nose and tried again. What at first looked like letters were a series of squiggles, dashes, and circles that made him think Nelson had written the responses in shorthand. Then, he found other pages filled with nothing but Xs meticulously crafted and perfectly straight and then on another page the word "outcast" had been repeated for half a page and the word "dog" filled the other half. He threw the papers in a loose pile on the desk, on top of H.H. Huckleberry's file and poked Nelson again. Nelson lifted his head and managed to stay awake long enough to lean back in his chair.

"That wasn't a very smart trick. We're not playing a game here," Dr. Joonce said with more force than he had intended.

"What do you mean?"

"I mean these hieroglyphics." Dr. Joonce picked up the papers and shook them. "I mean this gibberish. These are tests designed to understand what you are thinking, how have you interpreted the culture in which you live, what place you see yourself assuming. This test was a large part of my assessment. The only part of my assessment, since you refused to answer any of the questions I posed to you. The judge wants to know if you are competent to stand trial and you disrespect the process. You write "outcast" and "dog" as an answer? Do you think you can fool me by acting crazy? I've seen every trick, Mr. Huckleberry. I've had prisoners defecate on the very chair on which you sit. I've seen them eat ink pens and bite their own wrists. I've even seen them try to jump out that useless window above our heads." He pointed to the window above his desk. "They try to kill themselves, but the window doesn't open and can't be broken except by a small hand grenade. Do you think the judge will look kindly on this? She's a terror. When she sees in my report that you have been uncooperative, that you filled page after page with nonsense and hieroglyphics, what do you think she will do? She'll become your enemy in court. She'll favor the prosecution in subtle ways. She'll change her body language whenever your public defender speaks. She'll look like she's being loaded down with a heavy burden. Her shoulders will slump. Her face will screw up into a horrified scowl every time she looks at you. She will be the guide to the jury and they will be thankful to her for making sense out of the charges and willing them to hate and punish you. Why is it you wish to release the Furies? Do you not understand that nemesis always follows hubris? Who are you to stand up to the judge? Who are you to make a mockery of her requests? She is the avenger of victims. She is the daughter of Uranus and Gaea. She has bat's wings, black skin, snakes for hair and the head of a dog. In the distance you hear her barking. She is flying to you, for you. Born of castration, when Chronos sliced the balls off Uranus and his blood and ejaculate rained from the sky and sprinkled Gaea, the earth mother, with seed. Up rose the judge and her sisters. She will drive you mad with her pursuit. She will chase you over three lifetimes until you tire and she feasts on your organs."

Nelson leaned over and offered a hand to Dr. Joonce so he could inspect the papers himself. Dr. Joonce passed them to him reluctantly because he had just remembered the Sumerian god of justice, Shamash and his two servants Kittu (truth) and Mesharu (integrity) and while not a perfect match for the judge's demeanor, Shamash did serve the purpose of proving the idea of justice might be as old as civilization. He knew using a word as loaded with complexity as civilization was problematic, because who could pinpoint the starting point of civilization other than to say it had begun with the first family and that sounded much too soft-headed for metaphorical purposes. In any case, handing over the papers to H.H. Huckleberry diverted his mind from the Sumerians and to the problem of writing the report for the judge with no material on which to make the determination. He would do his best at assessing her intent. He believed he remembered some campaign literature with her picture on it. In the picture she wore the judge's robes, sat behind the bench, flanked by her two dogs, twin Pekingese caught mid-yap. The photo caused a minor flap in the political gossip columns and chatter because the question arose as to the propriety of setting the dog's asses on the polished bench of justice for a cheesy campaign photo, but the scandal caused no lasting damage. Dr. Joonce had jumped into the fray and wrote an anonymous but impassioned defense of the judge in which he first developed his Furies metaphor. Word came back to him that although the newspaper thought the piece well written they would not publish an anonymous letter unless it involved knowledge of corruption, salaciousness or some other whistle-blowing information and that the judge became more furious at having her head compared to a dog than the criticism of the campaign photo.

Nelson looked over his handwriting and it had no resemblance to anything he had ever written before. He found the page with outcast and dog written so closely together that barely enough white space could be seen to discern actual words. Nelson briefly remembered the narrative of the story before it slipped away. He wanted to tell the doctor he could recite his narratives in response to the cards, but he remembered his shaky control of spoken language had landed him in jail in the first place. He dropped the papers on the desk.

"I have no explanation for bread and fish. I am an ape agape," he said with difficulty, like he spoke through a mouthful of ice and sand.

"You have no explanation and you have nothing to say. If that is your only defense then things will go poorly for you. I believe I've tried my level best to make you understand the gravity of your situation and the likelihood that the judge will mete out a severe punishment. If she could cast herself a judge in the western territories she would sentence you to hanging by your neck until you're dead. But mutilating dogs is not a capital offense in our civilization, as of yet. Lucky for you, I suppose. You know she owns dogs and volunteers at an animal shelter when her schedule allows? You're sending your poor public defender to the slaughterhouse."

They rode the elevator down to the ground floor and walked across a mammoth expanse, disproportionate to human scale with a ceiling four stories high and constructed with nothing but stone and concrete so that their footsteps sounded like an army mobilizing in the night. During the day when the courts slogged through the backlog of cases and people paid parking tickets and detectives came in to testify and deputies transferred prisoners to downstate penitentiaries and reporters hustled in to take notes on the most salacious and violent of crimes (usually involving child pornography, domestic abuse in families with well known names or involving couples with high-profile jobs, traffic deaths caused by drunk drivers), neighbors who wanted to complain about other neighbors concerning fireworks or loud arguing or dogs that wouldn't stop barking or smoking near the property line and the smoke disturbing family dinners with the awful and poisonous stench and who were sent away with the knowledge that police reports had to be taken at the neighborhood police stations and not at the crossroads of county justice, and families of victims marching to the bank of elevators to the courts on the upper floors and sometimes riding the same car with the families of perpetrators and each trying not to look a the other and both sets might be thinking of the many hours they would have to sit in the courtroom and watch a young man barely out of childhood be sentenced for a string of years that they couldn't possibly imagine. When all of these people walked and talked and passed by each other in a moving tapestry, the lobby sounded like a waterfall of metal trash cans. The employees developed a hunch to their back when they walked through the waves and even the guards and deputies sometimes betrayed bewilderment on their faces when the noise grew so loud it seemed like it came from inside their heads.

They entered the jail side of the facility and were stopped by two guards who sat behind plexiglass, dulled and scratched in a halo around the vented opening used to speak through. Dr. Joonce identified himself and the prisoner, H.H. Huckleberry. He didn't tell them the guard hadn't showed up to escort the prisoner back to his cell, but, he hoped, they could surmise the fact just by his presence in front of their filthy station, even though they would not get one of their own in trouble. One guard looked up Huckleberry's name on a clipboard and eventually found him even though the pages had been clipped out of order and saw that he had been taken to the headshrinker but had not returned. After the first guard had gone off shift a second had never been dispatched. The guard wondered if that responsibility had been his.

"You should have called us, Doc. We would have come."

"I did call."

"Not this number. We've been sitting here the whole time."

The second guard looked up from his paperwork to affirm this observation.

"I called this number. I'm not an idiot. There wasn't even a voicemail prompt."

"I'm not calling you an idiot, Doc. I'm just saying you didn't call this number. We've been sitting here the whole time."

"I called the number in the directory."

"We haven't used that number in, like, two years."

"It's been at least two years," the second guard said.

"Besides, we don't have voicemail. We don't rate like the admin tower where you work."

"I'm surprised we have phones."

"Right, but we do have some lovely windows that look on the street. They're not bad for looking at the lady lawyers."

"I was never a big fan of that look when I started, seemed like all starch and creases, but I've learned to appreciate the power, money, and education that a business suit projects, not that any of them would ever talk to me, I'm not saying that."

"No, but you were saying you could see them through our *window.* Sometimes the sunshine and rain get me through the day."

"Yes, it is nice having a window."

Dr. Joonce waited for the babble of working class bitterness to subside. It would be more palpable, he thought, if they had an inkling of class awareness. These same troglodytes voted Republican, hated blacks and cradled their guns to their breasts, wishing the forged steel could take hold of their flabby breasts and suckle nourishment from their bodies. So, they lash out at the educated, the intelligent, the thinkers, and believe they are the cause of the world's plight. They would be the Khmer Rogue if not for television, football and fast food. As it is their rage is impotent, channeled into painting their faces with their team colors and raging at the field. If they collectively formed a fist and

494

smashed down the walls, stopped crawling on their bellies in search of crumbs, stopped acting like worms on a hook and bellyaching about slow computer systems and old phones and the inherent nonsense of their work and stood up for once. Maybe they could once slide on a pair of hobnailed boots and step on the throats of the ruling class. One time they could turn away from the fucking football field and paint themselves red, white, and blue and go to city hall and scream and beat their councilmen and mayor who grant tax breaks to the largest and wealthiest corporations on the planet in the name of development. Develop into what? A slave state. They think that's what the other countries are for. Hondurans making our clothes, the Japanese making our cars, the French making our wine, and the Chinese making everything else. A nation of slaves who think they are slave owners. A nation without workers because the workers have no class awareness. They have no idea what is in their best interest. They think living in a trailer, wearing Honduran clothes and bitching about the door of the trailer being too narrow for the new flat screen to fit or the walls being too flimsy to hold the flat screen is the life of a slave owner. And if ever this roiling mass of idiots ever did find its way clear of television and organized itself into something resembling an army, the Anasazi Red, for example, he, Dr. Joonce, would throw away his glasses and either have radial keratotomy or wear contacts, because his eyesight is terrible and getting worse, with the purpose of staying alive, because without a doubt the fist, once it is formed, will seek out the intellectuals, the wearers of glasses, the possessors of degrees and slaughter them, and Dr. Joonce in his new disguise will join the mob and punish the class of architects for their smugness and hubris. He personally would put a bullet in the brain of the Nazi who designed this jail and other disciples of sterility he had taken under his wing. First someone needed to blow up an electrical plant to stop the flow of drugs running through the electrical circuits and maybe their minds would clear enough for them to realize they live in squalor.

"Doc, we got it from here," the first guard said. Both were disappointed the doctor had not taken the bait or even knew the bait had been thrown in the water. Everyone knew the doctor babbled to himself and whoever was in earshot about windows and architects, but the guards had not yet been lucky enough to hear him speak on the subject. "Call us next time. Don't take chances with these people. They'll turn on you over a piece of gum."

Dr. Joonce watched Nelson and the guard walk through the door and he followed them through the scratched glass until they disappeared through another interior door. No question now that he would be sleeping in his office. He would catch a few hours of sleep and write the report in the morning. He walked back to his office through the deserted gloom of the center. The next post-apocalypse, last man on earth movie, no…the last man on earth meets the last woman on earth and they both happen to be beautiful, fashionable and unscathed by the apocalypse as they unearth a vast underground network of zombies movie should be filmed at this center, Dr. Joonce thought. At least the moviegoer would be made to choose which world they would prefer, the sterile modernist fancies of an unrepentant Nazi architect or repopulating the earth with a gorgeous Eve while zombies pounded on the door.

Dr. Joonce did sleep in his office that night and he did write the psych evaluation for inmate H.H. Huckleberry in the morning, in which he savaged Nelson for not cooperating and failing to participate in all of the finely honed assessment tools. Huckleberry, in his opinion, mocked the justice system and he showed a highly manipulative, cunning, and pre-meditated scheme, and could thoroughly understand the charges brought against him. He was, in Dr. Joonce's humble but professional opinion, capable to stand trial. He wrote the report in a fury and used an image of the judge, resplendent in her black robes and a glittering crown and standing on a sidewalk near a railroad tracks as a train filled with prisoners on their way to spending the next 10 to 20 years in a little cage in the foothills of the Appalachians rushed by, causing a gust of wind to lift her robe and reveal that the judge worked on the bench without the benefit of a skirt or panties, to push him forward and make him write the best report he had ever produced. Dr. Joonce wound himself up in such a state by the time he came to the end of the report he very nearly recommended execution for H.H. Huckleberry for his impudence and intransience. He would have executed Huckleberry himself if it meant a chance to stick his head under the judge's robe or to be a rush of wind brushing across her thighs.

The judge scanned his report, noted some excellent wordplay and recognized paragraphs where the doctor had written in her voice. The doctor had some literary ability and she liked his interpretation of her, mean and irascible, hawk-faced and predatory, but obviously the last, best hope of containing the burgeoning insanity of the world. The good doctor had delivered what she wanted and she had to remember to send him a note of thanks. She scheduled the trial. The public defender cursed under his breath through most of the proceedings and simply did not have the time, the staff, the energy, the ability or a defendant capable of garnering a modicum of sympathy from the judge or jury so he ended up losing the case on all counts to an assistant prosecutor with a misshapen left nostril who tried her first case. On the night of the victory the assistant prosecutor celebrated over drinks with a couple of male colleagues and one of them, probably both of them, fucked her through a vodka and cranberry haze, and if it had been both then she blew both of them and they took turns licking her pussy and trying different positions until they came. One liked looking at the nostril while he fucked and the other had to have it hidden to bring the session to a close. The legend of this night followed her through her twenty years as a prosecutor and helped her with male judges and hurt her with female judges, but she ended up with many more wins than losses and rose to the middle ranks of the office. So, years later the only three people who remembered the case of H. H. Huckleberry included the assistant prosecutor who remembered it because it had been her first trial, her first win and had led to a college-like indiscretion that forever tainted her time at the prosecutor's office, and her two colleagues, who both washed out of the office after a few years but remembered H.H. Huckleberry because his case led to a spontaneous threesome, which had not ever happened to them even in college and they liked retelling their story over beers to new colleagues and friends because the story, in their eyes, bestowed a form of magical ability on the pair who turned a case of animal abuse into a sexual fantasy of the highest order, even though they glossed over the fact the threesome involved two men and not two women and the woman had a misshapen nostril.

Dr. Joonce had been right about the judge's love of dogs, a love so deep she held a fantasy of opening a luxury kennel with heated sleeping mats, landscaped play areas, organic dog food and 24 hour attention with a veterinarian on site, but in the end she stayed content with Celaeno and Ocypete, her two Pekingese. She loved her dogs so much she thought of recusing herself from Nelson's case when it landed in her docket, but she didn't want the whispers and snickers to start again about her inordinate compassion for canines, a compassion and understanding severely lacking in her judgments and sentences of criminals. So, after the assistant prosecutor mopped the floor with the public defender whose defense began from two ends: 1) The victim's dog had never been seen since that night and there was no sign of struggle or violence, so the court and jury couldn't be sure if the dog hadn't just run away (and here the public defender tried a joke that proved to be disastrous) to join the circus or to become a roadie with a traveling rock band. Not a single juror smiled at the joke or probably even understood the references since running away to join the circus had ended as a career option in the 1920s and not a single juror knew anything about being a roadie of a rock band or why a dog would choose such an occupation, so even before the last word left his mouth the public defender knew he had fucked himself and his client; and 2) The report written by Dr. Joonce, while damning, held obviously prejudicial intent against his client, as Dr. Joonce based his conclusions on no real evidence or observations and refusing to participate in assessment tests could just as well be a manifestation of insanity as an indication of pre-meditation. Dr. Joonce had provided an incoherent diatribe based on his own anger directed at the client as he tried desperately to curry favor with the court. The judge rejected this line of defense and stifled the public defender from going further when he cross-examined Dr. Joonce. She agreed with the public defender's conclusions, but she couldn't stand to see Dr. Joonce's bald spot turn red as the questions became more aggressive and probing. She had to provide a small shield of protection for her admirers lest they become ridiculous fools and their attention thereby cheapened. So, the only defense the public defender had left maintained that no one knew what had become of the dog in question. The assistant prosecutor painted a picture of domestic bliss, of a newly pregnant wife, a stable if somewhat underemployed husband, a family pet for three years which had been a present from husband to wife after an emotionally wrenching miscarriage, of a wife who took her disappointment and created a deep and permanent bond with the dog, a dog they saved on his last day before being euthanized, a dog who became a loyal friend, a dog who once scared away a burglar who had pried the dead bolt out of its frame on the back door before the dog bit him on the ankle and suffered a busted jaw from a vicious, desperate kick from the burglar, a dog who had to have his mouth wired shut for a month so the jaw could heal (a procedure that cost the young family considerable expense), of a wife who fed the dog by liquefying dog food and blowing it through a straw between a small gap between the dog's teeth, because surprisingly dogs don't understand the concept of sucking, of a fractured and distraught family who turned their grief into more sexual activity and who by the grace of God would be welcoming a child into the world six months hence, the gender of which they are leaving unknown and they are not even discussing names until the baby is born given their horrific experience with the miscarriage, contrasting that story of love, compassion, faithfulness, and the indefatigable spirit of the young and pure with the story of H.H. Huckleberry, a man with no past, no social security number, with barely twenty words at his command, who writes his bizarre thoughts in a personal code, indecipherable even to a highly educated and trained psychiatrist, a sullen outcast, a drifter who follows his own whims and his own laws, a bogeyman who haunts our neighborhoods, who watches our windows and doors, who eats our trash and shrieks at the moon, a man whose very existence threatens the stability of the community, of a man quite capable of strangling the dog in its sleep while he slept in a handcrafted doghouse the husband had made on three successive weekends, a dog, mind you, that had only known the kindness of human hands since being adopted by the loving couple, startled from his sleep by the sudden pressure on his throat, but he relaxes when he realizes the pressure comes from human hands, a dog that trusted too much and dies from asphyxiation, his black tongue lolling from his mouth as his last thought held an image of the wife unlatching his cage and taking him in her arms, just hours away from the gas chamber, and, finally, of a man quite capable of eating the dog (here she apologized to the judge, the jury and the husband and wife for conjuring such an indecent image) because we don't know what happened to the dog, so H.H. Huckleberry could very well have made the dog a meal for his ravenous stomach.

The jury deliberated less than 15 minutes and could have decided sooner hadn't the jury foreman had to take a restroom break. When the foreman told the court their verdict of guilty on all counts, the judge remanded Nelson back to his cell and scheduled a sentencing hearing for the next week. At the sentencing hearing she cut all testimony short and sentenced him to the maximum number of months for every count: six months for animal cruelty (a first degree misdemeanor), six months for criminal trespass (a fourth degree misdemeanor), eighteen months for resisting arrest (second degree misdemeanor), and six months for public indecency (a fourth degree misdemeanor). The police report indicated that H.H. Huckleberry had been found nude when tied to the doghouse, a prejudicial image that weighed heavily on the minds of the jury because it spoke to bondage and sickness, perversion and debasement. Nelson did not contend the fact, even though he actually remembered wearing clothes, but the husband and wife held steadfast to the accuracy of the report and the whispers around the court advanced the theory the wife had not been able to look at her husband's naked body since the incident because she had been so traumatized. The remaining offenses manufactured by Hayes and Brankowski never made it past the assistant prosecutor's desk, but the result of the convictions meant that H.H. Huckleberry would be spending the next three years incarcerated. The husband and wife gasped and cried their approval. The wife repeatedly shook the assistant prosecutor's hand as the husband placed a paternalistic hand on her back and rubbed his fingertips over the polyester blend of her suit.

Nelson's expression did not change as the judge read the sentence and delivered a defense of animals speech in which she outlined the moral ground we human beings held and that our progress as rational stewards of the earth can be measured by our treatment of those beasts without opposable thumbs and without our capacity for cleverness and imagination. If she looked at the facts of this particular case as a barometer, human kind had miles to go before ascending to a higher state of being. The deputies came and handcuffed Nelson and for theater's sake clamped a set of leg irons around his ankles so he had to shuffle from the courtroom with a short chain between his legs.

The guards escorted him back to his cell. Daron and Delonte played cards on a bunk, using a greasy and dog-eared set that had been passed around the jail for years. Bear, the wife-beater, and Dan Evans, the embezzler, had both made bail. Bear's wife had collected the money and they had a tearful reunion in the courthouse parking lot where he promised to never touch her again and she promised never to do anything that would lead him to violence like having two hours of unaccounted time on a Thursday afternoon when he knew his ex-best friend malingered at home with a bee sting on his neck. Dan Evans persuaded a soft-minded cousin to post the bond, against his brother's wishes, by using an equity line against her house, because no one needed new windows and doors when a blood relative had a run of bad luck, she thought, until Dan skipped bail and moved to Arizona under an alias, Steve Future, and his cousin would lose the money she used to post the bond and she would think of Dan every time a draft blew across her bed or past her ears as she sat on the couch watching television. Steve Future would be caught seven years later after his brother hired a private investigator who tracked him to Phoenix, where he had opened a tanning salon that did remarkably well for being located in the desert. Dan and Bear had been replaced by three scofflaws, who sat close together on the floor against the far wall, so close they looked like itinerant farm workers in the back of a pickup truck or fully mature, weird brothers used to sleeping in the same bed. The guards unlocked Nelson's handcuffs and leg irons outside the cell door and pushed him inside. Spider had been taken to the infirmary the day before complaining of sharp chest pain and numbness in his left arm. The stress of the cell, of not seeing the sun, of hungering for chicken wing and noodle take-out, of not knowing the betting lines of the games and who threw games and who still took sucker bets on all those Vegas fixes, led to a minor heart attack, a precursor to a series of other attacks and strokes that led to Spider's death two years later at the age of 54, which everyone in his family agreed turned out to be unfortunate because Spider liked to tell the story of being wheeled out on a stretcher from the county jail with his left arm numb and he looked at his cellmates, drug dealers, wife-beaters, white-collar crooks and a crazy motherfucker who seemed to grow more body hair each day and who smelled worse after a shower than before, and he remembered asking himself why, as a man in his fifties, did he sit in jail with these freaks and right then he decided that instead of dying in the company of fuckups under the laughing eyes of guards, he would turn his life around and do something, anything productive, even if it meant working at a car wash for tips. The preacher, an amateur actor and director, who delivered the funeral service talked about second and third acts and how Spider lived a long first act but has ascended to heaven before he could apply what he had learned in the first act to the second and third acts. The family thought the preacher sounded fine and he stretched the service throughout the afternoon and into early evening which everyone expected, but they did think his theater analogies strange and incongruent with Spider's life since they believed he had never seen a play and only watched sports or the shopping channels when he did watch television. Now the sullen, dark brothers sat against the wall, touching shoulder to shoulder and collectively staring at their feet. They didn't acknowledge the noises of the door opening, the unlocking of handcuffs and leg irons and Delonte exclaiming, perhaps too exuberantly, that Florida had returned to the nest.

The attempted assassination occurred three days later around 3:00 am when the three men who called themselves Balto, Rover, and Rin Tin Tin pulled steel shanks from the soles of their orange slippers and crept up to Nelson as he lay on his cot dreaming of blood and frozen mud. Rover achieved the first cut, but he suffered from uncorrected astigmatism and mistook Nelson's arm for a soft chest lying over a beating and vulnerable heart. The shank did hit bone and the subsequent pain jolted Nelson to his feet. He jumped on the first shadow as two other shanks whistled past his body wildly. Nelson ripped off Rover's ear with his teeth and followed him to the ground as he collapsed. Several other wild swings of the shanks missed him or nicked his skin with the blade point. Balto rushed him, holding the shank above his head like he could cleave Nelson's skull in half with one downstroke. His arm came down in a fierce arc, but Nelson sidestepped the blade and Balto stabbed his own thigh. His moaning harmonized with Rover's curses as he patted the ground in search of the mangled cartilage that once made up his ear. By now Delonte and Daron had awakened and shouted encouragement to the assassins even though they couldn't tell what happened in the dark. As Balto pulled the knife from his thigh, he lurched toward Nelson who took the opportunity to sink his teeth into Balto's neck. He held the bite long enough to tear some of his flesh and begin to clamp down on an artery and a vein, but Balto recovered his senses enough to raise the shank high and sink it into Nelson's back. They broke apart, their hands searching for their wounds. An alarm had sounded. The other inmates swore at God, screamed the names of their mothers and taunted the guards as they came running past. Rin Tin Tin made one last attempt at the kill, but the floor ran slick with blood so when he tried to step over the fallen bodies of his two mates he slipped and fell onto Rover who held a used tissue to his face, thinking it his ear. Rin Tin Tin's legs split apart and he ripped both hamstrings simultaneously. The guards burst through the door and in a matter of moments they beat everyone no matter if they were bleeding or just observers. They knocked Delonte and Daron unconscious and repeatedly struck Nelson on or about the shank wound. The other inmates screamed, howled, and beat their fists against the walls and each other as if they watched a family being flayed alive. The guards hauled away the assassins first, dragging them by the ankles and beating as they slid across the concrete. Nelson had collapsed on the floor and two guards stood over him until a medical team came and lifted him onto a stretcher and applied pressure to the wound. His hands and feet were very cold and he couldn't move his hands. Someone pressed on the wound with an icy cloth. The gloves of the paramedics were slick with blood.

They took him to the infirmary, stabilized him with a bag of plasma and some bandages, then carted him to the county hospital so he could be checked for internal damage and be properly sewn up. On the way he thought he asked the attending paramedics to stop the truck, to wheel the stretcher down the asphalt and leave him at the side of the road. No more trouble should be made on account of his life. He thought the paramedics said, "You had enough fight in you back at the jail. You should have thought of giving up when you had a chance. You looked the angels of death in the face and bit the ear off one of them. Now, you talk of passivity and receiving death like a warm embrace of a child. The fight doesn't leave you that fast. You're just starting your time, Huckleberry. You're going to need that fight. No one can stand to just have it taken away." The paramedic checked his pulse and Nelson wanted to respond, but he didn't want to sound desperate. He thought they were afraid to lose their jobs if they left him by the side of the road to fend for himself. The paramedic started telling a story about a guy he knew who went into a bar, met a foxy woman with huge tits and a nice pooper and how this guy took the lady to his car and made out with her and the lady blew him right then and there in the car, but he didn't come. He saved his load for a motel tucked under the shadow of the mill and when they were there the lady started blowing him again to get him going and when they moved to the bed and took off all their clothes and there dangling between the fox's legs, or maybe by now standing at full attention, hung a full-sized rod and reel. The guy, the friend of the paramedic, jumped off the bed and ran out the door with his flag at half-mast and he hid behind his car. After he composed himself and realized he had left his pants he went back into the room and she had gone. She had slipped out the bathroom window with his pants, phone, wallet and keys. "Goddamn chick-with-a-dick," the other paramedic said. "Goddamn right," the first paramedic said. The second paramedic wanted to know how the guy got home with no pants, phone, keys or wallet and the first paramedic told him that he found no phone in the room, only a jack, so he had to knock on all the doors of the motel to assemble a working phone and most, if not all, the rooms were being used by whores so they didn't think twice about a naked man at their door asking for phone parts, because they had seen everything, every variation of depravity and weirdness the American society could cough up. The last whore, who possessed the cord that travels between the base and the receiver asked him why he stood naked and looked for phone parts and he told his story about the chick-with-a-dick. The whore called the chick-with-a-dick a little faggot who unwittingly ruined their business because now every experienced john wanted to see her pussy before she even started talking price. Either she did it or they suspected her of hiding a package in her panties. It used to be, she said, that a few years ago she could charge just for a look and now with chick-with-a-dick paranoia a sneak peek had become nothing more than the cost of doing business. He asked her for money or a ride and she politely refused to give him help. After all, he had not been her client and she felt no responsibility for his plight, only sympathy. He thanked her for the cord and walked back to his room. His wife had the only other set of car keys and he couldn't call his brother to ask him to retrieve the keys from her, because that would make her mad and she would come along anyway and he would be humiliated anew in front of his brother. So, he called his wife and told her the location of the motel and his plight of being without a phone, wallet, keys or pants and she could piece together the situation without much other explanation. He decided to tell her the chick-with-a-dick story because somewhere in the narrative if you looked hard enough a listener could glean a moral comeuppance for a man willing to pick up a woman at a bar while he being supposedly happily married. The guy thought maybe she would enjoy his humiliation enough to forgive his adultery. Nothing, of course, could have been farther from the actual outcome. His wife told her family and friends his story and the consensus became that either her husband had turned gay or bi-curious, and neither would lead to a happy and stable marriage.

"Isn't it bad enough worrying about every woman he works with or meets?" her sister said. "Now you have to worry about all the guys too?" That line had resonance and rotted the marriage from the inside out. Every time they had an argument she would invariably get around too calling him a faggot or she would ask him if the men in his life gave better blow jobs than her, so in a matter of months they were divorced. Now the guy will barely leave his house and he had to quit his job because the teasing became relentless. He ended up getting a security job in a lumberyard during the graveyard shift so he didn't have to meet anyone. He always talks about things not being what they seem. He's applied this experience to the rest of the world, the world without gender confusion that does not know or acknowledge the existence of chicks-with-dicks. He'll probably never be the same." The first paramedic stopped his ramble as Nelson's wound bled anew and needed attention.

"I don't want to think about a dude sucking my dick," the second paramedic said.

"But if it is a dude who believes he's a girl what difference does it make?"

"The difference would be having a man suck your cock compared to having a woman suck your cock."

"I know, but I don't think you understand the philosophy of what I am saying."

"There's no philosophy to what you are saying. You just want to include he-shes in your universe to increase your chances of getting laid."

Nelson passed out before he could hear the response and woke up again in a hospital bed. Above him hanging on the wall a television blared through a loose speaker so every voice had a harsh lisp and every other sound, including music, sounded like a chain saw or a lawnmower being run with no oil. Beds on either side of him lay empty. His mouth felt dry and abused, as if the doctors and nurses had passed the time by seeing how many objects could fit in his mouth at any one time, tongue depressors, cotton balls, syringes, clamps, tubes, needles, and anything else they could find. An IV snaked up from his arm. Caked blood hung on his knuckles and under his nails. The color of the walls looked like the inside of a colon. He watched the swirls and smears of the television until a nurse came in and checked his vital signs, read his current chart, and inspected the bag of urine slowly filling from the catheter. He asked the nurse her how his mouth compared to other patients in terms of volume and elasticity, but the words died before they could form. The nurse snapped her head around in the direction of the sound. Their eyes met and she stared at him for what felt like five minutes before she commented on his alertness. Nelson thought he recognized her extraordinary beauty from a magazine or film because she seemed too pretty to have been a part of his life. She asked Nelson if he knew where he lay and how he landed here. Her question felt like a gift. He wanted to hold the sound of her voice in his ear as a salve to soothe and forget his leaden body. She asked again and Nelson listened until the last syllables faded from his memory and he asked her who sent the assassins. Had Montenegro found him or had Zune or Gutterman risen from the dead? Had they pieced together their mutilated corpses with string and tape for the purpose of making one last zombie run at Montenegro? And if she could confirm if they had been sent by Montenegro, if word of Nelson's arrest had leaked back to his lair and he sent the three weird brothers after him, the follow-up question would be whether or not Montenegro would stop any time before Nelson's death had been confirmed by his head being delivered to his door? The nurse confirmed it had been Montenegro who had sent the assassins and no, he would not forget that Nelson had bungled the assignment, had lost the shipment to two kids and had tried to slink away with his tail between his legs. The nurse inspected the IV and Nelson asked her if she had any news about Jules. The nurse's lips curled in bitter mockery. Still Huckleberry? she said. Still you pine after that shallow waif whose plan in life was to live off a progression of worse men, a sliding scale of acceptability starting with the underemployed, sinking to the criminal, traveling through the jailed and ending with the psychotic, abusive and addled. You ask about a woman whose only assets are her weathered flesh, her shriveling skin, her clouding eyes, her sagging breasts and her calloused toes? Have you forgotten about Koo Koo? Didn't she give safe harbor, nurse you back to relative good health, give you shelter, ask nothing of you but a sliver of attention in the form of impersonal sex and sharing lunchtime meals, asked no questions about why you crawled nearly naked from the river, why you traveled with a dirty little man who wore no shoes or never acted too creeped out by you wearing her ex-boyfriend's clothes, who let you inhabit his room and who didn't run when you started, much like her ex-boyfriend, raving about dogs and fiends?

I have forgotten her, Nelson said. I can't remember what she looks like or what she smells like or the timbre of her voice. I've forgotten her acts of kindness or the possibility I had to stay with her until the valves in my heart loosen and wildly flap with each beat, until the crown of my skull pokes through my hair, until my liver bloats with unprocessed bile and I shut my eyes against the earth. I've forgotten her kindness in picking me up off the street when I felt close to death, when I despaired of losing the Captain's company. Nurse, is she well? Has she moved on to a more respectable man? Moved on, the nurse chortled, moved on from you? Seriously, Huckleberry, what did she move on from? Did she sleep soundly the first night you were gone, unafraid that you would come into her room and cut her throat or rape orifices that she preferred not to use? Did she smile all through the next week when she no longer had to cover-up your existence or feel shame of letting you have sex with her even though she felt nothing for you? Did she finally clean out the studio of her boyfriend's possessions and throw them in the dumpster, thinking they may be infused with evil spirits who were responsible for throwing her life off the tracks? She gathered up the mammoth painting on the wall and the dozens of studies that went into making the piece, meticulously taking out the staples around the frames and rolling the canvases into tight tubes and taking all those tubes to an art gallery on the eastside of town and leaving the paintings at the back door under a small awning with a hole, leaving a note that explained the artist of these paintings had died and the executor of his will, Koo Koo, had grown tired of looking at the images and even though she did not have an education in art or art history she thought the paintings worthy of display and if the gallery saw fit to display the paintings and sell them she asked that some of the proceeds be sent to a suicide prevention program or a dog rescue organization.

But how is Jules, Nelson asked. The nurse glared at him through eyes that had seen whole cities euthanized. Really, back to her? Are we reaching the dregs of your memory? Do I have to scrape it clean or powerwash the gray out of your matter for you to finally and irrevocably forget her? How is Jules? This is the burning question? At the moment there are a couple of possibilities. Either she is high or drunk and tangled and writhing in her bed sheets or considering letting a man with a tattoo of red puckered lips on his neck and a swollen and cloudy eyeball fuck her, and when I mean fuck her I mean this gentleman has a specific regimen he follows when he deigns to procure a dance partner for his perversions, on the rumor he has drugs in his pocket and for Jules a slim prospect of getting high is better than no prospect at all. She has forgotten about you. Not a remnant of you remains, not the trip to Bermuda, not the kindness you showed when she ingested E. coli from a tainted strip steak, not your braying laugh, not your wit or the books you've read, not your uncontrolled leering and subsequent erection when she sunbathed topless by the pool and all those men who passed, even the geriatrics, salivated over her tits and plotted your assassination so they could nuzzle between them. She doesn't remember Otter who pushed you out, gave you an assignment, set in motion a destruction you had secretly pined for, but that you couldn't pull off by yourself. You're not a trigger man. You need to be passive and let the doom roll over you. When he disappeared she wailed for a day and then the image of his face became smudged and distorted. Soon his head had the shape of a watermelon and then he had no head at all. His hands became lobster claws or pirate hooks. His penis shriveled to the size of an acorn. His body eventually deflated and his clothes fell in a heap on the floor and soon even the clothes turned to dust in the sun and wind. Why would you tell me about Otter? Nelson asked. The nurse folded her arms over her breasts. Nelson wished she wore one of the old time nurse's uniforms with a starched and brilliant white dress with a strange little hat perched amidst her curled hair. The dress should be so starched it should move independently of her body as if made of aluminum or sheet metal. She wore, incorrectly, blue scrubs, the kind that surgical nurses wear. The floor nurses wore lavender pants and loose tops riddled with cornflower blooms, comfortable pajamas that were horribly unattractive. Nelson thought all the nurses may live in trailer parks and feed their kids meals out of a plastic bag.

You have space in your thoughts to worry about my clothes and a socio-economic status based on a hospital-issued, unattractive fabric print? The nursed asked the question, looking ready to rip the IV from his arm.

But you're wearing surgical green. It's very becoming. When I see it I think you've seen inside my body. You've held my pumping heart or my secreting liver. You have been initiated in sacred and ancient rites. Tlazolteotl flows through your hands. You wear the flayed skin of a sacrificial victim, a

Huaxtec nose-plug and a headdress of unspun cotton. You weigh my kidneys in your hands like they were a pair of identical newborn twins.

She looked at her uniform. Why am I wearing green? The administration has cracked down on this sort of thing. They believe in color-coding their staff. I should be in lavender. Nurses have been fired for such transgressions. It's a way of slotting, of imposing a cheerful caste system on us, it's a control of ego by color. Without rank or slotting our egos would go wild and within weeks I would start believing I could perform surgeries myself and maybe even open a little surgical shop on the fourth floor specializing in splenectomies and rhinoplasty.

Nurse, what does this have to do with Jules, or Otter for that matter?

You asked why I would tell you about Otter, why would I point out that you are number 48 and Otter is 49 and Jules had already progressed to 54, so I ask you who ever remembers number 48? I am appalled that of all the mysteries of the universe you have become entangled in a thread of memory that involves a woman who gives vacuity a bad name. If these are your last thoughts, then you have misspent your gift. You were dropped onto this green and blue planet and you ignored delight and your curiosity turned to bitterness. You lived your life as a circuit on a grid.

Nurse, who ever said anything about last thoughts? I was unconscious. I think I may be still unconscious. Most of my old blood has drained out of the holes that have been opened in me, but now I am being fortified. How many bags lie at my feet? I can feel the donor's thoughts canoeing down my blood stream. I am rich in menstrual blood and emotion. I want to cry at my misfortune or because it is a cloudy day. My mind was blank and dim, but now my old life returns to me. With each moment I better understand how and why I landed here. I cling to Jules because at least she is a pleasant image in an otherwise relentless shitstorm. For months the only thing that could bring a smile to my face is the memory of her naked tits in the sun and you want to disparage even that? You want to mock and scoff at my base animal desire? What's left, nurse? Am I to be refused the smallest of pleasures?

The nurse closed her eyes to blot out Nelson's imploring face. Jesus, Huckleberry, she said. It would be easier to find my way to compassion if you included an ounce of pathos to your defense. How do you expect me to react when you tell me your life has boiled down, has been reduced to leering at a pair of tits on a drug-addled waif? Huckleberry, where was your engagement with the planet? Didn't you have at least a passing interest in something? Had you rejected everything? When you open your mouth and show me your lack of philosophy I want to see you ground down, tortured, whipped and imprisoned. I don't want to acknowledge your existence or the possibility of you. I want to know you've died, but I will never acknowledge it by reading your brief obituary or putting flowers on your grave. I won't come to the funeral. I will send the newspaper the wrong address of the funeral home, so if any of your friends and family still care enough to indulge the compulsion to see your dead body shrouded in a cheap suit and lying in a cheap casket they won't be able to find you. I'll send them to an abandoned field with poisoned dirt where a rusty fence with barbed wire strung along the top has been erected around the border. There, they can whisper their prayers for you and consider to what purpose H.H. Huckleberry lived his life. We can hope that the wind will stir and blow across the field and carry to their noses the acrid tang of chemicals that brews in the dirt. That would about sum it up. That would be a fitting memorial for you.

Nurse, my God. I have a wound in my back and I'm lashed to this bed. The knife missed my heart by millimeters but tore my lungs and muscle. I'm lucky to be alive. I've suffered through a spiral of degradation, pain and suffering.

Stop right there, Huckleberry. I have ceased to care. I never have cared, remember? Do you know that ten more shipments of roughly the same quantity and value have been carried by ten little mules to the doorstep of Montenegro without incident or accident since you tried your hand at it? Montenegro has taken control of the entire Midwest. He is in a frenzy of expansion and has designs on Maryland and Virigina. He is but a few steps away from making governors and corrupting legislators so thoroughly they will enact laws thinking they are rooting out the drug trade, when in truth the laws will provide protection and fertile ground for the trade's relentless expansion. Montenegro will wear a bearskin and sit on a throne of skulls. He gives the people what they want. They want television left on twenty-four hours a day. They want food in plastic bags that can be prepared in a minute. They want deep black coffee to blast them awake from any hangover. They want tidy little piles of powder on their nightstands or desk drawers in their offices to keep them functioning or little rocks clinking in their pockets as they walk down the street looking for a useful errand to perform or little pills in their cabinets to bring them up or down on a whim. So, your suffering does not interest me, because it is not interesting. Suffering should be for a goal, or a misguided belief, for an advancement of humanity, or a stand against brutality, regression and other misguided beliefs. You are a collection, a product, of your choices. You've failed, now die. Do us a favor and blot yourself out. We don't want to be reminded that you are one of our possible futures.

Are you a nurse or an undertaker?

The nurse smiled, but she kept the thought that made her smile to herself. The question assumes that the two inhabit opposite poles. The duties of the jobs are closer than you think and oftentimes the patient won't know which one they are talking to until it is too late.

I don't want to go to prison, nurse. I don't think I can stay in a cage all those years.

You should have thought of that before you eviscerated and ate that poor puppy. Huckleberry, we have standards of decency and guidelines of acceptable human behavior and that act falls well outside the norm of acceptability.

Besides, what difference does it matter what form the cage takes, whether it's real and has a physical manifestation or whether it's the limit to your own thinking. We always have lived within a boundary. Maybe you just never acknowledged it.

Would it make any difference if I told you that I remain innocent of the crimes of which I have been convicted?

Every criminal is innocent. Every husband is faithful. Every stripper is working her way through college, trying to earn a degree in botany, and she really wants to be your girlfriend.

I think I am suffocating, nurse. I can't swallow. I'm choking.

That would be the respirator, Huckleberry. Your lung had collapsed and hung against your ribs like a deflated balloon. You've been in a deep sleep, aided by a smooth sedative, and breathing just fine. Now the sedatives are wearing off and you're feeling the tube in your throat. Not very comfortable, eh? The nurse shined a small pen light in Nelson's eyes and watched them dilate.

"Don't cough. Don't try to take it out. You'll hurt yourself very badly."

Nelson found the tube lying on his chest and followed it with his hands near his mouth. He readied himself to yank it from his throat when the nurse pounced on his arm and pinned it against the bed. She called for help over the intercom and two blue-clad orderlies rushed in and strapped Nelson's arms in restraints as the nurse opened the valve in the IV and let flow another dose of sedative.

It's not necessary, nurse. I'll be fine if you take the tube out of my throat, if you let me breathe on my own.

Really, Huckleberry, if you are worried about breathing you'll never make it through your time in prison. The state controls your functions now. Within months they'll be able to get you to shit on command and they'll house you in cells with men they think will make good mates. They'll regulate your diet and let you join a pack. They'll let a certain amount of drugs circulate to keep you calm and from killing each other. They'll take you out in the yard for fresh air and they'll tell you when you need a shower. Sometimes they will slowly vacuum out the air of the building until everyone shuffles about, hallucinating and near death and other times they will pump in oxygen rich air, humid as a jungle, and they'll watch through their security cameras as you fuck anything or anyone in sight and your fear and depression will be washed away by tears and sweat. There will be times when they will illuminate your cell, the lunchroom, the weight room and the library with a dim light and you'll feel as if the world has been wrapped in gauze because of some terrible wound. Your thoughts will grind and plod and eventually stop or be so slow you will forget what you are saying before any given sentence is completed. To jolt you awake they will flood the rooms with light that is so close to sunlight you'll openly wonder if they have taken the roof off of the prison. A sense of buoyancy will pervade your thoughts and for a time the end of a sentence will feel in sight, easily accomplished. You may feel hope or what now passes for hope. At the very least you will experience thoughts that can be classified as positive. The state monitors your moods and they know when your thoughts have reached an apex and just as they teeter on that summit and you begin to actively wonder if you can achieve a higher status, they will plunge the prison into four days of darkness and cold. They will serve especially soggy meals and boil all meat until it turns gray. Canned green beans will be poured from the can directly on your plate, and the coffee, if they make coffee during this period of atonement, will taste like it has been made with bleach or that someone has pissed in it. They will experiment with all the tools they have at hand. Sometimes the prison will be oxygen-rich but cold, other times they will serve choice beef prepared by a decent chef in the dark. They will analyze the wave lengths of your mind before and after conjugal visits and be able to determine from the pattern how often you have lain with a man in the quarter before the visit. There is a plan to build a database of human behavior inside prison walls so that generations of prisoners to come will be able to be manipulated by a control room and one or two underpaid operators. The theory has been advanced that given a couple of small steps in technological advancement the control room and the prison need not even be at the same location. One control room could monitor and run several prisons, thus eliminating overhead and administration and introducing a replicable and competitive prison model into the market place. Prisons will be located in the desert, on uninhabited atolls, on floating platforms in the sea, in underground caves deep in the earth's mantle, anywhere the state can establish a data connection. So, you can assume they will have a detailed record of your breathing and heart rates as your days behind the walls, such as do you take rapid, shallow breaths when your asshole is being raped for the first time or how do you react when they plunge the prison in total darkness and pipe in the soundtrack of angry chimps eviscerating a rival. Your data will be invaluable and after you have been released and have another opportunity to produce and consume, you will wish the invisible hand guided your thoughts and bodily functions. You will come to believe that living under the master control is easier, more efficient and adaptable to shift work.

Nelson fell into unconsciousness and the nurse made a note to keep H.H. Huckleberry under heavy sedation until the respirator came out and he regained enough health to be shipped off to Mansfield Prison.

The Cathedral of His Life

Estonia's water broke in the middle of the night and when she awoke moments after it released she thought she had wet the bed so shame and horror crept into her thoughts. But Annie Marie had tutored her over and over on the stages of pregnancy and a couple of times even read aloud straight from a book she had borrowed from the library, so her brain processed this development quickly and as she lay blinking at the black ceiling she understood that she would be giving birth to her baby on this day. A small contraction rippled through her body and she wondered when fear and panic would set in, when she would begin to thrash and curse and spit on whoever made the mistake of standing close to her. Anne Marie had listened patiently to Estonia describe what she thought would happen in the birthing process. She let her unravel every fear and retell every silly movie she had ever seen that used births to inject action and screaming into the lame script. She even let Estonia tell her what curses she would likely use. Estonia had told her that she would most likely use the word cocksucker more than a few times because it somehow had lodged in her mind as a terrible curse, one brought out in the most severe circumstances, even though, in truth, she liked performing fellatio and had gotten used to the taste of dick, so she couldn't understand why the curse continued to have such power, except men hated being called a cocksucker more than just about anything, but she had even called women that and she remembered after she shouted it being as puzzled by its significance as was the receiver of the curse, so puzzled that both the curser and cursed exchanged a look to signify that no matter what disagreements they had they could agree that they were, in fact, both cocksuckers and proud to wear the title. I guess, Estonia told Anne Marie, it's the same reason men don't call each other cuntlickers. Anne Marie let her talk, did not betray a hint of the revulsion she felt at the thought of a young girl spending that much time analyzing a word like that, much less confiding with not a hint of shame that she performed the act with some regularity. So, after she determined Estonia had completed her thought, she told Estonia that her birthing experiences were not like that and if she wanted she could have a very different birth than what she had seen on television. She told Estonia that she knew two women who used to be nurses at one of the big corporate hospitals that built a new wing dedicated to a new disease funded by a dead or dying new corporate chieftain every year who forked over cash to have their names emblazoned on the walls and forever be linked to that disease for future generations, that they had performed over a thousand births between them and that they had now gone on their own to bring women back into the birthing process, that they had quit their corporate hospital jobs and even had written a thin, underground manual on birthing that no publisher would touch because of the hundred critical comments on the practices of corporate hospitals and the ingrained arrogance and denial of natural processes of the medical staff for fear of malpractice. If Estonia wanted a natural birth at home she could enlist their help and they could create the proper environment to welcome a new child on the planet.

Estonia had already convinced herself there would be a lot of screaming and even the doctors and nurses would show a little panic, that giving birth would be a kind of a test, the ultimate rite of passage for a woman, the transformation of a girl into a mother so that two new people were being born at the same time, a moment when a women could close the argument of who could endure more pain and suffering. What kind of rite or test would it be without cursing and being able to scream cocksucker at the doctors at the top of her lungs? She wanted to scream so many times the room would tremble under her violence. So, at first she refused the aid of the nurses, but Anne Marie kept up the pressure and finally convinced her by describing what treatment she could expect as an indigent teenage girl giving birth at a local hospital that certainly wouldn't be the corporate hospital gorging on huge swaths of land and neighborhoods for their state-of-the-art facilities. No, she would be in a room that had serviced the poor for the past hundred years and the first time she would meet her doctor would be in the delivery room and she would not know if the doctor moved up, collecting solid and usable knowledge that she would later use in her practice or whether she tumbled downward toward deterioration and confusion, fueled by anger or bitterness at being stuck serving a river of pregnant indigent girls in the inner city. The description fit Estonia's idea of birth: a dirty room and an incompetent doctor carelessly causing pain. She and Glover had left California with no money in their pockets. They had gone hungry for days at a time and slept in fields with insects and mice and fucked in abandoned buildings and fought the homeless psycho freaks for the right to be on the street, so why shouldn't giving birth fit on this spectrum of deprivation and anger? But Anne Marie could always get to the heart of the matter and she said, "Estonia, you have to do what's best for the baby. Stop thinking you need to be punished," which effectively set off an echo chamber in her head and killed her whole idea of birth as needing to be as dreadful and painful as possible because the baby had not, as of yet, made terrible choices and did not need to pay retribution. Anne Marie left unsaid that she thought Estonia a complete fool, a selfish, pig-headed little girl half-informed about life from television shows made to sell cars, beer, tampons and pharmaceuticals. Estonia relented and told Anne Marie she would accept the help of the two nurses.

The nurses, Suni and Jill, came to the house the next day and began the process by completing a room by room inspection. They ended up picking the living room as the most hospitable place to have a birth. The room ran the length of the house and had both east and west facing windows. They could imagine the room filled with pink morning light should the baby come in the morning or deep yellow light should she step out in the afternoon. Night births were rare, in their experience, but moonlight would work just as well, although one had to worry about a child born at night. The room could also accommodate a portable birthing tub, chairs and a bed. Acoustically, the room echoed and peaked, given the hardwood floor and drywall surfaces, but they assumed that now that the room had been selected, Jack would focus on completing it. Suni and Jill had never been able to design a room from the drywall, so they shot off a thousand possibilities concerning room color, style of drapes, the stain color of the floor, the brand of polyurethane, the furniture placement and pieces of art that projected a natural state of grace.

After they selected the room they sat down with Estonia and Anne Marie on the front porch. They brought a thermos of herbal tea and each of the four women had a cup. They remarked at Estonia's beauty and the radiance of her skin. They guessed Basque, but mixed with an American wholesomeness, a frank American sexuality propped up by good works and a solid work ethic, looking like a nude as painted by Norman Rockwell, if he had ever deigned to dip his toes in those waters. Estonia had expected something else from them, if she knew at all what to expect from two ex-nurses reclaiming the birthing process. The first, Suni, had a fair complexion and carried a stretched and soft quality from giving birth to five children. She told Estonia that she would have had a child every year if the family could have afforded it and found a reasonably priced house with enough bedrooms to cover her childbearing years. She loved being pregnant more than conception even though she had to tip her hat to her husband for his inventive and sometimes surprising variations on a theme. The edge had been buffed off of her voice and her personality, and Estonia wondered how she managed to corral five kids with such a soft persona. The second, Jill, thin and very beautiful, with a wave of red hair hanging to her shoulders and sporting perfect teeth, smelled the better of the two and came across as smarter and more analytical. Whereas Suni embraced and lived their theories, Jill carefully constructed, tested and ultimately implemented them, ending at the same place as Suni by taking a very different route. Suni asked about the father of the baby and Estonia negated Glover with a toss of her head. Suni told her that women of her age often experienced birth without the father and that they would welcome the child for her. They never asked about

Glover again and considered the topic closed. They told her stories of positive birth experiences and even brought along a portable DVD player and showed her a short documentary shot in Mexico that depicted a Mexican artist who gave birth at home in a tub that looked like a Roman pool with her husband and children in the water with her. Never once did she scream or shout cocksucker. Maybe a low moan came from her as the baby's crown passed through the vaginal canal, something more akin to pleasure than pain. Of course, the movie did not aid Estonia's understanding all that much, since the woman created amazing art and looked universally beautiful, with perfect skin and a body that could have been carved in stone for the ages to see or that her husband looked supportive and virile, something like Jack if Jack hadn't turned old, mean and insane, and that her children, impossibly beautiful and patient, didn't scream in horror as their new baby sister swam out of the vaginal canal and broke to the surface like a newborn Naiad, who cooed when she recognized her mother and began laughing when the rest of the family broke into smiles. That scenario seemed fine if you created art and you knew that life can be shaped and formed according to your desires and you were Mexican and you lived in an ancient looking valley with a sprawling stone house. Estonia had slept with mice and fucked in rotting rooms that smelled of piss and vomit. Her baby would not be born in the same world as the artist's baby in the sprawling stone house. So, Estonia listened to them and drank their tea, but she did not for a minute believe anything they said. She agreed to their whole plan without enthusiasm. Yes, she would try water-birthing. Yes, she would train with Anne Marie in guided imagery, relaxation techniques, and hypnosis. Yes, she would try to think of the experience in a positive light and try to push fear from her mind. Yes, she would deliver in the living room and understood that should something go wrong the baby could be taken to the hospital in a matter of minutes.

"What could go wrong?" Estonia asked.

They assured her that in the many births they had witnessed and assisted they had seen everything that could possibly go wrong and most could be categorized as either the woman being completely unprepared, untutored and enamored with the idea of birth as the ultimate in pain and suffering or plain, flat out doctor panic.

"Don't forgot vagina bias," Suni reminded Jill. "They look at c-sections like a zipper waiting to be made. The vagina takes its time, has its own rhythm, but the docs and their minions always want to push and force the baby before she is ready."

At one point in the conversation Estonia drifted away and thought they all may be talking about someone else who happened to be pregnant, a friend of Anne Marie's like Mary Kelly down the street, because none of this bizarre talk could have anything to do with her. They had left California and planned on making it to New York and maybe London and Paris after that. Once they were on the road less than a week and she and Glover had slept in a field and went hungry for a few days, she viewed the world as brutal and indifferent to suffering and fantasies alike and that knowledge felt freeing and intoxicating. Estonia remembered she had demanded they stay with Jack because she felt tired, hungry and sick of wandering and that began the problems between Glover and her. She also remembered that she really felt very tired and very hungry and she wondered if she had been pregnant the moment she had made the decision. If so, she could be exonerated. How could she have given birth in a field with mice and insects or behind a dumpster in a New York alleyway? What could Glover have done for her? He had no money, no skills, and everyone he knew he had left back in California. He would have left her and the baby in a ditch, maybe dead, or well on their way to starving. But as quickly as this fog had descended on her thoughts it cleared and the scene on the porch suddenly came into sharp relief and she could hear the syllable of every word scrape across the nurses' teeth and tongue as she remembered all this talk concerned her and her baby. She would deliver in the living room of a falling down house with Jack, Anne Marie, Suni and Jill in attendance. Glover had long gone and he would never return. She started laughing out of context to the conversation, because no one had said anything humorous for some time. The three women stopped talking and exchanged glances. She sounded on the edge of hysteria.

"What's so funny, Estonia?" Jill asked.

"Oh, I was just thinking…" she took a breath to let the laughter finally settle, "…about the artist's stone house sprawling in the countryside and I thought about this house with no walls, with maggots in the basement, and we've had an outhouse in the back for the longest time with no plumbing and we still really don't even have a kitchen. I thought maybe it just sort of fit my life. I'm thinking you won't be filming me to sell happy births."

The women smiled but didn't laugh, because they all thought it a little sad and true. Anne Marie patted her on the knee and poured her some more tea. Suni leaned back in her chair and hummed a tune one of her children had been singing in the morning and it had been looping in her head ever since. Jill started planning what needed to be done and how she would get Jack to do it.

Jack had been working on the kitchen because Anne Marie's brother had stopped by to tell them he had almost finished the cabinets, so Jack had to complete the thousand little details in order to make the kitchen ready, namely hanging the drywall, taping, sanding, wiring the switches and outlets, running the gas pipe to where the stove would sit, and hanging new light fixtures. Suni and Jill found him in the garage rummaging through his tools, looking for a drill bit for his cordless drill. He had become a maniac with his tools, leaving them on the floor where he worked, misplacing them in his tool boxes, carrying them to the garage or basement with every intent of putting them away in their proper place before becoming distracted and setting them down in some random place. He could be forgiven a little absent-mindedness given all that had happened in the course of the rehab, but he had hell to pay whenever we wanted to find a tool again after he had misplaced it. Jack had just completed a sting of epithets directed at his own inadequacy when Jill and Suni walked in. He heard their breathing and raised his head from his tangle of tools. He dropped a stray piece of sandpaper and a crescent wrench and ensnared his thumbs in his belt loops.

"I've never seen a garage with a turret before," Jill began. "That will make a lovely studio. Your technique looks magnificent."

"Could we have the birth in the loft?" Suni asked Jill.

"No, it's the wrong message to send to Estonia. I believe she would always remember that she had her baby in a garage. That might lead to guilt towards the baby that would manifest itself in her parenting like letting the child drink soft drinks or eat fast food or not setting proper bedtimes."

"It worked out for Mary and Joseph, though," said Suni.

"I would say extraordinarily well."

"The light must be amazing up there."

"True, but are you forgetting the magnificence of the living room. It has both east and west facing windows."

"You're Anne Marie's friends, right?" Jack butted in.

"Yes, and soon to be Estonia's friends and your friends and friends of the baby," said Suni.

Jack nodded because he could think of nothing else to say other than 'that's good' but he couldn't convince himself that friendship with the two women would be possible or good.

"What we need from you Jack is quite simple. All of your work now needs to focus on the arrival of the baby," Jill began as Jack squinted at her. "We've picked the living room as the most conducive space in the house for birthing, but it's far from ready."

"Obviously, the walls need to be fixed," piped Suni.

"You mean taped, mudded and sanded."

"Whatever will take those cracks away. It reminds me how fragile our edifices really are and how clever we have become in sheltering ourselves. Interesting philosophical questions for another day. The baby doesn't need to be introduced to fragility the first hour of her life, so the walls must be finished and painted. I think we would prefer a healing green, something along the lines of recycled glass- glittering prisms, but calming. We can pick the color and you're certainly allowed to paint over it after Estonia moves to her room, but I think you will end up keeping it. Suni has an extraordinary eye for color. I tell her she can find the right color from a room's spectrum as if she can peel the layers like an onion until she finds the perfect hidden color that's just been waiting for someone to find it. The room also has to be spotless. There is far too much dust in the house. I very nearly felt like I was suffocating when I was inside."

"It all has to be cleaned. Estonia is well into her third trimester and the house now becomes about her. She could have the baby anytime. It's not good that she's been breathing all that contaminated air during the pregnancy, but there's nothing to be done about past mistakes. Basically, Jack, what we are telling you is that once the birthing room is done all work has to stop. These old houses have more poisons in them than we want to know."

Jack thought about how long it took him to rid the place of the Nazi echoes, but he said nothing.

"It would be nice to have the birthing room floor refinished. That old wood will just gleam with life and we could make sure all the lead in the old varnish has been sealed. Can you imagine the stories the floor could tell once we properly prepare it."

"We'll also need water, lots of water. Estonia was talking about an outhouse?"

"A temporary solution. We have water and real plumbing. That girl knows better. She's been shitting inside for couple of month's now."

"We're not here to criticize your time management skills or your project management ability. Anne Marie has told us of your kindness toward Estonia, so we believe you want what's best for the girl and her baby. Once you consider the baby a blessing nothing will seem like an inconvenience. Are we right about the kindness you have shown?"

"I let them stay. One left. One stayed."

"It's been our experience that fathers of this age flee with resolve. He may never stop running or, better said, this probably won't be the last child he abandons."

"We haven't been able to pinpoint if it's a societal disease or a primordial instinct. We have the research but no clear conclusions can be drawn from it. There is a huge statistical difference if the baby is a boy or girl. The fathers will tend to stay involved at a forty percent higher rate if the baby is a boy."

"In this case he didn't wait to find out the sex. He just booked."

"That's a quaint old saying, 'booked.' You wonder where some of this slang comes from. We're always shaping language to fit our needs and at some point somebody made the decision that 'he left quickly' could no longer capture the nature or reason why he left or the speaker made up a variation that captured the attention of the larger population for a few years before the saying fell back to disuse. Here, we have a remnant of an earlier time. You're still a believer in its effectiveness although the world has long since moved on. Can you imagine what a dictionary from a hundred years ago must look like? Dictionaries try to bring order to the chaos, but sometimes you have to question their effectiveness. I mean, on some streets standard dictionaries are just ridiculous."

"Do you always talk like this?"

"Of course, we are curious people."

"Are you going to talk like this during the birth?"

"We're going to be friends, Jack. We know what we are doing. We started helping women because we are curious. We wondered if there was a better way than making women feel like they had a disease, a better way than cutting open their bellies and yanking out the baby because the doctor is too stressed and too incompetent to truly understand a woman's body, of not paralyzing their lower half to manage the pain. We've debunked so many things because we began looking at them. We need your help in creating the environment. That's all we are asking. Follow our specifications and Estonia will have a beautiful experience."

"I've got my own timetable. I've done alright up to this point."

"You're sure the plumbing is working? We're all about going back to the basics, but an outhouse is over the line. We don't go back that far."

"It's done. It'll give you a flood if you want one."

"And the cracks in the wall. And the paint. We'll drop off the paint later in the week."

"And the floor and the cleaning. We don't want lead dust in the baby's lungs now do we?"

"I got it."

"I told you he would be cooperative. The man has a heart," Suni said to Jill as she kept her eyes on Jack.

"He did let them stay."

"Let's trust his words."

"Trust but verify. We'll be back in a couple of days to see how you're doing. Let us know if you need help. I've painted my whole house three or four times."

Jack let his anger rise after they had left the house in a banana yellow compact car. He stomped around the garage and let fly a string of epithets created solely to demean women. He banged a monkey wrench against his tool table and cocked his arm to put his fist through the wall of the garage. The quick movement sent a shot of pain through his armpit and he had to lower his arm before it would subside. Those dykes come to his house, he thought, a house he pulled off the scrap heap and start bossing him around for the sake of that little slut? He immediately regretted thinking that about Estonia and his anger began to recede as quickly as it had risen. If he could have conjured Glover at that moment he would have choked him until he died. Where would Estonia go? Kicking her out would surely kill the baby and he had no reason to kick her out other than she had become an inconvenience to the reconstruction. Surely, inconvenience could not justify kicking her out, could it? He thought of burning houses, of fighting a naked Glover, of the poor sap with the mangled leg and broken neck in the backyard. Comparing his frustration with reality his thoughts felt like nothing but idle, impotent chatter. What choice did he have? If he made a move to put Estonia out, he would be terrorized by Anne Marie and her two dyke friends until he jumped off a bridge or a building, driven crazy and frenzied by their retribution.

The next day Jack began by inspecting the plumbing and making sure he wouldn't be embarrassed by a leak during the birth. His work looked good and all the soldering held. He inspected the gas pipes while in the basement, because he smelled a faint scent of natural gas. He found seven leaks in the pipes and motherfucked his luck, the nurses and the bastards who had let this house fall to ruin. He stood in the basement, confused. Had he not checked this when he fired up the hot water tank? The house could have exploded like a failed rocket on the launch pad and he could be standing in a pile of rubble had a few more cubic feet leaked. So, for two days Jack unscrewed every piece of gas pipe and resealed the connections. Suni and Jill stopped by the first day, but Anne Marie warned them at the door that Jack had been gripped by a foul mood because of the setback so they left a gallon of primer and two gallons of paint and left without speaking to him. He eventually found thirteen additional leaks and with each find he wanted to smash himself in the head with a hammer for being so stupid. He had forgotten that he had become a complete fucking idiot, but the house had reminded him, unmasked him, and paraded him down a wide and crowded boulevard in leg irons with "blowhard" tattooed across his forehead, the tattoo looking like it had been scrawled by an artist with a bad case of the shakes. But his ego settled when he opened the gas valve and lit the pilot under the hot water tank and a thick blue flame spread across the bottom and he checked the pipes joint by joint and he had solved all the leaks. Jack returned to the tank and the flame caught his eye. He could think of nothing but money burning. He could steal the gas for a while, maybe even a year, but gas, water and electricity would all eventually cost money and the household had moved in the realm of a permanent settlement while leaving behind its Bedouin simplicity. Structures and cages rose around him. Water and gas rushed through the bars of the cage. Dyke guards barked orders, telling him what to build and where to build and for what purpose. Why had he taken on the house in the first place? He had avoided planting himself in one particular spot on the earth his whole adult life and now he had done it to himself. His great and final statement turned out to be borrowed wholesale from the dreams of convicts.

Jack followed the nurses' orders. A chill developed between Anne Marie and him, because Jack blamed Anne Marie for converting his house into a maternity ward and Anne Marie, for her part, didn't grasp the depth of Jack's unhappiness. So, they worked side by side without the same enthusiasm or ease as Jack constructed doomsday scenarios in his head, projecting this perceived nugget of control into raging fights about how he spends his time, how many drinks he imbibes at a sitting, what women he can and cannot talk to, and how often he washes behind his ears. His face looked like he fought an argument with himself and he moved more quickly and impulsively than normal. Anne Marie snuck peeks at him to gauge the depth of his anger when it became obvious that he had been throttled by a dark and bottomless brood, but she decided not to engage or recognize his rage. Estonia needed a place to birth the baby. Suni and Jill were just trying to make the experience a little more positive and beautiful instead of medical and awful, she thought, so if Jack stayed too thick or stubborn to understand their intent he could go to hell, or maybe better said, he could slide back to hell, tumble head over heels back into hell, because all of his traveling, all of his wandering and fighting and screwing women looked like a land of torture and pain to her. At least she had stuck by Ben until she could absolutely take it no more. She had found the end of her endurance after nearly thirty years so no one could say she hadn't done her time, but Jack never stuck to anything and more than likely this anger of his would be the first sign of his not sticking with her. He's beginning to feel crowded and coerced. She thought he may still be mad at her for getting the kitchen cabinets made by her brother outside of his control and specifications. He resented the intrusion into his vision and now something in the house will not have been made by his hands. His house is becoming our house and he hates me for it, she continued. He would run like Glover if he had the energy and the knees. Glover couldn't stand the idea that his life would not be entirely his own as he would have to share it with the baby and Estonia. Jack pretends not to understand and says he tried to stop Glover, but he understands and he probably kicks himself for not leaving with him. How long will it be before Jack walks down to Mary Kelly's house and sleeps with her? Even though she liked and respected Mary Kelly she knew that she obviously could not turn down a man and that she obviously attracted her share with that runner's body of hers. What will I do when it happens? I could screech at him until I make him stop visiting her, but he'll do it again with someone else or even go back to Mary Kelly after the dust had settled, depending on how much he liked to lie with that runner's body. He'll never be faithful. I knew that. I accepted that when I moved in, no? Such an unrealistic word. Ben probably stayed faithful to me, but I would have been dead in a year had I stayed, choked by inertia. I don't want all of Jack. I don't need all of Jack. What did I think when I moved in here? Had he so completely changed from a lifetime of doing exactly what he wanted when he wanted to embracing family and understanding families survive by consensus and compromise? Jack has been faithful to his nature. He didn't spend nearly thirty years with a person he could barely stand. He didn't raise children who grew up to be morose and bitter, carrying on their father's personality and exterminating your own. Jack, you'll never completely understand the feeling of my heart, the rush of blood when you walked through my kitchen door. You were my past and my excuse to leave, for me to assume the title of whore in my husband's and children's eyes, and to give Ben yet another reason to drink and curse the blasted world. My God, even my transgressions are selfless. I've given my poor bitter children a gift. They can now blame their hatreds and failures on a lascivious mother. They can steel themselves against me even further and nurse poor Ben or feel justified in buying him bottles by the case, because he has to do something to forget that awful woman with whom he had spent his adult life. I'll help you with your house, Jack. I'll ride your tides of anger and violence. I'll remember that poor dough-faced guard and his mangled leg and broken neck. I'll plant flowers on his grave and mourn in my own way. We've committed murder together, which, by itself, may have been worth leaving Ben's house. I've never been able to kill anything for any reason, but for you it seemed like such an effortless enterprise. Did it never occur to you to submit to his pistol, give ourselves up, be convicted of burglary or breaking and entering and serving some short time? How is that possible? Where did you learn that? Why did you throw yourself into the abyss for me at that moment? For a moment you were faithful to me. Nothing else mattered. You considered no consequences and you didn't waffle on your devotion to me. So, Jack, should I give you Mary Kelly with her flat stomach, tight butt and winning smile because you murdered for me and my silence has made me a beneficiary and an accessory to the crime? Stay faithful to your nature, Jack. Stay faithful to your nature and violence. Tear it all down and build it anew. Set the house ablaze and sow the ashes for next year's crops, but I have my own decisions to make once the fire licks my eyes.

Jack, after the gas pipe fiasco, began work on the living room. He rented a floor sander from the lumberyard to refinish the floors. Anne Marie took Estonia and Ellen in the truck and drove around the city completing minor errands, having lunch and generally killing time until the floor dust settled and Jack could sweep and mop. The nurses had given strict orders that Estonia not be in the house when the sanding and sealing took place and they added that the dust probably could also cause problems with Ellen's overworked lungs. The nurses had given Ellen a physical and Anne Marie had told them about the doctor who had nearly killed her with morphine and who had misdiagnosed her with having gangrene. Suni and Jill burst out laughing, not at Ellen's misfortune, but at the predictable outcomes of traditional, corporate medicine.

"That wouldn't be the first time a doctor has used morphine to mask his own incompetence," Jill nearly shouted. "Some of them just don't know what to do and they're afraid to ask, so they throw their hands up and say death is inevitable. Let's make them comfortable. Morphine stops the screaming. The doc was probably trained by incompetents. He probably never stood a chance of becoming a real doctor."

"Do your legs hurt, hun?" Suni asked Ellen.

"They bear my burden. They are my pain. I would have had them cut off a long time ago, but what happens when you start giving away pieces of yourself? Soon, it would be like a half price sale at a department store or a chicken restaurant. The hordes will come and leave nothing but my teeth. You ask about my legs, but I can't help but ask what is your intent? Do you feel you can employ them more effectively than I?" said Ellen.

The nurses consulted Anne Marie and asked if Ellen had been prescribed psychotropic medication and when Anne Marie answered that she hadn't they mulled over the situation with expressions of horrified shock and weariness from having seen too much suffering in the world. They told her they would see what they could do, but psychotropic prescriptions could not easily be gotten outside the established routes and care needed to be taken. Ellen knew they were talking about her and remembered the last time she had taken medicine for her brain. She ended up riding the bus to the zoo every day she swam in the medication and sitting in the monkey house. She could find no better place that served as a metaphor for her drugged state: half-wild monkeys cavorting and screaming behind glass three inches thick so none of the observers could hear their chatter, understand their observations or feel guilt for trapping them behind glass for their amusement. So, after she realized her thoughts resembled trapped monkeys behind glass she stopped taking the medication and never returned to the monkey house. When Anne Marie asked her where she would like to go so they wouldn't breathe in the lead dust she reflexively said the monkey house at the zoo and both Anne Marie and Estonia smiled at the notion, because they had been expecting a more provocative and apocalyptic response.

Before Anne Marie left she gave Jack a kiss on the ear and bit his earlobe to help melt his core of ice. It worked for a moment or two as he smiled at her and suggested they go upstairs and solve their disagreements with a round or two of donkey fucking, but Anne Marie mistakenly sent another cold blast his way when she straightened up and considered the walls and floors. She asked him if he shouldn't have finished the drywall and painted before sanding the floors. His eyes narrowed and he sent a breath fluttering through his moustache.

"Of course I goddamn should. Those bitches have unscrewed my head. I'm out of synch. Once I go off plan I'm fucked. I had a plan and now I'm outside that plan. Goddamn! It's ridiculous to mud and tape and sand and paint over a newly finished floor! I'm losing my fucking mind!"

Jack stomped off, and, when he didn't return in five minutes and Anne Marie didn't know if he changed his tools to drywall finishing or had begun punching the basement wall, she left and figured they could sort it all out upon her return. She had to take Estonia and Ellen out of the house even if Jack did no sanding. She would scatter the audience of Jack's humiliation, and his anger might recede faster if he had the house to himself. She would try to think of something special for him to untangle his anger and frustration, but this particular version seemed deep and knotted, but, she hoped, nothing so deep that a steak and a blow job wouldn't fix. Maybe Estonia is rubbing off on me, she thought.

Jack found himself standing in the footprint of the house he had burned to the ground. He had punched and kicked the air as he stomped through his backyard and past the garage and the outhouse grave. The garage with its turret and nail perfect construction represented his best work of the entire project, completed when his vision had been strong and he had the energy to make it happen. In a few months it had all dissipated. His vision lay buried beneath a blanket of compromises, incompetency, tragedies and abandonment. The gas and electric meters would soon be running and he had tied himself inexorably to two monolithic corporations bent on squeezing every nickel from his pocket. Soon, goons from the government, insurance companies, and telephone companies would come knocking on his door. Politicians, reporters, salesmen, exterminators, repairmen, landscapers, policemen, plumbers and electricians would slink around the neighborhood looking for an opportunity to take his money or bury him under some other entanglement. First, they would come with their hands out, palms up, and if he refused the hand would turn into a fist, and if they couldn't beat it out of him, the hand would turn sneaky and slender and they would pick his pocket and spend his money before he even knew they had taken it. How had he lost his mind so quickly and completely that he couldn't sequence a basic rehab? The ground where he stood still smelled of charred wood. Most of the house had been hauled away, but some of it had been buried and they hadn't bothered digging up the basement, so the smell would be with them for a season or two. Would an archeologist find this house, this city, three thousand years hence and wonder what cataclysm had swept it from the earth? Would myths and narratives arise around its fate, placing the destruction in a religious or historical context but failing to translate the horror of its annihilation?

He could see a row of apple trees growing in a line from the outhouse grave to the street. Ten feet away would grow a line of pear trees and on the other end of the yard a line of peach trees would grow, crossing the spot where he stood. He would start the seedlings in spring or to speed up the process he could scout tree farms east of the city and load up his truck with an orchard one night. He could smell the blossoms as a breeze rippled through the young trees and carried the scent to his bedroom where he and Mary Kelly lay. How had she snuck up the stairs and pushed Anne Marie out of bed? he joked with himself. He knew very well how she got there, as he had carried her from her house, down the street, up the stairs and undressed her before even asking her if he had something she would like to try. He thought he might make a run at her just to see if could still bed a woman against her better judgment. A breeze did pick up at that moment and carried a scent of piss and shit from the contaminated dirt near where the outhouse stood. Two toilets now worked inside, using water, asking to be maintained and kept in proper working order. Jack looked around and wondered why he stood in his planned orchard. On the sidewalk across the empty yard a dog sat looking at him. The dog didn't look like a stray as its coat looked washed and well-tended and it didn't have that cowering, hunting gait that all strays seemed to have. Jack never remembered a stray sitting long enough for him to get a good look at him let alone sit this long and stare directly at him. He whistled to the dog. Its ears pricked up, a slight acknowledgement of receiving the sound, but it didn't move otherwise. Jack slapped his leg and asked the dog to come in an encouraging voice. Down the middle of the street came a second dog, its nose and tongue just above the asphalt as it followed a trail of oil and rubber. It spied the first dog and loped up to it. They sniffed each other's snouts and licked each other's cheeks. The second dog sat down next to the first and took up staring at Jack as well. Jack danced and begged the dogs to come, but they wouldn't move. He took three or four steps toward them and the hair on their backs slowly rose as their bodies rose, preparing for Jack's advance. Their lips drew apart and revealed glistening fangs. The second dog's teeth betrayed a hard life of scavenging on the streets even though its body looked relatively healthy. Jack stopped, tried to whistle and even held out his hand for the dogs to sniff, but they showed no interest in the offering. Jack lowered his head and walked back to the house, casting a few backward glances to see if the dogs followed. They stayed where they sat and when Jack gave one last look before collecting his drywall tools in the garage they had disappeared, ready to roam after their brief rest.

Jack taped and mudded all the drywall in the living room, dining room and kitchen, covering all the offending cracks and blotting out all thoughts of the temporality and fragility inherent in the human condition. We would have to wait until the next day to sand and apply a skim coat, so he washed his tools and considered his options. He thought to leave Mary Kelly for another day when he hadn't been fueled by anger and his hands didn't feel like two lobster claws. He could take a shower and maybe dig out one of the books he had accumulated on his travels and read and ultimately doze in bed. He laughed at the idea. How could he relax enough to concentrate on a book in a house half done? The only way he had been able to sleep the past couple of months was to work until he could physically work no more and more or less pass out from exhaustion. When had he last fucked Anne Marie? Fucking had been part of the day's routine a short while ago, but he thought their last coupling could not have been less than two weeks previous, and he couldn't remember the details. The outhouse had to come down, preferably in a ritual blaze, but he worried the neighborhood remained a little jumpy since the arson, so if he did set it on fire his yard would be swarming with firefighters. So, he picked up a sledge and made quick work of his terrible carpentry, blasting away the rotten wood and throwing it in a pile on the empty lot. He watched if the dogs had come back, but they had not. He half-expected to see a hand or a face rising from the shit, but at the time of the burial he had used enough dirt to keep the corpse buried. Jack liked to think the guard had been accepted by the earth, but to complete the thought he had to think what it would mean for the earth to reject a body and he conjured up an image of bodies being spit out of the ground like watermelon seeds and landing in the grass, so he tried to stay away from the concept of ritual burial and whether the earth ever really accepts anything or just acts as a passive player in the strangeness of man. He shoveled dirt into the hole and made a mound on top that looked like the crown of a bald man's head, because he knew that all the shit and piss and flesh would eventually be absorbed into the dirt and the ground would sink and he didn't want a low spot in the yard that would collect rain water and breed mosquitoes. He spent too much time breaking up the clods of dirt and raking the mound smooth, thinking through what Anne Marie would plant there. He realized he aped real work, performed a ruse, puttered, hoping the women would return before he found trouble.

When he tired of raking he went inside and checked the drying joint compound and thought about taking a shower in his newly heated water, but today could be the last time he would be able to see Mary Kelly without an invitation, so he gathered up his shower supplies and walked down to her house. He found her home alone, dressed in spandex bottoms, a top no bigger than a sports bra and running shoes. Sweat covered her skin in a sheen as Jack had obviously interrupted a session on the treadmill.

"You're dirty," she said as she noted the flecks of joint compound on his hands, face and clothes.

"So are you."

She looked at her skin and wondered if sweat equaled joint compound. "You haven't come in a few weeks. I thought either you finally finished your plumbing or let your hygiene severely lapse."

"I think both are true. The truth is that I finished putting in the gas pipes and water heater and I was all set to take myself a shower in my new house with my almost new pipes. Then, I thought maybe I'd go down to Mary Kelly's house and see if she was in one of her running outfits and I thought that'd raise my spirits and maybe she'd let me have one last shower and I would think of someway of repaying her generosity."

Mary Kelly laughed. She laughed so long that the laughter took a turn toward outright mockery. "Really, Jack? That's why you didn't take a shower in your own house? You're so good with women that I'll consider it a form of repayment? Jesus, you're an old fool. That's just about the last reason I would want to have sex. That might be just above rape on the scale of degeneracy. Sex for water. You are a crazy old man."

"You've twice called me old. I don't take offense lightly, but my pecker is shrinking to a little acorn under this tongue lashing." Jack had decided to fight through the humiliation and work until he could regain some ground, enough to leave doubt in her mind that he could use should they ever talk again. "You call me old to put me in my place, to knock me off my feet, but that's a bad defense, Mary Kelly, because I might be worn out and fat, but I'm not old. I still have a grip that can break a man's neck and even though my knees are grinding bone against bone I'm raising that goddamn house out of the dung heap all by myself. These two hands and two wobbly knees are doing that. You act like I'm a goddamn corpse. What are you thinking, Mary Kelly? Invite me in. There's a chill in the air and your bare belly must be getting cold. I can see it quivering. It's not good to stand in a draft after you've sweated."

"You're ridiculous. That belt buckle. That gut. Those hands that look like bear paws."

"Are you telling me you prefer boys to men? I've earned this goddamn belly. All I've done is work for a living and I haven't stopped working since I was ten years old. I don't give a good goddamn if I collected a few pounds of fat along the way. You don't think a man with a belly can have sex? Am I that disgusting in your eyes? Ya, I probably am to a hard body like you, but all you're looking at in this gut is wisdom and experience, you're looking at gallons of pretty good wine and buckets of beer, you're seeing my love of grilled cheese sandwiches and hamburgers. You're seeing a life lived. I imagine you liked that boy Glover with his thin hairless body and his big cock. Is that desire? Or a better question is was it desire fulfilled? Kissing pretty skin. Is that pleasure? All that energy, unfocused, random and untutored. You like the thought of having sex with him more than the memory of the sex. Chaotic and hurried. All cock and no technique. Is that really what you desire?"

"He really wasn't as bad as all that."

Jack winced a little as she confirmed their coupling even though he obviously had no claim to be first in. "He's younger than your own son, Mary Kelly."

"I'm young enough to be your daughter."

"We're both old enough to understand the difference."

"Are you saying I'm a pervert?"

"No, confused. You're trying to hang on to your fast fading youth, but you'll crumble just like me. Ok, maybe in me you are seeing the advanced stages of decay but look and see what awaits thee. All of your running and fucking of boys won't put the genie back in the bottle. You're old, so fucking what? Now's the time for you to fuck without remorse, without reservations, without worrying how it will look if the man measures up as a future husband or can withstand your litmus test of status, future prospects, and known genetic diseases in the family. You now know there will be no future husband that will stay with you and grow old together with you. The idea of me makes you sad. I make you think you are old and you're not ready to let go of ideas two decades old and embrace what is to come. You're trapped in nonsense. There's no going back, you know that, and no going forward if you're always looking back. It's about pleasure, pleasure now, pleasure the moment you say yes. I'm an ugly sonofabitch, but if you can get past the idea of a monster touching your taut skin, of allowing impulse to break through your regimen of starvation and exercise, then you'll have given yourself the opportunity to feel something other than thigh burn. I know what I'm doing. I know how to give pleasure to a woman. I've been practicing and paying attention for close to forty-five years so you'd think I'd pick up an idea or two. So when you say yes you'll get the best of my training and this old carcass will raise the pleasure inside you. A pleasure, I expect, that's been left for dead a long time ago. Why else would you burn off all traces of belly flab? Why else would you be in a cycle of transgression and repentance? Eat a cookie and run for an hour. Let an old monster touch you and consider plastic surgery, because surely if you smoothed out those crow feet the boys would come back flocking to your door. You're supposed to be fat, happy, walking around nude whenever you can and fucking like a bunny at your age."

Mary Kelly let the screen door close and she walked into the house. She left the interior door open, but she didn't ask him in or give a sign of what step she wanted him to take. Jack stared at the open door for a moment and considered it a passive invitation, working nicely both literally and metaphorically. He isolated a single square in the screen and imagined the hairy legs of a fly crawling past in search of the origin of the heavy scents pouring from inside. The poor bastard would search until he died on the concrete step, unable to leave because the smells held him close and promised such bounty. He waited another moment, giving Mary Kelly time to reconsider and close and deadbolt the door, but it remained open. He pulled the screen open and walked into the house. He walked through the kitchen and dining room, both scrubbed and impeccably clean although the scent of sweat and a lunch of baked fish hung in the air. In the living room the couch and chairs had been pushed against the walls to fit a massive treadmill still humming from Mary Kelly's interrupted workout. Jack guessed she didn't much care about company since the furniture looked stored and forgotten. He picked a couch and sat down, throwing his shower supplies on the cushion next to him.

She came into the room wearing a robe and sweats pants. The robe looked old and worn, like something a person would wear when they had the flu. She walked on the cuffs of the sweat pants, which had frayed from dragging along the ground. She sat in a big, overstuffed chair against the opposite wall from Jack, wedged between a coffee and end table on either side.

"You're getting my couch dirty."

"I came for a shower, but I was turned away. I was called old and ridiculous, so I remained dirty. I apologize for the stains and dust on your couch. I'm sure it won't take much to clean up after I'm gone."

"It's not going to happen, Jack. I'm friends with Anne Marie. I'm not going to do that to her. We'd both be betraying her."

"It must be hard living with so many rules, so many constructs and cages of your own making. I learned a long time ago that once you start living by what you think will happen or by the possible bruised feelings of other people then you might as well just sit in a corner and suck your thumb. I suspect you don't really give a rat's ass about Anne Marie's feelings. Who is she to you, really? To me, she's the woman I've always loved and was too stupid to make her my wife years and years ago, goddamn, a couple of dozen lifetimes ago. But it's too late for all that. We won't be married and we won't have a brood of children together and those are regrets and the central sadness of my life. She knows it's never going to happen or that I'd change my nature. I never promised her that. How can a man change his nature at my age? Fucking you won't make me love her less. I don't want to marry you, live with you, or even know about your life. I don't want to know how you came to be raising an idiot son or where the poor kid's father is. I don't care about your bundle of neuroses or your favorite flower. I don't care if you eat potted meat right out of a can or if you floss your teeth. I don't care if you have disease other than in your pussy and I don't give a shit about your philosophy of life. You could be a Nazi, well, no, not a Nazi, but you could be a nut job, a crazy, a full-blown wear-underwear-on-your-head-lunatic for all I care. That's all reserved for Anne Marie and I have no desire to replace her. I want to know every minute of the lives we spent apart. I want to know what she's thinking all the time even when she pisses me off by giving the perfect advice. I never get pissed off at her being right, but I do get pissed off that my mind is so inadequate, so simple and slow that I couldn't figure out the problem myself. Maybe I'm pissed at being humbled, of having my ego hacked apart until it lays at my feet in ruins, but that just binds me closer to her. I'd bite through a man's throat if he threatened her. So you don't have to worry about Anne Marie. You have no chance of ever alienating my affections from her. She knows me. I bet she knows I'm here at your house right now and I bet she also knows I will come back to her and worship her and do anything she wants. You, Mary Kelly, I want to fuck. I want to feel that runner's body in my hands. I want my hands to follow the slope of your tight ass and I want to see if those heavy breasts of yours are real or surgically enhanced. I want a moment of pleasure with your perfect body, crafted and toned by so much work and sacrifice. I have a curiosity if all that exercising and starving makes for a better fuck. You've created this offering, so you can't be offended when the requests pour in. You look fantastic, but I want to know if the contents measure up to the beautiful wrapping. I want to see you lose control and release yourself to pleasure. I want to taste your sweat. I want to feel you quiver as I lick that little bridge between your pussy and your asshole. Then, I want to leave and not feel an ounce of obligation. I want to know you won't show up on my doorstep asking for more, creating a scene and embarrassing yourself. In turn, I'll never ask again. I'll never work this hard again and I'll certainly never use as many words. I'll only try to convince you once. If we establish a routine, so be it. If there is some schedule, some number of times that we need to couple to work out our curiosity then I'll follow it. In the perfect world all this preliminary noise will be dispensed with and replaced by a pantomime no longer than a minute or two and then we'd fuck until our hearts felt ready to explode."

"I'm trying not to throw something at you, Jack. Do you suppose I think so little of myself that I would allow myself to become your whore? God Jack, if I had any flicker of an idea, any warm ember in the pit of my stomach that was considering accepting your bizarre invitation you pretty much extinguished it with that bucket of cold ice water that I suppose was meant to convince me. Really, did you actually think that I ever thought of you, that I ever placed you in my desires? You, with that broken down truck and rat infested house, with the belt buckle and western moustache. Really, this is who I think about and pine for? Have I sunk so low that I can only think that broken down old men will come to my door? "

"The lady has an insufferable ego. I could have guessed. Her body is not an offering but bait. You must choose from the line of suitors bearing gifts, stretching from your door to the corner of the street. One suitor has a diamond ring, another a sprawling ranch in the burbs, another saves idiot children who are doughy and white, and they all crawl on their knees hoping to catch a whiff of your pussy as they genuflect to your beauty and charm. Who will she bestow her vaginal gifts upon? Only the brave and well-heeled can enter her pussy hole, which she refers to as the Golden Comfort because she has a gift for marketing. The name hangs in their thoughts and drives them to delirium and fever. You'll never be my whore, because I'll never pay for your services. You'll get nothing in return from me. I thought you might be past all that fantasy and the need for tributes and gifts laid at your feet. I thought you might be in the mood for a little unencumbered fun. But if you're still waiting for that suitor line to form or there's a queue I don't know about I apologize. I wish whores were the answer, but once commerce creeps in the idea is ruined. Can you honestly tell me that you didn't use Glover for the same purpose that I'm proposing? You liked the idea of being older, of being in control, that you were getting over on him. You liked the feel of his nice young skin and his young cock with an erection so hard and tight you could have hung a closet full of laundry on it to dry. He wasn't hurt or humiliated by you sticking a wad of cash in his pocket. At best he'll have a memory and at worst he's already forgotten the older lady with a runner's body who fell into his lap and that he had no idea what to do with her."

"Jesus, the words don't stop. If I do this will you promise me that you will stop talking?"

"Immediately upon consent. I'm the best goddamn mime there is."

"Promise me you'll never come to my house again unless I invite you. Never come knocking at my door just because you're tired of Anne Marie that night."

"I already told you that this is my first and last attempt."

"You're really not much of a salesman. This is a gift from me to you. Mostly I want you to stop talking so your voice is out of my head."

"Think of it anyway you want."

"At least take a shower. I can smell your BO from here."

"No, you'll fuck me dirty."

"Fine, have it your way."

Mary Kelly would not have been able to pinpoint why she had acquiesced. She did want Jack to stop talking. She wanted the whole discussion to end. His insistence and her refusal had grown past the importance of the act. Were so many words really needed when two people were talking about sex? Jack would have never stopped. He derived his power from his surety about the right thing to do and his stamina for driving home the point. She remembered some men had actually courted her, had entertained and fed her, had slowly ratcheted up the heat until they could no longer bear to keep their hands off each other, usually months after they had first met. How many words, gestures, postures, advances and retreats, not to mention cold hard cash, had been used in these agreements? Jack had taken the opposite approach, barging into her life and beating her with words that felt like ingots, pummeling her half-hearted defense and just plain wearing her down. She already felt exhausted and used and they had never even been close enough to feel each other's breath. So, she stood with the thought that the most flexible trees survive thunderstorms. The thin and pliable trees can bend to the ground under the wind and spring back up once the storm has passed, while the oaks and maples that have grown too big, have grown past flexibility and pliability, will snap at their trunks and lie dead under the retreating clouds.

She disappointed Jack when she led him upstairs to her bedroom. He would have liked to fuck her on the floor next to the treadmill, sore knees and all. She undressed quickly and slipped under the sheets before he could get a good look at her, which became a second disappointment in the span of a minute. He undressed with difficulty and tried not to moan or wince when a certain movement of a limb caused him pain. He limped over to the bed and pulled the covers off her body. She tried to keep them on her, but Jack insisted and yanked them to the floor.

"I'm cold," she said.

"You won't be if you put your mind to the business at hand. I've never been able to fuck under covers. It feels like shame or insecurity. I'd rather have a cold ass."

"You don't live in a house that has holes the size of your head in the siding. Sometimes it feels like it's snowing inside this room."

"I'd offer to fix that for you but that would sound like something a boyfriend or a very interested neighbor would say."

"No, you won't be fixing my house."

The sex they had surprised Mary Kelly and disappointed Jack, his third and deepest disappointment of the adventure. When he crawled onto the bed and felt a surge of blood pressure at his temples and a corkscrew of pain at the base of his skull, he guessed he might encounter some performance issues. Maybe he would be quick or his dick would take too long to get hard or be uninspired when called upon. She, of course, would not make it easy so she passively lay there as if her body said, "You wanted to fuck me. You wanted to see my body without spandex wrap. I agreed against my better judgment, so here you go and good luck." At first she didn't respond to his touch or his kisses. Her body felt hard and smooth. She had burned away any trace of her distant pregnancy and any indulging she may have allowed in the interim. Her ligaments that played such an important role in the look and feel of her body disturbed him. Collectively, they looked like ropes holding together her skeleton, made of some unbreakable polymer and tasting of a sour chemical blend.

She relented, finally, when after he worked her clitoris and asshole with just the right amount of pressure and movement, not easy for a man who couldn't really feel his fingers past the second knuckle, but Jack thought her concentration wavered and stray thoughts of betrayal, humiliation, insecurity, chastity, disappointment, fear, probably terror, control, hunger, worry, and not a little disgust considering she had allowed a foul smelling monster into her bed, affected her performance. He opened up his arsenal by turning her over, spreading her ass cheeks that felt like stretching a taut rubber band, and slipping his tongue and part of his moustache into her anus. That proved to be the key and she moved to the waves of sensation and she forgot the image of his old, tattered body with the gray chest hair and his map of scars, the unpleasant pockets of fat and the muscles so strong he could crush her on a whim. She beat the pillow and raised her ass in welcome. Jack now lost his focus. Having achieved a level of success, he became distracted by his own thoughts and wished the session to be over. She looked pretty enough, of course, and now that she had allowed herself to respond she demonstrated a basic knack for sex. Her movements were lithe and in rhythm. She didn't shriek or thrash or otherwise make a listener believe he had impaled or eviscerated her, but she lost herself enough to pass pleasure back to him. But he wanted Ann Marie's thick thighs and her heavy, drooping breasts, her unruly pubic hair and her callused toes. He wanted to feel her accumulation of desire and misdeeds resident in her flesh, stretched, bloated and slightly abused. Where had the spider webs of veins and the brown and yellow bruises gone? What had happened to the laughter in the back of her throat and the tangle of hair falling over her eyes? She remained the girl in the black field picking up stones. He had come back for her and raised a house from the brink of demolition for her. What kind of delirium had led him to Mary Kelly's bed? What kind of destructive impulse did he still have to work out and how had it been planted so deep that exhaustion consumed his body and yet the impulse had not yet been extinguished? Had he been able to end the session at that moment, without orgasms, without fear of humiliation and the possibility, quite real, of Mary Kelly laughing at his retreat he would have jumped from the bed and run home without a word of explanation. He would have disengaged his mouth from her ass, and never, ever returned. But after seeking her out, walking to her door, barging in and bullying her and exhausting her until she accepted and getting her to raise her ass in acknowledgement of his right to be in her bed, how could he honorably retreat? He pushed on, but her lean body became more of a burden to his concentration. Her movements became athletic and aerobic. When he wanted to grind and writhe she thrust against him as if she practiced donkey kicks. He would have thrown her on top of him, but he worried she might do pushups on his cock and he would lose his erection. He finally came after he paraded a host of sensual memories past his mind's eye, highlights of his erotic life that often served as material for successful masturbation and the impetus for trying to bed new women, moments of lost glory that remained elusive, mysterious and confounding because he never knew when one of the moments might happen again or when one would be replaced by something better. Mary Kelly wouldn't make this hall of fame, but she would probably be remembered for her strange ligaments. He pulled out and came on her thighs. She had probably cum a couple of times, but he found that he didn't much care. He rolled off the bed and started dressing without cleaning himself off. She peered at him through a half-closed eye, the majority of her face buried deep in a pillow.

"Are you going to shower now?"

"No, I've got my own water. If Anne Marie's home she'll know something's up if I come back clean."

"Already thinking of how to cover your tracks?"

Jack let the comment die and finished dressing as he stared at the floor.

"Was I not what you expected?"

Jack analyzed her body. She spread her legs so she looked like a half-opened compass and he could see part of her pussy past her sculpted butt cheeks. The soles of her feet had been meticulously buffed and scrubbed so they looked soft and pink. Her torso began with strong, broad shoulders and tapered perfectly to a trim waist.

"You're a beautiful woman. It seems impossible to say, but I think I'm past all that. It's no longer achievable and not that appealing."

She raised herself onto her arms, but she remained lying on her stomach.

"Thanks, Jack, that's a wonderful parting sentiment."

"You know you're beautiful. I just have no vanity left. I'm all impulses and nerve endings. Your beauty is strange and it's from a part of the world I've passed from. Look at me. Not a goddamn thing is going to make me pretty. You are not my mirror. When I look at you I become grotesque, a fucking aging monster. It was a struggle for me to come. Sometimes you have to follow an impulse before you realize it was a mistake."

"You're out of your fucking mind. Why don't you just stop talking now? I was feeling good and buying into your sex without bullshit philosophy and then you change course and repeat the very thing I was feeling when this all started. You do look like a monster. You are ridiculous. You're twenty, thirty years past your prime, but you're still trying to convince yourself to follow the impulses of a young man. Think about it, Jack. Who in their right mind would take on a project like your house at your age and condition? Shouldn't that be left to young men still fighting and clawing to make a name and a place for themselves in the world? You wear your scars and past stupidity on your chest like a collection of medals. People only fuck a lot when they're trying to figure out what they want and who they are. Supposedly you've convinced yourself that Anne Marie is the love of your life and look where you're standing. You can blather all you want, but you like my ass and you liked touching me. Your impulses and nerves have led you nowhere except chasing my parts. For all your experience and technique you're still an adolescent enthralled with form. Just because you now repent means nothing. After your guilt dies down you'll be back, hopefully not at my door, but at the next woman's door, probably not a runner because you believe it's my body that trapped you and turned you off, when both of us know Jack your drama had nothing to do with me and my body. I don't need an explanation from you. I understand you. You had this big plan to come back to your hometown and make everything right, to put in place a plan that you should have followed thirty years ago, but that is an old and ridiculous plan, Jack. You want to come rolling back, pretending to be older, wiser, a veteran of life, blown in from the west on the back of dust and hallucinations. Poor Anne Marie waited so many years. She never thought she'd see a reformed Jack and she still hasn't. Put a notch in your belt and call it experience. You got me to fuck you, big deal. I suppose I'm not all the hard to get in the first place, but now you can believe yourself to be a colossus, randomly choosing women to service your needs. Can you just leave my house before I really start getting pissed off?"

"It's just something I realized about myself. It had nothing to do with you."

"I know. None of this had anything to do with me. I get it. I think I knew before your started, but you've more than confirmed it for me. Thank you and get the fuck out."

Jack walked out of the room and the house. He went home and checked his drywall work and went upstairs to take a shower. He realized he had left his towel, soap and shampoo on Mary Kelly's couch and briefly entertained the thought she might make a great show of returning them after Anne Marie came home as payback for his rejection, but he hoped and bet that he would not be worthy of her fury and retaliation. She would chock up the experience as something done in a fever dream, a ridiculous act performed in a fog of temporary insanity.

When the women returned from their day out both Estonia and Ellen had fallen asleep in the truck, no small feat given the rattling and the less than air tight seal between the engine and the cabin that allowed the air to bear the burden of poisonous fumes. Jack carried Ellen to her room. She felt no heavier than a bundle of sticks wrapped in canvas. Estonia staggered to her room and fell asleep. When Jack and Anne Marie stood alone in the living room and as Anne Marie inspected Jack's excellent work, he let fly his confession that he had bedded Mary Kelly while the women were out. She had been thinking that Jack had taken her advice and finished the walls before sanding the floors and in his way had admitted she had been right and he had indirectly apologized for his anger and some of the distance between them closed. His words cut her musing short, and she gasped, which sounded like a sudden death rattle. The joint compound smelled noxious and had made the air extraordinarily dry. She could feel her lips chapping as she stood in the room under the gaze of Jack's heavy lidded eyes.

"I didn't want secrets between us. I'm not going to cover my tracks. It was something I was thinking about for awhile and it all came to a head today. I regret it. I made a mistake. I knew it was a mistake while I was doing it."

Anne Marie narrowed her eyes and opened her mouth to speak, but a cold shudder stopped her and she wrapped her arms around her torso to stop herself from shivering. "I'm a fool. I'm a fool. I'm a fool," she whispered to herself and then she found her voice. "I'm here on my own. Nobody forced me. I left my husband to be with you. I said I'd come with you because I hoped you had gotten old enough to slow down, hoped that something had changed, that you could consider other people. I'm a fool. I feel like I'm wearing a donkey's head and naked from the neck down. I came with you because I owed it to myself to give you a try. I know my life with Ben had exhausted itself. I had nothing left to do in that house except weep for missed opportunities and die alone. I wanted to find the path I had long ago abandoned. I had abandoned you. You were barely a memory, a pleasant memory, because I had forgotten all the pain, but I wasn't waiting for you. I knew this was coming. I pretended I forgot the pain, but it all came roaring back the moment I left my husband's house. Fear on all sides. Insecurity. Waiting for the other shoe to drop. I wasn't waiting for you. You came back. You came back to my neighborhood. You told me you had come back for me. I wasn't searching for you. Of all the places in the world and all the women in your past you picked my neighborhood and me to act out this stupid game. Within a year you're fucking that whore. You know she slept with Glover and probably all the men still living on the street. The women gossip that she addled her son by sleeping with him. I made friends with her because I felt bad about all the rumors. I thought it was just vicious slander by women who couldn't keep their husbands in their own beds. 'How can anyone spread such vicious lies,' I said. 'How could anyone drag such a sweet woman through the mud because she has a weird son,' I said. But, I'm a fool, so you would expect a fool to defend the guilty, to be repaid for her kindness by this, because that's what happens to fools. But even fools can harbor a little pride and the only reason I'm not leaving is because of Estonia and Ellen. I know you won't be able to take care of them. I have a vision of you trying to deliver the baby using a pair of tin snips and rope. After Estonia delivers the baby and we get her back to her family and I figure out something to do with Ellen, I'll no longer be a burden to you. I won't be here to stand in your way. It's alright, Jack, not to want to have roots. Not everyone can live amongst the trees. Be honest with yourself."

"I'm staying. I made a mistake. Another one. Pretty soon I'll get to the end of them. I'll tap out and live like a normal person. I think it was one of the first times I realized I was making a mistake while I was making it."

"That's twice you've referred to the act of fucking that whore Mary Kelly. You say it one more time I'll kill you with the first sharp object I can find. I don't want to hear about your epiphany during the act. I don't want to hear that you thought of me while you fucked her. That almost puts me in the room watching the whole ugly affair. A little sensitivity might make this go better."

"Maybe I'm not as close to the end of my mistakes as I think. The point is I realized at her house…" Anne Marie screamed and picked up a putty knife and brandished it at Jack, who couldn't tell how serious to take the threat, but he took a few steps back just in case she had true murderous intent. "The point is I realized I had reached the end of the line. I missed you. I wanted only you. There was no other. There will be no other. She was the last exit. It's only you, from now on,"

"I thought that's where we were when you picked me up at my house. You told me then I was the only one, and I imagined you thought about me while working in the oil fields or in a cannery and that it took thirty years to answer the question, but the question was finally answered and you were coming home. I expected we would reclaim lost time. I saw us packing in three or four years of love and happiness for every year we had left together. I thought we knew that time no longer yawned before us and felt like infinity and that we had all the time in the world to fight, to betray, to sneak around and try to be three people at once and never really, totally tell the truth of who you are. I thought I had exhausted all that. I think I expected this to happen. God, I'm a fool. I had my thoughts about Mary Kelly and I told myself I would accept you for who you are. I want to be that person. I want to tell you that it doesn't matter and that I feel the same way about you than I did before you told me about the deed. I'm just not. A person can think all they want about who they want to be, but I'm not a swinger, Jack. I don't share and I'm not to be shared. I figure if you go down that road you've turned off your emotions. I suppose there's a certain interest in being a bonobo, the ability to satiate yourself unfettered without jealousy and possession, but that's not me, Jack. You had to know that. You had to remember that. But you followed your pecker anyway. Where does this leave us? How do we move forward or even backward? Where are you going to be sleeping while I'm here? Unless you don't want me here, unless you want to help deliver the baby and make a peaceful end for Ellen. If you move in with Mary Kelly while I'm in this house I'll burn it to the fucking ground. I'll take these two women back to Ben's house. I'll keep him in booze and make him feel like he won and he'll be happy enough."

"It's getting too cold to sleep on the ground. I can sleep in the garage."

"Good choice. Excellent choice."

So Jack retreated to the loft above the garage. He placed a chair within the round walls of the turret and slept in his old sleeping bag that had been used so much his toes sometimes poked through the holes at the end. For a pillow he used his arm or a wadded up shirt. Certainly Anne Marie would not have begrudged him his pillow from their bed, but Jack wanted something of himself in the room, something with his smell and discarded skin that would remind Anne Marie that he had once been there. He fired up a kerosene heater an hour before he went to sleep and turned it off when he turned off the light, just enough to take the chill out of the air. By morning he could see his breath.

He completed the living/birthing room and dining room. He meticulously applied a skim coat to the walls so they looked like the original plaster. The nurses had picked a soft green for the birthing room that looked like something a person would see at a fancy spa where the patrons wore short white robes and flopped around in hemp flip flops between kelp and eel wraps and whole body scrubs of sea salt and the ashes of a mangrove copse. Jack had to admit that the color gave off a calming and peaceful energy and gave him ideas of meditating or at least he found that when he walked into the room after it had been painted he invariably ended up staring at a wall and reviewing every mistake he had ever made and imagining his life without those decisions, which had sent him yawing and pitching through his days.

He sanded the floors and vented the dust using a dryer hose as homemade tube. He ran the hose out the window and with every pass of the sander a dusty cloud blew into the air and drifted into the neighbor's yard. Jack sanded off at least a half inch before he could get rid of all the stains, chips gouging and warping. He preferred a dark stain, but the nurses persuaded him to keep it blonde because of the natural light and the play of the wall color. He had burned through all his leverage with his dalliance with Mary Kelly so he agreed without a fight, even though the nurses knew nothing of him moving to the garage or the reason for it. He thought it better to agree than lose more ground over the tone of the floor, because, even though he never actually asked Anne Marie directly, he assumed she would agree with the nurses. So, it irritated and troubled him, when he applied a maple stain and Anne Marie said something to the effect that she had looked forward to a mahogany stain, something deep and almost black, but if Jack wanted something pale and light, she could live with the decision given the short time she would be residing in the house. Jack stood with his hands on hips and wanted to hack apart the floor with an axe, even though he had applied the stain perfectly. Instead he walked out of the house without a word with the intention of walking around the block to clear his head of the stain fumes and his anger, even though his knees felt like someone had poured gravel between the bones. He inadvertently passed Mary Kelly's house, but he kept himself walking and he made sure to return to his own house, if you could call it his house anymore, by a different route. He didn't fear passing her house and he would have liked to drop in for a visit, but he didn't want Anne Marie to think that every time they had a disagreement he would run to Mary Kelly to have his ego patched together. They lived on a relatively short block, thirty-five houses on his side of the street. If he added the lots behind his street he came up with seventy households interconnected, minus the four lots that sat vacant and weedy, where houses had been burned accidently or, in Jack's case, purposely, and never rebuilt and fifteen houses that stood vacant and had been hastily boarded up and inevitably trespassed against. The copper and fixtures had been stripped, some by Jack and Wood, or other roving bands of tramps and scrappers. Some of the fifteen had been outright abandoned, turned into drug houses where a group of friends could form a loose congregation and blow their minds on the chemical of their choice or makeshift brothels where one or two whores could easily supply a small circle of men. Other houses had fallen into foreclosure and no one knew the family had been kicked out until full-blown chaos erupted in the yard with waist-high grass or in the house itself as the windows were shattered one-by-one and the doors were busted down or clumsy and ignorant thieves stole the pipes and a vapor trail of natural gas rose up the chimney or out of the broken windows. Other houses had tidy yards and fertilized grass and trees that blossomed with whites and pinks in the spring. The neighborhood crumbled around them, but either the homeowners were too old to move away from the chaos or they hadn't noticed that half of their neighbors had disappeared and had been replaced by a harder, meaner, and out-of-control set or their parents had been buried in a small cemetery a few blocks away and they couldn't muster the will to leave them forgotten in the ground.

When he came to the two lots where the houses had burned he paused to look at his house from behind. Again, the image of an orchard of fruit trees popped into his head and he saw his house rising above the first buds of a lush spring. The turret of the garage gleamed. It had promised to be the first detail of his cathedral, but now it looked out of place as he had abandoned grandeur in favor of completion. Originally, he had planned to add a matching turret, possibly two, on the house, but somewhere the idea had been lost. Had he rushed through it? Had he given all of himself? He had taken his shot and come up with mediocrity? No wonder the world always seemed on the edge of collapse. Did anyone really have the talent to make anything work? He walked through the lot to the back of his house, more troubled than when he began the walk. He felt a presence behind him and when he turned around he saw the same stray dog that had watched him before. The dog sat on its haunches and watched Jack with a look of calm and disdain. Jack called to it again, slapped his thigh and whistled. The dog did not move. Jack walked into the kitchen and opened his vintage refrigerator, which now hummed with electricity. It tended to chill food to the brink of freezing because the thermostat has been jostled loose on his travels. He picked scraps of chicken off of a nearly clean carcass and walked back to the dog. The first dog had now been joined by two others. Jack's hands began sweating as he approached the three dogs. He thought he could smell other dogs on their way, loping in from behind, encircling him, but he didn't want to turn and face the possible menace. He threw a chunk of chicken at the feet of the first dog, but it did not acknowledge the offering in any way. Jack sprayed the rest of it in front of the other two. They would not take his handouts either, but as he turned to go back to his house the first dog alone advanced and followed him at his heels. Jack did not offer his hand or try to pet it, but he kept walking and the dog followed. He climbed the stairs to the garage loft and the dog followed him inside, where it sniffed at the kerosene heater then walked as far away as it could from the smell. The dog curled in a ball on the chair in the turret, falling fast asleep. Jack considered the dog's trust a little unsettling, since it had gone from mistrustful stray to contented pet with no transition other than an offering of food it hadn't eaten. He would leave the door open to the stairs should the dog want to continue its ramble.

When Jack descended the stairs to find what odds and ends he could do he saw a delivery truck pull into the driveway. Anne Marie came out of the side door and held up a hand to halt the truck before it came too far down the drive. She walked to the side door, stepped up on the running board and kissed the driver through an open window. She held onto the door and spoke in a whisper and even stole a glance or two at Jack standing in the garage. Jack decided to find out who had come, so he started walking toward the truck, but the truck pulled out as he approached and had backed into the street by the time he had come up to Anne Marie.

"How's Mary Kelly?"

Jack felt a surge of pity for her, since he had been the author of her destruction and pushed her to scorn and paranoia.

"I adopted a dog. I needed the company. Have you noticed all the strays in this neighborhood? I wouldn't doubt we'll start seeing packs."

"People are just leaving their dogs. Can't afford to feed them or take them wherever they're going."

"Who was in the truck?"

"That was my brother. He was going to deliver the kitchen cabinets, but I turned him around and told him to store them in his shop. We weren't ready for them."

"The kitchen is ready. The walls are done and so is the floor. The only thing left is the cabinets. Why didn't you come and ask me? I would have told you I was ready for them."

"Right. I have eyes, Jack. I can see the kitchen is done, but you're not listening to what I'm saying. I'm not having my brother put in cabinets in a house where I won't be living. That's my money, his work and your house. We have to be practical about the future."

She had stunned him like she had smacked him in the face with a shovel or he accidently cut through a live wire and had been shocked off his feet. He knew that Anne Marie had continued to be upset and hurt, but for the first time he let sink in the fact that she had begun making plans that did not include him or the house. Where would he get cabinets?" His copper money had all been spent and Wood's money had been used to buy a boiler and there remained so many other expenses yet to come that using anything beyond cardboard boxes and plywood for cabinets seemed unlikely.

"Are you going to stay mad at me?"

"I'm not mad. I'm just not stupid. I have decisions to make and I haven't made them yet. We don't need to complicate things right now with cabinets."

"If we don't have the cabinets I won't have any place to set the sink and we won't have water in the kitchen. I need something to set the sink on and finish the plumbing."

"I suggest you find something on a tree lawn or build it yourself, because my brother's cabinets are not going in this house until I say so. Or you could ask Mary Kelly if she has an extra cabinet or two you can borrow whenever you feel like it."

"You are mad. You can say you're not, but you are."

"Of course I am. Who wouldn't be mad? You reject me for that skinny little bitch with no ass. Why shouldn't I be mad? Do you actually expect me not to be? I am who I am. I hoped you would remember that."

"I'll go make a cabinet."

Jack walked away. She seethed over the fact that he left the battlefield before her anger could be spent, so she picked up a rock and threw it at his head. Lucky for Jack the ligaments in her shoulder had not been properly warmed up before the throw so her arm did not fully extend and the rock missed its target by an inch as it whistled past his ear. He turned in time to see the side door slam shut.

A car pulled into the driveway and Jack stopped to see if the driver had come to see him or wanted to turn around. He thought of Kaufman, but the car, a nondescript domestic five or six years old, had white government plates, and Kaufman didn't like to angle his deals through the government. Jack waited and the car idled. He could see movement through the windshield as someone tried to organize an unruly mess on the passenger side seat. Finally, the engine stopped and a lanky man in a white shirt and an unremarkable tie uncoiled himself from the car. He held a clipboard and pen in his left hand and as he made his way toward Jack he looked at the house and even paused his steps to mentally record some detail.

"Are you the owner of this house?" The man stopped about five feet away from Jack and obviously had no intention of covering the rest of the ground to shake his hand.

"I am."

"My name in Paul Newcombe and I'm a housing inspector with the City of Cleveland. You are Jack Cactus?"

"I am."

"That's the name listed on the deed. You had to make that up at some point, right? I mean no one is born with a name like that, right? I would think that Cactus had never been used as a surname until folks like yourself started adding it on to provide a sense of mystery and wonder."

"That's my name."

"And you became the owner just earlier this year?

"Right."

"You are the only person this year to buy into this block. That's quite an achievement. All the rats are running away from the sinking ship and you're the one rat who ran onto it. Here comes the hero. Here comes the hero rat."

"I'm guessing you think you can come onto my property and be a dick because you have City Hall behind you. I haven't ever given a fuck about any of that. I'm not some worm that you can frighten with your boot. I could give a fuck where you are from or who you think you are."

"Calm down, I'm here on a simple mission, really. I've come to see your permit for building that garage. That shouldn't be too hard for you. I know things can get misplaced during the chaos of building, but you look like an old hand at this construction game. I can tell right from the get go if someone knows what they're doing. I just bet my co-worker before I left to come here that even though we received complaints from some neighbors about a garage with a turret at this address and even though there are no permits on file at City Hall anywhere, not even an application, I bet him that when I came I would find an old experienced guy who knew the whatnots and the wherefores. My co-worker said I was a fool and an optimist. He said he's seen a hundred cases like this and he said he's always found that it's some scofflaw, some miscreant who thought he could skirt the law, who thought he could ignore community standards and building codes and all the other rules and regulations that generations of citizens have fine-tuned and argued about for decades. He said that I was going to find that kind of guy, and frankly, I told him he was full of shit. He laughed at me and said when it came out the way I said it would come out it would be the first time he's ever witnessed such a conclusion. I have to say he said he hoped he was surprised, that mistakes can be honest, and that paperwork simply is not filed in the correct file and major problems could be fixed with simple solutions."

"I pulled this house off the scrap heap. Nazis lived here. I beat back a cancer cell with these two hands. I've done more work on this place in six months than all the owners had in fifty years."

"Of course, and I understand the commendation is working its way through the Mayor's office as we speak and we're hoping you'll agree to the parade and the media coverage, because you are one of the first to buy an old, decrepit house and make is passably livable. Besides, this whole city is a scrap heap. I wouldn't doubt Nazi cells are popping up everywhere. There's gunfire every night. There's fire and death. What are you thinking?"

"You know there's no permit for the garage."

"I didn't know that until you just told me. That's an unfortunate development. Now I have to go back to work and pay twenty bucks to the guy that called me a fool. That's not a good feeling. I feel terrible about it really. I mean I was on your damn side and I clutched an optimist's dream that something simple could be done. Now I don't know what to think. I know that nothing good can now come of this."

"What do you want from me?"

"I want you to go inside your house and come out with a copy of a permit to build a garage with a ridiculous turret, an element that is not in any way reflected in the architectural elements of the house."

"You know I can't do that."

"Why can't you do that? Why would you build a garage without asking anyone if you could? Why wouldn't you draw up plans so that someone could check to see if the structure would stand for more than a month? Why would someone just build something from their head? Have you got a permit for any of the work on your house? The electrical, the plumbing, and the boiler, no?"

"I don't see what business the government has in my business."

"Really? The government doesn't have a stake when your wiring catches fire or your gas pipes leak and the government has to send over firefighters to extinguish your ineptitude. Are we supposed to just let it burn and have it take the whole block with it? Is that your idea?"

"We? So you've taken the whole of the government on your back?"

"I'm a representative. It's a legitimate use of the plural pronoun. I'm not speaking out of turn."

"My God, where do they manufacture dickheads like you?

"Sir, abusive language leads us to a bad place. Neither the government nor I made the mistake of building a garage and putting a house through major renovations without seeking permits."

"So how do I get the permits?"

"If it were only so easy. See, had you sought the permit before you started building your plans would have been passed to the architectural review board and they would have taken one look at that turret and struck it down. It never would have gotten passed. They don't like flights of fancy or grandiose statements out of context."

"So you're telling me I'm going to have to take it down?"

"That's one solution. Submit some reasonable plans and modify the structure to fit within the norms of the community. Nobody is going to respond to your iconoclasm. It's all fine inside your head, but once you've committed to building something there are other interested parties who have to weigh in. You need to enter into a discussion with your neighbors, your representatives and the administrators of the government they have chosen to rule. I know you're thinking I'm making an argument for collectivism, but it's not as bad as all that. You can express yourself all you want as long as it's inside the agreed upon parameters."

"Alright, let's cut the bullshit. How much is this going to cost me?"

"A thousand dollars in cash for me and another five hundred for the permit desk to certify the permit."

"I don't have it."

"You'll have to get it."

"I don't have any place to get it."

Paul Newcombe laughed. "An old pirate like you has a dozen sources to find that small amount of money. I'll give you a couple of weeks and if you don't come up with it I'll throw so much paper at you you'll spend the next year in court just trying to figure out what the charges are and in the end you'll have to tear that monstrosity down anyway."

"What does the cash buy me?"

"Everlasting peace and tranquility, unless you get the idea in your head to build a moat and drawbridge in your front yard. Then, I might be back. I can backdate the paperwork and the permit desk will stamp anything for a little cash."

"You're a fucking little bloodsucker."

"Sir, there's no need to complicate the transaction with emotion. I've provided you with a path out of your predicament. By the looks of you I thought you'd appreciate the unofficial solution, the straight out horse trade of cash for trouble, but if you want to go down the other road of official reports, housing court and fines then by all means we can proceed that way as well."

"Give me a couple of weeks and I'll get your cash."

"Here's my card. You can call me when you're ready. Don't send me an email or leave a voicemail other than stating your name. That's all public record and we want no tracks, agreed?"

Jack took the card and neither man offered a hand to conclude the deal, so an awkward moment of confusion and hesitation occurred before Paul Newcombe turned and walked back to his car. Jack jammed the card in his pocket and felt a rage he could not release, so he set to work on a makeshift cabinet. He used a piece of plywood for the counter and two-by-fours as the frame and cut a rough hole in the plywood large enough to fit the sink. He set the sink in the hole and roughly sanded the splinters off the edges. Then he found sturdy cardboard boxes to act as cabinets by rummaging through dumpsters after the morning deliveries had been made. He stacked the boxes on either side of the sink to make a cubed shelf. He connected the plumbing to the faucet and sink. The hot water came when summoned and the pipes didn't leak, so Jack gathered some food to eat in the loft, making sure to bring enough scraps for the dog.

When Estonia felt her water break she placed a hand on the wet spot and the bed felt warmer than she expected even though she knew that soon it would be cold and uncomfortable. She pulled the sheets back over her body and stared into the dark. The nurses had tutored her, drilled her really, in the birthing process and she knew enough not to panic at this early stage. She lay there until she counted ten contractions. In the intervals she dreamed of having the baby in the room alone, and the baby responded to her commands and inched down the canal at her pace, neither dawdling or rushing, responding perfectly to the slow stretching and expanding, and finally releasing when Estonia had her hands at the ready to catch her before she bounced on the bed. Glover hung in the shadows so she realized she had never been entirely alone in the room, but she didn't know of his presence until after the baby had been born. He handed her scissors and a clamp and she cut the umbilical cord even though she wished she could have been physically attached a few hours longer.

She stood up, pulled off her wet pajamas and slipped into a robe the nurses had given her, an incredible piece of material that felt both warm and soft as silk and closed with Velcro over her belly, because, as the nurses said, a belt would be impractical to get around a pregnant belly and "We don't want the baby thinking she's been born into a noose," they added in unison. Estonia had kept quiet, but she worried that even without the belt the idea rang truer than anyone wanted to admit.

She padded down the hall and knocked on Jack and Anne Marie's door and she expected Jack to answer not wearing any pants with his balls hanging down to his knees and his belly shading his penis as she had seen him several times making nighttime excursions to the outhouse or to get a drink of water while not bothering to clothe his lower half. But Anne Marie came to the door with red-rimmed eyes and her hair uncharacteristically mussed and greasy. Then Estonia remembered that Jack hadn't slept in the room for weeks. Jack had done something, of course, but Anne Marie had never told her any of the details. She saw Estonia's birthing robe and a big smile broke across her face.

"Do we need to get the nurses?" Anne Marie asked.

"Yes, she's coming today."

"I'll tell Jack to go get them."

They still didn't have a phone and the prospects for getting one had dimmed further since money had become so tight and winter utility bills loomed, not to mention the debt that Jack now owed to the housing inspector. Anne Marie walked to the garage, using a flashlight to lead the way. She climbed the stairs and swept the light across the floor until she found Jack lying in his sleeping bag with a dog curled near his head. From another angle it might look like Jack used the dog as a pillow for his massive head. The room smelled of kerosene and wet dog fur. A burst of pity flashed through her but died as her resolve strangled it with soft hands. She tiptoed around the dog, who had been listening to her since she came out of the side door, and leaned over Jack's ear and whispered that he needed to get up. It took five or six whispers, shaking his arm, flicking his ear, a stamp of the foot, nine loud claps near his ear and a kiss on the cheek before Jack roused himself and sat up. The dog had remained calm and curled in a ball but watched Anne Marie with one half-opened eye.

"Turn on the light. You don't need a flashlight."

"You have electricity out here?"

"I've had it. That's old news.

Anne Marie felt the last of her misplaced pity drain away. "Why don't you use an electric heater? Those fumes are going to kill you."

"It's not burning clean. Something wrong with the heating element, but it's cheap to run."

Jack hoped that Anne Marie's visit meant that she had relented some and she came to tell him that she needed him as bad as he needed her, but she doused his hopes when she told him the reason for her visit. He had thought she may have had a dream in which his pecker had a starring role and that she had awakened him in the throes of an urge, but his luck had run out. If Anne Marie didn't relent soon he would have to visit Mary Kelly again and that would be just one step closer to entanglement with her and one step farther away from Anne Marie, if he could get any farther away from her while living on the same property as they were now. He peeled off the sleeping bag and dressed as Anne Marie scratched the dog under its chin.

"What did you name him?" she asked.

"He hasn't been around long enough to earn a name."

"They like names. They respond better with a consistent salutation. I'm sure you can think of something that fits his personality or yours."

"Cerberus guarded the gates of hell. That'd be a good name. Maybe too regal."

"C'mon, Jack. He looks like a sweet dog."

"How about Barghest? Or Black Shuck?"

"I like Black Shuck. Maybe drop the 'black' part because people might think you're being racist. Why not just Shuck?"

"Shuck."

The dog raised its head and gave a limp wag of the tail. Jack said the name again and the dog stood up and walked over to him with its head down, supplicating. Once at Jack's feet the dog stretched its neck to get a scratch behind the ears before nuzzling Jack's leg.

"See, they like names."

"He shouldn't like that name."

"What does it mean?"

"Estonia might be giving birth already. Let me go fetch the nurses. Give me the addresses."

Jack drove to Suni's house, located in a suburb close to the city in a rambling, wooden house crammed with toys and children. Suni and her husband sustained on the wages her husband could earn as a landscape and snowplow contractor and whatever she could earn from women unwilling to give birth in corporate hospitals. In the neighborhood the children ran in a pack, showed fierce loyalty to their parents and siblings and scrapped over any injustice on the soccer field, basketball court or during imaginary play. Jack rang the bell in rapid-fire and her husband answered the door after five or six rings. He stared at the man standing on his front steps and couldn't imagine what he could want other than to invade his home, tie up his children, his wife and himself and steal every last piece of electronic equipment the family had managed to accumulate. Of course, the joke would be on the burglar because they bought crap to begin with since they couldn't afford the high-end stuff and all of it been smeared with jelly and cream cheese, beaten with plastic hammers, dropped into potting soil, squirted with water guns, and, in the case of the family digital camera, dropped in the toilet and two oceans. The camera still managed to take slightly skewed snapshots that looked like the records of someone whose eyeballs had been melted and reconstituted six or seven times.

When Jack asked for Suni and told her husband that a girl named Estonia had gone into labor and that her water had broken, the husband rolled his eyes and cursed himself for not connecting the man with the enormous, painted belt buckle, the unkempt hair and the prevalent look of craziness in his eyes with his adorable wife. A collection of strays, bums and teenage whores showed up on the doorstep constantly, asking for her wisdom and her help at all hours of the night or day. So many had come that an old woman across the street, after watching a week's worth of hysteria on the television, had become convinced that they were running a drug house and repeatedly called the police and screamed into the receiver to have the family thrown in jail before their disease spread to other streets. In truth the woman hated the children and once had seen Suni undress in a lighted bedroom window so further irregularity coming from the house sent her over the edge. The police had stopped coming to the house once they met Suni and saw the VCR smeared with peanut butter and tried to conduct an interview with the brood angry and active like a jostled hornet's nest.

Suni bounded down the steps dressed in what looked a first glace like hospital scrubs, but the material looked softer, more fragile and printed with muted lotus flowers.

"Still no phone, Jack? How long has it been since her water broke?"

Jack shook his head. He listened to the shrieks and laughter rumbling from upstairs. His arrival had awakened one of the children, who in turn roused the others and now all joined in a free-for-all game that involved jumping and stripping their beds clear of covers and sheets in what later would be described as a reenactment of the battle of Shiloh with pillows and broken light sabers used for guns and cannon. In addition to being a landscaper, Suni's husband spent his weekends studying the Civil War and he tried to impart his knowledge to his children whenever he could slip it in, over dinner, during a bath, embedded in a children's story before bedtime or between pitches during a baseball game. When he saw the children play their war games he thought of joining a reenactment squad, but ordering the uniforms and replica rifles seemed expensive and complicated so he never joined. Who knew who made the best replica rifle and he could just imagine dropping a bundle on one of them, joining the squad, finding out he had bought the least historically accurate brand and having to endure the mockery of his fellow soldiers and derision from the enemy.

Suni called Jill and left with Jack in his truck. Jill would meet them at the house and, given the state of Jack's rattling and smoking truck, would probably beat them even though she lived fifteen miles further away in the suburbs under a canopy of leaves with her children and husband, who obsessively listened to Uriah Heep albums and spent more time than he should have doodling with a fan website to keep alive the band's music and spirit. His interest could not be said to be purely nostalgia for his adolescence, because he believed the band had released some of the best music from the past decade. Jill gave him a spare bedroom to store his memorabilia and his extensive collection of vinyl Heep albums. The central piece of the collection had been added the year before, a pristine, never played copy of *The Magician's Birthday* framed in a museum quality frame with a ticket from the February 26, 1972 Akron, Ohio Civic Theater performance signed by the lead vocalist Gary Byron. Her husband was too young to have been at the show, but by all accounts the kids left with damaged ears that didn't stop ringing until days after. On the wall next to it hung a copy of *Demons and Wizards,* also from 1972, but he considered it an inferior album that paved the way for *The Magician's Birthday* but never reached its heights. Jill hoped to fill the room with another child soon and she wanted to convince her husband to build a loft like Jack's over the garage so they could both pursue their interests, he, his Uriah Heep collection and she, a house where the collection did not exist.

When they all arrived back at the house they found that Estonia had already climbed into the tub, a portable birthing tub the size of a hot tub that used inflation and a flexible superstructure to hold the water, which Jack had placed at the exact center of the room to the nurse's specifications. Jack had run a hose from the kitchen sink to the tub so he could screw in both ends at the intake valve of the tub and at the faucet to have a water supply. Suni had advised Estonia to use it at least a month before her due date so that her body and mind became conditioned to recognize it as a place of relaxation, but she had felt strange taking a bath in the middle of the living room with Jack roaming around so she forgot the advice. So, the tub sat empty when the first contractions started and Estonia had to wait for Anne Marie to connect the hose and watch 170 gallons of water flow through the hose. The tub had a thermostat, a built in heater and therapeutic wave action, but Estonia jumped in before the temperature rose to the optimal level and before the tub had completely filled. A couple of contractions had taken her breath away and she could feel her back and neck tensing against the onslaught, so she needed the water to work out the knots.

Suni's face looked green and her lips blue by the end of the truck ride and once she stepped into the house she paused and breathed deeply, trying to replace the exhaust in her lungs with some moderately fresh oxygen. Jill had adjusted the lights to just above darkness. Jack had installed dimmers in all the rooms downstairs, because the nurses wanted the control the amount of electricity introduced into the environment. Suni began mumbling about the tyranny of circuits and shrouds of confusion, but she didn't complete her thought because some task of preparation distracted her. Jill held up a hand to stop Jack before he came too far in the room.

"Estonia, do you want Jack it the room?"

Estonia craned her neck to see Jack standing near the threshold and she considered him a moment. In his gruff way he had been more kind than her father had ever been and she thought, again, of herself giving birth in a ditch, this time with murky water carrying a ribbon of oil through a dank woods and under and past her spread thighs as a rotting elm towered over her, as the baby ripped her in half, more clawing its way out than actually respecting the birth canal, as Glover cried and tried to beat it back with a stick. Jack acted lecherously, no doubt, as she had caught him looking at her body nearly every day since she had been with him, but it had remained a distant, admiring lechery and who could possibly get off on her now pregnant body flopping and thrashing around in a birthing tub?

"I want him here if he wants to stay. Without him I'd be fucked. I'd be on a garbage pile with my little garbage baby."

Jill smiled at Jack as Estonia turned back to a more comfortable position. Suni played a CD of music that very well could have been the soundtrack for a flock of green sprites who had gathered in a forest glen to sip the dew off of spring leaves and to make a lunch of freshly fallen walnuts and elderberries. Jack had to admit that with the wall color, the crepuscular light, the dim radiance of the wooden floor and the music that Estonia may have been a naiad relaxing in a meadow pool, guarded from above by a grove of ancient oak trees. Her breasts and belly bobbed near the surface and her skin looked translucent. He could have sworn he saw the baby patiently move into birthing position, preparing for a head first dive into the world. He found a chair in the corner of the room, distant enough that he could be a spectator, but near enough to watch the changes on Estonia's face and feel like the naiad had invited him to rest with her. Anne Marie sat in a chair facing Estonia on the other side of the room, so that all the activity happened between Jack and her, so they felt like they sat miles apart. They watched Suni and Jill walk around the tub, checking the temperature and the water level and preparing a small table behind Estonia that held clamps, a scissors for cutting the cord and a few towels. At the other end of the room sat a hospital bed decorated with faux wood grain to mask the lifting mechanism. The nurses had supplied it all at no cost.

"This is going to drive me nuts. I want to get out," Estonia suddenly blurted and the four attendants jerked their heads in her direction. "The water is making my skin crawl."

Jill and Suni helped her out of the tub and slipped on the robe, which she immediately threw off. "There is something wrong with my skin. Is there a rash or something?"

Jill pretended to check her back and arms and told her that she could find nothing wrong with her skin. Estonia paced between the tub and bed, dripping a path of water. Jack watched her make five or six circuits before he felt Anne Marie's eyes boring into the side of his neck, so he cast his sight toward his toes. Which suited him just fine, because seeing her whole form made him think that she may have been more beautiful than he had ever seen her and, since she had grown out of her teenage body and his lasciviousness could indeed gain a proper hold. If he watched her much longer, walking naked and wet, he very well may develop some ideas that would have to be acted upon in the future. What could he do when the world spit up such beauty right at his feet? To not acknowledge her, to kill the image with a blanket or reason and propriety, would be to renounce the world and forget its perpetual spin and its new bloom. Was he supposed to not want to nuzzle his face between those ripe breasts and ass cheeks? She was young enough to be his granddaughter by all figuring, but she didn't carry his blood and he wondered how the ladies would react if he climbed in the tub hard as pipe and kissed the translucent skin as the baby shot into the water with a flutter kick. He finally summoned the courage to look at Anne Marie, who smiled at him with a drowsy, heated, and inviting look. Estonia's nude and pregnant body must have had the same effect on her, like she performed the rites of a fertility goddess charm, filling the room with sexual energy and condensing science and philosophy into the touch between a vagina and penis, channeling the whole world into a single urge to reproduce or at least practice the method again and again until the participants passed out from lack of blood or just plain shock, because when Anne Marie looked at Jack her anger abated and she wanted nothing more than to feel his penis in her hand and then inside her, to smell his sweat close to her nostrils and taste his bitter skin, to pretend for a moment she would be the only one he would ever want. She stood up and muttered for Jack to follow her upstairs. Suni and Jill waited until they heard the creak on the stairs to begin a dialogue on the mating habit of wolves and then wander into a speculative conversation that had as its central question whether or not an orgy had ever broken out amongst the witnesses of a birth.

"What more could confirm a good fuck?" Suni said to Jill, who added, "Than a wee baby in your arms."

Jack and Anne Marie made it just beyond the threshold of their bedroom before tearing at each other's clothes and stumbling to the floor to engage in desperate and frantic sex. Their movements resembled trapped theater patrons clawing at a locked door as the auditorium filled with smoke and fire. They probably would have had sex on the staircase had they been two decades younger or on the landing or on the floor just out of sight of the nurses if they hadn't been momentarily chastened by the thought of Ellen, who sometimes now wandered through the house and yard, seeing them, and neither wanted poor Ellen to witness their conjoining.

Afterwards, Anne Marie felt enormously better about having Jack still in the house. She thought this may be the first step toward reconciliation, but only a single step and about a hundred more would be needed to approach the place where they had been. If nothing else, they had released a little pressure and she could genuinely smile in his presence without hating herself for relenting on her anger. Anne Marie thought of confronting Mary Kelly, telling her to stay away from Jack, berating her for abusing their friendship, and asking her why she seemed bent on becoming known as the street's most active whore, but she quickly decided against it because there would be others like Mary Kelly, as many as Jack could meet through chance or premeditation and she wouldn't spend her life chasing after every little bitch he managed to bed and making a glorious fool of herself and acting like their problem was the woman's problem and not an inherent flaw in Jack's character and a flaw in her character for loving him. She blotted out this possible line of action and tried to enjoy the moment with Jack as they lay with their clothes off and in a tangle around their legs. She hoped he could gather strength for another go because the first attempt had prepared the field, had softened the ground with an artillery barrage, and now she waited for Jack to jump out of the trench, hop over the barbed wire and make a dash across the dead man's land to bring her all the way to orgasm, something that would count for a few steps toward gaining their equilibrium. Jack did gather his strength and could go a second time, which satisfied Anne Marie, but Jack lost sensation soon after he started so the fucking didn't feel much more than sticking a dowel rod into a pre-drilled hole. He dribbled a thimbleful of semen from his cock as he rolled off of her. They ended with a long kiss that bespoke of their friendship and became the most obvious sign to Jack that he may have a chance to be forgiven and his banishment in the wilderness would end.

They dressed and walked downstairs to find that Estonia had returned to the tub. Suni sat at her side and led her through a progression of guided images, pulling her deeper into complete relaxation. She breathed into the contraction, letting go and trying not to interfere with her body's rhythm. Jill pointed for Jack and Anne Marie to sit in the chairs and from there they watched Estonia repeat the cycle of relaxing in the bath, walking around the room naked, leaning against the fireplace, closing her eyes to let the contractions roll through her before returning to the bath to relax all over again. She repeated the cycle fifteen or sixteen times. Jack drowsed in the chair, unable to keep his head from bobbing. Anne Marie watched him descend into sleep and couldn't help thinking of him as a giant orangutan with a giant full face and a gray beard, massive pot belly and arms coiled with thick ropes of muscle, a powerful, frightening beast at rest, who, she had to admit, had a powerful sway over her thoughts and feelings. She turned her eyes toward Estonia and found herself wishing that she had had Jack's children. As her life turned out she had propagated Ben's genes into three feckless and bitter boys who had run away to stew themselves in alcohol and rage, even though she suspected that by some of his talk the middle child had become born again, but she had suspicions about his piety because in her recollections born agains didn't keep quiet about their faith and didn't worship in solitude, as her middle son did. Jack's children probably wouldn't have been any more successful than her own with Ben, but at least she could have counted on them having some fire and curiosity about the world. Even if they had turned out to be lesser versions of Jack, if they carried forth a fraction of his spirit, if they had inherited a smaller and more fragile frame from her side of the family, they would have been better suited for life, more interested in the possibilities, and less damaged and crippled by a household pathology bordering on cruel and unusual. Ben had done them a disservice in having them and giving them a tangled and confused hierarchy of thoughts that led them down blind alleys, swampy paths and roads littered with trash and bad decisions. Their women thought for them, turned them this way and that and then discarded them when they had bored of their incompetency and drinking. Their jobs paid just above the poverty line and their prospects were more dim than their present situations. They remained childless so far and with any luck Ben's line would extinguish with them. If they all could walk into a black lake on a moonless night and collectively breath the black water some of her mistakes could be corrected, not that she wished suicide on her sons, but if they could find no way out of their misery, if they had learned no tricks to fool themselves into believing in something, if they had nothing they loved on the blue and green rock on which they stood, they could probably just as well leave the oxygen for someone else who had a purpose for using it. Selfishly, she would have been spared the sight of their long dissolution. But Jack had left then too and gave her, what seemed like at the time, few options. He took with him the possibility of sons strong enough to withstand the torrent of life. Jack always left, will always leave and probably was never really there. How long had he been thinking of Mary Kelly before he bedded her? He may have begun thinking about her even before he came and took her out of Ben's house. How quickly had he tired of her after his return? After he came and pulled me from that house and all that misery how long did it take him to start chasing his next conquest? How had she not seen herself as just piece in his collection?

Estonia's contractions intensified and the time between them shortened. She imagined a massive bronze gate with a scene of heaven on one door, of angels soaring through the air, of the souls of blessed people rising with jaws agape, with a bright white orb casting a pure light upon them. God, his will, or just a blue sun, she did not know. On the other door hung a depiction of hell with steaming foul pools of waste and naked people running amok with horrible lurid grins on their faces, fucking animals, drinking their own streams of urine, worshipping graven images of bat heads, donkey phalluses, and dung coils, fashioned out of solid gold that had been melted down from the crowns of deposed despots and their queens. The doors were guarded by the watchful and sinister eyes of a large ape with horns and a greedy smile. The gate slowly inched open, groaning and creaking, breaking rust off its hinges. Twenty men pushed on each door and revealed the light within. Sweat stained their backs and when a man fell from exhaustion another from the wings took his place. They worked hours before they could make the opening large enough for her to see through, but she waited until the gap increased enough for her to slip through if she turned her body sideways. She walked into a white land with no definition, so as she walked she could not discern the topography on the ground. There seemed to be gravity, but nothing else. She could see no horizon or edge and when she turned back the door had disappeared. The men must have quickly pushed it closed to keep her in the white land. She walked for miles and hours and passed new levels of exhaustion, but she couldn't stop moving in the white land. She felt that stopping meant something horrible, but she could not take the time or energy to articulate the thought. She let an inward propulsion guide her. Finally, a black dot appeared before her. The dot was either very small or miles more away, giving some definition to the breadth of the white land. She forgot her legs throbbed or that her back felt as if it had been kicked a hundred times. She looked down at her flat belly and she felt the sudden panic of loss. She grabbed her belly. It felt like it had never been stretched with a pregnancy. She screamed to the blankness and the dot and demanded to know what had happened to her baby and silence answered her. The light grew even brighter and now resembled the flash of whiteness that occurs just before the brain falls into an unplanned unconsciousness. She stopped and spread her arms, turning to steady herself but unable to grab anything of substance. She tried to let herself fall, but her brain rebelled and kept her body upright, tapping a reservoir of terror that would not let her give up, would not let her collapse into a white unknown. She remembered the black dot and continued walking. Her hopes rose that the black dot held her baby, was her baby, that they had taken her baby out of her belly and placed it far away on the horizon in a black box, testing her to see if she could rescue the child and prove herself worthy of raising and protecting her. She walked for hours more and the wind picked up, carrying hot, arid air from a valley of a desert. As she approached she could see movement and when she finally got close enough to distinguish detail she saw that a woman stood next to a leafless tree, probably a maple or oak, stolid, but not yet fully mature or impressively thick. The woman carried an enormous belly in front of her and she began pacing around the tree in a ragged circle. Sometimes, the tree changed into Glover, performing a cheap imitation of a tree with his legs spread and his arms raised, when the woman passed between Estonia's and the tree, as if the change could occur only when her sight had been blocked. Then, Glover turned back into a tree, which relieved Estonia because she couldn't figure out why the woman would be circling Glover. Besides, if she had to pick a symbol or metaphor for him a tree would be close to last on the list. She cast her mind for the right symbol, but she could only come up with a small puddle of iron-rich urine splashed on a gum-coated sidewalk or a pulpy mass of half-eaten grass swimming in a pool of stomach acid, but she thought the images too harsh and uncharitable for a boy she once loved and who had once loved her in a total and frightening way. She let Glover be a silly tree and left it at that. The woman acknowledged her, but she didn't speak. She hummed a tune, really just three notes, B, G and C, repeated over and over again in the same sequence with an inconsistent beat. Estonia let herself sit and watched the woman repeat the circle. Glover appeared once more in the same pose, but all humor had drained from his face. He looked like he had held the pose too long and now struggled to keep his arms up. Then, the tree remained a tree. The woman stopped, squatted and leaned against it. Estonia received a full view of her vagina and asshole and she looked away. Nothing else could hold her attention in the whiteness. Even the tree lost its color and she barely caught the rapidly fading brown and black. So, Estonia returned her gaze to the woman's exposed and brightly illuminated lower half when she saw the crown of the baby beginning to appear and before she could be excited and amazed the baby slipped out onto the whiteness and lay squirming and squalling. No umbilical cord connected the woman with the newborn baby. The woman turned and looked at the baby, then she flashed anger toward Estonia.

"Pick up the goddamn baby, girl. It's yours," the woman seethed.

Estonia held out her arms hesitantly, but she didn't move close enough to pick up the baby even with her arms fully extended.

"Pick her up! Are you going to let her die of exposure? Are you going to drop her down the stairs in Jack's rickety house? Are you going to let her walk into the street to be run down by a teenager high on pills and driving a stolen car, something you and Glover used to do when he had access to his mom's car and his father's pills? Are you going to feed her when she's hungry and know to wrap her up when she is cold? Are you going to stay up at night and listen to her breathing, making sure her breaths are regular and deep enough to carry oxygen to all her growing cells? Will you worry over every cough or gas bubble? Will you cry at the thought that she could be autistic or disabled or blind or deaf or crippled or that she has inherited Glover's weakness, his inability to face adversity, his cowardliness? Pick up the baby, you bitch! Pick her up!"

Estonia inched closer and touched the baby's feet. For a moment the baby's wandering eyes drifted toward Estonia before drifting back toward the whiteness. Estonia raised her head to ask the woman exactly what she expected her to do with the baby, but when she looked up she found the woman had gone and had taken the tree with her. She scooped the baby in her arms and held her to her breast. The fragility and lightness of her charge shocked her. The baby clawed at her breast and found the nipple without much effort. Estonia realized she sat naked and wondered if she had been naked during the whole trek or if the woman had taken her clothes with her when she took the tree. She could feel the plane of nothingness shrink to the limits of her imagination and she pulled the infant closer and promised to never let her lie on the ground again. What now could be more important in her life?

The four witnesses watched with interest as Estonia held her belly and smiled. They could tell she had left the room and her concentration had taken her to a meditative state. She stepped into the tub again with the help of Jill and Suni and everyone realized by the way she moaned that the baby would be born within minutes. Jill stepped out of her clothes and revealed she had been wearing a one piece bathing suit the whole time. Jack would have liked to see Suni do the same because her fleshy and curvy body suited his tastes, but she remained clothed in her silken scrubs. Jill helped Estonia get comfortable and sat at her side, talking in a low, even voice and telling Estonia that each part of her body now fell into peace and relaxation. At first, Estonia shut her eyes so tight creases radiated across her eyelids and temples, but soon after Jill started talking her eyes relaxed and her arms floated by her sides. The sunlight in the room turned bright and clear as Suni opened the curtains. She played another CD that sounded like a tune cherubim would whistle as they glided through the early morning mist looking for lovers asleep in each other's arms, not to wake them, but to spy on their post-coital contentment and intimacy so they could whisper about what they saw, who ended up with whom, and how they felt about it all. Jack tumbled into the fantasy, unaware he had become so vulnerable to suggestion and he looked at Anne Marie to see if she had answers, but she had focused on Estonia and both Jill and Suni would not acknowledge his silent entreaties because he had become entirely superfluous to the event.

Estonia fell inside herself and her breathing became deep and expansive. Jill hovered near her ear and whispered calming images that only she could hear. She spoke of the opening of a flower in the morning's first light, the slow rotation of Saturn, the most powerful and calming of the female planets, the birth of a wave in the middle of a warm ocean and its steady and unhurried advancement to shore, a hawk's glide through towers of warm air in a shaft of sun pouring through the clouds. She asked Estonia to remember the place she had felt the most safe and calm in her life, like a favorite chair or her mother's arms, a place of complete refuge. Jill had no idea how risky this request had been, because Estonia had very few options from which to choose. She could have picked her childhood bed in her little room next to the garage, but the mattress smelled of urine as it had been passed down through the siblings until it landed stained and foul in baby Estonia's room. Besides, the mattress represented night terrors and irrational fears of her parents dying in the night and leaving her alone in the world atop a piss soaked mattress. What else could she find from her young life? She thought of a spot outside of Bakersfield where the county government had piled a dozen concrete culverts from a stalled sewer replacement project. Kids found the network of tunnels to be perfect for activities best performed in the shadows, smoking pot and fucking being the two most popular sports. She had a memory of being calm, sitting inside one of the tunnels, shoulder to shoulder with Glover, watching the day fall into twilight. The image collapsed. It had all been a lie.. She thought they had been charting their future. She thought they would fight together and stay together forever. What a goddamn joke. In one last desperate attempt to latch onto something peaceful before she became angry and she lost all of the relaxation and flexibility of her body, she thought of Jack's house, of this moment, of the warm water lapping against her belly, of a pretty woman whispering in her ear and a room filled with fairy music so opposite of the thrash metal that she and Glover listened to that it may have actually been composed by a different species of animal, of the tremendous contractions that threatened to split her body in half, of Jack and Anne Marie, two down-and-outers themselves who held out their hands and opened their house to let her and this baby live. Anne Marie for the sake of her own big heart and Jack who also had the same big heart that was muffled and compromised by his compulsion to leer at her tits. In this specially made room just for her, of this moment with her as the complete focus, of the world stopping for her, of Saturn halting its rotation, of the baby's head earnestly making its way down the birth canal, her crown visible under the water, this moment became the moment in her life when she had been the most relaxed.

The baby came out in a swoosh into the water and both Estonia and Jill pulled her up to the surface and placed her on Estonia's chest, where she began to breathe on her own. Even though Estonia felt every last millimeter slide out of her, she acted surprised when the little creature appeared on her breasts. Her body became infused with a frightening love and for a moment she thought she might be going crazy or that she had bumped her head during the delivery. The world had never seemed so bewildering and beautiful, crushing and so expansive that hope extended to infinity and the white room, instead of shrinking, burst with color and engulfed the solar system in one sudden leap.

Jill asked Anne Marie or Jack if they wanted to cut the umbilical cord. Jack accepted and could barely hold the tiny surgical scissors in his giant paw, but he managed to cut between the clamps. When he looked at the baby his arms and feet felt numb and he wondered if she could fit into the palm of his hand. His eyes welled with tears on their own accord and he knew he had missed too many of these moments in his past. He may have sired five or six children who had grown up in various regions of the country. He probably had a mountain child, a desert child, a great rolling plains child, a couple of ocean children, and maybe even an across the border child. Boys, who probably now were growing into their mustaches and work boots and girls who were learning the difference between wants and needs, and all of them either chasing after the ghost of him, long gone, or running away from the tales of darkness and immorality. No doubt, given the tendencies of their mothers, his daughters lived either as nuns or whores, and his sons, if they carried a flicker of his fire, felt restless like their skin crawled with ants and looked for an escape from whatever temporary prison in which they lived. Jack also couldn't help thinking of Glover and wondering what he could be doing at this moment of his daughter's birth. Was he nursing a hangover with a cup of coffee and a bean burrito? Was he working the first shift in some factory that made tiny parts to complex machines that aided in the development of even more complicated machines that produced large quantities of plastic bric-a-brac? Was he still lying in bed with another waif who understands he is the latest entry onto a long and sad list of useless boyfriends? What could you be doing, Glover, that matches this? That comes close to this? That is even in the same ballpark or state as this fresh baby and this radiant girl in the tub? You should be curled next to her in the water, whispering that you are ready to step off into the universe and float lost and free with her and her baby until your last goddamn breath. Estonia watched him cry and felt glad and relieved for the tears. She knew she could trust Jack and that she and the baby would be safe. He reached out and touched her cheek. She recoiled at the roughness of his skin, as the softness and smoothness of her skin fought through his callouses and nerve damage.

Jack sat back down in his chair and brooded as they helped Estonia out of the tub, cleaned the baby, helped Estonia into her robe and onto the hospital bed. Suni laid the baby into Estonia's arms and she looked like she would never let her feet touch the floor or let her go until her arms failed from exhaustion. Jack couldn't help feeling that his purpose had been renewed. He had to bring this project to a close and figure out a steady source of income that didn't involve violating too many laws to keep a roof over the heads of Estonia and her baby. The gas, electricity and water all ran. The birthing tub would have cost him a few bucks to fill had he been on the meter. Even the Water Department, with its collection of dispirited and bitter employees who had been sent to work there by the chiefs of other departments, because they had failed in their previous jobs, because of incompetence, insubordination, thieving or alcoholism, as transferring them offered an easier and more efficient solution than fighting through the termination process with its grueling schedule of grievances, warnings, and appeals, even these castoffs would eventually figure out that he stole water and they were known for their vindictiveness in prosecuting people who tried to subvert their shaky system because what else did incompetent alcoholics have other than their bitterness on which to dwell?

"Why don't we let the young mother have a moment alone with her baby?" Suni told Jack and Anne Marie. "Anne Marie, what do you cook on?"

"The stove is working. I hooked up the gas weeks ago," Jack answered.

The three walked into the kitchen, leaving Jill in the room with Estonia to finish cleaning up.

"Never got around to figuring out the cabinets, Jack?" Suni lightly mocked.

Anne Marie and Jack let the comment clatter to the ground without a response and avoided each other's eyes.

"I need some fresh air. I've been sitting too long," Jack said to kill the silence.

"That's a good idea," Anne Marie chimed in.

They both slipped on jackets and walked out the front door to the porch. A dusting of snow had covered the grass. The wind carried arctic air on its back and the light shone so brightly they looked at each other through squints. They expected the landscape to be blooming with life, so the quietness and deadness surprised them. The cold dry air felt good in their lungs after breathing humid air all day.

"Does she count as a granddaughter?" Jack mused.

"I suppose it all depends on how it all plays out from here. If you want a daughter and granddaughter I'm thinking you can have a set, at least for awhile until Estonia gets on her feet or gets too homesick to stay."

"Maybe she'll find Glover."

Anne Marie laughed. "My God, Jack. You hold out too much hope for that boy. You of all people should know he's long gone and he's not coming back any time soon or when it will matter and she's not going to search to find him. What's she going to do? Check every gutter and burned out building for him? If anything, the baby will probably make him stay away longer, probably forever, or maybe after forty years he'll come rolling into town on a cloud of dust driving some old truck, making the same old tired promises he made decades before, promises he made right before he left."

"It appears you're going to stay mad. Are you making plans for leaving?"

"Not just yet. The baby is five minutes old and Ellen is still with us. I'm keeping my options open."

"As long as there is a chance for me to find my way back into your heart I can go on."

"That would be beautiful, it if didn't seem so goddamn empty. It's cold out here. I'm going back inside."

They found Jill and Suni in the kitchen. They had found a stockpot and had placed the washed and dried placenta inside of it. They discussed how to best cook it and what recipe they preferred. Jill felt partial to a stew, heavy on the potatoes and carrots, especially as the weather had turned cold and the body demanded hearty foods. Suni preferred making a sauce with it to be used over pasta or rice, foods that provided her with the most comfort. After each birth they almost always had the same conversation with a variation of competing recipes based on the season. In the early autumn they often agreed on a meatloaf with ricotta or a dish with green beans, pumpkin and basil in a coconut-tomato curry, but they were far apart throughout the rest of the year. They put the question to Jack and Anne Marie. Jack pretended to consider the question seriously, like pondering over a menu and gauging his hunger and his particular cravings of the day. Anne Marie had heard of this practice, but she had never been confronted with the possibility of putting afterbirth in her mouth, so she had a hard time hiding her rising disgust and bile. She put a hand over her mouth and shrugged.

"Ladies, I had planned to bury the placenta in the ground under that ancient oak in our backyard. I've seen that done before and I always liked the thought of something so fresh with new life being put into tired soil. A kind of regeneration of the earth, if you know what I mean," Jack conjured up on the spot.

Suni and Jill acted disappointed but respectful. They had buried the placenta before because families refused to partake, but it had been hard. For them it felt a little like burying a slab of filet mignon in the ground, but Jack's symbolism carried the day.

"As a compromise why don't I prepare a kebob and all of us can share. Something to eat before the burial. One cube for each us. There will be plenty left over to bury and perform your ceremony."

"I've only seen it where the whole afterbirth is buried. I've never seen a partial."

"You can hardly call this a partial. I'm talking about only four or five square inch cubes. Burying the whole thing is just wasteful. You'll feel twenty years younger."

"Every other mammal eats their placenta. It's a natural and common sense process. We ignore such nutrients at our own risk."

"I've never been particularly moved to act by the habits of other mammals. We have worries beyond their understanding. They don't have electricity and gas pipes to worry about. But I ain't going to argue about it anyway. If a cube takes twenty years off this body I'll eat it. I've eaten worse, far worse."

"Are you agreed Anne Marie?" Jill asked.

Anne Marie didn't know if she could answer because she worried if she took her hand from her mouth she may spray the kitchen with vomit. She nodded just to get them to stop looking at her and waiting for an answer. She agreed, knowing that once the placenta had been cooked she would avoid eating it and by agreeing she could take a few moments to compose herself and settle down the bile in the back of her throat. Jill flopped the placenta onto a piece of foil she had spread on the plywood countertop. It looked like a collapsed liver and the spider web of veins covering the outside looked like delicate hand-stitched lacework, intricate and hearty because they had just recently stopped pulsing. Jack wanted to put his hand inside the amniotic sac and see if the curing powers could heal his smashed up fingers and drive the arthritis from the joints. The more Anne Marie looked at it the less disgusted she became. She followed the umbilical cord to where it attached to the sac and she thought the whole of it looked like a little nest, comforting and warm

"Why don't you make two skewers?" Jack said.

"I'll make a skewer for each one of us," Jill said as she created the cubes using a slender and extremely sharp knife.

Jack had eaten just about everything Americans in their vast diversity had deemed fit to eat. He had seen television shows where forest tribes crunched on dung beetles or rats, so he couldn't make the claim he had sampled the whole of the world's cuisine, but he convinced himself that since he had been offered placenta and if other Americans scarfed it down, then he figured he should at least sample it for the experience.

They first decided to bury the majority of the placenta in yard. Jack, of course, had never seen such a ceremony or had taken part in one, and even though he would try eating a skewer he didn't want a full meal from it, so he continued pushing for the burial. He went outside and dug a hole at the base of the huge oak in the backyard. He called the women out after he made the hole deep enough to prevent scavengers, dogs, raccoons and possums, from digging it back up and lunching on it. Suni had wrapped a blanket around her shoulders as her silken pajamas offered little protection from the cold. Anne Marie and Jill wore heavy coats, but they both looked impatient for the ceremony to be over so they could return to the warmth of the house. Jack thought it a little strange that Estonia didn't take part in the burial since, in essence, they were burying a part of her under the oak. But she wouldn't be on her feet for a day or two and what would they do with the placenta in the interim? They could stick it in the refrigerator or freezer. Not only would it tempt Suni and Jill to come back and have another go at producing a meal, it also seemed to run counter to the notion of burying a pulsing, quivering mass of life to regenerate the earth, even though this remained a distant and secondary reason for the burial and one of dubious worth.

They stood around the frozen clods of dirt. Jill held the stock pot with the placenta she had not used for the skewers. They looked to Jack to lead the ceremony since every family had a different reason for the interment.

"World, we greeted a newborn this morning," Jack began. "Since she was born how many others have joined her and taken their first breath of air? We stand here celebrating the ongoing miracle of life and birth. We present to you this living cradle so that we give back what we take. Let the life feed this old tree, so the old man can exhale oxygen for the next generation of newborns. Let this neighborhood be filled with the screams of roving bands of children running through the yards like a squall. Let fire sweep away the rot and new young shoots break through the ground. Let these people forget about the sins of their past and may all the toxins leech away from the soil or evaporate and be carried to another state or fall headlong into the vast and rolling ocean plains. Let that baby girl in my house grow up with the tenacity of a weed. May she break through concrete and bow to hail, lifting her head when the storm has passed. May she not give a good goddamn what anyone else thinks of her life and may she fight extermination with her last root. May she understand that the world is an ever chewing jaw and that she'll be pulverized five or six times by the molars, ripped to her bone by unseen incisors, scored and lacerated by hungry eye teeth. May this baby girl crawl from the mouth each time, reconstituted and wiser, maybe degraded and not put back together as well she went in, but with a tougher engineering and solid underpinnings. May she show humility and help those broken and beaten by the jaw. Have her use her strength for good, but don't let the weak and defeated swamp her own resolve until she becomes one of them, bitter and lost. May she breed babies like herself, resilient and strong, a generation more capable of surviving with joy. They will be the generation or their children will be the generation that will get around to building machines or architecture or invent a politic that stops the jaws from their crushing and smashing so that their children will use the molars for fields of play or farms where they will grow rich and plentiful crops."

Anne Marie touched Jack on the arm. "Jack, it's cold out here. Maybe we can get to the burying part."

Jack looked at the other women and they did look blue and frozen, so he motioned for Jill to dump the placenta into the hole. It landed with a moist thud against the hard ground, but the mass had cooled to the point where it no longer steamed. The women all acknowledged the landing in their own way, Anne Marie even crossed herself, and they left Jack to fill in the hole. He smashed the frozen clods apart with his shovel to better fill the hole. Within a few minutes his adopted dog, Shuck, joined him and sniffed at the edges of the hole and licked his chops in anticipation of a fresh meal.

"I knew you'd be coming out."

Now that the dog knew where the placenta had been buried he would dig until he found it, so Jack really couldn't dig a hole deep enough to keep it from the dog's mouth. He shooed the dog away from the hole by brandishing his shovel and shouting long enough for him to retrieve some lye from the garage and sprinkle it into the hole. The lye effectively killed the scent and poisoned the meal, so when the dog returned to the hole he looked at Jack with a flash of anger and confusion. With a whimper the dog trotted off to his warm spot in the loft.

By the time Jack finished the burying, put away the shovel and walked inside, Suni had nearly finished braising the skewers with chunks of onion and red pepper. Anne Marie had turned pale and concentrated on her breathing, which became so shallow it looked like her breaths hardly made it past her mouth. They each took a skewer and Suni set the last aside for Estonia once she felt like eating. Jill raised a skewer in a toast and the three responded in kind but were careful not to touch the ends. Jack ate without thinking, although his brain could tell the difference between pepper, onion and afterbirth, which was chewy and tasted like blood since Suni preferred it cooked just above tartare. Anne Marie made the mistake of using her eye teeth as the vehicle for masticating, which kept the cube on her lips longer than necessary and really worked inefficiently compared to the set of flat molars just a few teeth away. Using the molars meant committing to the idea of eating the skewer, which after the placenta lay on her lips as she nibbled became harder to do. The other three finished their portions and washed it down with a celebratory glass of sulfite-heavy wine before Anne Marie had torn apart half a cube, which she wallowed back and forth between her cheeks, afraid to bite down with vigor should more flavor be released. She set the skewer down on a plate and drifted to the living room to check on Estonia and spit the offal from her mouth. The three clinked glasses and shared a moment of quiet fellowship. Jack thought that twenty years ago, before his knees started grinding bone on bone, before Randy Reamer had crushed his ankle into powder and before his back felt like his vertebrae had been scrambled by a drunken mechanic who had stuffed them back under the skin in no particular order to hide his mistake, and before he ever considered monogamy and virtue to be possible, much less achievable, he would have finished this bottle of wine with these two nurses and probably a second and third bottle and had both of them down on their knees with their pants around their ankles and slapping their asses and screaming to the sun, or, if indoors, to the plaster cracks on the ceiling. A hungry look must have passed through his eyes because Suni returned it briefly before catching herself. She knew from experience that almost anything could happen after eating the afterbirth. Jill balanced herself on the tips of her toes and felt ready to launch herself into the air. If she happened to land on Jack with legs spread and her pants on the floor she would chalk it up the luck of the draw and following where her urges took her.

"I'm going to start eating more onion," Jack joked.

They laughed, touched his arm, gave his belly a poke and drank more wine. Unfortunately, they remembered their responsibilities towards Estonia and checked on her and the baby, who both rested peacefully, and that broke the spell and adverted a threesome on the kitchen floor, or an orgy if Anne Marie had decided to join in. Estonia had not changed her expression since the birth, an intense look that carried boundless love, fear and exhaustion. Jack stayed in the kitchen and finished the skewer that Anne Marie had left and thought about digging the buried placenta back up, washing it and making it edible. But he remembered the lye and some story he had heard about a man who accidently ingested lye and who vomited blood for a week before dying between screams. Then he ate the skewer that had been set aside for Estonia after concluding that she would never want to eat one of her organs, even a temporary one. The top of his head felt ready to separate from the rest of his skull. He snuck Anne Marie, who had returned to normal color, upstairs and fucked her until he lost feeling. He picked up scrap pieces of wood and debris from the front and back yards. He walked through the house, making a mental inventory of all the odds and ends left to do and the house felt on the verge of completion. He had very little work left to do. He jumped in his truck, thinking he had a couple of errands to run, and told Anne Marie he would be back in an hour or two. He successfully passed Mary Kelly's house the first time, because he had finished with Anne Marie not that long before and his body had not completely regenerated, a process that seemed to have sped up to double time, fueled by the nutrients coursing through his veins. He bought a bouquet of flowers for Estonia and a newspaper so that the baby could know what had happened on her birthday. The main headline concerned a bank collapse with a picture of depositors lined up outside a locked door and two smaller front page stories about corruption in the Mayor's office and a random murder on the steps of the courthouse. He also bought a pair of pink pajamas, wildly too big for a newborn, with a matching hat that said "I can't bear to stay awake" around a stitched teddy bear with no eyes or chin.

On his return he turned into Mary Kelly's driveway and parked in the back should Anne Marie want a breath of fresh air and happen to look down the street. Mary had opened the side door when she heard his truck pull into her driveway and knew why he had come and knew they had both softened since the last time they had met. He walked in and found her in her bedroom, already naked and lying on the bed above the covers. He became hard before he could get his clothes off and when he started fucking her he thought he might be in the grips of a new strain of South American fever, because his brain remained devoid of thought except for the sensation radiating from his dick and he felt so alive he thought he could fuck for a month if they could keep themselves lubricated and fed. He surprised Mary Kelly because their first encounter had been so tepid and Jack had been so distracted that she had resolved to think of their fucking with a heap of remorse, with not much fondness or any memory of intense pleasure. This Jack, on the other hand, lived up to his myth. She understood a little more why when Anne Marie talked of him her eyes clouded over and her words became tangled and unclear. This Jack pushed her to the edge of madness and utter capitulation.

Jack rolled off the bed and dressed.

"Estonia had her baby today. A little girl."

"What's her name?"

"I haven't heard a final decision. She seems in no hurry to pick one."

"What are the popular names in the trailer parks and projects?"

"You're very nice."

"The baby shouldn't be given any false hopes. Might as well name her something appropriate for her sad existence."

"Jesus, I don't like you. What the hell am I doing here?"

"Just telling it like a see it."

"The baby hasn't lived through its first day yet. You might want to lighten up on the doom and gloom."

"Look at the odds, Jack. I'm basing my observations on math. If you stepped away and looked at the situation objectively you would come to the same conclusion. The girl stands no chance. By twenty she'll be pregnant, stupid and lost just like her mamma. Why do you care so much anyway? Is she your baby? Is that why you're feeling all proud and protective?"

Jack walked out of the house without answering, resolved to end the affair before it gathered steam and ruined the little he had left with Anne Marie. But by the time he started his truck the anger began to fade so his resolve really never had an opportunity to harden or take shape. So, over the next three months through the teeth of winter Jack made regular visits to Mary Kelly's house, usually after midnight and returning no later than 3:00 am. He sometimes worried about the tracks in the snow that connected his garage door to Mary Kelly's side door, especially his unmistakable boots prints in the newly fallen snow, but Anne Marie had no desire to track him and she had no use of a dog to help her. During this time Anne Marie inched closer to him, thinking that he had remained true to her and hoped that maybe his mistake with Mary Kelly had been an aberration afterall, a tip of his hat to his wild past, the final spark of a self-destructive comet trail.

One night in late March when Jack crept down his loft staircase and walked in the shadow of the house he noticed a white cargo van idling on the street directly in front of his house. The driver smoked a cigarette and Jack could see the orange tip glowing in the dark. Jack thought of the housing inspector. He had not heard from him since that day he tried to extort him for money and the two week deadline had long passed. No official notice had come from the building department outlining his violations. Jack hoped the inspector had thought better of going through with the shakedown, but he knew better. The inspector knew he had him by the shorthairs and he would not leave easy money on the table. He would come to collect or Jack would end up in court. Jack still had no money to give him, so all he could do would be threaten the inspector with taking him down with him, of exposing the bribery scheme in some way, but City Hall teemed with so many thieves he wondered who he would get to listen, something the inspector probably also knew. Jack approached the driver's side window, and the driver rolled down the window as he approached.

"You Jack?"

"Depends on who's asking?"

"Kaufman sent me for you. He wants me to bring you to his house. You ever been to his house?"

"No, I don't think I have."

"Did you ever think of getting a fucking phone like every other white man on the planet? A person wouldn't have to fetch you in the middle of the night with this bullshit weather raging."

"I'll follow you in my truck."

"No, Kaufman wants you in the van. He told me specifically not to let you drive the truck. He says it makes him nervous just looking at it and he doesn't want it leaking oil on his driveway.

"You work for him?"

"When I can stand it."

Jack climbed inside the van. The inside had been stripped of everything except the front two seats. The cargo area was just the steel of the outer skin so that every bump sounded like a cannon being shot through an aluminum valley. A hole gaped where the radio should have been, the door to the glove compartment had been taken off, and, gauging by the temperature inside, the heater had been disconnected as well. The driver hunched over the wheel and in the dim flashes of streetlights passing overhead Jack could discern an almost completely bald head with a few wisps of hair swirled across his crown, that he had broken his nose on a number of occasions and now it hung in a heavy and formless mass and looked ready to fall off his face altogether, that the ear closest to Jack hung like the nose and had been beaten into a twisted lump, that he fiercely hated the cold because his body remained coiled and braced against the drafts, and that he had stray, sometimes random and probably dangerous thoughts creating drastic solutions to his life's problems, because he also carried a grim and bitter visage that had nothing to do with the freezing air scraping across his skin and already numb face.

"So, do you know what Kaufman has in mind?"

"Right, Kaufman confides in me. He runs everything past me before he makes a decision. You could call me his right hand man, his number two, his goddamn chief o-fucking staff, his consigliere. I've got the pulse of that motherfucker. He doesn't make a move without me."

"Alright, I got it," Jack said with enough force to make the driver stop talking. "Is this his van?"

"Fuck, man. Are you the fountain of stupid questions? Who the fuck has a van without at least a goddamn AM radio? I drove this goddamn thing down to Kentucky and back last month and I thought I was going to lose my fucking mind. I started making up sports talk. I tried to fucking sing, but I found out I only know about two lines to every song so that got boring after like two minutes. And you hear that banging? I started thinking my brain had fallen out and the echo was inside my head. And my goddamn feet almost froze the fuck off. This goddamn van will only defrost the windows, using air that's about a degree or two above the freezing mark so by the time I crossed into Kentucky I had clear windows, but my fucking lips were blue. My goddamn car is loaded. I've got satellite radio, man, that beams me more music and talk than I could ever listen to in a lifetime. Why the fuck would I torture myself driving around in this stripped-down piece-o-shit van?"

"So, it's Kaufman's?"

"Why do you care? Kaufman told me to pick you up and approximately where to find you. I've been looking for two goddamn hours, because you don't have a phone. He told me to bring you to his house. That's all I know."

"That's not much to know. I don't know how long you've worked with Kaufman, but you have to keep asking questions until he starts frothing around the mouth. Otherwise he won't tell you a goddamn thing. And what he wants you to do usually isn't inside the law, so you better damn well know what you're getting yourself into."

"What do I look like? I know what I'm doing and I don't need advice from an old man like you. Your advice didn't get you very goddamn far, so maybe you could just keep it to yourself. I know, maybe you know more than two lines of a song. Would you like to entertain us so I don't have to hear that banging or your stupid advice?"

"Christ, I only know sea shanties and field songs. I'm not sure I've memorized anything from the past two centuries."

"Is there anything that's not ridiculous about you?"

Jack cleared his throat and launched into *Barnacle Bill* with a confident volume as he hit or approximated most of the notes.

"Who's that knocking at my door?
Who's that knocking at my door?"
Said the fair young maiden.
"It's only me from across the sea,
Says Barnacle Bill the Sailor.
My ass is tight, my temper's raw,"

Says Barnacle Bill the Sailor.
"I'm so wound up I'm afraid to stop.
I'm looking for meat or I'm going to pop.
A rag, a bone with a cherry on top,"
Says Barnacle Bill the Sailor.

"I'll come down and let you in,
I'll come down and let you in,"
Said the fair young maiden.
"Well hurry before I bust the door,"
Said Barnacle Bill the Sailor.
"I'm hard to windward and hard a-lee,"
Says Barnacle Bill the Sailor
"I've newly come upon the shore
And this is what I'm looking for,
A jade, a maid, or even a whore,"
Says Barnacle Bill the Sailor.

"Oh, your whiskers scrape my cheeks,
Oh, your whiskers scrape my cheeks,"
Said the fair young maiden.
"I'm dirty and lousy and full of fleas,"
Says Barnacle Bill the Sailor.
"My flaming whiskers give me class
The sea horses ate them instead of grass,
If they hurt your cheeks, they'll tickle your ass,"
Says Barnacle Bill the Sailor.

"Bill, there's something you should know.
Bill there's something you should know."
Said the fair young maiden.
"You have a mast where a hole should be"
Says Barnacle Bill the Sailor
"I thought you be a sweet young lass
My eyes may need the help of some new glass
But never you mind, I'll use your sweet ass"
Says Barnacle Bill the Sailor

"Tell me that we'll soon be wed
Tell me that we'll soon be wed,"
Said the fair young he she.
"You foolish boy, it's nothing but sport,"
"I've got me a wife in every port."
Says Barnacle Bill the Sailor.

"Off I go on another tack
To give some other fair maid a crack,
But keep it oiled till I come back,"
Says Barnacle Bill the Sailor.

By the end of the song the driver smiled and laughed and he asked Jack to sing some more. Jack ripped through *The Mermaid* and *The Banks of Sweet Loch Ray* and by the time he wrapped up the third song the driver had grown quiet and thoughtful and suggested that since he had gotten thirsty and he knew of a bar where the barmaid had big tits and wouldn't be stingy with the liquor. They pulled into the parking lot of a drab little building with a once colorful awning that had faded under the assault of rain, sun, snow and sleet. Cursive letters on the awning spelled out the name, The Otter's Head, but the barmaid who the driver hoped would be pouring had taken the night to care for her ailing father. In her stead the owner had taken over her duties and he kept the drinks weak. The regulars knew he poured cheaper liquor into the more expensive bottles, which ultimately didn't work much in his favor because the regulars would never buy top shelf because they didn't have the money or they couldn't taste the difference between the shelves anyway, so the doctored liquor sat in its adopted bottle unmolested. The owner thought of pouring the cheaper liquor back into its original bottle but now some of the more expensive brands had been mixed in and he couldn't stand the thought of his patrons getting something for nothing. The owner had a dead eye that he called a souvenir from his days as a welder and his clothes hung off of him like his skeleton had been wrapped in cloth with no flesh between the two.

Even though they were weak, the drinks came in a torrent and soon Jack had the driver singing songs he didn't know and using a voice that registered just under a shout. A few of the other regulars tapped the bar in a ragged beat. None of them sang for various reasons: one had lost his larynx five years before, another had left his teeth at home because he didn't want to stain them with whiskey, a third couldn't keep the tune or words in his head long enough to sing because his thoughts came to him in monstrous blasts of static and four others had been in the bar since noon and they were so drunk, really just hovering above consciousness, that they could not muster the energy to sing, even though the tuneless caterwauling that Jack and the driver produced sounded to them like a flock of birds had alighted on the bar and sang a joyful hymnal. One old woman cried a little and dabbed the corners of her painted eyes with a previously used tissue, saying over and over again that she had dreams of singing for a living, that she had more than a little encouragement from a host of musicians and agents, that you couldn't tell from the potato her body had turned into, but she once had tits and ass and she could make men twitch on beat, that the music business, like any business, turned out to be a rat hole filled with stinking rats and undependable piano players who would rather chase skirt than practice and bar owners who never wanted to pay and so many bad, really bad choices, that a lady can get lost without that ever being her intention.

So Jack and the driver didn't stop drinking until the bartender kicked everyone out a few minutes before closing time because his dead eye ached and he had become frankly sick of all the singing as his bar sounded like it had been invaded by a flock of crippled or diseased geese. They arrived at Kaufman's house past 2:00 am and as they approached they saw that every light burned like a silent party raged within. The lighted windows helped define the hulking shadow of the house, that seemed to tower above them and fall away to either side into the darkness of a forest of giant oaks. Jack rang the bell and Kaufman answered before the first cycle of the ring could be completed. He stood in his bathrobe that hung to his knees and revealed his white and hairless shins. He wore no shoes or slippers and his feet looked like talons of a scavenger looking for carrion, something Jack had not noticed at the schvitz.

"I knew you'd have to dig him out of a goddamn bar. Honest to God, Jack. That swollen liver of yours must think it's in the battle of Bull Run. You should use my nose and smell the two of you. I got nothing but alkies and hillbillies working for me," Kaufman said as he puffed himself up and made himself seem twice as large as his actual size.

"I didn't know I worked for you," Jack responded with a grin.

"You better get your goddamn memory straight. I'll call you when and where I want you. Remember what I did for you and remember your debt. It's a big goddamn debt, Jack. I'm telling you you're going to need two more lifetimes to get to the end of this debt. Honest to God you might want to start working full-time to accelerate the payments. Otherwise I'm going to have to track down every one of the little bastards your wild seed created and place the debt of their heads. Maybe I could get the whole goddamn brood working and we might make some progress on the principle."

"I never wanted to owe you nothing. I was a creditor of yours for a long time."

"That's right, until I took your debt over. Our man was going to make you do unsavory things, violent, brutal things that would have led to the corruption of your soul, like it hasn't been corrupted past recognition already, but I couldn't watch it happen again so I made a barter and took the debt and, believe me when I tell you, the payment was not small to get the anvil off your neck, honest to God. I still feel dirty and used like some pathetic broad when I start to think about how I got abused in the deal. I need a couple of big-assed broads and a quart of scotch to take my mind off the deal, because look what I got in return. I got a drunk, broken down old man for my cherry. I can't make a fucking deal anymore. I'm always the bitch. But the long and short of it is that you work for me. I bought a goddamn cell phone for you so when I need you I can find you. It's got unlimited minutes so you can chat with all your girlfriends as much as you like. And you know what the fuck it's costing me? Honest to God. Those slimy little fuckers at the phone store play that three-card monte with the charges and the taxes and the fees. I told the one little shit that I was going to eat his tongue if he didn't stop trying to confuse me with his telecommunications bullshit. I told him to give me the best deal he had or I was going to take out my pecker and piss on their floor samples. What the fuck do I care? I probably have cancer in seven or eight hot spots right fucking now. How long before the dots are connected and I'm fucking dead? Still, even that little phone store pissant bent me over the counter and rammed that phone, charger and all, up my ass and laughed with his buddies later that I had the fucking nerve to threaten him."

"I don't need a phone. Haven't needed one up till now."

"I can't afford to have these assholes," Kaufman used his thumb to point to the driver. "Chasing you down at every pisshole in town. I sent this fucker out at 9:00 pm. He comes back at two in the morning stinking of whiskey that was probably filtered by running it through three or four kidneys, livers and bladders of useless bums like him before it was bottled. I expected you to show up drunk, Jack, but not the driver of my fucking van, honest to God. Do you ever sit in your little rat hole of an apartment and wonder why you have nothing? Did you ever wonder why you don't have some broad with the haunches of a horse lounging about your rat hole in a pair of underwear too small to cover the tufts of pubes spilling over the elastic band, just waiting for you to say the word to suck the skin off your cock? Did you ever fucking think that there are alternate existences other than eating shit and drinking yourself unconscious every fucking night while watching some bullshit on the tube? Maybe if you lived like a human being and used your fucking head, maybe even worked a little, produced a little, then maybe you could evolve from your worm-like state. You goddamn cocksucker. Did you buy the drinks with my credit card too? Did you go and try to impress that big-titted bartender again?"

The driver kept his head down and wouldn't answer, so Kaufman took his posture and silence as a yes, that they had indeed gotten drunk on his money and his time. Kaufman knew though that no matter how bad the driver screwed-up he would keep him, because he liked him as an employee, a guy that would try to do anything, even murder and self-immolation if told to perform the task.

"I'm king of the fucking apes. Look, drink some coffee and slap your balls, whatever it takes to kill your buzz. I've got a problem. My wife is at a goddamn hotel right now, probably eating all that overpriced shit out of the convenience refrigerator and blowing the bellhops because I have rats in this fucking house. She opened a goddamn cupboard and the fucker was staring back at her. Ten fucking inches long. His fucking nasty bald tail lying across our plates. I thought she was going to have an embolism. Her face got blood fucking red and she wouldn't stop panting. I tried to stick my finger up her cunt, thinking that would distract her, but she slapped my hand away and called me a pervert for the millionth time. Getting pissed at me helped her get control of herself long enough to tell me she's not coming back until she sees that little fucker's head on a pike and you two need to find him. Find him quick because I don't want my wife to develop too strong of a taste for hotels and the cocks of bellhops."

"Call an exterminator. They'll catch it and kill it," said Jack.

"Fuck, Jack. I'm sure that's a job you had. I remember a couple of your stories that you were spraying so much poison your hands turned color and you thought they were going to fall off. No one is going to take the time you will. I need this fucker out of my house."

"It was my face," Jack confessed.

Jack had spent a couple of years being a bug man, spraying poison, setting traps, hanging fly catchers, digging out the queens of carpenter ant colonies, strategizing against armies of cockroaches, chopping down hives, filling in burrows, delousing couches and chairs and chasing bed bugs across pillows and mattresses. He learned that rats lived in the sewers and they usually entered a house through a grate or a broken pipe. Sometimes they burrowed through the dirt after they found a breech in a pipe, and he had seen where they had chewed through concrete and cinder block to get inside. What else did a rat have to do other than survive? He quit after accidently spraying some of the poison on his face, which at first hardened, then boiled, then died in patches and left scars that were still a part of his face's landscape.

"Do you have traps and a flashlight?"

Kaufman pointed to a bag lying on the floor that held thirteen traps that looked big enough to catch errant homo sapiens. Jack picked up the bag and Kaufman left to find the flashlight. They waited for him in a wide center hall. When Jack looked to either end of the house as the rooms rambled past where he expected walls. He calculated that five, maybe ten of his houses could fit inside the footprint of Kaufman's house. The rooms had been filled with sculpted furniture, thick, hand-knotted carpets, elegant paintings of moors and sinister landscapes, slender statues of nude women carrying water jugs or in thoughtful repose, gilded chandeliers hanging heavy and low, cabinets filled with three full sets of china with tasteful designs and a forest of crystal goblets and serving bowls, lamps with heavy shades, curtains that spilled to the ground and that looked thick enough to stop a bullet, and two silver candelabras that held thin white candles that could have been stolen from the table of a king. The walls had been covered in delicate rice paper creating a muted earthy tone throughout the rooms. Jack imagined a rat scurrying across the gleaming wooden floors and thought it might not be so out of place, that Kaufman should just adopt the creature as his talisman, his fetish or his ancestor and learn from its wisdom collected from a few millennia of battling with human beings.

Kaufman led them to the basement. Five traps had already been set on the stairs and baited with liverwurst and broccoli. They skirted past a pool table that looked so heavy that a crane would have to be used to move it. Two more traps lay on the green velvet amongst the remnants of an abandoned game of nine ball. Kaufman used apple slices in these traps, but the rat had not been tempted.

"These little fuckers are picky eaters. Honest to God, I think I'll have to cook a filet to get his little neck in one of these traps."

"They learn the traps. Sometimes you could swear the knowledge is passed along through the tribe," Jack said with a nod of respect.

"Well, Jack, I'm counting on you being smarter than a goddamn rat. Obviously, in addition to me being a cunt that everybody wants to abuse I've become an addled old man who can't get a goddamn rodent out of his house. So, I'm calling in the man who can think and act like a rat."

As Jack and Kaufman talked the driver drifted over to a framed black and white photo hanging on the wall.

"How long has your wife been gone?"

"A fucking month. I'd bring broads over here, but she's friends with the two crones on either side of us and they'd tell her every time a honey with hot pants pulled into the crack of her ass rolled into the driveway in her leaking car with a fake rag top. Then, it would cost me a diamond the size of my left nut to get my wife back in the house, honest to God. I thought about fucking one of the crones to give myself some cover, but those broads are so passed fuckable I'd rather have one of these rats suck my cock."

"You probably only have one rat. They're solitary. They prefer to live alone. They will live in groups if forced to, but they're always going off on their own. Mice live in families. If you see one mouse, you probably have a hundred."

"Who the fuck is in this photo?" the driver asked as he continued to stare at the image.

"Did I give you permission to use that kind of language in my house, you fucking little worm? It's one thing for me to motherfuck somebody or something, but it's another thing for you, entirely, because I can barely stand to hear you speak, let alone curse like a faggot sailor. The next time you say fuck I'll knock your teeth out with a pool stick. And since you're so goddamn curious about the photo I'll tell you it's a picture of me and the wife on a boat I used to own. My wife called it The Well-Tempered Clavier, but my name for it was The Moaning Lisa. That's when my wife and I were fucking like bunnies and it had a cabin underneath and sometimes we'd stay out on the lake all weekend, when some fucking squall wasn't trying to kill us, and we'd stay naked all the time and I'd flash my junk at passing barges or when we'd find a dead and calm spot we'd fuck right on the deck with my ass to the sun. I sank that fucker on a rock, split the fucking hull in half. By that time I was taking broads out on it and hoping the engine didn't blow up on me. Luckily it sank close to shore and the broad knew how to swim. She thought it was the funniest damn adventure, but I was thinking about the recovery cost and explaining to the wife how it sank and avoiding any kind of official inquiry. I want to remember her with an Alabama accent, but I can't imagine I went for a hillbilly, but you never know. I'll probably fuck one of the crones tomorrow and then I won't believe I could do it. Anyway, I got her ashore, back to her apartment and out of her wet clothes before the cops figured out anything. The last thing I needed was for her name to show up in some official report and the cops looking to make a hassle and looking to get paid, honest to God. My wife hung that picture up. Look at my fucking hair. It was so thick I could barely get a comb through it. My wife says she misses the boat and she says that was the happiest time of her life, Jesus God."

Jack turned on the flashlight and crept through a door that led to an unfinished portion of the basement where the furnace and hot water tank sat. He hoped he could surprise the rat as he sat on his haunches eating a piece of chocolate, stomp the fucker with a boot and go home to sleep off his drunk, but if the rat had remained somewhere in the house he had probably scrambled to safety at the sound of Jack's boots on the staircase. Jack inspected the tangle of waste pipes descending from the six bathrooms to the concrete floor of the basement. The pipes had no cracks or holes, but Jack swore he could smell sewer gas coming from somewhere. On the far wall hung a grate the size of a basement window. He walked across the length of the room and shined the flashlight through the lattice of the grate, revealing a crawl space with a dirt floor. This part of the house had been a later addition to the original plan and the builder sold the owner on not digging a full basement because how much underground space does a family really need, considering that outside the cement walls the worms constantly churn and emit heavy, choking vapors? The builder had an unspoken and crippling fear of being buried alive and throughout his short career never built anything underground. The smell of sewage tumbled out of the grate and that probably meant a waste pipe had been breached and the hole provided egress from the bowels of the sewer system for any rat looking to find shelter from a torrent of storm water or looking for a new source of food. The driver and Kaufman joined him and he explained the problem to Kaufman, who wanted Jack to check it out anyway.

"I can smell it from here," said Jack.

"But the problem is in there and I want you to look at it."

"Christ, I have a gallon of whiskey in my gut and I don't know if I can squeeze through there or not. You need sewer work. A backhoe. A yard of cement. Wire mesh. Blow torches. Hobnailed boots. You have to block his entrance and then you'll be rat free."

"I have to know what the fuck I'm talking about with my slimy contractors or they'll build me a new basement. Go in and fucking look."

"This is why I never wanted to owe you."

"Jesus, Jack, you're a dirty, filthy man. It won't be the first time you've crawled in the dirt."

Jack unscrewed the grate and hoisted himself through the opening. The driver thought Jack's belly would never fit through such a small space, but Jack wriggled until he dug his fingers into the dirt and pulled his legs through the opening. He crawled on his belly across the dirt toward the source of the sewer vapor because only about three feet of clearance existed between the floor and the ceiling, covered with a tangle of beams, electrical conduit, and water and gas pipes. Whiskey bottles, electrical switches, shards of glass, rusted pipe, splintered wood, stones, a handful of pennies, broken ceramic tile, fired bricks, a couple of porcelain cups, wine bottles, a square of tin, a road sign for a street called Walnut Walk, a moldering book on plate tectonics, a flattened trombone, a doll's head with missing eyes, a paper umbrella from a tropical drink served at a long since demolished tiki bar, a phone card, a dog collar and tags for a dog named Tippy, and a moldering leather shoe that had once stepped across parquet floors of downtown ballrooms and tread through the plush carpets of a well-connected law firm littered the dirt so Jack thought he had crawled across an archeological dig into the lives of the past owners of the house. Jack made it to the pipe and put his nose close to where it came out of the dirt. A couple of small tunnels and been dug the length of the pipe and when Jack flashed the light down one of them a small twinkle of sewage told him he had been correct in his diagnosis. Jack planned out how a crew might fix the pipe by laying a diamond grid of steel on the dirt and pour a yard of concrete on the grid and down the tunnels so that if the rats managed to break through again and made a new tunnel upward they would be met with an impenetrable barrier their teeth would not be able to gnaw through. He would have to convince Kaufman to call in some pros, spend some money and have the job done right, because solutions born from desperate circumstances were not part of the vocabulary. He'd seen rich families tear down whole garages because of a little mold and replace entire roofs with a lot of life left in them because some ice had backed up under a few shingles, so if Kaufman decided to have the crawl space dug out to get to the source of the breech he would let him.

Jack turned himself around and faced the opening, snagging and slicing his knees on a nail as he turned. He slid himself back along the trail he had made, trying not to shine the flashlight into the eyes of Kaufman and the driver who watched him from the opening. A few feet to the right of their heads he noticed the rat leaning against the brick of the wall. It sat incredibly still, but Jack could recognize its silhouette in the shadows. He shined the light on the form and saw that it had died some time ago. Its two front feet still held a nugget of poison and it looked like it had been overcome by a sudden heart attack while chewing. It had slumped against the wall and its chin rested on its chest.

"Do you have a pair of gloves?" asked Jack.

"What? You want some lace for your dainty hands? You're already dirty Jack, honest to God. Besides, why the hell would I have gloves that would fit those paws of yours? Look, I have women's hands. Good for finding a clit, but not much else."

Jack grabbed the rat with his bare hand and tossed it through the opening. The piece of broccoli hit the driver on the nose and the rat sailed between their heads and skidded across the cement floor. Kaufman shrieked and the driver very nearly wretched.

"There's your rat. Tell your wife she can come home."

"Jesus, Jack! Honest to God, if you would have hit me with that rat I would have bricked you up in that crawl space."

"Left me in here with all the other junk."

"What? Am I supposed to have my crawl space vacuumed?

Jack climbed out of the hole and started to dust himself. His chest, belly and thighs were covered in smears of dirt and wood chips.

"Don't brush yourself off in here. Go outside. Do you think I want a pissy maid? When I tell her to go to the basement and to sweep up your pile of shit and rat hair, her face will bleed contempt. Honest to God, I'd fire her, but she has a perfect ass. I can't stop thinking about it. Don't think I didn't think about popping her when the old lady was gone, but then there's drama inside your walls and what am I supposed to do? Make the wife look like a complete asshole in front of the hired help? Pick up the rat on your way out."

"Got anything else for me while I'm here? Jack said as he bent over to pick up the rat.

"One more thing, Jack. Don't think I forgot. You were going to leave here, thinking I would forget to give you the cell phone." Kaufman pulled the phone from his front pocket and handed it to Jack. "I'll pay for the plan. It'll be worth me being able to get a hold of you whenever I need you. When I call, you better fucking answer it. Keep it charged and keep the ringer on. You have electricity in that shithole of yours, right?"

Jack straightened his back and took the phone, so that the rat and the phone balanced him as he walked up the stairs, through the house, and out the front door. He admitted to himself that he preferred holding the rat. Even though the rat had gone stiff and showed the first signs of rotting and bloat, Jack felt more kinship with the rat than the little bundle of wires and speakers that would carry Kaufman's voice directly into his ear. He contemplated stuffing the rat in his pocket and throwing the phone in the bushes, but Kaufman would discover the switch within a few minutes because he would call Jack on his way home as his first test. He pitched the rat behind a bush, hoping it couldn't be seen from the front picture window and finally dusted himself off. The driver had already slumped behind the wheel of the van, inexactly whistling *The Saucy Arabella*, but he stopped when Jack slid onto the passenger seat.

"Jesus, you must have one hell of a debt."

"That's not something I'm going to talk about."

"All I know is I wouldn't let myself get that deep with Kaufman. Before it's over you're going to be wiping his ass and chewing his food. Hell, you might even have to bang his old lady."

"Like I said, I'm not talking about it. I'm sure you have your own story."

The driver backed out of the winding driveway and just as he hit the street and pulled the shifter into drive Jack's cell phone rang. After some maneuvering, Jack fished it out of his pocket, fumbled with the buttons and just answered it before voicemail kicked in.

"Jackie?"

"It's me."

"You answered."

"I did."

"Good boy."

Kaufman hung up and Jack rested his head fully on the back of the seat, hoping to sleep a little before the sunrise.

What diseases do dust specks carry? Or are they dissipated thoughts floating through the air, pulverized and lost, and they only become reconstituted once a person has breathed them into their lungs and from the lungs they take residence in a person's brain and that person starts having random, sometimes dangerous, sometimes violent, sometimes beautiful thoughts that have no discernible origin. These thoughts float in and out of shafts of radiation, slowly advancing towards my nostrils. Is it possible to only breathe in half of a thought and these half-formed thoughts take the form of dreams and hallucinations, disjointed, pieces erased, continuity ignored? How does one stop breathing and continue to live? They won't bring me a mask. A mask may keep out the thoughts. Or is it better to have the dust conjuring up my thoughts, because the collective wisdom of all who have thought and died floats though the air? Is father in the air? A pulverized rant waiting for receptive alveoli and an unsuspecting mind to inhabit. There is so little left of him here. The bellowing bull tromps up and down the stairs, ripping out walls and windows, releasing poor Papa to the currents. I'm left with a mumble, a whisper in the night trying to ease my fear and pain. Now the house is filled with the bull's snorts and his rutting. The bull is ten times the size of the butcher and I wonder what will drive him to smash me in two, spilling my blood on this cot and this gleaming wood floor. I fear he will eat me, rip out my heart with his teeth and suck the marrow from my bones. He rages against the currents, keeps them at bay with his roaring and his sex, even though Sister Bollo told me that the male member is often used as an antennae for the voices. Somehow he keeps them at bay.

What is she doing up so early? Maybe the sun is too bright and too warm for the day to be called early. Maybe I've eliminated time as a consideration. Maybe I am free to float between light and dark. What are you doing Sister Anne Marie? You've worked that patch of earth for a week, for a lifetime, I think. Isn't that where he buried our defecation? The earth is so black and smooth it looks like a carpet or a bedspread from this window. It will be a beautiful bed of flowers, Sister Anne Marie has said, when she is done and maybe some of the scent will reach up to this room and it will smell like sickly sweet funerals or when demons wed. She must have planted two or three hundred flowers on that patch of dirt. She won't stop working the earth.

The bull never helps her. He limps by, holding some machine with an electrical cord attached. I wonder if he plugs himself in at night? Always with that cur on his heels. Its black tongue always lolling from its black lips. They think I have forgotten their betrayal, their kidnapping, but I never sleep when that dog is awake. I want to be prepared for their next attack. Maybe this time they can carry me to my grave.

I've seen them bring their sex to the dirt and grass and couple like two animals in the woods. I blame him for his desires. Sister Anne Marie has to bend over to protect her garden and she can't defend every orifice from entry. Didn't I have my own butcher to contend with? The attack upon us is relentless. Drop your guard for a minute and the swarm will be upon you. I asked Sister Anne Marie, but she said she didn't mind and she apologized, poor thing, for her display and I told her I didn't think she was the one to apologize and that it was the bull, but she said, "The tango is performed by two partners." Or some such aphorism, which I take to mean that she was a willing partner in the act. I told her shamefully, but honestly, that there was a time I enjoyed myself with the butcher, but after his interest waned I found that I never thought much about it, so I questioned whether I ever felt desire in the first place. I empathized with the butcher's desire. I responded. I acquiesced to his entreaties and invasions, but I don't ever remember inviting him in. "Jack," Sister Anne Marie said, "understands he has an open invitation. We don't stand on formalities. We're too old." Which I thought was rather ugly of her to say. I hadn't expected her to embrace whoredom with such zeal, but surprises are boundless and cruel. I haven't seen them engaging in marriage after we spoke, but sometimes I hear the house moan and groan and shudder right down to the foundation. Whores and satyrs can't be embarrassed, so I imagine they've found another dark corner to do their business in front of a more willing and decadent audience.

I think my left ear, finally, is losing its hearing capability. When I lie on my left side I can hear the baby squalling, the house groaning and creaking just like it did fifty years ago, the wind scraping its fingers along the roof and the waves of anger smashing against the glass of the windows and dying a miserable and violent death in the grass. When I lay on my right side and expose my ear to the whipsaw world I hear nothing but what sounds like heavy-legged spiders tripping across the floor. No intrusions. No attacks. No assaults. If I could clear out both eardrums with an ice pick I could find my legs. I could stand up and again start walking and see the teeming world and know that I am immune to its surly advances and my own crystalline thoughts could rise and spire without the threat of being smashed by other people's fetishes, anger and boredom. So I sleep on my right side until my bones ache and when I have to move onto my left side I wrap a pillow around my head, but my hearing is too acute on the right side to make this technique very effective. I talk to the baby through the walls. I understand her cries. I register her hunger and her gas and her drowsiness the instant she emits a sound. This surprises me. I have never felt in tune with children and the butcher lamented we had remained childless. When mothers and fathers gushed at the possibilities of new life, I saw only sadness. What if the babe ended up like me? Sensitive to every tick and tock and cowering from the hurly burly of the street. Cast out from the hearts of my parents, looked upon with charity and condescension from my sister, and forgotten by my brother. When mothers saw the cries as opportunities to care for their children I could only imagine slinking away and letting the child shriek until it stopped, either unable to take another breath or so hardened against my cowardice as to never want the teat between their lips again. But this one calls to me in the night, tells me she has lived through her first dream, a confusing stew of images and sensations that had no form and I whisper comfort through the dark. I tell her the dream is the first of many, thousands of sleeping or waking dreams that will bemuse and bewilder. I tell her to carefully breathe the dust or the dreams will be from someone else and she could be lost in a sea of confusion before she even has a chance to understand her own mind. She may breathe in my father's dark rage and bellow at her mother for no good reason. When she cries for her mother's breast I tell her to enjoy the comfort and I tell her that I hope her mother doesn't take away the comfort until she is ready to sleep and dream without the memory of the breast on her cheek. I ask her about her name, but she doesn't know it yet or her mother can't get past calling her "baby" or "my baby girl." Understandable I suppose for one so young, but does this mean, baby girl, you have no discernible personality and that no name has jumped from the mist to attach itself to you? Are you both nameless and faceless? Will you remain a cry through the wall or will you creep along the floor and open my bedroom door and crawl into my bed. I will take you in my arms. I will kiss you on the forehead and cry for the pain to come. I have no milk to offer you, only disease.

Jack walked through his newly planted orchard of seedlings, standing no higher than his ankle. In six years time they would bear bushels of fruit, but he would have to figure out a way to keep the neighborhood from stealing it off the trees. In six years the dog would be too old to do much, let alone guard the orchard. Even old Cactus Jack might not be able to lurch from his chair in time to catch the thieves or he himself may be buried alongside the moldering corpse of the lumberyard guard. The air smelled of earth as Jack had turned over the ground and planted trees in both lots. He had piled the stray bricks, charred pieces of wood, broken toys, rusting bolts, splinters of glass, rocks, links of chain, chunks of concrete, split rubber hoses, mangled sunglasses and crushed aluminum cans in a pile on the tree lawn of the street behind his house. The pile had grown to over four feet high with a diameter of about seven feet, so Jack thought the pile would be the perfect ammunition if a riot ever formed over the brutality of the police, the shallowness of the city government's imagination or the general bankruptcy of the world. The pile also clearly represented a temptation to the neighborhood children to pick up the debris and hurl it against the standing houses, whether occupied or not. He first thought of drenching the pile in gasoline to deter the children from grabbing the weapons, but he quickly conjured up an image of flaming bricks smashing through windows and torching the entire block, his house included, so he determined he would have to spend an afternoon throwing the debris into the back of his truck and then take it to the dump.

Jack held a watering can that he had fashioned by soldering a split funnel onto coffee can. He made the act of filling the smallish can from a hose near his house, walking the length of his backyard to the orchard, and dousing each seedling with a gentle rain from the can, into a process so slow and formalized a witness would swear he had been performing some ancient spring ritual concerning water and trees that the druids had passed down. He made the circuit for all fifty seedlings he had planted. He had started the seedlings in his garage, first eating the fruit to the seed and conjuring the new shoots with a combination of nutrient laden dirt, fluorescent light and a constant electrical heat from a pad underneath. He had grown a second crop that he planned to keep growing in pots in the garage throughout the next winter because some of the planted seedlings were bound to succumb under blizzards or be tromped down by kids or dug up by dogs. Jack's dog walked at his heels each of the fifty trips, sometimes sitting on its haunches and waiting for Jack to finish a task and sometimes curling into a tight ball and catching a quick nap before Jack moved again. Jack thought the dog had perfected sleeping like a dolphin, shutting down one side of the brain at a time while the other remained alert for danger and opportunity. The dog never lapsed in following and stayed no more than two paces behind Jack no matter where Jack went or what task he performed. At night he slept at Jack's feet in the loft, because Jack had not made it back into Anne Marie's room, even though he made frequent trips there with ever lengthening durations. Anne Marie didn't like the dog in the house with the infant, but its obvious gentleness and obedience won her over and she allowed it to sleep on the landing outside her door until Jack completed his conjugal visit. A few times when both Jack and Anne Marie fell asleep from utter exhaustion and shared the bed in a kind of accidental intimacy the dog would nudge open the door that Jack still had not been able to get to latch properly and sleep underneath the bed until Jack roused. The dog followed Jack to Mary Kelly's house and waited outside on the driveway in the dark in all kinds of weather. Mary Kelly would not entertain the possibility of letting the dog in the house, so even when the snow flew and had accumulated in deep drifts around the house the dog stayed outside and kept itself warm by burrowing into the snow and creating a temporary cave in which to sleep while it waited for Jack. The dog ate little, exercised as much as the number of steps Jack took in a day, and managed its shitting on its own. Jack never had to clean a pile from the yard and could not remember ever even seeing the dog defecate. He figured the dog probably slipped out at night and left turds in the neighbors' yards, but he could never confirm his suspicions because no matter when he woke up in the night because of an aching bladder, an ugly dream or a fully formed erection that drove him to Anne Marie's or Mary Kelly's bed, the dog always waited for him to take the next step.

The dog even followed Jack on his errands that Kaufman summoned him via the cell phone. Kaufman had given Jack the use of a stripped-down white cargo van identical to the one he had given the other driver and it sat in the driveway behind Jack's old truck. Kaufman forbid Jack from taking the dog along on jobs, but if he knew he wouldn't be seeing Kaufman the dog rode shotgun and provided another layer of menace when needed. Kaufman railed about dog hair and gallons and gallons of ubiquitous saliva, which would lower the resale value of the van further, after his trained apes beat the living shit out of it and he was ready to trade it in. Jack didn't argue, because he liked to keep his conversations with Kaufman short, and as far as Jack could tell the dog did not shed or ever leave a mark where it had been. Jack had a number of jobs, including on-going skirmishes with rats inside Kaufman's house. Kaufman's wife had returned to the house only to have a foot long monster run across the kitchen floor during a dinner party. None of the guests saw the rat, but his wife and the cook did and the blood drained from his wife's face so demonstrably that the guests inquired if she felt ill and discreetly ended the affair earlier than expected to give her the opportunity to retire to her bed. She packed and left the house that night with only the vaguest idea of where she may end up. She told Kaufman she would call him when she settled, but at the moment she couldn't be sure in what country or continent that might be. Kaufman told her that every country has rats and every sewer everywhere teemed with their disgusting, furry bodies. She shrieked something incomprehensible at him and left in a cab. So, that night with dirty dishes still on the table and the kitchen loaded with abandoned pot and pans and serving dishes, Kaufman summoned Jack to the house to kill the rat and fix the problem. Jack told Kaufman about the hole in the waste pipe and Kaufman screamed for Jack to fix it. Jack had explained the crawlspace had to be cleaned of debris, that he needed wire mesh, concrete and that the pipe had to be dug out and replaced.

"Do the fuck whatever you have to do to keep rats out of my fucking house! I'm like a crazy person thinking of those little bastards eating my fucking food."

Kaufman went upstairs to watch television in his bedroom, some infomercial about a new colon cleansing process, and jerk off to a pretty lady with milky skin who read the script about the color and flexibility of her colon. Jack had fetched the dog from the van and led it to the basement where it trapped and killed the rat in a few minutes. The dog had no taste for rats and dropped it at Jack's feet.

Jack spent the next few weeks clearing out the crawl space and digging out by hand the pipe that lay seven feet under dirt. He replaced the pipe and created a wire and concrete barrier that no rat would be able to chew or tunnel through. And when he finished that job Jack worked other jobs, like picking up Kaufman's sister at the airport. She lived in Palm Springs and usually returned to Ohio every year around the anniversary of their father's death. She stayed long enough to argue with Kaufman's wife on a variety of topics that most often included Kaufman's awful house, their tacky and overwrought décor, the coldness of the air and the swill they tried to pass off as food. She had gotten wind that his wife had moved out of the house so she moved up the timing of the visit to benefit from her sister-in-law's absence. She acted less than happy to be picked up by Jack in a cargo van that boomed and echoed over every imperfection in the road. Her skin had been cured by the sun so that even her eyelids and palms looked leathery brown. She smoked four cigarettes from the airport to Kaufman's house, an hour's drive in the worst traffic and she rasped and snarled at Jack between drags that he was nothing more than an ape, a bandit, a sword swallower (Jack thought this might be an archaic reference to homosexuality, because it made no sense otherwise.) a reckless miscreant, a cobra with a pig's body, a vulture picking on her brother's carrion, a thief, a swindler, a cheat, a pickpocket, a gorilla with a driver's license, an oafish giant, a retard and a mental midget. Jack squeezed the wheel harder with every slur until the knuckles on his hand throbbed. After Jack carried her bags inside Kaufman's front door she thanked him for not raping her and tipped him a dollar for his trouble. Kaufman screamed at her to not tip his workers, that they got paid enough as it is, but she threw up a hand to block his arguments and said something to the effect that the house smelled better without the wife. Jack walked back to the van with the dollar still in his hand until he jammed it under the sun visor, considering the bill to be the hardest dollar he had ever earned.

Jack also became Kaufman's collection agent. Kaufman had stray pieces of property scattered around town, remnants of whims, inside tips, hunches and gut feelings that never amounted to much other than a small stream of rent that had become increasingly harder to collect. The first property turned out to be an industrial site with a working factory still smoking away. The owner had inherited the business from his father and grandfather and Jack knew after a few minutes of conversation that the last thing in the world the son wanted to do with his life was run a small manufacturing concern in a dying city in the middle of a ghetto with nothing to do but drink or jerk off. The son talked about cash flow and orders being down and how the Chinese beat the shit out of their business, but Jack stared through him as he talked to the posters of Paris, London and Milan hanging on the wall and he wondered how much longer the place would stay open. Kaufman bought the property off the old man thirty-five years before when he thought, based on an inside tip from a state transportation planner, a spur of the interstate would slice through that part of town. The planner had shown him the preliminary drawings and survey work for a small bribe and a night out at a steak restaurant. But by the time Kaufman worked up the lease with the old man to rent the property back until the highway came calling, the state announced that all new highway projects would be delayed until residents stopped fleeing and the economy stabilized. Thirty-five years later the plans lay in a drawer untouched and forgotten.

"What would you rather be doing?" Jack asked without enthusiasm.

"Ah, you've pried open the central question. I have no answer for it."

"Then do what's in front of you."

"What? Is Kaufman hiring sages now? I have no interest in boiling my life down to an aphorism."

"No, I've got eyes and sense enough to know that if you hadn't inherited a factory you'd be selling shoes in a department shoe. Maybe even in one of them new Shoe Horns."

"Jesus, now even goons are making fun of me."

The owner took Jack's disinterested stare and obvious disdain for him as a person as a real threat. He started parking his Porsche in the garage, had his secretary screen all of his calls, and he made sure to mail the rent check more or less on time every month.

The second property on Jack's list was a small grocery store run by two immigrant brothers from Laos located deep within acres of desolate property, where every business had hand-painted signs and boards over the windows, where rusted chain link fences protected squares of poisoned properties and where the residents looked like a dazed and fearful population who had just crept back into the damaged buildings after a cataclysm. After Jack introduced himself and told the brothers that he would be collecting the rent from now on they became obsequious, offered Jack a plate of freshly made noodles and started pulling cash out of their pockets, the cash register, under the counter, from hidden pockets in their belts and from a large dusty can of tomato sauce until they made the rent. Jack sat and ate their noodles and asked them how they had escaped Laos.

"We ask you to please take the dog outside. He is not supposed to be in the store."

Jack considered the dog and then stared through the brothers.

"The dog goes where I go."

"But surely, Mr. Jack, you understand the government does not allow animals in a food store."

"I certainly would like to start off on a better foot than this. It does not please me to argue about the dog."

The brothers exchanged glances and wanted to launch into a more vigorous defense of their rights to deny access to the dog, but they looked at Jack's massive hands and his broken face and took him to be both vengeful and violent so, instead of an argument, the story of their lives tumbled out of them against their will. They had been the sons of farmers in the high, northern part of Laos. They descended from ethnic Lua, a minority population of Laos that had been beaten, displaced and killed during the Vietnam war. They both had been born in a refugee camp, but their parents passed on the chance to emigrate to the United States in favor of returning to Xaisnabouli Province. Their aunts and uncles moved to Stockton, California, Iowa City, Iowa and Nashville, Tennessee. Uncle Payloth picked Nashville because he had heard a Johnny Cash song on an American radio station in the camp and thought a city that sang songs like that had to be better than war and famine. Upon their return to Laos their parents found the land and the people changed. Sadness and death had stricken the country and the few crops they raised grew tasteless and malformed and kept them barely above subsistence. They hadn't thought the earth would be poisoned or that the people would have turned away from peace so irrevocably. First, mother died from injuries and the shame of being raped by a gang of ex-military thugs who roved the region, taking what they wanted because they kept their military issue guns and gear, and father two months after from mourning and despair. Neighbors fed the brothers, Xok and Xay, until a representative of the government could take them to an orphanage. From the orphanage, their aunts and uncles in the United States would be contacted and they would go live with one of them, so their father planned as he lay dying. But a representative of the smashed and incoherent government never came because after so many years of war and it had no capacity to care for the nation's children, especially the sons of the dirty Lua of the north, so Xok and Xay suffered terrible beatings from the neighbors and hard, punishing labor forced upon them. Then, one day Xok, the eldest, decided they needed to run away and find Uncle Payloth in Nashville, Tennessee because they remembered him as kindly with a sweat smile and with an the ability to conjure up the most valuable presents in the middle of the crowded and chaotic refugee camp, a stick of American gum, an apple, a chipped croquet ball that would never break no matter how many times they threw it against the tin sheds that housed the camp's latrines and food supplies, and a piece of wood with a head of a bird carved on its face that Uncle explained was a totem of an ancient form of animism and that it would be very valuable outside of the economy of the camp. What wonders would he be able to conjure in the wilds and riches of America? So, Xok and Xay walked to the south. They had been educated enough to know the difference between China to the north, Vietnam to the east, Burma to the northwest, Cambodia to the south and Thailand to the west and south. They knew enough to walk into Thailand. They bribed the border guard with the totem, the most powerful possession they would ever own. By luck or through divine will the border guard trafficked in drugs and antiquities so he spotted the craft and age of the object, smiled at his good fortune that two dirty orphans would be carrying such a treasure, and he let the boys walk into the country, instead of shooting them and giving nothing in exchange for the bird.

Over the next four years they worked their way across the country doing odd jobs, hiding from the police and soldiers, and stealing food when their hunger drove them to the point of unconsciousness. Xok would often tell his younger brother Xay that the Lua were born to suffer and live short lives like their parents had, but that they shouldn't complain or forget the beauty of the world and that helped Xay sleep when hunger gnawed at him or he strained under the burden of brutal work. Eventually they washed up in a newer section of Bangkok where the rich walked as if they were asleep and the doormen and police used violence against them to keep them off the gleaming streets and away from the golden doors of the buildings. One day they asked a beautiful lady with sculpted and shiny hair if they could carry her bags. She glared at them as predator to prey but softened when she saw the same open grin repeated on each of the brother's faces.

"What are two Lua doing in this crazy city?" she asked, using their language. It had been such a long time since they had heard someone other than their brother speak it.

"The wind blew us here, ma'am," Xok said. The wind picked us up from our homes and landed us at your feet like two seeds from a flower or a tree. We are presents from the sky. Lost and looking to find root." Xok had not made up the image or really understood the metaphor because he had no chance to study either flowers or trees, but he had picked it up from a farmer's wife who always carried a bemused look on her face like she had been dropped on her head from great height. They had spent a month working for her and her husband planting rice. The couple who were childless and getting older thought Xok and Xay as gifts sent to them to relieve their burdens and heavy hearts.

The woman let them carry her bags and she paid them handsomely. They readied themselves to race through the streets to the nearest vendor to fill their stomachs with whatever treats he sold as soon as the women formally released them from her service. But the woman paused before letting them go and posed a question after a long period of formulation.

"Where are you parents, Lua?"

"Ma'am, they died a long time ago. Their hearts were broken by the war and the rape of their land. Uprooted flowers wither and die, but their seeds live on," Xok said, again parroting the farmer's wife, who in a month's time shaped their story into a poetic narrative that they used to their great advantage since she had created it.

"So many people on the move. But hasn't there always been diaspora, young Lua?"

Both Xok and Xay repeated and memorized the syllables of diaspora because it sounded like an important word that could be useful in the future. The woman brought them into her apartment and had them sit in a large entryway with ochre walls, two large flowering plants, and a plush carpet with a motif of water buffalo, antelope and falcons. She disappeared and came back with two cokes, but they were too polite to tell her that they didn't really know how to drink it since they had never seen anything like it before. Xay thought she could be a witch and that she offered them poison. Xok could read his thoughts and glared at him to stop being so foolish. A witch would have no reason to poison and eat them, because they did not have enough meat on their bones. They told her about their Uncle Payloth in Nashville and his bewitchment by the singer Johnny Cash. She disappeared again and within a few moments the apartment vibrated with a thumping sound and the twanging of strings. A man's voice began to wail an incomprehensible string of syllables, but the voice sounded friendly and not unlike Uncle Payloth himself. Xay became so confused he asked if Uncle Payloth screamed from the next room, and the woman laughed at him and told them she was playing a Johnny Cash record for them. They looked at each other and exchanged a communication with their eyes that they thought the woman may be mad, because anyone could tell Uncle Payloth sang even though the lyrics may be gibberish.

Jack squirmed in his stool and Xay filled up his bowl with more noodles. They were spicy and wholesome and Jack thought he might be able to eat five more bowls if the brothers had cooked enough. He had a reason for sitting through their story. He had Kaufman's money in his pocket, but he had to find a way to make his own money. He still had the threat of the housing inspector hanging over his head. The inspector had not come back on the two week deadline, but that did not mean the matter had been closed. Jack knew he could come back anytime, and when he did Jack better have the cash ready or the garage would be coming down or he could expect to be in court for the rest of his life. The inspector could unleash paper and bureaucracy whenever he pleased and once that started even harpies would quake with fear. He couldn't ask Kaufman for a loan, so he had to resort to shaking down Kaufman's tenants if the opportunity arose. The brothers continued their story as Jack thought through his predicament.

So, the woman cleaned and fed them and called a friend who worked at an international relief agency. She either used the promise of future company or cashed in a pleasurable memory with the man because in the next few months he worked to get them classified as war refugees, had his agency make contact with Uncle Payloth and had him agree to be their sponsor and guardian in America. The woman saw them off at the airport, hugged them goodbye, called them her little seedlings carried away again by the wind and walked out of their lives as coolly as she had entered.

Uncle Payloth greeted them with an enormous smile and an extraordinary present for each of them, a Spiderman comic book for Xok and a hand puppet that looked like it wanted to eat human flesh for Xay. Weeks went by before Xay could summon the courage to stick his hand in the sleeve and make the puppet speak, and even then he moved tentatively and made the puppet speak in the voice of a monster, bent on hunting human beings. Uncle Payloth lived in a one bedroom apartment in downtown Nashville above a store that advertised itself as a Christian bakery with a blue and red neon cross in the window. The cross acted as a beacon for the newly arrived homeless who thought it might be a street mission where they could eat a cup of soup in exchange for listening to a sermon about the wonder of Jesus in the free market economy. Uncle

Payloth began by telling them two of his observations. One, that he could not understand what made the bread in the shop below Christian bread, but he warned about eating too much of it because it gave him horrible indigestion and it may alter their religious beliefs from the stomach outward. Two, that Johnny Cash no longer lived in Nashville and his music had fallen out of favor with the locals who now liked singers with thin, reedy voices who made music that sounded like it had been pumped with air and drained of all of its blood. Xok spotted a guitar in the corner of the small kitchenette tucked in the back of the apartment and asked Uncle Payloth to play. Uncle smiled broadly and told them they would be his first audience and even though he missed half the notes of the song he played, *Hellhound of My Trail* by Robert Johnson, he mesmerized Xok and Xay who thought Uncle Payloth might have transformed into a bird by breathing American air and eating Christian bread. Xok asked Uncle Payloth to translate the words and he had dreams of mongrels and flight through thickets and dense forests the rest of the week.

With the boys encouragement Uncle Payloth continued practicing everyday for years during the time most families settle down in front of the television after dinner but before bed. He worked in a warehouse and starting calling Xok and Xay his sons because he acted as their guardian and the prospects of finding a wife and creating a family for himself were dim. A small Laotian community existed in Nashville at the time, so he had only a small number of available women from which to choose a mate. His steady job and the responsibility he demonstrated by raising his two nephews indicated he had the raw material for making a good husband, but his love of country music and, as he learned the culture of the city and the music scene, his preference for cowboy boots, tight jeans and black cowboy hats disconcerted his prospective brides. One woman, Damang, went so far as to go to the library and check out a dozen classic country albums, Buck Owens, Merle Haggard, Dolly Parton and George Jones among them, but she could not get through an entire record without weeping and suffering paralyzing migraine headaches. Her interest in Payloth dissipated as she contemplated a life under that kind of assault.

Jack found himself with a third bowl of noodles sitting on his lap. Neither the story or the food had changed the menacing look on his face even though he liked Xok and Xay and their cooking. Xok told the story and Xay watched the movements of Jack's face and his hands. Xay could account for every thought behind a man's eyes; he knew what a scratch of the temple meant or a whistle of air out of the left nostril. They had developed their act soon after running away from the graves of their parents. Xok, naturally loquacious, could spin words as fast as he could think of them and Xay honed and practiced his talent until he became something of a wizard at reading people. He would sit very still during one of Xok's stories, and the story of their lives often changed, sometimes it included Uncle Payloth and sometimes it didn't, sometimes Uncle Payloth acted kindly and sometimes he became a tyrant who beat them and made them work in dangerous jobs until they were old enough to escape.

Sometimes their parents still lived in Stockton, California and other times their parents had been killed by an American bomb, the Viet Cong or by a soldier of the communist Pathet Lao and no matter what version Xok dished off, Xay would wait until the exact moment to either embellish the story with a burst of description or repeat the same questions that formed in the minds of the listeners. So, if Xok had made it halfway through the narrative and the listener started mulling over the truthfulness of what he heard, Xay may burst out with, "Many of us have lived incredible lives. Once war begins anything and everything is possible. Diaspora will lead you down many paths." If he timed the remark correctly and delivered it with enough conviction the last of the listener's defenses could be dismantled and he would be left open to Xok's mastery. At that moment as Jack scratched his chin and opened his mouth to launch into his demand for money for his own pocket to pay off the inspector, Xay launched his strike.

"Mr. Kaufman not a friendly man. He never ate a bowl of our noodles. He has never sat down in this store ever. He only calls and yells at us on the phone. Threatens to blow up the store or make me have sex with animals. We always pay. Even if we eat our own inventory and keep the heat down to forty degrees at night, we always pay. We fight to keep our money and food out of the hands of our customers. They try to steal and sometimes shoot us, but we're still alive and paying Mr. Kaufman. We can't understand why he hates us so much."

Jack broke out into a wide grin and told them he didn't believe in that kind of intimidation and as long as they paid the rent on time and they made him noodles that tasted this good they would have no problems. Xok looked at his younger brother with awe and wondered if he could read his own thoughts and if they had been molded and manipulated by Xay like the evil puppet Uncle Payloth had bought them in one of his stories. Jack set the third bowl of noodles on the counter uneaten and padded his belly to indicate they had stuffed him. He had no way of backing away from his magnanimity and looking worse than Kaufman, so he decided to leave the request for extra cash for another day.

"One last thing Mr. Cactus," Xay said. "Do you know why Mr. Kaufman owns this building?"

"I don't know. I would be afraid to ask him."

A few of the old neighborhood people, the last remnants of the first immigrants, told Xok and Xay say that Kaufman grew up in this neighborhood and this store had been owned by the father of a girl he loved. That Kaufman was the son of a peddler and tinker and that they could never stay very long in any one house because they were very poor and Kaufman's father didn't have the personality or talent to make more than starvation wages. When he got old enough he asked the storeowner for his daughter's hand in marriage and the father laughed and told him that he didn't slave away his life, scrimping and saving, fighting customers and collectors, just to watch his daughter marry a tinker's son. "We might as well let her marry an ape or throw her on the street and let her marry any man with an urge," the father said. The scolding went on for a year. Every time the storeowner saw Kaufman or his name happened to come up in conversation the storeowner would say something like, "Oh, Kaufman, my son-in-law. The one with no knees in his pants. He found his pecker one night and now he thinks he can be a husband," or "Hello, Kaufman, I'm still thinking about your proposal. It's between you and the garbage can."

The daughter became betrothed to another man who was the son of a sporting goods storeowner, but a robber killed him on the street. One of the thieves had an old gun with a tricky trigger and he accidently discharged it into the poor boy's face. They gave him the chair anyway because the jury knew nothing of guns. The tragedy disappointed the storeowner, but he could not yet accept Kaufman, but he suffered a horrible stroke not six months after the boy's death and he died within a year. The mother kept the store going and the patrons said she made the place cleaner and friendlier than when her husband had run it.

The neighborhood began to change. The old families began to move out to the edges of the city or the suburbs and the new families had less money and no loyalty to her or her store. So, just about the time her books became horribly unbalanced and she contemplated closing and getting a job as a bank teller or in the office of one of the unions, she received a visit by Kaufman who had come back from wherever he had gone when he learned the daughter had become engaged to someone else. He offered to run the store for a fifty percent ownership stake, but he demanded that the mother could not work in the store and the girl, even though she had started taking business courses to learn shorthand and typing, had to work in the store at least two days a week. The mother agreed and Kaufman raised all the prices on the food and started featuring cigarettes, beer and wine. He screamed at his customers and one shot him in the shoulder, another stabbed him in the hand and several beat him with fists a number of times until he made a deal with a thug with a harelip and a head the size of an H-bomb, who ran a loose confederacy of thugs formed to scratch money from the street in any way their dull minds could conjure. They became Kaufman's gang and they firebombed or stinkbombed other competitors who wouldn't agree to fix their prices a notch higher than Kaufman's prices. They bullied delivery drivers to leave an extra pallet or two of merchandise and mark it as waste, they chased down and beat anyone who smashed a bottle in the parking lot, tried to steal from the store or hung around the building looking to hassle the other customers. They worked for a salary of free wine, use of the storage rooms for dice and poker games and tips on the horses at the track.

The store flourished. Kaufman diversified his business into coin-operated jukeboxes, because money could be made now that all the restaurants and bars walked away from live entertainment in favor of vinyl hits. He needed the right muscle and a little luck so as not to be killed before he made his fortune.

He kept the store and Xok and Xay were the latest in a long line of renters. Kaufman said that one day they would be killed by a crackhead. Xok told him they wanted peace, but they had seen the slaughter of villages and watched both their dear mother and father strangled inside their small home. They knew how to take care of themselves

"The soldiers and the farmers who beat us did not hate with the depth Mr. Kaufman can achieve."

"Xok, no one left in this neighborhood would know that story. Where did you pick it up from?"

"My brother is sometimes too discreet. We heard the story from Kaufman's wife. She used to collect the rent before you. She liked the noodles also. She liked to walk the aisles and remember her father, but she often said that she could find nothing left but nostalgia and sentimentality conjured up by an old woman. Kaufman had killed any good there ever had been, of that she remained confident. Finally, they married and the money started pouring in and they ended by buying a succession of ever bigger houses in more exclusive neighborhoods and she finally realized that her husband did nothing for love or money. Kaufman liked to remind her where she came from, liked to prod her into remembering that he saved her from being a typist for some sleazy lawyer or some lecherous bank president. He likes driving into the neighborhood of crumbling houses and staggering drunks on the sidewalks. He wants to remind her what she could have been and that it had been his wit and his balls that rescued them from the jungle. I asked her if she didn't like life in her mansion and that maybe her husband had a point to always remember where they came from so they would never take their good fortune for granted. She looked at me a long time and I thought she would cry or commit some act of violence. 'The house is full of rats. They've eaten away the foundation and sleep in my bed. Sometimes I wake up and they are trying to stick their slimy heads between my lips. We never had rats in the store of my father's house. You can never escape a bad decision. Then, Mr. Cactus, you've shown up and we wonder what we've done to deserve you. We liked Mrs. Kaufman very much. She's not like Mr. Kaufman in any way."

"Mrs. Kaufman is tired of living with rats. She's living in a hotel. Obviously, her duties in the Kaufman empire had to be picked up by someone else."

"But Mr. Cactus is now the man we must pay. I will tell you how under the tutelage of our Uncle Payloth we grew up to be men in Nashville and made our way to Cleveland where we both have wives and children and how very soon we will be buying houses farther away from this violent place."

Jack held up his hands and stopped Xok before he got wound up.

"I'll see you next month. You can tell me then."

"Fine, Mr. Cactus, fine."

"And you can tell me then if a war ever stops."

Xok and Xay looked at him thoughtfully.

"No, it's like a haunting. The ghosts are always there," said Xok.

"Here, Mr. Cactus, something for the road," said Xay. He handed him an off-brand soda and a package of cupcakes a month past their expiration date. They shook hands and they assured Jack they would always have the rent on-time, or would at least be close to accumulating it when the first of the month rolled around. When Jack started the van and Xok's voice had cleared from his head, he thought about going back in and demanding his money, but the opportunity had been missed. Next time Jack would have to come out with his demand before Xok started one of his stories and he started feeling kindly and paternal toward the brothers.

Next, Jack visited a 70 suite apartment building that hung on a cliff overlooking the lake. The building had once been considered elegant and a place to aspire to, but over the years the suites were halved and the renters changed from the tony rich who wanted a weekend place to breathe the fresh air of the lake to a mob that included students studying gastronomy and paleontology, filmmakers who began a project with the best intentions of making something personal and profound and who, in the course of filmmaking lost control of the script and ended up making karate or superhero movies with questionable special effects, pensioners eking out a living on social security and flea market booths or with jobs stocking pharmacy or grocery store shelves or missing every third meal or indiscriminately suing the largest corporations for a host of grievances and injuries, lesbian poets who discovered their taste for vagina and their love of poetry at the same time so now the two are inextricably linked, bitter clerks who worked at mail order houses and direct marketing firms who could not see past the personal politics of their workplaces to find joy in their lives, divorced moms with tattoos on their lower backs whose bodies held the remnants of a curvy youth and who wished they could have the resemblance of their ex-husbands surgically removed their children's faces, divorced men who retreated into booze, televised sports and internet porn and who spied on the divorced moms with tattoos on their lower backs, but they had neither the energy or inclination to make a move in their direction, an apprentice plumber who practiced the accordion four hours every night because he believed the polka music of his grandfather would find an audience of young people because he never felt angry, depressed or agitated after listening to a polka tune, a banker who had lost his understanding of the world, who once thought that his knowledge could be stitched like a thread into the larger fabric of society, philosophy and family, but who had suffered a series of blows professionally and personally so that now he sometimes found himself standing naked and dripping from a shower, holding a piece of dental floss and wondering what thread of knowledge he would now clean his teeth with, a cohort of Russian immigrants taken with group sex and bourbon because they had tired of monogamy and everyone asking their opinions on the best brand of vodka, young married couples with bad jobs, few prospects and less understanding of how the economy is organized and how it punished young people who didn't understand the value of skills or that the next gang of leaders, bosses and managers had already been culled and trained in distant neighborhoods and private schools and would rule their lives in ways they did not understand or would ever know existed, and even a smattering of thieves lived in the building who preyed on young retail mangers that involved scams of stealing items, returning the next day or later in the same day and acting out emotional scenes in which they demanded justice, promised vengeance and used not a few stolen identities to demand ownership rights to merchandise that had just been dropped off by a delivery truck and cash for items returned with no receipt.

When Jack arrived he found the manager of the building holed up in his apartment, who did not collect the rent on a consistent basis and did not fix minor maintenance problems so half the toilets did not flush properly and some of the rooms sat dark from blown fuses. Jack saw broken windows, uncut grass, abandoned cars in the parking lot and he felt himself sinking into the same general malaise the building had fallen. He looked at Kaufman's cell phone and wanted to smash it against his forehead until he cracked the circuit board, but the manager stood beside him with five days worth of beard on his face, mussed hair and a t-shirt that announced him as a volunteer at a fish fry banquet held in support of the fight against tooth decay six years previous to meeting Jack, and Jack thought that demonstrating an act of unhinged rage so early in their working relationship might be detrimental to getting the building in shape. He figured he would have to smash the phone on the manager's head in a month's time and if he survived he would have Kaufman fire him and if he died he would drag him into one of the empty apartments they couldn't rent because of a broken stove or a water leak that had been fixed by shutting off the water and Jack would leave the corpse there to molder until someone complained about the stench.

"I'll be back tomorrow and we'll start at the top floor and work our way down," said Jack as he eyed the manager and wondered if he would show. "The repairs should only take this lifetime and part of the next. No problem, right?"

The next day Jack arrived around 6:00 am and pounded on the manager's door with no luck. Either he slept off a binge or the thought of work, being anathema to him, had driven him to stand in his bedroom closet with his hands pressed against his ears until Jack became discouraged and went to work on his own. On average Jack finished an apartment per day by himself, and for a week he pounded on the manager's door, but the manager would never answer the knock or come out of the apartment while Jack's truck sat in the lot. He ran whatever errands he had during the night and always kept the blinds drawn. Kaufman had given Jack a master key and at the end of the first week of working alone and hearing the tirades from the renters, kicking out a group of young squatters from an apartment with no running water and fully understanding the state of the building had deteriorated further than he first expected, he decided to use the key and rouse the manager into action. He opened the manager's door, cut the chain with a pair of bolt cutters and strode in with purpose. He found the manager in bed watching television with the sound turned down and the covers pulled up to his chin. He lay awake and he knew that Jack had just walked into his bedroom unannounced, but he refused to take his eyes off the television or otherwise acknowledge his presence. Jack turned on the light and stepped over a trail of dirty clothes to turn off the television. More dirty clothes lay scattered and twisted on the bed, on top of an unstable dresser, and hung from the edges and knobs of the closet and entry doors.

"How do you know Kaufman?"

"I'm his son-in-law, ex-son-in law, I guess."

"You married his daughter?"

"I did."

"For how long?"

"Seven years."

"Nothing lasts forever."

"She ran off with a chick-with-a-dick. She's calling herself a lesbian, but that's ridiculous because there's a dick involved. The last thing she said to me is that she liked the culture of women, but she needs a flesh and blood dick. Imagine that being the last thing your wife says to you. Kaufman was mortified, not any more than me, but I don't think he's talked to her after she brought her he-she to dinner with Kaufman and his wife. My mother-in-law said she thought Kaufman had several minor strokes through the course of the dinner and eventually stopped talking and wouldn't eat his food or even pick up his fork."

"So he gave you this job?"

"Out of pity, I guess. Or maybe to make sure I didn't completely bottom out. If I ended up on the street then his daughter and the he-she would have won some battle, some battle in his mind. There was no way he was going to let me completely fail."

Jack looked around the dirty bedroom and back to the manager with the covers pulled up to his chin and wondered what losing would have looked like.

"What did you do before this job?"

"The real question is what did I do before my wife told me that she was in love with a chick-with-a-dick."

"OK, that question works just as well."

"Financial advisor. My clients dropped me en masse once the story got out. I mean you lose your wife to a chick-with-a-dick and after they see her for the freak she is and the initial shock and titillation is over they start looking at you. They start obsessing about what could possibly be wrong with you to be the loser in that tug-of-war. After a period of brief reflection they come to one conclusion out of the whole mess. You are not going to manage their investments and their retirement money, even if you pulled a 15% return the past five years. No way, no how. In that business once you've acquired the taint of freakdom you're shot. Not even Kaufman will throw me an account and he raised her. He thinks there's something seriously wrong with my dick to drive his daughter to that extreme, but he just can't accept her way of handling it."

"So you know nothing about maintenance or managing a building?"

"Nothing."

"What do you do when a renter calls with a problem?"

"I erase the messages. When they see me in the parking lot I tell them I'm just the manager and that the owner has to approve all maintenance expenses. I've told them he's serving time at a medical clinic in Haiti, that he's connected to a heart-lung machine and can't communicate, that his finances are in freefall because he invested heavily in a company that invented self-cutting grass that was engineered to snap off once it reached the height of two inches, but that the company could not get EPA approval because there was concern the modified gene might migrate to trees and the corn crop and within a generation we would be without shade and ears of corn you had to hold with two hands. I've told them he was mauled by dogs, chimps and a bobcat. Now, they don't even ask or acknowledge me as a source of information or influence."

"Do you want to learn or should I drag you out of that bed and leave you on the sidewalk?"

The son-in-law began chewing the corner of the blanket and tired to sink lower in the mattress to avoid the decision that Jack pressed.

"What would Kaufman say?"

"Never mind about Kaufman. If I told him the state of his building and how much money he was losing in lost rent he would order me to publicly flog you or flay the skin off your body."

"He's a mean man."

"Yes, this act of pity is completely out of character."

"What the hell else am I going to do? I can't think of a place where I could go where the story won't follow me. I'm my own worst enemy. For some reason I can't get out of a loop in my thinking. I can't stop analyzing and reanalyzing. Get a few drinks in me, ask me if I've ever been married and my story will inevitably come tumbling out, so I'm a long way from reinventing myself. I'm still in the open wound stage."

"So, I am supposed to guess that you are interested in staying on?"

"And learn my wrenches and circuits?"

"Whatever. Maybe we'll start with how to unclog a toilet and replace a fuse."

"I am your apprentice."

"Jesus, this deal just keeps getting better and better."

Over the next two months Jack and the manager, who now insisted on being called AKA Blindersmith, fixed all the outstanding problems with the apartments. Black Shuck came with him every day and sniffed the hallways before sleeping in a corner in whatever apartment Jack worked. They implemented a rent collection process, began evictions for renters who had no hope of ever finding a job or paying their past debts and for a few no hope of even lifting their heads from a muddle of drugs, obesity or bad decisions long enough to remember they had bills, a landlord or rent due every month. Jack did most of the work and Blindersmith assisted. He remained attentive and he didn't try to fix something he didn't have firsthand knowledge how to fix, which included very nearly every task except for replacing the broken handle of a toilet, because, besides falling in love with a chick-with-a-dick, his ex-wife had the habit of slamming down the toilet handle after she finished eliminating because the sight of her own waste gave her, as she said, "the creeps," and after calling the plumber three or four times and shelling out a couple of hundred bucks each time he decided to learn how to fix the toilet handle by himself. So, whenever they came to a broken or loose handle during the maintenance sweep, Blindersmith took charge and completed the task himself. Also, Jack liked him because Blindersmith knew when to talk and when not to talk during the long hours they worked together. Jack considered there to be nothing worse than an apprentice or partner who rattled and blathered all day about nothing so that his ears ached more than his knees. The worst of curses to a working man.

Jack came to like AKA Blindersmith and hoped he would stay on as manager now that he had trained him, that he had driven out all the squatters, and that all the renters could now cook, turn on their lights and flush their toilets whenever they pleased. Jack also liked hearing some of the stories of the Kaufman family from an inside perspective. The more he knew about Kaufman the better. Before, he had parlayed information into a debt that Kaufman owed him, until the debt had been obliterated by the stupidity of the dough-faced guard at the lumberyard, and the more Blindersmith talked the more likely he might stumble on some new piece of information that could reduce some of his own debt load that Kaufman hung over his head. But Blindersmith's stories involved his ex-wife and Kaufman only played a minor role in most of them. Kaufman had treated the ex-son-in-law like a putz, Jack surmised, and kept him at arm's length from his business and his schemes. He may have used his financial services to launder some money, but the son-in-law had never been taken into Kaufman's confidence. So, Jack listened to the tales about the ex-wife and her betrayal and when he considered the whole of her history and the rap sheet of her misdeeds, the fact she had run off with a transgender person did not seem particularly out of character. Some stories from school included her adopting the persona of a virginal Algonquin maiden rife with hallucinations and missives from the Creator and she casting her teachers, parents and a few rude boys as Jesuit priests bent on crushing the fragile globe of her spirit and raping the joy out of her. Of her being thrown from a car her boyfriend had been driving and landing in a muck-filled ditch, escaping with a scraped ear and a broken wrist. Of watching her boyfriend and best friend be burned alive as the car burst into flames upon terminating its flight on the trunks of two thick oaks. The Jesuit onslaught and the horrible screams of the two people she most loved in the world dying by flame drove her to perform fellatio on a history teacher in the school parking lot every morning for a month until a security guard caught them and the superintendent fired the teacher and expelled the Algonquin maiden. Then, she aced her equivalency exam and enrolled in a community college but dropped out after a semester and disappeared into Appalachia for two years before emerging with a nasal twang and a fondness for fishing and marshmallow pie. Blindersmith knew it all before he married her and considered her free spirit as a counterpoint to his dull and plodding advancement through school and his quiet and respectful family life that included Sunday evening family reading circles when everyone had to recite a piece of writing that moved them from the previous week. He listened to her frequent and impassioned declarations against foreskins, people with limps, grocery stores, automobiles in general, but Volkswagens in particular, genetically modified food, newscasters, summer Hollywood movies, poems about cancer, wall-to-wall carpeting, purple ink, squirrels without bushy tails, any music in a dentist's office, anything carbonated that wasn't straight-up coke, dogs with black tongues, any type of shoe that shined, Wallace Stevens, members of Congress from even numbered districts, sideburns, lousy toilet handles, and Jesuits. The vagaries of her whims could take her just about anywhere and she could conjure just as impassioned and voluminous pleas for penis' with foreskins, bears, strategically placed stuffed animals near her pillows, milkshakes, disabled people without limps, Rimbaud and Verlaine, the thighs of basketball players, the idea of mobsters casting a rival's feet in cement and dropping them into a lake or ocean, her breasts, which were the perfect size and shape for her body, crepes, a world without electricity, the human genome project, the Indian Ocean, open marriages, walking barefoot through shopping malls, the way a morning mist hangs in a holler, the knuckles on a person's thumbs, coffee, marshmallow pie, and bacon. None of this signaled trouble to Blindersmith through the courtship and eventual marriage. He had been young and inexperienced and didn't know the difference between a red flag and charming uniqueness. Jack picked up on the fact that Blindersmith didn't have many stories of his own that didn't involve studying and a grim focus on money. Jack thought about taking him under his wing and showing him a side of life the boy had missed thus far, but his insistence on being called AKA Blindersmith bothered Jack to the point of distraction. He had known plenty of people who lived under pseudonyms and several simultaneous identities and it had been his experience that not a one of them could be trusted. Jack asked him at least ten times for his real name and ten times Blindersmith answered with a premeditated statement that his previous name had been retired due to misuse, neglect and moral bankruptcy and while AKA Blindersmith might not be the perfect transformative name it suited him for now in this period of transition. Jack resisted calling Kaufman and asking for Blindersmith's real name, because he wanted to hear it from his lips with his own inflection and his own facial expression and then he would be able to tell if the name had, in fact, died in Blindersmith's imagination of himself. As it was Jack felt like he worked next to someone with a poorly fitted mask or a corny disguise of big horned-rimmed glasses and a bushy mustache that did not coordinate with his hair color, and working next to someone like that for eight to ten hours a day he eventually found it to be as exhausting as someone who chattered inanely. The eleventh time Jack asked him his name, very near the end of the cleanup of the building, Blindersmith stopped his work and squared off to Jack as if preparing for a fight.

"Do you prefer Puddin' Tain?"

"At least pick something that sounds like it's from this century."

"I live on Strawberry Lane."

"You best back down. You're risking a beating."

"How about Pudd'Nhead Wilson? It's Twain."

"How about shutting your mouth?"

"How about In the American Grain? Not much of a name, but just the same, ask me again and I'll tell you the same. Got it?"

"Christ, stick with Blindersmith. It suits you."

"Thank you. Step away from the man deconstructing. I know what I'm doing."

One evening after Jack had finished a day's worth of apartments, he stepped from the van and stretched his back with a groan. The cell phone rang in his pocket and without seeing the caller ID he knew who would be calling, because only Kaufman called the phone. He had not given the number to either Anne Marie or Mary Kelly, because the thought of another person having unlimited access to his ear made him agitated and angry. He fished the phone out of his pocket and answered it. Kaufman would have kept calling over and over again until Jack answered the phone and depending how many times he had to dial before Jack answered would dictate how much his anger had frothed and then the anger would have to be mollified by Jack performing some mundane task or errand for him, like picking up his dry cleaning or driving to an Asian supermarket to buy fish heads so his cook could make fish head soup. Kaufman wanted to talk to him about the apartment building, the significant rise in rent collections, the son-in-law who seemed to have been raised from the dead, and the calls from a building inspector hinting at cash payments, steak dinners, football tickets, strippers and a hefty account at Shoe Horn for the building to continue passing inspection.

"What was the inspector's name?" Jack asked.

"You know the son-of-a-bitch."

"Newcombe?"

"The same."

"He's been around to see me."

"I know. Honest to God, Jackie, you get your dick in more ringers than any man alive. Why the hell would you build without a permit? You know those pudwhackers wait for us honest folk to trip up like that. Your ass would have been in court, but I took care of him for you."

"What did you do?"

"There's only one thing to do in a case like that. Pay the motherfucker and make sure your thoroughly lubed because peckerheads like Newcombe are always trying to figure out new ways to violate your ass."

"I never talked to you about it. I never asked you."

"Consider it a bonus, Jackie. I suddenly got money flowing in from my properties like the old days when I collected with a .38 in my pocket and a hard-on a foot long. That's when I collected all the money my wife is now spending on hotels and poolboys, honest to God."

"It's not on my debt?"

"Jackie, Jesus, what do you think I am? A pimp? A goddamn Nazi? I shared a little of what you brought in, so if that inspector comes snooping around you have the green light to beat the piss out of him."

"That sounds fine."

Jack stood at the side door of his house and was about to enter when he saw a truck skid to a stop on his tree lawn, almost clipping a fire hydrant. A figure fell out of the driver's side door and disappeared behind the truck. Jack told Kaufman he would call him back as some bullshit had been dumped on his front lawn. The figure stayed unseen until he staggered to his feet and braced himself against the hood. He held something at his side and tried to catch his breath. Jack closed the phone and slipped it back into his pocket. The man turned and Jack recognized Ben, Anne Marie's ex-husband. They hadn't yet divorced on paper, but to Jack's knowledge Anne Marie had not once seen him since she had left. After Ben had failed to show up at Jack's house in the first months of their life together he faded from Jack's memory and concern.

Ben caught sight of Jack standing in the driveway and pointed a finger at him, shouting something unintelligible. He stepped away from the truck and he carried a shotgun loosely with his left hand. Jack took a couple of steps toward him. Ten years prior he would have sprinted toward him, wrestled the gun from his hand and beat him with the stock until he fell unconscious, hurtling toward a coma, but his back had seized up on him and his knees still throbbed with every step, so a sprint now would look more like a crawl, giving enough time for Ben to collect himself, count to twenty and shoot him through the heart. Ben took three staggering steps forward, almost crashed headlong onto the cement the driveway, but he caught himself with a desperate step and balanced with his feet wide apart and the gun pointing in Jack's general direction.

"Seems a little late for this kind of display, Ben."

"What are you telling me sonofabitch? Did you say something?"

"I said it's a little late to come fetch Anne Marie. She's been gone almost a year."

"Who said I came to fetch her? Who said I want her back?" Ben had difficulty focusing his eyes and keeping his head from swaying side to side. "She's long gone. Long gone." He raised the shotgun and tried to point it at Jack, but the best he could manage was three feet above his head or five feet in front of him or at the front door of the house. "I've come to shoot you."

"For what purpose?"

"Satisfaction and justice. Maybe a little delayed. Seems to me you shouldn't just get away with whatever your dick wants. Sometimes there should be a price to pay."

Jack tried to take a few steps forward, but Ben caught the movement, swung the gun around with a quick and instinctive aim and fired. Ben had loaded the gun with birdshot, so a swarm of pellets rushed toward Jack. The main cluster just barely missed him, but the periphery caught him in the shoulder, cheek, scalp and ear in a hundred simultaneous stings. Jack spun around and fell to his knees. For a moment his back lay exposed to Ben and a sober assassin would have stepped up behind Jack and finished the job with a blast to the skull and neck, but Ben had more than a fifth of gin sloshing around in his stomach and confusing his synapses, so instead of moving in for the kill he paused to admire his shot and revel in Jack's vulnerability. By the time Ben regained his purpose, aimed and fired a second shot, the chances of hitting Jack were greatly reduced. Jack had been reduced to half of his previous height and Ben had a tendency to aim high even when sober and the sight of Jack's blood dripping out of his body further weakened his ability to aim. The third force working against Ben turned out to be his failure to imagine himself at this point. His thoughts during the time of his drunken rage coursed over many scenarios and ultimately gave him the impetuous to right a wrong that Jack had done, but he had not imagined what he would do in the case of a wounding. He thought he could shoot Jack and he witnessed him falling dead away countless times and he even imagined himself walking to Jack's corpse and kicking him in the head to confirm his death. But now Jack kneeled in front of him with about half of his strength shot out of him and Ben wouldn't take one more step forward to ensure a more accurate shot. So, the second shot sailed to the right and terminated in the chest and face of Black Shuck. The dog flew backwards and landed on his back. He died within three shallow breaths. Ben cracked open the gun to reload two more shells, but he lost his balance and fell backwards. He smashed his head against the cement without otherwise breaking the momentum of the fall and gasped once or twice before losing consciousness.

Jack's left arm had gone numb. He still had movement in the arm, but he could feel nothing from where he had been shot in the shoulder to his fingertips. He also couldn't see from his left eye and he didn't know if the shot had blinded him or that blood clouded his eye from the wounds on his scalp. He tried to get to his feet, but suddenly Anne Marie's hand held him down.

She cried and told him to relax, to breathe, that an ambulance would by now be on its way, to hold on anyway he possibly could. Jack looked up at her and smiled even though the left side of on his face felt like it had been stuffed with marbles.

"Now I've got my Anne Marie scar," Jack laughed even though the peals of laughter shook his body and aggravated the hundred or two hundred wounds and sent fresh pain through the nerve endings that hadn't been destroyed.

Anne Marie stared at him in disbelief and not a little wonder.

Jack sat at the head of the dining room table. Brown Shuck lay in a ball under the table, resting his head on Jack's feet. Anne Marie sat on the other end, wearing a new dress and looking a little flushed from getting a traditional Thanksgiving meal on the table. Estonia sat on the left next to her baby, who she named Lucy, who slumped in a high chair, playing with a spoon. Ellen sat on the right. Anne Marie had washed her hair and styled it with a blow dryer. She had also dabbed makeup on her cheeks as well as a touch of lipstick. Ellen wore a floral dress that Anne Marie had picked up at a resale shop. The print of the dress looked tasteful, but the sleeves were overly large and creased, so the whole dress looked anachronistic, like it had been created for a woman living on the prairie, who needed a dress both fresh and formal.

Anne Marie had made the meal from memory, with some small assistance from Estonia. In her life with Ben they had ceased celebrating any holiday when their children stopped returning home. Ben would take advantage of the day off and the relative quietness of his favorite bar and drink himself to the periphery of a coma, sometimes ordering Wild Turkey as a tip of the hat to the pilgrims and their wives. All of them, even the baby, stared at the turkey, which lorded over a heap of mashed potatoes, the apple celery stuffing, the fresh cranberry sauce, the candied yams and the green beans with almonds. Jack wondered how Anne Marie and Estonia had made the meal with a gimpy stove, a plywood counter that had slightly warped from months of being splashed with water, and having to spread the ingredients on the floor in bags because they still had no cabinets. The shooting and Jack's subsequent rehabilitation had softened her and drawn them close to where they had been during the first few days after Jack had fetched her from Ben's house, but Jack knew she held off on installing the cabinets to see if he would return to Mary Kelly's house once he had healed. He had guessed right, because Anne Marie had decided that if the affair started up again she would buy her own house and have her brother install the cabinets there. Clearly, the decision of whether they would stay together remained in Jack's control. She would wait until his wounds fully healed and until then enjoy reliving those first heady days of rekindled love. She looked upon the table with pride. The meal looked close to perfect, even though she knew once she started eating she would taste every misstep she had made, but for a moment she could enjoy her work. She asked Jack to say grace.

Jack arched an eyebrow and wiped saliva from the corner of his mouth. He had some paralysis on the left side of his face and oftentimes couldn't tell if he drooled or not. What could he say that could be an appropriate summation of his thankfulness and benediction for this table laden with food? Where lay the entry point into that stream of thought? Was it baby Lucy who caught a glint of her blue eye in the reflection on the spoon and thought she stumbled upon a miracle? Was it Ellen who somehow survived a relentless beating from the world and came out the other side as crazy as a loon, remembering nothing of the fight or its purpose? Was it Estonia who had transformed from a child into a woman in the two years he had known her, who had grown serious and calculating as she plotted a path for her child and who had reached the absolute zenith of her beauty and sexuality and all he had to do was look at her to ache and feel regret for not being able to hold her in his arms. Was it Anne Marie? Shouldn't his thankfulness be wrapped around her like a second skin? Hadn't she kept all the threads together and sublimated her own happiness until the roar of his heart and his head had quieted? How could he construct a prayer to life that avoided a bow of the head toward a supreme mirage, a primitive's projection of joy, love and unspeakable sorrow? He hadn't thought of God in any serious way since he had outgrown night terrors and prayed his parents would be alive in the morning, so he thought it ridiculous to start now that the end had suddenly come in focus. He thought of flinging out random words until they congealed and formed a thought, but he couldn't even find words to describe the ride he had taken, fueled as it was by the roar, by rage, by a burning that could never be extinguished. There must be a kernel of it in baby Lucy, a drive, a propulsion, a gear that will grow and get louder and spin faster as the combinations and truths of the world reveal or obscure themselves to her, and her curiosity is fueled by delight, wonder, and the need to know what has been covered from her view. The roar would push her body to the limits of its endurance until she too had a panoply of scars and a dead arm and an uglier face than she could think possible, the muscles of the left side torn by birdshot and slowly healing into permanent hardness near the lip and under the eye. Give Ben credit, Jack thought, for at least trying to alter a few circumstances. At least the poor sonofabitch can think of himself as someone who acted, who didn't stand by and let another man swoop in and steal his bride without a fight, but whatever credit had been granted him he soon spent when he woke up in the hospital and learned the police held him in custody and he started moaning for a drink. He had to be sedated six times because every time he woke up the panic became greater, the pain more intense. The doctors figured a detox would kill him and they couldn't very well prescribe whiskey, so they kept him in twilight until the police sorted out the crime. Jack refused to press charges. He said Ben had been showing him the shotgun because he had been thinking of buying it and the gun accidently went off, twice. The cops figured out that Anne Marie legally remained Ben's wife, so they could spot the lovers' triangulation even before they stepped out of the car. When they asked Jack about it as he lay in the hospital with bandages covering most of his face, he told them the triangle had been resolved long ago and even though new triangles may have formed Ben had fallen out of the equation.

"Did he know that?" asked Hayes.

"I suppose not," answered Jack.

"Are you sticking with the accident story, Mr. Cactus?" asked Brankowski.

"What does Ben say?"

"He's says 'I want a drink. Goddamn, somebody get me a fucking drink in a dog bowl.'"

"I'm sticking to my story."

"Case closed. You know he's going to try again."

"If it gnaws on him that he missed me."

"This is missing?" Brankowski held his hands over Jack's body like a performance of last rites.

"I'm not dead. If he comes again he won't have a chance to pull the trigger."

"Right, because now that you've been filled with birdshot you're even faster than before."

"Let me worry about that."

"Well, we'll figure out something to charge him with. A person can't unleash that kind of mayhem without paying some price."

If Ben had it in him to try again Jack would be waiting and he didn't want the law to interfere with the rightful outcome of the struggle, but the chances of Ben mustering the energy and courage again were slim. He would probably be content with leaving a mark on Jack's face and maiming him and seeing his bartender and the regulars at his bar treat him with more deference and respect. Maybe baby Lucy would understand that there are consequences, always consequences, for your actions, and unless you want to go through life without rearranging any furniture or disturbing the dust you were liable to stir up anger and resentment against you. But you can't react against the resentment or let the anger under your skin. Fight through the consequences, baby Lucy, and move on. You may end up with a dead arm and face that haunts the dreams of children or you may sail through life, looking for the disturbances and finding none. But what words, baby Lucy, are left? How do you compose a sentence from the vast mewing and whipsaw of a man's life? How can you express that he had been sung into the world by his mother and his songline had been revealing itself to him every day since, sometimes unrecognizable in the industrial wail of steel and paper valley, sometimes atonal, sometimes so transparently melodic his hands twitched at the desire to make the melody manifest. How, baby Lucy, do I explain that the propulsion in you sometimes resembles a scream more than a song or that sometimes the world feels like clay that you can manipulate into any shape you want and sometimes it feels like a stone being pounded against your skull?

The time that had elapsed from when Anne Marie had asked for the prayer to this point in Jack's reverie lasted but a few seconds, no more, and just as Jack cleared his throat to attempt to shape something other than a whoop or a holler there came a knock on the door. Anne Marie moved to get up, but Jack stayed her with the arm he could raise. He lurched out of the chair and steadied himself with some effort before making his way to the door. He knew they watched him with pity and horror, but that would pass as they got use to his face and if the feeling ever came back into his arm. He expected to open the door and find Glover, returned from his walkabout to be with Estonia and raise the baby the best he could, but instead he found a black teenager standing on his porch. His face looked freshly mauled and his shirt had all but been torn off his back and hung in shreds from his shoulders. One eye had swollen shut. For a moment they looked at each other's faces and wondered if they were looking into a mirror, then they broke out in a simultaneous laugh. Brown Shuck yawned and sauntered to the door, where he sat at Jack's side and waited for direction.

"It looks like I came to the right place."

"For what?" Jack held onto the door to keep himself from falling over.

"People say this is where Wood was living."

"Another exile?"

"Pretty much."

"Son, we were about to eat Thanksgiving dinner."

"Alright. Can I come back here tomorrow? I need work and a place to stay."

Jack looked at the smooth hairless skin of the boy's chest and figured the air temperature to be somewhere in the mid-40s.

"Christ, we've got more turkey than we'll ever eat. I'll get you a shirt. We ain't formal around here, but we eat Thanksgiving with shirts on."

"Tomorrow is fine."

"Son, get the fuck inside the house. This heat costs plenty of money and its pouring out my door. I'm guessing you're starving and, not to disparage your momma or grandma in anyway, you've probably have never had a meal like the one we are about to eat? Get inside and tell me your name."

"Blizzard."

Jack pointed the way in and Blizzard walked tentatively like he treaded across plush carpet with filthy shoes. Anne Marie, anticipating his thoughts, had already set down a fork and plate and dragged another chair to the table. When she saw his face and his ripped clothing she made a trip to the basement to find an old shirt and to the refrigerator to fetch ice she could wrap inside a towel to help reduce the swelling. She had forgotten to put the reusable ice pack back in the refrigerator after Jack had last used it on his shoulder. The damaged arm always swelled and changed color. She hoped he didn't lose it, but how much abuse can a body take? Blizzard slipped on the shirt, a faded plaid, that instantly changed his status from feral exile to dinner guest. He sat down on the chair between Jack and Ellen, who scanned his figure up and down and found him surprisingly free of demons and static electricity. The ice went over his eye, but with his good eye he watched Estonia and her baby. He had to blink several times to determine if Estonia actually looked as beautiful as he thought or if her initial beauty had been some effect from his sudden change in fortune, from being hungry and freezing and cast out from his friends by 365 Everyday to eating a feast in a warm shirt with an angel sitting across the table from him. He knew they would probably try to fuck him in some way, but he would worry about that after the meal. Jack sat back down and just missed stepping on Brown Shuck's nose as he put his feet underneath the table. Brown Shuck, so named because he bore a striking resemblance to Black Shuck, except in the lighter coloring and less massive build, had shown up the day Jack returned from the hospital and had yet to leave his side.

"I think we were about to carve the turkey. I need an assistant to hold down the bird while I wield the knife. I can cut to order, everything from paper thin to a slab of meat."

"Jack, the blessing," Anne Marie reminded him.

"That's like telling a man to stand on the head of a pin. How can I compress all of my joy and wonder into a sentence, or even a paragraph, if you want something from the heart and not some rote brainwash? How am I going to tell you that you can find a family just about anywhere? You take a small step toward putting down roots and pretty soon you have a brood. How am I going to tell you that when Ben shot me, right at the moment the birdshot broke the skin a thousand times over, I thought my best days had come back to sting me for forgetting their import and their perfection. A swarm of avenging fireflies or minor furies come to remind me that each day is a jewel to be polished and admired. Should I tell you that a man can make the same mistake over and over again until he establishes a routine of bad decisions and forgets he's making decisions at all until he's shaken awake by an act of simple kindness or maybe an act of love and devotion and suddenly his path of errors is revealed and he suddenly understands why he is standing alone in a deep forest, his voice muffled to the edge of muteness by the thicket of trees around him? Maybe I'll make it simple and say you've got to hack out a place for yourself in the world before it mashes you with its teeth. I could tell you all we're just a bunch of drifters walking in the desert, looking for crusts of bread, but the metaphor might be lost as we sit in front of this feast. I could tell you how a man can stop wandering and how he digs himself a hole on a dirty city street. He hunkers down. He lets the storms pass overhead and the winds rage. Maybe he builds a garage with a turret and thinks in his head he can build the perfect house. He sees it. Sometimes when he closes his eyes he thinks he's living inside this perfect house, completely done and sparkling. The house is filled with a wooden gleam. But when he opens his eyes he sees a half-done kitchen, some sloppy drywall taping on the living room walls, floors that didn't come all the way back to their original luster, windows that let the cold air pour through like they stood open, some seeping where the wall meets the floor in the basement, and a whole house that has settled and turned and looks like it's trying to look back over its shoulder, a posture that doesn't quite fit my personality. I've got some paint peeling already along the eaves and birds have shit on my new siding the length of the house. Remember that cloud of crows that terrorized the neighborhood last month? Well, they didn't leave our house untouched. I had a grand scheme, a fantasy, the idea of one last great act, but really it all amounted to me saving the house from the wrecking ball for a few years more and that's hardly the palace I imagined in my head. But I can't say that's the first time that's happened in my life. I suppose we need to be thankful for small things, for baby Lucy, for the ability to conjure up dumb ideas that have no chance of succeeding because you're probably doomed by your own limitations even before you start. Let's be thankful that we don't know that or that we refuse to remember it. So, grab a fork everyone. Baby Lucy, you can use a spoon." They all acquiesced, even Ellen. "Raise them high. Hold them to the light. Lord, Goddamn!"

Jack stabbed the turkey. The congregation responded to his prayer with a chorus of mumbled amens.

In the Pack

The wind sliced across the cold lake and roared through the canyons between the dark and silent buildings. The world had been muted except for what the wind could disturb, a loose stop sign, the rattle of trash on the sidewalk, a flapping dumpster lid, the creak of a traffic light swaying on a wire. The city would have looked like a ruin except for the still pulsing electricity. The wind and the agitated and angry lake seemed poised to blast the brick and mortar apart, scattering the debris across barren fields and submerging it all under cold, black water until the small pulse had been extinguished.

A lone figure staggered along the sidewalk. He may have been the last man awake or alive in the city because in an hour of walking through the brutal wind he had met no one and had not seen a single moving car. He wore a blue and gold coat from a marching band uniform over a housecoat. A stocking cap rode high on his head and the cuffs of his pants had been stuffed into four layers of socks. His shoes looked like a combination of leather, laces and duct tape. They hadn't been off his feet for months. A swirl of whiskers lay matted against his jaw and his exposed nose had turned purple from the cold and decades of alcohol. He leaned against a building and took three or four deep breaths with his face averted from the force of the wind. He fought an urge to lie down, because he surely would freeze to death if he fell asleep on the sidewalk exposed to the wind. His instinct of avoiding obvious situations where he could freeze to death and his swollen bladder, now throbbing because it had passed an expansion previously unknown, had kept him from sleeping. The very act of urinating required great skill because under his housecoat he wore several layers of pants, sweatpants, long underwear, boxer shorts and briefs that all had different angles and paths of access so finding access to his penis begged for dexterity, concentration and determination. He steadied himself against the brick wall, which radiated cold through his coats and shirts and right to the core of his spine, and scouted with one hand. He barely touched flesh then lost it in the swaddle. He thought maybe he could just pull the whole construction down, but he worried if he could ever pull it back up and in place and he certainly didn't want to end his life with his bare ass in the air for all the commuters to see, lying next to a pond of frozen urine. He continued digging until he caught the knob and yanked it through a tight path, cursing his undersized penis again, which sported a respectable girth, but not much length, so getting it through the layers called for some stretching and positioning. Finally, a meager stream came forth and the man coaxed the urine past his swollen prostrate by exhorting his penis with "C'mon dog. Get a move on dog. You're killing me dog. C'mon dog!" because the penis, because of its disappointing dimensions, often found blame for issues not directly related to it. As the throbbing of the bladder began to subside and the man began to breathe more easily, a shriek echoed down the street. The man couldn't very well stop the stream, because once he stopped it the prostrate could clamp down and it could take hours to open again. The shriek sounded, louder, closer, and more distinct.

"Ain't fit for bladder or beast," the man whispered to the puddle of urine growing at his feet.

A third shriek slashed through the tail of the second shriek's echo.

"Best find me a box or a hole to sleep this off."

He started shaking and milking his penis to aid the flow, but nothing would make the stream go faster or become more hearty. Another cry shook him. This time it sounded like it came from a few feet behind him. He thought he heard panting, but it could have been his own breathing or his heartbeat throbbing behind his ear. His neck itched in anticipation. Anticipating what he could not say, but he concluded the menace behind him meant no good. He let go of his penis and it snapped back into the swaddling, spurting whatever urine it held into the cloth. The man turned and saw Nelson standing in the street behind him. He wore blue pajama bottoms, rain boots that looked like they had just come from a box and two sizes small for his feet, and a thick wool sweater with gaping holes at the elbows and neck.

"Why you robbing the someone who ain't got nothing? Nothing to steal here," the man said as he took a couple of steps backwards, a dangerous feat even when sober, but next to impossible when fear and booze competed in his veins. "Goddamn, made me piss myself. What chance does that have of drying on a night like this?"

Somehow he pulled off the backwards steps, but an attempted pivot, a preparatory move to turning tail and running, undid him. The pivot itself went smoothly, but the other foot, once lifted, could not find the ground again, sending him into a reel and he crashed to the sidewalk with his chin pointing the way. An explosion of white light blinded his eyes and he groaned horribly as he took inventory of his body after this fresh assault. Had he not lost his front teeth years before they surely would have been lying helter-skelter on the cement before him. He touched his chin. A large scrape had been opened and blood seeped from several spots of the wound. When he rolled over he saw that Nelson loomed over him, offering him a hand to get to his feet. The man closed his eyes for a moment and collected his consciousness with a few deep breaths before accepting the offer and rising to his feet. Nelson grabbed a handful of the man's coat and wouldn't let go. He steered the man down the sidewalk, giving encouragement to him by nodding his head and grunting. The man leaned heavily on him as they walked in a broken dance.

They entered a vacant apartment building through a splintered plywood door. They walked up three flights of stairs littered with trash and pieces of the building that had fallen inward. Vandals had hacked the walls and pissed in the corners. They went inside what had been apartment 3G and in the middle of what had been the living room a fire burned inside an oil drum. A section of the roof had fallen in over where the fire burned so the smoke escaped into the night. Around the fire sat three overstuffed chairs in three distinct phases of decay. One looked like it could have been taken from a pensioner's home, an old chair with an outdated plaid pattern, but it had been cared for and prized for its ability to pitch a person into spontaneous sleep. The second resembled the first except the fabric on the arms had been worn away and the padding had fallen out of various weak spots, but it somehow had managed to keep its shape and a hint of its past stateliness. The third chair had had pieces ripped from its structure and burned in previous fires. Two or three springs had worked themselves through the fabric and two legs had splintered so that the next person carrying over 150 pounds of weight would surely end up on the floor amidst the wreckage of the collasped chair. Nelson dropped the man in the best chair and knelt at his feet. He found the end of the duct tape on the right foot and began unwinding it. The man protested but Nelson stayed him with a hand, then continued unwinding. He worked until he had extracted two gnarled feet with discolored nails and angry blisters on the knuckle of each toe from the rubbing of his makeshift shoes. Nelson touched the feet tentatively, let his fingers dance over the curled and bent nails, marveling at their grotesqueness.

"What you fixin' to do pajama?"

Nelson, his concentration broken, stood up and threw more fuel on the fire: three lumps of coal culled from the fields near the steel mill, slats from orange crates, a smashed high chair and scraps of molding from another vacant apartment. He rubbed his hands just out of range of the tongues of flame. Slowly, he peeled his lips apart. His mouth stayed open and he looked like he had been frozen mid-stutter before he could force words to escape.

"I.....I....am....a desperate noodle."

"Sad, sad truth...damn noodle," the man answered as he became aware of the chair and the fire creating a leaden drowsiness that felt like it could be permanent. Nelson sat in the second best chair and kicked off his rain boots. He touched a raw spot were the too small boots had rubbed, then propped his sore feet and inch from the hot barrel. Thick black smoke curled from the mouth from burning creosote.

"Cold night to be wearing pajamas. Don't make no sense robbing a man, knocking down a man to the ground and bust up his chin and wearing sleep clothes. What's your aim pajama?"

Nelson stared at the tips of the new green flame as through the apartment door came a single file of dogs, heads down, tongues lolling from their jowls and dripping saliva. The first wave filled the living room, but the line kept coming. They twirled in tight circles, looking for a comfortable place to lie on the floor. The man drew his legs to his chest and wrapped his arms around his knees. Two dogs quickly filled the space he vacated. They curled around each other and leaned close to the fire. Soon, a hundred dogs lay in the apartment. As they lost consciousness, they began breathing in unison and it sounded like a huge, lazy bellows rising and falling. The man could spot a serpentine path from his chair to the door and he thought he had a reasonable chance of escape if the dogs remained asleep. He moved to the edge of the chair and looked for a landing spot for his feet. Nelson held up two hands, palms outward, with a look of irritation on his face.

"Nothing…out there….for a noodle," he stammered.

"I ain't a noodle. You's the noodle."

With a rigid index finger Nelson ordered the man back in the chair. The man leaned back and drew his feet back on the cushion. Nelson squirmed in his chair and fished out a dog-eared square of typing paper from a hidden pocket under his sweater. The paper had been folded and unfolded so many times the folds threatened to become fissures. He flicked it onto the man's lap, just avoiding the current of heat and spark rising through the hole in the ceiling. The man carefully unfolded the paper. Scrawled between the folds and written in blue ink it read:

Welcome to Me

The man folded the paper just as carefully back to the original square, but he did not attempt to flick it back to Nelson near the heat. He let the square rest on his thigh and wondered what to do with it.

"Much obliged Pajama. I certainly appreciate the hospitality."

One of the dogs stood up and caught the note in its mouth and returned it to Nelson. He scratched the dog behind the ears and slipped the note back into the hidden pocket. The temperature of the room began rising with the heat of so many bodies and the fire. They sat in their chairs, watching the flames, and drowsing among the dog pack.

CPSIA information can be obtained at www.ICGtesting.com
Printed in the USA
BVOW012011200912

300999BV00003B/5/P